The MAGICIAN'S Apprentice

Something began to squeeze her from all sides. Looking around, she could not see any sign of the force pressing against her. A relentless pressure at her back pushed her forward. It forced her against the Sachakan, who laughed.

"Lord Dakon," she coughed out. "He won't let you—"

"He's not here. And what's he going to do when he finds out? Punish me? I'll be halfway home by then. How many people do you want knowing, anyway?"

As he plucked at the front of her tunic she tried to move her arms, but some invisible force held them still. She could not move her legs, either. She could not move anything. Not even her head. And as she opened her mouth to yell she felt something invisible envelop it and force her jaw closed again. The Sachakan's grinning, leering face loomed over her. Her skin crawled. Her skull throbbed as if it would burst.

Is he inside my head? She closed her eyes, concentrated on the feeling and tried to push it away.

Get off get off get off GET OFF!

Suddenly the force holding her melted away and she fell backwards. At the same time she felt a sensation of something pouring out of her. A bright, bright light behind her eyelids was followed by a resounding crash.

TRUDI CANAVAN

The MAGICIAN'S *Apprentice*

orbit

www.orbitbooks.net

ORBIT

First published in Great Britain in 2009 by Orbit
This paperback edition published in 2010 by Orbit

Copyright © 2009 by Trudi Canavan

Excerpt from *The Ambassador's Mission* by Trudi Canavan
Copyright © 2010 by Trudi Canavan

Excerpt from *The Edge of the World* by Kevin J. Anderson
Copyright © 2009 by Kevin J. Anderson

The moral right of the author has been asserted.

A CIP catalogue record for this book is available
from the British Library.

ISBN 978-1-84149-590-3

Typeset in Garamond 3 by Palimpsest Book Production Limited,
Grangemouth, Stirlingshire
Printed and bound in Great Britain by Clays Ltd, St Ives plc

Papers used by Orbit are natural, renewable and recyclable
products sourced from well-managed forests and certified
in accordance with the rules of the Forest Stewardship Council.

Mixed Sources
Product group from well-managed
forests and other controlled sources
www.fsc.org Cert no. SGS-COC-004081
© 1996 Forest Stewardship Council
FSC

Orbit
An imprint of
Little, Brown Book Group
100 Victoria Embankment
London EC4Y 0DY

An Hachette UK Company
www.hachette.co.uk

www.orbitbooks.net

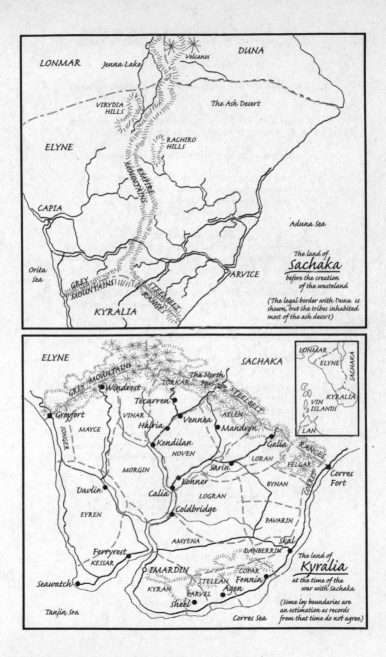

LONMAR

Jenna Lake

Volcanos

DUNA

ELYNE

VIRYDIA HILLS

The Ash Desert

RACHIRO HILLS

EMPIRE MOUNTAINS

CAPIA

Aduna Sea

Orita Sea

GREY MOUNTAINS

STEELBELT RANGES

ARVICE

The land of
Sachaka
before the creation
of the wasteland

(The legal border with Duna is
shown, but the tribes inhabited
most of the ash desert)

KYRALIA

ELYNE

SACHAKA

GREY MOUNTAINS

Windrest

TORKAR

The North Pass

STEELBELT

Greyfort

Tecurren

VINAR

Halria

Vennea

AYLEN

Mahdryn

JONGER

MAYCE

Kendilan

NOVEN

Sarin

Galia

RANGES

LORAN

FELGAR

MORGIN

Lohner

Calia

LOGRAN

BYNAN

CORREL

Corres Fort

Davlin

Coldbridge

PAVARIN

EYREN

AMYENA

Skal

Ferryrest

KESSAR

DANBERRIN

IMARDIN

COPAR

Fennin

Seawatch

KYRAN

STELEAN

Agen

TARVEL

Sheel

Tanjin Sea

Corres Sea

LONMAR

ELYNE

SACHAKA

KYRALIA

VIN ISLANDS

LAN

The land of
Kyralia
at the time of the
war with Sachaka

(Some ley boundaries are
an estimation as records
from that time do not agree)

"Found a book describing the Sachakan War written soon after the event. It is remarkable in that it portrays the Guild as the enemy — and it paints an unflattering image indeed!"

Letter from Lord Dannyl to Administrator Lorlen

"The history of magic is a tale of accidental discoveries and deliberate concealments. It would be impossible to write an accurate history of magic without scraping away the dirt under which unpalatable facts have long been buried. Twenty years ago the Guild was scandalised to discover that what we know as 'black magic' was once called 'higher magic' and was practised by all magicians — who were all known as Higher Magicians. It was as much a shock to learn this as to comprehend that so much of our recorded history has been altered and destroyed. But there are stranger truths to be uncovered. I have unearthed no mention of the destruction of Imardin in the accounts of the Sachakan War, for instance. Yet it is an accepted part of our basic historical teachings. And the greatest mystery of all is how the wastelands of Sachaka were created. The people of that land hold the Guild responsible for that terrible act. Yet no record has ever been found to explain how it was done."

Extract from the preface of Lord Dannyl's
A Complete History of Magic

"History is written by the victors."

Winston Churchill

PART ONE

CHAPTER 1

There was no fast and painless way to perform an amputation, Tessia knew. Not if you did it properly. A neat amputation required a flap of skin to be cut to cover the stump, and that took time.

As her father deftly began to slice into the skin around the boy's finger, Tessia noted the expressions of the people in the room. The boy's father stood with his arms crossed and his back straight. His scowl did not quite hide signs of worry, though whether it was sympathy for his son or anxiety about whether he'd get the harvest finished in time without his son's help, she could not tell. Probably a bit of both.

The mother held her son's other hand tightly while staring into his eyes. The boy's face was flushed and beaded with sweat. His jaw was clenched and, despite her father's warning, he watched the work being done intently. He had remained still so far, not moving his wounded hand or squirming. No sound had escaped him. Such control impressed Tessia, especially in one so young. Landworkers were said to be a tough lot, but in her experience that was not always true. She wondered if the child would be able to keep it up. Worse was to come, after all.

Her father's face was creased with concentration. He had carefully peeled the skin of the boy's finger back past the joint of the knuckle. At a glance from him she took the small jointer knife from the burner and handed it to him, then took the number five peeler from him, washed it and carefully set the blade over the burner so it would be seared clean.

When she looked up, the boy's face was a mass of wrinkles, screwed up tight. Tessia's father had begun to cut through the joint. Looking up, she noted that the boy's father was now a pasty grey. The mother was white.

"Don't watch," Tessia advised in a murmur. The woman's head turned abruptly away.

The blade met the surgery board with a clunk of finality. Taking the small jointer from her father, Tessia handed him a curved needle, already threaded with fine gut-string. The needle glided easily through the boy's skin and Tessia felt a little glow of pride; she had sharpened it carefully in readiness for this operation, and the gut-string was the finest she had ever fashioned.

She looked at the amputated finger lying at the end of the surgery board. At one end it was a blackened, oozing mess, but there was reassuringly healthy flesh all through the cut end. It had been badly crushed in an accident during harvest some days before, but like most of the villagers and landworkers her father serviced, neither boy nor father had sought help until the wound had festered. It took time, and extreme pain, before a person could accept, let alone seek, removal of a part of their body.

If left too long, such a festering could poison the blood, causing fevers and even death. That a small wound could prove fatal fascinated Tessia. It also scared her. She had seen a man driven to insanity and self-mutilation by a mere rotten tooth, otherwise robust women bleed to death after giving birth, healthy babies that stopped breathing for no apparent reason and fevers that spread through the village, taking one or two lives but causing no more than discomfort for the rest.

Through working with her father, she had seen more

4

wounds, illness and death in her sixteen years than most women did in their lifetimes. But she had also seen maladies remedied, chronic illness relieved and lives saved. She knew every man, woman and child in the village and the ley, and some beyond. She had knowledge of matters that few were privy to. Unlike most of the locals she could read and write, reason and—

Her father looked up and handed her the needle, then cut off the remaining thread. Neat stitches held the flap of skin closed over the stump of the boy's finger. Knowing what came next, Tessia took some wadding and bandages from his healer's bag and handed them to him.

"Take these," he told the mother.

Letting the boy's other hand go, the woman passively let Tessia's father lay the bandage across one palm, then arrange wadding on top. He placed the boy's hand over her palm so the stump of the finger rested in the centre of the wadding, then took hold of the pulse binder on the boy's arm.

"When I loosen this the blood in his arm will regain its rhythm," he told her. "His finger will begin to bleed. You must wrap the wadding around the finger and hold it firmly until the blood finds a new pulse path."

The woman bit her lip and nodded. As Tessia's father loosened the binder the boy's arm and hand slowly regained a healthy pinkness. Blood welled around the stitches and the mother quickly wrapped her hand around the stump. The boy grimaced. She smoothed his hair affectionately.

Tessia suppressed a smile. Her father had taught her that it was wise to allow a family to take part in the healing process in some small way. It gave them a sense of control, and they were less likely to be suspicious or dismissive of the methods he used if they took part in them.

After a little wait, her father checked the stump then bound it up firmly, giving the family instructions on how often to replace the bandages, how to keep them clean and dry if the boy resumed work (he knew better than to tell them to keep the boy at home), when they could be discarded, and what signs of festering they should watch for.

As he listed off the medicines and extra bandages they would need, Tessia removed them from his bag and set them on the cleanest patch of the table that she could find. The amputated finger she wrapped up and set aside. Patients and their families preferred to bury or burn such things, perhaps worrying what might be done with them if they didn't dispose of them themselves. No doubt they had heard the disturbing and ridiculous stories that went around from time to time of healers in Kyralia secretly experimenting on amputated limbs, grinding bones up into unnatural potions or somehow re-animating them.

Cleaning and then searing the needle over the burner, she packed it and the other tools away. The surgery board would have to be treated later, at home. She extinguished the burner and waited as the family began to offer their thanks.

This was also a well-practised part of their routine. Her father hated being trapped while patients poured out their gratitude. It embarrassed him. After all, he was not offering his services for free. Lord Dakon provided him and his family with a house and income in exchange for looking after the people of his ley.

But her father knew that accepting thanks with humility and patience kept him well placed in the local people's opinions. He never accepted gifts, however. Everyone under Lord Dakon's rule paid a tithe to their master, and so in effect had already paid Tessia's father for his services.

Her role was to wait for the right moment to interrupt and remind her father that they had other work to do. The family would apologise. Her father would apologise. Then they would be ushered out.

But as the right moment neared the sound of hoofbeats drummed outside the house. All paused to listen. The hoofbeats stopped and were replaced by footsteps, then a pounding at the door.

"Healer Veran? Is Healer Veran there?"

The farmer and Tessia's father started forward at the same time, then her father stopped, allowing the man to answer his own door. A well-dressed middle-aged man stood outside, his brow slick with sweat. Tessia recognised him as Lord Dakon's house master, Keron.

"He's here," the farmer told him.

Keron squinted into the dimness of the farmer's house. "Your services are required at the Residence, Healer Veran. With some urgency."

Tessia's father frowned, then turned to beckon to her. Grabbing his bag and the burner, she hurried after him into the daylight. One of the farmer's older sons was waiting by the horse and cart provided by Lord Dakon for her father to use when visiting patients outside the village, and he quickly rose and removed a feedbag from the old mare's head. Tessia's father nodded his thanks then took his bag from Tessia and stowed it in the back of the cart.

As they climbed up onto the seat, Keron galloped past them back towards the village. Her father took up the reins and flicked them. The mare snorted and shook her head, then started forward.

Tessia glanced at her father. "Do you think . . . ?" she began, then stopped as she realised the pointlessness of her question.

Do you think it might have something to do with the Sachakan? she had wanted to ask, but such questions were a waste of breath. They would find out when they got there.

It was hard not to imagine the worst. The villagers hadn't stopped muttering about the foreign magician visiting Lord Dakon's house since he had arrived, and it was hard not to be infected by their fear and awe. Though Lord Dakon was a magician, he was familiar, respected and Kyralian. If he was feared it was only because of the magic he could wield and the control over their lives he held; he was not the sort of landowner who misused either power. Sachakan magicians on the other hand had, scant centuries ago, ruled and enslaved Kyralia and by all reports liked to remind people, whenever the chance came, what things had been like before Kyralia was granted its independence.

Think like a healer, she told herself as the cart bounced down the road. *Consider the information you have. Trust reason over emotion.*

Neither the Sachakan nor Lord Dakon could be ill. Both were magicians and resistant to all but a few rare maladies. They weren't immune to plagues, but rarely succumbed to them. Lord Dakon would have called on her father for help long before any disease needed urgent attention, though it was possible the Sachakan wouldn't have mentioned being ill if he didn't want to be tended by a Kyralian healer.

Magicians could die of wounds, she knew. Lord Dakon could have injured himself. Then an even more frightening possibility occurred to her. Had Lord Dakon and the Sachakan fought each other?

If they had, the lord's house – and perhaps the village, too – would be ruined and smoking, she told herself, *if the tales of what magical battles are like are true*. The road descending from the farmer's home gave a clear view of the houses below, lining either side of the main road this side of the river. All was as peaceful and undisturbed as it had been when they had left.

Perhaps the patient or patients they were hurrying to treat

were servants in the lord's house. Aside from Keron, six other house and stable servants kept Lord Dakon's home in order. She and her father had treated them many times before. Landworkers living outside the village sometimes travelled to the Residence when they were sick or injured, though usually they went directly to her father.

Who else is there? Ah, of course. There's Jayan, Lord Dakon's apprentice, she remembered. *But as far as I know he has all the same physical protections against illness as a higher magician. Perhaps he picked a fight with the Sachakan. To the Sachakan, Jayan would be the closest thing to a slave, and—*

"Tessia."

She looked at her father expectantly. Had he anticipated who needed his services?

"I . . . Your mother wants you to stop assisting me."

Anticipation shrivelled into exasperation. "I know." She grimaced. "She wants me to find a nice husband and start having babies."

He didn't smile, as he had in the past when the subject came up. "Is that so bad? You can't become a healer, Tessia."

Hearing the serious tone in his voice, she stared at him in surprise and disappointment. While her mother had expressed this opinion many times before, her father had never agreed with it. She felt something inside her turn to stone and fall down into her gut, where it lay cold and hard and uncomfortable. Which was impossible, of course. Human organs did not turn to stone and certainly could not shift into the stomach.

"The villagers won't accept you," he continued.

"You can't know that," she protested. "Not until I've tried and failed. What reason could they have to distrust me?"

"None. They like you well enough, but it is as hard for them to believe that a woman can heal as that a reber could

9

sprout wings and fly. It's not in a woman's nature to have a steady head, they think."

"But the birthmothers . . . they trust them. Why is there any difference between that and healing?"

"Because what we . . . what the birthmothers do is specialised and limited. Remember, they call for my help when their knowledge is insufficient. A healer has learning and experience behind him that no birthmother has access to. Most birthmothers can't even read."

"And yet the villagers trust them. Sometimes they trust them more than you."

"Birthing is an entirely female activity," he said wryly. "Healing isn't."

Tessia could not speak. Annoyance and frustration rose inside her but she knew angry outbursts would not help her cause. She had to be persuasive, and her father was no simple peasant who might be easily swayed. He was probably the smartest man in the village.

As the cart reached the main road she cursed silently. She had not realised how firmly he'd come to agree with her mother. *I need to change his mind back again, and I need to do it carefully*, she realised. *He doesn't like to go against Mother's wishes. So I need to weaken her confidence in her arguments as much as reduce Father's doubts about continuing to teach me.* She needed to consider all the arguments for and against her becoming a healer, and how to use them to her benefit. And she needed to know every detail of her parents' plans.

"What will you do without me assisting you?" she asked.

"I'll take on a boy from the village," her father said.

"Which one?"

"Perhaps Miller's youngest. He is a bright child."

So he'd already been considering the matter. She felt a stab of hurt.

The well-maintained main road was less rutted than the farmer's track, so her father flicked the reins and urged the mare to quicken her pace. The increased vibration of the cart robbed Tessia of the ability to think. She saw faces appear in windows as they reached the village. The few people walking about stopped, acknowledging her father with nods and smiles.

She gripped the rail as her father tugged on the reins to slow the mare and turn her through the gates at one side of the lord's Residence. In the dim light of the building's shadows she made out stable workers coming forward to take the reins as the cart stopped. Her father jumped down from the seat. Keron stepped forward to take her father's bag. She leapt down to the ground and hurried after as they disappeared into the house.

Tessia caught glimpses of the kitchen, storeroom, washroom and other practical spaces through the doorways of the corridor they strode down. Their rapid footsteps echoed in the narrow stairwell as they climbed up to the floor above. A few turns later and she found herself in a part of the building she had never seen before. Tastefully decorated walls and fine furniture suggested a living area, but these were not the rooms she had seen a few years before, when her father had been summoned to tend a rather vapid young woman suffering from a fainting fit. There were a few bedrooms, and a seating room, and she guessed these were rooms for guests.

She was surprised, then, when Keron opened a door and ushered them into a small room furnished with only a plain bed and a narrow table. No windows let in light, so a tiny lamp burned in the room. It felt mean and dingy. She looked at the bed and suddenly all thought of the décor left her mind.

A man lay there, his face bruised and swollen so badly one

eye was a bloodied, compressed slit. The white of the other eye was dark. She suspected it would appear red in better light. His lips did not line up properly, possibly indicating a broken jaw. His face seemed broad and strangely shaped, though that might have been an effect of the injuries.

He also cradled his right hand to his chest, and she saw instantly that the forearm bent in a way it shouldn't. His chest, too, was dark with bruises. All he wore was a pair of short, tattered trousers that had been roughly mended in many places. His skin was deeply tanned and his build was slight. His feet were bare, and black with dirt. One ankle was badly swollen. The calf of the other leg looked slightly crooked, as if it had healed badly after a break.

The room was silent but for the man's rapid, laboured breathing. Tessia recognised the sound and felt her stomach sink. Her father had once treated a man whose ribs had been broken, puncturing his lungs. That man had died.

Her father hadn't moved since entering the room. He stood still, back slightly bent, gazing at the beaten, broken figure on the bed.

"Father," she ventured.

With a jerk, he straightened and turned to look at her. As he met her eyes she felt understanding pass between them. She found herself shaking her head slightly, and realised he was doing the same. Then she smiled. Surely at moments like these, when they did not even need to speak to understand each other, he could see that she was meant to follow in his footsteps?

He frowned and looked down, then turned back to the bed. She felt a sudden, painful loss. What he should have done was smile, or nod, or give her some sign of reassurance that they would continue working together.

I must regain his confidence, she thought. She took her father's bag from Keron, placed it on the narrow table and opened it. Taking out the burner, she lit it and adjusted the flame. Footsteps sounded outside the room.

"We need more light," her father muttered.

Abruptly the room was filled with a dazzling white light. Tessia ducked as a ball of brightness moved past her head. She stared at it and immediately regretted doing so. It was too bright. When she looked away a circular shadow obscured her sight.

"Is that enough?" a strangely accented voice asked.

"I thank you, master," she heard her father say respectfully.

Master? Tessia felt her stomach spasm. Only one person currently staying in the Residence would be addressed so by her father. Yet with the realisation came a feeling of rebellion. *I will not show this Sachakan any fear*, she decided. *Though I guess there's no risk of trembling at the sight of anyone when I can't actually see properly.* She rubbed at her eyes. The dark patch was receding as her eyes recovered. Squinting at the doorway, she realised there were two figures standing there.

"How do you rate his chances, Healer Veran?" a more familiar voice asked.

Her father hesitated before answering. "Low, my lord," he admitted. "His lungs are pierced. Such an injury is usually fatal."

"Do what you can," Lord Dakon instructed.

Tessia could just make out the two magicians' faces now. Lord Dakon's expression was grim. His companion was smiling. She could see enough to make out his broad Sachakan features, the elaborately decorated jacket and pants he wore, and the jewelled knife in its sheath on his belt that Sachakans wore to indicate they were magicians. Lord Dakon said something quietly, and the pair moved out of sight. She heard their footsteps receding down the corridor beyond.

Abruptly, the light blinked out, leaving them in darkness. Tessia heard her father curse under his breath. Then the room brightened again, though not so fiercely. She looked up to see Keron step inside carrying two full-sized lamps.

"Ah, thank you," Tessia's father said. "Place them over here, and here."

"Is there anything else you require?" the servant asked. "Water? Cloth?"

"At the moment what I need more than anything else is information. How did this happen?"

"I'm . . . I'm not sure. I did not witness it."

"Did anyone? It is easy to miss an injury when there are so many. A description of where each blow fell—"

"Nobody saw," the man said quickly. "None but Lord Dakon, this slave and his master."

Slave? Tessia looked down at the injured man. Of course. The tanned skin and broad features were typically Sachakan. Suddenly the Sachakan magician's interest made sense.

Her father sighed. "Then fetch us some water, and I will write a list of supplies for you to collect from my wife."

The house master hurried away. Tessia's father looked at her, his expression grim. "It will be a long night for you and me." He smiled faintly. "I have to wonder, at times like these, if you are tempted by your mother's vision of your future."

"At times like these it never crosses my mind," she told him. Then she added quietly, "This time we may succeed."

His eyes widened, then his shoulders straightened a little.

"Let's get started, then."

CHAPTER 2

Playing host to a Sachakan magician was never easy and rarely pleasant. Of all the tasks required of Lord Dakon's servants, feeding their guest had caused the most distress. If Ashaki Takado was served a dish he recognised as one he'd eaten before he would reject it, even if he had enjoyed it. He disliked most dishes and he had a large appetite, so at each meal many, many more courses had to be prepared than were normally required to feed two people.

The reward for enduring the fussiness of this guest was a great surfeit of food, which was shared among the household afterwards. *If Takado stays for many more weeks I will not be surprised to find my servants have begun to get a little rotund,* Dakon mused. *Still, I am sure they would much rather the Sachakan moved on.*

As would I, he added to himself as his guest leaned back, patted his broad girth and belched. *Preferably back to his homeland, which I presume is where he is heading since he has travelled through most of Kyralia and this is the closest Residence to the pass.*

"An excellent meal," Takado announced. "Did I detect a little bellspice in that last dish?"

Dakon nodded. "An advantage to living close to the border is that Sachakan traders occasionally pass this way."

"I'm surprised they do. Mandryn isn't on the direct road to Imardin."

"No, but occasionally spring floods block the main road

15

and the best alternative route brings traffic right through the village." He wiped his mouth on a cloth. "Shall we retire to the seating room?"

As Takado nodded, Dakon heard a faint sigh of relief from Cannia, who was on duty in the dining room tonight. *At least the servants' trials are over for the evening*, Dakon thought wearily as he stood up. *Mine don't end until the man sleeps.*

Takado rose and stepped away from the table. He was a full head taller than Dakon, and his broad shoulders and wide face added to the impression of bulk. Beneath a layer of soft fat was the frame of a typical Sachakan – strong and big. Next to Takado, Dakon knew he must appear pathetically thin and small. And pale. While not as dark as the Lonmars of the north, Sachakan skin was a healthy brown that Kyralian women had been trying to achieve with paints for centuries.

Which they still did, despite otherwise loathing and fearing the Sachakans. Dakon led the way out of the room. *They should be proud of their complexion, but centuries of believing our pallor is evidence that we are a weak, barbaric race can't be turned around easily.*

He entered the seating room, Takado following and dropping into the chair he'd claimed as his own for the duration of his stay. The room was illuminated by two lamps. Though he could easily have lit the room with a magical light, Dakon preferred the warm glow of lamplight. It reminded him of his mother, who'd had no magical talent and preferred to do things "the old-fashioned way". She'd also decorated and furnished the seating room. After another Sachakan visitor, impressed with the library, had decided that Dakon's father would gift him with several valuable books, she had decreed that such visitors be entertained in a room that appeared full of priceless treasures, but actually contained copies, fakes or inexpensive knick-knacks.

16

Takado stretched his legs and watched Dakon pour wine from a jug the servants had left for them. "So, Lord Dakon, do you think your healer can save my slave?"

Dakon detected no concern in the man's voice. He hadn't expected care for the slave's well-being — just the sort of interest a man has in a belonging that has broken and is being repaired. "Healer Veran will do the best he can."

"And if he fails, how will you punish him?"

Dakon handed Takado a goblet. "I won't."

Takado's eyebrows rose. "How do you know he will do his best, then?"

"Because I trust him. He is a man of honour."

"He is a Kyralian. My slave is valuable to me, and I am Sachakan. How do I know he won't hasten the man's death to spite me?"

Dakon sat down and took a sip of the wine. It wasn't a good vintage. His ley didn't enjoy a climate favourable for winemaking. But it was strong, and would speed the Sachakan towards retiring for the night. Dakon doubted it would loosen the man's tongue, though. It hadn't on any of the previous evenings.

"Because he is a man of honour," Dakon repeated.

The Sachakan snorted. "Honour! Among servants? If I were you, I'd take the daughter. She's not so ugly, for a Kyralian. She'll have picked up a few healing tricks, so she'd be a useful slave, too."

Dakon smiled. "Surely you have noticed during your journeying that slavery is outlawed in Kyralia."

Takado's nose wrinkled. "Oh, I couldn't help but notice. Nobody could fail to see how badly your servants attend to their masters. Surly. Stupid. Clumsy. It wasn't always that way, you know. Your people once embraced slavery as if it was their own idea. They could again, too. You might regain the prosperity your great-grandfathers enjoyed." He downed the wine in a few gulps and then sighed appreciatively.

"We've enjoyed greater prosperity since outlawing slavery than we ever had before," Dakon told his guest as he rose to refill the Sachakan's goblet and top up his own. "Keeping slaves isn't profitable. Treat them badly and they die before they become useful, or else rebel or run away. Treat them well and they cost as much to feed and control as free servants, yet have no motivation to work well."

"No motivation but fear of punishment or death."

"An injured or dead slave is of no use to anyone. I can't see how beating a slave to death for stepping on your foot is going to encourage him to be careful in the future. His death won't even be an example to others, since there are no other slaves here to learn from it."

Takado swirled the wine in his goblet, his expression unreadable. "I probably went a bit too far. Trouble is, after travelling with him for months I've grown utterly sick of his company. You would, too, if you were restricted to one servant when you visited a country. I'm sure whichever of your kings came up with that law only wanted to punish Sachakans."

"Happy servants make better companions," Dakon said. "I enjoy conversing and dealing with my people, and they don't seem to mind talking to and working for me. If they didn't like me, they wouldn't alert me to potential problems in the ley, or suggest ways to increase crop yield."

"If my slaves didn't alert me to problems in my domain or get the best out of my crops, I'd have them killed."

"And then their skills would be lost. My people live longer and so gain proficiency in their work. They take pride in it, and are more likely to be innovative and inventive – like the healer tending your slave."

"But not like his daughter," Takado said. "Her skill will

be wasted, won't it? She is a woman and in Kyralia women do not become healers. In my country her skills would be utilised." He leaned towards Dakon. "If you let me buy her off you, I'll make sure she gets to use them. I suspect she'd welcome the chance." He took a swig of the wine, watching Dakon over the rim of the goblet.

For a greedy, cruel man with too much power and too little self-restraint, Takado can be disturbingly perceptive, Dakon noted. "Even if I would not be breaking a law, and she agreed to such a thing, I don't think it's her healing skills you're interested in."

Takado laughed and relaxed in his chair. "You've seen through me once again, Lord Dakon. I expect you haven't tasted that dish – or have you?"

"Of course not. She is half my age."

"Which only makes her more appealing."

Takado was goading him again, Dakon knew. "And more likely that such a liaison would make me look a fool."

"There's no shame in seeking a little entertainment while looking for a suitable wife," Takado said. "I'm surprised you haven't found yourself one yet – a wife, that is. I suppose there aren't any females in Aylen ley worthy of your status. You should visit Imardin more often. Looks like everything worth being a part of happens there."

"It has been too long since I visited," Dakon agreed. He sipped the wine. "Did you enjoy your stay there?"

Takado shrugged. "I don't know if I'd use the word 'enjoy'. It was as barbaric a place as I expected."

"If you didn't expect to enjoy it, why did you go?"

The Sachakan's eyes gleamed and he held out his empty goblet again. "To satisfy my curiosity."

Dakon rose to refill it. Every time they came close to discussing why Takado had toured Kyralia the Sachakan became flippant or changed the subject. It had made some magicians nervous, especially since rumours had reached them that some of the younger Sachakan magicians had met in Arvice, the capital of Sachaka, to discuss whether regaining the empire's former colonies was possible. The Kyralian king had sent secret requests to all landowners that any lord or lady Takado stayed with seek the reason for his visit.

"So has your curiosity been satisfied?" Dakon asked as he returned to his seat.

Takado shrugged. "There's more I'd like to see, but without a slave . . . ? No."

"Your slave might yet live."

"Much as I have appreciated your hospitality, I'm not going to stay here only to see whether a slave I'm tired of recovers. I've probably been too great a drain on your resources already." He paused to drink. "No, if he lives, keep him. He'll probably be crippled and useless."

Dakon blinked in surprise. "So if he lives and I allow him to stay, you grant him his freedom?"

"Yes. Of course." Takado waved a hand dismissively. "Can't have you breaking your own laws because of me."

"I thank you for your consideration. So where will you go next? Home?"

The Sachakan nodded, then grinned. "Can't let the slaves back in my domain get any foolish ideas about who is in control, can I?"

"Absence, as they say, tempers the bonds of affection."

Takado laughed. "You have some strange sayings here in Kyralia. Like 'Sleep is the cheapest tonic'." He stood and, as Dakon followed suit, handed over his empty wine goblet. "You haven't finished yours," he noted.

"As you are no doubt aware, small bodies make for quick drunks." Dakon set his half-empty goblet next to the empty one on the tray. "And while there is an injured man in my house I feel a responsibility to remain sober, even when that man is only a lowly Sachakan slave."

Takado's stare was somewhere between blank and amused. "You Kyralians are truly a strange people." He turned away. "No need to escort me to my room. I remember the way." He swayed slightly. "At least, I think I remember. Good night, Lord Dakon, as you strange Kyralians say."

"Good night, Ashaki Takado," Dakon replied.

He watched the Sachakan stroll down the corridor, and listened to the man's footsteps receding. Then he followed as silently as he could manage. Not to make sure that his guest went where he intended, but because he wanted to check on Veran's progress. The slave's room was, naturally, not far from his master's and Dakon did not want the Sachakan noticing where he was going, and deciding to accompany him.

A few corridors and a stairway later Dakon watched as Takado walked past the door to his slave's room without glancing at it, and disappeared into his own chamber. Muffled sounds came from within the slave's room. The light spilling under the door flickered. Dakon paused, reconsidering whether he should interrupt.

The slave will either live or he won't, he told himself; *it won't make any difference whether you visit or not.* But he could not find the cold practicality with which Takado regarded all but the most powerful of humans. Memories of the slave pinned to a wall, recoiling from relentless invisible blows dealt by the Sachakan magician, made Dakon shudder. He could still hear the crunch of breaking bones, the slap of impacts upon vulnerable flesh.

Turning away, he headed towards his own apartments, trying not to hope that Veran would fail.

Because what in the name of higher magic was he going to do with a freed Sachakan slave?

Early morning light illuminated the village when Tessia and her father emerged from Lord Dakon's house. It was a thin, cold glow, but when she turned to look at her father she knew the greyness of his face was not just a trick of the light. He was exhausted.

Their home was across the road and along it for a hundred steps or so, yet the distance seemed enormous. It would have been ridiculous to ask the stable workers to hitch a horse to the cart for such a short journey, but she was so tired she wished someone had. Her father's shoe clipped a stone and she tucked an arm round his to steady him, her other hand gripping the handle of his bag. It felt heavier than it ever had before, even though most of the bandages and a substantial amount of the medicines usually contained within it were now wrapped around or applied to various parts of the Sachakan slave's body.

That poor man. Her father had cut him open in order to remove the broken piece of rib from his lung and sew up the hole. Such drastic surgery should have killed the fellow, but somehow he had continued to breathe and live. Her father had said it was pure luck the incision he'd made hadn't severed a major pulse path.

He'd made the cut as small as possible, and worked mostly by feel, his fingers deep within the man's body. It had been incredible to watch.

Coming to the door of their house, Tessia stepped forward to open it. But as she reached out for the handle, the door swung inward. Her mother drew them inside, her face lined with worry.

"Cannia said you were treating a Sachakan. I thought at

first she meant *him*. I thought, 'How could a magician be that badly injured?' but she told me it was the slave. Is he alive?"

"Yes," Tessia's father said.

"Will he stay so?"

"It's unlikely. He's a tough one, though."

"Didn't hardly yell at all," Tessia agreed. "Though I suspect that's because he was afraid of attracting his master's attention."

Her mother turned to regard her. She opened her mouth, then closed it again and shook her head.

"Did they feed you?" she asked.

Her father looked thoughtful.

"Keron brought some food," Tessia answered for him, "but we didn't have time to eat it."

"I'll heat up some soup." The woman ushered them into the kitchen. Tessia and her father dropped into two chairs by the cooking table. Stirring up the coals in the fire, her mother persuaded some fresh wood to catch then hitched a small pan over the flames.

"We'll have to check on him regularly," Tessia's father murmured, more to himself than to Tessia or her mother. "Change his bandages. Watch for signs of fever."

"Did Cannia say why he was beaten?" Tessia asked her mother.

The woman shook her head. "What reason do those Sachakan brutes need? Most likely he did it for fun, but put a bit more force into it than he intended."

"Lord Yerven always said that not all Sachakans are cruel," her father said.

"Just most of them," Tessia finished. She smiled. Lord Dakon's father had died when she was a child. Her memories of him were of a kindly, vague old man who always carried sweetdrops to give to the village children.

"Well, this is clearly one of the cruel ones." Tessia's mother looked at her husband and her frown returned. "I wish you didn't have to go back there."

He smiled grimly. "Lord Dakon will not allow anything to happen to us."

The woman looked from him to Tessia and back. Her frown deepened and her expression changed from concern to annoyance. Turning back to the fire, she tested the soup with the tip of a finger, and nodded to herself. She brought out the pan and poured its contents into two mugs. Tessia took both and handed one to her father. The broth was warm and delicious, and she felt herself growing rapidly sleepier as she drank it. Her father's eyelids drooped.

"Off to bed now, the both of you," her mother said as soon as they had finished. Neither of them argued as she ordered them upstairs to their rooms. Intense weariness washed over Tessia as she changed into nightclothes. Climbing under the covers, she sighed contentedly.

Just as she began to drift into sleep the sound of voices roused her again.

The sound was coming from across the corridor. From her parents' bedroom. Remembering her conversation with her father the previous day, she felt a twinge of anxiety. She pushed herself into a sitting position, then swung her feet down to the floor.

Her door made only a thin, quiet squeak as she opened it. The last time she had listened in on a late night conversation between her parents had been many years before, when she was only a child. Padding slowly and silently to their door, she pressed her ear to the wood.

"You want them too," her mother said.

"Of course. But I would never expect that of Tessia if she didn't want them," her father replied.

24

"You'd be disappointed, though."

"And relieved. It is always a risk. I've seen too many healthy women die."

"It is a risk we must all take. To not have children out of fear is wrong. Yes, it is a risk, but the rewards are so great. She could deny herself great joy. And who will look after her when she is old?"

Silence followed.

"If she had a son, you could train the boy," her mother added.

"It is too late for that. When I have grown too old to work the boy would still be too young and inexperienced to take on the responsibility."

"So you train Tessia instead? She *can't* replace you. You *know* that."

"She might, if she shared the task with another healer. She could be . . . I don't know what to call it . . . something between a healer and a birthmother. A . . . a 'carer', perhaps. Or at least an assistant."

Tessia wanted to interrupt, to tell them that she could be more than half a healer, but she kept silent and still. Bursting into the room, after having obviously eavesdropped, would hardly do anything to change her mother's mind.

"You have to take on a village boy," her mother said firmly. "And you must stop training her. It has filled her head with impossible ideas. She will not even consider marriage or raising a family until she stops trying to be a healer."

"If I am to employ a new apprentice he will take time to train. I will need Tessia's assistance in the meantime. The village is growing larger, and will keep growing. By the time I have trained this boy we may need two healers here. Tessia could continue her work – perhaps marry as well."

"Her husband would not allow it."

"He might, if she chose the right man. An intelligent man . . ."

"A *tolerant* man. A man who does not mind gossip and breaking tradition. Where is she going to find such a one?"

Tessia's father was silent a long time.

"I'm tired. I need to sleep," he said eventually.

"We both do. I was up most of the night worrying about you two. Especially with Tessia being in the same house as that Sachakan brute."

"We were in no danger. Lord Dakon is a good man."

The few words that followed were muffled. Tessia waited until the pair had not spoken for some time, then carefully crept back to her bed.

Last night I proved my worth to him, she thought smugly. *He can't ask me to stop assisting him now. He knows no foolish village boy would have had the nerve or knowledge to deal with that slave's injuries.*

But I did.

CHAPTER 3

At the soft tap on the door, Apprentice Jayan smiled. He turned and sent out a small surge and twist of magic to the handle. With a click the door swung inward. Beyond the doorway, a young woman bowed as best she could, laden as she was with a large tray.

"Greetings, Apprentice Jayan," she chimed as she entered the room. Carrying her burden over to him, she set it on one ample hip and began transferring bowls, plates and cups onto the desk.

"Greetings to you, Malia," he replied. "You're looking particularly cheerful today."

"I am," she said. "The lord's guest is leaving today."

He straightened. "He is? Are you sure?"

"Quite sure. I guess he can't cope without a slave tending to his every need." She sent him a sidelong, thoughtful look. "I wonder, could you get by without me?"

Jayan ignored her question and the obvious hook for a compliment. "Why hasn't he got a slave? What happened to the slave he arrived with?"

Malia's eyes rounded. "Of course. You wouldn't know. And you wouldn't have heard anything, hidden here in the back of the Residence. Takado beat his slave almost to death yesterday afternoon. Healer Veran worked on him the full night." Despite her matter-of-fact tone, her quick gestures betrayed her uneasiness. He guessed all the servants would be unnerved by the Sachakan's behaviour. They knew that, to him, there was little difference between them and a slave.

But Malia's smile had quickly returned, and it was a sly one. She knew what the Sachakan's departure would mean for him. He looked at her expectantly.

"And?"

The smile widened. "And what?"

"Did he live or die?"

"Oh." She frowned, then shrugged. "I assume he's still alive, or we'd have heard something."

Jayan stood up and moved to the window. He wanted to seek Dakon and discover more, but his master had ordered him to remain in his room while the Sachakan was staying in the Residence. Looking out of the window, down at the closed stable doors and empty yard, he chewed his lip.

If I can't find out myself, Malia will be more than willing to get information for me.

Trouble was, she always wanted a little more than thanks in return for her favours. While she was pretty enough, Dakon had long ago warned him that young female house servants had a habit of taking a fancy to young male apprentice magicians – or their influence and fortunes – and he was not to take advantage of them, or allow himself to be taken advantage of by them. While Jayan knew his master was forgiving of the occasional mistake or misbehaviour, he had also learned over the last four years that the magician had subtle and unpleasant ways to punish unacceptable conduct. He did not believe Dakon would resort to the ultimate punishment for such misconduct – send an apprentice back to his family with his education unfinished and without the knowledge of higher magic that marked him as an independent magician – but he didn't fancy Malia enough to test that belief. Or any young woman of Mandryn, for that matter.

The trick with Malia was never to actually *ask* for anything. Only express a wish to know something. If she provided information he'd *asked* for, she considered he owed her something in return.

"I wonder when the Sachakan will leave," he murmured.

"Oh, probably not till dusk," Malia said lightly.

"Dusk? Why would he travel at night?"

She smiled and slipped the tray under her arm. "I don't know, but I like the thought of you stuck here, all by yourself, for another whole day. After all, you don't want to risk he'll take a fancy to you, and take you home with him in place of his slave, do you? Enjoy your day."

Chuckling, she left the room, pulling the door closed behind her. Jayan stared at the back of the door, not sure if she'd seen through his ploy or was merely seizing an opportunity to tease him.

Then he sighed, returned to his desk and began his morning meal.

At first Jayan hadn't minded Dakon's decision that he must stay in his room for the duration of the Sachakan's visit. He had plenty of books to read and study, and didn't mind being alone. He wasn't worried that Takado would attempt to kidnap him, as Malia had suggested, since Sachakans didn't make slaves of anyone who had access to their magical abilities. They preferred slaves with powerful *latent* talent, who could not use magic yet would provide their master with plenty of magical strength to absorb.

No, if any conflict arose between Takado and Dakon it was more likely the Sachakan would try to kill Jayan. Part of an apprentice's role was to provide his master with a source of extra magical strength, just as a slave did, except that apprentices gained magical knowledge in return. And were free men, or women.

Conflict between Takado and Dakon was unlikely, though. It would have diplomatic repercussions in Sachaka and Kyralia that neither magician would want to face. Still, it was possible Takado might stir up some minor trouble, knowing he was little over a day's journey from his homeland, only to make a point about Sachakan superiority and power.

Like beating his own slave to death?

I guess he has made his point already. He's shown us he still has power over other human lives, and he's done so without breaking any Kyralian laws.

That thought made Jayan feel oddly relieved. Now that the Sachakan had made his point he would leave – was leaving – and soon Jayan would be out of danger. He could leave the room. And the Residence, if he wished. Life would return to normal.

Jayan felt his mood lighten. He had never thought he would get sick of his own company or of reading. It turned out he could reach a point where he began to long for sunlight and fresh air. He'd passed that point a few days ago, and since then he'd been restless.

Only so much of magic could be learned from reading. To gain any skill took practice. It had been weeks since he'd had a lesson from Lord Dakon. Each day that passed was a lesson delayed. Each delayed lesson meant it would be longer before the day Lord Dakon taught him higher magic and Jayan became a magician in his own right.

Then Jayan would enjoy the respect and power due him as a higher magician, and begin to earn his own fortune. He, like his older brother, Lord Velan, would have a title, though "Magician" would never surpass "Lord" in importance. Nothing was more respected in Kyralia than ownership of land, even if all it encompassed was one of the city's grand old houses.

But ownership of a ley was rated more highly than

ownership of a house, which was ironic since magicians who lived in the country were considered backward-thinking and out of touch. If Jayan stayed on good terms with his master, and Dakon did not marry and sire an heir, there was a chance the lord would nominate him as his successor. It was not unheard of for a magician to favour a former apprentice in this way.

It was not just the thought of surpassing his brother in land ownership that appealed to Jayan, though. The idea of retiring to Mandryn someday was also very attractive. He had found he liked this quiet existence, far from the social games of the city he'd once enjoyed watching, and far from the influence of his father and brother.

But Dakon isn't too old to marry and have children, he thought. *His father did both quite late in life. Even if Dakon doesn't, he's got several years in him yet, so I have plenty of time to explore the world first. And the sooner I learn what I need to become a higher magician, the sooner I'll be free to travel wherever I want.*

The light spilling around the window screens of Tessia's bedroom was all wrong. Then she remembered the work of the night before, and how she and her parents had gone to bed in the morning. Of course the light was wrong. It was midday.

For a while she lay there, expecting to fall asleep again, but she didn't. Despite having slept only a few hours, and still feeling a cloying weariness, she remained awake. Her stomach growled. Perhaps it was hunger keeping her from sleep. She climbed out of bed, dressed, and tidied her hair. Stepping quietly out of her room, she saw that her parents' door was still closed. She could hear faint snoring.

At the bottom of the stairs she turned in to the kitchen. The hearth was cold, the fire of the morning having burned itself out. She helped herself to some pachi fruit in a bowl on the table. Then she noticed her father's bag on the floor.

31

The slave, she thought. *Father said the first day of care after treatment was the most important. Bandages will need changing. Wounds will need cleaning. And the pain cures will be wearing off.*

Looking up at the ceiling, toward her parents' room, she considered whether to rouse her father. *Not yet*, she decided. *He needs sleep more than I do, at his age.*

So she waited. She considered trying to cook something, but doubted she could do so without rousing her parents. Instead she went through her father's bag. Slipping into his workroom, she topped up and replaced medicines, thread and bandages. Then she carefully cleaned and sharpened all his tools, while the sunlight streaming through the windows crept slowly across the room.

Her work kept her busy for a few hours. When she could not think of any new task to do, she returned to the kitchen, leaving her father's bag by the front door. Creeping up the staircase, she listened to the sound of snoring and deliberated.

We must check on the slave soon, she thought. *I should wake Father up – which will wake Mother up in the process. Or I could go myself.*

The last thought sent a thrill of excitement through her. If she tended to the slave by herself – if the servants at Lord Dakon's house allowed her to – wouldn't that prove that the villagers did have confidence in her as a healer? Wouldn't it show that she might, given time, replace her father?

She backed down the stairs and moved to the front door. Looking at her father's bag, she felt a twinge of doubt.

It could make Father angry. Doing something he didn't ask me to do isn't as bad as disobeying an order, though. And it's not as if I'm doing anything more than the simple routine of care after treatment. She smiled to herself. *And if I get one of the Residence servants to stay with me, I can show I at least took Mother's worries about my safety into consideration.*

Taking the bag's handles, she lifted it, opened the front door as quietly as possible, then slipped outside.

Several of the villagers were about, she saw. The baker's two sons were slouching against the wall of their house, enjoying the sunny afternoon. They nodded to her and she smiled back. *Are they on my mother's list of prospective husbands?* she wondered. Neither of them interested her. Though they were polite enough now, she could not help remembering how annoying they'd been as boys, calling her names and pulling her hair.

The former metal worker's widow was walking with slow, deliberate steps down the main road, steadying herself with two canes. She'd walked the length of the village and back every sunny day for as long as Tessia could remember. When Tessia was a child, and the widow less withered, other older women of the village had joined her and much gossiping had transpired during their circuit. Now the other women said they were too old to venture out, and feared they would trip or be knocked over by the village children.

Faint childish screams and laughter drew Tessia's attention to the river, where small figures swarmed around the broad, flat curve of the waterway where she had played as a child. Then she heard her name spoken, and turned in time to see a local farmer nod at her as he passed.

He had come from the direction of Lord Dakon's house, now only a few dozen steps away. Entering the alley beside the Residence, she walked up to the side door she and her father had entered the previous day, and knocked.

The door was opened by Cannia. The woman smiled at Tessia, then glanced around the alley.

"Father is still resting," Tessia explained. "I'm to check on the slave and report back."

Cannia nodded and beckoned Tessia inside. "Took him

33

some broth this morning. Tried to feed it to him, since he can't in the state he's in. Didn't take more than a few mouthfuls, I reckon."

"So he's awake."

"Sure is, though I dare say he wishes he wasn't."

"Could you or someone else assist while I tend to him?"

"Of course." She lit a lamp and gave it to Tessia. "Go on ahead and I'll send someone to help you."

Tessia felt her skin prickle slightly as she climbed the stairs to the slave's room. She could not help wondering where the Sachakan was, and hoping she wouldn't encounter him. When she reached the slave's room and found it empty but for her patient, she sighed with relief.

The man stared at her, his pupils wide. She could not tell if it was from fear or surprise. Nobody had told her his name, she realised.

"Greetings again," she said. "I'm here to change your bandages and check if you're healing properly."

He said nothing, and continued to stare. Well, she could hardly expect him to speak, since his jaw had been broken and his head was bound up to prevent it from moving. This was going to be a one-sided conversation.

"You must be in a lot of pain," she continued. "I can give you medicine to dull it. Would you like that?"

The man blinked, then nodded once.

Smiling, Tessia turned to her father's bag and brought out a syrup her father used to treat children. The slave would have trouble swallowing, and a draught of powder mixed in water was likely to leave bitter-tasting grit in his mouth if he couldn't drink it easily. She would have to thin out the syrup with some water, too, and dribble it through a siphon inserted between his lips.

As the medication ran into the man's mouth he stiffened,

then swallowed. But he didn't relax again and his eyes were wide as he stared over her shoulder.

He looks terrified, she thought.

A small gust of air told her that the door was open.

Pulling the siphon out, she stepped back and looked up to see who Cannia had sent to her. The man who gazed back at her was tall, bulky and wearing exotic-looking clothing.

Her heart froze in horror.

"I see you've come back to check on Hanara," the Sachakan said, with a smile that lacked any genuine gratitude. "How good of you. Is he going to live?"

She drew in a breath and somehow found her voice. "I do not know . . . master."

"It won't matter if he doesn't," he told her in a reassuring tone.

She could not think of anything to say to that, so she said nothing. *Where is the servant Cannia said she'd send?* she thought. *Where's Lord Dakon, for that matter? Surely he doesn't let the Sachakan roam the house unsupervised . . .*

"I suppose he's a good patient to experiment on," the Sachakan said, looking at his slave. "Perhaps you'll learn something new." The slave avoided his master's gaze. The Sachakan looked at her again. "Enjoy yourself."

He backed out of the doorway and closed the door. Tessia let out a sigh of relief, and heard another exhalation follow her own. She looked at the slave and smiled crookedly.

"Your master has a strange idea of fun," she murmured. Then she set to work replacing his bandages.

He made no noise as she worked, only occasionally catching his breath as those bandages that had stuck a little to the wounds came away. His injuries were looking remarkably good – minimal swelling and redness, and no festering ooze.

She wiped all carefully with a purifier and replaced the soiled bandages with clean ones.

When she had finished at last, the Sachakan's visit was a distant, unpleasant memory. She packed her father's bag and picked it up. Pausing at the door, she nodded at the slave.

"Rest well, Hanara."

The skin around his eyes crinkled slightly, the closest he could get to a smile. Feeling pleased with her work, she stepped out of the room and started down the corridor to the servants' stairs, wondering if her parents were awake yet.

From one of the doorways drifted a voice that sent her heart sinking to her knees.

"Have you finished, Tessia?"

The Sachakan. She stopped, then cursed herself for doing so. If she hadn't, she could have pretended not to have heard him, but now that it was obvious she had she could not ignore him without being rude. Drawing a deep breath, she took two steps back and looked into the room. It was a seating room, furnished with comfortable chairs and small tables on which a guest could rest a drink or a book. The Sachakan was sitting in a large wooden chair.

"I have, master," she replied.

"Come here."

His request was spoken quietly, but in the steely tone of a man who expected to be obeyed. With heart racing, Tessia moved to the doorway. The Sachakan smiled and waved a hand.

"All the way here," he said.

Stepping inside the room, she stopped a few paces away from him and concentrated on keeping her face as expressionless as possible.

From behind her came the sound of the door closing firmly. She jumped, her heart skipping a beat. Then she cursed, because she knew she had let fear show on her face. *Let's hope he thought it was surprise*, she told herself. She realised she was breathing too fast, and tried to slow her breaths.

The Sachakan rose and walked towards her, all the while staring into her eyes. Someone had told her once that meeting a Sachakan's eyes was to show him you thought yourself his equal. Unless you were a powerful magician, he might decide to teach you otherwise. She looked down.

"There is a private matter I wish to discuss with you," he told her quietly.

She nodded. "Your slave. He is—"

"No. Something else. I've been watching you. You've got some unique qualities, for a Kyralian. I've noticed nobody here knows your true worth. Am I right? I could change that."

He moved a little closer. Too close. She took a step back. *What game is he playing?* she thought. *Does he think he's so powerful that he can change the way we live here in Kyralia? Or does he think I'd fall for something as stupid as an offer of a better life in Sachaka?*

"If I can't convince anyone here that I can be a healer, I doubt it'll be any different elsewhere, where people don't know me," she told him.

He paused, then chuckled. "Oh, the healing is only part of your worth. The rest of you is being wasted even more. Look at you . . ."

Coming closer again, he reached out and touched the side of her face. She flinched away.

". . . those fine bones. That sleek hair and such pale skin. When I first came here I thought Kyralian women were ugly, but now and then I'd see one that changed my mind. Like you. Your foolish men . . ." His voice had been growing quieter and more intense, and she found herself backing away

37

from hands reaching out to touch her hair . . . snaking round her waist.

"Stop it!" she said, dropping the bag and pushing his hands away.

He paused, then his expression darkened. "Nobody wants what you have, girl. So nobody is going to care if I take it."

Something began to squeeze her from all sides. Looking around, she could not see any sign of the force pressing against her. A relentless pressure at her back pushed her forward. It forced her against the Sachakan, who laughed.

"Lord Dakon," she coughed out. "He won't let you—"

"He's not here. And what's he going to do when he finds out? Punish me? I'll be halfway home by then. How many people do you want knowing, anyway?"

As he plucked at the front of her tunic she tried to move her arms, but some invisible force held them still. She could not move her legs, either. She could not move anything. Not even her head. And as she opened her mouth to yell she felt something invisible envelop it and force her jaw closed again. The Sachakan's grinning, leering face loomed over her. Her skin crawled. Her skull throbbed as if it would burst.

Is he inside my head? She closed her eyes, concentrated on the feeling and tried to push it away.

Get off get off get off GET OFF!

Suddenly the force holding her melted away and she fell backwards. At the same time she felt a sensation of something pouring out of her. A bright, bright light behind her eyelids was followed by a resounding crash.

Tessia felt her back meet the floor. The impact hurt, and her eyes flew open. She scrambled up into a sitting position and then froze as she took in the scene before her. One corner of the room was now a mess of broken furniture. The walls were cracked. Black marks radiated away from her, and she smelled the acrid scent of smoke.

Rapid footsteps echoed from the corridor outside the room.

The Sachakan rose from among the broken mess in the corner. He looked at her, scowling, then down at himself. His clothes were as scorched as the walls, the stitchwork and beading blackened. After brushing at the marks with no effect, his face twisted into a snarl.

The door to the room flew open. Tessia jumped as Lord Dakon stepped inside. He stopped, looking from her to the Sachakan, then at the damage.

"What happened?" he demanded.

The Sachakan said nothing. He smiled, stepped over a broken chair, and strode from the room.

Lord Dakon turned to her. His eyes slid from her face to her chest. Looking down, she realised the front of her dress was unbuttoned to the waist, exposing her undershift. Hastily, she sat up and turned away so he could not see her buttoning it up again.

"What happened?" he asked again, this time more gently.

Tessia drew in a breath to answer, but the words would not come out. *Your guest tried to force himself on me*, she silently told him. But she found the Sachakan had been right. She didn't want anyone to know. Not if there were the slightest chance her mother might hear of it. As her father had always said, there was no such thing as a secret in this tiny community.

And nothing *had* happened. *Well, nothing like what the Sachakan appeared to intend*, she thought. She stood up and glanced at the scorched walls. *I have no idea why he did that.*

Turning back to Dakon, she did not meet his eyes. "I . . . I was rude. He took offence. I'm sorry . . . about the mess, Lord Dakon." She picked up her father's bag and began to turn away, then stopped to add: "The slave is healing well."

He watched her as she walked past him into the corridor, and said nothing. Though she did not risk looking too closely at him for fear of meeting his eyes, there was something odd in the way he stared at her. She hurried to the servants' stairs, and down them. Cannia was in the doorway to the kitchen. The woman said something as Tessia left, but Tessia did not hear properly and did not want to stop.

The late afternoon sunlight was too bright now. Suddenly all Tessia felt was an immense weariness. She hurried along the road to her home, paused to gather her courage before she entered, then opened the door.

Her parents were in the kitchen. They looked up as she entered. Her mother frowned, and her father appeared to suppress a smile as she dropped the bag at his feet.

"The slave is doing well. I'm going to take a nap," she told them, and before they could say anything in reply she strode out of the kitchen and up the stairs. Nobody pursued her. She heard low voices from the kitchen but didn't pause to try to make them out. Entering her room, she threw herself on her bed and, to her surprise, a sob escaped her.

What am I doing? Am I going to cry like a child? She rolled over and took a deep breath, forcing tears away. *Nothing happened.*

But something could have. Her mind veered away from that possibility to a memory of blackened walls. Something else had happened. Not what the Sachakan had intended. Something powerful and destructive. But *what?*

Magic?

Suddenly it all made sense. Lord Dakon. He must have heard something and come to rescue her.

But he didn't arrive until after it happened.

That didn't mean he couldn't have reached out from wherever he had been. It would explain the destruction.

The magician would not have made such a mess of the room if he'd been able to see where he directed his power. He'd been working blindly.

I owe him gratitude for doing so, she thought. *He broke a lot of expensive things to save me. No wonder he stared at me so strangely. He was expecting thanks, and all I did was rush off home.*

After drawing in a deep breath, she let it out slowly. At least she had managed to treat the slave first. Next time she would not be going to the Residence alone. She would stay by her father's side, every moment she was there. Closing her eyes, she surrendered to exhaustion and slept.

CHAPTER 4

Now that the pain had receded a little, Hanara was able to think, though his thoughts were slow and sluggish from the drug the healer woman had given him. He was not sure being able to think was to his advantage, though. There was no direction in which he could set his mind without finding fear and pain.

He never liked to look backwards. The past was stuffed with bad memories, and the good ones left him full of bitterness. His current situation was hardly one he could find pleasant distractions from. Even if moving didn't send agonising pain through his body he couldn't have got out of bed. He was so trussed up with bandages, he might as well have been tied up and gagged.

Considering the future was even more unpleasant. The servant woman who fed him had told him during her last visit that his master had left. Takado was gone, she'd said, declaring he was headed for Sachaka and home.

She had told Hanara he was safe now.

She has no idea, he thought. *None of these Kyralians do, except perhaps the magician, Lord Dakon. Takado will come back. He has to.*

Sachakan magicians never freed ordinary slaves, let alone source slaves. They never left them behind in enemy territory. Not alive, at least.

When he comes back, he'll either take me with him, or kill me.

If Hanara hadn't healed enough by then to be useful to

Takado, then the latter was more likely. No Sachakan magician was going to waste time tending to the wounds of a slave, or wait while that slave struggled to keep up, or put up with a slave too weak or crippled to serve their master properly.

Would the healers have worked so hard, if they knew there was a chance their efforts would be wasted?

Remembering the young woman, Hanara felt a strange constriction inside. Her touch had been gentle, her words kind. A person like her could not exist in his homeland. Only in this country was it possible for a woman her age to be so lacking in guile and bitterness.

She was like all the other good things he had seen in this land, which filled him with longing even as he despised them. He wished Takado had never visited Kyralia. The healer woman and Kyralia were the same: young, free, blissfully unaware of how lucky they were. It was hard to imagine she could ever defend herself against the cruel power of Sachakan magic, yet even his master had admitted that Kyralians could be "annoyingly feisty" when faced with a threat.

Takado. He will be back.

While slaves of Hanara's value weren't common, they were not impossible to replace either. Takado would test all his slaves when he returned home, and would probably find one with enough latent ability to be his new main source of magic. After all, once the man had discovered Hanara's latent ability, he'd made sure his source slave had sired plenty of offspring.

Hanara felt only a faint pity for whichever of his progeny would be chosen. He'd never had the chance to know any of them. He was not even sure which of the child slaves were his. A working slave's life had as many disadvantages as that of a source slave. All slaves' lives were equally likely to end abruptly, whether by accident, overwork, the cruelty of a slave controller or the whim or violent mood swing of their master.

Why should I care who replaces me, anyway? When you're dead, you're dead, he thought. *And if Takado finds another source slave, he'll be more likely to kill me when he returns, if I haven't healed fast or well enough.*

But he couldn't prevent that from happening. He could barely even move. All he could do was lie still and wonder, as he had all his life, if he would survive the next day.

The miniature paintings were quite amazing. Jayan peered at them closely, wondering why he hadn't noticed them before. The woman's tiny eyes even had eyelashes and he wondered what sort of brush could have produced such impossibly thin lines. There was a subtle blush to her cheek. She was quite pretty, he decided.

Where did Lord Dakon find the time to purchase art while entertaining Takado? Or has this always been here, and I've never noticed it?

He nudged a frame with one finger, swinging it slightly across the wall. Beneath was a faint dark shadow where the paint hadn't faded as much as the exposed area around the miniature.

They've been here for years, he mused. *It's as if I've been away for a while. I'm noticing things I've become so accustomed to that I don't see them any more.*

But he hadn't been travelling the country, he'd been stuck in his room. Now, according to Malia, the reason for his imprisonment had ended. The Sachakan magician, Takado, had packed up his few belongings, ordered his horse saddled and his pack horse loaded, and left.

As soon as Jayan had received the news, he had gone in search of Lord Dakon. Moving through the house, he noticed the excited chatter of the servants, adding to the impression that an oppressive force had been lifted from the place. In one room he saw silver tableware being packed away in an ornate cabinet; outside another on the guest floor he passed house servants carrying bedding away to be cleaned.

One of them nodded to a closed door and mouthed a word. *Slave.*

Jayan had looked at the door. So there was still one grim shadow remaining in the Residence. He had been surprised to hear the Sachakan had left his man behind. Perhaps Malia's reports that the slave was healing well were wrong.

He had left searching the guest floor until last. It was possible Malia had been wrong about the Sachakan's leaving. It was also possible Takado had come back, having forgotten something.

I won't feel completely at ease until Dakon confirms Takado is well and truly gone.

The smell of something burnt reached his nose as he continued down the corridor, adding to his growing anxiety. He peered through an open door – and stopped.

"What . . . ?" he muttered.

One corner of the room was a mess. The walls were cracked, and the floor and furniture scorched. He moved to the threshold and stared at the destruction.

"What would you say did this?"

Recognising the voice, Jayan turned to see that Lord Dakon was sitting in a chair facing the mess, his head resting on one hand and his elbow on the arm of the chair. His expression was one of absorbed thoughtfulness.

That side of the room, Jayan noted, hadn't suffered any damage at all. He turned back to examine the damage critically.

"Takado," Jayan replied. The destruction must have a magical

45

cause, and Dakon wouldn't have asked the question if he'd done it himself.

"I thought so too, at first. But it doesn't make sense."

"No? You weren't here at the time, then?"

"No." Dakon rose and looked down at the floor rug. One corner of it had been scorched. He stepped onto the burnt patch and turned round. Then he pointed to the floor a few steps away. "Stand there."

Mystified, Jayan obeyed.

"That's where Tessia was lying."

"Tessia?" Jayan asked. "The healer's daughter?" Then he added. "*Lying?*"

"Yes." Dakon backed away, looking over his shoulder as he stepped over a broken chair. When he was nearly in the corner of the room where the scorching was the worst, he stopped. "This is where Takado was standing when I arrived."

Jayan raised his eyebrows. "What was Tessia doing in the room with Takado?"

"She had come to tend to Hanara."

"Hanara?"

"The slave."

"The slave was in here?"

"No — a few doors down, in the servant's closet."

"So why was she in here, on the floor? Or . . . why was Takado in here with her?" Jayan looked down at his feet, then over at Lord Dakon, and felt a shiver run across his skin as he realised which direction all the scorch marks ran in. "Oh."

Dakon smiled and stepped back over the chair. "Yes. The answer to those questions may be less relevant than their consequences. Whatever the reason those two were in here alone together, with the door closed, the result was something neither expected."

"It left her on the floor and . . ." Jayan look pointedly over

46

Dakon's shoulder, "did that. From the looks of it, I'd say she didn't much like Takado's company."

Which meant Tessia used magic, he thought. *Surely not . . .*

The magician sighed. "We can't dismiss the possibility that the Sachakan arranged this to look that way, so we would jump to conclusions about her. I can't see why – except as a joke. But if he didn't . . ." He shrugged and let the sentence hang.

If he didn't, then Tessia is a natural.

Jayan watched his master closely, trying to judge what the man felt about this unexpected turn of events. By law, Kyralian magicians had to train naturals, no matter who they were, or what social status they had. Dakon did not look dismayed, but he didn't look particularly pleased, either. Instead, he seemed worried. Lines Jayan hadn't noticed before marked his forehead and each side of his mouth. That bothered the apprentice on another level. He had always been smugly relieved to have a teacher young enough to still be active and, well, not a boring, lecturing old man. Though Dakon was eighteen years older than Jayan, his mind was still youthful enough to be interesting, while knowledgeable enough to be a good resource. Jayan enjoyed Dakon's company as much as his lessons.

And what do I think of Tessia joining us? He tried to imagine having the same sorts of conversations with a woman – and commoner – in the room, and couldn't.

Tessia was by no means Dakon's social equal, so perhaps she would not always be a part of their social evenings. *No*, he decided. *She will have lessons separately, too, because they'll be so basic there won't be much point my being there. But she'll demand a lot of Dakon's time.* Abruptly, Jayan realised there was much he disliked about this turn of events. If Dakon had two apprentices, his time would have to be split between them. Unless . . .

"You don't have to take her on," Jayan said, making his tone reassuring. "You could send her to someone else."

Dakon looked up at Jayan and smiled crookedly. "And send her away from her family? No, she stays here," he said firmly. "But her family may not like it. The news must be delivered with some delicacy. Her father is obviously attached to her. To frighten her would be disastrous. Above all we must not give them high hopes then dash them. I have to test her, to be sure she is what she appears to be."

Jayan nodded and turned away to hide his dismay. *I suppose if anyone in the village must turn out to be a natural, at least it's someone who doesn't have to be taught to read and write.* He moved to the chair Dakon had occupied and sat down. Then he smiled. "I wish I could have seen his face."

"Veran's?"

"No, Takado's."

Dakon chuckled and moved to another, slightly scorched, chair. "He wasn't pleased. No, he looked disgusted."

Sachakans hated naturals, Jayan knew. They didn't fit into Sachakan social structure, a problem which was usually more dangerous for the natural than for the master. A person's powers had to be particularly strong to surface on their own, yet no ordinary magician, no matter how powerful, could hope to match the strength of a higher magician, who had taken and stored magic numerous times from their slaves or apprentices. But a trained magician was much more dangerous to keep as a slave than an untrained latent. Sachakan naturals were too much trouble, and therefore doomed to die, if not killed by a magician then when they eventually lost control of their powers.

"It's fortunate that I discovered them when I did," Dakon added. "I suspect he would have killed her, and expected me to thank him for doing me a favour."

Jayan shuddered. "And risk the uncontrolled release of her power when she died?"

"No risk if he drained her of power first." Dakon sighed. "Takado knows I would have dealt with her before now if she had already shown signs of natural ability, so he could safely assume her power must only just be surfacing, and not be particularly dangerous."

Jayan looked at the scorched and cracked wall. "That's not dangerous?"

"It would be to a non-magician," Dakon agreed. "It's mostly cosmetic, though. Not much force behind it, or she'd have blown a hole in the wall."

"How much damage would she have done if she'd been at the point of losing control completely?"

"The whole house. Maybe the village. Naturals are usually stronger than the average magician. Some have even suggested that those of us who would never have gained access to our power without help from our masters were never meant to be magicians."

"The whole village." Jayan swallowed, his throat suddenly dry. "When are you going to test her?"

Dakon sighed, then rose to his feet. "The sooner the better. I'll give her a little time to get over the shock of what happened, then pay her family a visit, probably after dinner. I suspect she'd think me neglectful if I didn't at least check to see if she was all right." He strode to the door.

"Do you want me to come with you?"

"No." Dakon smiled in gratitude. "The fewer scary magicians in her house the better."

Then he turned and headed down the corridor.

CHAPTER 5

The house in which Healer Veran lived with his family was one of three that Dakon's father had ordered constructed over thirty years before, to attract skilled men to the village. Looking at the simple, sturdy building with a critical eye, Dakon was happy to see it was showing no outward signs of decay. He relied on the occupants to tell him when repairs were needed. Sometimes villagers were too shy, proud, or even ignorant to ask for work to be done and as a result some of the houses hadn't been as well maintained as they ought to have been.

Dakon's and Veran's fathers had been close friends for many years. Lord Yerven had met the opinionated Healer Berin in Imardin, and been so impressed by him that he offered him a position in his ley. Dakon had grown up not realising that their friendship was unusual for two men of different status and age. The twelve years' difference in age was the lesser barrier since both men were in their middle to later years, but a close friendship that lasted when one was a subordinate and the other the local magician and lord was rare.

Dakon's father had died five years ago, at the age of seventy-seven, and Berin had passed away less than a year later. Though Yerven had children late in life, and the difference in age between Dakon and Veran was smaller than that between their fathers, they had never been more than acquaintances.

We may not be close friends but we have a respect for each other,

50

Dakon thought now. *At least, I hope he knows how much I value him.* He lifted a hand to knock on the door, then froze. *Should I tell him what I suspect brought about Tessia's possible use of magic?*

No, he decided. *I can't be sure what she and Takado were doing, although I doubt Tessia initiated or welcomed it. Even so, I should leave it to Tessia to decide how much anyone learns of the matter. And I might be wrong. It's always possible, though highly unlikely, she approached him.*

He knocked, and after a short wait the door opened. Tessia's mother, Lasia, answered. She lifted a small lamp.

"Lord Dakon," she said. "Would you like to come in?"

"Yes, thank you," he replied. Stepping inside, he looked through an open door to the right and saw a homely kitchen with freshly washed dishes on the table. The door opposite was closed, but he knew from past visits that Veran's work-room was beyond. Berin had used the room for the same purpose. Lasia knocked on the door and called out to her husband. A muffled reply came from within.

"Come into the seating room, Lord Dakon," she urged, leading him to the end of the short corridor, where she opened another door and stepped back to let him pass through. He entered a small, slightly musty-smelling room containing a few old chairs and some sturdy wooden chests and tables. Following him in, Lasia bade him take a chair, then lit another lamp. Footsteps in the corridor heralded Veran's arrival.

"Is Tessia here?" Dakon asked.

Lasia nodded. "She's asleep. I looked in on her before dinner, but she didn't wake up. She's clearly exhausted."

Dakon nodded. *Should I ask them to rouse her? If I tell them without her, I'll have to explain it all again to Tessia.* But she probably needed the sleep, after all the work of the night before, and the surprises of the day.

"Tessia came to the Residence earlier," he began.

"Yes. We're sorry about that," Lasia interrupted. "She should have waited for her father, but we were asleep and I expect she thought she was doing Veran a favour. Sometimes I think she has no grasp of proper manners, or, worse, she knows but chooses to—"

"I have no problem with her coming alone to the Residence," Dakon assured her. "That is not why I am here."

Veran had laid a hand on his wife's arm during her outburst. Now he looked at Dakon, his eyebrows rising.

"Is it the slave? Has his condition worsened?"

"No." Dakon shook his head. "He is awake and has managed to eat some broth. Tessia said he was healing well." He paused. "It is what happened afterwards that I must talk to you about."

The couple exchanged a glance, then looked at Dakon expectantly.

"On her way out of the Residence Tessia was . . . surprised by my guest," Dakon continued. "The Sachakan. I think he gave her a fright. She may or may not have done something quite extraordinary in reaction."

Lasia's eye widened. Veran frowned. "What do you mean?"

"I think she used magic."

For a long moment the couple stared at him, then as realisation came a grin broke out on Veran's face. Lasia had turned pale, but suddenly she flushed a bright red and her eyes brightened with excitement. By then, Veran had smothered his smile and become serious.

"You're not sure, are you?" he asked.

Dakon shook his head. "No. It is possible Takado made it appear she had used magic, as some kind of strange joke. But it is—"

"I thought *you* did it!"

Everybody jumped. The voice, female and full of surprise,

came from the doorway. They all turned to find Tessia standing there. She stared at Lord Dakon. "So it was *him*?"

"Tessia!" Lasia exclaimed. "Use Lord Dakon's name when you address him."

The young woman glanced at her mother, then gave Dakon an apologetic look. "Sorry, Lord Dakon."

He chuckled. "Apology accepted. Actually, I'm here to establish whether or not *you* used magic this morning."

She looked suddenly uncomfortable. "It wasn't me . . . was it?"

"It is possible. We'll know for sure if I test you."

"How . . . how do you do that?"

"An untrained natural magician cannot prevent magic from straying from their mind. I should be able to detect it with a light search."

"Mind-reading?" Her eyes widened.

"No, there's no need for me to enter your mind, just sit at the edges and look for leakage."

"Leakage?" Veran looked at his daughter. "You magicians have some interesting terms. Not particularly reassuring ones."

"They shouldn't be, in this case," Dakon told him. "There is another way to learn whether Tessia can use magic: wait until she uses it again. It tends to lead to expensive house repairs and redecoration costs, so I don't recommend it."

Tessia looked at the floor. "Sorry about that — if it was me."

Dakon smiled at her. "I never liked the colours in that room, anyway. The pink was too . . . orange." She did not smile, and he realised she was too nervous to find any humour in the situation.

"So . . . what do I do?" she asked.

He looked around, then with magic drew one of the smaller chairs round to face his. Veran chuckled and gave Dakon a knowing look. The small reminder of what Tessia might be able to do if she co-operated wasn't lost on the healer.

"You'll find it more comfortable if you sit," Dakon invited. Tessia obeyed. "Close your eyes and try to still and calm your mind. That's probably not easy right now, but you must try. It helps if you breathe slowly."

She did as he suggested. Aware of her parents watching, he placed his fingers gently on either side of her brow and closed his own eyes. He sent his mind forth.

It took only a moment to find what he sought. Magic was flowing from her, gently but with occasional small bursts suggesting greater power within. Truly the term "leakage" was a good one to describe what he sensed. It wasn't meant to suggest the drip from a small vessel, but instead the escaping water from cracks in a dam. Cracks that warned of imminent failure, and of flooding and destruction of all in its path.

Releasing Tessia, he opened his eyes. Her own flew open and she stared at him expectantly. As always, it amazed him that a mere person, a human, could contain such power. Like all new apprentices, she had no grasp of her own potential. Not even the most educated, ambitious apprentice truly appreciated the limitless possibilities it offered, or the inescapable limitations it imposed.

"Yes, you have magical ability," he told her. "Plenty of it, from what I saw."

Her parents both let out the breaths they'd been holding, then Lasia burst into chatter.

"Of all the things . . . what amazing luck! This couldn't have come at a better time. She's not ready to marry, sweet thing, and this will give her the time to – and what a husband she might attract now. Oh! But how long until she can marry? I expect she has to become a magician first. What—"

"*Mother!*" burst from Tessia. "Stop talking about me as if I'm not here!"

Lasia paused, then patted her daughter's hand apologetically. "Sorry, dear. But I'm excited for you. No more . . ." She looked at her husband. "No more silly ideas about you becoming a healer."

Veran frowned, then turned to Dakon. "I expect Tessia will have to move into the Residence."

Dakon considered, then nodded. "It would be better if she did. Especially at the beginning, when she has little control over her power. If I'm there when she uses it, I can minimise the damage."

"Of course," Veran said. "I would ask a favour, though. I was considering taking a boy of the village to be my apprentice. It seems I must, now. But it will take time to train him to even half of Tessia's level of skill, knowledge and experience. Might I borrow her now and then?"

Dakon smiled. "Of course. After all the good work you've done, I can hardly begrudge you that."

"Could . . . ?" Tessia began, then faltered at a stern look from her mother. When she didn't continue, Dakon gestured that she should. She sighed. "Can a magician still study and practise healing?"

"No, Tessia, it's—" her mother began.

"Of course," Dakon replied. "Most magicians have personal interests, and pet projects. But," he added, "your first priority at this point is to learn to control that power of yours. It is what we magicians call the price of magic. You must learn control because if you don't, your magic will eventually kill you. And when it does it will destroy not only you, but a great deal of whatever surrounds you. With the strength of your power, it's unlikely it would be just a room."

Tessia's eyes went wide. Her parents exchanged a grim look. She swallowed and nodded. "Then I had better learn fast."

Dakon smiled. "I'm sure you will. But I'm afraid you won't have many chances to indulge interests or pet projects fully until you are an actual magician, and that usually takes years of study."

Her shoulders dropped a little, but her lips compressed into a smile of determination. "I'm good at study," she told him. "And fast. Aren't I, Father?"

Veran laughed. "You do well enough, though I think if you saw how much study an entrant to the healing university had to do, you wouldn't be so sure of yourself. I don't know if a magician's apprentice faces as much hard work?" He looked at Dakon questioningly.

"I doubt it," Dakon admitted. "We prefer a steady pace. It's vital to ensure every lesson is well understood before proceeding to the next. Hasty learning can lead to mistakes, and magical mistakes tend to be more spectacular than healing mistakes. My father used to use that reasoning to explain why apprentices of magic drink far less than the students of healing."

Veran grinned. "'Healers wake up with a sore head', he used to say; 'magicians wake up with a sore head, our toes burned black and the roof on the floor.'"

"Oh dear," Lasia said, rolling her eyes. "Here they go. Just like their fathers."

Tessia was looking from Dakon to her father and back with a bemused expression. Dakon sobered. The girl was probably still stunned by the news she was going to be a magician. She needed time to think about her future, and would probably appreciate some time with her family before stepping into her new life.

"So, when do you want to take my daughter off my hands?" Veran asked, his thoughts obviously following the same track.

"Tomorrow?" Dakon suggested. Veran looked at Lasia, who nodded.

"Any particular time?"

"No. Whenever it suits you all." Dakon paused. "Though it would be a fine excuse for a celebratory meal, I think. Why don't you bring her over a few hours before dusk? Tessia can settle into her new home, then you can all join Jayan and me for a meal."

Lasia's eyes brightened and she looked eagerly at Veran. The healer nodded. "We would be honoured."

Dakon rose. "I'll leave you to make your arrangements, then. I must let the servants know there'll be a new pupil in the Residence tomorrow, and Cannia will probably want plenty of notice to plan the meal." As the others stood up, he smiled. "It's an unexpected turn of events, but a pleasant one for all, I hope. Don't worry about Tessia's gaining control of her powers. It's a part of the training that we all begin with, whether our powers develop naturally or with help." He looked at Tessia. "You'll have mastered it in no time."

Sitting in the window casement, Tessia watched her mother carefully folding clothes and arranging them with numerous other things in a trunk. The room smelled of the trunk's fragrant, resinous wood, which was not unpleasant but still alien, like a stranger come into her private space.

Her mother straightened and regarded her handiwork, then huffed and waved her hands as a thought struck her. Without an explanation, she bustled out of the room.

Tessia looked outside. The world glistened as afternoon sunshine set droplets from the recent rain shower alight. Below, the vegetable patch looked near empty, but if she looked closely she could see that the beds containing winter crops had a thin green pelt of new shoots, the plants within them happy to get a regular soaking.

Hearing footsteps coming up the stairs, Tessia looked

towards the doorway. Her father smiled and came into the room. She noted the wrinkles round his eyes and mouth, and the slight stoop of his shoulders. It wasn't the first time she'd noticed them, and as always they roused a wistful sadness. *He isn't growing any younger. But neither is anyone, really.*

His gaze moved to the trunk. "Are you ready, do you think?"

She shrugged. "Only Mother could tell you that."

He smiled crookedly. "Indeed. But are *you* ready? Have you got used to the idea of becoming a magician yet?"

Sighing, she moved from the casement to the bed.

"Yes. No. I don't know. Must I move into the Residence?"

He looked at her silently for a moment before answering. "Yes. If your magic is as dangerous as Lord Dakon says, he probably wants to put you somewhere others aren't at risk. It will be easier for him to protect everyone if you're close by."

"But I won't be coming back after I've learned to control it," she said.

He met her eyes and shook his head. "I doubt it. You have much to learn."

"I could still live here and visit the Residence for lessons."

"You're a magician's apprentice now," another voice replied. Tessia looked up at her mother, who stood in the doorway of the room. "It's appropriate to your status that you move into the Residence."

Tessia looked away. She didn't care about status, but there was no point arguing. Other people did, so it had to be taken into account. Instead she turned to her father again. "You will send for me if you need me, won't you? You won't hesitate because you're worried about interrupting lessons or something?"

"Of course not," he assured her. Then he smiled. "I promise

to send for you when I need you so long as you trust me to judge whether I truly need you – and you promise not to skip lessons."

"Father!" Tessia protested. "I am not a child any more."

"No, but I know you'll find perfectly adult reasons to place higher priority on helping people than on learning magic." His expression became serious. "There are other ways to help the village, Tessia, and magic is one of them. It is more important because it is rare, and because we live so close to the border. You may one day save more locals by defending us than by healing us."

"I doubt it," she scoffed. "The Sachakans wouldn't bother conquering Kyralia again."

"Not if there are powerful magicians protecting our borders."

Tessia grimaced. "I don't think any amount of training would make me a fighter, Father. It's not what I'm good at."

I'm good at healing, she wanted to say. But though she would have expected to be dismayed at discovering she must become a magician, she wasn't. *Maybe because it doesn't mean all my hopes of becoming a healer must end*, she thought. *They've been delayed, that's all. All I have to do is learn everything I need to know to become a magician, then I'll be free to become a healer. Much freer than I was before, because magicians can do whatever they like. Well, so long as they're not breaking laws.*

Perhaps learning magic would show her other ways to help people. Perhaps magic could be used to heal. The possibilities were exciting.

"It's not up to you to decide what you're good at now," her mother said sternly. "Lord Dakon could hardly have planned to end up with another apprentice. You are not to waste his time or resources, you hear?"

Tessia smiled. "Yes, Mother."

Her father cleared his throat. "Time to carry this down-stairs yet?"

"No." Her mother's frown disappeared. "There's this to go in." In her hand was a flat box, the size of a thin book. Instead of putting it in the trunk, she handed it to Tessia.

As Tessia took it she felt a shock of recognition. "Your necklace? Why? For safe-keeping?"

"For you to wear," her mother corrected her. "I was going to wait until you showed some interest in attracting a husband before giving it to you . . . but it looks as if that will have to wait. You'll be needing something to wear now that you'll be associating with rich and influential people."

"But . . . it's *yours*. Father gave it to you." She glanced at her father and saw that he had an approving, almost smug, look on his face.

"And now it's yours," her mother said firmly. "Besides, it looks ridiculous on me now. It suits a younger face." She took the box from Tessia and placed it in the trunk, then shut the lid.

Tessia opened her mouth to protest, then closed it again. She knew she would not win this argument. Perhaps another time, when her mother was in a different mood, she would persuade her to take back the necklace. It was ridiculous, this idea that she would need it to impress rich and influential people. Nobody in the village could be considered that way except one person: Lord Dakon.

Then an uncomfortable feeling came over her.

Surely Mother isn't . . . she couldn't be . . . there's no way she would . . . the age difference is . . .

But she knew her mother all too well.

It's too obvious to deny. She closed her eyes and cursed silently. *Mother is hoping I'll marry Lord Dakon.*

CHAPTER 6

"Well, don't you look fancy."

Jayan turned to find Malia standing in the doorway of his room. She looked down at his clothes and her eyebrows rose. "Is that the latest fashion in Imardin, then?"

He chuckled and smoothed his clothing. The robe was nearly long enough to touch the floor and all but covered the matching trousers he wore underneath. Both were dark green and the fine material they were made from had a slight shine to it.

"It's what's been worn there for the last twenty years," he told Malia. "Hardly the *latest* fashion."

"By both men and women?"

"No, just men."

Her eyebrows managed to rise even higher. "I'd love to see what the women wear, then."

"You wouldn't believe what your eyes were seeing – and don't ask me to describe it. I'd have to learn a whole new vocabulary first."

Her brows finally came back to a normal level as she grinned. "If I hadn't seen Lord Dakon wearing much the same thing, I'd have wondered about you, Apprentice Jayan. Don't go walking out in the village like that or people will be talking about you from here to the mountains. As for your guests . . . they hid their surprise very well when they saw Lord Dakon." She paused. "They're all in the dining room, by the way."

In other words, "You're late", he thought. "I was about to join them," he said. "Until I was delayed by a nosy servant, that is."

She rolled her eyes to the ceiling, then took the hint and strode away.

Looking down at himself, he adjusted the sash, tugged a few creases out of the robe, then followed her down the corridor. He eyed the doorway at the end. Earlier that morning the servants had opened up the unused room beyond, cleaned it and moved furniture in and out. Later in the day Jayan had heard voices through his own closed door. He hadn't gone out to greet Tessia and her family. They had more immediate things to be concerned about than meeting Dakon's apprentice. Dakon's *other* apprentice.

The truth was, Jayan hadn't wanted to go out and meet them. He was not sure why. *I don't dislike Tessia or her family personally. Nor do I particularly like them, or want to gain their favour.* It was more important, he had decided, that he spend his time studying than being sociable. The sooner he became a magician the more time Tessia would have from Dakon, after all.

It wasn't as if she was from some important and powerful family that he might want to establish and maintain friendly relations with. She wasn't a land servant or crafter's daughter, thankfully, but she wasn't a woman of influence or connections either. Becoming a magician would elevate her, but it wouldn't make her the equal of other magicians.

Which is why this is unfair on Dakon. He won't be gaining any of the good connections or favours owed from training her as he did by taking on my training . . . except, perhaps, respect for what might be seen as an admirable act of charity. If not that, then sympathy for having to obey the law on naturals.

Would people be as sympathetic towards Tessia? With no influential or wealthy family behind her, she would hardly attract much favour among the powerful men and women of Kyralia. It was unlikely that the king or anyone else would give her any important position or task to perform. Without such a wage or work she'd never make much of an income. All this would not make her a desirable wife, so she wasn't going to attract a husband of influence or wealth either.

She might, with hard work and time, gain a few allies and friends, and slowly prove herself worthy of work with a decent income. And someone might marry her hoping her offspring would prove magically strong.

But neither would ever happen if she stayed in isolated Mandryn.

Another option came to Jayan's mind, then. There were cases in history of apprentices who did not become higher magicians. She could choose to remain in service to Dakon, giving him magical strength, and in return he would give her a place to live and possibly a small sum to live on after he died.

Jayan felt an unexpected sympathy for her then. She probably had no idea where her natural powers were going to lead her. She could become trapped in a social limbo, caught between the advantages of magic and its inescapable limitations.

At the bottom of the stairs it was a short walk down a corridor to the dining room. Entering, Jayan was amused at the relief he felt on seeing Lord Dakon wearing the same style of dress as he. Dakon's robe was black with fine stitch-work. The magician was standing with his guests. He looked up and acknowledged Jayan with a nod as he finished what he was saying to Veran's family.

Healer Veran wore a simple tunic and trousers typical of the local men, but made of a finer cloth. His wife – *what is her name?* – wore a plain dark blue tunic dress that did nothing to make her look womanly. Tessia's dress was almost as ugly, its severity tempered only because it was a more appealing dark red. The young woman's necklace, though simple, also relieved some of the unflattering impact of her garb.

Dakon now gestured to Jayan. "This is my apprentice, Jayan of Drayn. Jayan, you know Healer Veran. This is his wife, Lasia. And this is Tessia, your new fellow apprentice."

Jayan made a short, polite bow. "Welcome, Apprentice Tessia," he said. "Healer Veran, Lasia. A pleasure to have your company tonight."

Dakon smiled approvingly then directed the guests to their seats. Lasia and Tessia started in surprise as a gong positioned on a side table rang.

Soon the room filled with servants carrying plates and bowls, jugs and glasses. A generous spread of food covered the table. Dakon picked up a pair of carving knives and began to slice the meat for his guests.

The kitchen servants had done a fine job, Jayan noted. As Dakon sliced through a glistening roll of roasted, golden skin he revealed many-layered circles of different meats and vegetables. Once he had finished he urged his guests to help themselves, then turned to a larger haunch of enka. Ribbons of dark marin fruit syrup oozed from within the rare meat. Next, he expertly chopped up cakes made of different root vegetables, layered to form decorative patterns when cut, and quartered juicy yellow and green cabbas stuffed with a frothy herbed mix of bread and eggs.

This is such a strange tradition, Jayan mused. *I wonder if it was introduced by the Sachakans, or harks back to an earlier age in Kyralia. It's supposed to be a demonstration of humility from the host, but I suspect it's really meant to show off his prowess with knives.*

Dakon certainly gave the impression of being well practised, which was surprising considering how rarely he gave formal dinners. Watching his master closely, Jayan decided the man actually enjoyed the task. He wondered if this love of chopping things up would surface should Dakon ever find himself in a fight.

At last Dakon had finished. Conversation as they ate was sporadic and concerned the quality of local and imported produce, the weather and other general topics. Jayan glanced at Tessia now and then. She was not pretty, he decided, but neither was she ugly. Young women in the ley were likely to be either slim and hard-muscled from work, or buxom and generous like some of the Residence's house servants or crafters' wives. Tessia was neither skinny or curvaceous, as far as he could tell.

She did not speak, just listened and watched Lord Dakon with obvious restrained curiosity. The magician might have noticed this, as he began to ask her direct questions.

"If there is anything any of you wish to know," he said as the meal ended, "be it about magic or magicians or apprenticeship, please ask. I will do my best to answer."

The healer and his family exchanged glances. Veran opened his mouth to speak, then closed it and looked at Tessia.

"I think my daughter's questions should come first, since she is the one who is to learn magic."

Tessia smiled faintly at her father, then frowned as she gathered her thoughts.

"Where does the body generate magic?" she asked. "Is it stored in the brain or the heart?"

Dakon chuckled. "Ah, that is a question asked often and never properly answered. I believe the source is the brain, but there are some who are convinced it comes from the heart. Since the brain generates thoughts, and the heart emotions, it makes more sense that magic comes from the brain. Magic responds to our mental command and control. We have little control of what we feel – though we can control how we act in response to our feelings. If magic responded to emotion we'd have no control of it at all."

Tessia leaned forward. "So . . . how does the body generate magic?"

"An even greater mystery," Dakon told her. "Some believe that it is the result of friction caused by all the rhythms in the body: blood pulsing through pulse paths, breath through the lungs."

Tessia frowned. "Does that mean people with magical ability have a faster pulse and breathing rate?"

"No," Veran answered for Dakon. "But since some substances create friction more easily than others, perhaps a magician's blood is different somehow and more able to create friction." He shrugged. "It is a strange idea, and one my father didn't think much of."

"Nor of the theory of the stars," Dakon said, smiling.

"Even less so," Veran agreed, chuckling. "Which almost lost him his membership of the Healers' Guild."

"How so?" Jayan asked, noticing that everyone wore the same knowing smile. Either losing membership of the Healers' Guild wasn't as grave a downfall as he'd thought, or there was more to this story.

Dakon looked at Jayan. "Healer Berin declared that the timing of the stars and seasons had no bearing on health, illness and death, but was only useful as an excuse for healers to fall back on when incompetent."

"I can see how that might upset a few people," Jayan said.

"It did, and a few of them made life so difficult for Berin that when my father offered him a position here he was happy to take it."

"It also helped that they were friends," Veran added.

Lasia cleared her throat. "There is something I'd like to know."

Dakon turned to regard her. "What is that?"

"Is there any difference between a natural magician and a normal one?"

"Other than the natural's power developing spontaneously, and that it is usually stronger than the average magician's, there is no difference. Most magicians' ability is discovered when they are tested at a young age, then developed with the help of another magician. If any of those magicians are naturals, we'd never know because their power never gets the chance to develop without assistance. For magical ability to surface with no intervention, it must be strong, but ultimately that strength will not matter much. Higher magic adds to a magician's natural ability, so in the end it's how many apprentices a magician has taken power from, and how many times, that dictates his strength, not his natural ability."

"So you don't usually know a person has magical ability until you test them?" Veran asked.

Dakon shook his head. "And magic does not favour rich or poor, powerful or humble. Anybody you pass on the road could be a latent magician."

"So why don't you teach them?" Lasia asked. "Surely having more magicians would make Kyralia better able to defend itself."

"Who would teach them? There aren't enough magicians to teach all the latent magicians among the rich, let alone commoners as well."

"You might not want to teach all of them, anyway," Veran added, his expression thoughtful. "I'm sure you consider character when you select an apprentice, even if he or she is from a powerful family." He glanced at Tessia. "When you have a choice, of course."

Dakon smiled. "You are right. Fortunately Tessia is of excellent character and I'm sure will be a pleasure to teach."

Everyone looked at Tessia. Jayan saw her face flush and she dropped her gaze.

"I'm sure she will be," Lasia said. "She has been a great help to her father." She looked at Dakon. "What does being a source for a magician involve?"

Watching Dakon, Jayan saw the humour in the magician's eyes vanish, though he remained smiling.

"I can't give you details, of course, as higher magic is a secret shared only between magicians. I can tell you it is a quick, co-operative ritual. Magic is transferred from apprentice to magician, and stored by the magician."

"This giving of power is the only payment Tessia makes in exchange for apprenticeship?"

"Yes, and as you can imagine it is more than payment enough. By the time an apprentice is ready to become a magician, he or she will have made their master many hundreds of times stronger than he would be without their help. Of course, we aren't usually hundreds of times stronger by then, because we will have used that power in the meantime, but it does allow us to do many things."

"Why don't magicians have several apprentices?" Tessia asked. "Then they would have even more power."

"Because it would take even longer to train each of them," Dakon replied. "One magician has only so much time to spend teaching, and we have an obligation to instruct our apprentices well and thoroughly. Remember, most of our apprentices come from powerful families who can influence whether or not we are given well-paid work to do, or remain the lords of our leys. We don't usually want to annoy them." He paused and grimaced. "And I think having several apprentices, no matter how well I taught them, would make me feel too much like a Sachakan magician, with a crowd of slaves to abuse." He looked at Jayan. "No, I much prefer the Kyralian method of mutual respect and benefits."

The others nodded in agreement. Dakon looked at each of them in turn. "Any more questions?"

Tessia shifted in her seat, attracting his attention.

"Yes?" he asked.

She looked at her father, then flushed again. "Can magic be used to heal?"

Dakon gave her a knowing smile. "Only by helping in the physical tasks of healing work. It can move, hold, warm or sear. It can provide constriction in place of a pulse binder and I've even heard of it being used to jolt a heart into beating after it stopped. But it cannot assist the body to actually heal. The body must do that itself."

Tessia nodded, and Jayan thought he detected disappointment in her eyes. *I'm surprised she's still interested in healing, now that she has magic to learn.*

"On the other hand, it might be possible and we just haven't discovered how yet," Dakon added. Tessia looked at him, her expression thoughtful. "I don't think we should ever stop trying."

Jayan looked at Dakon in surprise. *He's actually encouraging her. What point is there in that?*

As he watched, Tessia's shoulders relaxed and she gave Dakon a smile of gratitude. It occurred to Jayan then that Dakon might only be making the transition easier for her by holding out the promise of something familiar in the strange new world she was entering. Something to interest her.

But surely he didn't have to. Surely she was as excited to be learning magic as any new apprentice. The thought that she might not be sent a thin ripple of anger through him. *That would be incredibly ungrateful, both to the natural luck that has given her such a chance, and to Lord Dakon for taking her on.* He found himself scowling and quickly relaxed his face. *Once she begins to use magic, and realises how wonderful it is, she'll soon put her old life behind her. Healing will be nothing in comparison.*

Immensely tall trees surrounded Hanara. He looked up. The straight, narrow trunks swayed, slow and heavy, in winds high above their heads. A warning cry. One began to fall. Someone screamed as it broke through the branches of neighbouring trees and slammed onto the forest floor, splinters from where the axes hadn't quite cut through the trunk flying through the air. The screaming continued. He rushed in. Branches parted, and he saw. A slave – his friend – pinned to the ground, his legs crushed. The other slaves ignored the injured man and his screams, and set to work cutting.

Hanara jolted awake. For a moment he blinked at the darkness. The air smelled wrong.

Kyralia, he remembered. *I'm in Kyralia, in the house of a magician. I'm hurt. Must heal quickly so Takado doesn't kill me when he comes back.* He closed his eyes.

He was cutting and shaping wood. He loved how it peeled away under the blade. Once you understood the patterns of the grain, how it resisted some cuts and welcomed others, it was easy work. All the information you needed was there, written in the grain. He imagined reading was the same.

He heard the timber master come up behind him to watch. He couldn't see the man, but he knew who it was. If he stopped to look, the man would whip him, so he kept working. Perhaps if Hanara demonstrated how he could read the wood, the man would teach him how to do the decorative work on the mansion rather than making palings for the slavehouse fences.

A few more cuts and the paling was done. It was perfect, too good for a mere slave fence. He turned to show the timber master.

It wasn't the timber master standing behind him. It was Ashaki

Takado. Hanara froze, his heart suddenly beating wildly, then dropped to the ground. The magician, owner of the house and slaves and forest and fields, stepped close and ordered Hanara to stand up, then stared into his face. Hanara lowered his eyes. The magician grabbed his jaw and lifted it, his gaze boring into Hanara's. But the magician's gaze didn't meet Hanara's. It went beyond. Inside. Takado's eyes blazed.

Then the master was gone. The plank was removed from Hanara's hand and he was taken away from the slave yard. His arms hurt. The world whirled around him. Looking down, he saw that his skin was criss-crossed by countless scars and new bleeding cuts. Takado was looming over him, laughing.

Are you a good slave? *he asked.* Are you? *He raised an arm, in his hands a glittering curved blade . . .*

Hanara jolted awake again, but this time he found himself stiff, in pain and breathing hard. *Kyralia. House of a magician. Hurt. Must heal before Takado—* He heard voices and a shiver ran down his spine. The voices came closer. Stopped outside the door to his room.

He took slow, deep breaths and willed his heart to stop racing. It refused.

The door creaked open and light spilled in. Hanara recognised the healer, the young woman who assisted him, and Lord Dakon. He sank into the bed with relief.

"Sorry for waking you, Hanara," the healer said. "Since I was here, I thought I'd check on you. How are you feeling?"

Hanara looked at all the expectant faces, then reluctantly croaked an answer.

"Better."

The healer nodded. His daughter smiled. Seeing the warmth in her eyes, Hanara felt his heart constrict again. Looking at her was not unlike watching a newborn slave child, vulnerable and ignorant. But when looking at the slave child, he

71

also felt sympathy and sadness. He knew the hardship and pain it would face and hoped that it would be strong enough, and lucky enough, to achieve a feeling of long-life.

Hanara did not yet feel he'd reached long-life. It was a state, slaves said, where you felt satisfied you had lived long enough. Where you didn't feel cheated if you died. You might not have had an easy life, or a happy one, but you'd had your measure. Or you had made a difference to the world, even a small one, because you had existed.

He'd known slaves who had said they'd reached that state in under twenty years, and old slaves who still didn't feel they'd achieved it yet. Some said it came when they'd sired or birthed a child. Some said it happened when they had completed the best work they'd ever done. Some said it was an unexpected benefit of helping another slave. Some even said it came from serving their master well and loyally.

It was said most slaves never felt it. Hanara hadn't felt it even when a child he suspected he'd fathered had been born. He'd never had a chance to make his best work with wood. He'd helped other slaves in only minor ways, which didn't give him any great feeling of satisfaction. Serving Takado was probably the only chance he'd have of feeling long-life. Ironically, it was also likely to lead to his dying before he had that chance.

And what chance was there now that he was stuck in Kyralia?

As the healer fussed and poked at Hanara he asked many questions. Hanara said as little as possible. Though none of the questions were about anything but his wounds and his health, he could never be sure whether he was revealing anything he shouldn't. Takado had warned him of that, before they came to Kyralia.

Eventually the healer turned to the magician.

"He's healing fast. Better than I expected. I have no doubts now that he'll recover. It's quite extraordinary."

The magician's lips thinned into a wry smile. "Hanara was Takado's source slave. Though he cannot use his magic, it still gives him the same advantages of fast healing and resilience that all magicians enjoy."

The healer nodded. "Lucky man."

"So this healing is automatic?" the young woman asked. "Unconscious?"

The magician smiled at her. "Yes. You have this ability, too. Have you not always healed quickly, and rarely sickened?"

She paused at that, as if it had only just occurred to her, then nodded. "So if we could find a way to consciously heal, could we apply it to others?"

"Maybe," the magician replied. "Magicians must have tried it before, but with no success, so I doubt it is easy – if it is possible at all."

Her eyes shifted to Hanara. He could tell her attention was more on whatever thoughts this discussion had stirred than on himself. The magician followed her gaze, then met Hanara's eyes.

"Sounds like you'll be up and about soon, Hanara," he said. "Takado said that if you recovered I could do whatever I wished with you. Since slavery is outlawed here, that means you can no longer be a slave." He smiled. "You are free."

A thrill ran through Hanara. Free? Could he really stay here, in this dream-like land of gentle people? Would he be given reward in return for work, and choose what to do with it – to travel, to learn to read, to form bonds with people . . . have friends, a woman who wasn't indifferent to him, children he could raise in kindness and have some hope of protecting from—

No. A wave of sickening realisation brought him back to reality. *Takado only said Lord Dakon could do whatever he wanted with me because if he had revealed he was coming back for me, Lord Dakon might have tried to hide me away.*

He might still, if Hanara told him the truth.

He wouldn't do it well enough, because he doesn't know Takado. Takado loves a hunt. He will track me down. He'll find me. He'll read my mind and find out I ran away from him. Then he'll kill me. No. I'm better off waiting until he returns.

And enjoying what freedom he could have in the meantime. But at that thought his stomach sank again.

Or does he expect me to go home as soon as I'm able to? Will he only return here if I don't? Only punish me if I stay here?

The visitors were leaving now. Hanara watched them go, envying them their freedom, yet at the same time despising them for their ignorance. They knew nothing. They were fools. Takado would return.

CHAPTER 7

After opening her eyes the next morning, Tessia spent a long moment lying in bed gazing at the room she had slept in.

She could not quite believe it was hers.

The walls were painted the colour of a summer sky. A nightwood screen covered the enormous window. The large chests, cupboards, desk, chair and bed were made of the same rare and expensive timber. The covering on her bed was quilted and made of the softest cloth she had ever touched, and the mattress beneath was even and slightly spongy.

Framed paintings hung from the walls. All were landscapes, and she recognised most of the settings as local. A small vase contained some field herbs, their zesty fragrance lightening the air.

The fireplace was as large as the one in the kitchen of her home.

This is my home now. That she should have to remind herself of this now seemed terribly predictable, but also incredible. *I bet I have to say that to myself many, many more mornings before this place starts to feel like home.*

She sat up. Nobody had told her what routine she should follow or expect. Lord Dakon hadn't even told her when she should present herself for her first lesson.

Lying in bed was not her habit so she got up and wandered around the room in her nightshift examining its furnishings and unpacking some of her belongings from her trunk. One of the room's chests held books, a folder of parchment and writing tools. The books were histories, magical texts and even a few of the novels written for entertainment that her father had once described to her.

He'd had a low opinion of the latter. She'd never read one, so she picked up the first and started to read.

When the knock came at the door she found she was already a quarter of the way through the book. It was as frivolous as her father had described, yet she was enjoying it. While the escapades of the characters were unbelievable, she found the minor details of life in the city of Imardin fascinating. The lives of these men and women did not hang on the success of crops or the health of livestock, but on wise alliances with honourable men and women, the favour of the king, and a good marriage.

Replacing the book in the chest, Tessia rose to answer the door. She opened it a crack to see who was there. A buxom young serving woman smiled and stepped inside as Tessia opened the door for her.

"A good morning to you, Apprentice Tessia," she said. "My name's Malia. I've been looking after your new friend down the other end of the corridor for a few years now, so I'm used to the ways and needs of young apprentices. Here's your wash water."

Malia had a large jug in one hand and a broad basin in the other, and bundles of cloth wedged under one arm. She set all down on the top of one of the chests.

"I'll bring your morning meal up for you in a bit," she continued. "Is there anything you would like?"

"What do you usually have?"

From a long list of foods, some of which she had never heard of anyone eating first thing in the morning, Tessia chose something simple and the servant left. Tessia washed and dressed, then combed and plaited her hair.

"Lord Dakon will see you in the library when you're done," Malia said when she returned with a tray laden with food. "No hurry. He's always in there in the mornings, reading."

At the thought of this impending meeting, perhaps her first lesson, Tessia's appetite lagged, but she forced herself to eat the food the servant had brought, knowing she'd feel guilty about wasting it if she didn't. Picking up the tray, she carried it out of the room, encountering Malia in the corridor outside.

"Oh, you should just leave that there," the servant exclaimed. "Bringing it down is my job." She took the tray from Tessia.

"Where is—" Tessia began.

"Down the main stairs to the first floor, turn to your right," Malia answered. "Can't miss it."

Following the servant's instructions, Tessia found herself standing in an open doorway, gaping. Inside was a room twice the size of the Residence's dining room – which was almost the size of her father's entire house. This room was lined with shelving crammed with books. Lord Dakon was sitting in a large cushioned chair, his eyes scanning the pages of a large, leather-bound tome. He looked up at her and smiled.

"A good morning to you, Tessia," he said. "Come in. This is my library."

"I see that, Lord Dakon," she murmured, staring around the room as she entered.

"I thought we could start your control exercises today," he said. "The sooner you attain it the sooner we can avoid any more unintentional magical strayings – and get to more interesting lessons. We'll work in the mornings, then I'll give you books to read in the afternoon."

She felt her stomach flutter. "Yes, Lord Dakon."

He nodded to the chair next to his. "Take a seat. Learning is always easier when you're comfortable and relaxed." He paused. "Well, as relaxed as you can be when confronted with something new and strange."

Moving to the chair, she sat down and took a deep, calming breath. Lord Dakon put aside his book and looked at her thoughtfully.

"I haven't taught a natural before," he told her. "But nothing I've read or been told indicates the lessons need to be done any differently, which suggests to me that if we do encounter something unusual it will be small and easily worked around. Are you ready?"

She shrugged. "I don't know. I don't know what 'ready' is when it comes to magic. But I don't feel *un*ready, I suppose."

He chuckled. "That sounds good enough to me. Now, lean back in your chair, close your eyes and breathe slowly."

She did as he asked. The broad back of the chair had a slight backward tilt, encouraging her to rest against it. She let her hands lie on the chair's arms and her feet sit flat on the floor.

"Let your thoughts wander," Dakon murmured. "Don't be too anxious for the lesson to work. It'll happen when it happens. One week, two, perhaps three, and you'll be ready to learn to use magic."

He kept talking, his voice gentle and unhurried.

"Now I'm going to put my hand over yours. This will enable my mind to communicate with yours with less effort."

She felt fingers gently press on top of hers. They were neither hot nor cold, the touch neither too firm nor too light. It was a little odd and *personal* having the ley's magician touching her hand like this. For a moment a memory of a

78

Sachakan face leering over her flashed through her mind. She pushed it aside, annoyed. *This is nothing like that. Lord Dakon is nothing like Takado.*

Then she remembered her suspicion that her mother wanted her to marry Lord Dakon. She couldn't imagine he would ever consider her as a potential wife. Surely he'd rather marry someone more important than a commoner like herself. She was nowhere near pretty enough to make up for her low status, either. No matter what her mother thought, she was not going to try to seduce the magician. For a start, she had no idea how. But more important, she didn't even know if she—

"Think about what you can see," Dakon instructed, his voice calm. "Nothing, am I right? Just darkness behind your eyes. Imagine you are standing in a place with no walls or floor or ceiling. It may be dark, but it is comfortable. You are standing within it."

She felt something then. A sensation that was not physical. A feeling of personality . . . of Lord Dakon's personality. It seemed to emanate reassurance and encouragement. And certainly not romantic interest. She was surprised at the relief she felt. She didn't need such distractions when she was trying to learn something this important.

"I am standing behind you. Turn round."

Whether she had turned round, or the dark place in her imagination had revolved, she couldn't tell. Lord Dakon was there, a few paces away. Yet he wasn't completely distinct. Only where she looked did he come into focus completely: his face, his feet, his hands. His smile.

—*Good, Tessia.*

She understood that he had spoken into her mind. Could she do the same in return?

—*Lord Dakon?*

—*Yes. You are doing well.*

79

—Oh. Good. What next?

—Can you see what I'm carrying? It is a box.

His arms lifted, and she saw that there was something in his hands. As he said *box* it immediately resolved into a small nightwood container with gold corners and latch.

—Yes.

—This contains my magic. If I want to use it, I open the box. All other times I keep it closed. You, too, have a box. Look down at your hands and let the box take shape.

Looking down, she realised she could see her hands. Holding them palm up, she thought *box*.

A slim, flat box appeared. It was old and plain, and a little dusty. It looked just like the one that held her mother's necklace.

—Open it, Dakon bade her.

She undid the latch and lifted the lid. Inside was the necklace, glittering softly in the dim light. For some reason this filled her with disappointment. She looked up at him, confused.

—My mother's necklace is my magic?

The magician frowned.

—I doubt it, he said slowly. *More likely this box was recent in your thoughts. Put it behind you. Let's try this again.*

She did as he said, laying the box down on the invisible ground behind her. Straightening, she looked down at her hands again.

—Try to imagine a box worthy of magic. Your magic.

Magic was special. It was power and influence. And wealth. It was grand. A large box formed. The whole box was gold, glittering brightly. Its sides were thick and it was very heavy. She looked up at Dakon. He looked amused.

—Better. I don't think either of us will mistake that for anything but a box of magic, he said. *Now open it.*

A thrill of expectation and trepidation ran through her as she unlatched the lid. What would she find inside? Power? Uncontrolled power, most likely. As the lid hinged up a dazzling white light assailed her eyes.

It was too bright. She felt a force pour out, knocking the box from her hands. A crashing noise shocked her back into an awareness of her real surroundings and she opened her eyes. She blinked as she searched the room for the source of the disturbance. Then she saw the broken glass shards covering a nearby table.

"Oh."

Lord Dakon stirred, opened his eyes and turned to look at the broken . . . whatever it had been.

"Sorry," she said.

He frowned. "I think maybe we should conduct these lessons somewhere less . . . vulnerable."

"I'm very sorry," she repeated.

"Don't apologise," he told her firmly. "I should have realised there was a possibility of stray magic being loosed. I guess I did, but didn't take it seriously enough. I've never taught a natural before. Why don't we——?"

A knock came at the door. His eyes moved to the doorway. Following his gaze, Tessia saw Keron peering through the opening.

"Lord Dakon," the servant said. "Lord Narvelan of Loran ley has arrived."

Dakon's eyebrows rose in surprise, then he stood up. He turned to Tessia. "That will do for today. Practise entering that mental state when you can, and visualising the box, but do not open it."

She smiled. "Not a chance of that."

"The books on that table by the door are for you to read." He pointed. "Let me know if anything doesn't make sense."

She nodded.

Turning away, he strode out of the library. Noting his haste, she could not help feeling an intense curiosity stirring. Was it a habit of the Lord Narvelan to come visiting Lord Dakon without warning? She had rarely seen the magician of the neighbouring ley, and then only at a distance. It was said, in the village, that he was a handsome man. Maybe he would be at dinner tonight.

I suspect that if I keep my eyes and ears open, I may learn more here than how to use magic. I might learn a lot more about the world of magicians and of wealthy and influential people.

Which was something she had half expected anyway. She just hadn't expected to do so straight away.

Dakon envied the man pacing the library his youth. Having received Dakon's message that Takado had left late the day before, Lord Narvelan had ridden through the night to Mandryn, yet he was still alert and restless. But then, politics always energised the magician. If Dakon hadn't known better, he might have dismissed Narvelan's interest in the Sachakan as that of a bored young man living in the relatively unexciting countryside. But he did know better.

Three years before, Dakon had been amused and surprised to find himself being "recruited" by his neighbour. Narvelan and several other country ley owners, and a few sympathetic city lords, had agreed to meet a few times a year to discuss issues that affected country leys. It had begun as an informal arrangement, meant as much to strengthen relations between magicians living in their isolated leys as to reach any binding agreement. They called themselves the Circle of Friends.

As it was informal, and not entirely secret, King Errik had learned of it within a few months. Narvelan had been among the members who had travelled to the city to reassure the king that their intentions did not conflict with the interests of the crown. Dakon didn't know what had been said or agreed to. Sometimes Narvelan referred jokingly to the group as the king's favourite country gossips.

But their group and its purpose had evolved into something else when news and rumours began to reach them suggesting that young Sachakan magicians wanted to reconquer Kyralia. Dakon hadn't shared their worries until he had received an order from the king, some weeks back, to seek from Ashaki Takado his purpose for visiting Kyralia if he should pass through Mandryn. Narvelan had received a similar command.

The young magician had ridden all night for nothing, unfortunately. Dakon had no information to relay, as he'd indicated in his message.

"I know, I know," Narvelan said when Dakon reminded him of this. "I want to hear all about him anyway. Has the slave survived?"

"Yes . . . and not a slave any longer," Dakon pointed out. "Takado acknowledged that I must free Hanara once he left the country."

"Did you read his mind?"

"No. It would hardly be a convincing introduction to freedom."

The younger magician turned away from the window and frowned at Dakon. "Surely you don't trust him?"

Dakon shrugged. "As much as any man I don't know."

"He is more than that. More than just a stranger. He is Sachakan and an ex-slave. Loyalty is bred into him, if not loyalty for his master then for his country."

"I'm not going to lock him up or read his mind unless there is a strong reason to."

Narvelan pursed his lips, then nodded. "I guess not. But

if I were you I'd keep a close eye on him, for fear of him harming himself as much as others. It can't be an easy adjustment, changing from a source slave to a free man."

"I won't be forcing him out of my house before he's ready," Dakon assured him. "But it would not be appropriate to keep him here as a guest for ever. I'll find employment for him somewhere I can keep an eye on him."

The other magician nodded. "Do you think Takado had a reason other than curiosity for visiting Kyralia?"

"I can't say." Dakon grimaced. "I don't know if it was something in his manner that betrayed him, or merely the slyness of his nature giving me the wrong impression, but it's hard not to suspect he had ill intentions. Will we receive confirmation when he has left the country?"

"I don't know." Narvelan frowned, then shook his head. "The king should have a few guards at the pass, keeping watch on who comes and goes."

"If it's any consolation, I doubt Takado will want to spend a day more than necessary without a slave to serve him." Dakon chuckled, then made his expression sober. "He did attempt some mischief before he left, however. Tried to force himself on a woman, but was interrupted before he could do anything more than frighten her."

Narvelan's expression darkened. "Was that why he left?"

Dakon shook his head. "No, it happened after he decided to leave. I think he wanted to remind us that the Sachakans once had such power over us – as if beating his slave near to death hadn't already."

"I don't know why we have to allow any of them into the country," Narvelan muttered. Then he sighed and sat down. "No, I do understand why. Diplomacy and good relations, trade and all that. I just wish we didn't have to. Especially not when . . ." He looked at Dakon, his young face suddenly

84

creased with the lines of an older man. "I suppose I should get on with telling you the gossip."

Dakon smiled crookedly. "Please do."

Narvelan put his elbows on the arms of the chair and pressed his fingertips together. "Where to start? Lord Ruskel's story, I think. Ruskel had heard several reports of strangers being seen in the southern end of the mountains. Usually small groups of young men. He investigated and found a group of three Sachakan magicians and their slaves camping within our border. They claimed to have become lost in the mountains."

Dakon couldn't help feeling a chill run down his spine. Stumbling alone upon three Sachakan magicians would not be pleasant for any Kyralian magician, if they had mischief in mind.

"They apologised and returned the way they came," Narvelan continued. "Lord Ruskel called on a few neighbours for support and followed a few days later. He found a path that at first was natural and probably used by hunters, but as they moved deeper into the mountains it was clear some magical effort had gone into extending the path. As obvious as cutting a shelf into a sheer cliff face, and moving immense boulders into place to form a bridge."

"So, a path for non-magicians. Or magicians who don't want to use up too much of their power," Dakon said.

"Yes. Hunters and their families also approached Lord Ruskel and his companions, telling them of men who had hunted for decades in the mountains disappearing, on days of fine weather."

"Have the Sachakans been seen since?"

"No, and there have been no more reports of missing people either. Perhaps the young drumbloods have been put off." Narvelan smiled grimly. "Which brings me to the next

85

subject: what's going on in Sachaka. Our friend over there managed to contact us again."

Dakon smiled. He had no idea whether this "friend" was Kyralian or Sachakan, but Narvelan had vouched for the honesty of the man – or woman – and the quality of their information.

"Our friend says there is a split forming between the younger and older Sachakan magicians. There are too many young magicians without land, relying on the sibling their father chose as heir to support them. The number of landless magicians has been slowly growing for years, but only now have they begun to unite and cause trouble. Emperor Vochira doesn't seem able to do much about them.

"There are reports of landless magicians tormenting and killing slaves that don't belong to them. This in itself isn't remarkable, so they must be causing a lot of economic damage for their actions to be protested against. Some have turned to thievery, occasionally daring to attack and rob other magicians. Others have even raided the homes of landed magicians, attacking their families and killing slaves.

"The worst offenders have been banished and declared 'ichani' – outlaws. A few were hunted down and killed, but not enough to make a difference because the emperor needs assistance to overcome the offenders, and too few of the older magicians can risk losing alliances with the families the offenders are related to." Narvelan sighed and shook his head. "There is some satisfaction in knowing the Sachakans have as much trouble getting magicians to unite with and support each other as we do."

Dakon chuckled, knowing that the young man referred to the habit of some magicians to hoard magical knowledge to themselves. Like Lord Jilden, who had discovered a way to harden stone with magic, but refused to share the knowledge with anyone else. He claimed it was only useful for his small sculptures – which were exquisite and fragile – and that like most artisans he had a right to keep his methods secret. King Errik could not risk ordering Lord Jilden to reveal his secret, because most magicians would not support it. Though they wanted the knowledge, their freedom to do as they wished, so long as it did no harm to the country, was more valuable to them. The king could only force Lord Jilden to divulge his secret if he could prove withholding it was harmful.

"Our Sachakan friend says that the younger magicians talk of the past," Narvelan added. "They glorify the days when the Sachakan empire spread from coast to coast, bringing in wealth from other lands. They feel the empire is declining and believe they could revive it by reconquering the lost territories."

Dakon frowned. "That doesn't sound promising."

Narvelan smiled. "Ah, but the older magicians call the young ones fools and dreamers. They recall that the empire relinquished Elyne and Kyralia because the two countries were no longer bringing in the wealth they once had. Which is what happens, when you rob a land," Narvelan added darkly. "They also say that Kyralia would cost too much to conquer now, and isn't worth the trouble."

"But the young magicians want land," Dakon guessed. "The lack of it drives them to see Kyralia as a greater prize than it is. They tell themselves they aren't going to rob and run, but stay and rule."

The younger magician's gaze became thoughtful. "I fear you may be right. The question is, will the older magicians convince and control their younger opponents, or will they let them invade Kyralia?"

"It always seems easier to do nothing, when the harm is done elsewhere," Dakon said. "They know their young ones will either learn a lesson and limp home – or die and stop being a problem – or prove successful. The worst that could happen is a bit of a diplomatic hiccup in history."

"Are the youngsters right?" Narvelan asked, though more to himself than to Dakon. "Are we as weak as they think we are? Would we win or lose such a war?"

Dakon considered. "The king's war masters would know better than we do." He looked at the young man. "But your friends are already trying to find out for themselves, aren't they?"

Narvelan grinned. "Trying to. There is one more question to be answered, though. One as important as those two."

"Yes?"

"Would we unite against them?"

"Of course. We managed it a few centuries ago, in order to force the emperor to grant us independence."

"But how long would it take? *What* would it take? How much land could the Sachakans overrun before the city magicians decided it was time to act? One ley? Two or three?"

"Only if the Sachakans moved quickly."

Narvelan shook his head. "You don't know the city magicians as I do. They fear confrontation far more than they care for some remote leys at the edge of the country." He looked towards the window and frowned. "We are close to the main pass – you closer than me. Even if you are right, our land and people will still be the first to go."

Dakon felt his skin chill, as if he had been sitting outside and a cloud had just blocked the sunlight. He could not argue against what Narvelan said. He could only hope that the Sachakans never managed to convince themselves Kyralia was worth invading, or that their attempts to organise and form alliances failed.

And if my hopes are in vain, that I can evacuate the villages of

Aylen ley in time, and get my people to safety. Surely Narvelan is wrong about the city magicians. Beside, such decisions are not theirs to make.

"The king would not allow the city magicians to delay," he said, feeling his mood lighten a fraction. "He won't want to lose one handful of his land to Sachaka, let alone a few leys."

Narvelan looked at him and nodded. "I hope you are right. I think . . . and our circle of friends believe . . . that we can better our chances. That the king is more likely to act promptly if he has met and reassured us he will. He should *know* the people most in danger if such a crisis should occur. People like you. It's much harder to let people die if you've met and liked them, and promised to help them."

"You want me to meet the king?" Dakon exclaimed. He laughed. "Why would he agree to meet me? I doubt he'll do so just to ease my mind. More likely he'll think I'm a nervous rassook jumping at every suggestion of a threat and most likely inventing half of them."

"He won't," Narvelan said, with a shrug and a glint of amusement in his eye. "Not with your reputation. And once he meets you, he'll know you're not easily frightened."

"Reputation?" Dakon stared at the young man. "What reputation?"

Narvelan's gaze began to roam around the room. "Is it too early for wine, do you think?"

"Only for those who mention a man's reputation and fail to supply the details."

The young man grinned. "Is that a bribe or a punishment?"

"That depends entirely on how it affects my reputation."

Narvelan laughed. "Very well. We've made sure you're known as a sturdy sort of man who is unimpressed by frivolity. Which is why you have no wife — or so the assorted wives and daughters of our circle of friends have concluded."

Dakon opened his mouth, then closed it again. "I do hope this reputation you have arranged for me will not prevent my marrying at some point in the future."

The young magician smiled. "I'm sure it won't." Abruptly his eyes widened and he laughed. "You can tell people your reason for visiting the city was to find a wife. That would provide plenty of distraction from—"

"No," Dakon said firmly.

"Why not? We magicians often marry late, but you're leaving it a bit later than most."

"It's not a matter of leaving it," Dakon said, shrugging. "Or of meeting appropriate women. While I have met women I would have liked to marry – and the feeling was recipro-cated more than once – I have not yet met a woman who liked the idea enough to leave the city and her friends and family, and live in Mandryn. You haven't discovered this for yourself, having married before you moved here. Young women of the country are desperate to move to the city, and those in the city are not keen to leave it. Your idea is hardly going to cause the distraction you hope for. They're more likely to make a point of ignoring me."

"Oh." Narvelan looked disappointed. "Now that you mention it, Celia does often complain about how boring it is in the country."

"I travel to the city every year to visit friends and deal with trade issues. There is no need for anyone to suspect another agenda."

Narvelan nodded. "So, when do you think you'll leave?"

"Not for a few weeks." As the young magician opened his mouth to protest, Dakon raised a hand to stall him. "Something else happened this last week. I have a new apprentice."

"Ah. An apprentice. I suppose I shall have to think about

taking one on soon. Should I approach a likely family? Is that how you found yours?"

"No, this one is special. A natural."

Understanding entered the magician's gaze. "A natural! How exciting!"

"It certainly has been."

Narvelan nodded. "You are stuck here. You can't leave him behind untrained and taking him with you would be unfair on the people you stayed with. So, will I get to meet him?"

"You'll get to meet *her* at dinner, if you are planning to stay."

"Her?" Narvelan's eyebrows rose.

"Yes. My healer's daughter."

"Well then, I'm definitely going to stay for dinner."

"Hopefully it will be her charming personality that provides the entertainment, not a stray bit of magic. I don't mind having to repair and redecorate one of the seating rooms, but the dining room could be a touch expensive."

Narvelan's eyes widened. "Repair a seating room?"

"Yes. The signs of her first use of magic are rather hard to miss."

"Can you show me, or has the work already been done?"

Dakon smiled. "Not completely. It's still fairly impressive. I'll show you later tonight."

CHAPTER 8

"While most people say the law allows magicians to do whatever they like, the truth is we are still restricted in what we can do," Lord Dakon said.

Tessia watched him pace the library, as he usually did when lecturing. Her lessons for the last few weeks had consisted of short attempts at control, much like her first lesson, and these longer ones in which he taught her about the laws of Kyralia, some history which she had already learned from her father but was interested to hear from the perspective of magicians, and how her learning would be structured over the years to come. He often diverged from the chosen subject, moving into Sachakan culture and politics, or telling her about trading his ley's goods with other landowners in the country or the city, and the convoluted world of Kyralia's most powerful families.

"The first restriction is that nothing we do harms Kyralia," he continued. "Now, what is harmful and what is not can be subjective. Building a dam may solve water storage problems, but it also floods land above it and restricts how much water flows below it. A mine, kiln or forge upstream may bring prosperity there, but it may foul the water and poison fish, crops, livestock and people downstream." Dakon stopped pacing to regard her.

"Ultimately the king decides what is classed as harmful. But before the matter can be brought to his attention, a long and formal process must be carried out and mediation between the complainant and the magician attempted. Without this process he would face an impossible number of cases to decide." He grimaced. "I won't go into detail on the process right now, or we'll be stuck on the subject for the rest of the afternoon. Do you have any questions?"

Tessia was ready for the enquiry. If she didn't ask questions, Dakon would lecture her on how necessary it was for her to do so. No question was too silly or irrelevant, he had assured her.

But Apprentice Jayan clearly didn't agree. Whenever she had lessons with him in the afternoon to make up for being called out to help her father in the morning – fortunately only three times so far – she would return cheerful only to spend an uncomfortable afternoon conscious of Jayan's half-hidden snickers, sighs and disdainful looks.

It made her reluctant to ask questions, and determined to only ask ones that didn't sound foolish.

"The king is a magician," she said. "Does he face the same restrictions? Who decides whether what he does is harmful or not?"

Dakon smiled. "He is, indeed, a magician and he does face the same restrictions. If he is ever accused of harming his kingdom, the lords of Kyralia must decide if the accusation is correct – and we must all agree, if action is to be taken."

"What action would you take?"

"Whatever is appropriate for the crime, I imagine. There is no set action or punishment scribed in law."

"The king isn't a strong magician, is he?"

She heard a snort from where Jayan was sitting, but resisted turning to look at him.

"That is a rumour and is incorrect," Dakon said. "A magician's natural ability may be small or large, but that is irrelevant once higher magic is learned. Then his or her strength is based entirely on how much magic has been taken from apprentices. Of course, a magician may choose to not have an apprentice and to rely entirely on natural strength – not every magician has the time or inclination to teach. The king does not have time to train apprentices because his prime responsibility is the state of the country. He is allowed to receive magic given by other magicians – usually from a small group of loyal friends, sometimes as payment for a debt or favour."

Tessia considered this quietly. Sometimes the city sounded like a completely different world rather than the capital of her country.

A soft cough from Jayan caught Dakon's attention. He smiled crookedly. "I will tell you more another time. Now, I think we've covered enough law and history. It is time we tested your control again. No, stay where you are."

She stopped, having half risen from her seat. "We're not going out into the fields?"

He nodded. "You are past the most dangerous stage, I think. Can you recall using magic unintentionally at all in the last week?"

She thought back, then shook her head.

"Good. Now, let's get into a more comfortable position."

He took a seat beside her, and the two of them turned their chairs so they faced each other. She could see Jayan now, sitting in the corner of the room. He was watching them, his brow creased by a faint frown.

She held out her hands to Lord Dakon. As the magician took them in a light grip, she closed her eyes. Then she opened them again, looking at Jayan, and caught an undisguised curl to his lips – a sneer of disdain or displeasure that was quickly hidden. She felt a stab of dismay, followed by curiosity.

He really doesn't like me, she thought. *I wonder why.*

Possible reasons ran through her mind, upsetting her ability to calm it and focus. Was it her humbler upbringing? Was it because she was a woman? Did she have some habit that disgusted or irritated him?

Or, she suddenly thought, was it resentment? Had he lost something when she had become Dakon's apprentice? Status? No, her presence here wouldn't prevent him from becoming a magician or endanger any connections or influence he or his family had.

Whatever it was, it must concern Dakon. The magician was the only person in Mandryn that Jayan might want something from. Then a solution finally dawned on Tessia. Dakon did not have children. She had assumed that if he never did, the ley would go to another relative, as had been the case for Narvelan's predecessor, Lord Gempel. But maybe apprentices could inherit leys.

Even so, surely Jayan, being older and from good bloodlines, would be chosen over her. The possibility that she could inherit a ley was so strange and ridiculous, she almost laughed aloud. *That can't be it*, she thought. *It must be something else.*

She would have to think about it later. For now all she could do was ignore him. Though not if he was openly obnoxious, she decided. Then she would stand up to him. After all, she had faced a Sachakan magician. She had dealt with grown men made difficult by pain and sickness. No mere Kyralian apprentice was going to cow her.

That decided, she was able to clear her thoughts and concentrate on Dakon's control lesson. As always, she visualised a box and nervously opened it. Inside lay her power, a swirling, bright ball of light. She touched it, held it in her hand, even gave it a squeeze, then put it back and closed the lid.

When she opened her eyes, Dakon sat back and smiled at

her. Then he stood up, walked to a shelf and took down a heavy stone bowl that had been wedged between two rows of books. He put it on the floor in front of her, then tore up a scrap of paper and dropped it into the bowl.

"Look at the paper," he told her. "I want you to remember what it felt like to hold your power. Then I want you to take a tiny bit of it – just a pinch – and direct it at the paper. At the same time, think about heat. Think about fire."

This was nothing like the lessons she'd had before. She looked at him questioningly, but he just nodded at the bowl.

Taking a deep breath, she leaned forward and stared at the paper. She recalled how it had felt to hold and squeeze her magic. The sensation was still there, even though she had her eyes open.

It was not unlike the feeling she had experienced when her magic loosed itself without her meaning it but . . . not as *slippery*.

She dared not blink.

Still staring at the stone vessel, she plucked at the magic she sensed and felt it respond. Scared that if she waited too long the bit of magic she had taken would slip from her grasp, she directed it towards the torn paper.

Her forehead burned as the air before her suddenly grew hot. The vessel slid away from her a few strides, then flames began to flicker from within.

"You did it!" Dakon exclaimed. His tone was half surprised, half pleased. "I thought you might be ready."

"So she has."

Tessia jumped as she realised Jayan was standing beside her chair, peering over her shoulder at the burning paper. The smell of smoke stung her nose. Jayan grimaced and made a small gesture with one finger.

Looking back at the bowl, she saw that the smoke was

now contained within it by an invisible shield. After a few moments the flames shrank and disappeared. She felt a vague disappointment as the result of her first controlled use of magic was extinguished.

Dakon, she noted, was looking at Jayan with a thoughtful expression. The young apprentice shrugged and walked back to his seat, picking up the book he had been reading. Dakon said nothing and turned back to Tessia.

"So, I think I can officially say you have gained control of your power, Tessia," he said. "We need not fear any further destruction, though I must say the room we had to refurnish is looking a lot better than it did before."

She felt her face warm and looked away. "What happens now?"

"We celebrate," he told her. Across the room a small gong set within an alcove in the wall rang. "After all, I've never heard of any magician gaining control in just two weeks. I took three. Jayan took four."

"Three and a half," Jayan corrected, not looking up from his book. "And we lost three days when Lord Gempel dropped in for a chat and decided to hang around and deplete your wine store."

Dakon chuckled. "He was old. How could I deny him a rest and a little company now and then?"

Jayan didn't answer. At a tap on the door, Dakon turned to look at it. Tessia noted the way his gaze intensified as he used magic. The door swung open. Cannia stepped into the room.

"Bring us a bottle of wine, Cannia. A good one, too. Now that Tessia's control lessons are over she had best start learning something all respectable Kyralians must know: which of our wines are better than others."

As the servant smiled and left, Tessia drew her attention

back to her own magic. This new awareness she had of something within her, discovered during her first lessons and reinforced by numerous exercises, reminded her of something. Then she remembered how she had become acutely conscious of the position and rhythms of her heart and lungs after her father had shown her sketches of those organs within a body and started teaching her about them.

But her magic was different. She did not need to be in control of her heart and lungs. She could forget about them and trust that they kept working. Though Dakon had assured her she would eventually stop noticing that she was exerting control over her power, that control must always remain.

Now, for the first time, the prospect no longer scared her.

Jayan yawned as he crossed the yard to the stables. The grass in the surrounding fields was white with frost, and his breath misted in the air. As the cold penetrated his clothes he created a shield about himself and warmed the air within it.

Magic could do something about the cold, but it couldn't fix the early hour. Why had Dakon sent for him? Malia hadn't been able or willing to tell him anything except that he'd find Dakon in the stables.

A man leading a roan horse emerged from the blackness behind the open stable door and Jayan felt his mood darken further. Dakon had given Hanara a job in the stables, which Jayan had to admit was a wise move. It kept the former slave out of the house but not out of sight. But it did mean Jayan had to deal with the man whenever he wanted or needed to go for a ride.

Hanara kept his eyes to the ground, his shoulders hunched. The apparent meekness only made Jayan more uneasy.

"For you, master," the man said.

Jayan bit back a reminder that the title was not appropriate.

He should not be called "master" until he was a magician, and then only by his own apprentice. The one time he had tried to explain this Hanara had stared at the ground, saying nothing, and later resumed using the term.

Hanara turned the mare to the side ready for mounting, then positioned himself at her head. Jayan paused, then took the reins from the man and held them as he swung up onto the horse's back. Hoofbeats to his right heralded the emergence of Dakon from the stable, leading his favourite gelding, Sleet.

"A good morning to you, Apprentice Jayan," Dakon said. "Care for a ride?"

"Do I have a choice? Can I get down and go back inside to study?" Jayan asked, a touch snappier than he intended.

Dakon's mouth twitched into a smile. "That would be a pity, when Hanara spent so much time readying Ember for you."

"Wouldn't it just," Jayan replied sarcastically. "So where are we heading so early in the morning?"

"The usual circuit of the village," Dakon said, placing a foot in Sleet's stirrup. He swung up and settled into the grey's saddle, then nudged the horse into motion. Jayan sighed and urged his mount after them.

As they emerged from the Residence's gates Jayan saw that a few villagers were already out and about. The baker, of course, was doing his usual early deliveries. A few young boys carried bundles of firewood from a cart to the doors of the houses, leaving them beside the doorstep.

It did not take Dakon and Jayan long to reach the edge of the village. Crossing the bridge, they headed southward.

"You don't trust Hanara, do you?" Dakon asked.

Jayan shook his head. "No. I don't think you should, either."

"I don't, but perhaps not as little as you." He turned to

regard Jayan. "I may not expect his loyalty, or trust him with secret information – not that I have any – but I do trust him to hold the head of my horse when I mount. It would be petty and stupid of him to try to spook a horse we were mounting. He knows I would cast him out of the village if I thought it was deliberate."

"And if you weren't sure?" Jayan asked.

"I'd give him another chance. And probably another. Once is a mistake, twice is bad luck or a coincidence, three times is either deliberate or a bad habit and would at least prove him incapable of the job I've given him."

"Even if someone was hurt?"

"That would force me to read his mind."

Jayan frowned. "You haven't already?"

"No. I'm no Sachakan ashaki." Dakon lifted one eyebrow. "Do you feel no sympathy for the man?"

Looking away, Jayan let out a sigh. "A little. Well, I suppose more than a little. But that doesn't mean I trust him. If Takado turned up I'm sure Hanara would scurry back to his master's side without hesitation."

"Would he? He's a free man now. Takado said I could do what I wished with his man. Hanara knows that. Would he willingly go back to the life of a slave?"

"If he has known nothing else. If he feared to do otherwise."

"Nobody is forcing him to stay. He could leave and return to Sachaka if he wanted to." Dakon smiled. "He is trying out a different life now. The longer he has his freedom, the more he may like it. And he will like it even more if he is not treated with distrust by every Kyralian he meets."

Jayan nodded reluctantly. "But that will count for nothing if he does not respect you," he pointed out. "Should Hanara face Takado again, his reaction will depend on who he fears and respects the most, you or Takado."

"True."

"And he may never respect a man he doesn't fear, if that's the only way he knows how to judge. Fear may mean a lot more than trust to him."

Dakon frowned and fell into a thoughtful silence. They turned off the road onto a cart track which climbed steadily up and along a ridge overlooking the village. Jayan stared down at the double line of houses extending from the river to the end of the little valley. Dakon's house was a storey higher and several times larger than the rest of the buildings. Whenever Jayan looked at the village from this viewpoint, he wondered how the villagers managed to live and work in their tiny homes.

"Your distrust of Hanara is reasonable," Dakon said. Jayan resisted the urge to sigh with exasperation. *Isn't he finished with this subject yet?* he thought impatiently. "But I don't quite understand the issue you have with Tessia."

Jayan's stomach lurched disconcertingly. "Tessia? I have no issue with her."

Dakon laughed quietly. "Oh, it's clear you do. Your dislike of her is as obvious as your distrust of Hanara. I'm afraid you aren't good enough at hiding your feelings, Jayan."

I ought to turn and meet his eyes, and state that I am happy that Tessia has joined us and look forward to many years of her company, Jayan thought. But not yet. He wasn't ready. Dakon had surprised him.

"If I'm so bad at hiding my feelings, then shouldn't it be obvious what my 'issue' is?" he countered. "Maybe you don't understand because there's nothing to understand."

"Then explain to me why you sigh or scowl at half her questions, and listen to her lessons when you say you want to read, and ignore her unless she speaks to you directly, then give her the shortest and often least helpful response?" Dakon chuckled.

"From the look on your face when she's present, anyone would think she gave you a stomach ache."

Jayan glanced at Dakon then looked away again, thinking hard. What possible explanation could he give? He certainly couldn't tell Dakon that he resented every moment of time Tessia took away from his own training.

"She's just so . . . so ignorant," he said. "So slow – I know she's learning fast but it doesn't feel like it." He grimaced, sure that his answer wasn't clever or evasive enough. *Make it sound as if you actually want her around for some reason.* "It's going to be a long time before we can have a conversation about magic, or practise together, or play a game, or . . . something." *Now look at him.* He turned to face Dakon, meeting the magician's eyes and shrugging helplessly.

Dakon smiled and turned to regard the track ahead of them, which was leading to a fence and a gate.

"Watching her must remind you of your own beginnings, of the awkward questions and failed attempts at magic, of mistakes and difficulties. You know," he looked at Jayan again, "I'm sure she'd welcome your help. You've put her a bit on edge, but a little assistance now and then would reassure her. Not that you should try to teach her anything new entirely on your own." Dakon grew serious. "Apprentices are not supposed to be teachers. It's seen as an abuse of the magician–apprentice exchange of duties."

Jayan nodded, hoping it looked like agreement and not a commitment. Their conversation ceased as they navigated the gate. Then, as they continued on their way, Dakon looked at Jayan expectantly.

"Promise me you'll be nicer to Tessia."

Jayan suppressed the urge to sigh in relief. It could have been worse. Dakon could have asked him to dedicate time to assisting Tessia.

"I promise," he said. "I'll be nicer to her. And try not to 'put her on edge', as you say."

"Good." Apparently satisfied, Dakon nudged Sleet into a trot. Watching his master moving away, Jayan surrendered to the sigh. Then he grimaced and urged Ember to follow.

If I am so easy to read, then I need to work on changing that. Perhaps I should think of Tessia as an opportunity to gain some skill in this area. After all, what's a minor fault here in Mandryn could be a fatal weakness in Imardin.

He might as well try to gain some advantage out of the situation. It didn't look as if Dakon was going to send her to another teacher. Tessia was here to stay, and he would just have to get used to it.

CHAPTER 9

Tessia stared at the bowl of water and reached for magic. She felt her power respond, obediently, flowing out to take the form she wanted and going where she directed it. Bubbles welled up and burst, droplets splashing her. She flinched and rubbed her skin. Too hot.

Dakon had suggested she practise turning magic into heat by warming her washing water each morning. Using magic for everyday tasks was good practice and kept a magician's mind sharp, he told her. Nevertheless, she could not help thinking that magicians were a lazy lot every time she saw him or Jayan using magic to open doors, or to fetch something from across a room.

She knew better now than to warm the water *before* washing, however. Her most common mistake in any magical task was to employ too much magic, and to begin with there had been a few mornings she'd had to wait for some time before the water cooled enough to use.

A knock at the door attracted her attention.

"Come in," she called.

The servant, Malia, strode in, and glanced from the steaming bowl to the empty dishes from Tessia's morning meal stacked on the desk. She moved towards the latter, taking the tray she was nearly always carrying out from under her arm. "Good morning, Tessia."

Tessia rose and stretched. "Good morning, Malia."

"Practising again?"

"Yes. Give the bowl a moment to cool down before you take it."

"I will." Malia chuckled ruefully. "Believe me, I won't be ignoring your warning a second time. What are your plans for today?"

"Stables first." Tessia picked up the small bag of bandages and salves her father had left for her to use when tending Hanara. "Then lessons."

Tessia headed to the door, then paused to look back at Malia. She had expected the servant to ask how Hanara was, but the woman said nothing.

"Malia, do you know how well Hanara is fitting in? What do the stable servants think of him? What about the villagers?"

Malia straightened from tidying the bedcovers and looked thoughtful. "Well, people generally find him a bit strange, but that's expected, right? It would be weird if he behaved like a Kyralian."

Tessia smiled. "Yes, it would be. And the stable servants?"

"They say he works hard enough – more than what he's supposed to what with the mending he still has to do. They say he's tough. Almost admiringly." Malia hesitated. "But he keeps to himself and doesn't always answer questions." She shrugged, indicating that was all she had to convey.

"Thank you." Tessia smiled and continued on her way. Thinking about what Malia had said, she decided things were going as well as anyone could expect for the former slave. He probably wasn't used to friendly chatter, and it would take time for him to learn how to befriend people.

Leaving the house, Tessia crossed to the stables and slipped through the open door. Then she stopped, surprised by the scene before her.

Two of the stable servants were peeing into a bucket.

Before she could look away, the young men glanced up. Expressions of horror crossed their faces, and streams of urine veered from their intended paths – one across the trousers of the other – as they hastily covered themselves.

"Having a good look?" Birren jeered, recovering from his embarrassment enough to try to joke about it.

"Yeah." Ullan followed. "Looked to me like she was checking us out. Impressed, were you, Tess? Want a closer look?"

She suppressed a laugh. The banter was typical of young men their age, and what she'd have expected in this situation – before she'd become an apprentice. She didn't have the heart to increase their discomfort by reminding them she wasn't Tessia the healer's daughter any more. "I was wondering if it's true that all boys get bigger when they get older. Didn't look like you'd grown much since that time my father and I treated you two for . . . what was it again? Warts?"

They winced.

"We can make them get bigger," Birren told her, grinning. "You'd be scared."

She snorted derisively. "I've seen much scarier things helping my father. Where's Hanara?"

Ullan began a cheeky reply, but Birren stopped him with a low hiss, then nodded towards the end of the building. Hanara was sitting at a table, cleaning and polishing a saddle. She walked towards him. Harnesses and tools were lying nearby, waiting to be mended or cleaned. He looked up as she approached, and his frown faded a little.

Though the man's face was typically Sachakan, broad and brown-skinned, it was quite different from his master's. It was finer and more angled, youthful but scarred. She was glad of this, because while it was impossible not to think of Takado whenever she thought of Hanara, at least looking at the former slave did not stir unpleasant memories of his master's face leering at her.

"I'm here to change your bandages," she told him.

He nodded. "You've not seen anything scary," he told her, standing up and taking off his tunic. "Nothing truly scary."

Realising he had overheard the youths, she sighed and began removing the bandages around his chest and shoulder. "Probably not, but don't be too quick to judge. I've seen more of the insides of people than most Kyralians have. Some nasty injuries and a few fatal ones that I doubt I'll ever forget."

"The dead are not scary. They cannot do anything to you."

"But they smell almost as bad as those two back there."

He smiled faintly, then grew serious again. "You should not let them speak to you like that. You are a magician now."

"Apprentice," she corrected. "You're probably right. But then, I should have knocked or called out, not just walked in on them."

"You should not have to knock."

She gave him a level look. "This is Kyralia. Even magicians are expected to have good manners."

He met her eyes for the briefest moment, then quickly looked down.

The wounds he'd suffered, even the cut her father had made to reach his broken ribs, had sealed into red, raised scars. She probed where the breaks in his bones had been, asking if he felt pain. He shook his head each time, and didn't look as if he was trying to hide any reaction.

"You look completely healed to me," she told him. "I don't think you need any more bandages. Be careful not to pick up anything heavy, or strain bones that were broken." She shook her head. "It's amazing how fast you heal. I'm not sure you even needed our help."

"I would have healed badly – crooked. Your father stopped that happening." He paused. "Thank you."

Tessia smiled, her heart lifting. "I'll pass your thanks on to my father."

"You, too," he said, pointing to the discarded bandages. "You're . . ." He frowned, and gestured vaguely towards the stable door. "Not like . . ."

Was he talking about the stable boys, or had his gesture been meant to encompass more? The village, perhaps. She felt a stab of concern.

"Are the villagers treating you well?" she asked.

He shrugged. "I am a stranger."

"Yes, but that is no excuse for . . . bad behaviour. Hanara." She waited until he looked up and met her gaze. "If someone does anything mean to you – anything, ah, un-Kyralian – you tell me. It's important. Just as you must live like a Kyralian now, by our laws and ideals, *they* must not start behaving like . . . like Sachakans. Do you understand? You mustn't put up with it because you did before."

He gazed back at her.

"You do understand me, don't you?"

He nodded.

Letting out a sigh of relief, she gathered the old bandages into a bundle. "I must go. I have lessons to learn."

He nodded again and suddenly seemed glum.

"I'll come here to talk to you now and then, if you like," she offered.

Though his expression did not change, a warmth entered his gaze. As she left the stable, she imagined she could feel his eyes on her back.

I hope I'm not giving him romantic notions, she thought. *I can imagine Mother's horror. She'll barely forgive me for not trying to get Lord Dakon to fall in love with me, but if I end up with a Sachakan former slave writing me poetry she'll disown me.*

She considered the likelihood of Hanara's writing poetry for her as she re-entered the house and headed back to her room to drop off the bandages and her bag. He probably couldn't even write. But if he could, would she welcome it?

He's quite attractive, in an exotic way, she decided. *Now that the swelling has gone. But . . . no. I don't think I know him well enough yet to even decide I like him. There's too much about him that is secretive.* Then she chuckled. *I guess those novels in my room have it all wrong. Secretive men with mysterious pasts aren't irresistibly attractive at all.*

Reaching the stairs, she heard her name called and turned to see Malia hurrying towards her.

"Your father's here, Apprentice Tessia," the servant said. "Says he needs your help this morning – something urgent in the village." Her brow furrowed. "I hope it's nothing serious."

"Tell him I'll be right there. And could you tell Lord Dakon?"

"Of course."

Hurrying upstairs, Tessia quickly deposited her burden in her room then backed out again. She checked her stride as she nearly collided with Jayan at the top of the stairs. The young man paused and looked at her, the annoyance in his expression changing to the smooth politeness he had adopted around her of late.

"You look eager for your lessons this morning," he said.

"I'll have to miss them today," she said, wishing he'd move aside and let her past. "Father's here and it's urgent."

"Ah, skipping classes again, are we?" He smiled and shook his head with mock disapproval – or was it really mocking? Was that a hint of true disdain she detected in his tone? She felt anger rising.

"At least I'm doing something useful with what I know," she snapped, meeting his gaze and silently daring him to object.

His eyes widened in surprise. Stepping back, he let her pass, and watched her hurry down the stairs. She heard him mutter something, catching the word "idiot".

So he thinks I'm an idiot, she mused. *Arrogant fool. I bet he doesn't know more than a handful of the people in the village, let alone care about whether they live or die, are sick or in pain. So long as they do the work of the ley he's not interested. He's no better than a Sachakan.* She resolved to put him out of her mind.

No matter how many times Dakon urged her father otherwise, Veran always came to the servants' door and today was no exception. She found him pacing in the corridor outside the kitchen. When he saw her he frowned and she realised she was still scowling at her encounter with Jayan.

"Are you missing a particularly important lesson today?" he asked, picking up his bag.

She shook her head and smiled. "No. Don't worry. It's nothing to do with Dakon or magic or lessons. Just a petty annoyance. Where's Aran?" She had grown used to the presence of her father's new assistant, a quiet boy with a missing lower leg who had grown up on one of the more distant farms. The boy's deformity prevented him from joining in with more robust tasks in the field, despite being remarkably agile on the wooden leg his father had made for him, but he had a quick mind and, she grudgingly admitted to herself, was proving a good choice for assistant.

"Visiting his grandmother," her father replied. "She's broken her arm and he's helping her out."

"Ah. So who are we treating today?"

He led her out of the Residence before he answered.

110

"Yaden, Jornen's son. Pains in the belly early this morning. Worse now. I suspect an inflamed appendix."

Tessia nodded. A dangerous condition. Her father might have to attempt surgery to remove the organ and the chances of infection were high. The boy could easily die.

Reaching the main road, they strode down to one of the last houses in the village, belonging to Jornen the metal worker. The man's workshop was a small distance from the rear of his home, down by one of the streams that flowed into the river. On most days the smoke from his forge blew away from the houses, but occasionally what was known locally as "the smoke wind" gusted distinctly metallic-smelling clouds over the village.

Tessia's father stepped up to the door and knocked. The sound of running feet echoed inside the house, then the door opened and two small children stared up at them; a girl and a boy. The girl ran back into the house, crying: "They're here! They're here!" while the boy took Veran's hand and led him upstairs to where Jornen and his wife, Possa, were waiting. A baby in the woman's arms quietly snuffled its displeasure.

"He's in here," the metal worker said, gesturing to a bedroom.

It was a tiny room filled with a metal-framed three-tier bunk bed. Yaden, a boy of about twelve, was curled up on the bottom mattress, moaning loudly.

Tessia watched her father inspect Yaden, prodding his abdomen gently, timing the rhythm of his heart and breathing and asking questions. The two children who had greeted them at the door appeared, with two older boys in tow. One of the newcomers was leading the other by a rope around his neck.

"What's this?" Possa said, her voice strained. "What are you doing with that rope?"

"We're playing master and slave," one of the boys said.

Tessia and the mother exchanged a look of dismay.

"Take it off," Possa ordered. "We're not Sachakans. We don't enslave people. It's wrong."

To Tessia's amusement, both boys looked disappointed as they removed the rope.

"What about the slave Lord Dakon has?" the one who'd worn the rope asked.

"He's not a slave any more," Tessia told him gently. "He's free now."

"But he still acts weird," the other boy said.

"That's because he's not used to being free. And he doesn't know our ways yet. But he'll learn them. He's actually nice, when you get to know him."

The children looked thoughtful. Hearing a sniff, Tessia turned to see a doubtful look on Possa's face. The woman quickly looked away. Veran made a low noise of concern. He straightened, knocking his head on the middle bunk.

"There's not enough room for me to work here. Can we move him somewhere with more space?"

"The kitchen?" the metal worker suggested, looking at his wife. She shook her head.

"Too dirty. The cellar's got more room."

Her husband entered the bedroom, lifted his son and carried him down the stairs, the small crowd of family following. Tessia and Veran trailed behind them down to the lower floor and along the corridor towards the back of the house.

Glancing through an open door, Tessia glimpsed a kitchen table overflowing with utensils, vessels and baskets filled with the familiar shapes of edible fungi. She nodded to herself, approving of Possa's reluctance to take Yaden to a place covered in dirt and manure. Perhaps her father's and grand-father's efforts to instil a respect for hygiene in the villagers hadn't been as futile as they had often suspected.

More likely she doesn't want to disturb her work when there's an alternative place to take her son.

The long column of bodies descended another staircase. They reached a cold room smelling of damp and mould, with a time-darkened old wooden table covered in grime in the middle, and Tessia felt her heart sink. This was barely healthier than the dirty kitchen table.

"Get the lamp," the metal worker ordered, but to which child Tessia couldn't guess in the dimness. She felt someone smaller than her trip over her shoe and heard an exclamation of pain. Backing away, she heard a protest as she stepped on someone else's foot.

Argh! We need light now*!* she thought, exasperated. *Well, I can fix that . . .*

She concentrated and abruptly the room filled with brilliance. All sounds ceased. Guessing the family and her father were all as dazzled as she was, Tessia reduced the ball of light floating up near the ceiling to a softer glow.

Looking around, she realised the metal worker and family were all staring at her. Even her father appeared astonished. She felt her face warming. Then Yaden groaned with pain and all eyes returned to him. Tessia sighed with relief. The boy was placed on the table. Tessia's father handed her his bag then moved to Yaden's side. She removed the burner and began to set it up on an old stool. The metal worker's wife eyed Tessia warily, then gathered all the children and drew them from the room.

Almost as though she was removing them from danger rather than out of the way.

The next few hours were a mix of familiar methods and routines, and the less familiar demands of surgery. Once, her father glanced up at the globe of light and asked Tessia to bring it closer to the table. She felt heartened by his

113

acceptance of her use of magic. The metal worker made a strangled noise as Veran made the first cut, then hurried out of the cellar.

Finally they were done. Tessia replaced the last of the tools, seared clean, in her father's bag. Yaden was now unconscious, but the rhythm of his breathing and blood was steady and strong. Her father gave the child one last thoughtful look, then turned to Tessia.

He smiled, then glanced meaningfully at the globe of light.

"Handy trick, that one. It's good to see you've been paying attention to your lessons."

She shrugged. "It's like learning the right way to use bandages. Once you know how, you don't think too much about it. I'm sure there's much harder magic to learn."

Something shifted in his gaze, removing the humour from his smile for a moment.

"It might . . . I suspect it would be unsettling for the villagers if you kept surprising them like that, though."

She nodded. "Yes. I think I might have scared them. Now I've seen how they react . . . I don't think I'll be drawing attention to myself like that again."

"Not unless it's necessary." He shrugged. "I'm sure they'd understand if you had to defend the village or save a life. You better let the family know we're finished."

She handed him his bag, then moved to the doorway. A lamp was sitting on the floor in the corridor. Picking it up, she moved it to the floor beside the boy then extinguished her light, leaving the room lit only by the comforting glow of the lamp.

"*There were strangers.*"

Tessia and her father stopped and looked at each other. Then she picked up the lamp and held it to one side of Yaden's head. His eyes were open. They moved to Veran.

"*Strangers in the hills,*" the boy whispered. "*Hunters' boys told us. Father said not to bother Lord Dakon, but it might be important. Will you tell him?*"

Tessia's father glanced at her, then looked at Yaden and nodded. "Of course. He probably knows already."

The boy grimaced. "*Hurts.*"

"I know. I'm about to give your mother something for you that will keep the pain away. Be patient. She'll bring it to you soon." He patted the boy's shoulder gently, nodded at Tessia and followed her to the doorway.

"Could be he's a bit delirious. Still, if his father knows something we'll know it's nothing to do with the illness. If he does, would you . . . ?"

She nodded. "I'll mention it to Lord Dakon."

He smiled, then turned back to the boy. As Tessia started along the corridor the metal worker's wife peered out of the entrance to the kitchen.

"Is he . . . ?"

"He's fine," Tessia told her. "Could you bring some more clean water?"

As the servants removed the empty plates, Lord Dakon opened the second bottle of wine and refilled Tessia's and Jayan's glasses. The apprentices looked surprised, and raised their glasses in a salute of thanks. Both had been unusually quiet this evening. Usually one or the other conversed with him during the meal, Tessia with more ease as the weeks passed, even though they rarely spoke to each other.

The division between them dismayed Dakon. It had started with Jayan. The young man was no extrovert, but he was sociable and cheerful enough to get along with most people. Yet he had clearly disliked Tessia from the moment she arrived.

It had taken Tessia a week or two to realise it. Jayan was

not the type to be petty or cruel. His impatient and disdainful manner did eventually give him away, however, and since then she had been quietly defiant, ignoring him when she could and occasionally retaliating with a delightfully biting remark when provoked.

Dakon was almost enjoying watching the pair. Almost.

Tonight there appeared to be something on Tessia's mind. Jayan, on the other hand, appeared to be unusually interested in Tessia, looking thoughtfully at her from time to time. It was a good thing Tessia was so distracted, as Dakon was sure this behaviour from his older apprentice would have made her irritable and suspicious.

"I have an announcement to make," he told them, then smiled as they straightened and looked at him with expectant curiosity. "In a week we will be travelling to Imardin."

Tessia's eyes opened wide. Jayan, in contrast, relaxed back in his chair, smiling with obvious pleasure.

"Imardin?" Tessia repeated.

"Yes. I travel there every year," Dakon explained, "to deal with matters of trade, buy what we can't get here in Mandryn and visit friends."

She nodded. That much wouldn't be a surprise to her, he knew. Like all the villagers she must have noted his yearly absences, and that he usually brought back cures and ingredients for her father. Her surprise was at the news that she would be travelling with him, and her next question confirmed it.

"We're both going with you?" she asked, glancing at Jayan, who frowned at the question.

"Of course. Jayan usually visits his family. The king requires all magicians to notify him of their intention to take on an apprentice. Though you are a natural and nobody can stop you learning magic, not even the king, I should at least give him the opportunity to meet you."

She glanced at Jayan again. "I hope this is a silly question, but what would happen if the village was attacked while you and Jayan were gone?"

It was not the question Dakon had expected, but if she was worried about the safety of her family it would naturally be a more pressing concern than the prospect of meeting the king.

Jayan's frown had disappeared, Dakon noted. He looked as though he was carefully keeping his face expressionless.

"Lord Narvelan would deal with it," Dakon assured her, "just as I deal with any trouble in his ley whenever he is absent."

She nodded, but there was still a crease between her eyebrows. Her fingers drummed softly on the table, and then she drew in a deep breath and looked up at him again.

"When we were treating the metal worker's boy today, he told us that hunters' children said they'd seen strangers in the mountains – and that you should know." She spread her hands. "It might be nonsense. The metal worker dismissed it as stories made up by the children to scare each other."

Dakon kept his expression neutral as he considered her words. It was possible this was just a piece of gossip, or a scary story as she'd suggested. Or the strangers might simply be Kyralian travellers, or even lawless bandits. It might only be Narvelan's fears of invasion that made the news sound sinister.

Or Hanara's belief that Takado would return for him. Dakon had read the man's mind this morning, deciding it would be foolish to leave the village without at least making sure the ex-slave wasn't planning some mischief. Fortunately the slave had submitted to the mind-read willingly. Dakon was not sure what he would have done if he hadn't. It had heartened him to find he was right: Hanara had no terrible plans for Mandryn. In fact,

Hanara's fear that his master would return indicated how badly he wanted to stay in Kyralia, and how unlikely he was to run back to his master. Dakon could not find any evidence in the ex-slave's memories that the Sachakan magician had spoken or indicated an intention to return.

Still, these rumours make me glad Narvelan is as diligent as he is. I should have it investigated. And have any news sent to him.

"I'll send someone to the hunters to see if there's anything to it," he told Tessia.

She nodded and looked away. For a moment he waited to see if she recalled what he'd said about the king, but she remained silent, having either not heard it or forgotten it.

"Any other questions?" he prompted.

Tessia frowned. "How long will we be gone for?"

"At least a month. It takes a week to get to the city at this time of the year, when the roads are still wet."

Her frown deepened. Knowing how she still worried about her father managing without her, he smiled. By all accounts, the healer's new assistant was learning fast. He decided to change the subject.

"You've never travelled before, have you?"

She shook her head.

"It will be a novel experience for you, then. I'll continue your lessons during the journey. It'll keep us entertained as well as add to your education. I'm afraid Jayan and I have made the journey so often enough that we'll probably only notice the rain and the cold.

"We'll stay with two other country lords as we pass through their leys. Otherwise we'll stop overnight in whatever town we manage to reach, with the town master. In Imardin we'll stay with a friend of mine, Lord Everran, and his wife Lady Avaria. He inherited one of the city's great Houses – a rather large half-empty building. They're both magicians – you may find it interesting to talk to another female magician, though Lady Avaria will probably be more interested in taking you round the shops in the city, and visiting her friends, each of whom will encourage you to spend all the allowance I give you, and more."

Tessia's eyes widened. "You don't have to—"

"Oh, believe me, I do," he told her, "or I will never hear the end of it from Avaria. Besides, I could hardly give Jayan a little spending money without doing you the same favour." He turned to look at Jayan. The young man shrugged. "Anything you wish to ask?"

Jayan shook his head, then hesitated. "Is there any more wine?"

Dakon laughed and reached for the bottle. "I'm sure we'll get one half-glass each from what's left. Then perhaps we can share a few of our travel stories."

"Are you sure that's wise?" Jayan asked, glancing at Tessia. "We don't want to make her wish she wasn't coming."

Dakon waved a hand dismissively. "Oh, nothing has ever happened that was truly dangerous or unpleasant."

"No?" Jayan asked, his expression clearly showing his disagreement.

"Nothing that didn't make for a good story afterwards, that is."

As Tessia's eyebrows rose, Dakon grinned. "Well, there was that time I was helping Jayan practise making fireballs . . ."

CHAPTER 10

Tessia slipped through the main door of Lord Dakon's house into the well-lit greeting hall. Lately the magician had insisted she use the front entrance, pointing out that he and Jayan used it, and the villagers would think he was neglecting to grant her the full benefits of her new status if she kept using the servants' door.

Everything was much fancier in this part of the house. A staircase wide enough for two or three people to ascend together, with gracefully carved railings, led up to the next floor. Broad openings on either side beckoned visitors into side corridors, from which they could access the dining room and a formal seating room.

As Tessia closed the door a head appeared from within one of the corridors. Keron smiled and nodded politely, and his head withdrew again. Tessia crossed to the stairs.

At the top of the staircase she paused. Dakon had suggested she have her last dinner before leaving Mandryn with her parents. Veran and Lasia had expressed their excitement over her coming journey in their individual ways, her mother exclaiming with delight and her father quietly giving advice on how to behave in the city. It had been nice, but exhausting. She was tempted to slip up to her room and bed.

Light spilled out of the library doorway and voices drifted to her ears. Tessia found herself moving towards the door instead of heading to her room. She doubted she would fall asleep despite her weariness. More likely she would lie awake, as she had the last two nights, thinking about the journey ahead, and what might happen in the city. Dakon might have last-moment instructions, too.

When she stepped into the doorway, Dakon and Jayan looked up. Both held books, she saw, but from the chatter she'd heard she guessed they had stopped to talk. The magician smiled, but a frown, quickly smoothed away, creased the apprentice's brow.

"Ah, Tessia," Dakon said. "How was your evening with your parents?"

"Good, Lord Dakon. They had a lot of advice." She shrugged. "I'm not sure how useful it will be, even if it was given with the best of intentions."

He chuckled. "I'm sure it was. Your mother hasn't visited Imardin, has she?"

"No. Father has, but not for over ten years. That seems to bother him now. I fear you have put ideas into his head."

"Hmm. Perhaps I should have invited him to join us. I expect it's too late for that now."

She caught her breath. It would have been wonderful to travel to Imardin with her father. He would have enjoyed it, she was sure. But it was likely he would have turned down the opportunity, not wanting to leave the village without a healer.

A short silence followed. She searched for something to say. "Is there anything else to be done before we leave in the morning?"

Dakon shook his head, but his expression as he regarded her was thoughtful. "There is one matter." He paused. "Now that you have gained control of your power, it is time we began the ritual of higher magic."

Tessia blinked, then felt a thrill of both excitement and dread. "Tonight?" She felt her heartbeat quicken. "Now?"

"Yes."

"Well then." She moved into the room. "How does it . . . work?"

"Perhaps it would be easier to show her," Jayan suggested. Tessia started in surprise. She had almost forgotten he was there.

Dakon turned to regard the apprentice. The pair exchanged unreadable looks, then Dakon slowly nodded. "Perhaps it would."

He rose from his seat and stepped into the space between the chairs. Jayan put his book aside, yawned and got to his feet. He smiled faintly, then an expression Tessia had never seen before smoothed his face and he looked older and more dignified. Moving towards Dakon, he stopped in front of the magician, his gaze fixed on the floor. Then he knelt and lifted his hands, palms upward, to the level of his head.

A shiver ran down Tessia's spine. Jayan was no longer just a young, disdainful man but a submissive, obedient apprentice. Dakon was no longer the benevolent lord of ley and village, but the master magician. *This is the world of magicians that ordinary people do not see*, she thought. A world they had kept private until now. A world she was a part of. The idea seemed unreal. Unbelievable. But perhaps after she took part in the ritual she would feel more like someone who belonged in their world.

Dakon reached into his shirt and took out a small, slim object. As he slid the object apart into two pieces, Tessia realised it was a tiny blade. Dakon touched the palms of both Jayan's hands with the point of the knife. If it hurt, Jayan hid it well. Then the magician put away the knife, placed his palms over Jayan's and closed his eyes.

Tessia held her breath, her heart still beating quickly.

A moment later Dakon lifted his hands from Jayan's, smiled and murmured something. The rite was over.

That's it? she thought. *No, of course that isn't it. There's always much more going on, when magic is involved.*

Jayan stood up, reflexively brushed the knees of his trousers with the backs of his hands, then took a cloth from within his clothing and wiped his hands. He glanced at her and shrugged.

"See? Nothing to it."

Nothing obvious to the eye, she thought wryly. But seeing him cheerfully survive the ritual was reassuring. She suppressed a sudden reluctance and swallowed her nervousness, then stepped forward. Jayan moved away as she approached, and Dakon gave her his usual encouraging smile. Facing him, she looked up, then away again as she realised it would be more uncomfortable the longer she prolonged the next part. She quickly dropped to her knees and held up her palms, keeping her eyes on the floor and trying not to visualise herself looking as submissive as Jayan had.

Submissive and yet respectful, she suddenly thought. *There is a dignity to the rite, I suppose. I wonder how the Sachakans do it. There's probably no ritual at all. They just rip the power from their slaves whenever they want to. So the fact there's a ritual at all for Kyralian magicians is a good thing. A sign of respect to the apprentices . . .*

She felt a sting of pain in one palm, and resisted the urge to look up. The second pinprick came. Then Dakon's hands met hers.

A faint feeling of dizziness came next. Then not so faint. She felt herself tilting and tried to recover her balance, but couldn't get her body to obey her. Hands grasped her shoulders, supporting her. The sensation of weakness became something more distinct and as she concentrated she felt another will drawing on her power. Though she recognised Dakon's presence linked to the will she instinctively resisted . . . in vain. For the first time since she had learned to harness her power she had no control over it.

Then, abruptly, it was given back to her. She felt her body jerk as it overreacted to her desire to regain her balance. Once again, hands steadied her.

"Don't worry. You'll work out how to stop yourself falling over."

The voice was Jayan's and came from behind her. He was the one supporting her. Suddenly, she only wanted to be on her feet and doing anything but kneeling on the floor relying on Jayan to keep her upright. Slipping out of his grasp, she stood up, reaching out to a chair to steady herself as a wave of dizziness came.

"Slowly," Dakon said. "You did well, but it can be a shock to the body until it grows used to it."

She turned to him. "That worked, then? I didn't do anything wrong?"

He smiled. "No. It worked. As Jayan said, your body will work out how to support itself. Your mind will adjust as well. How do you feel?"

She shrugged. "Fine. It was . . . interesting. Manageable." She glanced at Jayan, who was watching her with a faint smile on his face. "I'll be fine."

Dakon reached into his jacket again, but this time produced a small white cloth. He handed it to her. As she took it she realised that a thin trickle of blood had streaked her palm.

"Any questions?" he asked expectantly.

"Why is the cutting necessary?" she asked as she wiped her hands, pressing against the tiny cuts on each palm. They had already stopped bleeding.

"The skin of humans and animals is a boundary of sorts," he told her. "Everything within our skin we are in control of. That is why a magician cannot reach into another human's body and damage it, no matter how powerful he or she is. He can attack it from outside, but not influence anything within." Dakon moved back to his chair and sat down, and Jayan followed suit. "To gain control, we must break the barrier."

Tessia considered that information as she moved to her usual seat. "Is the magician taking power always in control? What happens if the person he is trying to control is a higher magician too?"

"The one taking power still has an unbroken barrier," Dakon pointed out. "Even if he did not, once he begins drawing magic he can also weaken the body. How much depends on the skill and intent of the magician using higher magic. If it is a benevolent exchange, as little as possible. If it is malevolent, the higher magician can paralyse his victim, making it difficult to even think."

Tessia shuddered. The ritual of higher magic was simple, but it was a tamed version of an act of violence and death. It was akin to asking apprentices to bare their throats to the thrust of a sharpened sword blade by their masters, trusting that the blade would not cut.

But no sword took strength from its victims. No sword, even used gently, could benefit its wielder the way higher magic did. The ritual was also an exchange of power, and of trust and respect. In return apprentices learned to use magic. They gained years of training and knowledge that they would otherwise have to gain from experimentation. They also had food and a home to live in while they learned, as well as nice clothes . . . and the occasional visit to Imardin to socialise with the powerful and influential. Perhaps even the king.

Suddenly it didn't seem that Dakon received much in return for his time and energy. Just magic. Unless he had a particular need for that extra magic, it must feel as though the effort and time were not worth it. No wonder that some magicians chose not to take on apprentices.

But as the cuts on Tessia's palms began to itch faintly, she ruefully acknowledged that there would be times she gave him plenty in return for her training, and made a mental note to herself to get hold of some wound balm before she left.

Under the light of an oil lamp and the half-moon, Hanara and two of the younger stable servants carefully rubbed grease into harness leathers and polished the trim of Lord Dakon's wagon.

Since he'd accepted Lord Dakon's offer of work and moved into the stable quarters, Hanara had felt much more comfortable with his surroundings. He felt less at ease with the stable servants, however. They constantly exchanged a teasing banter that no Sachakan master would have approved of. Hanara did not know how to respond to it, so he had decided to pretend that he understood their accent and ways less than he did. Whenever they played their foolish pranks on him he shrugged off the laughter. He'd endured far worse indignities, and his weary acceptance appeared to make them respect him in some strange way.

I was a source slave to an ashaki, he reminded himself. *They'll never understand what that meant – how few slaves gain that status.*

One in a thousand might. It was somewhere between being a Kyralian lord's personal, favourite servant and his apprentice. Except he was still a slave.

Now he was a commoner. But he was free. Surely what he had gained was better than what he had lost.

Like the other stable servants, he received coin each week from Lord Dakon – though it was handed out by Keron, the house master. Hanara hadn't known what to do with it at first. The women servants from the main house brought out food each morning and night, so he didn't need to purchase any. Boots and clothing had been given to him the day he'd moved into the stable. They were warmer than his old slave garb, but rough compared to the fine cloth Takado had provided. He slept on a pallet up in the stable loft, thankfully away from the other workers – who seemed to enjoy sleeping close to the horses – so he didn't need to pay for a roof over his head.

Eventually, by watching the others, Hanara gathered that the stable servants liked to spend their fee on frivolities in the village. The baker made sweets as well as bread. The metal worker's wife sold preserves, dried foods, scented candles, oils and balms. One of the old men carved scraps of wood into utensils and vessels that would have been better made of metal or pottery, as well as game pieces, bead necklaces and strange little figurines of animals and people.

At first Hanara did not see why he should waste his money on such objects. He watched the other workers compare their purchases when they returned to the stables, and noted whether they kept the item, or gave it as a gift – usually to one of the women of the village.

Slowly he came to realise that buying such items would give him an excuse to explore more of the village, so one day he followed some of the workers out on one of their excursions. They noticed him and insisted he join them. It might be that they accepted and wanted to include him, or they might have wanted to keep an eye on him. He had noticed how he was never left alone, and sometimes caught them watching him.

The villagers were welcoming to the stable servants, but each time they noticed Hanara their smiles became forced.

They continued to be friendly, even when he came forward to buy something, but when they turned away he saw their expressions turn to fear, wariness or dislike.

On their return to the stable, he noticed children peering from around the sides of houses, staring at him. Some ran away when he noticed them. It was ironic that they should fear him, who had once been a lowly slave.

The stable servants had also passed a gathering of four young women, who whispered and grimaced with distaste when they noticed Hanara. Two young men who saw this turned to regard Hanara with narrowed eyes as he and his companions went by.

Hanara was not surprised by the villagers' reaction to him. He was a foreigner. He was from a country that had once conquered their people. A member of a race they feared.

Tessia had told him that if any villagers bothered him, he was to tell her. She had assured him there were laws and rules that would protect him. He smiled as he remembered her visits. She, of all the villagers, did not fear or distrust him. The person who came closest to understanding him did not hate him.

Here, in the stables, it was easy to be amused by the haughtiness of some of the villagers. They weren't slaves, but they weren't as free as they thought they were. Most worked hard all the same. They might have their fee and their freedom, but they were bound to the lord they served because he owned the land they cultivated and the houses they lived in. They were subject to his whim as any slave was to his or her master. It just didn't feel like slavery to them because Lord Dakon was a benevolent and generous man.

He even asked if I would let him read my mind. I think he felt guilty about it, too. How can anyone be that scrupulous? That squeamish? It had been tempting to refuse, to see if Dakon would insist or apologise and leave, but Hanara had wanted the magician to know of the danger. Takado would return for him.

I don't think he believed it. He looked for evidence. I don't need evidence. I know Takado. What good is it being given my freedom by a man who can't protect me because he won't believe it when I say I'm in danger?

Perhaps he'd have been better off working for another, tougher magician. Or perhaps not. He'd noticed unhappy, fearful servants during Takado's travels through Kyralia. He'd heard stories and rumours. Kyralian magicians could be cruel, and there was not a lot their servants could do about it.

Not all ashaki are as cruel as Takado, he told himself. *Some of them are far worse, of course. But there are stories of ashaki who treat their slaves well.*

Takado was a cruel man, but rarely without reason. He did not hurt or kill a slave unless that slave had failed or offended him in some way. The punishment usually fitted the crime. Hanara had never heard of Takado harming a slave for entertainment, though it was not uncommon among other ashaki.

Hanara shifted in his seat, suddenly uncomfortable as a now familiar uneasiness stole over him again, as it had every night since he woke up bandaged head to foot in the Residence.

He could not understand why Takado had beaten him so badly and left him behind, when his mistake had been so small. *If Takado is not cruel without reason, then I just haven't seen the reason yet.*

But if Hanara hadn't earned such a savage punishment, what other reason might Takado have for beating him? Had he been trying to impress Lord Dakon? Had he intended for Hanara to be too badly injured to accompany him home?

What possible use was Hanara to his master while stuck here in Kyralia?

The most obvious answer was that he was meant to spy on Lord Dakon. Why Lord Dakon rather than any of the more powerful magicians, Hanara couldn't guess.

And how am I supposed to spy on him if I'm out here in the stables, and he's always in the Residence? If I go creeping around inside it'll make people suspicious. Not that they aren't suspicious already.

Dakon would be gone soon, too. How could he spy on the magician if he wasn't here?

How could Lord Dakon protect Hanara if he wasn't here? Hanara's heart began to race as it had when he first heard the magician was going to journey to Imardin.

Can I persuade Lord Dakon to take me with him?

He shook his head and sighed. Lord Dakon had been kind and generous, but Hanara knew the man was not a fool. The last place he'd take a possible spy was the city, where Hanara might learn something useful. He'd want Hanara here, watched by his own people, where he couldn't do any harm.

I am no spy. I have nothing to tell Takado. Soon I won't even know where Lord Dakon is.

But even before he'd finished the thought he realised that he was wrong. He knew where Lord Dakon *wouldn't* be. He also knew that a magician living nearby would protect the village if it was threatened.

He knew that while Takado could take this information from his mind, he had to reach Hanara first. For now all he could do was hope the precautions Lord Dakon had put in place would work.

PART TWO

CHAPTER 11

The magical shield encompassing the wagon kept the rain and wind at bay, but the only known methods of using magic to smooth the road surface were too slow or too laborious to be worth applying. Rutted mud, sometimes submerged under pools and puddles, the road was a torment to both horses and humans, sucking at the hoofs of the former and shaking and jolting the latter.

Someone needs to invent a better wagon, Dakon thought. He'd had the cover removed from this one because he found being enclosed in a rocking vehicle made him feel sick. Tanner, the driver, had stowed it away in case it was needed later.

Protecting himself and his companions with magic took little effort, and Lord Dakon had no trouble sparing attention for lessons. Two objects were moving through the air between the four passengers. One was a metal disc, the other a small knife. The knife kept shooting towards the centre of the disc, while the disc dodged away. Malia made a small noise and flinched as the knife whizzed past her ear.

"Wouldn't this be safer if I used something other than a knife?" Tessia asked, her voice strained.

Jayan stared hard at the disc. "It gives you the incentive to concentrate."

Her frown deepened, then Dakon saw it suddenly ease. Her eyes flickered towards Jayan. A faint smile touched her mouth. The knife wove through the air, then suddenly headed straight towards the disc.

A metallic clink was followed by a muttered curse from Jayan.

Dakon laughed at his older apprentice's expression of surprise.

"What did you do, Tessia?" he asked.

"I imagined what Jayan would see if the disc was between him and the knife. It blocked his view."

Dakon nodded. "Good. You used reasoning and imagination. You're no match for him in control and reaction speed yet, and until you are it is thinking like this that will win the game for you. Either that, or his laziness." Jayan frowned at Dakon in protest. "But it is dexterity that you need to learn. Now swap places."

Tessia's gaze remained fixed on the disc as she dodged and evaded the pursuing knife. They had played this game many times now. Jayan was running out of tricks to surprise her with and she was becoming more skilled at manipulating objects with magic and her will.

Dakon suppressed a smile. Travel was exciting only when venturing somewhere new, not when enduring the same bad roads that had jolted his bones every time he made this journey. How many times had he travelled to Imardin? He'd lost count.

As always, his apprentices provided distraction and alleviated the boredom. However, Dakon missed the conversations that had kept him entertained on previous journeys, as Jayan was reticent around Tessia and Tessia wasn't making up for the lack of talk, either. She was not the type of woman to chatter incessantly, thank goodness, but she, too, was disinclined to speak around her fellow apprentice.

Really, Dakon thought, *the two of them were a right pair of sulks when they were together.*

So he kept them both occupied with lessons. Even Malia appeared to draw some entertainment from the exercises, watching with fascination and sometimes a worried frown as she witnessed more magic being used than most country people saw in their lifetimes.

The servant had become more subdued and respectful as the days passed, Dakon noted. Perhaps she was intimidated by the display of power. Or perhaps it was exhaustion. She was the only house servant accompanying them – Cannia had asked him to take Malia instead of herself, saying she was getting too old for such journeys and the young woman needed the "maturing" effect of travel.

A cry of triumph from Jayan told Dakon the apprentice had finally got the knife to touch the centre of the disc. Dakon made a small gesture, and the two swapped roles again.

Jayan made a small chuckling noise. His disc abruptly halted, poised between himself and Tessia, and began to spin in circles. When she tried to send the knife at it, the spinning sides of the disc knocked it away. She looked at Dakon.

"Is that allowed?"

He shrugged. "No rule against it."

"But that's not fair. How am I supposed to get the knife in?"

He didn't answer, just looked at her expectantly. She turned her gaze back to the spinning disc.

"I suppose if I got the knife to spin around the disc at the same rate . . ."

Dakon smiled. "Let's see if you can, then."

The knife began to revolve round the disc, point always directed toward its quarry. But though its speed increased, it never matched the disc, which now spun so rapidly it had blurred into a sphere.

"I can't," she said and, frustrated, abandoned her attempt. "I can't see how fast it's going, so how can I match the speed?"

Jayan was trying hard to not look smug, Dakon noticed. "You can't," Dakon told her.

"So why did you have me . . . ?" She caught herself and looked thoughtful. "To learn that it's impossible," she concluded.

"Yes," he confirmed. "The most powerful magician in all history would still be vulnerable if he were blind. Our physical form is our greatest limitation."

She rubbed her temples. "I didn't need the demonstration," she said wryly, but without reproach. "I have a headache that's reminding me of my physical form very effectively."

"Then rest," he said. "It'll go away soon."

He looked at Jayan, considering what activity to suggest next. Jayan needed to hone his fighting skills, both magical and strategic. It was all too easy to skip battle exercises when settled in a peaceful and safe environment. The magical ones could be dangerous, both to magician and apprentice and to local buildings and people. Now that there were hints of a threat from Sachaka, he ought to make sure that Jayan, at least, was well prepared. But clearly they couldn't start throwing magic about while travelling.

A hopeful look had entered the young man's gaze. "Kyrima?"

Dakon nodded.

As Jayan dived into the baggage for the box of game pieces, Dakon smiled. He remembered playing the game with his own master. Kyrima had been banned by the Sachakans when they had occupied Kyralia, which was proof of its effectiveness in teaching battle strategy. Once independence had been regained, the game resurfaced, though after three hundred years of secret practice the rules had to be re-established, as so many different variations had evolved. Most magicians took the opportunity to play against new opponents whenever they could, because a player eventually learned the habits and mannerisms of those he or she regularly played against.

Malia and Jayan swapped seats in the wagon so Dakon and his apprentice were sitting opposite each other. They selected their pieces – a magician each and a number of "sources" decided by the roll of three dice. Another dice throw decided the strength of the magician. Jayan looked at Tessia and held out a waxed tablet and scribe.

"Score for us?"

She sighed and took the items. "Why is it that so many of your games are about war and fighting?"

"Conflict challenges us to extend ourselves – to stretch the limits of our skills and power," Dakon replied.

"Being able to defend our people and our country is part of our responsibility as magicians," Jayan told her. "To neglect to learn to fight is . . . well, it makes us the useless, glorified parasites that some say we are."

Dakon blinked and stared at Jayan, wanting to ask where the apprentice had heard such things said, but he did not want to be distracted from answering Tessia's question so he turned back to her.

"What we learn from these games we can apply elsewhere. The control you need for the disc and knife game might come in handy if you are occupied with something that takes more than two hands, and you do not have an assistant – or an assistant with the appropriate skill for the task."

As he'd expected, a familiar expression of comprehension came to her face, then an almost secretive thoughtfulness. He knew she was thinking how such a skill could be used in healing. That same expression had crossed her face when their discussions had touched on healing and magic too many times now for him to not recognise it.

Would she ever lose her interest – perhaps obsession –

with healing? Was there any harm in it? He hoped the answer to both questions was no. While her apprenticeship might have benefited if she had been as captivated by magic for its own sake, she was absorbing his lessons and gaining skills at an acceptable rate. More than acceptable, he was pleased to see. For an apprentice forced to learn while travelling, and sharing her master's time and attention with another, she was learning with impressive speed.

What was most startling was *how* she learned. She saw everything in reference to her physical self. He had been telling himself that this was because she had already learned to think from the perspective of a healer, but he had a nagging feeling that there was more to it than that. When shown how to use magic in a certain way, she grasped the concept immediately and understood all the variations, almost as instinctively as a newborn enka knows how to walk and then run and then jump.

He had no doubt that one day she would surpass him not just in strength, but in ability. It was going to be interesting to watch.

But when it came to battle training she showed a strong reluctance. Perhaps it was natural that someone so focused on mending was repelled by actions designed for harming. She needed to see the value of defensive skills. It was better to prevent an injury in the first place, than to have to treat it.

Turning back to the game, he gave his pieces their own tiny protective shields and suspended them. Jayan followed suit. Various items were positioned between them to act as obstacles, and they took it in turns to block the other's view by holding up a travel rug while they arranged their pieces. Then the rug was lowered and the game began.

At the end of the first round they had both used up most of their source pieces' value. Dakon took a risk and elevated one of his sources to a magician. This meant he had lost a source, but had two positions from which to attack. The start of a new round re-energised the sources, as it represented a night's rest.

"Why do your magicians have so many sources?" Tessia asked. "Kyralian magicians don't have that many apprentices."

"We don't," Dakon agreed. "But in war people can volunteer to be sources."

"Do you ever play with one or both sides arranged as if they are Sachakan magicians?"

"Yes."

"How is that different? Do you have to take the sources out of the game once they are used?"

"Not necessarily, though when playing 'Sachakan' you're allowed to kill sources and give your magician extra points. Sachakan magicians are not as inclined to kill their sources as they are rumoured to be. Sources are more valuable in an extended battle if they are alive to be useful again the next day."

"But not in a short battle."

"Or in a desperate situation," Dakon added.

"Why don't you represent non-magicians in the game? Ordinary people – or fighters."

"Ordinary weapons aren't much good against magicians," Jayan pointed out.

"Not unless the enemy is exhausted," she said. "If weapons are always ineffective, why do ordinary people make and learn to use them?"

"Ordinary people are a potential source of power during battle," Dakon told her. "They're best kept well out of the reach of the enemy. Non-magicians who use ordinary weapons are usually guards, and their purpose is mainly to protect or control ordinary people. It's been many hundreds of years since Kyralia had soldiers as part of its defence. Not since the times when magicians were few and expensive to hire. Hey!"

Taking advantage of Dakon's distraction, Jayan had struck one of the lord's magicians. Dakon didn't manage to strengthen its shield in time, and the piece glowed and began to melt. Sighing, and ignoring Jayan's triumphant grin, he drew it out of the game, carefully reshaped it while it was still hot, and held it to one side to cool before he put it in the box.

"Lord Dakon."

Tanner had spoken. Dakon looked up. The driver jerked his head in the direction of something further down the road. As Dakon looked beyond the man and took in the scene they were approaching, his stomach sank. Jayan turned and glanced behind, then looked back at Dakon. Without saying a word, they returned the pieces to the box, discarded the "obstacles" and, as the wagon slowed to a stop, climbed out.

Once the wagon was still, Tessia stood up to get a better view of the scene before it. A stream or small river, bloated from the rain, crossed their path. The water's flow was fast, swirling around the broken wooden supports of a bridge and the remains of the carts that must have been crossing it when the bridge gave way.

On both sides of the stream people milled about, suggesting that the bridge had failed some time ago and plenty of travellers had arrived since to find their way blocked. Most were locals, Tessia guessed. All were staring at Dakon and Jayan, no doubt taking note of their expensive clothing. Several carts were lined up along the road – most on the opposite bank – piled high with goods of various kinds. There was even a small herd of reber, their woolly coats dripping and their bellies dark with mud.

Suddenly she felt a soft but insistent tapping on her shoulders and head. As cold moisture penetrated her dress she hastily created a shield to shelter herself, Tanner and Malia from the rain. Dakon and Jayan were striding towards the fallen bridge, taking their own shields with them.

Should she follow? There was nothing she could do that they weren't more capable of handling. But it was possible someone had been hurt. Taking care to make sure Malia was still sheltered by a shield, Tessia began to climb out of the wagon.

"Oh, Apprentice Tessia, should you be leaving the wagon?" Malia asked anxiously. "What if someone tries to take something?"

Tessia paused, looked around and smiled. "What? While you and Tanner are on board? They wouldn't dare."

It wasn't easy climbing off a wagon wearing a dress — at least with any kind of dignity. The hem caught on a protruding piece of wood, and she paused to tug it free.

"But it's a mess," Malia said anxiously.

"All the more reason to have a look," Tessia replied, stretching a leg towards the ground. It didn't quite reach, but she was close enough. She let herself drop.

And felt her foot sink deep into mud.

Looking down, she lifted her skirt enough to see that she had sunk well past the top of the dainty boots Malia had dug up from some store of feminine clothes in the Residence — possibly Dakon's mother's. They had been a compromise. Tessia had wanted sturdy boots for the journey, while Malia had wanted her to wear delicate shoes worthy of palace courtiers.

Holding on to the wagon for support, Tessia reached out with her other foot, seeking firmer ground. Fortunately she found it a mere step away. With one leg now on a solid base, she pulled her foot from the mud.

And it slid out of her dainty boot, leaving the mud free to slowly slump and cave in over the top. Malia sighed.

"See what I mean?" she said sadly. "Probably ruined them. Should I dig it out?"

Tessia looked up at Malia and felt a stab of guilt. The poor girl would have quite a job cleaning mud off clothes and shoes tonight. Then she looked at the shrinking hole. Muddy shoes shouldn't put anyone off helping others. Still, there was no need to make Malia's life any harder than necessary.

Ignoring the lingering headache from Dakon's lessons, Tessia focused her mind on the ground and exerted her will. Mud now flowed away from the hole. As the edge of the leather appeared she concentrated on building a magical force down and around the shoe, cupping it and drawing it up. It came free with a sucking sound. She grabbed it and felt liquid sloshing around inside, tipped it upside down to let the water out, then slipped it back on her foot. Malia made a wordless protest.

Tessia looked up and shrugged. "If I walk around without a shoe I'm going to get my stockings just as dirty."

Malia wrinkled her nose in reply.

Turning away, Tessia headed towards the bridge. A large horse stood tethered nearby, broken harness still hanging from flanks and neck. Jayan and Dakon were standing on one side of the bridge, hands on hips and, from the looks on their faces, arguing. She caught a few words as she approached.

"—me do it."

"No, it's too easy to break a rib or—"

As she rounded the remains of the bridge she saw what they were discussing. A man was clinging to one of the broken support columns, midstream. He wore the typical leather vest of a metal worker. *I can't believe they're arguing about this. He could fall in at any moment.*

"How long has he been there?" she asked, moving quickly to Dakon's side. "He looks tired."

Jayan's mouth closed with an audible snap and he looked away. Dakon glanced at her, than back at the stranded metal worker. His eyes narrowed.

The man's eyes flew open as he began to move away from the column. He gave a shout and clawed at the beam; then, as he was drawn too far away to reach it, scrabbled at the air. Then he belatedly realised he was moving upward, not falling downward, and he went limp. It was a strange sight, this sodden, stunned man floating slowly through the air towards the bank of the stream.

When his feet met the ground his legs folded and he collapsed. Tessia moved to his side. He didn't appear to have any wounds. His gaze was unfixed and he was breathing rapidly. She felt for his pulse and counted. His skin was cold. He needed warmth and dry clothing.

Looking up, she found a ring of people standing around her, their expressions full of curiosity and puzzlement. Dakon stood within the ring, watching her with an unreadable expression.

"He's dazed," she told him. "He needs drying out and warming up. Is there anyone here who knows him? A relative? Friend?"

"Boy was with him," a man in the crowd said, stepping forward. "Washed up downriver. Drowned."

A son? Or apprentice? She grimaced and looked down at the man, whose distant expression hadn't changed. Perhaps he hadn't heard. She hoped so. That was the last piece of information he needed right now.

"I'd take him home to his wife." The speaker glanced at the bridge. "I'm headed that way, but . . ." He waved at the broken bridge.

Home is on the other side, she guessed.

"I'll deal with that," Dakon said. "Stay here." As he walked away the small crowd parted to let him through. Jayan hurried after. The pair approached the trees that grew on one side of the road, part of a forest maintained by the local lord, and disappeared in the undergrowth.

Tessia looked at the man who had spoken, then glanced down at the prone metal worker.

"You know him?"

The man shrugged. "I've bought wares from him. He lives in Little Smoketown, a way down past the stream."

"Serves him right," someone in the crowd said. "Took too much weight over the bridge."

"Didn't wait, either. Travellers aren't supposed to cross more than one cart at a time," someone else argued. "Lord Gilar said so."

"How're *we* supposed to know that?" another said. "If your lord knew the bridge might break, he should've fixed it."

"Have to now," the first speaker said quietly.

"Won't," said a short, stocky man who had come up to peer at the metal worker. "Too miserly. He'll make us use the southern bridge."

Groans came from several onlookers, and a few muttered curses. The crowd had crept forward, drawn by curiosity and the conversation.

"This road is the most direct route for Lord Dakon to take to the city," Tessia told them. "If Lord Gilar is resistant to local voices, maybe my master's need for a safe bridge will persuade him."

The crowd fell silent and she guessed they were wondering whether she would repeat what they'd said to Lord Dakon. Expressions became wary. She could not help wondering if people living on Dakon's land spoke as resentfully of him.

Would he leave a dangerous bridge in place? But Lord Gilar had left instructions to prevent the bridge's fall, and perhaps he was in the process of dealing with the problem. Perhaps he was waiting for materials or skilled workmen to arrive, or for safer weather to be working in.

A distant thud drew everyone's attention to the forest. She felt it in the ground, through her soggy boots. People turned to stare expectantly. Small trees quivered as something disturbed them, each one closer to the road. Finally the undergrowth parted and a huge log slid forward onto the mud.

It was as thick as a man was tall, and longer than three wagons and their horses standing end to end. The bright pale fresh wood where branches had been cut away stood out from the darker, wet bark. Dakon and Jayan stepped out of the forest. They paused in discussion for a moment, then Dakon moved closer to the trunk. He stared at it intently.

A crack split the air, and the log fell into two halves, split down its length.

Tessia heard gasps from all around. Possibly from her own mouth as well. *Well, that* was *impressive*, she thought.

All watched as magician and apprentice slid the log halves forward, curved side down like the hulls of boats. They pushed them across the bloated stream to settle beside each other, making a flat platform with a small gap between. Dirt around the end of the logs swelled outward, allowing the new bridge to sink into the ground and raising the road surface to meet the flat top of the logs.

Jayan crossed the new bridge and balanced on the other end as he repeated the embedding process on the other side.

One day I'll be able to do that, Tessia thought. *Clearly they used their power to shift the log, but what sort of magic did they use to split it? Or cut it down in the first place?* The ends of the trunk hadn't been split or burned. Clearly, she had a lot to learn. Suddenly the knowledge that she would one day be able to use magic in such impressive and useful ways was exciting and appealing. *It's not all about fighting after all.*

Jayan returned to Dakon's side, then the pair turned to look at her. Dakon nodded towards the wagon meaningfully. She realised he intended to cross the new bridge first, to demonstrate that it was safe. People had begun to head for their carts, and soon a queue would form before either end of the bridge.

She looked down at the metal worker. With magic she could dry him out and warm him up, but in the state he was in it would only terrify him further. She looked up at the man who had volunteered to return him to his home.

"Have you got any blankets?"

The volunteer met her gaze, and nodded. "I had better get my cart." Then he grimaced and looked at the river. "And I suppose I'd better fetch the boy, too," he added.

She gave him a grim smile of thanks. "Do it quickly and I might be able to arrange for you to follow us across the bridge."

He hurried away. Tessia headed for the wagon. Though she would have preferred to accompany the metal worker to his home and make sure he was treated properly, he appeared to be in good hands. She was not the local healer and the man had no serious injuries. Her father always knew when to insist and when to let people take care of themselves.

Still, if Dakon was willing to wait a little, the metal worker might get home sooner. And if his helper crossed the bridge after them, he would probably remain behind them until he turned off the road. If the sick man took a turn for the worse, she would be close by and still able to assist.

CHAPTER 12

The only objects Tessia could see were the sphere of light floating above them, the wagon, its occupants, the horses that pulled it, and a circle of constantly shifting ground below them. Nothing broke the darkness on either side, though occasionally a tiny pair of eyes flashed in and out of sight. If it weren't for the endless flow of rutted road surface passing below them, she'd have wondered if they were moving at all, or simply bumping up and down on the spot.

Dakon's games had ended hours ago. Much earlier they had said farewell to the metal worker's helper, as he pulled up before a shop in a small village. The incident at the bridge might have happened days before, it felt so long ago.

Travelling was not as exciting as it ought to be, Tessia decided. It involved long stretches of discomfort and boredom. And hunger. The delay at the broken bridge meant travelling in darkness, well past their usual mealtime.

The evenings were usually much more pleasant. They'd stayed with a village master the first night. Every village and town had a master who oversaw the work of the locals, and the houses they lived in contained a few extra rooms for when their own or any passing lord visited. The next night they'd stayed with a town master of Lord Gilar's, and tonight they would be staying with Lord Gilar himself.

Suddenly Jayan straightened in his seat. Moments before he had been snoring softly, in danger of slumping against

Dakon – she had been half hoping he would, just to see his embarrassment, but also hoping he wouldn't as it would embarrass Dakon. Now his eyes widened with hope.

"A light," he said. "We're nearly there – at last."

Tessia turned to see a single, lonely light ahead of the wagon. It flickered in the misty air. As they drew near she saw it was a simple oil lamp hanging from a pole where another road intersected with the main thoroughfare. Tanner directed the horses onto the side road.

Watching the light shrink behind them, Tessia wondered whether they would have found the turn if it hadn't been signposted so effectively. She figured their host must have sent a servant out to light it.

The new road was less rutted and bumpy. The horses slowed as the road slowly and steadily rose along the side of a hill. She was looking forward to reaching their host's house, but was not looking forward to meeting the man himself. What if the bridge *had* failed out of neglect? She had been steeling herself these past few hours, expecting she would have to show a respect she didn't feel, and resist the urge to speak her mind.

The wagon turned a sharp corner, leading them into a treed valley. Turning around, Tessia saw that, at the far end of this valley, a wide stone façade glowed with the light of many, many lamps.

It was bigger than the Residence. Bigger than any building she'd seen before. A high wall stretched between the two arms of the valley, broken by two towers. The only windows were tiny slots in the towers, high up. In the middle of the wall was a huge pair of wooden doors.

"Lord Gilar's Residence," Lord Dakon said. "It was built before the Sachakans conquered Kyralia, when there were few magicians and fortifications like this, which can only really repel non-magical attack, were worth the time and expense of construction."

As the wagon approached the doors they began to swing open. They rolled through into a narrow courtyard. Another wall towered before them. They passed through a doorless entrance and into a covered, cobbled area.

There a short, thin man with grey streaking his black hair stepped out from between another pair of wooden doors, smaller than the ones at the front but still large.

"Lord Gilar," Dakon said, climbing to the ground.

"Lord Dakon," the man replied. The pair grasped each other's upper arms briefly. As Jayan, Tessia and Malia disembarked, servants emerged from a side door. One stepped forward to murmur something to Tanner, who was now holding the halter of one of the horses. Another beckoned to Malia, who smiled and moved to the woman's side.

"You have met Apprentice Jayan before," Dakon said.

"Indeed I have," Gilar said in a slightly husky voice. "Welcome back, young man. And this is your new apprentice?" He turned to smile at Tessia. "The one you mentioned in your letter?"

"This is Apprentice Tessia," Dakon told him. "A natural – the daughter of Mandryn's healer, Veran."

"Welcome, Apprentice Tessia," Gilar said.

"Thank you, Lord Gilar."

He turned back to Dakon and gestured towards the double doors. The two magicians moved inside. Jayan followed. Tessia trailed after, noting that Malia had disappeared with the servants. She felt suddenly unsure of her place.

I've never been a part of a servant's world, attending to the needs of people more important and wealthy than me. I've not been part of the world of powerful people either. She suddenly felt lucky to have grown up in that comfortable state between the two opposites, answering to a powerful man, but of a higher status and with greater freedoms than a servant. Though now that she considered it, the purpose of a healer was to attend to the needs of all who needed him or her, including servants. They served the servants. That ought to put them on the bottom of the service hierarchy.

"You were delayed?" Lord Gilar asked.

"Yes. I made you a temporary bridge today. When we came to the second bridge after the border post, we found it had collapsed."

Gilar nodded slowly. "I know the one. I've been undecided whether to replace it for a while now. It was strong enough for light usage, but the road has been getting busier in recent years."

"The rain and swollen stream probably contributed, too. A metal worker's cart fell when it collapsed. A boy drowned."

Gilar grimaced. "I'll have to find out the details. I have to confess, I was hoping the bridge's weakness would act in our favour if we were ever attacked."

Attacked? Tessia thought. *By who?*

Dakon's eyebrows rose. "More likely it would prevent locals from fleeing." He shrugged. "The temporary bridge I made is rough and narrow. You'll need to replace it with a proper bridge wide enough for vehicles to pass each other, and with railings for safety."

Gilar shrugged. "Of course. But let's leave the planning for later. Right now you and your companions would probably appreciate a bath and a meal. I've had the servants prepare rooms for you all."

They'd entered a greeting hall that, despite the scale of the place, was modest in size. Gilar led them up a staircase to a corridor, then indicated rooms on either side for Lord Dakon, Tessia and Jayan.

"I'll leave you to your baths," he said. "I'll see you at dinner."

A servant girl stood waiting outside Tessia's room. As Tessia moved to the door the girl opened it for her. Within the room was the usual bedroom furniture, Tessia's travel trunk, and a tub full of water. Two servants bent over the tub, one pouring water out of a large jug and the other holding a similar, empty vessel. The women turned, bowed to Tessia, lifted their burdens and filed out of the room.

The servant girl drew Tessia's attention to scrubs and oils, combs and drying cloths.

"Would you like someone to help you, Apprentice Tessia?" she asked.

"No. Thank you."

"Come out when you are ready and I'll take you to dinner."

After the girl had left, Tessia heated the bath water with magic, then peeled off her travelling clothes. The hem of her dress was caked with dried mud. Her stockings were stained and her boots were a sad shadow of their former selves. The warm water soothed muscles aching from the jolting of the wagon and she lay quietly for a short while, glad to be still again, before climbing out and drying herself. Looking into the bath, she saw that the water was a soupy brown clearing slowly as sediment settled at the base of the tub.

I had no idea I was so dirty, she mused. *And how did I manage to get mud as far up as my elbows?*

She changed into a clean dress, then combed out her hair and tied it neatly back. Then she opened the door to her room and peered out. The girl servant was waiting outside. She nodded to Tessia.

"Follow me, Apprentice Tessia."

"Have Lord Dakon and Apprentice Jayan left already?"

"Yes, Apprentice Tessia."

They embarked on another journey through the house, down to the lower level. The servant stopped at a doorway and with a graceful gesture indicated that Tessia should enter.

"The Lady Pimia and her daughter Faynara await within," she said.

Moving through the door, Tessia saw that two women were seated at a small round table. One was older, though perhaps not as old as Lord Gilar. Tessia guessed she was Lady Pimia. The younger woman was short and curvaceous, with a pretty face. Both looked up at Tessia, then rose to greet her.

"You are Apprentice Tessia?" the older woman asked then, not waiting for an answer, continued, "I'm Lady Pimia and this is Faynara. Please sit down. You must be starving. The servants are ready and will bring the first course immediately."

Tessia let herself be ushered to a chair. As she sat, the other two women returned to their seats. Tessia looked around the room, though more to confirm her suspicions than to examine her surroundings. There were no other tables or chairs.

"Thank you for arranging the bath, Lady Pimia," Tessia said. "Will Lord Gilar and Lord Dakon be joining us?"

Lady Pimia waved a hand. "No, no. The men will be eating together. They have important things to discuss. Magic. Politics. History." She shrugged dismissively and Faynara made a face. "We would hardly get a word in if we all ate together."

Tessia felt a pang of disappointment. Was it usual for women apprentices – or even magicians – to be excluded from "important" discussions? She felt a twinge of jealousy and annoyance. Why should Jayan get to talk about magic, and not she? *Well, I can't be sure Jayan is there. It might just be Gilar and Dakon, two magicians nattering about whatever magicians natter about, while Jayan is eating somewhere on his own.*

"So how did you come to be an apprentice magician?" Faynara asked.

Without warning, Takado's leering face flashed into Tessia's mind. She ignored it and the contempt it roused. "By accident. I didn't even know I'd used magic until Lord Dakon told me, and then he wasn't sure until he tested me."

"You're a natural!" Faynara exclaimed, smiling with delight. "How lucky for you. What did you do before then?" A tiny crease had appeared between Lady Pimia's eyebrows.

"I assisted my father, who is a healer."

"Ah," Pimia said approvingly. "That would explain why you speak so well."

"I have magical ability," Faynara said proudly.

Tessia looked at the girl with interest. "How many years have you been learning?"

"Oh, I'm only a latent," Faynara shrugged.

Tessia frowned. "Latent?"

"We decided not to develop Faynara's powers," Lady Pimia said, smiling at her daughter. "She wasn't interested in becoming a magician, but her ability should bring a fine choice of suitors. Her older brother is apprenticed to Lord Ruskel of Felgar ley."

"So . . . does learning magic deter suitors?" Tessia asked hesitantly.

The two women laughed quietly. "Perhaps," Pimia said. "Mostly, learning magic would take up too much of Faynara's time and she would gain little benefit from it, apart from a few useful tricks. She's better off learning the arts of running a home and being a good wife."

"You can't become a magician just for a few useful tricks," Faynara added, grimacing. "You have to go all the way. That takes *years*. There's no point marrying and having children until you're finished, and you have to go wherever your master goes."

Tessia thought about Jayan's view that a magician has a

responsibility to protect his people and his country. She wondered what he would think of Faynara's dismissal of her opportunity to become a magician. Gilar's daughter would be of no use to Kyralia if it was attacked.

Or would she? As a latent magician, she would be a powerful source of magic. Listening to the young woman list the advantages of not learning magic, which included the ability to shop and visit friends in Imardin whenever she wanted, Tessia found it hard to imagine Faynara being a dedicated student.

Then she remembered Lord Dakon's lesson about physical limitations restricting what a magician could do with his or her power. Perhaps there were mental limitations as well. While teaching someone who did not apply himself would be difficult, teaching someone who simply did not take her power seriously could be dangerous.

"Gilar informed me that you will be staying a day, then leaving the morning after," Pimia said. "We will have to think up an entertainment for you to enjoy tomorrow."

Tessia smiled and nodded. *I wonder what these women consider entertainment?*

"Is this your first visit to Imardin?" Faynara asked.

"Yes."

"Oh!" Faynara clapped her hands together. "How exciting for you. I must tell you who the best jewellers, shoemakers and tailors are!"

Although she doubted Dakon's allowance would extend far enough for such luxuries, Tessia decided she might as well take the young woman's advice. Even if she did not need it herself, she might be socialising with women who felt such things were important.

After all, if I'm not going to be included in important discussions, I might have to have unimportant ones with women like Pimia

154

and Faynara. It will be useful to know what they consider good conversation . . . and entertainment.

The night before they had set off for Imardin, Dakon had told Jayan about the Circle of Friends and the true purpose of his visit to Imardin. The information had left Jayan feeling both shock and pride. He was pleased Dakon had decided to entrust him with the secret, but horrified by the possibility that their fears might be proved justified, and Kyralia be invaded by Sachaka again. Annoyingly, he couldn't enjoy his new status as confidant because every time he thought about it, he inevitably wound up worrying about the future. Was he ready for battle, if it came? Was Kyralia?

When he considered the possibility of Dakon being killed he felt a tightness in his chest. He hadn't realised how much he had grown to respect and like his master and teacher. He found himself worrying about Tessia, too. If they faced an attack, Dakon would need his help. But Tessia was too new to magic to be an effective fighter. She did not have the time or inclination to become one, either. She would need protecting. But his loyalty must be to Dakon first. He had to trust that the magician would protect Tessia, or else send her away somewhere safe.

Dakon didn't want Tessia knowing the real reason for his trip to Imardin. Travelling far from her parents for the first time would be challenging enough, without adding to it the fear of an attack from Sachaka. This first trip to Imardin ought to be an enjoyable one.

So, not surprisingly, she had not been admitted to the dinner conversation tonight. Apparently she'd eaten with Lord Gilar's wife and daughter. *That would have been a new experience for her. It's obvious Gilar chose Pimia to be his wife for her magical bloodline, not her intelligence, and Faynara isn't much better. Still, they're well mannered. They wouldn't look down on Tessia openly, or try to manipulate or trick her.*

Conversation between Dakon and Gilar had been almost solely about the threat from Sachaka and Dakon's coming meeting with the king. Lord Gilar had switched between declaring that no Sachakan would ever dare to invade Kyralia to believing they were all doomed, then back again. These shifts from confidence to despondency confused Jayan at first, then disappointed him.

Lord Gilar is a bit mad, I suspect. He's got no grasp on reality. I can't imagine him being a help during battle – more a hindrance. Dakon had to talk Gilar out of battle-training his farmers or getting them to abandon their crops and animals to spend months building walls around his borders. Jayan wondered if Gilar's education had included any battle strategy at all. The man overestimated how long a physical barrier could delay a magician. One moment he couldn't see the value of his people as sources, the next he was excessively concerned about not letting them become a resource for the enemy.

By the time dinner ended Jayan was exhausted from suppressing the desire to tell the man what an idiot he was, and immensely grateful to have a teacher as sensible as Lord Dakon. *I pity any apprentice who finds himself receiving lessons from Lord Gilar.*

They finished late in the night, long after the women of the house had retired to bed. Instead of heading to his room, Dakon indicated he wanted Jayan to follow him into the small seating room next door.

"Not tired?" Jayan asked.

Dakon grimaced. "Of course, but we don't get much opportunity to talk privately at the moment. What did you think of Lord Gilar?"

Jayan sat down. "I'm surprised he's a member of the Circle of Friends."

"Oh? He's a country magician. Why wouldn't he be?"

"He's hardly the reliable type. Constantly changing his mind."

Dakon chuckled. "I think if all doubts of an invasion were allayed he would be much more . . . decided."

"All doubts allayed meaning an invasion taking place?"

"Yes."

"Until that happens can you rely on his support?"

"Oh, yes. But he's a man who finds it easier to follow the guidance of others than decide on action himself. The trouble is, within the Circle there are conflicting opinions on whether we need to make preparations, and what they should be." Dakon stretched and yawned. "Gilar does have good intentions, he just isn't always consistent in carrying them out."

Jayan thought of the bridge, and nodded.

"Whereas there are some in Imardin who are quite the opposite," Dakon continued. "Their intentions are not so good, and they are astute at carrying them out. We will have to tread carefully."

"But surely it is in their interest to help us. There can't be much benefit to letting the enemy invade, unless . . . do you think some are traitors? Most Kyralian families contain some Sachakan blood, if you look back a few generations."

"No. Not yet, at least, and I doubt it would be for that reason. After two hundred years I don't think there are any who would not consider themselves Kyralian. They would rather think of themselves as descendants of the Kyralians who gained us independence than of the Sachakans who conquered and ruled the previous generations."

"You should hear my father talk." Jayan grimaced. "He says it was only breeding with Sachakans that brought toughness into the Kyralian race. Sometimes I think he'd like to thank them personally."

Dakon smiled. "Yet is he still proud to be Kyralian?"

"Stiflingly," Jayan replied. He sighed. "I don't think he'd like to see Kryalia invaded. Surely to suggest allowing such a thing would be considered traitorous?"

"Some will reason that if only the country leys are overtaken they will not be affected. They will be tempted to strike a bargain, give the Sachakans some land in exchange for avoiding a war. We must convince them that, in the long term, they will suffer for it."

"Do you think they're expecting us, and have prepared?"

"Perhaps. It is no great secret that the country magicians have formed an alliance of sorts due to fear of invasion."

No great secret. "Gilar didn't seem particularly careful. Tessia was a bit puzzled by his comments about the bridge being a barrier to invasion."

Dakon frowned, then sighed. "I'll have to tell her eventually. It's just . . . it's a bit cruel so soon after she's discovered her powers. One moment she has a wonderful gift, the next she might have to use it to fight in a war."

Jayan felt a stab of alarm. "Fight?"

"Well . . . be a source, not literally fight. But it still involves risk." Dakon looked over at Jayan, his face suddenly thoughtful. "I've noticed that while you are being nicer to her, she still appears wary of you."

Jayan grimaced. "Yes, I don't think she's forgiven me for being so tough on her when she first arrived."

"Has your opinion of her changed?"

"A little," Jayan admitted grudgingly.

"What changed it?"

Shifting in his seat, Jayan avoided Dakon's gaze. "Something . . . happened. Before we left. I was trying to be friendly, but instead sounded like an idiot. She got all defensive. I don't remember exactly what . . ." He paused, remembering the moment and feeling an echo of realisation and admiration. "It wasn't what she said, but the way she said it." He shook his head. "And then it was as if I could see into the future. When she knows what she's talking about, she has such *conviction*. I imagined what that would be like, when she was older and more confident, and it was almost . . . scary."

Dakon chuckled. "You're right, of course. She is a natural. It's possible she'll surpass us both in power, and she has the focus and discipline of someone already used to study."

Jayan paused. Dakon hadn't quite taken in what he had been trying to say. *I wish I was better at explaining things like this.* But he wasn't sure how to. Once he'd found something to like in Tessia, her fixation on healing and demands on Dakon's time had suddenly become unimportant. And he began to find more things about her to like. Her practicality and lack of fussiness. How she was more inclined to hide discomfort to the point of her own detriment, rather than complain. The hints he had caught of a great store of healing knowledge, which in itself was amazing in someone so young.

But he had no idea how to communicate this, or to apologise for his earlier behaviour. So she continued to assume he hated her, and she hated him in return. *How am I supposed to let her know I no longer resent her, when I'd have to admit why I resented her in the first place? And when she ignores me all the time anyway.*

"Do you think she'll ever lose this interest in healing?" he asked.

"I hope not. Plenty of magicians waste their spare time on worse things."

"Would the Healers' Guild accept her?" Jayan wondered aloud. He'd not heard of any magician receiving training through the Healers' Guild, or any other trade guild for that matter. Maybe they gave some assistance to magicians, but the idea they'd take one on as a student was, well, ludicrous.

"Maybe. She may not want to join them, since she won't need their endorsement in order to earn a living."

Jayan frowned as he considered, again, his earlier assessment of her future. He'd doubted that she would be given highly paid magical tasks due to her lowly origins and lack of connections to powerful families. Perhaps he could help her, when the time came. Perhaps she would make some influential friends while they were in Imardin.

"So how are you going to keep Tessia occupied while you're meeting the Circle and the king?"

Dakon smiled. "Oh, Everran's wife will keep her well and truly distracted."

Jayan winced. "You're going to leave her in Avaria's hands?"

"She'll be fine." Dakon sighed and rose. "Best get some sleep. Lady Pimia is bound to have some foolish activity planned for us tomorrow, and Gilar will no doubt want to talk more."

Jayan stood up and moved towards the door of his room. Would the women Tessia spent her time with in Imardin accept her? They could be cruel, when they took a dislike to someone.

Then I'll make it known that I don't approve. There are, at least, some benefits to being the son of an influential, if unlikeable, Kyralian patriarch. Perhaps it will be a way to make up for being mean to her at the beginning.

He stepped into his bedroom and closed the door.

I just have to learn to stop saying things that she can take the wrong way.

CHAPTER 13

A t first Tessia caught a glimpse of a strange flat area in the dip between two hills and wondered what it was. It looked like a second sky, but darker, and it lay where there should have been land.

Then the wagon rolled around the curve of a hill and a great expanse of blue appeared. She knew it must be the sea. What else could it be? Flat, yet constantly stirring as if alive. Rippled like the surface of a pond tickled by the wind, occasionally foaming like a river running fast. And there were objects on the water she had only seen in paintings. Tiny, tiny ships, and even smaller boats.

She hadn't yet grown used to the sight when Imardin came into view.

It had been clear they were drawing close. The road had grown busier, populated with a constant flow of people and their carts, wagons and domestic beasts. It wound alongside the wide Tarali river towards a range of southern hills. She had been told the city sat at the foot of the first hill. She had also been told that it lay where the river flowed into the sea, allowing safe mooring for ships at its docks.

As the wagon continued past the hill, a blanket of stone and roof tile appeared and she stared in amazement.

"You look surprised, Tessia," Jayan observed, smiling smugly.

"It's bigger than I expected," she admitted, quashing her annoyance.

161

"Imardin is a third the size of Arvice, Sachaka's main city," Dakon told her. "But Sachakans prefer sprawling single-storey mansions. Kyralians build two- to three-storey houses, closer together so they fit more in a smaller space."

She turned to look at him. "Have you been to Arvice?"

He smiled and shook his head. "No, but the description came from a friend not given to exaggeration."

Looking back at the city, Tessia tried to match landmarks with those she'd seen on maps and drawings. The road they were travelling on, which had been paved for some time now, crossed the city in a gentle curve, then continued along the coast.

On the side we're approaching from it's called the North Road, within the city it's the Main Road, and on the other side it becomes the South Road, she reminded herself. *All very simple and logical.*

Five wide streets ran parallel to the Main Road, each a measure further up the hill. From the docks another wide thoroughfare climbed upward, crossing all six roads, to the Royal Palace. This was King's Parade, and where it met the Main Road there was a wide area called Market Square.

The tangle of buildings before her hid most of these features. She could see that some rooftops followed the line of the roads, but mainly they were a muddle of different shapes and sizes. Only the towers of the Royal Palace, at the high side of the city, were distinct. As the wagon reached the first structures along the road it became even more obvious that this was not the ordered, clean city that the maps had suggested.

These first dwellings were hovels clearly made from salvaged materials. They were half hidden behind droves of dirty, thin people in ragged, tattered clothes. A woman whose wide grin exposed a few remaining blackened teeth limped up to the wagon, holding up a basket of wrinkled fruit. She did not come too close, Tessia noticed. Others approached as the wagon passed, offering wares no fresher or more appealing. Looking beyond them, Tessia saw that arms were rising in appeal among an endless row of people huddling by the hovel walls, like a flowing salute to the passing wagon. Beggars, she realised, holding out hands or vessels for coin. Looking closer, she saw sores that should be cleaned and covered, signs of illness caused by bad diet. Growths that could be cut away easily enough by a skilled surgeon. She smelled refuse and excrement, infection and stale sweat.

She felt paralysed. Shocked. These people needed help. They needed an army of healers. She wanted to leap out of the wagon and do something, but with what? She had no bag of medicines and tools. No burner to sear a blade clean. No blade to sear clean. And where would she start?

A wave of depression swept through her, like a squall of ice-cold rain chilling her to the core. As she sank into her seat she felt eyes close by, watching her. Lord Dakon. She did not look up. She knew she'd see sympathy and right now she resented that.

I ought to be grateful that he understands. He knows I want to heal these people, but can't. I don't want his sympathy, I want the knowledge, resources and freedom to do something to help them. And an explanation of why they live like this – and why nobody else has done anything about it.

The road widened abruptly and they entered an open space. To one side she could see ships and boats tied up to long wooden walkways that extended into the river. On the other a broad road ascended between large stone houses. This, she realised, must be Market Square.

"Should there be stalls here?" she asked.

"Only on market day – every fifth day," Dakon replied.

The wagon turned and slowly moved with the flow of other vehicles making their way towards King's Parade. Progress was slow. Occasionally a large and spectacular covered wagon would force its way through, gaudily dressed men using short whips to enforce demands that other travellers move aside. Tessia wondered why nobody protested against this casual brutality. The finely dressed couple and three children she glimpsed inside one such wagon didn't seem aware of it. Lord Dakon said and did nothing, but she was relieved when he did not order Tanner to speed their way with his whip, either.

She also noticed that most traffic avoided the centre of the road. Even the fancier wagons only dared swing out into the middle if they could leave it again immediately. When two riders came cantering up the centre gap, wearing identical clothing, she guessed that they were servants of some sort headed for the palace. There must be a law against blocking the path of anyone using the road for royal business, and the penalty or punishment must be severe if even those within the fancier wagons were keen to avoid it.

"See these buildings to the left?" Dakon said, drawing her attention from the traffic to the large, pale-stoned walls nearby. "They were built by the Sachakans during their rule here. Though they embraced the Kyralian way of building multiple-storey homes, they imported the stone from quarries in the mountains of their land."

"How?" she asked; then, as she realised the answer was obvious, she shook her head. "Slaves."

"Yes."

"Who lives there now?"

"Whoever was lucky enough to inherit or wealthy enough to buy them."

"People *want* to live in houses built by Sachakans?"

"They are well designed. Warm in the winter, cool in the summer. The best of them have bathing rooms with piped hot water." He shrugged. "While we consider Sachakans barbaric for enslaving others, they consider us so for being unsophisticated and dirty."

"At least we learned when exposed to their ways. We adopted their technologies, but they remained slavers," Jayan said.

"They gave us back our independence," Dakon pointed out. "Through negotiation, not war, which was a first for Sachaka. Did that willingness to talk rather than fight stem from our influence?"

Jayan looked thoughtful. "Perhaps."

"What was Kyralia like before the Sachakans came?" Tessia asked.

"A lot of independently ruled leys that were in conflict with each other as often as they were at peace," Dakon told her. "No one ruler controlled all, though the lord of the southern ley was by far the most powerful. Everyone came to Imardin to trade, and he grew rich on the wealth that came from controlling the centre of commerce."

"Is King Errik descended from that lord?"

"No, the southern lord died in the invasion. Our king is descended from one of the men who negotiated our independence."

"How did magicians live before the invasion?"

"There weren't many, and most sold their services to ley lords. No more than seven are mentioned in the few records left from that time. There is no description of higher magic, either. Some people believe the Sachakans discovered higher magic, and that was why they conquered so many lands so quickly. But eventually they lost them again as the knowledge of higher magic spread in those lands and local magicians began to equal them in strength."

The wagon turned into one of the side streets. Realising she had forgotten to count the streets, Tessia glanced around for some indication of which one they had entered. On the wall of one of the corner buildings was a painted metal plaque.

Fourth Street, it read.

Remembering her lessons on Imardin, Tessia knew that people living in houses closer to the palace were usually more important and powerful than those living further down the hill, although it wasn't always true. Some powerful families lived closer to Market Square because they or their predecessors had lost their wealth but not their influence, or perhaps because they simply *liked* their house and didn't want to move. But the opposite did not happen: no poor or insignificant families lived above Third Street.

Tessia had wondered, back when Dakon had told her of the social structure in Imardin, if there was a constant shuffle of householders as wealth and influence waxed and waned. He had told her that houses changed owners only rarely. The powerful families of Kyralia had learned to hold on to what they had, and only the most dramatic of circumstances wrested it from their hands.

If Dakon's hosts lived on Fourth Street they must be important. Most of the houses that Tessia could see were Sachakan-built – or perhaps facsimiles. The wagon pulled up before a large wooden door within a recessed porch. A man dressed in uniform stepped forward and bowed.

"Welcome, Lord Dakon," the man said. He nodded stiffly to Jayan, "Apprentice Jayan," and then, to her surprise, towards herself. "Apprentice Tessia. Lord Everran and Lady Avaria are expecting you, and bid you enter and join them for afternoon refreshments."

"Thank you, Lerran," Dakon said, climbing out of the wagon. "Are the lord and lady well?"

"Lady Avaria has been a bit low and slow, but much better this past month."

166

Tessia smiled. "Low and slow" referred to the assumption that someone who appeared pale and tired probably had a cool body and a slow heartbeat. It was not always the case, and the saying had more to do with ideas the uneducated had come up with from overheard comments by healers.

When they had all alighted, the driver took the wagon away, steering it through a much larger opening in the house's façade. Lerran led them through the doors. Instead of a grand greeting hall, they entered a wide passage. Dakon looked back at Tessia.

"In Sachakan homes this is known as the 'approach'," he told her. "The room at the end is known as the 'master's room' as it is where the owner of the house greets and entertains visitors, and serves meals."

The room they entered was huge. Benches covered in cushions were spread around the floor, and where large cabinets did not cover the walls, paintings, hangings and carvings hung. Doors led away in all directions. There was no stairway visible, so Tessia assumed access to the upper floor must be located elsewhere in the house.

In the middle of the room stood a couple, smiling at their visitors. *This must be Lord Everran and Lady Avaria.* They were younger than Tessia had expected, probably in their twenties. Lord Everran was a tall, thin man with typically black Kyralian hair, but his skin was darker than the norm – a pleasant golden hue. He was quite handsome in a sleek, groomed way, she decided.

Tessia had never seen a woman like Lady Avaria. Her hostess was attractive, but in a restrained way. *She is what Mother meant when she tried to describe "elegance" to me,* Tessia mused. But there was something in Avaria's face – a glint of mischief in her eye, a quirk in her smile – suggesting something playful underneath the restraint. *And this woman is a magician,* she reminded herself.

Everran's expression was openly pleased as he greeted Dakon, slapping his guest's upper arms in what Tessia now concluded was some sort of greeting among important men. She noted that he did not favour Jayan with the same gesture. Lord Gilar hadn't either, she recalled. Perhaps Jayan would not be considered important until he was a higher magician.

Lady Avaria did not follow suit. She smiled and touched Dakon lightly on the cheek.

"It is good to have you back, Dakon," she said in a warm, low voice. She turned to Jayan. "Welcome back, Apprentice Jayan of Drayn."

Both host and hostess had an alertness to their gaze, Tessia noted. As they turned to regard her she had the distinct feeling she was being examined with astute care. *It is a good thing I'm not the sort to babble when I'm nervous*, she thought as she answered their questions, *and have nothing to hide. I have a feeling they'd never miss a slip of the tongue.*

"A healer's assistant?" Avaria said. "I have a friend who is in training to become a healer. I should arrange a meeting, over lunch or something."

Tessia blinked in surprise. "I was only an assistant. They may find me, ah, rather wanting."

"Oh, I'm sure you'll be fascinating," Avaria assured her. "And I've been looking forward to a new shopping companion." She turned to Dakon. "Now, have you given your apprentices the usual allowance?"

Dakon chuckled. "Just as soon as we have all unpacked."

"Prices have risen considerably since your last visit," Avaria warned. "Since this is Tessia's first visit she has more than the usual stocking up to do."

Tessia felt her face warming. "I don't—" she began then stopped as Jayan put out a hand to stall her.

168

"Oh, yes you do," Jayan told her quietly, "if you're going to survive Avaria's company for more than five minutes."

The lady looked back at him and narrowed her eyes. "I heard that."

"She also has very sharp ears," he warned Tessia.

"Five minutes." Avaria clicked her tongue, her eyes flashing with amusement. "A whole five minutes. I shall have to do something to salvage my reputation."

"Hanar!"

Suppressing a grimace, Hanara straightened and looked towards the voice. No self-respecting Kyralian man had a name ending in a, as their women did – or so the stable servants had told him – so they had shortened his.

The stable master, Ravern, was standing at the door. He beckoned, so Hanara put aside his shovel and walked over.

"Take this to Bregar, the store master," Ravern said, handing Hanara a waxed tablet with writing scrawled over it. "Bring back what he gives you. And be quick, or you'll interrupt his dinner."

Hanara nodded his head as the other stable servants did to show respect to the man, and strode out into the late afternoon light. He tucked the tablet into his tunic, where it sat wax-side outward against his belt. Hurrying down the cartway to the gate, he paused to quickly scan the village.

No people about. It was not surprising. The air had a chill to it that promised a late snow.

Stepping out onto the road, he strode purposefully towards the large store building. It was both a shop and the place where produce made in the ley, or brought in from outside for the use of the ley's populace, was kept. The stable master had sent him out on errands like this a few times now. Hanara suspected his trustworthiness was being tested. And his usefulness.

Reaching the store, Hanara entered and removed the tablet

from his tunic. The store master was absent, so he rang the bell. Bregar shuffled into the room from a door at the back, his scowl softening into a frown when he saw Hanara. The man didn't trust Hanara, but he never mocked him either. He reached out to take the tablet.

Bregar was a big man for a Kyralian. Hanara suspected there was quite a bit of Sachakan in his bloodline. As he watched, the store master piled up solid blocks of a glossy substance on a table, then bags of grain and a heavy ceramic jar, its stopper sealed generously with wax. All the items were for the stables, which made sense, but Hanara had noticed that he had never been sent – as other stable servants often were – to collect food for the Residence or to take items to be sharpened to the metal worker.

Bregar handed back the tablet. The pile on the table was large, and the store master set about packing everything into a wooden crate. Seeing this, Hanara dropped the tablet down his tunic front again. He would need both hands to carry the crate. As Bregar lifted the container, Hanara bent over and indicated that the man should place it on his shoulders. He straightened up, and the man frowned and made a questioning grunt.

Hanara nodded. The store master shrugged and opened the door.

Outside the light of day was failing. As Hanara started back towards the Residence, he mused that the grunt had been the closest thing to a conversation that he'd ever had with Bregar. He didn't mind. Slaves tended to be as reticent. Chatter got you into trouble.

Halfway to the Residence something stung Hanara's arm. He flinched and kept walking. This often happened when he was out in the village alone. Usually when the two young louts were about.

He hadn't gone much further when he heard footsteps coming closer. As the two young men approached he felt his stomach sink. They were an irritation most of the time, but if they made him drop his burden and something broke there would be trouble back at the stables.

He kept walking. The pair moved to either side, keeping pace.

"Hanara," one said. "Do you have a wife back in Sachaka?"

As always, he stayed silent. Kept walking.

"Do you miss her? Do you miss *bedding* her?"

"Does your Sachakan master do that now?"

One foot in front of the other. Their taunting was meaningless. They knew too little to hurt him. The benefit of not being allowed to care for anyone was that there was nobody that could be used against you.

"Or did he do that with *you*?"

It was a strange saying, this "bedding". As if the act of human breeding was done with mattresses rather than body parts.

"I bet he'll get into trouble if he drops those boxes."

"That's stuff for the Residence," the other said.

"So? Lord Dakon can afford to replace it if it breaks. But Hanara here can't afford to do anything wrong, or he'll get kicked out."

The cartway entrance was only a hundred paces away. Hanara felt a shove from one side. He swayed, keeping the load balanced. There was a shove from the other side. This time he stepped on one of the lout's feet as he swerved. The young man swore.

"Stupid slave," he snarled. Stepping in front of Hanara, he slammed his fist into Hanara's stomach.

There was a crack. The young man recoiled, his face distorted in open-mouthed pain. Hanara felt the tablet shift

171

as broken pieces fell downward to settle against his belt. He stepped round the lout and continued on his way.

From behind he heard the other lout asking what had happened.

"Don't know. It's like he was wearing *armour*. Ouch! My thumb feels like it's *broken*."

Hanara smiled. He stepped into the cartway, then couldn't resist turning and looking back towards the village. But before he could make out the two louts in the gloom, something else caught his eye.

Beyond the village, on the ridge above, a blue light was blinking slowly in and out of existence.

His blood went cold.

Turning, he fled down the cartway to the stables, his heart racing. He couldn't read the writing on the broken tablet down his shirt, but he was able to decode the pulsing light on the hill. The pattern represented one word. One order.

Report.

Takado had returned.

CHAPTER 14

The master's room of Everran's house smelled of marin flowers, a crisp yet rich scent that gave the space a mood both lively and meditative. Dakon and Jayan had settled onto one of the bench chairs. They hadn't seen Tessia or Avaria yet today. The two women had left early to explore the city, and would spend the afternoon with one of Avaria's friends.

Everran had vanished, but now he re-entered the room rubbing his hands together eagerly.

"Our visitors should begin arriving soon."

Dakon nodded. His father and Everran's grandfather had been cousins, so they had a link through family ties, albeit a distant one. Dakon had continued his father's custom of staying with Everran's father when visiting Imardin. Then, when the man died five years ago from a seizure of the heart, his son insisted on taking over the role of Dakon's host when he visited Imardin.

Everran was a likeable and smart young man. He had come into his inheritance too young, but he had shouldered the burden with admirable maturity, and had a good grasp of politics. It had pleased Dakon when Everran had joined the Circle of Friends, and not just because he liked the young magician. It was heartening to see that some city magicians were as concerned about the threat from Sachaka as the country lords, and willing to support their cause.

"What are they expecting?" Dakon asked. "Will they be wanting information? News?"

Everran shrugged. "No. It's unlikely you'll know anything they don't already. We'll be discussing how you should approach the king."

"All advice is welcome." Dakon grimaced wryly. "It's been a long time since I met the king, and then it wasn't on official business."

"It's in all our interests that you succeed. They – ah, here's the first of them now."

Footsteps drew their attention to the passage leading from the front entrance of the house. Everran rose and Dakon and Jayan followed suit. A short, slightly overweight man with grey in his black hair appeared, escorted by Lerran the doorman. He paused to smile and nod to Everran, and then to Dakon as Everran introduced him.

"This is Magician Wayel of the Paren family, the new trade master."

"Congratulations. I hope it has been a smooth transition."

Wayel shrugged. "As smooth as can be expected."

"What is Lord Gregar up to now?" Dakon asked.

"Resting at home." At Everran's urging, they moved to the benches and sat down again. "I've heard he isn't well. Some say he gave away the position too early and is expiring of boredom, but I've been told that he might have quit because he was unwell. Perhaps dying."

Thinking of the energetic old man whose task it had been to settle trading disputes between the leys, Dakon felt a pang of sadness. Men like Lord Gregar, efficient and intelligent, were hard to find. He hoped Magician Wayel would live up to his predecessor's standards, though he didn't envy the man the demands of the job.

Laughter echoed down the corridor. Two men were ushered into the room. All rose to greet the newcomers.

"Lord Prinan is here on behalf of his father, Lord Ruskel," Everran told Dakon. "Lord Bolvin is from Eyren ley."

Lord Ruskel's ley was located at the south-eastern end of the mountains bordering Sachaka. It had been Ruskel who had stumbled upon the three "lost" Sachakan magicians in his land, Dakon remembered. Prinan was a young, newly independent magician, trained by his father. He greeted Dakon with nervous deference. Dakon noted that Everran had adopted the new habit of using the title "Lord" for an heir to a ley or house, helping to indicate which offspring would inherit. It was a new custom, which he'd noticed becoming popular during his last few city visits. He wasn't sure he liked it.

He had met Bolvin some years before, but the man had changed considerably. Several years older than Prinan, and a full head taller, Bolvin had an air of maturity not usually found in one so young. He, like Everran, had inherited too young when his father had disappeared with his ship during a storm; he had an entire ley to manage as well as the family fortune.

Eyren ley was on the west coast, far from any immediate danger in the event of an invasion, yet Lord Bolvin's expression was serious and sympathetic as he greeted Dakon. *This one understands that the threat will not be over if a few border leys are overrun*, Dakon thought.

Before they had finished their greetings another voice came from the room's entrance.

"Ah, good, I'm not the only early arrival."

A tall, slim, middle-aged man walked gracefully into the room. Dakon recognised the man with surprise.

Everran laughed. "You're actually on time for once, Lord Olleran."

Olleran was very much a city lord, who had admitted in the past (when turning down invitations to stay with lords outside the city) that he found the country boring and dirty. But it wasn't that which made his presence at this meeting so surprising. He was also married to a Sachakan. He came forward to grasp Dakon's arm.

"Welcome back to Imardin, Lord Dakon," he said. "In case you're too polite to ask, it was my wife who convinced me that I should join your cause. She says she likes Kyralia just how it is and ordered me to find and help anyone who was doing something to keep it that way."

Dakon smiled. He had heard it said that Lord Olleran's early failures in courtship stemmed from a preference for difficult women. When the man married a Sachakan most people thought he'd finally overcome the tendency. But it turned out that this was no ordinary Sachakan woman. Though brought up to be quiet and obedient, she had thrown off her stifling upbringing upon arrival in Kyralia and had worked on a string of charity projects. Dakon had never met her, but she was popular among Avaria's friends.

"So she believes there is a threat from Sachaka?"

"Her family does. They ordered her home. She refused, of course." He shook his head sadly. "Which forces me to be glad she is such a disobedient wife."

More guests arrived. Some, like Lord Gilar, Dakon knew. Some he had heard about but never met. A few were unknown to him. They included a handful of country lords or their representatives, and two more city lords. Of the latter, Dakon knew Magician Sabin by reputation. He was a skilled sword master who had studied warfare extensively. *That one will have good advice if we ever face a battle*, Dakon decided. *But I'm not sure if he'll be useful to me now.*

Soon the room was echoing with voices and no one bothered

sitting back down after greeting a new arrival. They stood in small groups, talking. Once the last magician was ushered into the room and introduced, Everran rang a small gong to get everyone's attention. Voices fell silent. Everyone looked towards their host.

"As you know, I've called this meeting with a purpose other than good conversation and food – which will arrive shortly. Lord Dakon has journeyed to Imardin from distant Aylen ley to approach the king on our behalf. What we need to decide today is: what should he say to the king? What shouldn't he say? What do we want to gain? What do we hope to avoid?"

A short silence followed as the men exchanged glances, looking to see who would speak first.

"We need an assurance that he will send out a force of magicians to retake and protect border leys if they are over-come," Prinan said. "At least, that's what my father said."

Everran nodded. "And he is right." He turned to Dakon. "This is what Lord Narvelan asked you to do?"

Dakon nodded. "Yes."

"But isn't it insulting to the king to suggest he wouldn't retake leys?" Bolvin asked.

The magicians' reaction to this was a mixture of shrugs and nods. Dakon noted how several heads had turned towards Sabin. For some reason they thought him a greater authority on the king than anyone else here.

"He would find it so," Sabin agreed. "He would know there is more to the request than what you ask for, and be annoyed that you think him fool enough not to see it."

"It's all in the way you ask for it," Olleran said, looking round. "You would have to say: 'There are some, in the city, who have been heard to express the opinion that the outer leys aren't worth fighting for in the event they are taken. What is your opinion, your majesty?'"

Sabin chuckled and looked at Olleran. "How many times have you practised that little speech?" he asked quietly.

Olleran shrugged modestly. "A few . . . hundred."

"And if he wants to know who expressed this opinion, what do I say?" Dakon asked. "Will I need names?"

"Tell him lords who won't act unless it brings them direct benefits," Wayel growled. "Magicians unwilling to put their lives at risk, through selfishness or cowardice."

"We must make them see a lack of action will cost them more in the long term," Bolvin said. "The Sachakans won't stop at a few outer leys. They will see a lack of a resistance as a sign of weakness, and take all."

"Some will not believe that. Not until it is too late," Sabin predicted. "Magical ability does not come only to those with foresight."

"Or common sense," Everran agreed. "But most of the reluctant would change their minds if an attack did come. For now they hold higher the opinions of their most powerful allies because they feel they have to, but faced with the news of an attack they might decide that, if we proved to be right about an invasion of the outer leys, we might prove to be right about the consequences of not driving the Sachakans back out."

"They had better change their minds," Bolvin muttered. Others nodded and a small silence followed. Dakon held his tongue. They had not answered his question, but perhaps the digression would come back round to the subject again if he waited.

"Would the more resistant help us for a fee?" Prinan asked.

The room vibrated with noises of protest.

"The king would not condone it!" Bolvin declared.

Dakon shivered. "If he allowed the Sachakans to hold our land without resistance, he would have sunk so low that allowing others to demand a fee to help us will seem a minor crime."

"We will only buy help if we are desperate," Everran assured him.

"If we get to that point I'm not sure I'd have much regard left for my own countrymen," Sabin said, sighing.

Gilar nodded in agreement. "Are the Sachakans in the city a problem?" He smiled at Olleran. "Aside from your lovely wife, of course."

"Oh, she's a problem, just not in the way you mean," Olleran said, with an unconvincing grimace. "More my own private little problem."

"You do long-suffering very badly, Olleran," Sabin said, shaking his head in mock disappointment.

"Most are traders," Wayel said, ignoring the banter. "And there's Emperor Vochira's representative. A few women who married Kyralians." He nodded to Olleran. "I expect if they are a danger it will be only in the usual ways: they may be spies, and might attempt to bribe or trick Kyralians into doing harm here."

"The people we have to worry about," Sabin said, "are the more powerful Kyralian families, especially those who have troubles a rich offer from Sachaka could help to solve. Debts. A lack of buyers for produce. Competitors."

Ah, good, Dakon thought. *Back to the subject of who might speak against us . . .*

"Who?" he asked. "Are they the same people speaking out against us now?"

Wayel shook his head. "It may be unwise to start pointing fingers at anybody in particular. That is not a wise approach."

Sabin nodded. "What the lords think is irrelevant. They will not be making the decision to regain the border leys if they are taken. The king will."

"So should Dakon try to convince the king that the leys are worth keeping?" Prinan asked.

Everran shook his head. "That should only come if we are convinced he believes otherwise. Wayel is right. Mentioning adverse opinions is a dangerous justification for seeking his assurance of protection. He is bound to ask who expressed those opinions, and who passed that information on, and hesitate to believe any of it if we have no proof, and it just sounds like gossip." He sighed. "No, it is by presenting the latest evidence we have that we can justify seeking reassurance from him."

The others nodded. Dakon suppressed a sigh of relief. At last they were agreeing with each other.

"Plainly and simply, so he doesn't think we're jumping to conclusions," Wayel added quietly.

"I don't think there's any danger he'll think that of Dakon." Everran smiled and nodded to his guest. "And if Dakon appears to need reassuring for his own benefit, rather than for the benefit of us all, it may be enough of a prompt to extract promises from the king."

"A promise to Dakon, not us," one of the other ley magicians pointed out.

"Would there be a difference, ultimately?" someone else asked.

"King Errik is hardly going to make such a promise to one ley magician and not others," Sabin said quietly. "Unless, of course, he *wanted* to show favour – but in this case it would be foolish to risk jealousy among the country magicians. He wants them united, not competing with each other."

"Are you sure?" Wayel asked. "He might want to use such a ploy to divide us, to stop us pestering him."

"He won't," Sabin said. The others nodded in acceptance, once again demonstrating to Dakon the respect the others had for the sword master.

"So if he makes a promise, it will be to all of us?" Prinan asked.

Sabin nodded. "But I will be surprised if he makes any promises. He does not give any ground if he does not have to. At least, not in a practice bout."

Suddenly the source of the respect the others showed the sword master was obvious. *Sabin must spar with the king*, Dakon thought. *That* would *give him some insight into the man's intellect and character.* Then another possibility occurred to him. *I wonder if he is one of the magicians who give magical strength to the king?*

Everran sighed. "No doubt it is too much to expect, but if Dakon can extract or spark some discussion on the form and timing of the king's aid, it would be easier for us to make plans – ah! Let's talk about that later. Here's the food!"

As servants entered the room carrying platters of food, glasses and flagons of wine and water, the visitors moved to the benches. Some struck up conversations with their neighbours as they ate, rehashing what they'd already covered. Dakon considered what he'd heard so far. He didn't feel as though he'd gained much insight into how to approach the king yet. The talk had gone in circles.

As he looked at Everran, the man smiled and tilted his head toward his friends slightly as if to ask "Are you listening to this?"

Suddenly it became clear to Dakon what Everran expected. These powerful men did not like to be pushed or interrupted, especially when caught up in passionate discussion. No, it was up to Dakon to take note of what was said by whom, and select which men to approach later and ask more specific advice about the coming meeting.

And what would he ask? What he needed to know was how King Errik might react to certain approaches and suggestions. Sabin appeared to be, unexpectedly, the man closest to the king. Dakon would have chosen Wayel at first, but the man had asked some questions Dakon had expected him to know the answer to, so perhaps he was too new in his position. And the others?

When the discussions began again, Dakon decided, he would insert a few comments and questions designed to reveal more about these men. He waved away the offer of wine, opting for water instead.

As on every visit to the city Dakon had made before, it took some time to adjust to the more subtle ways matters were tackled here. This time he had to adapt fast, because the level of politics the king was involved in was a complicated and tortuous one indeed, and soon he would be meeting with the man himself.

Through the window flap of the wagon's cover Tessia saw a frightening and thrilling sight. A great crowd of people and wagons filled the streets, all pushing in different directions. More people than wagons – and there were plenty of those. More people in one place than she'd ever seen before. The mass of them, the sense of gathered force, the roar of voices, set her heart racing.

The reason the Parade was so crowded lay at the foot of it. A mass of people had gathered there, and the sound of music rose faintly above the crowd. Flashes of colour promised strange sights.

The market.

"We should have left earlier," Avaria said for the fourth time, sighing and smoothing her carefully pinned hair.

They had talked about Tessia's childhood and upbringing, the reason her father had moved to Mandryn, how Tessia had discovered her powers (Avaria accepted that Takado had merely "given her a fright") and all the interesting incidents on the journey to Imardin. Tessia was beginning to wonder if she'd used up all the significant stories of her life within her first day in the city.

She also felt as if she was talking about herself too much. But when she asked Avaria the same sorts of questions, the woman would begin an anecdote about her childhood or apprenticeship, only to be reminded of something else she wanted to ask Tessia.

"It might be faster on foot." Tessia peered at the crowd passing the wagon.

"Not a good idea, I'm afraid. Aside from all the shoving and pushing, we'd be robbed before we got there," Avaria said, shrugging gracefully.

"Robbed?" Tessia looked at her hostess in alarm.

Avaria smiled crookedly. "Indeed – though it is unlikely we'd notice at first. Pickpockets are very skilled in Imardin. And most are children – small and fast in a crowd. Even if you see them, your servants have no hope of catching them."

"Children?" Tessia looked more closely at the crowd. She'd seen some appallingly thin, dirty children the day before. No surprise they were desperate enough to turn to thieving.

Her father had told her about the poor of Imardin. When she had asked him why they had no money his explanation had been long and complicated. He'd offered a list of reasons – too little work for too many people, nobody willing to offer work to people who were a bit strange in the mind, or crippled. Some people had nobody to care for them when they fell ill, and if their illness led to their no longer having work they might starve before they recovered. Some people were injured while working, and if their employers didn't care for them they ended up in a similar situation.

It was not the first time, and certainly not the last, that

she'd been told that few lords were as caring of their people and conscious of their responsibilities as Lord Dakon and his father had been. Some were fools. Some only saw their people as commodities. Some were downright malicious.

"Poor things," Avaria said. "Born into poverty, raised to be thieves. If the city is plagued by such ills, it serves it right for not taking better care of its people."

Tessia nodded, wondering at this way of referring to the city as if it were a person.

"But it can't be as easy to care for a whole city as it is a village."

"No." Avaria smiled and her eyes glowed as she looked at Tessia. Perhaps in approval. Tessia wasn't sure.

The wagon began moving. Tessia braced herself, expecting it to stop again, but it rolled on. Then it swung round a corner and came to a halt again.

"We're here!" Avaria announced happily. Rising, she pulled the wagon cover open and climbed out. One of the two male servants who had ridden on the back of the wagon was already there to help her down to the ground. As Tessia stepped down the tiny ladder built against the side of the vehicle, the second servant moved forward to offer a hand. She didn't take it, but smiled at him in gratitude anyway.

He smiled back politely and followed as she moved to join Avaria, who hooked an arm through hers.

Tessia looked around and blinked in surprise. They weren't in the market, as she'd expected. They were in a busy side street, narrower than the main roads and lined with small shops.

"Welcome to Vanity Street," Avaria said, patting Tessia's arm. "Where most of the best shops in Imardin can be found."

"Not in the market, then?"

"Oh no. That's full of vegetables and grain and smelly

animals. The only cloth you'll find there is for making grain sacks or saddles, and the closest thing they have to books is wax accounting tablets."

Avaria guided Tessia to one side of the street. The closeness of the other woman was unexpected, but reassuring. The street was crowded with finely dressed men and women. Musicians in pairs and trios played and sang at the side of the road and occasionally a passer-by tossed a coin into the iron cups at their feet. The cups, Tessia noted, had numbers painted on their sides.

"Come in here," Avaria said, drawing Tessia through the door of a shop. Inside, the street noises were muffled. Two women were examining rolls of cloth laid out on a table. More rolls leaned up against the walls, in a dazzling range of bright colours. A man was standing in the doorway to another room. As Tessia looked at him he smiled and nodded politely.

"Oh, look," Avaria suddenly exclaimed. "Isn't this beautiful!"

She led Tessia to one of the walls and tugged off a glove so she could run her fingers lightly over some smooth cloth in a deep, vibrant blue.

"I must have some of this. What colours do you like, Tessia?"

Looking around at the range of brilliant colours, Tessia couldn't help thinking they were all a bit too gaudy. She tried to imagine each individually forming a garment, and found herself drawn to a dark green. It reminded her of one of her father's favourite wound-salve ingredients, an oil from a tree that grew in the mountains, which smelled delicious.

Avaria picked up the bolt and held it up to Tessia's face.

"You have a good eye," she told her. "That will suit you very well." She turned to the seller. "We'll take both. Oh, and that would look wonderful on Everran." She picked up another bolt of dark red then winked at Tessia. "Thankfully, the only bit of Sachakan bloodline left in his veins is the good one – he has such enviable skin."

So that explains the golden tone of his skin, Tessia thought. She'd noticed interesting physical differences between the rich and powerful men and women in the city and the commoners. There was a greater variety in their height, stature and colouring, whereas commoners were more likely to be slight and pale-skinned, the more typical Kyralian characteristics.

Avaria beckoned over the man and much haggling ensued; then, from the embroidered bag tucked into the waist of her dress, she counted a sum that made Tessia slightly breathless. The cloth was wrapped and given to the servants to carry. With a satisfied sigh, Avaria led Tessia outside, hooked her arm round Tessia's again, and continued down Vanity Street.

"What else can we buy? I know! Some shoes."

Several shops later Avaria had bought more cloth, some shoes that were going to make Malia squeak with admiration, a bag for Tessia to store her coin in because "that thing Dakon gave you is too manly", and some hand mirrors. When Tessia hesitated before a shop window filled with fine writing tools, paper and books, Avaria wordlessly pulled her inside. Tessia bought her father some quills and ink in a box inlaid with different types of wood. Avaria complimented her on her choice of gift.

"He'll think of you every time he uses it."

Next a shop filled with books caught Tessia's eye and she was glad when Avaria headed towards it. A quick examination told her there was nothing that her father didn't already have among the healing tomes, though. Lord Yerven had always brought back a book or two for her grandfather, after his trips to Imardin.

"Do you read novels?" Avaria asked.

"I found some when I first moved into Lord Dakon's house," Tessia answered, moving to join her. A small row of slim volumes sat within a long narrow display box.

"Did you like them?"

"Yes – they're a bit . . . unrealistic."

Avaria laughed. "That's what's so fun about them. What have you read?"

"*Moonlight on the Lake. The Ambassador's Daughter. Five Rubies.*"

"Old ones." Avaria waved a hand dismissively. "Honarand has written much better ones since then. You'll find his island series quite enchanting."

"The author is a man?"

"Yes. What's so strange about that?"

"They're always from a woman's point of view."

Avaria smiled. "You'd not think that so strange if you knew him. Here." She handed over two books. "These are his best."

Taking the two books, Tessia looked at the bookseller. "How much are they?"

"For you, twenty silver for the two," he said.

She stared at him in astonishment. "Twenty silver? That's more than a year's wage for—"

Avaria laid a gloved hand on her arm and leaned close, her expression serious. "Those books are copied by hand. It takes weeks to make one. Books are expensive because they take time and paper – which is also time-consuming to make."

Tessia looked down at the slim volumes. "Even something as, well, frivolous as this?"

The woman smiled and shrugged. "Whatever there's a market for is worth making. There are plenty of love-lonely women in Imardin with way too much spare money to spend, stuck in marriages arranged by their parents." She shrugged. "How much is a comforting daydream worth? But don't pay more than ten silver for the two. I'd start haggling at five."

Unused to bargaining, Tessia only managed to argue the man down to twelve silver, but she bought the books anyway. It pleased her hostess. Avaria had already bought her several expensive items and, Tessia suspected, would buy these as well if Tessia didn't. And there might be times when Avaria wasn't free to entertain Tessia while Dakon and Jayan were occupied with their important meetings.

As they left the shop Avaria gasped. "Oh, look! There's Falia!" Suddenly she was pulling Tessia by the arm, her wandering steps lengthening to strides. "Falia sweet!"

A blonde woman in a pale pink and cream dress turned, her face lighting up with a wide smile as she saw Avaria.

"Avaria sweet!"

"This is Apprentice Tessia, who is staying with us at the moment, along with Lord Dakon from Aylen ley and Apprentice Jayan of Drayn. It's Tessia's first visit to Imardin."

Falia's eyebrows rose. "Welcome to Imardin, Apprentice Tessia." Still smiling, she tilted her head to the side and narrowed her eyes. "Are you apprenticed to Lord Dakon?"

"Yes."

"With Jayan as your co-apprentice." The woman's nose wrinkled. "Poor you! He was such a brat as a child. I hope he's improved." She regarded Tessia expectantly.

"I'm hardly able to judge since I didn't know him as a br— ah-child," Tessia managed.

Falia laughed. "Our families were close back then. Now they're not." She shrugged. "That's life in the city. So what is he like as a young man?"

Tessia tried to search for the right word and failed. "Older."

Both Avaria and Falia laughed, this time knowingly. "I

guess not much has changed," Avaria concluded. "Though he isn't a strain to look at."

"Really?" Falia's expressive eyebrows rose again. "Not all bad, then. Are you two coming to the party at Darya's?"

"Of course."

"I was just going to buy some conecakes, then go. Would you like to come with me? There's room in my wagon."

"Why not?" Avaria smiled at Tessia. "I think we've spent all we need to spend for today, haven't we?"

Tessia nodded. She hadn't yet bought a present for her mother, but she was sure there'd be more shopping trips to come.

They followed Falia along the street to a shop selling spices and other food ingredients, as well as a multitude of sweet treats. Conecakes turned out to be little cone-shaped frothy breads dusted in fine sugar. Inside, Falia told her, was a little surprise of sweetened fruit puree. You could never tell which type of fruit it would be until you bit into it.

Somehow Tessia found herself holding a bag of salted tiro nuts while they waited for Falia's wagon to arrive. When it did, Avaria sent one of her servants back to her wagon driver, who was apparently waiting on First Street, to tell him to return home without them and then be ready to collect them from Falia's house later. The other piled their purchases inside Falia's wagon and climbed onto the back.

The two city women chatted about people Tessia did not know during the ride to Darya's house. Tessia was relieved that they did. She felt exhausted. Though she had only walked a distance she estimated was the length of Mandryn twice or three times over, she felt as if she'd run across the entire length of a ley.

She wasn't so tired that she didn't notice when they turned into Fourth Street, and drove along the opposite side of King's

Parade to the one on which Avaria's house was situated. It wasn't much later that the wagon stopped and the two women gracefully stepped out, making the awkward stepladder seem no more difficult than a mansion staircase. Tessia followed them to the door.

Once inside, Avaria hooked her arm in Tessia's again. For a moment Falia looked disappointed, but then she gave a little shrug and led the way into the house.

Darya's home was set out in what Tessia now recognised as the Kyralian style, like Lord Dakon's Residence. The entrance opened into a greeting hall, from which stairs led up to the second storey and openings on either side invited access to the ground-level rooms.

A servant guided them to a room on the first floor with large windows overlooking the street. Three women were sitting about a round table, and rose to greet the newcomers. Tessia was surprised to see that the hostess was short, a little rounded, and clearly Sachakan. But when Lady Darya smiled her green eyes shone with friendliness.

"Avaria! Falia!" She lightly touched both cheeks of the women with her fingertips, then turned to Tessia. "And this must be Apprentice Tessia. Welcome. Sit down. Relax. Oh! You brought conecakes!"

The other women made appreciative sounds as the cakes were laid on the table. More chairs were brought by servants, and a silver platter to arrange the cakes on.

The conversation that ensued was every bit as noisy, gaudy and disorientating as the market. Tessia settled on listening, and for some time it seemed everyone had forgotten she was there. The other two women were Kendaria and Lady Zakia. Darya had married the magician son of a rich trader – and his entire family, she joked. Zakia's husband was a city lord and magician. Kendaria's was cousin to the king, and they lived with his older brother and their family. They spent a lot of time making fun of their husbands, Tessia noticed.

Then, when a piece of gossip had been milked of all its possibilities and everyone had fallen into a speculative silence, Avaria nodded to her guest.

"Tessia's father is a healer, and she was his assistant before she stumbled on her powers."

"You're a natural!" Zakia nodded approvingly. "You must be very strong."

Tessia shrugged. "I don't know yet, but I'm told that is the way things work."

"Kendaria is training to be a healer," Avaria said, giving Tessia a meaningful look.

Tessia blinked in surprise, then looked at the small, slim woman sitting beside her. "You are?" She paused. "I thought . . . aren't women . . . ?"

Kendaria laughed quietly. "Money," she said. "Power. And the fact that there is no actual rule or law anywhere that says we can't *train* to be healers. Work as one?" Her shoulders lifted, but her eyes were sharp with determination. "We'll see about that one when we get there, though I only started because I wanted to use my skills to help friends and family."

Hope and bitterness swept over Tessia. If her father had been rich and powerful, would she have been able to train as well? Was Kendaria the first woman to defy tradition?

The woman leaned closer. "If you like, I'll take you to watch a dissection. Would you like that?"

A thrill ran through Tessia. She remembered her father wistfully describing what he'd seen and learned watching dissections, the few times he'd visited Imardin and the Healer's Guild in order to improve his knowledge. His descriptions had been both horrifying and fascinating, and she'd always wondered whether she, in that situation, would faint, or would lose herself in the mysteries of the human body as he had. She liked to believe she wouldn't faint, and wondered every time they treated a gory injury or encountered a corpse if that was test enough.

"Eugh!" Zakia said. "I don't know how you can stand it. Don't go if you don't want to, Tessia. Nobody would blame you."

Tessia smiled and looked at Kendaria.

"I'd love to.".

CHAPTER 15

Dakon's wagon pulled up in front of the imposing grey stone building, home of the Drayn family for four centuries. Jayan sighed and forced himself out of his seat. As always happened when he visited his childhood home, mixed feelings arose at the first sight of it. Memories washed over him of childish games played with his brother, teasing his younger sisters, the warmth and smell of his mother, and celebrations both formal and informal. They brought a wistful fondness, inevitably followed by a gut-sinking resentment and remembered fear, grief and bitterness as he recalled punishment for mistakes that still seemed too harsh, the terrible feeling of loss and being lost and alone after his mother had gone, and the sour realisation of what being the second son meant.

Magic had offered him an escape in more ways than one. It took him from a home that had become stifling and humiliating, and gave him the means, if needed, to be independent of his family's wealth.

Wealth? Or is that charity?

Still, he wasn't stupid. He hadn't cut himself off from them. His father's nature might never soften, but with the weakness of age it was a blunt weapon. His brother's arrogance in youth had also faded a little with maturity, perhaps because he knew Jayan, as a magician, would not be the dependent and obedient little brother he'd anticipated pushing around for the rest of his life, perhaps because he'd learned that other people – people he wanted to impress – were repelled by his maliciousness.

The door servant bowed and opened the door. Walking inside, Jayan looked around the greeting hall. Nothing had changed. The same paintings hung on the walls. The same screens framed the windows. Another servant greeted him and led him through the house. Jayan breathed in the sight and smell of familiarity. It was like dust laced with old perfume.

Finally they reached a small room at the back of the house, furnished with two old chairs. This was his father's favourite room, into which he had always retreated "to think". It had been a place forbidden to small children, where stern talks and punishments were given to older children, and orders were given to adult children. The significance wasn't lost on Jayan. His father was in the mood for imposing his will. Jayan would have to be careful.

Yet Lord Karvelan, head of family Drayn, looked smaller and more lined than Jayan remembered, as if he had dried out slightly in the year since Jayan had seen him. There was still strength in the set of his shoulders and the directness of his gaze, though. Jayan met that gaze, smiled politely, and waited for his father to speak. You always waited for Lord Karvelan to speak. It was a right he insisted on.

"Welcome back, Apprentice Jayan," Karvelan said.

"Thank you, Father," Jayan replied. "Did you get my message?"

Karvelan nodded. "I gather our notes crossed each other."

"It appears so," Jayan replied, holding up the brusque summons he had received that morning, not long after he had dutifully sent his own note informing his father of his presence in the city and enquiring if he should visit.

"Sit down," Karvelan said, nodding at the other chair. Jayan obeyed. Karvelan was silent a moment, his expression thoughtful. *Strange how I never call him "Father" in my mind. Always "Karvelan". But Mother was always "Mother".*

"How is your training going?" Karvelan asked finally.

"Well."

"Any closer to finishing?"

"Yes, but I can't say how close. Only Lord Dakon can answer that question."

"You were almost done when you last visited." Karvelan scowled. "Is it true he has another apprentice?"

Jayan nodded. "It is."

The scowl deepened. "This will surely delay your training. He should have waited until yours was finished."

"He had no choice. She is a natural and dangerous if left untrained. By law he must train her."

His father's eyes narrowed and Jayan almost expected a scolding. Instead the old man grimaced. "Then he should have sent her elsewhere."

Jayan shrugged. "He probably would have, if I were not close to independence. Even so, I don't presume to question my master's decisions. He does, usually, know best."

Karvelan's expression changed from approval at Jayan's subservience to another scowl.

"Does he? What of this group he has joined? This 'Circle of Friends'. Do you not find it an unwise move? It smells of rebellion."

Jayan gazed at his father in surprise, then realised he was staring and looked away.

"You didn't know I knew, did you?" There was satisfaction in Karvelan's voice.

"Oh, the group isn't a secret."

"Then what?"

195

"That anyone . . . this idea that . . ." Jayan stopped and shook his head. It was never wise to phrase anything in a way that might be taken as a criticism of his father's opinion. "Rebellion is a strong word. I assure you, the group has the encouragement and support of the king. Or . . . do you suggest rebellion against someone else?"

A sullen darkness had entered his father's eyes – a look Jayan knew all too well. It was the look that Karvelan wore whenever he had reason to dislike his younger son.

"Rebellion against the city *is* rebellion against the king," he growled. He shifted, his gaze sliding away for a brief moment. "I don't want you associating with this Circle," he said. "Links to them could reflect badly on your family."

Jayan opened his mouth to protest, but stopped himself. He wanted to assure his father that the Circle of Friends was only concerned with the defence of the country. The *whole* country. That he could not, in good conscience, oppose the defending of his homeland. But there was no point in arguing.

So he sighed. "Until I am a higher magician I must obey Lord Dakon. If he associates with the Circle then I have no choice but to do so as well. But . . . I will do what I can to remain a mere observer."

"You should find yourself a new teacher," Karvelan said, but without conviction. He knew that the choice, again, was out of his son's hands. Jayan didn't test his patience by pointing that out.

"I will do what I can," he repeated.

"Finish your training," his father said. "Don't let that girl take all of Lord Dakon's attention. She has no good reputation or alliances to lose." He shook his head. "It is irresponsible of your master to drag you into this."

Jayan said nothing. A silence fell between them, and when he judged it long enough to justify changing the subject, he asked how his brother was faring. While his father proudly described Velan's conquests in trade and of women who might be acceptable marriage prospects, Jayan found himself thinking about Tessia.

No reputation to lose? he mused. *No annoying family obligations to shake off, more like it. And alliances . . . from the way she and Avaria were talking last night, after their party, I suspect she's doing a very good job of making friends here. With some particularly powerful women of the city, too.*

And he'd been worried about her being accepted.

Suddenly he could see the attraction Tessia might have for city socialites. There were no alliances to endanger by befriending her. As a village healer's daughter, she was educated enough to be acceptable company, different enough to provide entertainment. He could even see that her interest in healing, and determination to pursue it, made her an exciting person for city socialites to watch and admire.

Even if she failed, she would provide entertainment for the rich and bored. And, like Jayan, at least her magic would ensure she could not fall too far or too hard.

We have more in common than I thought, he mused wryly. He liked the idea that, if either of them ever fell from grace, the other might be there to offer support. *It's always easier to become friends with someone you have something in common with. I just hope it doesn't take some socially disastrous fall before she'll consider the possibility I might be a friend.*

The healers' university looked exactly as Tessia had imagined. Her father had described it as an "old but strange building that has adopted and absorbed surrounding houses as opportunity and funds allowed". It sounded confusing and intriguing, and it was.

Though a muddle of interconnecting buildings, all had

been built in the Kyralian style so there was a unifying look about the exterior. Inside, it was like walking through somebody's home without ever finding the back door. Narrow corridors led to more narrow corridors. The doors on either side of the corridors were nearly all closed, so there was little natural light in the passages. Instead they were lit with the warm glow of oil lamps. The few rooms Tessia managed to look inside were no larger than the kitchen in her parents' house, and furnished in a similar way with shelving on the walls, a table in the middle, and a fireplace at one end.

Kendaria was leading her to the dissection room. Tessia could not help wondering where in this place the healers would find a room big enough to hold both an audience the size her new friend had described *and* a dissection table.

Then they stepped from a doorway into a strange space. It was like the underside of a wooden staircase, except it was a very wide staircase. She could hear footsteps and voices above.

Ahead a narrow break in the "staircases" allowed access beyond, and Kendaria led her forward. They emerged into a large room. Looking around, Tessia realised that the wide stairways were actually tiered seats that sloped up to plain brick walls – some with bricked-up windows. Several young men were already sitting on the steps. They eyed her and Kendaria with interest.

The walls look like the exterior of houses, Tessia thought. She looked up. The beams of a wood and tile roof stretched overhead. *This must have been a small street or a garden. They just built those seats and covered it over.* Which explained why it was so cold.

In the middle of the room was a generous stone bench. From the grooves carved into it to carry fluids into buckets she guessed it was the dissection table. On another, smaller table nearby several tools had been arranged. She knew what

198

most of them were and wondered if the rest were specifically for dissections.

"We don't have to stay, if you're having second thoughts," Kendaria murmured.

Realising the woman must have noticed her looking at the tools, Tessia smiled. "No, I'm looking forward to it. Where do we sit?"

"First I need to introduce you to Healer Orran. I don't think there'll be any problem with my bringing you here, especially as your father is a healer and you've been his assistant, and we've paid our fee. But it's good manners to ask, and to introduce you."

She led Tessia to two men of about the same age as Tessia's father. The men were talking, as far as Tessia could tell, about the pregnancy of a colleague's wife. Just idle chatter, but though the pair both glanced at Kendaria and Tessia when they approached, they continued talking as if the two women were not present.

Kendaria waited, her gaze on the face of the taller man. Her expression was one of patience and determination. The two men still did not halt their gossiping – which was what it was, Tessia decided, when it became clear that there was nothing about the pregnancy that should concern the healers professionally. They repeated what they were saying several times, each time phrased in a different way.

Were they, by ignoring Kendaria for the sake of this pointless chatter, being deliberately rude? The longer and sillier the conversation become, the more convinced Tessia became that they were. But the woman remained calm and expectant, her eyes never leaving Healer Orran's face. At first Tessia was puzzled, then angry at this treatment, then fascinated. Clearly a social game was taking place here, and she couldn't help wondering why, and what the rules were.

Finally the two men's talk became so inane it faltered into an awkward silence. The taller man sighed and turned to smile coldly at Kendaria.

"Ah, I see you have decided to join the crowd today, Kendaria of Foden," he observed. Tessia swallowed the urge to laugh. There hadn't been a crowd when they had arrived, but now the room echoed with the voices of many more occupants.

"Indeed I have, Healer Orran," she replied. She nodded at Tessia. "I have brought a new friend from out of town: Apprentice Tessia from Aylen ley. Her father is healer to Lord Dakon, and she has worked as his assistant most of her young life." She smiled. "That is until recently, when she became Lord Dakon's apprentice."

Both healers' eyebrows rose.

"A magician with a touch of healer's training," Healer Orran said. "How interesting. What is your father's name?"

"Healer Veran," Tessia replied.

The two men frowned thoughtfully. "I have not heard of him," the other healer said.

"You wouldn't have," Tessia told him. "He did not study here, though he has visited from time to time. His grand-father was a member of the guild. His name was Healer Berin, though he worked here so long ago I imagine you wouldn't—"

The two men's mouths had opened in identical circles.

"Ahh," they both said.

Healer Orran chuckled. "Now the pieces fall into place. Good old Healer Berin. Stirred up the guild then vanished to the country."

"We owe your grandfather a small debt for questioning our over-reliance on the star code and steering us back towards rational observation," the other healer said. "Berin's granddaughter, eh?"

200

His gaze slid over Tessia's shoulder and his eyes brightened. "Ah! Here is our corpse!"

Tessia turned to see a stretcher being carried in, a pale figure lying upon it. She felt a thrill of excitement. Most of the corpses she had seen had been of old people. This was a young male, the pale skin of his chest marred with a wound.

"Have you seen a dissection before, Apprentice Tessia?" Healer Orran asked.

"No, but I have seen a few corpses, and more of the inside of a body than most people do," she replied. "This should be very interesting," she added quietly.

She heard Kendaria chuckle.

"Well then," Healer Orran said. "You had better find yourselves some seats. Most are taken, and you won't want to sit up at the back or you might become giddy. You there!" He waved an arm at two young men sitting in the front row. "Find your manners and make space for the ladies."

There was laughter all around as the two young men grumbled and left their seats, resignedly moving up to the back of the staircase. Kendaria smiled and winked at Tessia as they sat down.

"I think he likes you. Any time you want to see a dissection, let me know."

Cloth sheets were brought into the room and handed to those sitting in the front row. Kendaria showed Tessia how to drape hers across her shoulders and over her knees.

"Sometimes there's a bit of splatter," she whispered.

The corpse was half lifted, half rolled from the stretcher onto the table. Healer Orran moved to the collection of tools, then looked up at the crowd.

"Today we will be examining the heart and lungs . . ."

As he explained the purpose of the dissection and told the audience what to look for, Tessia sighed happily. *Father would have loved this. What will he say when he hears I was here? And he won't believe that grandfather is now remembered with gratitude!* Then she sobered. *Will there be anything I can tell him that will be useful to him? I wonder . . . I had better pay close attention.*

CHAPTER 16

From his pallet in the stable loft, Hanara could see the signal light. For three nights now it had appeared, slowly flickering dimmer and brighter in a pattern all slaves were taught to read. Each time it shone from a different location, so that if anyone in the village did notice and looked for the light in the same place the following night, they would not see it. Each time it pulsed the same message.

Report. Report.

Every waking moment since first seeing it – and there had been far too many waking moments and not enough sleeping ones – Hanara had been sick with fear. There was only one person in the village that message could be for: himself. And only one person who would expect Hanara to report to him: Takado.

So far Hanara hadn't obeyed. For three nights he had curled up on the pallet, unable to sleep until exhaustion claimed him, trying to pretend he hadn't seen the signal or didn't know what to make of it.

But I have seen it and I do know. When Takado reads my mind he'll know I disobeyed him.

He was not Takado's to order about any more, he reminded himself. He was a free man. He served Lord Dakon now.

But Lord Dakon isn't here. He can't stop Takado coming to get me.

It was possible Takado would conclude that the lack of

response to his signal meant that Hanara had, indeed, been freed. Or had left the village. He might give up and leave.

Hanara almost laughed aloud.

What will he do, really? he asked himself.

Takado did not like to waste magic, so he would try to avoid conflict. He'd enter the village with the intention of asking Lord Dakon to give Hanara back to him.

Lord Dakon would say that the choice was Hanara's to make. It was too easy to imagine that moment. Takado would then look at Hanara. So would Lord Dakon. So would everyone in the village. They would all know terrible consequences would come of Hanara's refusing. If Takado attacked the village and anyone died as a result, they would all blame Hanara.

But Lord Dakon was not in the village. He would not emerge to meet Takado. When Takado realised there was no magician to protect Mandryn, what would he do?

He will kill me for disobeying him.

Would he then leave? Or would he, having already killed one of Lord Dakon's people, attack the villagers as well? It was possible that, despite their dislike of Hanara, the villagers might try to protect him on Lord Dakon's behalf. If they did, they would die.

The only other choice I have is to go to Takado.

Then Takado would read his mind and learn that Lord Dakon was absent. Would he still attack the village? Not if he wanted to avoid conflict.

Beside, he'll also learn from my mind that there is another magician nearby ready to defend Mandryn if needed.

Hanara managed a smile, but it quickly faded. The trouble was, Takado wouldn't learn this if he didn't read Hanara's mind. The one piece of information that would deter Takado from coming to get Hanara was the one piece of information that he could only learn from Hanara.

That's not entirely true. He could learn it from other villagers, if he had reason to talk to them or read their minds.

But Takado would never deign to talk to commoners, and reading the minds of anyone here would be seen as an act of aggression. He'd only do it if he had decided to attack the village, at which point he would act swiftly and wouldn't waste time with mind-reading.

Hanara sighed and resisted the urge to sit up and look through the loft window to check if the signal was still blinking in the distance.

Hasn't anyone else noticed? He hadn't heard the men in the stables or people in the village say anything about it. If they had seen it, surely someone would have investigated. They would not find Takado unless he wanted them to. If they found nothing, would they still send a warning to this other magician who was supposed to protect Mandryn? *Where is this other magician, anyway?* The signal was coming from the ridges and hills surrounding the village. From what Hanara had learned during Takado's travels, villages in the outer leys were usually a day's wagon ride from each other. The only other habitations were small farmers' cottages and shacks.

He doubted this other magician lived in a cottage. So where did he live? And if Mandryn was attacked, how long would it take him to arrive?

There had to be some way he could find out. Moving to the edge of the loft, he looked down at the stables. A lamp had been set on a table where the servants had been playing a game using small pottery tokens and a board. The men were gone, their game unfinished.

He could hear faint voices somewhere behind the stables. "Hanar!"

He jumped and looked at the stable doors, where the stable master was standing.

"Come down," Ravern ordered.

Taking a deep breath to calm himself, Hanara stood up, dusted straw off his clothing, and climbed down the ladder to the stable floor. He followed the stable master out. Ravern led him behind the building, to where three familiar figures were standing, the two stable boys and Keron, the servant master. Their attention was fixed on something beyond the stables.

His stomach sank as he realised they were looking at the signal.

Keron turned towards him. It was too dark for Hanara to make out the man's expression. An arm rose and a finger pointed towards the signal.

"What do you think, Hanar? Know what it is?"

The servant master's tone was friendly, but there was a hint of worry in it.

Hanara turned to regard the signal.

Report. Report.

If he told them what it was, they would send for the other magician. But if they had seen the signal on other nights, they might wonder why he hadn't told them earlier. They might grow angry, and throw him out of the village.

They were already worried. They might send for the magician anyway, if prompted.

"I don't know," he told them. "Is it not normal?"

Silence followed, then Keron sighed. "No. Not normal." To the others he said: "Someone should take a look."

A longer silence. Hanara could make out enough to see the two youths exchanging looks. The stable master sighed again. "In the morning, then."

Fools, Hanara thought. *Cowards, too. They're too scared to do anything. They're going to pretend it doesn't exist and hope it goes away.*

Just as he had.

They weren't going to seek the other magician unless they were sure they needed to. Trouble was, once they knew Takado was here and a threat there'd be little time to seek the other magician's help. Was there a way he could convince them to call for help sooner? Perhaps there was.

"Is there danger?" he asked the stable master in a low voice.

"I don't know," the man admitted.

"You said another magician would come and protect us. Would he know if this is something bad?"

The man stared back at him, then nodded once. "Yeah. Don't worry about it. Go get some sleep."

As he walked away he caught snatches of conversation. A protest came from one of the younger workers. Climbing back up to the loft, Hanara listened carefully. Sure enough, when the men returned a horse was brought out and readied.

"It's dark so take it slowly, but the moon will be up soon and then you can step up the pace," the stable master advised. "Deliver the message and come straight back. Lord Narvelan will give you a fresh mount. I expect you back tomorrow night."

Hanara's heart froze. *Tomorrow night? The other magician must live a full day's ride away!*

Takado was much closer than that. Much, much closer.

As the sound of galloping hoofs faded into the distance, Hanara rolled onto his back, his heart racing. *This changes everything!* Did Takado know that the only other magician nearby lived a full day's ride away? *He probably does*, Hanara thought; *he paid attention to those sorts of details while he was travelling here. He probably took note of where all the Kyralian magicians live.*

So the only thing that was keeping him from entering

Mandryn and killing or reclaiming Hanara was the belief that Lord Dakon was here.

He was going to work out that this wasn't true eventually. Hanara could hope he didn't before the other magician arrived, or Lord Dakon returned. Or he could leave and go to Takado. Takado might not kill Hanara, if he came willingly.

Yet Hanara could not make himself move. He could not yet abandon the hope that by waiting a little bit longer he might not have to confront Takado. After all, there was still a chance that Takado would kill him anyway, for disobeying his signal for so long. He lay still, waiting, as time crept by with excruciating slowness.

Then a sound below caught his attention. He rolled over and looked down. Ravern was standing with arms crossed, the other young stable servant emerging from an empty stall. They were both staring at a sweat-stained horse pacing the length of the building. The same horse that had left with the messenger had returned, riderless.

Terror rushed through Hanara, leaving him gasping. *He's here. Takado is here. And now he knows everything!* He barely heard the stable master ordering two more horses to be saddled, cursing and mumbling that the messenger had probably just fallen off the horse. He couldn't bring himself to watch the men prepare themselves with futile weapons, and leave.

But once they were gone, he climbed, shaking, down the ladder and slipped out into the night. He told himself he was leaving to save the village, but he knew with a familiar certainty that he was leaving to save himself.

It had surprised and impressed Tessia to learn that Everran and Avaria owned two wagons, one for their own everyday use and one kept for visits to the Royal Palace. Since the journey to the palace consisted of half the length of two streets, it seemed frivolous to own a vehicle especially for it.

But she had to admit the palace wagon was spectacular, and using it for ordinary journeys, bumping up against people and other vehicles, would mean constant repairs. Made of highly polished wood and gold fittings, with a cover of fine leather impressed and painted with the family's incal – a revived heraldic fashion from before the Sachakan invasion – it declared to all around it that the occupants were rich and important. The four guards in uniform carrying whips also made it clear that such a wagon should not be delayed.

Inside the wagon a tiny globe light kept the chill of the night air at bay as well as providing illumination. Everran and Avaria sat opposite Dakon, Jayan and Tessia. All wore fine clothes in the latest fashion. Everran was in a long over-robe, the same style of clothing that Jayan and Dakon had worn when Tessia and her family had come to dinner at the Residence, made of the red cloth Avaria had bought in Vanity Street. Avaria wore a purple dress cinched in closely at the waist, with a narrow opening below the buttoned collar that would have been scandalously low if the glimpses it offered beneath had been of bare flesh, not a layer of red cloth. The skirt also had been "slashed" down each side, revealing more of the red cloth underskirt.

Tessia was as tightly clad in a dress of the green cloth bought by her hostess a few days before. To her relief, it was plain at the front, and while it did have slashes in the skirt, and along the sleeves, the cloth beneath was a demure black.

Dakon and Jayan wore over-robes, too, in black and dark blue. Back in the village the fashion had seemed extravagant and a little silly, but now it looked dignified and appropriate. It suited them both, she decided, then wondered if that meant they suited the city life better than life in Mandryn.

Perhaps Jayan, she thought. *But maybe not Dakon.* Her master did not look particularly relaxed. Black clothes and a frown combined to give an impression of distracted moodiness. In city clothes, Jayan looked calmly confident and she could even see a hint of why Avaria and her friends thought him handsome.

Sensing her gaze, he turned to look at her.

Just because I can admit he's good-looking doesn't mean he's not also annoying and arrogant, she reminded herself, meeting his gaze coolly, then looking away.

The wagon slowed to a stop and the flap was opened by one of the guards.

"Lord Everran and Lady Avaria of family Korin," he called out.

Rising from his seat, Everran climbed out of the wagon and Avaria followed, holding the skirt of her dress carefully to prevent it from catching on anything or rising above her ankles as she stepped outside. As his name was announced, Dakon rose, followed by Jayan. Last to leave, Tessia climbed out carefully. Unused to the dress, she took Dakon's offered hand gratefully and managed to reach the ground without baring too much of her ankles – or so she hoped. Apparently showing the bare skin of any part of your feet or legs was uncouth and common.

Looking up at Avaria, she felt relief as she saw the woman nod approvingly. Then Tessia turned to regard the Royal Palace and caught her breath.

She had seen glimpses of it before, but never an unbroken view or from this close. In front of them was an enormous gate, held suspended by huge chains above the men and women strolling into the palace. On either side of the gate were two tall towers, lamps burning in their narrow windows and between the crenellations of their roofline – and along the walls stretching on either side.

Everran and Avaria led the way beneath the suspended gate onto a bridge spanning a gap between the outer wall and an inner one, the space between filled with water that reflected the lights all around. The inner wall was breached by another entrance, this time graced by a pair of heavy iron doors standing open in grand but sober welcome. Tessia noted the markings on the doors, depicting King Errik's family name and incal.

Once through, they entered the palace greeting hall, which mirrored the one in Dakon's Residence, but on a bigger, grander scale. Servants were meeting each visitor and directing them through an archway between the stairways on either side. Tessia saw that these stairways had been blocked by free-standing paper screens and beside each stood two guards.

At the archway Everran repeated the names of the group to the servant who greeted them, then waved them through. As she moved into the room beyond Tessia felt her heart skip a beat.

She had never seen a room this large. It could have contained the whole Residence, she suspected. Maybe two Residences. Slim stone columns in two rows helped to support the cavernous ceiling. Instead of lamps, floating globes of magical light illuminated the room.

Enormous paintings and hangings covered the walls, but it was the people who caught Tessia's attention. Hundreds of men, women and even some children milled about, in couples, families, small groups, and larger circles. All wore fashion-able, expensive and, in some cases, extravagant clothing. Jewels glittered under the globe lights. As she followed the others into the room more people came into sight, while others were obscured. *It's like a landscape of people. As you move about your viewpoint changes, constantly offering a different vista containing something you haven't seen before.*

Even as she thought this, the view changed again and a well-dressed man of Jayan's age, surrounded by a half-circle of men, appeared. Her companions stopped and she realised they were all looking at the group.

"That is King Errik," Jayan murmured, leaning close.

She nodded. As she watched, the young man looked up in their direction, his eyes skimming across their faces, then turned his attention back to the men beside him.

"Well, he's seen us," Everran said, then turned to Dakon. "If he wants to talk to us he'll summon us. In the meantime, you and I should talk to Lord Olleran."

Dakon nodded. As he and Everran began to move away, Jayan following, Avaria hooked her arm in Tessia's.

"Let them talk politics and trade on their own," she whispered into Tessia's ear. "I've just spotted Kendaria. Come on. This way."

Tessia swallowed her frustration and disappointment. While she was eager to talk to Kendaria again, once again she would be excluded from whatever business Dakon was undertaking. Surely it was part of what being a magician entailed, and therefore something she needed to know, no matter how boring. Besides, what Avaria found boring Tessia might find interesting. Or vice versa.

Kendaria was watching a male acrobat performing graceful and impressive contortions. The young man was wearing loose trousers gathered tightly round ankles and waist, but his chest was bare and rippled with muscles. His performance was drawing a lot of female attention, Tessia noticed. Kendaria winked at her.

"Wouldn't mind dissecting that body," she murmured. "I wonder if his joints would be any different from the usual cadaver's? They're so flexible."

"Kendaria!" Avaria scolded. "Don't be so grotesque!"

But Tessia couldn't help looking at the acrobat in a different way, seeing the ribs pressing against the man's skin and remembering what the inside of a chest cavity looked like – where the heart was positioned, and the spongy masses of the lungs. She had learned so much, and was hoping Kendaria would take her to more dissections before Dakon left Imardin.

But Avaria was determined to head off any further anatomical conversation and soon the gossiping began in earnest as they were joined by Darya and Zakia. Time passed slowly. While Tessia listened politely, she watched the huge room filling with people and noted how the sound of voices grew exponentially as people needed to speak louder to be heard above the din. The acrobat left and a woman nearby began to sing, accompanied by a man plucking the strings of a strange box-like instrument he rested on one knee. Avaria's friends began a detailed assessment of other women's clothing, jewellery and romantic entanglements. Tessia found herself listening to the conversation of some men standing nearby.

"– healer told him to stop, but he keeps on drinking and it's only going to make him –"

"– Sarrin said we should raise our prices, but I'm afraid it will –"

"– Mandryn, I think, but –"

The name of her village caught her attention, but the following comment was lost behind her companions' laughter. She edged to the right, closer to the speaker and his listeners.

". . . sorry for . . . leys on the border. Wouldn't want to be living there myself."

The reply was inaudible.

"Oh, of course. Someone has to. Otherwise those blood-thirsty Sachakans would be even closer to us, wouldn't they? Still, maybe they will be soon if what we've been hearing proves—"

Suddenly the man's voice quietened so that she could not hear it. Then Tessia noticed that the crowd around them was stirring. Heads had turned in one direction. Searching for the source of the distraction, she peered round Avaria's shoulder.

The king was walking towards them. He paused to speak to someone, then smiled and moved on, his gaze on Avaria and the other women.

Tessia leaned close to her hostess's ear.

"Lady Avaria," she murmured. "Look to your left."

The woman glanced idly in that direction, then turned back to Tessia. "The king?"

"Yes. He's coming this way."

"He was bound to eventually," Avaria said, shrugging. "What with an attractive young new apprentice waiting to meet him."

Tessia's heart lurched. "I'm not . . ." she began, then stopped. The king was close enough now to hear her. *He wouldn't be here just because of me,* she told herself. *Avaria is teasing me.*

He moved into the circle of women, smiling and speaking their names. For each he had a question, often an enquiry as to the health or trade of a relative. When he reached Tessia his smile widened and he moved across the circle to stand before her.

"And you must be Apprentice Tessia, Lord Dakon's new student."

"Yes, your majesty," she replied, conscious that the other women had turned away and were moving off in pairs and trios. Even Avaria. Had the king made some signal that he wanted to talk to her privately?

He watched her with alert eyes. *I hope I don't say anything wrong or do something against protocol.* "You are a natural, is that right?"

She nodded. "Yes."

"It must seem a little frightening, perhaps bad luck, to discover your gift at the time and place you did."

Tessia frowned. Was he referring to her desire to become a healer? Surely he hadn't heard about Takado . . . no, Dakon wouldn't tell him that.

"No," she said slowly. "Well, it was frightening at the time. I didn't know what I'd done. But later it was . . . exciting, I have to admit."

He paused, a line appearing between his brows then disappearing as he smiled again. "You are referring to using your power for the first time, not to living close to the border?"

"Yes . . . but I suppose living close to the border has always been a little . . . worrying. Unless . . ." Her heart skipped. "Is there a special reason we should be concerned just now, your majesty?"

He blinked, then an expression of realisation crossed his face. "Ah. I must apologise. I did not mean to suggest such a thing. To those of us who live in the city the idea of living on the border with Sachaka always seems frightening, but you must be used to it."

His tone was soothing and she suddenly knew, with certainty, that he was hiding something.

"Is Sachaka likely to invade?" she asked bluntly, and immediately regretted it. He looked utterly taken aback. She began to apologise.

"Don't," he said, cutting her off. "It is I who should apologise to you. I should have been more careful not to alarm you." He moved to her side and took her arm, leading her slowly across the room. "There have been rumours," he told her quietly. "Of a possible threat. No doubt you will hear of them whether I tell you or not – it is hardly a secret here. But do not fear. No great armies await over the border.

215

The concern is that a few disgruntled Sachakan magicians might decide to make trouble for the emperor."

"Oh," she said, turning to stare at him. Even a few Sachakan magicians could do great damage in a village like Mandryn – especially with Dakon absent. "Is my village safe? My family?"

He met her gaze, his own glance wary and searching. Then his expression softened into a smile.

"It is safe. I assure you."

She drew in a deep breath and let it out slowly, willing her heart to stop racing.

"That is a relief, your majesty," she said.

He chuckled. "Yes. It is. I'm sorry to have alarmed you with all this rumour-mongering. I'm afraid those of us who spend too much time in the city tend to gossip far too much without thought for the consequences, and that even I am guilty of the habit from time to time."

She smiled at his admission. "Lady Avaria did warn me not to take city gossip too seriously – but gossip and rumour may be quite different things."

He laughed, then turned to face her. "Indeed they are. Now, I have a message for you to pass on to Lord Dakon." His expression became serious. "Tell him to meet me tomorrow at the training ground, an hour after midday."

She nodded. "Training ground. Hour after midday," she repeated.

He bowed, and she belatedly replied with the womanly dip that Avaria had taught her, hand modestly pressed to her chest. "Charming to meet you, Apprentice Tessia. I hope it will not be long before you visit Imardin again."

"I'm honoured and pleased to meet you, your majesty," she replied.

He smiled, then turned away. As he moved across the room a uniformed man strode forward to meet him.

"How did it go?" a familiar and breathless voice spoke at her elbow.

Tessia turned to look at Avaria. "Well. I think. Maybe. I have a message for Lord Dakon."

The woman nodded and smiled. "Then we'd better deliver it – discreetly, if we can."

CHAPTER 17

The Royal Palace was quiet, yet Dakon detected hints of activity all around. He caught the faint sounds of footsteps from time to time, or the hushed murmur of voices. Servants flitted into view and then out again.

The further his guide led him through the building, the more obvious the signs of activity became. He heard the sound of chopping and caught delicious aromas, and guessed he was near the kitchen. Then the neigh of a horse told him the stables were to his right. And finally the clang of metal against metal, and barked calls, warned him that he was nearing the training ground.

The guide brought Dakon out of a cobbled road between two buildings into a wide, gravel-covered area. Two men stood several paces from each other. Dakon recognised both instantly: Magician Sabin and King Errik. Around them, at a safe distance of several paces, stood a handful of men, watching the combatants.

Two were uniformed guards, whose role appeared to be to hold weapons. Two were servants, one carrying a bowl and towels, the other balancing a tray bearing a jug and several goblets. The other two men he recognised from the previous night as friends of the king, both from powerful families.

The guide indicated that Dakon should stand next to the latter, then left. Dakon exchanged polite nods with the men, but when they turned back to the king without speaking he took the hint and remained silent.

First the king, then Sabin, uttered a hoarse word which Dakon couldn't make out, then began to advance on each other. Both were already sweaty, but neither was out of breath or tired. Watching them, Dakon thought back to the gathering the night before.

It has to have been, aside from a few failed attempts at courting, one of the most frustrating nights of my life, he mused. The king had ignored them, and once even appeared to go out of his way to avoid them. This had been taken by some of the Circle's detractors as an indication that Dakon and his host were out of favour. They had closed in like scavengers, their mockery carefully phrased in the politest of language. Everran appeared to enjoy the challenge, replying with equal slyness and wit. Dakon, knowing this was a game he couldn't possibly win, stayed silent, took note of who their opponents appeared to be, and tried to guess if they were in earnest or playing along for the sake of politics.

It was the ringleader, Lord Hakkin, who had intrigued Dakon the most. Though the man's comments were by far the sharpest, he hadn't delivered them with the conviction the others had. Yet at times he had almost sneered at his supporters' jibes, repeating and embellishing them if they failed to be witty or cutting enough.

By the time Dakon and the others climbed into the wagon to return to Everran's home, he had been exhausted, despondent and angry.

When Avaria had suggested to Tessia that it was now safe to deliver the king's message, Dakon had barely heard. Poor Tessia had had to repeat it twice before he took it in.

The training ground. An hour past midday. King Errik *did* want to meet him. Just not with several hundred witnesses.

And that is something Jayan must be glad of, he thought. The apprentice had been uncharacteristically silent and nervous throughout the gathering. Eventually – perhaps too slowly – Dakon had worked out why. Among the detractors had been a man Dakon hadn't seen in years – Jayan's father, Karvelan of family Drayn.

Jayan had said nothing about his visit to his father and Dakon had assumed that was simply because nothing of interest had been discussed. Now he could see the conflict the young man faced. He was caught between loyalty to his master and his powerful and wealthy family. Dakon knew how little Jayan thought of his family, and he was fairly sure he had his apprentice's respect and even affection, but these things did not always matter in the face of money and politics.

I bet old Karvelan wishes I'd hurry up and release his son. Then Dakon frowned. *I wonder if Jayan wishes I would. It would free him to choose where his loyalties lie. But then, perhaps he'd rather have an excuse not to make that choice just now.*

A grunt of dismay brought his attention back to the fighters. Sabin and Errik were backing away from each other.

"You win, again," the king conceded with cheerful annoyance. Sabin bowed. Chuckling, the king handed his sword to one of the guards, then filled the goblet with clear water from the jug and downed it in one go. Then he took a towel and walked towards Dakon, wiping his brow as he came.

"Lord Dakon of family Aylendin. What did you think?"

"Of the fight, your majesty?" Dakon found himself searching for the appropriate response. He knew nothing about swordplay. "It was energetic."

"Would you like a bout?" Errik offered.

"Me?" Dakon blinked in surprise. "I, ah, I'm afraid I wouldn't make a good combatant."

"A bit rusty, eh?"

"No. I've, er, never picked up a sword in my life," Dakon admitted.

The king's eyebrows rose. "Never? What would you do, in a real war, if your magic ever ran out?"

Dakon paused to consider it, then decided he'd rather not. "Cheat?"

Errik laughed. "That's not very honourable!"

Dakon shrugged. "I've heard it said that real war isn't particularly honourable."

"No." The king's smile faded. He turned and waved at the others. All bowed, then walked away. The guards took away the weapons, followed by Sabin. The courtiers vanished through a doorway but the servants took up positions by another door, still holding their burdens, but out of earshot. Within moments Dakon was virtually alone with the king.

"So, Lord Dakon," Errik said. "You want to know what I will do if the wayward, rebellious Sachakan magicians who are causing our neighbouring emperor so much irritation decide to begin their own little invasion of Kyralia."

Dakon met the king's eyes and nodded. Sabin had warned him that the king preferred to be direct. Errik smiled crookedly, then sobered.

"So does everyone else. I tell them exactly what I tell you now: an attack on or invasion of any ley is an attack on or invasion of Kyralia. It is not to be tolerated."

"I'm glad to hear that," Dakon said. "I'm getting the impression, however, that others would not be."

The king's gaze flashed. "The trouble with Kyralians gathering together to support one cause is that other Kyralians then feel they must then gather together to oppose it. Not that I'm saying your Circle should not have formed." He shrugged, though his expression remained serious. "Just that the consequences were unavoidable."

"Would they still oppose each other if a greater enemy appeared?" Dakon asked.

"If they become too strongly opposed. There are plenty of examples of this happening in our history."

"So you can't appear to support either side, or they may not join forces when needed." Dakon nodded as he saw the king's dilemma.

The king's gaze warmed with approval. "I am making sure *I* can defend my kingdom when and if the need arises."

Dakon resisted a smile. "Are your plans too great a secret to be shared with a humble country magician?"

"Humble?" Errik rolled his eyes, then sighed and looked at Dakon levelly. "Not too secret. I will discuss some of them with you, and you must tell me if you see any flaws."

"I will do my best, your majesty."

"Good. Now, any Sachakans planning an attack will want to be sure they have the numbers to win. They don't form alliances easily, however. Their numbers are likely to be small at first, so their target is likely to be too. Unfortunately we have plenty of small targets – the villages in border leys protected by one or two magicians, too far apart to be of any use to each other.

"Evacuation is the only option in these leys," he continued. "Once a ley falls it must be regained immediately. The Sachakans will be relying on news of their success to bring them more allies. We must counter this with news of their failure, as quickly as possible."

Dakon nodded, pleased at the king's assessment.

"How would I do this?" Errik asked. "Speed will be important, so those magicians closest to the invaded ley will be ordered to respond. But at the same time I will send city magicians out, in case the first response is not sufficient."

Errik stopped and looked at Dakon, eyebrows raised. "Questions?"

"You would not post magicians out at the borders now?" Dakon asked. "To deter the Sachakans from attacking to begin with and prevent the outer leys being taken at all?"

"Magicians," the king said, his voice heavy with irony, "do not like being told what to do. If you can persuade some of your city supporters to return with you, by all means do so. But don't be surprised if they are too concerned with keeping an eye on their adversaries here to leave. It would cause me more trouble later if I order any to go, no attack comes to justify it, and they suffer some setback."

Dakon could not help frowning. The king nodded.

"Petty, I know. Rest assured, once an attack comes no magician will dare protest against defending their country. However," his eyes narrowed, "your new apprentice managed to extract a promise from me last night that I feel I must keep."

"Tessia?" Dakon frowned in dismay. "She demanded a promise?"

Errik chuckled. "No. I'm afraid it was my fault. I thought to test her and instead made a fool of myself."

Dakon's alarm grew. *What did she say?* He tried to read Errik's expression. *Well, the king doesn't look too annoyed. Perhaps annoyed at himself*, he corrected.

"I spoke of the threat, which she clearly knew nothing of," Errik explained. "And ended up promising her that her village was safe."

"Oh. I apologise for that," Dakon said. "I have tried to keep her from learning of the Sachakan threat, so that worry would not spoil her first visit to Imardin."

Errik smiled crookedly. "That was considerate of you. I'm afraid I now feel obliged to keep my promise, so I am sending one of my most loyal magician friends home with you." He turned and waved at the building the courtiers had disappeared into. One of the men stepped out and started walking towards them.

"This is Lord Werrin. He will live with you for now, officially there to assess Kyralia's defences but also conveniently rumoured to be keeping the country magicians in their place. It will meet everyone's requirements of me, I hope."

The man was short but lean, his hair flecked with grey, but his face as smooth as the king's so it was impossible to judge his age. He returned Dakon's gaze steadily as he stopped beside Errik, his eyes dark and intelligent but his face devoid of expression.

"I look forward to being your host, Lord Werrin," Dakon said.

The man smiled. "And I shall enjoy exploring the country leys in spring, Lord Dakon."

Dakon felt a moment of panic and worry. Did the king think he needed to keep an eye on Dakon and his neighbours? He pushed the feeling aside. He had nothing to hide. And having an extra magician in Mandryn would go a long way towards helping protect the village and ley, should it be attacked.

Then he felt sympathy for Werrin. The man would have little to do but travel the rounds of border leys, over rough roads, with none of the comforts and entertainments of the city. *I must find out his taste in books, and stock up*, Dakon thought. *And see what sort of—*

—WE HAVE BEEN ATTACKED! MANDRYN HAS BEEN ATTACKED!

For a moment, Dakon, Werrin and the king blinked at each other in surprise. Then Werrin placed a hand on the king's shoulder as if to steady him and did not remove it.

It was a notably personal gesture, indicating how close they were.

"That was Lord Narvelan," Werrin said. He looked at Dakon. "Am I correct?"

Dakon nodded. His stomach had sunk at the voice and its news. Mandryn. His home. Attacked. His head spun as the truth sank in.

—*Attacked by whom?* the king asked.

—*Sachakans*, Narvelan replied. *One of the villagers recognised the magician who passed through here a while back.*

"Takado," Dakon hissed, horror turning to anger.

—*How many survivors?* he asked.

—*Not many. We are still count—*

—*Cease communication*, the king ordered firmly. He looked at Dakon. "There are good reasons why speaking with the mind is forbidden by law. Do you want more Sachakans knowing how successful your former guest's attack was?"

Dakon shook his head. Errik glanced at Lord Werrin, who let his hand fall from the king's shoulder. "I doubt Narvelan intended to give away that he is there now, most likely alone and vulnerable." He grimaced and looked at Dakon. "I expect you want to return as quickly as possible – will probably leave tonight?"

Dakon nodded.

"Lord Werrin will go with you. He'll join you at Lord Everran's home in an hour." Errik looked at his friend, who nodded, then turned back to Dakon. "I will gather more magicians to follow as soon after as I can arrange. Go – and be careful. And . . . please convey my apology to Apprentice Tessia and my hope that her family is among those who survived."

There was genuine concern in the young ruler's face and voice. Dakon bowed.

"I will. Thank you, your majesty," he said.

Then he hurried away, unable to stop the images of death and destruction his imagination was conjuring up. How many had died? Who? He would not find out until he returned home. And home was at least three or four days' ride away, if he changed horses and rode through the night, and the road hadn't worsened . . .

Then he remembered Narvelan's last communication. The king had said Narvelan was in Mandryn. *We are still count —*. The last word had been "counting", surely. Counting the dead. Dakon shuddered.

But it also meant Takado — if the villager who recognised the attacker was correct — had left after his attack. That was unexpected. The Circle had always assumed Sachakans wouldn't attack unless they intended to possess a village or ley.

It was strange, and he would have plenty of time to ponder it on the ride home, but he would not find any answers until he got there.

"What is it, Tessia?"

Tessia started and looked at the faces of the women, all staring at her. She hesitated, worried that if she told them what had happened they would think her mad.

But the content of the message she'd heard was too shocking. She had to say something.

"I . . . I just heard someone talking," she said. "In my head."

Kendaria's eyebrows rose. "That's not good. Mental communication is forbidden by law. Magicians can only do it if the king approves or orders it. Did you recognise who it was?"

"It was . . ." Tessia frowned. "He didn't say, but it sounded like Lord Narvelan. And Lord Dakon replied. And another man . . . the king? It sounded like his voice." She shook her head. "Narvelan said Mandryn had been attacked by Takado — the Sachakan who visited us a few months ago." She looked at the women. They exchanged horrified looks. They clearly believed her. "Are you saying this is *real*?"

"Yes." Kendaria looked at Avaria. "Is this the beginning?"

Avaria shrugged. "I wouldn't dare guess." She was frowning at Tessia in concern. "Lord Dakon wouldn't have taught you about mind-speaking, I'm guessing, because it's not something you're supposed to do. But if Lord Narvelan used it, the need must have been urgent. We had better go home."

The others murmured sympathetic farewells and Kendaria, their hostess today, offered the use of her wagon so they would not have to send for Avaria's. Feeling dazed, Tessia followed Avaria out of the house and into the vehicle.

"So Mandryn has been attacked?" she asked as the wagon began moving.

Avaria looked grave. "Yes."

How many survivors? Dakon had asked. *Not many*, Narvelan had answered. She felt a rush of cold and fear. *Mother? Father? Are they alive?*

Takado's leering face flashed into her memory and she shuddered. *He came back.* Did he come back to punish her for humiliating him by repelling him with magic? Then she remembered Hanara. *Did he come back to reclaim his property?*

"Tessia, there is something I should tell you."

She looked up at Avaria. Dread filled her. Did the woman know something? Did she know that Tessia's parents were dead? How could she?

She might. All of this felt so unreal, it seemed anything was possible.

"Lord Dakon didn't come to Imardin just to sort out some trade matters and see some friends," Avaria told her. "He is part of a group of magicians known as the Circle of Friends, made up of country magicians and the city magicians who support them. We're all concerned that Kyralia may soon be invaded by Sachakan magicians. He came here to gain assurance from the king that if any of the outer leys were taken, the city magicians would help to regain them."

Tessia nodded to indicate she understood. She found she was not surprised. It explained the king's conversation with her the previous night. And why she hadn't been included in the gatherings Dakon and Jayan had attended. Dakon would have wanted as few people to know about the threat as possible. He wouldn't have wanted her worrying helplessly about the safety of Mandryn and her parents while she was in Imardin.

My parents. Perhaps I should have been worried. Perhaps I shouldn't have left . . .

Was her father treating injured villagers right now? Or was he one of the injured . . . or dead. *No.* She could see him, determined and exhausted, working away. She held on to that image. It was true until it had to be otherwise.

"None of us thought an attack would come this soon," Avaria said, staring out of the wagon through the cover flap. Then she cursed. "The king must be wondering if we set it up."

Tessia said nothing. Every word Avaria uttered solidified this new reality. Made sense of it. Tessia did not want it to be real. She wanted to go back to Kendaria's house, back to her seat, and start time again from that moment.

But I can't.

Suddenly she didn't care if she never saw Kendaria or Avaria or any of the women who had befriended and welcomed her again. She didn't care if she never saw another dissection. She just wanted to go home. To rush back to Mandryn and learn the truth, whether it was good or terrible.

And Dakon will want to as well, she realised. *We'll probably leave tonight. It'll be a fast, exhausting journey. Probably on horseback rather than by wagon.*

By the time the wagon stopped it was all she could do to stop leaping past Avaria and rushing inside the house to find Dakon. Gritting her teeth, she climbed out decorously. Once inside Avaria strode directly to the master's room. Dakon, Jayan and Everran were there, talking.

"– volunteers," Everran was saying. "They'll be no more than a day behind you."

They looked up as Avaria and Tessia arrived. Dakon opened his mouth.

"Don't worry, Dakon," Avaria said. "I've told Tessia your real reason for visiting Imardin. I expect you'll all be leaving as soon as possible."

"Yes." Dakon looked at Tessia, his expression full of concern and apology. "I am sorry, Tessia. I don't know if your parents are alive or not. I hope so."

She nodded, suddenly unable to speak.

"Jayan and I are leaving as soon as Lord Werrin, the magician the king has sent to accompany us, arrives. You will stay here."

She opened her mouth to protest, but he raised a hand to stop her.

"It will be a rough journey, Tessia. We have the use of the king's messenger horses, so we will be riding from dawn each day until it is too dark to ride. When we get there we don't know if we'll find Takado and his allies waiting for us or not. It will be dangerous, especially for a new apprentice."

"I'm no soft city woman," she told him. "I can ride, for long hours if needed. And *you* taught me that apprentices, new or not, are not supposed to stray from their master's side

229

during times of conflict. You should have the extra strength of a second apprentice to call on."

Dakon paused, then frowned and began to speak, but Avaria cut him off.

"Take the girl, you fool. She has healing knowledge. We can only hope it won't be needed."

Tessia winced. If it was needed then her father . . . no, she must not think about that. She must not lose hope.

Dakon stared at Avaria, then looked at Everran and Jayan. Both men nodded. He sighed and his shoulders slumped.

"Very well then. You have many tough days ahead, Tessia. If you find you are unable to bear them, say so and I'll arrange . . . something."

"Not as tough as what the people of Mandryn just went through," she replied quietly.

As he met her gaze, she saw the same worry she felt, and suddenly her heart filled with love for this man. He truly cared about his people, and she had come to appreciate how rare that was.

She only hoped those people were still alive to be cared for.

CHAPTER 18

Jayan was sure there was no word to properly describe the weariness he felt. He was beyond "tired". He was long past "exhausted". He was sure he was on the brink of passing out completely. It took all his will to convince his legs to continue gripping the saddle, and his back to stay upright.

Some time in the last day or so his awareness had begun to shrink. First he became oblivious of their surroundings unless someone drew his attention to them. Then he was aware of Dakon, Tessia and Werrin only as shadows that should always be near; he would only rouse from this state if they weren't. Then, as the soreness of his body increased and he endeavoured to ignore the pain, he eventually became wrapped up solely in himself for most of the long hours on the road, trusting his horse to keep up with the others without his direction.

A strange feeling crept over him as they descended into the valley he'd called home for so long. A premonition, perhaps. He was certain something bad was about to happen. But as Dakon rode on in front, crossing the bridge and entering Mandryn, Jayan found he was incapable of speaking. Unable to move, to tug on the reins and stop his horse. Unable to stop himself looking at the corpses strewn everywhere: on the road, in doorways, hanging out of windows. He looked, but he could not see details. Exhaustion made his sight blurry, his awareness frayed. His ears were deaf. Or perhaps it was just the stillness and silence of a village occupied only by dead people.

Then he did hear something. Footsteps. The sensuous metallic slide of a blade. He looked at Dakon walking in front. (When had they dismounted? He was so tired, he must have done it without realising.) The magician did not appear to have heard anything. Jayan opened his mouth to shout a warning, but no sound came out. *It's an ambush!* he wanted to shout. *Watch out!* From shadows emerged indistinct figures. There was a flash of dazzling light and—

"*Jayan.*"

Startled, Jayan opened his eyes and blinked at his surroundings. He was back astride the horse. He was not in Mandryn. The road climbed a ridge before him, but the horse had stopped.

"*Jayan! Wake up!*"

Tessia. The first voice had been different. Dakon's. He straightened and turned in his saddle to see the pair several paces behind, staring at him. Werrin, the king's magician, was frowning.

I fell asleep in the saddle, he thought. *Lucky I didn't fall off.* Then he smiled wryly. *I finally master the skill of sleeping in the saddle and what do I do? Have that same nightmare.*

Turning his mount round, he directed it back down the road to join the others. Dakon's expression was grim. Dark shadows hung under his eyes. Tessia was pale but her eyes were bright.

For the first few days of their journey, to Jayan's annoyance, he had worried constantly about Tessia. As he had expected, she hadn't complained once and rode silent and determined throughout each day. Because he knew her now, he'd worried that she wouldn't speak up if she was suffering, and would fall behind. But in the last few days he'd been too caught up in his own weariness to do more than check now and then that she was still with them, and he felt guilty about that.

"Lord Werrin and I will go on from here," Dakon said. "You and Tessia will wait here."

Jayan frowned, then looked round again and felt a shock of recognition. This was a part of the road near Mandryn he and Dakon had occasionally ridden along on their morning rides. The village was not far away.

Tessia looked as if she would have protested, if she hadn't been too tired to argue. Jayan felt the same. If there were more than one or two Sachakans watching the village, ready to attack any magicians that might approach, the chances were the four of them wouldn't survive. Dakon no doubt felt that there was no point in risking Jayan and Tessia's lives as well as his own and Werrin's. Perhaps he also wanted to make sure there were no nasty sights for Tessia to stumble upon. Jayan watched as Werrin nudged his horse after Dakon's and the pair rode up the ridge, then disappeared over the top.

"I'm supposed to stay near, aren't I?" Tessia asked quietly. "Safer for me and him, or something like that."

"Perhaps," Jayan replied, thinking of his nightmare. "But it won't make any difference if there are Sachakans waiting in ambush."

She said nothing to that, just sat staring at the ridge.

"I guess we could get off and walk around a bit," he suggested after a while. "Get our legs working again."

She looked down at her horse, then smiled grimly at him. "I suspect if I did I'd never manage to get back on again. Dakon would come back to find me lying on the side of the road, my legs no longer working."

Jayan nodded in agreement. "We should be ready to flee if any Sachakans turn up, too."

"Well, at least this time I can be sure none of them will want to seduce me." She ran a hand through the hair that had escaped her braid and grimaced. "I'm filthy, and I have riding sores on top of riding sores."

He gazed at her wearily, amazed that she was still able to make light of their situation when her home and confirmation of the fate of her parents was a short ride away. She looked back at him and her smile faded, then she looked away.

Embarrassed, he realised. *I should say something clever and reassuring.* But everything that came to mind sounded trite or likely to give her the impression he was romantically interested in her – which he certainly wanted to avoid.

So he said nothing. The haunted look that had come into her eyes so many times during the ride had returned. Definitely better to say nothing, he decided.

When Dakon and Werrin appeared on the ridge Tessia felt a wave of nausea. Part of her desperately wanted an answer, to be released from the suspense of not knowing the fate of her parents. The other part didn't want any news, if it were bad news.

The two magicians wore grim expressions. As they slowed to meet her and Jayan, Dakon looked straight at her. His expression was sympathetic. He shook his head.

For a moment she searched for another meaning – something else he might be trying to communicate to her. Then she took a deep breath and forced herself to face the truth. Dakon was not fool enough to make such a gesture and not know how she would read it.

They're dead, she told herself. *Father. Mother. Gone. Just like that.* It felt unreal, as had the news of the attack so many days ago. *What will it take to make me believe this? Do I even want to?*

"The village is safe for us to visit," Dakon told them. "Locals say the Sachakans headed for the mountains after the attack. Most of the buildings are burned or damaged so I'd advise against entering them in case they collapse. The dead . . ." He paused to draw in and then let out a deep breath. "The dead have been buried. Narvelan's people did not know how long it would take for us to get here. The few survivors – some children who managed to hide – were able to provide names for the markers."

They came to the top of the ridge. Tessia hadn't realised they were moving. In the distance a thin thread of smoke marred the sky.

"Narvelan has returned to his village to evacuate his people," Dakon continued. "We are to join him once we are finished here. It is possible, despite what we've been told, that the Sachakans have returned in stealth to await our return."

They continued in silence. It was easier for Tessia to concentrate on the tension and fear of the others than think about her parents. She eyed distant clumps of trees or houses, looking for movement or human shapes. Was Takado watching? The leering face flashed through her memory and she felt a rush of fear.

Then she remembered her mistake earlier. Her quip about Sachakans seducing her. Jayan had given her an odd look and she had realised what she had revealed . . . *this time I can be sure none of them will want to seduce me.* This time. Unlike last time. He must have understood what had prompted her to use magic the first time. Did he think she had encouraged Takado? Did he wonder how far Takado's "seduction" had gone?

At least I don't have to worry about Mother and Father finding out.

She felt a wrench inside at the thought. Suddenly all the things they would never find out came to her. They would never see her become a higher magician. Her mother would never attend her wedding – if she ever married. Her father would never hear about her visit to the Healers' Guild, or the dissection she'd watched. She'd never assist him in healing patients again.

The pain was almost too much to bear. She felt tears threatening and, conscious of the three men riding beside her, swallowed hard and blinked them away. She forced herself to think of something else and ended up worrying about the dangers of visiting the village instead.

Cresting another rise, the magicians reined in their horses. Tessia and Jayan joined them. She looked down at the village and caught her breath.

Dakon had been right. Most of the village was in ruins. Many buildings looked like toys smashed by a giant two-year-old child, and smoke still trailed out of a few of them. Where the Residence had been there was only a large pile of rubble. She searched for her parents' house. It was hard to make out where among the ruins it had been.

As Dakon nudged his horse into motion again, they followed him down into the valley. Only when she reached the bridge did Tessia realise that Takado had torn it down. They rode down the bank beside the ruined spans, and the horses easily waded through the shallow flow of water. Once they'd climbed the other side a youngster Tessia recognised as one of the metal worker's older boys emerged from behind a broken wall and jogged up to them.

"Lord Dakon," he said, bobbing his head respectfully.

"Tiken. Would you show Apprentice Tessia and Apprentice Jayan to the graves," Dakon asked.

The graves. Tessia felt her stomach sink, and shuddered.

The boy nodded, then looked up at Tessia and gave her a sympathetic smile. "Welcome back, Tess. Follow me."

Silently, Tessia and Jayan rode behind Tiken as he led them down the main road. Finally Tessia was able to recognise the pile of rubble that had been her home. She paused to stare, searching for some sign of familiar furniture.

"I found your father's bag," Tiken said. "And some other things that weren't broken. Been putting everything that might be valuable or useful where it won't get rained on."

She looked at him. "Thank you. I'll need the bag, and if the other things are cures and tools I should take them too. They might be needed, if there's another attack."

Tiken nodded. Jayan was frowning. She indicated that the boy should continue on.

Moving between two buildings with smoke wafting from their windows, Tiken led them out into a small field. Long furrows of disturbed earth bulged from the grass. Each had a short, thick plank of wood protruding from the ground beside it, and names had been roughly carved into the surface.

Jayan cursed under his breath. "So many," he muttered.

Tessia didn't look at him. She felt fragile and suddenly resented his presence. Dismounting, she paused to stretch and let her legs recover a little, then walked stiffly towards the graves. So many. Dakon had said only a few children had survived. All the rest were dead. Old Neslie the widow. Jornen the metal worker and his wife. Cannia, the kitchen servant at the Residence. Whole families had perished. Mothers, fathers and children. Young women and men she had grown up with. The frail and weak along with the robust and strong. None of them any threat to Takado, but all a source of a little more magic.

Tiken walked toward one corner of the field. She followed him. As she had expected and dreaded, two of the planks of wood were carved with her parents' names.

So. It's true. No denying it now.

"Nothing was done to them beforehand," the boy told her.

She looked up at him, puzzled by his comment. His expression was grave and his eyes haunted. He looked twice as old as she knew him to be. She shuddered. *What has he seen?*

"Probably 'cause they were old," he told her. "And maybe . . . maybe because your father helped the slave."

She heard Jayan curse again, but ignored him. In her mind she saw Hanara's thin face and frightened eyes. She looked at the other graves. "Is he . . ."

"No. He's not here." The boy's expression darkened. "Never found him."

She frowned, feeling suspicion like some parasite hatching inside her. *The boy believes Hanara betrayed us*, she thought. *Why would he give up his freedom? No, he would only have turned against the village if he thought he had no other choice.*

"What did they do to the others?" Jayan asked quietly behind her.

The boy hesitated. "What Sachakans do," he answered evasively.

Leave it at that, she thought at Jayan. *Knowing the details will torment you as much as not knowing them will. I'd rather not know.*

Jayan asked again. She moved away, closer to her parents' grave, hoping to get far enough away to not hear. Kneeling in the dirt, she placed a hand on the soil over her father's body and let grief come and drown out their voices.

CHAPTER 19

I should have run away, Hanara thought. *But how could I have known what was going to happen?*

Nothing had worked out quite as he'd expected, or as he'd feared. After leaving the stables, the former slave had run across fields and along roads, searching and searching. The signal light had disappeared, but he explored the area it must have shone from . . . and found nothing. He'd circled the village, looking in all the places he'd seen the signal flash from before, but in vain.

When he finally found Takado, the magician was sitting on a tree stump beside a path, at an intersection Hanara had passed several times in his search. Takado had laughed when Hanara threw himself at his feet. He'd laughed, then read Hanara's mind. Then he'd laughed again.

Did you not like freedom, then? Takado had asked. *Did you miss me? Admit it, you like being my slave. None of this humble shovelling of horse manure for you, Hanara. Deep down, you know you are better than that. You vain little man. You are only loyal to the most powerful master.*

Hanara had thought of Tessia, then. Unexpectedly. Was that why Takado had attacked the village? Had he been angry that Hanara thought another – a Kyralian – might be worthy of his loyalty? But Hanara had only thought of her briefly – and not convincingly. All he had done was realise that it was possible he might feel loyalty to her . . . in another life . . . if Takado hadn't already been his master.

When Takado had attacked the village Hanara had been shocked and puzzled. But his master never did anything without a reason. So why had he done it?

Hanara looked up at the men sitting around the fire and felt his empty stomach sour. *Ichani*. Exiles and outcasts. Company unworthy of his master, who owned land and was a respected ashaki. Some were familiar. All had been Takado's friends for years. In the beginning none of them had been outcasts. But after the first had found himself homeless after a feud with his brother ended badly, the others slipped out of respectability one by one. Sometimes by their own doing. Sometimes not. Takado had helped them in secret, sending supplies and hiding them from their enemies.

A faint whistle nearby brought all heads up, eyes searching the darkness. Footsteps told where to look. Then magical globes of light weaved into the clearing close to the ground, casting an eerie glow on the undersides of the faces of the men approaching.

Takado. As always, Hanara felt a thrill of both fear and relief. He never felt safe around other Sachakan masters if Takado was not present, yet he also feared Takado. His master had not yet punished him for ignoring the signal for so long. He might yet do so. He might yet have plans to kill Hanara, or send him to his death.

Hanara would have assumed Takado had not killed him because he needed a source slave, if his master hadn't returned to Kyralia with a new source slave. He looked back at the thin young man waiting by Takado's tent. Jochara hadn't said a word to Hanara, but his unfriendly stares made it clear he had not expected to be sharing his role with his predecessor.

As Takado and his two companions joined the Ichani,

Hanara hurried forward and placed the low wooden stool he'd been holding on the ground. His master sat down, not sparing him a glance.

The Sachakans who had left with Takado to see the ruins of Mandryn were unfamiliar. Like the Ichani, they wore knives in jewel-encrusted sheaths on their belt to indicate they were magicians. Their own slaves brought stools for their masters to sit on.

"Well?" Rokino, one of the outcasts, asked. "What did you think, Dachido?"

"Looks like it was an easy target," the newcomer replied. Kochavo, his companion, nodded in agreement.

All turned to look at Takado, who smiled. "They're all easy targets. Some easier than others. We could take a quarter of the country for ourselves with no real resistance. No immediate resistance, that is."

"Could we hold it?" Dachido asked.

"To do so permanently we will have to take the whole country, which I believe we can do, with careful planning."

Kochavo looked thoughtful. "The whole country. Reconquer Kyralia. If the emperor wished this, he would have done it already."

Takado nodded. "The emperor believes it is not possible. He is wrong."

Dachido frowned. "How can you be so sure?"

"I have examined Kyralia's defences for myself," Takado told him. "They have perhaps a hundred magicians, many of whom have never been trained to fight – except in some silly game they play. Most of the time they bicker with each other, never agreeing on anything. Those who live in the city despise those who live in the leys, who distrust them in return. Their king is young and inexperienced with about as much authority over his people as our emperor has over us. The commoners

241

hate the ruling class and are uncooperative and defiant. Their magicians are only allowed, by law, to take strength from apprentices – and many do not even have those." He smiled. "They are foolish and weak."

"Some would say much the same of us," Dachido said, chuckling. Then he sobered. "You are asking us to defy the emperor's wishes. He has made it clear he will punish anyone who threatens the peace between Sachaka and its neighbours."

Takado said nothing. He rose and paced around the fire, frowning, then he stopped before the two newcomers.

"The emperor knows that Sachaka may face civil war. Better the landless and disinherited unite to gain new land than fight over the old. If we win enough support, and demonstrate that victory is possible, Emperor Vochira will be forced to endorse a conquest of Kyralia. He may even join us."

"More likely he'll send someone to kill us," Dachido said darkly.

"Only if there are too few of us. The more of us he has to kill, the more allies he has to apologise to and compensate, and the weaker he will appear." Takado's teeth flashed in the light of the fire. "Some will join us without much urging, because they have nothing better to do, or love a good fight. Others will join us once they hear how much support we have gained. Even more will come when we have a few victories to our name. Still more will want some of the prizes – land, wealth, fame, power."

Dachido frowned. He was older than the other outcasts, Hanara saw. His eyes were not afire with excitement at the thought of real battles, of conquest or power. The suggestion they defy the emperor clearly worried him.

The man looked down at the fire and sighed. "I am not the only one who believes Sachaka is in danger of turning on itself," he said heavily. "Whether we act or not, we face conflict within. This . . . this may be what we need to minimise that."

"You see now why I, an ashaki, propose this?" Takado asked quietly. "Not for land or wealth; I have my own. I am no outcast, though I am not ashamed to fight with outcasts."

Dachido nodded. "You have everything to lose."

"I do this not just for my friends," Takado gestured to the two Ichani. "But for all Sachaka."

"I see that now," Dachido acknowledged. "Kochavo and I will talk." He looked up at Takado. "We will give you our decision tomorrow morning."

Takado nodded, then glanced at Hanara. "Then let me offer you a cup of raka to refresh your bodies and minds."

Even before he had finished speaking, Hanara was hurrying towards Takado's pack. But then he skidded to a halt. Another was there already. Jochara held the raka powder. With a smug gleam in his eyes, the young man hurried to serve the visitors. Takado said nothing, not caring who served him so long as his needs were fulfilled.

Hanara watched the other slave. The man was young, lithe and unhampered by the stiffness of healed muscles and scars. He was also a source slave, judging by the scars on his palms, but too old to be one of Hanara's progeny.

Hanara watched and felt worry and resentment stir inside him.

The ride to meet Narvelan seemed to take the whole night. The only light they had was the moon, which kept retreating behind clouds, and a tiny dim globe light created by Lord Werrin that hovered over the ground in front of them. When lights abruptly appeared ahead the relief that swept through Tessia was so powerful she felt tears spring into her eyes. She blinked them away, annoyed at herself. There were more appropriate things to cry about than the prospect of food, sleep and finally getting off a horse.

The lights were held by four men on horseback. One rode forward and held his light high.

"Lord Dakon," he said.

"Yes," Dakon replied. "This is Lord Werrin, Apprentice Jayan and Apprentice Tessia."

"Lord Narvelan told us to wait here for you. I am to escort you to the camp."

"Thank you."

Their guide led them off the road into a forest. After several paces of ducking branches and weaving through undergrowth, they came upon a track and began following it.

Time stretched out, slowed by anticipation.

Then, without warning, they entered a clearing. Small fires ringed a knot of makeshift tents. Well-laden carts rested among the tents and animals grazed, tethered to stakes or within rope-and-stake fences around the grassy area. At the edges of the clearing stood men and women, staring into the forest in all directions. Keeping watch, Tessia guessed. Nobody looked surprised to see Lord Dakon.

A tall shadow emerged from a tent and hurried towards them.

"Lord Dakon." Narvelan's voice was so strained it took a moment for Tessia to recognise it. As his face came into the light she saw unhidden grief and guilt. "I am so sorry. I came as soon as I could, but it was already too late."

Dakon swung down from his saddle. "You did everything you could, my friend. Do not apologise when the fault is not yours. If anything, it is mine for not seeing the danger and making better preparations."

"We were aware of the threat long before I recruited you. We should have posted a watch on the pass. We should—"

"And you would have, had you known this would happen," Dakon said firmly. "You didn't. Don't waste your energy and clever mind on regret. We cannot change the past. But we can learn from it – something I suspect we will have to do quickly." He turned to Werrin, who dismounted as Dakon introduced him.

Watching Narvelan, Tessia was wearily impressed with the young magician. He clearly felt badly about the fate of Mandryn. She quietly absorbed the implications in Dakon's heartfelt reply. Dakon had called him *my friend*. What else had he said? . . . *your energy and clever mind*. And Narvelan had said *before I recruited you*.

So Narvelan had been the one to draw Dakon into the Circle of Friends. And he was smart. She filed away these bits of information for consideration when she wasn't so tired, and forced her aching body to dismount, and then stay upright.

"You don't have an apprentice, do you?" Werrin asked Narvelan.

"No," Narvelan replied. "I'll have to do something about that."

Tessia noted the reluctance in the young magician's face and wondered at it. The magicians' conversation was interrupted as a young man rode out of the trees and approached them.

"Lord Narvelan," he said, stopping close to the magician.

Narvelan turned to face the young man. "Yes, Rovin? Did you find them?"

"Dek did. He spotted three of them heading north and followed. Lost them in the High Valley forest. They were on foot and not carrying supplies, so he reckons they're camping up there somewhere."

"Has Hannel returned?"

"No, but . . ." the young man paused to grimace, "Dek found Garrell's body. No deep wounds on him, just the sort of cuts you said to look for."

Narvelan nodded, his expression grim. "I will tell his family. Anything else?"

The young man shook his head.

"Go and get some rest then. And thank you."

Rovin's shoulders rose briefly, then he steered his horse away. Narvelan sighed.

"Not the first scout they've killed," he told them. "Now, would you like some food? We've packed as light as possible, but there's plenty of fare that won't travel well that we may as well use up."

"That would be much appreciated. We haven't eaten since morning," Dakon told him.

At Narvelan's orders, two men from the camp emerged to take care of the horses. Tessia warned the man who took hers to handle her father's bag carefully and not let it tip over. Then she followed the magicians to where blankets had been spread out in front of one of the fires. Cold, charred meat, slightly stale bread and fresh vegetables were brought out for them – a simple but welcome meal. Tessia felt her attention slipping as the magicians talked – Dakon about the journey and how the metal worker's boy refused to leave Mandryn, Narvelan about what he had and hadn't brought in the carts and how he'd had to be firm with the villagers about what and how many possessions to take.

Her thoughts slipped to a memory of two graves. *I didn't even get to see them dead*, she thought. *Not that it would have been pleasant. It's just . . . the last time I saw them they were healthy and alive. It's so hard to accept that they're—*

"I know what you're feeling."

Tessia blinked in surprise and turned to see Jayan watching her. His expression was serious and earnest.

"Just . . . if you need to talk about it," he told her.

Then he smiled, and she felt a sudden and unexpected anger. Of all people, why would she ever talk to *him* about something so . . . so . . . He'd only laugh at her weak nature, or use it against her later. She wasn't sure how. Maybe he'd consider it a favour she had to repay.

"You don't know how I feel," she found herself saying. "How could you know? Were your parents murdered?"

He flinched, then he frowned and she saw a flash of anger in his eyes. "No. But my mother died because my father would not let her see a healer, and wouldn't pay for any cures she needed. Does your father letting your mother die count?"

She stared at him and felt all her anger drain away, leaving a nasty feeling of shame and horror.

"Oh." She shook her head. "Sorry."

He opened his mouth to speak, but thought better of it. They both looked away. An awkward silence followed, then Narvelan asked if they minded sleeping by the fire. All the tents were occupied and at least the magically gifted had the ability to create a shield to shelter themselves if it rained. Dakon assured him they didn't mind.

Soon Tessia was trussed up in blankets on the hard ground, staring up at the stars and wryly wondering how she had managed to make herself feel even worse than before. Shame at what she'd said to Jayan overlaid the constant ache of grief.

His father let his mother die for want of a healer? she thought. *Is that why he disapproves of my wanting to be a healer? But surely such a tragedy would have the opposite effect.*

Clouds flowed across the moon, and darkness closed in round the fires. *He was trying to be nice. Maybe I shouldn't be suspicious of him all the time, but how am I supposed to know when he's being friendly?* She grimaced as she remembered his explanation. *His mother died and it was his father's fault.*

He might still have a father, but he did lose both his parents that day.

247

CHAPTER 20

E xhaustion's blessing was that it brought a sleep that Tessia did not wake from, despite grief, shame and fear, until long after the sun had risen. The stirring of the camp roused her, and she threw herself into helping Narvelan's people pack and prepare for the day's journey. They were travelling, Dakon told her and Jayan, to a village in Narvelan's ley that was notoriously hard to find even by those invited to it. Small and unimportant, it was unlikely to be considered a strategic target by Takado and his allies – if they even knew it existed – unless they realised it was being used as a meeting place. There, other Circle magicians would join Narvelan, Dakon and Werrin to discuss what they should do next.

The journey was made after dusk the next night, with shadowy figures emerging at intervals to assure the magicians the way ahead was safe. All remained in as close a state to silence as a lot of creaky old carts, harassed domestic animals, and the occasionally fretful baby would allow.

The villagers were mainly strangers to Tessia, but in the darkness the impression that she was surrounded by the people of Mandryn kept sneaking into her thoughts. The grumble of an old woman, the laugh of two young boys who'd forgotten the order of silence, the stern reproach of their mother – all reminded her of the people she had grown up among. People who were now dead, but for a few.

Other than Tiken, the metal worker's boy, who had

remained in Mandryn, the survivors had joined Narvelan's people. They now included one of the young stable workers, Ullan, who had run away when Takado had begun attacking villagers, and a few of the children who had hidden themselves successfully. Salia, the baker's daughter, had been visiting a sister on one of the farms. She was doubly lucky, because Takado and his allies had killed many of the surrounding farmers and their families after attacking the village.

Tessia glanced back and located Salia walking beside a cart laden with barrels and sacks. At once the young woman dropped her gaze to the ground, biting her lip. She looked guilty, but that didn't make any sense. Even if Salia had been in the village, she couldn't have prevented what happened. Ullan, in contrast, did not seem at all bothered about having run away.

Why should he? Tessia thought. *He would have died too, if he'd stayed. If he hadn't taken a horse and ridden to tell Narvelan, it would have taken longer for news of the attack to have reached us.*

He was scathing in his assessment of Hanara, though, saying the man had run off to join his master. But nobody had seen Hanara return to the village with Takado, so Tessia suspected he'd done no worse than the stable boy had — fled to save himself. She wondered where he was now. With news of a Sachakan attack spreading it was unlikely anyone would take him in.

They had been climbing a gentle slope, but now the ground levelled and abruptly descended again. Dakon looked at Tessia and smiled.

"Nearly there," he murmured.

The words were picked up by someone close behind, and relayed in a whisper back through those following. A scraping sound disturbed the night as cart drivers were forced to lower brakes to counter the steepness of the road. Tessia found herself leaning back in the saddle, her back resting against the solid shape of her father's bag strapped securely behind her.

The slope levelled off as abruptly as it had turned steep, and the trees on either side retreated to reveal a handful of small houses, windows glowing with welcoming light. Men and women carrying lamps stood waiting to greet them. Tessia heard sighs and murmurs of relief all around.

Some of Narvelan's people had ridden ahead to inform the village of their impending arrival, and help the villagers to prepare. Quietly and efficiently, the visitors were divided up among the houses, which were filled with makeshift beds. Animals were penned. Carts were taken into the shelter of stables.

The magicians and apprentices were taken in by the village master, Crannin, who owned a house not much bigger than Tessia's childhood home. After a hearty but simple meal everyone retired to bed. Crannin and his wife, Nivia, gave up their bedroom for the magicians. The village master and Jayan slept on the floor of the seating room, while Tessia and the man's wife shared the children's bedroom. She saw no sign of the children. Perhaps they were being cared for by a neighbour.

Though tired, Tessia did not fall asleep for a long time. She lay awake listening to the breathing of the woman sleeping nearby and thinking about all that had happened since she had visited Dakon's Residence on her own and unwittingly used magic to fend off Takado.

If she hadn't slipped away, hoping to impress her father, would she have discovered her ability anyway? Lord Dakon believed so. But maybe it wouldn't have happened until much later. Maybe she would have still been in the village when Takado attacked. Maybe she would be dead.

And from Tiken's description, probably taken and used by Takado or one of his allies beforehand. But I guess it's likely I'd have reacted the same way, and used magic to defend myself. Only he wouldn't have left me alive after using magic against him, and I'd have been too weak and unschooled to save myself.

If she hadn't discovered her magic when she had, it was likely she would be dead now along with her parents. Everyone would be dead anyway, whether she had stayed behind when Dakon left for the city or not.

Then she considered what might have happened if Dakon hadn't left. Tiken hadn't been sure how many magicians had attacked Mandryn, but there had been more than Takado. He'd run away to hide after seeing only two of them, but he was sure there had been more than that.

Dakon was just one magician. Two Sachakan magicians could have defeated him easily, if they'd prepared themselves by storing lots of power from their slaves. Once he was dead Takado and his allies would have gone on to slaughter the villagers anyway. She and her family would still be dead.

She had to be thankful, though bitterly, that the attack had occurred while she was away. No other scenario she could think of would have allowed her to survive the attack. And no scenario could have saved her parents.

Unless, of course, Lord Dakon and a few other magicians had learned of the attack in time to prepare a defence against it. But there was no point imagining that scenario. Nobody could see into the future. Not even magicians.

Once she fell asleep she slept deeply, and when she woke Crannin's wife was gone and the smell of cooking filled the house. A dim light suggested early morning. Her stomach grumbled. A basin of water lay on the floor a few steps away, and a clean dress, and she felt a surge of relief and gratitude. Washed and draped in the oversized dress, she bound her hair back and followed the cooking smells to the kitchen.

She found Nivia there assisting a servant to prepare a meal. The pair wouldn't let her help them, but asked questions about what had happened in Mandryn. Tessia skipped over the more gruesome details, instead telling of Narvelan's mental call, the subsequent gruelling ride, and the state of the village when they got there.

"What do you think the magicians'll do?" the servant woman asked.

"I don't know exactly," Tessia admitted. "Kill the Sachakans, most likely. I guess they have to find them, and there'll be a fight."

The woman's eyes widened. "Will you be fighting?"

Tessia considered. "Not exactly, but I'll probably be there. Lord Dakon is bound to be fighting, and he'll need Jayan and me to add to his strength. We can't let ourselves be separated from—"

She stopped as she heard a shout outside. Nivia dropped the knife she had been chopping vegetables with, wiped her hands and hurried out of the room. Tessia followed her to the front door. The woman opened it a crack and peered outside, then pulled it wide open and stepped outside. Tessia could now see several men on horseback entering the village. Kyralians, from the look of them. And by their clothing and manner she guessed these were the magicians come to help them.

Footsteps echoed in the corridor behind them, then Dakon, Werrin and Narvelan pushed past Tessia and Nivia, stepped outside and strode towards the newcomers.

"They're here, are they?"

Tessia turned to see Jayan emerging from the seating room, running hands through dishevelled hair. He grimaced and began to rub a shoulder.

"I expect so," Tessia replied. "Do you recognise them?"

She stepped back as he moved to the door.

"Ah. Lord Prinan, Lord Bolvin, Lord Ardalen and Lord Sudin. And their apprentices, by the looks of it. And a servant each."

Peering over his shoulder, she saw the men dismount. The more plainly dressed riders immediately took hold of the horses' leads. The young men hung back as their masters greeted Dakon, Werrin and Narvelan.

"Well, shall we meet our new allies?" Jayan asked. He didn't wait for an answer, but stepped outside and strolled towards the group.

Tessia reluctantly followed. Suddenly she was all too aware how different she was. A woman among all these men. A natural from a humble background among rich young men chosen from powerful families. A beginner among the well trained. It was too easy to imagine them all being like Jayan.

The magicians barely glanced at her and Jayan, but the apprentices eyed Jayan with interest. A few gave her a puzzled look, then seemed to dismiss her. It was not until the magicians had finished their greetings that Dakon paused to introduce her and Jayan. All looked at her in surprise.

Belatedly she realised the oversized dress Nivia had laid out for her would have given them the impression she was one of the villagers. *The woman is hardly able to offer up the sort of rich, elaborate clothing that city women prefer.* Tessia straightened her shoulders and replied with as much dignity as she could muster, hoping nobody could see how embarrassed and self-conscious she suddenly felt.

Crannin had emerged from his house now, and invited the magicians to eat with him as they discussed plans. He apologised that there was no room for the apprentices now there were so many here, but a table and food would be brought outside as soon as possible.

So once again I'm left out of the important discussions, Tessia thought wryly, *but this time at least I'm not the only one.*

As the magicians disappeared inside Crannin's house, the apprentices hovered by the front door, eyeing each other and saying nothing. They looked exhausted. Tessia guessed they had ridden here as quickly, or near to it, as Dakon had to reach Mandryn.

After a few minutes some men from the village emerged from another house and brought benches and tables out of a stable. They washed them down then threw cloths over them. Women emerged from Crannin's house carrying food and wine and laid out a small feast. The apprentices sat down to eat and soon quiet conversations began among them. They directed all their questions about Mandryn and the Sachakans at Jayan, but Tessia was happy to stay silent and let him deal with them. To her surprise, he was less descriptive than she had been when telling the village women about the attack.

"I don't think we should tell anyone too much," he murmured to her after a while. "I'm not sure how much Dakon wants people to know."

Tessia felt a pang of worry. Had she told Nivia anything she shouldn't have?

"Like what?" she asked.

"I don't know," he replied, a little irritably, turning to face one of the villagers as the man approached. She realised the man was looking at her.

"Apprentice Tessia. Forgive me if this is too bold," the man said. He paused, then hurried on. "You carry a healer's bag."

"Yes," she said when he didn't continue. "How do you know that?"

"I'm sorry. I thought it smelled of cures so I had a look inside. Who does it belong to?"

"My father," she answered. "Or it did. He . . . he was Mandryn's healer."

The man's face fell. "Oh. I am sorry. I had hoped . . . sorry."

As he began to back away she reached out towards him. "Wait. You don't have a healer here, do you?"

The man shook his head, his expression grim.

"Is someone ill?"

He frowned. "Yes. My wife. She . . . she . . ."

"I was my father's assistant," she told him. "I may not be able to do anything, but I can have a look."

He smiled. "Thank you. I'll take you to her. And have someone bring your bag."

To Tessia's surprise Jayan stood up and followed her. When they were out of the hearing of the other apprentices he caught her arm.

"What are you doing?" he said quietly. "You're not a healer."

She turned to stare at him. "So? I might still be able to help."

"What if Dakon calls for you? You're an apprentice now, Tessia. It's not . . . not . . ."

"Not . . . ?"

He grimaced. "You can't go off playing healer whenever you want to. It's not . . . appropriate."

She narrowed her eyes at him.

"What's more or less 'appropriate', Jayan: letting someone sick or in pain stay that way – or perhaps even die – because you're worried about what the other apprentices or their masters might think, or sitting around being a useless waste of space and food?"

He stared back at her, his expression intense and searching. Then his shoulders sagged.

"All right. But I'm coming with you."

She bit back a protest, then sighed and hurried after the man whose wife was ill. Let Jayan see the woman he would have abandoned to whatever ailment she suffered, for the sake of being "appropriate". Let him see that there was more to healing than being able to call a person a "healer". Let him see that the skill and knowledge she had was valuable, and know it shouldn't be wasted.

She grimaced. *I had better be able to help this woman, or I won't be letting him see much at all.*

The house the man led them to was at the edge of the village. Their guide only paused once to ask a boy to fetch her father's bag. Once in the house, he led them up the stairs to a bedroom, where a woman was dozing on the bed.

That the woman was ill was undeniable. She was so thin the skin of her shoulders, neck and face was stretched over her bones. Her mouth was open and as Tessia entered she quickly and self-consciously wiped away a line of drool.

Tessia moved to the side of the bed and smiled down at the woman.

"Hello. I'm Tessia," she said. "My father was a healer and I was his assistant most of my life. What's your name?"

"Paowa," the man said. "She can't talk easily."

The woman's eyes were wide with fear, but she managed a faint smile and nod in response.

"Let me have a look then," Tessia said.

The woman opened her mouth. At once Tessia felt a shiver of sympathetic horror. A growth filled one side of her mouth.

"Ah," Tessia said. "I've seen this before, though most often in men. It hurts when you eat, or even smell food, right?"

The woman nodded.

"Do you chew or smoke leaves?"

The woman looked at her husband.

"She used to chew dunda until this stopped her," he said. "Her family were hunters a generation back, and they kept some of the mountain ways."

Tessia nodded. "It's a hard habit to break, I've heard. This is called 'hunter-mouth'. I can cut out the lump and stitch you up, but you have to promise me two things."

The woman nodded eagerly.

"Use the mouthwash I give you. It tastes utterly foul and dries you out so much you'll swear you'll never have any spit ever again, but it'll stop the cut fouling."

"She will," her husband said, smiling. "I'll make sure of it."

Tessia nodded. "And stop chewing dunda. It'll kill you."

A glint of rebellion entered the woman's gaze, but Tessia stared back, keeping her expression serious, and after a moment it faded.

"I'll make sure of that, too," her husband said softly.

"Now, let me see how much there is." Tessia gently probed inside the woman's mouth. Lumps like this had been treated by her father before. While removing them was usually successful, some of the patients sickened and died within a year or two. Others lived to old age. Her father had a theory that this was related to how strongly the lump had "stuck" to the flesh around it.

This one felt loose, like a large, slightly squishy stone inserted under the skin. Promising. Tessia removed her fingers and wiped them on a cloth that the woman's husband offered her. She considered briefly whether she should attempt to cut the lump out.

As Jayan said, I'm not a healer. But I've seen this done. I know how to do it. It won't be long before the lump grows so large she'll either starve to death or suffocate. I have all the equipment . . . well, except the head brace. Her father used a brace he'd devised and had the metal worker make for him to hold open the mouth of patients when working on teeth and such. It prevented them from biting him out of pain or panic.

A knock at the door took the husband away, and he returned a moment later with her father's bag. She asked him to clear the table beside the bed and, while he did so, performed her father's routine check of a patient's heart and breathing rhythms. When the space was clear she opened the bag and began to remove tools, salves and a calming tonic.

"Take this first," Tessia told the woman, giving her the tonic. "I need you to lie on your side. Right on the edge of the bed. Arrange pillows behind you and under your head. Any blood and spit will drain out, so you'll want to protect the bed with cloths and put a basin underneath." The couple obeyed her instructions without question, which for some reason made her less certain of herself. They were relying on her. What if she got it wrong?

Don't think about that. Just act.

Remembering her father's advice about involving family members, she instructed the husband to rub a numbing salve inside and outside the woman's cheek. This had the added benefit of making sure Tessia's own hands weren't affected by it.

She took several blades out and checked their sharpness, but as she began to remove the burner she heard Paowa whimper. Looking up, she realised the woman's breathing had suddenly become rapid. Paowa's eyes were on the blades. Tessia felt a pang of sympathy.

"It's going to be fine," she told the woman. "It will hurt. I'm not going to lie about that. But the salve helps and I'll work as quickly as I can. It will be done and over with soon, and all you'll have is a cut in your mouth all stitched up neatly."

The woman's breathing slowed a little. Her husband sat

on the bed behind her and began rubbing her shoulders. Tessia took a deep breath, picked a blade and realised she hadn't yet seared any of them.

And realised if she delayed much longer fear would overtake the woman's reason.

No problem, she thought, and with a slight flexing of her will she seared the blade she was holding with magic. Then she set to work.

It was not easy, but nothing unexpected or disastrous happened either. After half an hour she had coaxed out the lump, sewn up the cut and applied a protective paste. Then she checked the woman's rhythms again and pronounced her work a success. As the woman rolled onto her back, exhausted from pain and fear, Tessia rose and swayed, suddenly dizzy with weariness.

"Sit down."

She blinked in surprise at Jayan's voice, having forgotten he was there. He was offering a small wooden stool. Gratefully, she sat down and immediately her head cleared. Drawing her father's bag closer, she rummaged inside and drew out a familiar wound cleanser.

"Have you a small clean jar with a lid?" she asked the husband. "And a bowl of clean water?"

The man produced the items, and she set about ensuring the jar was clean by steeping it in water she set boiling with magic. The man watched calmly without comment, as if water boiling by itself was an ordinary and regular occurrence.

Into a measure of water she counted drops of the cleanser. As she gave it to the man she instructed him how it should be used, and when he should cut and remove the stitches. He drew out a pouch and she heard the sound of coins clinking.

"No, you don't need to pay me," she told him.

"But how else can I repay you?" he asked.

"Your whole village is feeding and accommodating us. That's got to be cutting into everyone's food stores and stock. My master would not approve of me taking money for this, either."

He reluctantly pocketed the pouch again. "Then I'll make sure you two have one of my fattest rassook each for dinner," he said, smiling.

"Now *that* I could not easily refuse," she replied, smiling ruefully. "We'd best get back in case our master needs us." She looked down at Paowa. The woman was asleep, her mouth closed and face relaxed. "And remember, no more dunda."

"I will. Whether she does . . ." He shrugged. "I'll do what I can to help her stop."

They walked in a weary, comfortable silence back towards where the apprentices were waiting. From the shadows cast by the trees, she guessed only a few hours had passed. Paowa's husband left, at her request, to take her father's bag to Crannin's house instead of the stables. Next time someone took a peek inside they might not be as sensible or respectful of the contents.

As they came in sight of the apprentices she realised Jayan was watching her, and glanced at him. He was looking at her with a quizzical expression.

"What?" she asked.

"I, ah, I'm impressed," he said, his face reddening. "What you did back there . . . I'd have given her up for dead."

She felt her own face warming. He was acknowledging her skill as she had wanted, but for some reason it didn't feel triumphant. Just . . . embarrassing.

"It just looked impressive," she told him, looking away. "But it was simple, really. Routine work."

"Ah," he said, in a tone that was too accepting.

No, it wasn't simple! she wanted to say. *I don't know why I said that!* But his attention had moved away, to the apprentices, and even if she could think of a way to correct herself without sounding a fool it was too late to try.

The last rays of sun tinged the highest leaves of the forest when the magicians emerged from Crannin's house. A feast began, served on makeshift tables outdoors and lit by numerous torches and lamps. When Tessia and Jayan were served a large, fat rassook each, Jayan had smugly commented that Tessia certainly had a way with villagers and he would not be surprised if she could charm pickpockets into putting money *into* her wallet.

Only after the meal was done did Dakon find a moment in private to talk to his apprentices. He led them away from the main table, walking down to the end of the village, then turning back. From there the sight and sound of laughing and drinking gave the impression of a festival day. It only made the ache and guilt at the loss of Mandryn harder to bear. He turned to Tessia and Jayan. Both looked tired despite not having spent the day in the saddle.

"So what can you tell us?" Jayan asked, the tension in his voice obvious despite the quiet pitch.

Dakon sighed. *How much can I tell them?* The magicians had agreed that secrecy was necessary for their plans to work, but from what some had said it was clear they intended to let their apprentices know at least the general gist. Dakon too did not think it fair or wise to drag apprentices into danger without their knowledge.

"We're going to rebuild Mandryn," he said.

Two pairs of eyebrows rose.

"But . . ." Jayan paused to glance at Tessia. "But who is going to live there? Nearly everyone is dead."

"People will come from other parts of the ley, or other leys, once it is known that there is no further danger. And we will eventually need a place to live."

"Eventually," Jayan echoed. "And in the meantime?"

"We deal with the Sachakans." Dakon shrugged. "Which involves finding them, of course, then driving them out of Kyralia and making sure, by placing a watch on the mountain passes, that they do not return."

"Drive them out?" Tessia looked surprised. "Not kill them?"

He looked at her, wondering if she was disappointed or angry. If she wanted revenge. She stared back, her expression growing uncertain.

"No, not killing them unless they force us to," Dakon answered. "Werrin says the king fears doing so will stir up more support for Takado. Even if it didn't, relations of those we kill may seek revenge. And we will be obliged to seek justice for further deaths. It could begin a cycle of vengeance – them retaliating for what we do in retaliation for what Takado and his allies have done." He grimaced. "A cycle like that could start a war."

His two apprentices nodded in what he hoped was understanding.

What would I prefer? he asked himself. *Would I risk war for the sake of avenging the loss of Mandryn? Oh, I want justice for the deaths of my people, for the ruin of the home I grew up in.* The thought of the rare, irreplaceable books that had burned stung, but not as much as the thought of the ordinary men, women and children who had been tormented and slaughtered while he was absent. Servants he had known so long they were more like family. People who had known and loved his father. *Such a cowardly act, to wait until I was gone. Or did Takado not realise I wasn't there? Well, I'm sure the king wouldn't have been so reluctant for us to kill any*

262

Sachakans if a member of one of Kyralia's powerful families had been murdered. That would have been an act of war.

Dakon understood the king's caution, however. Sachakans would most likely be amused if Kyralians caught a few of their misbehaving Ichani and threw them out of the country. But if Kyralians dared to kill Sachakans for merely attacking one little village and slaughtering a few commoners, the Sachakans might decide the empire needed to put their neighbour back in its place.

And if the Sachakan emperor's grip on his own people was as weak as it was rumoured to be, he would not be able to stop them.

PART THREE

CHAPTER 21

The sun warmed Stara's back as the wagon climbed the shoulder of the hill. As the horses hauling the heavily laden vehicle reached the top of the rise, the view beyond was revealed, and the young woman caught her breath.

A great city fanned out over the land before her. At the limit of its spread was the coast, and the dark sea lay beyond. The apex of the fan was the mouth of a river. The buildings and roads that radiated from that point were linked by the concentric curves of connecting thoroughfares.

Arvice. She smiled. *The largest city ever built. I'm home at last.*

She had waited fifteen years for this. Fifteen long years since her father had taken her and her mother to Elyne and left them there. Now, at last, he had sent for her, as he had promised so long ago.

As the line of wagons continued down the other side of the rise it moved into shadow. She shivered and drew her shawl up around her shoulders. For fifteen years of her life the sun had set over water, painting the city of Elyne gold and red. Now if she wanted to see a spectacular meeting of sun and water she would have to wake early enough to catch the dawn.

It feels like I've travelled from one side of the world to the other.

The climate was similar in Elyne and southern Sachaka, however. She almost wished it wasn't. The same kinds of plants fed the same kinds of animals. The same types of trees

267

bore the same kinds of fruit stolen by the same kinds of birds. The same views of fertile farmland surrounded her. Only occasionally did she notice something unfamiliar and exotic – an unknown bird, or a strange tree.

The mountains had been more exciting and interesting, with their cold stone precipices, towering spires, and trees that sprang stunted and twisted from impossibly steep inclines. The wind had sung with the voice of a demented, ageless woman and the air had been crisp and clean.

Once or twice the wagon drivers had spotted distant figures on unfeasibly high paths above. Ichani, they said. They had assured her there was little chance they'd be robbed. The Ichani had no use for the dyestuff her father traded, and even if they had been tempted to steal it to sell, the pottery jugs it was transported in were too heavy and fragile to be worth carrying along those precarious mountain tracks. They knew there'd be no money on the wagon, and minimal food.

The wagoners had given Stara men's clothing to wear, however. A woman of her beauty was worth stealing, they told her, using flattery to persuade her to co-operate.

They hadn't needed to flatter her. She had liked dressing in the trousers and shift. Not only were they more practical than the dresses she usually wore, but she felt almost as if she was actually working for her father already as she helped the men with the lighter duties to enhance her disguise – much to their amusement.

She doubted her father would give her this sort of work to do when she arrived in Arvice, though. As the daughter of a Sachakan ashaki, she would be set to more dignified tasks. Like making trade deals and entertaining clients. Or overseeing the dye-making process and ensuring orders were filled and delivered.

She was well trained for the responsibility. Her mother had

performed such work in Elyne for years, and included her daughter in every part of the process. Stara had hated it at first, but one day it had occurred to her that her father might want her back sooner if she was useful to have around, and from then on she had dedicated herself to learning everything she could about his trade.

Stara smiled to herself as she imagined listing her skills to her father.

I can read and write, do sums and accounts. I know how to talk a client into paying twice what he meant to, and be happy to. I know where all the dyes are made, and how, which minerals set them and what kinds of cloth take them best. I've learned the names of all the important families in Elyne and Sachaka, and their alliances. And most useful of all . . . I can . . . I have . . .

She felt her heart skip. Even in her mind it was hard to imagine telling him her greatest secret. One she had never even told her mother.

A few years after arriving in Capia, Stara had befriended the daughter of one of her mother's friends. Nimelle had just been apprenticed to a magician, and was disappointed to find how few other girl apprentices there were. The girl had tested Stara for magical ability and found plenty. But when Stara had asked her mother what she would do if her daughter had magical ability the woman's answer was firm and unhesitating.

"I need you here with me, Stara. If you became a magician's apprentice you'd have to live with your master for many years. Do you want to be separated from your mother as well as your father?"

Stara could not bring herself to abandon her mother. When Nimelle had heard this, she had called it a "waste". She offered to set loose Stara's magical ability herself, and teach her the basics – but she must keep it a secret. Stara had eagerly agreed. Since then Stara had taught herself to use her magic, borrowing Nimelle's books and practising with her friend.

I'm going to miss Nimelle, she thought. *She was the only person who never treated me differently for being half Sachakan.*

They'd both blinked away tears at their last meeting. But Stara suspected Nimelle would soon be too busy to miss their friendship. Granted her independence as a higher magician last summer, Nimelle had married in the autumn and was now expecting her first child.

I'll be too busy helping Father to pine for her, either, she told herself firmly. *We have both started new lives.* Yet she was already looking forward to Nimelle's first letter.

The wagon was now travelling along a long, flat road shrouded in the gloom of dusk. Now and then walled enclosures appeared, bringing back memories of the typical Sachakan mansions, with their endless sprawl of curved walls coated in white render.

She also noticed the slaves working in the fields. She felt slightly discomforted whenever she saw them. Too many years in Elyne had taught her an aversion to slavery, yet she could also remember adoring the slaves who had looked after and indulged her as a child.

I'm sure life is a lot better for a house slave than a field slave, she told herself. *But as Mother said, "slavery is slavery".* She had hated it, and Stara knew it was part of the reason her parents had parted and her mother had returned to Elyne.

There were other reasons, Stara knew. Some she had been told, some she had worked out herself. Her mother had run away from her family in order to marry the man she loved, then discovered that he was a different person at home from the one he'd been in Elyne. He needed to be, she had explained to Stara. You have to be tough and cruel to survive Sachakan politics and make slaves obey you. Yet she couldn't bear to see the effect it had on him. Eventually he had allowed her to return to Elyne. A harder man would have made her stay, she had admitted. Or kept both of their children.

The man who visited them every year had always been the same: loving and generous. Stara had watched him carefully, looking for some hidden monster, but never saw it.

Perhaps because he never had to whip a slave when he was in Elyne.

Her brother, Ikaro, had visited Elyne a few times. Younger than Stara by three years, he had always been reserved to the point of being rude. She had admitted to her mother years before that she was jealous of him for being the one who stayed behind, but also felt sorry for him for growing up without his mother. But when she had expressed the latter to him during one visit, he'd sneeringly told her it didn't matter as much for a man to grow up without women around, as they weren't as important as men.

She lost a lot of respect for him that day. The expectation that he would feel the same way about her as he did about other women, especially in regard to her value in the trade, soured the anticipation and excitement of finally reaching her destination. But she was determined not to let him spoil her new life.

The fields between the mansions on either side had been shrinking, and now they disappeared entirely, to be replaced by unending walls broken by the occasional broad alleyway. The wagoners' cheerful whistling had stopped and their expressions were alert and unsmiling. Slaves hurried back and forth along the road, their eyes downcast. The only light now came from the wagoners' lamps and those carried by slaves, or the glow of hidden light sources on the other sides of the walls. Stara felt both excitement and disappointment as she realised they had entered the city, and it wasn't anything like she'd expected. Unlike Capia, Elyne's capital, the buildings didn't spread themselves around a great harbour in a glittering display. Instead they hid behind walls in an unending, secretive sprawl.

The wagon slowed as they approached a large wooden gate and Stara's heart skipped a beat as she realised this must be her father's mansion. The vehicle stopped and the head wagoner called out. No answer came, but there was a clunk, and then the gates began to swing open, revealing a wide paved courtyard lit by several lamps. The walls around her were white, broken only by doors and the ends of dark wooden beams. Stara's heart was beating fast. As the wagon moved inside her eyes searched the courtyard for her father, but all the people she saw were strangers.

When the vehicle stopped they threw themselves to the ground. Looking around, she realised that all their heads bowed toward her, and all their feet pointed away, so that bodies radiated away from her in all directions.

Slaves, she thought. *Do they always do this? What should I do now?* She looked towards the house. No familiar paternal figure appeared. Sagging back in her seat, feeling a little confused and disappointed, she waited to see what would happen next.

"Nobody is going to tell you what to do, mistress," a voice murmured close by. She glanced down to see a wagoner leaning up against the vehicle, his attention apparently elsewhere. "You give the orders now."

Understanding came in a rush. Nobody was going to tell her where her father was unless she asked. Nobody would even get up. In Elyne a woman was supposed to wait until she was met by her host – or a senior servant at the least – before alighting from a wagon. This was not Elyne. Here she was not a guest, but part of the family that ruled the estate.

"Go back to what you were doing," she called out.

The slaves slowly rose from the ground and resumed their tasks, but with a deliberate caution. She noticed that one, a man in a red cap, was ordering some of them about. Rising, she climbed down off the wagon with as much dignity as she could manage. She turned to the man in the red cap.

"I wish to see my father, if he is at home."

He bowed, this time bending at the waist, then gestured to a shirtless slave standing near the doorway.

"Your wish can be fulfilled, mistress. Follow this man and he will take you to Ashaki Sokara."

As she followed the slave into the interior she breathed deeply. A familiar scent hung in the air, but she could not identify it. The slave's thin silhouette led her down a narrow corridor coated in the same white render as the exterior. They emerged into a large room. Stara recognised the floor plan. This room was the centre of the house: the "master room", where her father met, entertained and fed guests. Doorways led from it to other parts of the house. Her mother's home followed the same design, as did other Sachakan-built houses in Elyne.

She took all this in with one glance, because a man sat on a large wooden chair in the centre of the room. Recognising him, she felt her heart leap with joy.

"Father," she said.

"Stara." He smiled and beckoned.

Walking across the room, she was disappointed when he didn't rise to greet her. She hesitated, unsure what to do next.

"Sit," he suggested, indicating a smaller chair next to his.

Taking it, she sighed with appropriate and not entirely faked appreciation. "Ah. You'd think after sitting down all day I wouldn't want to even look at a chair."

"Travelling is tiring," he agreed. "How was the journey? Did my men treat you well?"

"Interesting, and yes," she replied.

"Are you hungry?"

"A little." In truth, she was ravenous.

He made a small gesture and a gong on the other side of the room chimed. A moment later a slave ran into the room and threw himself on the floor.

"Bring food for mistress Stara."

The slave leapt to his feet and hurried away. Stara stared at the doorway he had vanished through. His arrival and departing had been so dramatically performed that Stara could not help finding it comical. She had to suppress the urge to laugh.

"You will grow used to the slaves," her father told her. "Eventually you forget they are there."

She looked at him and bit her lip. *I don't want to get so used to them I forget they're there*, she thought. *The next step might be forgetting that they're people.*

The conversation turned to her mother. She told him of the latest deals and of new customers, as well as an idea her mother was considering: developing a trade in sail dyeing.

"Sailcloth has always been undyed, but if we can suggest the benefits of dyed cloth to the right people, and the idea becomes popular, we might open up a whole new market." She grinned. "That was my idea. I was watching some children playing with toy boats, and—"

Annoyingly, slaves chose that moment to enter the room with food. She had hoped for some expression of admiration, or even just an opinion, from her father, but he was completely distracted now. From a box next to his chair he drew two small but deadly-looking knives, one of which he handed to her.

Sighing quietly, she watched as a strange ritual unfolded. The slaves took it in turns to fall to their knees before her father. He selected a few morsels of whatever was presented, picking them up with a stab of his knife then lifting the food to his mouth. Then he gestured that she should sample the dish, and the slave would shuffle sideways until he knelt before Stara.

Her mother had described Sachakan meals to her, and warned her that the master of an estate always ate before anyone else. Stara wasn't sure how much to try, as he wasn't taking much from each platter and there appeared to be quite a few dishes coming.

Whenever she had finished eating from a plate the slave remained in place until her father spoke. "Done," he said each time, then he glanced at her and told her to dismiss the slave when she had had enough.

Before her hunger was quite satisfied, but long after the ritual had lost its novelty, he abruptly waved a hand and simply said: "Go." The slaves hurried away, their bare feet making no sound on the carpets. Her father turned to regard her.

"In a week I will entertain some important visitors and you will attend. You will need some training in Sachakan manners. The slave who nursed you as a child will teach you what you need to know." He smiled, his expression becoming a little apologetic. "I wish I could have given you more time to settle in first."

"I'll be fine," she told him.

He nodded, his gaze moving over her face. "Yes. Any mistakes you make will be easily forgiven, I think, especially since you have the excuse of a part-Elyne upbringing." His smile faded. "You should know that I have one of the men in mind to be your husband."

Stara blinked, then found she could not move. Husband?

"A link between our families would strengthen an alliance

275

that has been tested these last few years. Your slave will tell you what you need to know, but be assured they have plenty of land and the favour of the emperor."

Husband?

He scowled. "And unfortunately your brother's wife is incapable of bearing children. If you do not bear us an heir our land will be passed on to Emperor Vochira when your brother dies."

"*Husband?*" escaped her throat.

Looking at her, he narrowed his eyes. "Yes. You are a little old to still be unmarried and childless, but your Elyne blood should counter that – unlike Elynes, Sachakans believe a little foreign blood is a strength, not a weakness."

A little *old*? She was only twenty-five!

"I thought . . ." She heard the indignation in her voice and stopped to breathe in and out. "I thought you wanted me here to help run the trade."

His face broke into a smile and he chuckled, at which she could not help bristling. Just as quickly the smile faded into an expression of realisation.

"You really did, didn't you?" He shook his head and grimaced. "Your mother should not have let you come here with such a misunderstanding. In Sachaka women do not trade."

"I could," she said quietly. "If you give me a—"

"No," he said firmly. "Not only would clients laugh at you, they would stop trading with me. It is not done here."

"So instead you sell me off like another pot of dye?" she exclaimed. "Without any say in who I marry?"

He stared at her, his expression slowly hardening, and her heart sank.

He means to do this. It was his intention all along. Mother can't have known. She would never have sent me if she had. All the hopes she'd had of working for her father, of making a new life here with him, crumbled into ashes. She stood up, moved away, then turned to face him.

"I can't believe it. You sent for me – you tricked me – into coming here. So you can sell me off like stock."

"Sit down," he said.

"Surely you didn't think I'd be happy about it?" she raged. "That after living in Elyne for fifteen years, working for your benefit most of that time, I'd be delighted to become some stranger's *wife*? No, a *whore*. No, a *slave*, since at least whores get paid for their serv—"

"SIT DOWN!"

She could not help flinching. Still breathing heavily, she closed her eyes and willed the fury inside her to cool and shrink. When it had, she opened her eyes and looked at him.

"Is this truly why you sent for me?"

His eyes were dark with anger now. "Yes," he growled.

She walked to the chair and sat down with what she hoped was resolve and dignity.

"Then I must, respectfully, refuse. I will return to Elyne."

He regarded her with narrowed eyes, then a wry smile pulled at his mouth.

"On your own, with no guards and protectors?"

"If I have to."

"The mountains are full of Ichani. They're outcasts – they don't care what family they offend or harm. You would never make it back."

"I'm willing to try."

He grimaced and shook his head. "You are right. I shouldn't have left you in Elyne for fifteen years and expected you to return without some foolish ideas in your head – though I'm not sure why you think your future would be so very different in Elyne. Your mother has been telling me for years that it is long past time for you to marry, and that most women your age have already produced more than one child." He straightened. "You should rest and think about your future, and I clearly need to reconsider my plans for you. Do bear in mind that I still expect you to behave like a proper Sachakan woman for our visitors."

She nodded. While a part of her wanted to rebel, to leave for Elyne before this meeting – or at least to convince the man her father had picked as her fiancé that she was a crazed shrew he'd never want to live with – she couldn't help feeling a twinge of hope. Perhaps there was a way to convince her father her value was in trading, perhaps in ways acceptable to Sachakan society other than as a womb with legs. She had to try.

He made a small gesture. The gong rang again. A woman with streaks of grey in her hair stepped into the room and prostrated herself, her movements stiff with age.

"This is Vora. You may remember her from your childhood. She is sure to remember you. She will take you to your rooms."

Stara managed a smile and turned away to look at the woman. There was something familiar about the name, but the wrinkled face did not raise any memories. Vora's eyebrows rose, but she shrugged and said nothing as she led Stara out of the room.

Twenty horses and their riders made their way up the steep track as quietly as twenty horses and their riders could hope to travel. The chink and flap of harness, the equine snorts and the occasional smothered human cough or sneeze were so familiar to Tessia now that she barely heard them. Instead she heard – or didn't hear – the lack of sound in the trees surrounding them. No birds chirruped or whistled, no wind rustled the leaves, no animals barked or bellowed or howled.

278

Perhaps the others had noticed the unusual quiet, or perhaps they felt a strangeness without recognising the source, but they were all searching the trees or staring ahead or behind. Frowns marred foreheads. Nervous glances were exchanged. A magician crooked a finger and his apprentice rode closer so they could have a murmured conversation. Signals like this were becoming a kind of language throughout the group, developing through necessity.

Tessia checked that the magical shield she was holding around herself and her horse was strong and complete. They all rode with barriers in place each day, ready in case of an unexpected attack. At night they took it in turns to shield their camp, if they were forced to sleep outside, or patrol whatever village or hamlet they had reached.

A figure appeared on the track ahead, jogging bravely in full view. Tessia recognised one of the scouts who were sent ahead each day. She knew Lord Dakon was not happy about them using non-magicians to do this work, as they were defenceless if the Sachakans found them, but if any of the magicians ventured out alone and encountered more than one of the enemy, or a Sachakan of greater power, he was just as likely to perish. Magicians were in much shorter supply than non magicians.

The man's expression was grim. He met the first of the magicians and spoke quietly, pointing back from where he'd come. Slowly the news was passed on, in a murmur, from one person to the next.

"There's a house ahead," Dakon told Tessia and Jayan. "All but one of the occupants has been murdered recently. The survivor is not likely to live much longer."

"Shall we go ahead and see?" Tessia asked. "Perhaps I can help this person."

He looked thoughtful, then nudged his horse forward. Lord

Narvelan and Lord Werrin had become unofficial leaders of the group, though this mainly involved putting questions to the others and offering advice rather than actually making decisions, Tessia had noticed. The others would accept any overriding decision Werrin made, as he was the king's representative, but they tended to become uncooperative if he didn't let them debate it among themselves first.

Some of them are so worried that someone will usurp their authority, it comes close to taking precedence over finding and getting rid of the Sachakans. I shouldn't be surprised if the Sachakans managed to overcome all of Kyralia during one of these "discussions".

After several minutes, Dakon returned.

"Just us and Narvelan," he said.

To Tessia's surprise, two other magicians and their apprentices broke away from the others to follow them up the road: Lord Bolvin and Lord Ardalen. Dakon nodded his thanks.

Seems not everyone is willing to huddle in the protection of the group while some poor ordinary Kyralian dies. Though I suppose Ardalen will want to know more. We are getting close to his ley now.

"Did the scout say what the injury was?" she murmured.

Dakon shook his head.

Several nervous minutes later they came upon a tiny stone building at the side of the track. Insects buzzed around the prone forms of two men, one with grey at his temples, the other much younger. Dakon, Tessia and Jayan dismounted, but the others remained on their horses, forming a protective ring around the front of the house.

Removing her father's bag, Tessia followed as Dakon cautiously stepped through the open doorway. A light flared into existence, revealing a table that filled most of the room. They stopped and glanced around, looking for the survivor.

As Tessia moved towards the back of the room she felt

something snag her foot. Looking down, she saw a leg, then squatted and found a young man lying under the table.

He stared at her with frightened eyes.

"You're safe now," she told him. "The house is surrounded by magicians – Kyralian magicians, that is. Where are you hurt?"

Dakon brought the light lower and Tessia felt her heart sink as she saw how pale the man was. His lips were blue. He was shivering. She could see no sign of blood, however. Was it an internal injury? The man hadn't moved. He just stared at her, his eyes wide.

"Show me where you are hurt," she said. "I can help you. My father was a healer and taught me much of what he knew."

When he didn't move, she began checking his rhythms. The spaces between his heartbeats were impossibly long. His breathing was painfully shallow. Dakon reached out and turned over one of the man's wrists. A thin cut already sealed by congealed blood stood out against his deathly pale skin.

"That's not enough to kill him," Tessia said.

The staring eyes were now fixed on the underside of the table. As she watched, they lost their intense focus. A last slow breath escaped the man. Dakon cursed. He reached out and placed a hand on the pale brow. After a moment he removed it. "Most of the energy within him was taken. He didn't have enough strength left to keep breathing."

"Could . . . could you have given him back some strength?" Tessia asked.

Dakon frowned. "I don't know. I have never tried – never needed to. Never heard of anyone doing it, either." He looked regretfully at the man. "I'd try now, but I suspect it is too late."

Tessia nodded. "My father always said it was foolish and wrong to try to reverse death. He'd read of a man whose rhythms were restarted after they'd stopped, but whose mind was never the same."

"If we encounter another like this," Dakon said, "we will try."

Tessia smiled and felt a wave of gratitude and affection for him. This willingness to help even the lowliest of people was one of the traits she most liked in him. In the past weeks she had come to the realisation that this sense of compassion was rare among magicians.

"Is that wise? You will need all the strength you possess if you have to fight the Sachakans," Jayan asked. As Tessia looked at him reproachfully he grimaced. "Saving one man might cost us our lives, which might cost many more."

He had a point, she grudgingly admitted. The harsh practicality of his remark only highlighted how different he was from Lord Dakon. Cold, truthful common sense was harder to like than warm, hopeful generosity. Yet it had replaced Jayan's former disdain and arrogance, giving him a maturity that hadn't been apparent before, and she had to admit she disliked him a little less now. Only a little, though.

Dakon straightened and sighed. "I suspect it would not take much energy to bring a man dying this way back to a state from which he could recover. A tiny portion of what I take from either of you each night – and so easily replaced. I wouldn't consider it dangerous unless we were in a desperate situation."

Jayan nodded, satisfied. As they stood up and left the house Tessia felt a weary sadness. Messages had been sent out to all the people living in villages, farms, forest and mountain cottages in the leys bordering Sachaka, advising an evacuation to the south until the Sachakans were driven out. But many people had stayed, their lives depending on the sowing of spring crops, hunting or other sources of income. They were easy targets for the invaders.

As she, Dakon and Jayan mounted and started back to rejoin the others, Tessia listened to the magicians quietly discussing how long ago they thought the house had been attacked. They had found several campsites of the enemy as well as their victims, but no sign of the Sachakans. She suspected that the magicians had expected the Sachakans to attack them weeks ago and were puzzled why they had not. Some speculated that there were too few of them. They wanted to split into smaller groups themselves, remaining close enough to help each other if attacked, in order to lure the Sachakans out.

But, as Jayan had pointed out, the Sachakans weren't going to attack unless they felt they could win. They wouldn't attack a smaller group if another was close enough to reinforce it.

So they let us follow them along the mountains, constantly giving us the slip and killing commoners as they go. Growing stronger while our magicians have only one apprentice each to draw from – those that have them.

All of the apprentices were expected to stay close to their masters, as much for their own protection as to be a ready source of extra power if needed. Strength was another constantly discussed issue among the Kyralian magicians. They could not know if they had as much stored magic as the Sachakans had. They considered how much power one might gain from slaves, and how many slaves the Sachakans might have with them. They tried to calculate how much power they each held, examining how many times they'd drawn it from their apprentices and how much they used, either habitually or on demanding tasks.

A routine had formed each night, when all the magicians took strength from their apprentices. Neither Werrin nor Narvelan had an apprentice, though apparently Werrin had sent for a young man he had promised to take on when the youth reached the customary age to begin training. The apprentice would travel with a group of magicians who had volunteered to help in the search.

The nightly ritual of higher magic made it clear how much magician and apprentice relied upon each other. One was vulnerable without the other. It was strangely comforting to know that, despite being otherwise untrained and of little use to the group, Tessia was contributing to both her own and Lord Dakon's protection. And Jayan's. And thus the whole of Kyralia's.

And it had one other benefit. It ensured Tessia slept well, despite anger, grief and a nagging fear that if the Kyralian magicians were incapable of tracking down and dealing with a few renegade Sachakans, they had no hope of repelling an invading army.

CHAPTER 22

A small exertion of will and magic increased the ambient temperature, and stirring the air helped dry Jayan's skin. Another gust of artificial wind chased dampness out of his clothes, and he dressed quickly so the next apprentice could use the room.

Part of a mill at the edge of Lord Ardalen's ley, this room had been a welcome find. Someone had set up an ingenious system which, at the pull of a lever, diverted water from the river through pipes into a large tub. Another lever opened a rather leaky plug and allowed the water to flow out again, probably back into the river.

Without any need for much discussion, the entire group – magicians, apprentices and servants – was taking it in turns to wash themselves and their clothes. Or rather, the servants were washing in the river while the magicians and apprentices enjoyed a much-needed bath.

Jayan picked up his second set of clothes, now also freshly washed and dried, and carried them out of the room. A short corridor led outside, where tents had been erected. Though they could have taken shelter inside the millhouse, both magicians and apprentices preferred to stay together in the open, ever watchful for attackers.

The mill had been deserted when they arrived. A careful inspection had revealed empty cupboards and, to their relief, no corpses. The occupants must have received Ardalen's message and moved south to safety. There were signs of looting, however. A storeroom had been broken into. A locked trunk had been smashed open, and the contents – mostly clothing, worth nothing to the thieves – had been strewn about. It was impossible to tell if they had been Sachakan or ordinary thieves. Stories of ransacking of abandoned villages by opportunistic locals had reached them.

Inevitable, I suppose, Jayan thought. *The fools probably don't understand or care that if they're caught by the Sachakans, their deaths will strengthen the enemy.*

Jayan paused in the shadows of the corridor and looked out. Tessia was not with the apprentices, he saw. The other four young men were aged from fifteen to twenty-two. Mikken, the next eldest after Jayan, was slim and confident and the best-looking. Leoran was a watchful type who made up for his quietness by always having a witty observation or play on words to offer. Refan was enthusiastic, and always went along with whatever the others said or thought. Aken, the youngest, needed to grow out of a habit of saying what he thought without first thinking about whether it would offend anyone, or make him look a fool.

They tended to ignore Tessia most of the time, though if she spoke they did listen and respond politely. He knew they were unsure how to behave around her. The young women they were used to were easy to categorise: either rich and from powerful families, or servants, or beggars and whores. Those female magicians they had encountered would all have come from the first category, and some of them had quite a reputation for being adventurous, especially in their attitude towards men.

The four laughed, then glanced to one side. Following their gaze, Jayan saw that the magicians were standing in a circle several paces away, probably discussing yet again all the reasons why they hadn't come face to face with any Sachakans and wishing they could find a risk-free way to lure out the enemy.

Now the apprentices were all looking in the other direction, and Jayan saw where Tessia had got to. She was picking small fruits off a tree and filling a bowl with them.

Probably some cure ingredient, he thought, suppressing a sigh. *Does she ever think of anything else?* Though her obsession with healing didn't bother him as much as it used to – not since he'd seen her work on the woman with the growth in her mouth – she was single-minded about it to the point of being predictable and, perhaps, a little bit boring.

As Jayan watched, Mikken rose and sauntered over to her. He held out his hands and she, looking mildly surprised, gave him the bowl. As she continued picking, he talked to her, all smiles.

Jayan's skin prickled. He didn't have to know what the apprentice was saying to know what he was up to. Stepping out of the doorway, he strode towards the pair. Mikken looked up and saw Jayan coming, and his expression became both guilty and defiant.

"It's your turn, Mikken," Jayan said. He paused, sniffed and smiled. "I wouldn't put it off much longer if I were you."

The young man frowned and opened his mouth to retort, then glanced at Tessia and thought better of it. He handed Jayan the bowl.

"I bow to the wisdom of my much, *much* older peer," he said mockingly, gave Tessia a parting smile and headed towards the mill.

Tessia raised an eyebrow. "You two still establishing a pecking order?"

"Oh, it's clear who's at the top," Jayan said. "The lesser hordes need to sort out their own hierarchy. Are you enjoying being the prize they're fighting over?"

287

"Me?"

"Yes, you. I'm afraid female magicians have quite a reputation. My young, naive subordinates are trying to work out if any of them stands a chance with you."

"A chance?" She turned and began picking fruit again. "Am I to expect a marriage proposal, or something much shallower?"

"Definitely shallower," he said.

She chuckled. "So how do I make it unarguably clear, without offending their sensitive male pride, that I will never accept such a proposal?"

Jayan paused, considering. "Be clear and unhesitating. Give them no reason to doubt your meaning. But don't insult them, of course. We do have to travel with them."

Tessia turned back to him, dropped another handful of the small green fruits in the bowl, then took the bowl from him. "Then I had best be unhesitating and clear up this matter."

She strode toward the apprentices. Jayan paused, suddenly doubting his own advice. He hadn't meant her to confront them straight away. The eyes of the three younger apprentices brightened as she approached, though Jayan could not tell if it was from apprehension or hope.

But Tessia did not launch into a speech on her unavailability, or reproach them for even considering it a matter for discussion. She sat down on the blanket they were relaxing on and handed the closest – Refan – the bowl.

"Try them. They're delicious."

Refan picked up one of the fruits. "But it's not ripe."

"It is. People make that mistake all the time. See the dark spot on the end? That's how you tell they're ripe. But they're only like that for a few weeks. When the fruit starts to change colour it's too late. They go all pithy and dry inside."

She began peeling the fruit she had retained. Reluctantly,

the others began to copy her. As they bit into the flesh under-neath Jayan saw the looks of surprise on their faces. Curious, he took one for himself and discovered she was right. They were tart, but sweet.

Soon, Mikken emerged from the mill, his hair glistening with water.

"What's this?" he said as he joined them. "What are you eating?"

"Ah, Mikken," Tessia said. "Good. Now you're here, there's something I apparently need to make completely and devas-tatingly clear to all of you." She glanced at Jayan. "You, too."

To his horror, Jayan felt his face warming. He sighed, rolled his eyes and affected boredom, all the while hoping his face wasn't red.

"I'm not planning to bed anyone during this trip, or after it," Tessia said. "So get the idea out of your heads now."

Jayan watched as the four boys bowed their heads and began looking anywhere but at Tessia. Aken sent Jayan a brief glare, though.

"We weren't—" Mikken began, spreading his hands, using the tone of someone trying to explain something.

She cut him off. "Oh, don't think I'm fool enough to believe that. You're all male – and young. I'm the only woman around. I'm not being vain; just not stupid." She chuckled. "I also know if there was a better-looking girl around, the situation would be different. Anyway . . . put the thought out of your minds. Not going to happen. After all, I'd hardly want to fall pregnant right now, would I?"

The apprentices didn't answer, but she caught the looks they exchanged.

"What?" she asked, a small measure of anger slipping into her voice. "That didn't even *occur* to you?"

"Of course not," Aken blurted. "You've got magic. You can stop that happening."

Tessia blinked in surprise, then, suspicion in her eyes, she looked at Jayan. "That's possible?" she asked him quietly.

Not quietly enough, it turned out. Even as Jayan nodded, the others had lifted their heads. They were grinning.

"That changed your mind, by any chance?" Aken asked slyly.

She gave him a withering look. "Not if you were the last man in Kyralia."

The others laughed. Tessia's mouth twitched, then relaxed into a smile. "Well, we've all learned something today, haven't we?" She picked up another fruit, and as Mikken examined one for himself she began explaining how to judge when it was ripe.

After a while she looked at Jayan and raised an eyebrow questioningly. *Did I convince them?* he imagined her asking. He shrugged and nodded. She leaned closer, her gaze moving to the magicians still talking several paces away.

"What do you think they're discussing? The same old things over and over?"

He nodded. "Probably."

"It's such a waste of time. If they didn't keep going over it, Lord Dakon could spend some time teaching us. I haven't learned any magic since before we arrived in Imardin."

Jayan gave her a disbelieving look. "I didn't think you were that interested."

She snorted softly. "Amazing what a bit of threat to your life and others' can do. Not to mention the death of your parents."

"Well, if it's any consolation, I haven't had any lessons either."

"It's all very well for you," she retorted. "You've had years of training. I've only had months."

"I could teach you," Jayan said. Then he gulped a mouthful of air and looked away. Where had *that* come from?

Then he remembered Lord Dakon, months ago, telling him to help Tessia practise. That helping another learn would benefit Jayan, too. But Dakon hadn't meant Jayan to *teach* Tessia, which apprentices weren't supposed to do.

The thought that she might die simply from lack of training was *wrong*, however. Surely the circumstances were extreme enough to justify bending the rules a little.

Tessia was staring at him now, but as he met her gaze again she nodded quickly.

"Now?"

He looked at the others. They were stuffing themselves with fruit, too occupied with their feasting to pay much attention to what Tessia and Jayan might do. He stood up. She followed suit and looked at him expectantly. Thinking hard, Jayan moved away from the others, considering what he could possibly teach her.

"More sophisticated defence methods," he said aloud. "That's the obvious thing to teach you first."

"Sounds sensible to me," she replied.

So he began to teach her ways to modify her shield. Lord Dakon had taught her basic shielding, since that was all a new and powerful apprentice needed to know at first. What had he said? *"There's no point confusing a new apprentice with complications. Just get into a good habit of strong shielding to begin with; then, when you can do it without thinking, start refining."*

Jayan hadn't noticed that they'd gained an audience until a voice spoke near his shoulder.

"I've never tried that. Would you show me?"

He turned to find Leoran standing behind him. He considered the boy, then shrugged and gestured for him to join Tessia. "Of course. This sort of thing could save your life, too."

"And mine?" Aken asked. The young apprentice didn't wait for an answer, but jogged to Leoran's side. Jayan smiled wryly and turned to look at Mikken and Refan. They shook their heads.

"Already know it," Mikken said.

As Jayan continued teaching the different forms of shielding he knew, Mikken stepped forward and began to help. The older apprentice revealed a method that Jayan hadn't heard of before, though it had some serious flaws. They began debating the advantages and disadvantages, each demonstrating using the other apprentices.

"Stop! Stop right now!"

All jumped at the shout. Turning, they saw Mikken's master, Lord Ardalen, striding towards them.

"What are you doing?" the magician demanded. "You're teaching each other, aren't you?" Reaching them, he laid a hand on Mikken's shoulder, his expression sympathetic but his voice revealing anger as he looked at Jayan. "I expect you think you're showing initiative and co-operation – and you are – but you should not be doing this. Apprentices are forbidden to teach apprentices. You are not allowed to teach until you become higher magicians."

"But why?" Aken asked, his frustration clear.

"It is dangerous." This came from Lord Bolvin, Leoran's master, as he reached them. The other magicians were coming closer, Jayan saw. Dakon was frowning. He felt a pang of guilt and fear that he might have offended his master.

"What is going on?" Lord Dakon asked as he came up to them. When the situation was explained his frown deepened. "I see. Be assured Jayan here has been trained to teach others safely. He is close to the end of his own training, so I have begun preparing him for the day he takes on his own pupil. Your apprentices were quite safe."

To Jayan's amusement, the magicians now began debating the issue, forming a new circle that excluded their juniors.

He looked over at Tessia, who wore a wry smile. She met his eyes, shrugged, then walked back to the blanket and the near empty bowl of fruit. As Jayan followed, the other apprentices tagged behind.

"That stinks," Aken said as he dropped sullenly onto the blanket.

The others nodded.

"Well . . ." Jayan began. "Do you think they'd protest if we started playing Kyrima? That's supposed to be good at developing battle strategy skills."

The others looked up eagerly. Tessia's shoulders sagged. "Oh, how wonderful," she muttered sarcastically.

Jayan ignored her. She'd play if he badgered her. And she wasn't too bad at it, either. As the others paired off he turned to face her.

"Can't leave me partnerless," he said.

She pulled a face, grabbed the bowl and stood up. "Forgot my little speech earlier, have you, Jayan? Not if you were the last man in Kyralia."

It was reassuring to Hanara to find that many of his master's new allies had brought more than one slave with them. Some had as many as ten, though not all were source slaves. Knowing this, he was able to tolerate Jochara, and it helped that Takado appeared to prefer to give Hanara the more complex tasks since Jochara, not yet used to their master's ways, was slower to grasp what was being asked of him.

If Takado had urged them to battle each other for his favour, then it would have been clear he didn't want two source slaves and would kill the loser. But since they were constantly on the move, there was so much work to do that both Hanara and Jochara were exhausted by the time Takado allowed them to sleep.

If every new ally presents him with gifts, we're not going to be able to carry everything, Hanara thought now as he shifted the weight on his shoulders.

Takado's allies had swelled to twelve. Slaves at the pass directed the new arrivals to slaves stationed at intervals along the mountains, all of whom only knew where the next and previous positions were. When Takado made camp at the end of each day he sent a slave to the end of the line, to inform arriving allies where to find him.

Two more had reached them last night. Fortunately the gifts they'd brought had been consumable. Takado needed food for his followers and slaves more than he needed heavy gold trinkets. Though they raided local farms and villages, the habitations were often far apart and most occupants had now left, taking what little food they had. Even those foolish enough to stay didn't have much in their stores, winter only just having ended.

Sometimes they came across domestic animals to slaughter and cook; otherwise there were wild animals to hunt. Fortunately, they didn't have to worry about cookfires or smoke revealing their location, as usually one or another magician roasted the meat with magic. Slaves skilled in tracking for hunts kept them informed on the Kryalian magicians' location and numbers.

As Takado began to climb a steep slope, angling across the incline, Hanara leaned forward and followed. He could hear Jochara panting behind him. Sweat ran down his back, soaking the shirt the stable master had given him. That life – his time in Mandryn – already seemed like a dream. It had been foolish of him to think it might last. There was a reassuring familiarity about serving Takado again. It was hard, but he knew the rules. He fitted in.

He was breathing heavily by the time he reached the top

of the slope. Takado, unburdened, had gained some distance and was standing further along the ridge listening to a slave belonging to one of the other magicians. The boy was fast and agile, so he was being used as a scout rather than a carrier.

". . . saw the light. Heard the boom, boom," the boy was saying, pointing towards where the road to the pass could be seen, like a wound cut in the forest, below them.

"A magical battle," Takado said, frowning at the distance. "How long ago?"

"Half a shadow line," the slave said. "Maybe more."

How the boy could estimate the time this way without a shadow dial was a mystery. Takado glanced at Hanara and the rest of his group, but said nothing, turning back to stare down at the forest again. Hanara could guess what he was thinking. Had the slaves at the pass failed to meet some potential new allies? Had the newcomers encountered the Kyralians instead? Had they won or lost?

Takado and his allies hadn't considered the group of Kyralians following them a serious threat, as there were only seven of them against the twelve Sachakans. But Takado wanted to avoid killing Kyralian magicians until the numbers at his side were much greater, and they could withstand whatever retaliation was sure to follow.

Waving the scout away, Takado started down the slope towards the road and the battle's location. Hanara felt his stomach sink and heard Jochara curse behind him. The other three of Takado's allies did not protest, though they did order their slaves to be silent and not make any noise.

Time slowed then. With every step Hanara scanned the forest ahead as well as the uneven ground in front. He listened for voices, or the whistling calls the slaves sometimes used to signal each other. Takado set a cautious pace, every step taken carefully. They reached the bottom of the slope, and set out across the valley the road followed. Time stretched on.

The closer they drew to the road, the more Hanara's heart raced. He kept trying to quieten his breathing by keeping his breaths shallow, but the exertion of carrying Takado's belongings was too much and he soon found himself gasping for breath.

Then Takado stopped and raised a hand to indicate the others should follow suit. Hanara realised they were now in sight of the road. They waited in silence.

Voices drifted to them from somewhere ahead. Takado didn't move. Slowly his shoulders relaxed. He shifted his weight to one leg. He crossed his arms.

Around a bend in the road rode two men. Before them walked a man dressed in fine clothing, bound with rope and bleeding from the temple. Behind them followed four slave girls, hunched and thin.

The hairs on the back of Hanara's neck prickled as he recognised the riders. They were two of Takado's Ichani friends, Dovaka and Nagana. Both had been outcasts for some years now, and were tanned and toughened from surviving in the northern mountains and ash desert. There was something about the older one, Dovaka, that made Hanara's stomach quiver and his skin prickle. It was not just that his slaves were always starved, cowed and terrified young women. His conversations were full of such eagerness for violence that even other Ichani were repelled by him. As Takado moved forward, out of the trees and onto the road, Hanara's stomach sank. The rest of the group followed.

"Takado!" Dovaka called as he saw them. "I have a gift for you." He leapt off his horse, grabbed the bound man by the collar and pushed him forward, then onto his knees in front of Takado. "Emperor Vochira's messenger. We heard he'd gone through the pass ahead of us, so we caught up with him to see what he was hoping to deliver."

"Messenger?" Takado repeated.

"Yes. He was carrying this."

Dovaka's eyes gleamed as he handed over a metal cylinder. Taking it, Takado slid the end off and pulled out a roll of parchment. He uncurled it and read, and his mouth twitched into a crooked smile.

"So the emperor is sending magicians to deal with us," he said, looking over his shoulder at his allies. "Or at least he wants the Kyralian king to believe so." He turned his attention to the messenger. "Is it true?"

"Would you believe me if I said it was?" the man replied defiantly.

"Probably not."

Takado grasped the man's head in his two hands and stared at him intently. All was silent but for the occasional bird call, and the distant bellow of some animal. Then Takado straightened.

"You believe it to be true." He paused and considered the man. "I will let you live if you join us."

The man blinked, then his eyes narrowed. "What makes you think I won't slip away at the first opportunity?"

Takado shook his head. "Because, Harika, you failed. Your task was to take the message to the Kyralian king, but, more important, it was to prevent that message from reaching *us*. Emperor Vochira may not have said as much, but you know it to be true. Even if you manage to get to the Kyralian king and convince him that you aren't lying about the contents of the message we took from you – even if you manage to return home – Vochira will have you killed or outcast." Takado smiled. "I'm afraid no matter what happens, you will be dead or an Ichani."

The messenger looked down, his brow furrowed.

"You may as well join us," Takado said. "I can promise what the emperor can't, that if we succeed and you survive, you will no longer be a landless, slaveless lackey. You can claim land for yourself, regain the status you have lost, and have something for your son to inherit."

Taking a deep breath, the messenger sighed and began to nod. "Yes," he said. He looked up and stared back at Takado. "I'll join you."

"Good." Takado smiled and the bindings fell away from the man's wrists. "Get up. My slave will take a look at that cut."

Takado turned and waved at Hanara. Pushing aside a strong desire to go no closer to Dovaka, Hanara hurried forward, set his burden down and brought out some clean water and cloth to clean Harika's wound. As he worked, he watched Takado and Dovaka move away from the others a little, their conversation too quiet for him to hear, their stance and gestures relaxed and friendly. But there was a deliberation to Takado's movements, as if he was forcing an impression of calm.

He's angry at them, probably because they didn't go where the slaves told them to, he thought. *He is not going to have an easy time keeping Dovaka and Nagana under control. Eventually Dovaka is going to challenge Takado's authority, and when he does I hope I'm a long way away.*

CHAPTER 23

I t worried Dakon every time he saw an empty village, farm-house or unploughed field. It worried him despite the fact that they were no longer his empty villages, farmhouses and unploughed fields but Lord Ardalen's, because he knew the situation was the same in his own ley.

It worried him on two levels: hundreds of people he was responsible for were homeless and dozens of them dead; and part of his land – from which he must earn the money to maintain his ley, pay his servants and rebuild Mandryn – was lying abandoned and neglected at the time of year crops should be planted and domestic animals set to breeding.

People and land, they're the same, his father used to say. *Neglect one and the other suffers eventually.* At the moment, while searching in vain for Takado and his allies, Dakon felt he was neglecting both. Fortunately, the area the Sachakans were moving through was mountainous and covered in forest, so it was sparsely inhabited. People living in these areas were likely to be hunters or woodcutters, their quotas negotiated with and agreed to by men Dakon or Ardalen employed for the job, who also did what they could to prevent and deal with poachers.

Fewer people had been killed or displaced than there would have been if the lowlands had been invaded, and there were few fields to be left unplanted. Even so, he wished he was in the lowlands, ensuring those driven from their homes were being given food and shelter in the southern villages, and that resources were not being wasted.

But he also knew his time was better spent dealing with the invaders. The sooner he and his colleagues drove the Sachakans out, the sooner people could return to their homes. He was not the only magician frustrated by their failure to do that. An understanding had grown between them as the weeks had crawled past. All were annoyed by their situation, all tempted by the knowledge that change could be forced if they were willing to take risks. None complained, though, because none wanted to urge anyone else to endanger his life. All were waiting and hoping for some benign influence to shift the balance of power, hopefully in their favour and not the Sachakans'.

Perhaps that benign influence has come today, Dakon thought, looking at the new magicians in the group. Five had arrived the previous night, bringing much needed supplies and Werrin's new apprentice.

Two were magicians from the Circle of Friends, Lord Moran and Lord Olleran. The other three were city magicians, Magician Genfel, Lord Tarrakin and Lord Hakkin. Magician Genfel had neither supported nor opposed the Circle as far as Dakon or Narvelan knew, but the other two city magicians were detractors. The most surprising of the latter was Lord Hakkin, who had openly mocked Dakon and Everran at the Royal Palace.

Dakon was not sure why Hakkin and his friends had come. Perhaps at the king's request. Narvelan had suggested a sense of duty, or there being nothing more interesting happening in the city, as possible motivations.

Lord Hakkin appeared to have assumed the leadership of the five during their journey here. Dakon suspected the man would have tried to take over the leadership of the entire group if the king hadn't already chosen Lord Werrin for the role.

Over the morning meal, the newcomers were coming to understand what they were now a part of.

"We haven't even come close to what we set out to achieve," Lord Werrin concluded as he finished describing their search so far.

"What were you hoping to achieve, exactly?" Lord Hakkin asked.

"To drive them out of Kyralia," Narvelan replied. "Preferably without anyone being killed. Driving them out requires us to find them first, and the trouble is, even when we do gain an idea of where they are, they move before we have a chance to confront them. We have to approach carefully, sending scouts ahead to discover their numbers, because we can't confront them until we know there is a chance of winning if they decide to fight us."

"Do they know you're hunting them?" Magician Genfel asked.

"Yes," Werrin replied. "They have caught and killed enough of our scouts to know what our intentions are. Those scouts that have returned have given us conflicting reports of their numbers, but we are gaining enough from their descriptions to recognise individuals."

"We suspect there is more than one group," Narvelan continued. "Each time a scout has seen the enemy they have counted seven or eight magicians, plus slaves. But the physical descriptions of the individuals are inconsistent. We get different combinations. They may be changing the members of each group around to confuse us."

"Presumably they meet from time to time," Lord Olleran said.

"I expect so," Narvelan agreed. "Though we have to consider

that they may be independent of each other, perhaps even competing. The only benefit to us, either way, is that each group appears to be small enough for us to tackle now."

"Yet we should still be careful," Werrin said. "Because if we are to avoid killing the Sachakans, and then escort them to the border, it is likely they will call on the other groups for help. And then we *will* be outnumbered."

"So we need more magicians?" Lord Tarrakin asked.

"Yes."

"More than five, from the sound of it," Lord Hakkin concluded, glancing around the group. "How many Sachakans do you think there are in total?"

"A few short of twenty."

"Were there that many to begin with?"

"I doubt it."

"So others are joining them. Is anyone watching the pass?"

"The scouts we sent haven't returned."

"So there must be Sachakans there, too." Lord Hakkin pinched his bottom lip between two fingers. "A magician should check. He may succeed where a scout would fail."

"So long as he doesn't encounter any Sachakan magicians," Narvelan pointed out.

"One would not be a problem."

"One can call for assistance. The road to the pass is exposed and surrounded by sheer rock slopes. It is difficult to approach in secret and it would be easy to become trapped between the pass and any Sachakans returning to help their allies."

"But you said earlier that the Sachakans are avoiding a confrontation with us," Lord Moran reminded him. "Because they don't want to risk killing a Kyralian magician for the same reason we want to avoid killing one of them."

Prinan shrugged. "Yet if they're relying on new allies coming through the pass to join them, they will have to deal with anyone trying to prevent that. They may prefer to wait until their numbers are large enough to take and hold land before killing any Kyralian magicians, but if we block the pass we may give them no choice."

The other magicians nodded in agreement.

"All the more reason for us to strike them before they grow that strong," Lord Hakkin said. "If we must be the ones to spill magician blood first, so be it. They are the invaders, after all. We are defending ourselves."

Werrin smiled crookedly. "Until the king decides otherwise, we must endeavour to achieve our aims without shedding Sachakan blood."

Hakkin frowned. "So even if we do manage to find one of their groups, they'll call for the help of another group and we'll find ourselves outnumbered. We are unable to prevent their numbers from continuing to grow by stopping allies coming through the pass, while our numbers are not growing as quickly. But even if we were enough to face them it wouldn't help because we can't find them." He shook his head. "Why did I bother coming out here? I may as well go home and wait for our new Sachakan masters to arrive."

Dakon couldn't help a small smile at the man's use of "we". Lord Hakkin hadn't been riding day after day, for weeks, searching for the Sachakans and finding only cold campsites and dead Kyralians.

"We need to change our tactics," Lord Olleran said. "Draw them out. Trick them into making a mistake."

"How do you suggest we do that?" Werrin asked. Dakon smiled at his patience. The group had discussed this many times already.

"Herd them into a corner. Bait them."

"Herding them would require us to split into smaller, more vulnerable groups."

Olleran shrugged. "More dangerous than staying in one, but that danger would be minimal if we stayed close enough together to help each other if one group was attacked."

"How do you suggest we communicate instructions to each other in order to co-ordinate our movements, or call for help?"

"We could use mental calls – if the king would allow it."

"And alert our quarry to our intentions, or our vulnerabilities?" Werrin shook his head. "It would only work if we already had them trapped. To do so we'd need to split into many different groups. The more groups, the more likely it is that communications will become confused."

"What of baiting them?" Lord Moran asked.

Werrin looked around the group. "Someone would have to volunteer to be the bait."

Lord Ardalen shook his head. "I may be willing to risk my own life, but I won't risk my apprentice's." Dakon was pleased to see that many of the newcomers were nodding.

"Of course, we wouldn't take any risks unless success was certain," Hakkin said.

"If it was certain, it wouldn't be a risk," Narvelan pointed out.

There was a long pause after that, and Dakon noted the signs of suppressed amusement among his colleagues, especially those who had travelled with Lord Hakkin.

"Surely it will not be long before more substantial re-inforcements arrive," he said. He turned to Hakkin. "Last night you said that others were planning to join us."

Hakkin's gaze, which had locked onto Dakon's, slid away. "Yes. I know of, ah, at least five magicians who said they would come – but I couldn't tell you when they were going to leave or how long they'll take to get here."

"We need more than five," Bolvin muttered, scowling.

Prinan gave a sharp huff of anger. "If they'd seen what

we've seen – the bodies of murdered men, women and children – our fellow magicians might not be so slow to get off their backsides and help defend their country!"

"Or maybe it would convince them to lock themselves in their homes," Narvelan said quietly.

Hakkin's back straightened and he scowled. "They will come. They will attend to their duty. But this invasion has caught many unprepared. Trips to the far reaches of Kyralia to engage in magical warfare are hardly a commonplace activity."

"I have a question," Magician Genfel said.

Everyone turned to look at him.

"If we did manage to overcome these magicians, how are we going to get them to the border?"

Werrin smiled. "We keep them drained of power."

"Of course, but they will regain it with time. We can't keep them tied up. They only need regain a little power to be able to burn their bonds away. Do we have some iron manacles, or something similar?"

"We'll take turns holding them imprisoned with magic."

"I see. And what happens after we take them to the border? What is going to stop them coming back?"

Werrin frowned. "The border will have to be guarded."

As the conversation moved in this new direction, Dakon found his attention wandering. He looked over to the circle of apprentices, now doubled in size. Three of the newcomers were only youngsters, probably new to their powers, including Werrin's apprentice. He worried that too many magicians were taking on the training of an apprentice out of a sudden need for a magical source to draw from, and would find themselves neglecting their responsibility later.

Yet I also worry about Narvelan, who has no apprentice to strengthen himself with. He'd suggested Narvelan take power from Jayan or Tessia, but the young magician had refused.

None of the new apprentices was female, he noticed. The powerful families of Kyralia might risk their sons' lives in the defence of their homeland, but it would take much more desperate need before they sent their daughters. He looked at Tessia. She was smiling, sitting on a blanket between Jayan and Ardalen's apprentice. Though he had occasionally seen a tear in her eye or a glimpse of pain and grief in her face, she had borne the journeying and rough living without complaint. He could not imagine the daughters of powerful Imardin families, brought up with all the comforts money could buy, coping nearly as well.

Even so, I should ask how she is getting on more often. It can't be easy being the only young woman among so many young men – many just boys – who have been brought up thinking people of her background are little better than servants.

She and Jayan appeared to be getting along better now. He didn't think there was much liking or affection between them, but neither went out of their way to obstruct or annoy the other, and they helped each other with practical tasks, like erecting tents, without hesitation. He was relieved at that, as the last thing they needed was bickering to add to what was already a tense, unpleasant situation.

If only he could say the same thing of the magicians. Sighing, Dakon turned his attention back to the debate.

Sachakan women's clothing had always fascinated and scandalised Stara. First they wrapped and tied a long, bright rectangle of colourful fabric, decorated with stitching and all manner of decorations from beads to coins to shells, around the typically voluptuous Sachakan chest, leaving their shoulders and legs bare in a way that would have been regarded as scandalous in Elyne. Then, if they ventured outside, they covered it with a short cape of thick fabric tied at the throat.

The cape did not cover bare legs and gaped open at the front to reveal the chest, so Stara wondered why they bothered. But the truth was, they did not bother often. Women rarely ventured beyond the walls of their homes, except in covered wagons when visiting friends. They were supposed to avoid the stares of men.

It would have been far more practical, and an easier way to avoid the stares of men, to wear one demure but feminine layer as women did in Elyne. But Stara had to admit she loved the wraps. They were much more comfortable, and she looked so good in them. Nobody in Elyne wore such bright colours.

As if the wraps weren't decoration enough, Sachakan women also wore a lot of jewellery. Their chests, wrists and ankles were covered by multiple strings of beads, shells or chains festooned with metal discs. Their dark hair provided a contrast against which elaborate headdresses draped and glittered. All this Stara embraced with feminine glee, except for one thing.

A part of the womanly habit of wearing half her body weight in jewellery involved piercing. Vora had told her that most Sachakan women wore several earrings in each ear, at least one ring in their nose, and even rings in their eyebrows, lips and navel.

Stara had flatly refused to let Vora put holes in any part of her body, much to the slave's consternation.

Father had better not have ordered her to, she thought. *I don't care how little it hurts, it's barbaric.*

At the thought of her father, she felt her stomach clench with nerves. She had seen nothing of him all week. For the first few days she had thought little of it, reasoning that he must be busy. But as the end of the week neared she grew annoyed. After so many years seeing him only on occasional visits, she wanted to get to know him better. Surely he wanted the same. After four days she sent Vora to him with a request for a meeting, but he didn't respond.

The previous morning she had ignored Vora's warning that it was inappropriate and left her rooms to seek him out. When she reached her father's apartments a slave had tried to stop her entering. Knowing that he couldn't touch her, she pushed past him.

Her father wasn't there. She had returned to her rooms disappointed and frustrated.

Tonight, however, she would see him – in the company of her prospective husband. Smothering a scowl, she leaned forward so Vora could drape several heavy strings of beads over her head.

"So tell me, mistress: when can you leave the master's room?" Vora asked. The slave had been teaching Stara local customs all week, and testing her all afternoon.

"After my father and the guests have left."

"When *must* you leave the room?"

"When my father tells me to. Or if I find myself alone with other men. Unless there are other women present – though that doesn't include slaves. And unless my father tells me to stay."

"Correct, mistress."

"What if my father says I must stay, but there are only other men in the room?"

"You do as Ashaki Sokara bids."

"Even if I feel I am in danger? Even if one of the men acts, er, improperly?"

"Even then, mistress, but Ashaki Sokara would not put you in that situation."

"That is stupid. What if he misjudged them? What if he left in a hurry and told me to stay without thinking it through? Surely, as my father, he'd rather I took steps to protect myself than let his mistake lead to a . . . a misunderstanding or tactical error. There's got to be a point where even he sees that unquestioning obedience would be foolish."

Vora did not answer, just pressed her lips together in disapproval as she always did when Stara spoke against the Sachakan customs or her father. It invariably made Stara angry and defiant.

"Unquestioning obedience is for slaves, the uneducated and the pathetic," Stara declared, moving to the jug of water on a side table and pouring herself a glass.

"We are all slaves, mistress," Vora said in reply. "Women. Men, in their own way. There is no such thing as freedom, just different kinds of slavery. Even an ashaki can act only within the restrictions of custom and politics. And the emperor is even more bound."

As Stara drank she looked at the woman and considered her words. *What a sad state this country is in. Yet it is the most powerful land in the region. Is that the price of power? But I suppose what she says about women and men being slaves to custom and politics is true in Elyne as well. And commoners, though not slaves, answer to the landowner or employer. Maybe we're not so different.*

But in Elyne, nobody — not even commoners — could be forced to marry anyone they did not wish to. They could leave the service of a landowner or employer and work for another. They were paid for their labour.

"Mistress, it is time," Vora said. As Stara turned to face her the woman's eyes narrowed. "You look acceptable." Then the corner of her mouth twitched upward. "No, you are beautiful, mistress — and lucky to be so."

Stara scowled. "It has only ever brought me trouble, and is likely to again tonight."

Vora snorted softly, then gestured to the door. "I'm sure

you've never used your looks to manipulate others, especially not in trade."

"Once, but it had entirely the opposite effect from the one I hoped for." Stara strode to the door. "If your appearance is all people see, they have no respect for your mind."

"Then they underestimate you, mistress. That is a weakness you can exploit," Vora said as she followed.

Stara weaved through the corridors of her father's mansion. For a slave, Vora was unexpectedly forthright. And bossy. Stara knew she was letting the woman get away with it because she was unused to dealing with slaves, and couldn't bring herself to snap at them as her father did.

Now, as she reached the master's room, she felt the knot in her stomach tighten. *How will Father behave towards me? Can I do anything to change his mind? And what will this suitor be like? Should I try to put him off marrying me?*

Her father sat in the same chair as he had the day she arrived, but other seats had been arranged around it and were occupied. Two men in richly decorated jackets sat to one side. She noted the knife sheaths at their belts that indicated they were magicians. On the other sat another stranger, in less colourful clothes and with no knife, and a man she recognised. As she realised who he was she felt her stomach sink. As if sensing her dismay, her brother looked up at her and frowned.

Then her father glanced towards the door and saw her waiting. He beckoned. Remembering Vora's lessons, Stara lowered her gaze and crossed to the only empty chair, directly across from her father, and waited for his permission to sit down.

"This is my daughter, Stara," he said to his guests. "She has recently returned from Elyne."

The men looked at Stara appraisingly for a moment,

then away. She took care not to meet their eyes, warned by Vora that it was considered rude.

"It must be a balm to your heart to have such beauty and grace in your home, Ashaki Sokara," the man in the plain jacket said.

All formality and charm, she thought. *Though if I'm a balm to my father's heart, then it's clear his heart hasn't needed any soothing this week.*

"Yes, you are lucky to have bred such a jewel," added the younger of the garishly dressed men. Stara swallowed a bitter laugh. That was more accurate. Jewel. Asset. Stock to trade. Something you lock away in a safe place and only take out to show off to guests.

"Stara has been away for many years, and is still learning our customs and manners," her father said. He met her eyes and frowned, and she realised she had been looking directly at him. Suppressing a sigh, she set her gaze on the floor.

"How old is she?" the older garish man asked.

"Twenty-two," her father replied. She opened her mouth to correct him, then stopped herself.

"And she has never been married?" the young man asked, surprise in his tone. "Nor bred any children?"

"No," her father replied. She could feel his eyes on her. "Her mother was instructed to prevent either, and did an admirable job."

"Indeed she has, considering how the Elyne women behave."

Stara resisted a smile. It hadn't been her mother's efforts that had prevented marriage or pregnancy. Stara's determination that nothing would prevent her becoming a trader had led her to refuse the few offers of marriage that had come her way, and magic had ensured that her enjoyment of lovers' company hadn't resulted in any awkward consequences.

"Sit down, Stara," her father said.

She obeyed. To her relief, the conversation now turned from herself to political issues. She was to sit silently, only speaking if questioned, and then only after looking to her father for permission to speak. Eventually food and drink was brought by slaves, served first to her father, then to her brother, then to the guests and finally to her.

Throughout the meal she pretended moments of forget-fulness, nearly speaking or eating out of turn then quickly catching herself. The young man must be her father's choice of husband, so she took to tapping her feet quietly when he spoke, and stifling the occasional yawn, in the hope that it would irritate him.

Aside from that first glance, her brother did not look at her again during the evening. His expression remained aloof and indifferent. He only spoke when the guests sought his opinion.

Little trade was discussed, to Stara's disappointment. The talk was all about politics. She listened, knowing that such matters could affect trade, especially in Sachaka.

"Sachaka needs to fight Kyralia," the older garish man declared at one point, "or it will turn on itself."

"Invading Kyralia will only delay the inevitable," the sober man disagreed. "We must solve our problems here, not compli-cate them by involving other lands, and giving those bold enough to disobey the emperor more power than they deserve."

"If we defeat them, the Kyralians will hardly be in a posi-tion to involve themselves in our politics," the young garish man pointed out. "And anyone who manages to conquer it will earn respect and power."

"But a freshly conquered land needs controlling. As do conquerors, if their ambition is not satisfied but instead increased by their success."

"The emperor would never—"

"Kakato," the older garish man cut in, silencing his son. "Let us not presume to know what the emperor would or wouldn't do."

At last, a name, Stara thought. *So my prospective husband is called Kakato.* She made up some rude rhymes to entertain herself. When she turned her attention back to the men their conversation had moved on to a broken agreement with the tribes of the ash desert, and whether it was an unwise or an unlucky move.

The night wore on, long past the meal's end. Stara found herself not having to fake her yawns. When her father finally dismissed her she rose and bowed with genuine relief before she left.

In the corridor outside, Vora was waiting. The woman's lips were pressed into a thin line, but she said nothing until they reached Stara's rooms.

"So, mistress," the slave said, as always with no trace of subservience, but Stara could not bring herself to correct the woman. "What did you think of your prospective husband?"

Stara sniffed dismissively. "I wasn't impressed. He's a bit young for me, don't you think?"

Vora's eyebrows rose. "Young? How old do you like your men?"

"Old?" Stara paused, then narrowed her eyes at the woman. "It isn't Kakato?"

The slave shook her head.

"Then one of the old . . . you must be joking! Which one, then?" The soberly dressed man had spoken the most intelligently, Stara noted, whereas the older garish man had seemed little smarter than his son.

"Master Kakato's father, Master Tokacha."

"Why didn't you tell me?"

"You didn't ask, mistress."

Stara gave the woman a withering look.

"I was ordered to teach you customs, nothing more." Vora spread her hands. "To do any more than ordered is to disobey."

"If I order you to tell me anything that might be useful or important, unless that information is specifically restricted by my father, would you be able to?"

The woman smiled and nodded. "Of course, mistress."

"Then tell me. Everything that might be useful or important." Stara lifted the necklaces from her neck. It was amazing how tiring the weight of so much jewellery could be. One of them caught on the headdress and she cursed. She felt Vora's hands plucking at it and soon she was free.

"How was Master Ikaro?" Vora asked as she stowed the headdress in a wooden box.

"I have no idea. He only looked at me once."

"Your brother is a kind man. And talented. But like you, a slave. You should ask to see him. I think Master Sokaro would allow it."

"I doubt my brother would. If he cares that I'm here at all, it's more likely he wants me married and out of the way." Stara peeled herself out of the wrap and gave it to Vora, who handed her a sleeping shift.

"Why would you say that?" the old woman asked.

"He made it pretty clear what he thought of women the last time he visited us in Elyne."

"That was some time ago. You may find he has changed. He would be a good ally. Shall I arrange it, mistress?"

Stara turned away. "I don't know. Ask me in the morning."

"Yes, mistress."

Moving to the bed, Stara sat down and relished a full, unsuppressed yawn.

"I know what you were doing tonight," Vora said from the doorway. "It will take more than that to put off your prospective husband."

Her lips were back in that narrow line. Stara frowned in annoyance. "Sachakans may treat women like stock, but we both know women aren't dumb animals or mindless objects. We have minds and hearts. Nobody can blame us for wanting, at the least, to influence who we are sold to."

Even as she said the words, Stara knew she had given herself away. If not by her behaviour during the evening, which Vora must have been able to see or hear, then by responding to Vora's accurate guess.

The woman lips softened and quirked upward.

"You're not going to influence anyone by being so obvious about it, mistress." Then she turned and vanished into the corridor beyond.

Stara stared at the empty doorway and considered a possibility she hadn't thought of before. *Could Vora actually be on my side?*

CHAPTER 24

As Tessia replaited her freshly combed hair she noticed that the voices of the magicians and apprentices outside the tent walls had grown from a few occasional murmured comments to a full, multi-voiced discussion. After tying off the plait, she crawled outside and stood up.

The morning sun filtered through the forest, striping the small abandoned field they had camped in with shadows. A knot of magicians had gathered between the tents, their apprentices hovering close by. All wore expressions of worry or annoyance. Spotting Jayan, she moved to his side.

"What's happening?"

"Lord Sudin has gone, taking Aken with him."

"Does anybody know why?"

"No, but Lord Hakkin has admitted that he and Lord Sudin discussed strategies for luring Sachakans into revealing themselves last night, or possibly scouting for themselves. He thinks Sudin might have left to try out one of his own ideas."

"We are getting closer to Sudin's ley," Mikken added, moving to her other side. As she turned to regard him he smiled briefly. She found herself noticing, not for the first time, that he was rather good-looking. *And nice, too*, she added. *Cheeky when the other apprentices are around, but never in a mean way.*

"When did he leave?" she asked him.

"We're not sure, but probably not long ago," Jayan replied.

She turned to see him scowling. Annoyed that a magician should so foolishly disobey Lord Werrin, she guessed. He saw that she was looking at him and his expression abruptly became neutral.

The knot of magicians broke apart.

"Pack up," Werrin ordered. "Make it quick."

At once the camp filled with activity and noise as all hastened to dismantle tents and stuff belongings into the saddlebags of the pack horses. When all were ready and mounted a scout led the group away, his gaze on the ground. Magicians and apprentices followed close behind, Werrin at the front. Servants followed nervously at the rear, but Werrin was reluctant to split the magicians up in order to keep the servants protected between them, especially as they were often forced by the terrain to travel in single file and a group of servants in the middle would be just as vulnerable to a surprise attack as one at the end.

Tessia heard Jayan's stomach growl, and smiled grimly. She doubted they'd be eating any time soon. At least their supplies of food would last a little longer. The fresh supplies Lord Hakkin and the other newcomers had brought with them had only lasted five days, and with a larger number to feed and so much of the local area looted by Sachakans, the magicians were finding it ever harder to gather enough food for people and horses. Werrin had sent a scout south requesting that regular deliveries of supplies be organised. Dakon had expressed his worry to Tessia and Jayan that, if not arranged carefully and without magicians as escort, those supplies would only end up feeding the Sachakans.

The mood of the group had changed with the arrival of the newcomers. The magicians' debates were more heated. Dakon had not revealed what the disagreements were about, but from watching closely Tessia was sure a battle of some sort was going on between Hakkin and Narvelan, and the rest of the magicians had either taken one side or the other, or were undecided.

Whatever the conflict was, she was not surprised to learn it might have led to Sudin's leaving the group. *Has he left to return home? Or is he planning some sort of attack on the Sachakans? I'd have guessed the former, since it would be madness to confront the enemy alone.* But soon it became clear that the tracks of Sudin's and Aken's horses weren't heading south. They were heading north-east, away from the city.

Confrontation might not be Sudin's plan, though. He might have decided to scout for himself. Perhaps make his way to the pass, from which no scouts had returned. Or maybe he intended to find a high place from which he might spot the Sachakans, then guide the rest of the group with mental instructions. It would be risky, as the Sachakans would hear the same communications and no doubt send someone to stop him.

Jayan's horse drew alongside hers. She glanced at him, wondering what he was thinking. His brow was creased in a frown. Had he guessed what Sudin was up to? She could not ask him. They were not to speak while travelling, unless necessity demanded it.

Looking ahead, she saw that they were moving into a narrow valley, and the horses, once again, were forced into a line. A new hierarchy had formed to include the newcomers, and she smiled wryly as she watched magicians hesitate or push forward to take their place in an order of rank only they understood.

The walls of the valley drew together and she found their closeness oppressive. She checked her shield to make sure it was strong. As time passed, they climbed ever higher. Up and up, steeper and steeper, until she began to worry that they would have to dismount and lead the horses.

Finally, the line of riders visible before her began to shorten as those at the front reached a crest of some sort and moved out of sight beyond it. As her own horse reached the end of the ascent she sighed with relief. They were riding along a ridge now. Through the thin spread of trees she could see the face of higher slopes. She realised they could probably be seen as easily in this scant cover.

—*Lord Werrin*!

She jumped. The mental voice was Sudin's, and it carried a hint of panic. Looking around, she saw heads turning as magicians and apprentices glanced about the forest as if the call had reached their ears rather than their minds.

—*Lord Sudin?* Werrin replied. *Where are*—

—*Too late! We're*—

A pause followed.

—*Help! Heeeelp!* Tessia flinched at Aken's voice in her mind, and the echo of his terror. She found herself staring at Jayan, who gazed back at her in horror.

—*We took the track north-east*, Sudin said quickly. *Over the ridge and to the left . . . into . . . a . . . valley. Two . . . Sacha*—

A faint thin cry filtered through the forest. It took Tessia a moment to realise her ears had heard it, not her mind. Something flashed before her mind's eye. An impression. Of blood. A lot of blood.

"Left!" Werrin exclaimed. The scout was already running back long the column, his expression stiff with shame. Werrin urged his horse after the man. After a moment he stopped and called out. "Four with me," he said. "The rest stay."

That meant five magicians and their apprentices. Dismay mingled with relief as she saw Dakon move to the side of the track, indicating that she and Jayan should too. Narvelan, Hakkin, Prinan and Ardalen and their apprentices hurried after Werrin.

319

I want to help, she thought. *But what if it's a trap?*

The sound of hoofbeats faded rapidly. For a long moment the rest remained still and silent. Then Dakon moved along the line and, finding that the servants were still on the steep track, brought them up onto the ridge to wait next to the remaining magicians.

The wait was not long, but it was slow and strained and full of dread. At every sound in the forest all jumped or searched the trees fearfully. Every exchanged glance was full of unspoken questions. Tessia realised she was no longer hungry. In fact, she felt a little queasy. She checked her shield again.

When the sound of approaching hoofbeats reached her Tessia held her breath. Dakon moved forward. Jayan urged his horse after, and Tessia nudged hers to follow. Heart racing, she gazed down the track.

Then Narvelan appeared and she let out a sigh of relief. But as she read his expression she felt her stomach sink. The young magician looked pale and grim. As Werrin came into sight she flinched at the fury in his face. Then Hakkin appeared. He hung his head, his expression tortured and bleak.

Narvelan looked up at those waiting.

"They're dead," he said.

None said a word for a long moment. The only sound was the movement of the horses returning to the group.

"Both of them?" a weak voice asked. Tessia turned as she realised Leoran had spoken.

"Yes," Werrin replied.

"You buried them, then?" Bolvin asked.

Werrin and Narvelan exchanged glances. "Yes."

Tessia felt a chill run down her spine. There had been more to it than that, she suspected. The glance between the two magicians hinted at something bad. Something they felt was better left unmentioned. She looked at the other magicians and their apprentices. Lord Ardalen looked ill. Lord Prinan's eyes were haunted but there was determination in the set of his jaw. The apprentices . . . they were pale and their eyes were wide. They kept glancing back over their shoulders. Mikken met her gaze, then looked at the ground.

"This changes things," Werrin said, addressing them all. "They have killed a Kyralian magician. Even by their standards, retaliation is justified. We must camp and discuss our next move, and notify the king of Lord Sudin's death. And Apprentice Aken's." He shook his head.

"I must accept responsibility," Lord Hakkin said. "I encouraged Sudin to contemplate the action he took today. I can see now that such risks are not worth taking. Should never be taken again. I . . . am sorry." He bowed his head.

"We have been only guessing the extent of the danger we face until now, balancing caution with courage," Narvelan said. "But now we know the truth, and it is a hard and bitter lesson for all of us. We know what we risk, both magician and apprentice."

"I have been thinking about that," Lord Bolvin said. "Since they share the risk, should we include the apprentices in our discussions? They may not have the experience to offer suggestions or insight, but they deserve to know what they are fighting against, and how."

To Tessia's surprise, all of the magicians nodded.

"Then let's get away from this place and return to somewhere less exposed and more protected," Ardalen said.

Without another word, the magicians led the group back down into the valley.

There were some truths you didn't need to know, but *had* to know, Jayan believed. He didn't need to know anything more than that Lord Sudin and Aken had been killed by the Sachakans. But something in him wanted to know the details. Wanted to know exactly how sadistic the Sachakans could be. Maybe there was a part of him that needed the details in order to prove that what he'd been told was true, and not something invented to encourage everyone in the group to co-operate, or to justify killing the invaders.

Or perhaps just because he couldn't quite believe he was never going to talk to, or tease, Aken again. Or play Kyrima against him. The young man he'd barely got to know was never going to grow into a higher magician, with power and authority. Never take on his own apprentice.

So at the first opportunity, as they were making camp, he sidled up to Mikken and asked.

The young man looked at Jayan in disbelief, then annoyance, but then his gaze became thoughtful and he nodded in understanding.

"They were in pieces," he said, then went on to describe what must have been the result of a planned, deliberate sequence of torture. Since then, whenever Jayan thought about what Mikken had told him he felt cold right down to his bones. He realised that, for most of his life, he'd imagined the Sachakan magicians as being not so different from Kyralians. They kept slaves instead of lording it over commoners. They maintained land and trade, as Kyralian lords did.

He'd reasoned that these invaders were merely bored young men with high ambitions – of which there were plenty in Kyralia, though none held ambitions as high as conquering another land. But now Jayan knew better. Now he knew they were savages. No ambitious young Kyralian magician would have killed with such deliberate, undeserved cruelty. Not unless he was dealing out revenge for a truly atrocious act.

And even then . . . Jayan had to acknowledge that if anyone he'd known had shown he was capable of such savagery he would have regarded them with disgust and wariness from then on.

What the Sachakans had done to Sudin and Aken took planning. And *practice*. That's what angered and frightened Jayan the most.

"Don't tell Tessia," Mikken said.

Though Jayan appreciated that Mikken had Tessia's well-being in mind, he wasn't going to keep anything from her just because the young man fancied her. Besides, Tessia had seen plenty of gruesome things as a healer's assistant. As the set-up of camp finished and Tessia approached Jayan to ask what he had learned, he considered telling her everything. And immediately decided against it. She would wonder if such things had been done to the villagers of Mandryn, or her parents. She was also more trusting than he. It probably wouldn't even occur to her to question whether she'd been told the full truth.

So he glossed over the details, only saying that Aken had been killed first, and that their bodies had been left in a state meant to shock and scare anyone who found them. Then the magicians called everyone to their meeting, rescuing Jayan from any further questions.

The decision to include apprentices in the meeting had surprised Jayan, and now he felt a twinge of excitement. The magicians sat in a wide circle and their apprentices settled beside them. The sound of the forest around them faded as Werrin raised a shield to prevent their words from being heard outside the group. Jayan glanced beyond, to where scouts and servants kept watch, holding the lanterns they were to signal with if anything suspicious was seen or heard.

Jayan glanced at Dakon, who smiled knowingly.

"Don't say anything unless invited," he murmured.

Nodding, Jayan suppressed a fleeting annoyance. Normally he had a chance to talk to Dakon before the magicians met. Dakon always asked if Jayan had anything to suggest or comment on. But there had been no time today.

Lord Werrin began by going over the events of the day, glossing over the gory details much as Jayan had for Tessia. Once again, Lord Hakkin admitted his part in encouraging Lord Sudin to risk venturing out on his own, and then all tried in vain to guess what the magician's plan had been.

When the possible reasons and consequences had been fully covered, Werrin sighed and straightened.

"Sudin's death changes much. A magician has been killed. This frees us to consider strategies that may result in Sachakan deaths. But we must consult the king first."

"Surely he will not prevent us from killing them now," Prinan said.

"I doubt it, but he will still expect some restraint," Werrin replied. "Every Sachakan we kill has a family who may feel obliged to seek revenge or compensation, whether that death was justified or not. The more Sachakans we kill, the more Sachakan families will have the obligation to strike back in common. If they unite . . . this could become a war."

"But we can't sit back and let these invaders kill and loot for fear of war," Lord Ardalen protested.

"If the choice is to be conquered again by these people, or face a war, I'd choose the war any time," Lord Bolvin said firmly.

"But would we win?" Narvelan asked.

The magicians exchanged frowns. Jayan's heart sank. *They're not sure.* He shivered. *Us against the might of the Sachakan empire. Does Kyralia have any hope of surviving the next few years?*

"Would the Elynes help us?" Prinan asked.

324

Hakkin grimaced. "They would not want to make themselves a target."

"But they could be brought to see that if Sachaka conquered Kyralia, Elyne would be next," Magician Genfel said. "And that if Sachaka was occupied in fighting us both it is more likely to lose."

"Best we avoid having to ask them at all," Bolvin said. "We must halt this invasion now. Drive out the Sachakans. Make it clear we will not be easily conquered again. We may try to avoid killing too many in the process, but it is more important to demonstrate that we will not tolerate these incursions. And murders."

The others nodded, and Jayan felt the same determination that was written on all their faces.

"Nevertheless," Genfel said, "if we wait too long to ask for help, it may not arrive in time. Someone needs to seek the promise of assistance, at the least." He paused. "I have friends in other lands who might be able to persuade magicians in their homeland to join us if we are not successful in driving the invaders out ourselves."

"Discovering that other lands are willing to join us might make Takado reconsider his plans," Narvelan said, his expression thoughtful. "And dissuade other Sachakans from joining him."

Werrin looked at Genfel. "You will need the king's endorsement."

Genfel shrugged. "Of course."

"If I may speak?" Hakkin looked at Werrin, who looked amused as he nodded. Hakkin turned to regard the other magicians. "Chasing the Sachakans with such a small party is ridiculous. We need more magicians and we need them now. With enough support, we could fan out across the north and sweep them out like the scum and dirt they are."

"With respect, Lord Hakkin," Dakon said – speaking for the first time, Jayan noted, "but the area you speak of is extensive and mountainous. It would take more magicians than we have in Kyralia to spread across it as you suggest, and even if we did they would be stretched so thin it would be no effort for the Sachakans to break through."

Hakkin looked at Dakon thoughtfully, and then, to Jayan's surprise, nodded. "You're right, of course. I am not familiar enough with this part of Kyralia and am only just coming to understand the challenges of moving in this type of terrain."

"We should, as you have suggested before, Lord Hakkin, regain control of the pass," Narvelan said.

Hakkin admitting his ignorance? Narvelan supporting Hakkin? Jayan resisted a wry smile. *If only it hadn't taken the gruesome death of a magician and his apprentice to get these men to co-operate.*

"I agree," Werrin said. "I suspect a large part of the Sachakans' plan is that news of their continuing existence here – and now the killing of one of us – should inspire their countrymen into joining them. We must make that as difficult as possible. But controlling the pass will have to become a separate task from ours."

"Then I volunteer to gather the forces necessary," Lord Ardalen said, "and to take them there and hold as best we can."

Eyebrows rose, then all nodded. Werrin smiled. "We must, as always, seek the king's approval, but I will also suggest that he would not err in granting the responsibility to one as capable as yourself."

Ardalen flushed. "Thank you." He grimaced. "I think."

"I'll send a scout south. We should have a reply in four or five days. I will suggest he replies with mental communication, using code words to indicate approval or disapproval, as Lord Olleran suggested a few days ago."

326

"If we block the pass," Prinan said quietly, "then I suspect any Sachakans determined to enter Kyralia will attempt to use the new pass in my father's ley. He should be warned and . . . and action taken to prevent access that way."

"Yes," Werrin said. "You are probably right." He paused, a thoughtful frown creasing his brow. "I will also suggest this to the king." He glanced around the group. "It would not hurt to have one who saw today's crime with his own eyes speak of it to those who do not yet grasp the situation we are in, and the future we face if we lose."

"In the meantime, we are too few and too weak," Bolvin said. "Is there any way we can strengthen ourselves more effectively?"

"We cannot speed or increase the rate at which we gain magic," Narvelan said, spreading his hands. "Even if we were allowed to seek power from commoners, most in these parts have fled or been killed."

"The king cannot grant us access to the strength of commoners, no matter how willing, until we are officially at war," Werrin said. "But . . . I know he has been considering how he might make exceptions."

"There is power and there is knowledge and skill," Dakon said. "We can, in the meantime, hone our skills. And improve our abilities, if we are willing to share what we know and practise working together."

"But that will use up magic we may need to deal with the enemy," Werrin pointed out.

"We do not have to use full-strength strikes," Dakon said. "Only beams of light. It would be considerably safer, too. Other magical applications . . . I'm sure we can come up with ways to teach or demonstrate to each other without overly tapping into our resources."

Werrin looked at the other magicians. "What do you all think?"

Shoulders lifted and heads nodded. "I doubt I have anything new to add," Prinan said wryly. "I'm no keeper of any great magical secrets."

"I may have something to offer," Ardalen said, smiling crookedly. "A little trick my master taught me that may prove useful, which I'm more than willing to share if it helps to protect Kyralia."

"I think that must be the aim against which we must all weigh any ownership of magical knowledge," Werrin said. "Secrets may be lost for ever if we lose. And you can be sure no Sachakan master will be paying any Kyralian magician for his unique talents — if we survive being conquered."

"I doubt there will be any Kyralian magicians left, should the Sachakans be in charge," Narvelan muttered darkly.

A long silence followed, then Werrin looked around the circle again, this time meeting the eyes of the apprentices.

"Now, do our young charges have any questions, or suggestions?"

Magicians looked at their apprentices, who shook their heads or shrugged. Jayan bit his lip. He realised Dakon was looking at him, one eyebrow raised in question. As Werrin opened his mouth to announce the meeting over, Jayan cleared his throat.

"I have one suggestion," he said.

All eyes turned to him, and he had to push aside a sudden nervousness.

"Yes, Apprentice Jayan?" Werrin said.

"I know this has come up before, and been rejected, but I would ask that it be reconsidered," Jayan began, choosing his words carefully. He glanced at Tessia to draw their eyes to her briefly. "Apprentice Tessia and I have had little training from our master since leaving Imardin. For me this is not such a loss, since I have many years of training behind me.

Tessia and many of the other apprentices here have had almost no training – perhaps only rudimentary instruction in defending themselves, if any." He paused to take a breath. "Could we begin training each other now?"

Werrin had already begun to frown in disapproval, anticipating Jayan's request. He looked at his fellow magicians, most of whom appeared as unimpressed as he with the idea.

"Might I make a different suggestion?" Dakon said.

Jayan looked at his master in surprise, and not a little disappointment. He had been hoping for support, not an alternative.

"I'm sure we all acknowledge how unfortunate it is that we must neglect the training we are obliged to give our apprentices in exchange for strength," Dakon said.

"Strength they should not be using up needlessly," Ardalen injected.

"No," Dakon agreed. "They should not need to protect themselves unless in an unusual or desperate situation. In that case, it would be better to have a weakened apprentice than a dead one, wouldn't you agree?"

Ardalen nodded and shrugged in agreement.

"Apprentices do not teach apprentices, however," Dakon continued. "It has been a rule for as long as we remember. We do not have time to spare in instruction. Or do we? How much time does it take for seven magicians to teach the same lesson to seven apprentices? The same time as it would take for one magician to teach the lesson to seven apprentices? I think not." He smiled. "If we are in agreement on what is taught, is there any harm in one of us teaching a group of apprentices, perhaps sharing the responsibility by teaching in turn, a different magician each time, as the opportunity comes?"

For a while none of the magicians spoke. All looked

thoughtful, their gazes moving about the circle and finally settling on Werrin.

"That is a suggestion we may have to think on," he began.

"No," Hakkin interrupted. "I think we can decide on this now. So long as these lessons do not take time or power from more immediate and important matters, and we are in agreement over their contents, I am in support of them. I think it will raise our spirits. Help us to feel we are achieving something, at least."

"Very well." Werrin looked around the magicians. "Does anyone disagree?"

None of the magicians responded. Jayan felt as if his heart was singing some kind of victory song. It wasn't what he had been hoping for. It was better, since he had suspected that, as the most experienced apprentice, he'd have been doing most of the teaching if the magicians had agreed to his suggestion.

"Then we shall begin group lessons," Werrin decided. "Before we discuss the contents of these lessons, and agree on a roster of teachers, let's attend to the matter of food. I believe the meal is ready."

Following Werrin's gaze, Jayan saw that some of the servants were stirring the contents of three large pots, which were sitting on a flat rock that one of the magicians had heated with magic to avoid the smoke of a cookfire.

Soup again, Jayan thought, groaning quietly. *It wouldn't be so bad if the ingredients weren't mostly shrivelled vegetables and the occasional bit of hard, overly salty dried meat.*

But he doubted anybody would be complaining. And he knew he'd be too hungry to care anyway.

CHAPTER 25

As Hanara swung the pile of dead branches and twigs off his back he felt the chill air of the night turn his sweat ice-cold. He dropped them beside the fire. Takado was seated before the flames and was staring into them, his expression thoughtful but with hints of the suppressed annoyance that only Hanara knew well enough to recognise.

Jochara squatted beside Takado, ready to leap up and do his master's bidding. It had taken the new source slave a long time, in Hanara's opinion, to learn not to interrupt Takado when in one of these moods. The burn across his cheek must hurt. Hanara felt a faint pity, but no great sympathy. Having seen how some of Takado's allies treated their slaves, he knew he and Jochara were lucky.

And I'm luckier than all of them, because for a short time I was free.

He resisted snorting aloud at himself. The freedom he'd experienced had never been true freedom. He'd known from the start that Takado would return for him. If his freedom had been real, it would not have been temporary. It had been like a small reward. Maybe just a concession – time to recuperate.

The rest of the magicians and their slaves were busy setting up their tents and bringing out food. Since Takado did not indicate otherwise, Hanara returned to the forest. It was getting dark and finding firewood was growing more difficult. At one point something dark slithered across his hand.

331

He dropped the branch he'd picked up, heart pounding, then continued to gather wood while trying to ignore the memory of multiple tiny legs running over his skin.

The fire was a luxury. Takado had chosen to camp in a twisting valley that hid the light of the fire from all but those about to stumble upon it. This far up in the mountains it was still chilly at night. The magicians could keep themselves warm with magic, but they preferred to save their strength.

Just as he had tied the first bundle of sticks together and hoisted it onto his shoulders he heard a voice. Looking further down the valley, he saw floating globes of light appear and several shadows approaching. The glimpses he caught through the trees were fleeting, but there was something familiar about the way these people walked. He abandoned his bundle of sticks and bolted back to the camp.

Takado looked up as Hanara hurried to his side. One eyebrow rose.

"Dovaka," Hanara panted.

A fleeting scowl darkened Takado's face, then his expression became calm again. He nodded to the ground.

Hanara huddled down beside Jochara and waited. *This is going to be interesting*, he thought. From what Hanara had overheard, some sort of confrontation had happened between some of Takado's allies and some Kyralians. Takado had been quiet since. And not a good kind of quiet. His voice had been calm and measured in a way Hanara had learned to dread.

Takado was angry. Very angry.

The other magicians in his group had been cautiously enthusiastic, phrasing their words carefully. One fewer Kyralian, they said, meant one more success to attract supporters to Takado. But mostly they kept their opinions to themselves. Takado had said little, and nothing to indicate his approval or disapproval.

After the camp was established and slaves were sent to the end of the line of communication so that the other group of magicians could find it, they had settled down to wait. Eventually the second group arrived, minus two members, Dovaka and Nagana. None knew anything about the confrontation.

Calls of greeting preceded Dovaka's arrival, then the man and his friend appeared and slaves of his group followed him into the clearing. Takado rose.

"I hear you have had a busy day," he said.

Dovaka grinned. "Yes. One of those weak white barbarians came sniffing, all on his own."

"He found you?" Takado's eyebrows rose.

A line deepened above Dovaka's brows at the suggestion he'd failed to remain hidden. "No. He came snooping so we taught him better manners."

"A lesson I'm sure he'll have plenty of opportunities to put into practice in future." Takado finished with a smile.

Dovaka hesitated, then grinned. "No chance at all."

A silence followed. Hanara noted that the rest of the magicians were watching Takado closely.

Takado's smile broadened. "Then congratulations on being the first of us to kill a Kyralian magician. You may go down in the records for that. Here." He glanced down at Jochara. "Let's sit and celebrate your achievement." The slave dashed away to the packs and brought back a bottle of spirits, while the magicians all sat down round the fire. As Takado offered Dovaka the first drink his smile faded. "I hope you don't go down as the man who spoiled our chances of conquering Kyralia."

Dovaka shrugged. "By killing one Kyralian?"

"Which we all know will have consequences," Takado replied. "They will have been restraining themselves for the

333

same reasons we have been. Now that we've killed one of them they'll be free to kill us. Their tactics will change. So must ours. Don't tell me you didn't realise this? It was why I asked that no Kyralian magician be killed until we were ready."

"We're ready," Dovaka scoffed. "We have the numbers and strength to take over ten villages. You would wait until all of Sachaka was roaming the mountains in hiding."

"Ten villages." Takado chuckled. He didn't say anything more. The bottle had come around the circle, so he offered it to Dovaka again.

"The Kyralians are few and they're stupid," Dovaka said, then drank deeply. His gaze moved from Takado to the other magicians, moving from face to face. "We could take a third of their land now. Their villages are spread too far apart for them to be defended."

"By them or us," Takado replied. "Why waste time and energy, and Sachakan lives, taking a village that you would lose again?"

"We could leave as easily as we could arrive – and once news we have taken land reaches home, those joining us will increase tenfold. Hiding and skulking in the forest is not going to inspire anyone to leave the comfort of their mansions. Taking land will. And when they join us we could take more land, until we have only Imardin to make our own." Dovaka took another swig of the spirit.

"Are you inspired?" Takado asked.

Dovaka blinked, looked down at the bottle then passed it to the next magician. "I am more than inspired. I have a goal, and a plan."

"Hmm," Takado said quietly, nodding. "So do I. What is yours? What do you want from all this?"

Dovaka's eye gleamed. "Kyralia."

"All to yourself?"

"No! For Sachaka." Dovaka grinned. "Well, with a part of it mine. I'd want something in return for taking the lea— all the risks."

"Yes," Takado said. "We all do. Every one of us has something to offer, whether they be risk takers or cautious planners, in this enterprise, as we all have something to gain. We must all act as our good sense tells us to."

As food was brought out and shared, including a magic-roasted leg of a reber brought by Dovaka's group, talk moved on to more practical subjects. Takado's bottle of spirits was emptied, then another produced. It felt like a celebration, and though Hanara was relieved the meeting of Dovaka and Takado hadn't turned into a confrontation, he knew all was not well.

The night deepened. Magicians yawned and began to retire for the night. Dovaka and Nagana stagged off to their beds and their slave women. When they were gone, Dachido leaned closer to Takado.

"What will you do?" he murmured.

A small crooked smile tweaked Takado's lips. "Nothing. In fact, I'm glad the first death has occurred, as some parts of my plan may now be set in motion." He nodded. "Our risk-taking friend has his uses."

Dachido looked doubtful, then considered Takado again. "I'd ask what you were up to, if I didn't already know there was no point. We'll find out in time. Sleep well."

As the man left Hanara felt a weight on his shoulder and realised Jochara was falling asleep on him. He elbowed the young man awake, getting a sullen scowl in return for the favour. Then Takado stood up and walked away to his tent, and they both hurried to follow.

*　　*　　*

Somewhere behind the thick cloud, the sun was slowly climbing up from the horizon. Only a dim natural light seeped through to the clearing, so a few globe lights had been created to illuminate the camp. Most of the magicians were still asleep – only a few early risers had emerged from their tents to relieve those on watch.

The apprentices standing before Dakon looked mainly puzzled or sullen, though more and more were blinking with sudden realisation and looking more enthusiastic.

"Some of you have guessed why I've woken you all up so early," he said. "A few nights ago we decided that your training must not be neglected, but the only practical way for your lessons to continue was for one magician to teach all of you simultaneously. I volunteered to be your first teacher."

He examined each of them, noting which apprentices looked worried, doubtful or eager. The death of Sudin and Aken might have forced everyone to see how dangerous the Sachakan invasion was, but he knew that some magicians still disagreed with and feared the sharing of knowledge.

To reassure the doubters, Dakon had a plan. They all agreed that apprentices ought to be able to defend themselves. So lessons should be all about magical fighting skills, with a heavy emphasis on defence.

He'd thought about it long into the night. He'd imagined lessons rather like games of Kyrima, but there were great differences between real life battles and the way Kyrima was played.

"We're going to start with a game of Kyrima where you are the pieces," he told them. "Before we begin, there are some basic rules that you should all follow. All strikes must be harmless bolts of non-continuous light. Do any of you not know how to do this?" None of the apprentices responded, so Dakon nodded. "We'll consider an apprentice's shield broken if it is struck once, but if he or she hasn't given strength to their magician yet that round, they get two strikes. When your shield is broken you must leave the game. Be honest: what we're trying to do here is learn, not achieve high individual scores.

"One of each side will choose someone to play the magician. A magician may shield, but can only be struck five times plus once for every apprentice he or she manages to take strength from. Magicians can elevate apprentices between rounds. Of course, those playing magician will not have to cut their apprentices, but they do need to touch for at least a count of thirty. If I catch anyone cutting someone or using harmful or painful strikes, they will be excluded from training."

He walked between them, effectively separating them into two near-equally sized groups. "Those to the left of me will form one group; those on the right the other," he continued. "As you play, note the ways in which Kyrima does not reflect real magical battles. We'll come back together and discuss them, and how to deal with them."

Most of the apprentices were smiling now, thinking that their lesson was going to be an easy, fun game. *I hope this doesn't turn out to be pointless, or end up with anyone getting hurt.* He'd never tried setting up a real life game of Kyrima. *But then, I've never taught more than two apprentices at once before. I'll just have to work it out as I go along.*

"Which rules do we follow, Lord Dakon?" Mikken asked.

"Standard." Dakon had considered using no system of rules, but many of them were intended to make the game easier or more interesting to play. Those that weren't could be removed once they'd played a few games and worked out which of the rules weren't practical.

"Are we going to roll dice to decide how strong the magicians are?" Leoran asked.

Dakon shook his head. "Since we're using harmless bolts of light, strength won't matter. We could give each magician a different number of bolts they could use up, but it will be hard to keep count. Still, we might try that later."

"Will you be keeping score?" Tessia asked.

"No scoring." Dakon smiled grimly. "The game ends when one magician's shield has broken."

At that their expressions turned sombre. *They know that means he is "dead". This is good; they will take the game seriously and question rules that don't work.*

He raised his eyebrows, waiting to see if anyone had more questions to pose, but everyone was silent and expectant. "Shall we start? Choose your leader, then."

Even as the two groups separated and began debating who should be their magician they began to point out differences between what they were doing and real life. Apprentices didn't get to choose their masters. Most magicians had one apprentice and, from what they'd been able to discover, the invaders did not have more than four or five slaves on average.

Once the "magicians" had been nominated, one group turned its back so the other could position itself around the camp, then the hidden group were trusted to avert their eyes as their opponents arranged themselves. Dakon noticed that some magicians had emerged from the tents and had stopped to watch.

There was much laughter and cursing as the "battle" unfolded. Dakon noted how vulnerable apprentices were once their strength had been taken. Their best strategy was to hide or keep close to their master, staying behind his shield. One "magician", frustrated at being the only one attacking his opponent, elevated an apprentice to "magician", but chose a friend rather than the apprentice who would have suited the role best.

When the game ended, they all came together to discuss the battle. Aside from a few accusations of dishonesty – apprentices who hadn't sat down after their shield was "broken" – they buzzed with ideas. All agreed that there should be more "magicians" on each side, with no more than two apprentices each, and they should have a limited number of strikes, all decided by the roll of dice. They started another game.

This was dramatically different. Suddenly there were more attackers and more targets. Immediately all had problems with communication and co-ordination. Both sides began to use signals to indicate their intentions, but these were spotted by the opposing side. Having no particular magician in charge led to arguments and the actions of some countering and hampering others.

At one point two "magician" friends tried to co-ordinate their attacks by striking at their opponent simultaneously, and several bolts were wasted because of bad timing.

Suddenly Dakon realised Lord Ardalen was standing at his side.

"There is a trick I should teach you before I leave," he murmured. "Once the game is finished."

Dakon glanced at him in surprise, then nodded. Looking around, he realised that all the magicians were awake and watching now. He began to wish the game would finish quickly so he could avoid their scrutiny, but he forced himself to keep analysing the battle. What could Lord Ardalen know that he was sure Dakon didn't? *He definitely said "you", not "them".*

When one side finally fell, Dakon restrained the temptation to dismiss them straight away. He told them to debate what they had done and learned, and whether the game needed more modifications. Then he turned to Ardalen.

"About that trick," he said.

"Yes," Ardalen replied. "I need two apprentices in order to demonstrate." He looked at the small crowd of eager faces and pointed at Refan and Leoran. "You'll do. I want one of you to strike at that old tree trunk." He patted Refan's shoulder and indicated an enormous broken stump at the edge of the clearing. "Now strike at it – using enough power to produce a visible result."

The air shivered and splinters of wood burst from the side of the trunk.

"Now, Leoran. Put your hand on Refan's shoulder. I want you to send magic to him. Don't form it into heat or force. Just let it seep out as unshaped magic. Refan. See if you can sense and draw in that magic."

Dakon's stomach sank with dismay. This was too much like higher magic. He saw other magicians moving closer, frowning with alarm.

"I feel it but I . . . I can't hold on to it," Refan said.

"No, you won't be able to," Ardalen confirmed. "Because until you learn higher magic you won't be able to store it in yourself. But you can channel it. Take the magic but use none of your own and strike the tree again."

Once again the air shimmered and splinters burst from the tree. Refan gasped. "I used Leoran's magic!"

"Yes," Ardalen said. "When my master was an apprentice, he and a friend couldn't wait to become higher magicians. They tried to teach themselves, and instead of higher magic they discovered this. It is useful if one magician is uniquely skilled, or a task needs a singular, accurate direction of magic, but more strength is needed than one magician can provide – then other magicians can add their own magic to the strike. I can see now that it would be useful in battle for the same reason."

Dakon felt a thrill of excitement. "I've had the apprentices playing magicians count to thirty while they pretend to take an apprentice's power. This eliminates the need for that – oh, my! Our apprentices don't need to be cut at all, do they?"

Ardalen shook his head. "Not in these circumstances, but I suspect magicians will continue the tradition of cutting because it keeps control in their hands. There are disadvantages to losing that control. Without it, the giver must send power exactly when the channeller is ready to take it, or the magic dissipates and is wasted." He paused. "But one great advantage is that, done correctly, a shield made with the magic of two or more magicians will allow the strikes of all of them through rather than react as if struck from the inside by the one not making the shield."

The other magicians had drawn close to hear Ardalen's instructions. All looked thoughtful and no longer suspicious or worried.

"Moving about with an apprentice or magician holding your shoulder could be awkward, too," Narvelan said. "But I can see much potential in this. Two apprentices could protect themselves with a double-strength shield if attacked by an enemy, for example."

Other magicians began discussing ways that they could use Ardalen's method. Dakon looked at the magician and saw the man look across the camp to where servants waited with several horses.

Ardalen sighed. "I wish I could stay to help refine and discuss my master's discovery, but Lord Prinan, Magician Genfel and I must leave now." The others quietened. "I have a pass to retake." He smiled grimly. "Genfel has foreign magicians to woo and Prinan has another pass to protect. And you have Sachakans to hunt. Good luck."

"I suspect you'll need it more than us," Narvelan replied. "Be careful."

"I will."

"And thank you," Dakon added.

Ardalen looked back at Dakon and smiled, then moved away. Farewells were murmured among the apprentices as Mikken, Refan and Genfel's apprentice extracted themselves and followed. Those remaining behind watched silently as the smaller party mounted their horses and rode away.

"Will they be safe?" a small voice whispered at Dakon's side. He looked down to see Tessia frowning anxiously.

"They are heading south to raise their forces and as far as we know the Sachakans are still in the mountains," he told her quietly. "Nobody can say whether they'll be completely safe, but travelling in a group is definitely wiser than alone. What did you think of my lesson?"

Her mouth quirked into a half-smile. "I think I enjoyed Kyrima for the first time. Though I'm not sure 'enjoyed' is the right word. It made sense for once."

Dakon nodded. *Because it reflects the grim reality of war. A shame it took that to make us question how we train our magicians.*

CHAPTER 26

Stara found she was pacing the room again and stopped. She clenched her fists and turned to Vora.

"How long am I going to be cooped up in here? It's been two weeks! The only time I've seen my father was the night he entertained his guests. Why doesn't he come to see me, or grant me a visit?" *Isn't he at all interested in knowing how I am?* she wanted to add. *In spending time with me? In finding out if I felt anything – liking, hate, indifference – for my prospective husband?*

Vora shrugged. "Master Sokara is very busy, from what I have heard among the slaves, mistress. A load of dyes sent to Elyne has disappeared. And the troubles the Ichani are making in Kyralia have lost him some buyers in Elyne too."

Stara stared at the slave woman. "Mother has lost goods and trade? Do you know how bad it is?"

"That is all I heard. Except that your father is trying to make deals here to make up for his loss there."

"*His* loss?" Stara sniffed. "She does all the work in Elyne." She began to pace the room again. "If only he would *talk* to me. Not knowing what is going on is driving me mad!" Stopping, she looked around the room and scowled. "I'm sick of these walls. If I can't see him, I will go out. Is there a market in the city?" She stopped. "Of course there is. Even if I have no coin to spend, I can at least find out what I might buy in future. And I might learn more about the situ-

ation in Elyne." She moved to the chest she knew Vora kept
her capes in, and opened it.

"You can't leave, mistress," Vora said. "Not without his
permission."

"Don't be ridiculous. I'm a grown woman, not a child."
Stara selected the least garish cape and swung it around her
shoulders.

"That is not how things are here," Vora told her. "You
need guards and the protection of a male. I could ask Master
Ikaro if—"

"No." Stara cut her off. "Leave my brother out of this. I'll
take some slaves. And a covered wagon. If anyone asks, we
can tell people my father is in it but doesn't want to speak
to anyone. Or my brother." She knotted the ties of the cape
and started towards the door. Vora hurried after her and she
felt a tug. Cloth bunched up behind her back came loose and
rustled down to her ankles. "Thank you," she murmured to
the woman. "And stop arguing with me. I'm going. We're
going. If something happens I'll just . . ." She paused and
finished silently, *zap them with magic.* "We'll be fine, I promise.
As Elyne traders like to say, all you need in life is confidence,
knowledge and a lot of bluff."

Ten minutes later she and Vora were in a covered wagon
rolling out of the mansion and into the streets of the city,
with four burly slave men as protectors and one as a driver.

"See?" Stara said. "Nobody stopped us."

"This isn't very fair on the slaves," Vora told her disapprovingly. "They will be punished."

"For obeying orders? Surely Father wouldn't be that cruel."

Vora's eyebrows rose, but she said nothing.

Yet disappointment diminished Stara's triumph at getting
out of the mansion without opposition. She would rather her
father had emerged to prevent her, so she could have asked

344

him about trade and her mother. Sighing, she leaned back in the seat of the wagon and watched the high white walls move past.

Is all the city like this? she wondered. *I don't have many memories of Arvice. Maybe I never went out. I can't imagine Mother wanting to be cooped up inside all the time. But I suppose that might have been part of the reason she hated it here. Maybe it wasn't all to do with Father having to be mean to his slaves.*

Maybe he had had to be mean to her, to make her comply with Sachakan ways. Stara felt her stomach sink. If that was so, he would probably be the same to her. And any man he chose to be her husband. She shuddered. *I have to find a way to avoid being married off. And then convince him I can work for him in some way.*

She began to imagine herself finding him new customers at the market. It was highly unlikely, she knew, but the idea kept her entertained as they travelled. Then the scene outside the wagon changed so suddenly that it took her a moment to grasp what she was seeing.

The white walls fell away, and then they were crossing a wide avenue, giving her a view down avenues of perfectly shaped trees and beds of brightly coloured flowers to a grand building. Instantly she recognised the white curved walls and domes of the Imperial Palace from pictures and paintings – and perhaps even a twinge of memory.

There isn't a straight wall in the whole place, she remembered her father saying. *You go around and round and it's easy to get lost – which is the point. Anybody trying to invade would be utterly confused. The walls are very thick, but I've heard they're hollow and defenders can unplug holes and attack intruders from inside.*

Just as abruptly, the wagon reached the opposite road and the view of the palace was replaced by boring high walls again. Stara closed her eyes and held on to the memory of the palace for a moment, and the feeling of love and connection with her father. It faded slowly and was replaced by anxiety and sadness.

Perhaps if I had lived with him all my life things would be different. But then I wouldn't have known my mother. Or enjoyed so many freedoms. Or learned magic.

The wagon turned and slowed to a stop, and as it did, muffled through the cloth walls of the canopy came the sound of voices mixed with the twitter and snort of animals combined with the clang and creak of metal and wood. Stara looked at Vora.

"The market?"

Vora nodded. "You should take two slaves, mistress."

Wrinkles of worry and a shadow of fear in Vora's eyes made her look even older than her years, Stara saw. "Should we go at all?" she asked.

The woman's lips pressed together and her eyes flashed with annoyance and perhaps a little defiance. "Go back now, mistress? That would be a waste of a trip."

Stara smiled and called out to the guards to open the flap.

Emerging, she saw that the market was surrounded by yet another high white wall. The entrance was a plain archway. Guards stood on either side, but their expressions were of boredom and they ignored Stara, Vora and the two slave guards passing through into the noise and bustle inside.

At once Stara noticed that there were other women there. Wearing capes, as she was, they were each accompanied by a man, though she saw one chaperon who was so young she'd have called him a boy if it weren't for the spotty skin on his forehead. Reassured, she strolled slowly up and down the rows of permanent stalls, looking at the wares and the prices, and often seeing women and children huddled or working in the dim rear of each stall.

There were traders of many races here. Dark-skinned Lonmar in their drab clothes selling dried fruit and spices. Pale, tall Lans covered in skin drawings offering up all manner of things made of carved bone. Squat brown Vindo were most frequently seen, selling a range of wares from all around the region. A few Elynes were selling wines and the bitter drink Stara had gained a taste for, sumi.

There were no Kyralians, she noted. A few grey-skinned men wearing only short skirts of cloth were selling gemstones.

"Who are they?" she asked Vora.

"Duna," Vora replied. "Tribesmen from the ash desert in the north."

As she walked around the market, examining goods and fending off sellers with a polite smile and a shake of her head, she listened to the talk, moving closer if she saw two traders in conversation. She caught half-hearted curses aimed at the Ichani who were disrupting trade with Kyralia. Some enthused about the opportunities that would come once Kyralia was conquered. Others worried that the Ichani would then turn on the emperor and throw Sachaka into a war with itself.

Stara thought about the opinions of her father's guests. They had argued that Sachaka had been heading for an internal battle already.

Trust my luck to end up in Sachaka at the wrong time.

As she and Vora turned a corner she saw a man glance at them, then give Vora a second look. His gaze immediately moved back to Stara and he smiled. She gave him a polite but distant nod, lowered her eyes and continued past.

She was amused to find her heart was beating a little faster, and not because she felt threatened. *What a handsome man! Really, if father chose him as a husband for me I'd have a hard time refusing.*

After a moment she glanced over her shoulder. Vora tugged

on her arm, but not before Stara saw that the man was still watching her.

"Stop it!" the woman muttered. "He'll take it as an invitation."

"An invitation for what?" Stara asked. Was there any way a woman could have a lover here in Sachaka? Probably not after marriage, but she wasn't married yet . . .

"To talk to you," Vora hissed. She pulled Stara round the next corner.

"Just talk? What's wrong with that?"

Vora gave a short sigh of exasperation, her gaze flicking about at all the people. "I can't tell you here, mistress. Until you learn who it is safe to talk to, you shouldn't speak to anyone. You may end up conversing with one of your father's enemies, or offending one of his allies."

"How am I going to learn who it is safe to talk to, when I never meet anybody?"

"I will tell you the names and families." Vora frowned and glanced over her shoulder. As she did so, the handsome man stepped out of a stall a few steps ahead of them. He turned and smiled as he saw Stara again. "There is much for you to learn. We will get to—"

"Forgive me, but would you be the daughter of Ashaki Sokara?"

Stara smiled and nodded. "I am."

"Then I am honoured to meet you," the man said. "I am Ashaki Kachiro. My house is next to yours, on the southern side."

"Oh, you are our neighbour, then." She glanced at Vora, who was keeping her eyes to the ground. "I am Stara – and honoured to meet you, too, Ashaki Kachiro."

"I see you have not bought anything," Kachiro said. "Does nothing here please you?"

"I am merely looking to see what is available. It is interesting to note the products that are hard to find in Capia but plentiful here, and the opposite, as well as the differences in prices." As she stepped up to a stall he moved aside to let her past, then fell into step beside her. She was amused to find herself flattered by this. *I'm getting more attention from him these last few moments than I've had from my father since arriving.* "Clearly some wares are too prone to spoiling to be a viable market item, but there are some trinkets here I think would sell well in Capia."

"You have an interest in trade, then?"

"Yes. My mother taught me to help her with the Elyne end of Father's trade."

She was sure that did not give away too much. She had kept her and her mother's involvement vague. If Sachakan men did not like dealing with women, saying that her mother ran part of her father's business might humiliate him and turn customers off.

"Can I ask which trinkets you believe would sell?"

She smiled. "You can ask, but I would be a fool to answer."

He chuckled. "I can tell you are no fool."

Feeling a tug on her arm, she sobered. To completely ignore Vora's warnings would be foolish, too.

"It is lovely to meet you, Ashaki Kachiro; but I must return home now. I hope we will meet again in future."

He nodded, looking thoughtful. As she began to turn away, he took a small step towards her.

"I, too, am about to leave. Since we are neighbours . . . I invite you to return with me, in my wagon. It is safer for a woman to travel with company – even in the city – and I would hate to see you come to harm."

Stara hesitated. Was it safer to refuse or accept? Would it be rude to turn him down? The chat had been nice, but she wasn't so susceptible to a good-looking and charming man that she'd jump into his wagon at the first invitation. She glanced at Vora. To her surprise, the woman looked undecided. Then Vora gave a small nod followed by a warning look. Stara turned back to Kachiro.

"May my slave travel with me?"

"Of course. And I am sure you will want your wagon to follow."

"Then I accept, Ashaki Kachiro."

The conversation remained reassuringly comfortable as they strolled out of the market, gave their orders and then settled into his wagon. He was flatteringly interested in her life in Elyne and appeared impressed by her knowledge of trade, and wasn't coy about his own life and business. She had learned a little about yellowseed crops and the uses for the oil by the time they arrived at the door to her father's mansion.

He stopped there, however, and politely escorted her and Vora to their wagon before continuing on to his own house. As the slaves drove them through the gates Stara gave Vora a questioning look.

"So. Why didn't he come inside?"

Vora's brow was wrinkled, but she looked only a little worried. "Ashaki Sokara doesn't like him much, mistress. I don't know why. He's not an enemy or an ally." Her lips thinned. "Expect him to be displeased, though."

"What's he likely to do? Stop me leaving again?"

"Probably, but he would have anyway."

Stara considered that, and how she might convince her father otherwise, as they climbed out and entered the mansion. Had she learned anything from Kachiro that might be of interest to him? She didn't think so. Unless he needed to know about yellowseed.

As they neared her rooms she found she was pleasantly tired and looking forward to relaxing for the afternoon.

"That was just what I needed," she told Vora. "A change of surroundings, some fresh air, and—" She stopped as she realised someone was standing in her room. Her father. His face was dark with anger.

"*Where have you been?*"

She paused before answering, registering the fury in his voice but catching herself before she could flinch. *I am a twenty-five-year-old woman, not a child*, she reminded herself.

"To the market, Father," she told him. "But there's no need to fuss. I didn't buy anything."

He looked at Vora. "Leave us now. Stara, you should have sought my permission."

"I'm not a child now, Father," Stara reminded him gently as Vora backed away. "I don't need anyone holding my hand."

"You are a woman," he snapped. "And this is Sachaka."

"Nobody bothered me," she reassured him. "I took slaves—"

"Who could not have done anything to protect you," he interrupted. "You forget: most free men are magicians here."

"And lawless savages?" she asked. "Surely there are laws against harming others here. If not, wouldn't the fear of retaliation from family deter criminals?"

He stared at her. "Is it true what the slaves tell me: that you let Ashaki Kachiro bring you home?" he asked softly.

She blinked at the change of topic. "Yes."

"You should not have done that."

She considered all the excuses she could give: that Kachiro had wanted to protect her, or that she hadn't known whether it was correct to refuse or accept, or that the man was their neighbour, or that Vora hadn't told her not to. Instead she decided to let him reveal what her best defence was by telling her what concerned him most about Kachiro. "Why not?"

He crossed the room to stand in front of her. Strangely, his gaze focused above her eyes, as if he was looking inside her head.

"What did you tell him?"

She shrugged. "A little bit about my life in Elyne. That Mother and I helped with your trade – but not that Mother was in charge. That there were products at the market that would sell well in Elyne, but not which products. That . . . you're not even listening, are you?" His gaze was still fixed on her forehead. She shook her head and sighed. "I find a possible source of profit but you're not even listening."

"I have to know what you told him," he said, more to himself than to her. He reached out and took her head between his hands.

"Father," she said, trying to pull his hands away, but his grip only tightened. "Ow! Father—"

Suddenly all her attention was drawn inward and she became conscious of something inside her mind that didn't belong there. A sense of him, laced with suspicion, anxiety and anger. At his direction her memories of the day began to play out – every bit of her frustration at his absence, every shred of her worry for her mother, all the information she had gathered at the market, all of Vora's advice and futile warnings, and, finally, every word between her and Kachiro. Even her attraction to the man.

He's reading my mind! I can't believe he'd do that. Without even asking me if I would let him. Would I, if he asked? Of course not! He's my father. He's supposed to trust me. All I did was talk to his neighbour. I don't deserve to be treated like this!

He delved deeper, seeking more personal information. Had she ever bedded a man? Had she ever been with child? How had she prevented it? Information that was private, that he had no business seeking.

She knew at that moment that she would never trust him again. Love shrivelled and was replaced by hate. Respect died in the face of a burning, raging anger. The bond of loyalty that she'd felt all her life, tested again so recently, broke.

He must have seen it. Felt it. But she sensed no shame or apology. Instead he kept looking, looking, and she knew she had to make him stop. *I have to get him out of my mind NOW!*

She reached for magic. He recoiled as he realised what she was doing, letting slip both his control of her mind and his grip on her head. She backed away, and as he reached out to grab her again she knocked his hands back with a slap of power.

He stared at her, his gaze calculating. She felt a rush of fear as she realised he was deciding whether to try again, this time with magic. It would go badly for her, she knew. He was a fully trained higher magician. She had learned magic as opportunity presented itself, and did not know how to draw power from others, let alone have a reserve of stored strength.

The fire in his eyes faded. She hoped that meant he had decided not to pursue her thoughts and memories again. Perhaps he hadn't seen enough to know the extent of her abilities . . .

"Your mother should have told me you had learned magic," he said, his voice laced with disgust and a hint of threat.

"She doesn't know."

"Why didn't you tell me?"

"I was waiting for the right moment."

His expression didn't soften.

"You have made yourself next to valueless as a wife and a daughter," he told her. His face set in a cold, hard expression and, not looking at her, he strode past her towards the door.

"I learned it for you," she told him. He paused in the

doorway. "Like everything else. Always for you. I thought it would allow me to help you in the trade."

Without turning, or speaking, he strode away.

The silence that he left her in was empty and full of hurt. She felt a loss, deep inside. But at the same time she felt a hard, cold anger growing to fill the void. *How dare he! His own daughter! Did he ever love me at all?*

She felt tears fill her eyes, ran to the bed and threw herself on it. But the sobs she expected didn't come. Instead she hammered the pillows in frustration and anger, remembering his words: *"You have made yourself next to valueless as a wife and a daughter."* She turned onto her back and stared up at the ceiling. Marrying her off for profit was all that he cared about. *In that case, I've just delivered the best revenge I could have managed in this stupid country.* She didn't care if nobody wanted to marry her.

But that was not true. She did dream of finding the right man, who would appreciate her talents and tolerate her flaws. Just as any woman did.

And if she did not marry, she might be stuck here – locked up in her rooms – for the rest of her life.

Footsteps echoed in the room. She lifted her head and found Vora approaching. The woman's expression was calm, but Stara caught hints of both anxiety and concern before the woman prostrated herself. *I'm beginning to read her better*, she thought. She dropped her head back to the bed.

"Ah, Vora. I have just experienced the joy of learning I am not just a chattel, but a *useless* chattel."

The bed shifted slightly as Vora sat on the edge of it. "What is useless to one person can be precious to another, mistress."

"Is that your way of telling me a husband might turn out to be more loving than my father? It wouldn't be difficult."

"Not exactly, though I wouldn't object to your taking it that way." Vora sighed. "So. You have magic."

Stara sat up and considered the old slave. "Listening in, were you?"

Vora smiled faintly. "As always, only for your benefit, mistress."

"So you heard what he said. Why does having magic make a Sachakan woman useless as a wife?"

Vora shrugged. "Men aren't supposed to like powerful women. The truth is, not all of them are like that. But they must appear not to, in order to gain respect. Remember what I said: we are all slaves."

Stara nodded. "If I am useless to him . . . I guess I can't hope that he'll let me help in the trade now. Do you think he'll send me back to Elyne?"

There was a flicker of something in Vora's eyes. Surely not dismay. "Perhaps. It is too dangerous to do so now, with the border closed and the Ichani doing as they please. He might merely reconsider who to marry you to. Hopefully not someone who likes to break a woman's spirit – just someone who fancies having such a beautiful wife enough to overlook the annoyance of a bit of magical resistance."

Stara winced and looked away. "Can't it be someone I wouldn't want to resist?"

"Do you think you can mend things with your father?"

His own daughter . . . Stara felt anger stir inside again. "Maybe on the surface."

"Do . . . do you know how to kill a man while bedding him?"

For a moment Stara could not believe what Vora had just asked. Then she turned to stare at the woman. Vora searched Stara's eyes, then nodded.

"I guess not. I believe it is a skill linked to higher magic."

Vora rose and moved towards the door. "I will have some food and wine brought in."

As the slave's footsteps faded, Stara considered what the woman had asked her. *So it's possible to kill someone that way. Trouble is, to do so you'd have to allow yourself to be bedded by someone you hated so much you wanted to kill them. But I guess if someone forced themself on you, you might want to kill them that much.*

She cursed Vora silently. The trouble was, once Stara knew something was possible with magic, she itched to know how to do it. And considering the situation she was in, she had more than just curiosity to fuel her desire to learn this particular skill.

But who was going to teach her?

Tessia yawned. For the last week the apprentices' day had begun early, with a lesson from one or more of the magicians. Usually the lesson began with one teacher, but often the other magicians would emerge from their tents to watch and comment, and this sometimes led to one of them taking over to contribute something that enhanced the original teacher's lesson, or, in one case, starting an argument.

". . . some way of continuing after we deal with the invaders," a voice said. Tessia resisted the temptation to turn and look at the magicians riding behind her in case it alerted them to the fact that she could hear them.

"I doubt it. Nobody co-operated to this extent before and I expect we'll revert to our old suspicions and secretiveness again after."

"But it is so much more efficient. *I've* learned new skills. I never realised there were such gaps in my knowledge."

"Or mine." There was a wistful sigh. "If there was a way to sustain . . ."

"We will have to find a way. The healers have their guild. I've heard it suggested we should start our own, so . . ."

As the voices faded Tessia looked at Jayan to see if he'd heard. He was smiling, his eyes bright.

"Do you think one of the apprentices passed on your idea to their master?" she asked.

He looked at her and his shoulders straightened. "Maybe."

Tessia shrugged. "Perhaps the magicians came to the same conclusion by themselves. They were bound to eventually."

He frowned at her reproachfully. "Do you think so?"

She smiled. "It would be too much of a coincidence, wouldn't it?"

"Yes," he said firmly. "Besides, they haven't had the time to think it through."

A few nights before, Jayan had told her of his ideas for a guild of magicians, where knowledge was shared and apprentices were taught by all magicians, not only their masters. They would have badges to identify them as members of the guild in the same way that members of the healers' guild did, to assure customers that they had been well trained.

His plans had included separating members of the guild into two or three groups and encouraging competition between them in order to spur on invention and the development of skills. She'd pointed out it might also cause division and conflict and suggested a tiered system for the apprentices based on skill and knowledge levels. Perhaps one for each year of learning. Jayan then decided that those on the same level could compete individually or in teams.

She had suggested that magicians might concentrate on one type of skill in order to explore and develop it further. Some might study fighting and defence, others construction techniques for bridges and buildings. She could see potential in the latter for ensuring all constructions in the country were safe, by encouraging magicians to oversee their creation.

Other apprentices had come to join them then, and she'd felt vaguely disappointed. It had been the first extended conversation she'd had with Jayan that she'd truly enjoyed, in which they'd agreed with each other and shared a mutual excitement. When he'd told the other apprentices about his idea she'd been taken aback, though she was not sure why.

I don't think it was because he put it forward as entirely his idea, she thought. *Or that it went from being something just between us that he suddenly shared with everyone else. No, it was more a feeling of worry than annoyance. Worry that if he told people about it too early, before it was fully developed, they would forget who came up with it in the first place.*

Ahead, the forest receded from the edges of the road and they rode into a small valley divided into fields. The state of the crops dismayed Tessia. Some fields had been left unharvested; others were covered in patches of weeds, having never been planted or maintained. Many of the crops were dry and brown, dead for lack of irrigation. The frustrating side to this wastage was that the Sachakans had never ventured this far south. The people had fled for no reason.

The magicians had abandoned their pursuit of the Sachakans for now, and were returning to the lowlands to meet re-inforcements sent by the king. Tessia was looking forward to sleeping on a real bed again, and eating better food. Above all she was looking forward to not having fear constantly nagging at her. She could relax, knowing that they wouldn't have to worry about being attacked by Sachakans at any moment.

Seeing dark shapes in the field ahead, Tessia grimaced. They had encountered animals dead or dying of starvation or thirst throughout their travels. She heard curses from the magicians and apprentices and silently added her own.

Then she realised that the leaders were urging their horses forward. She felt her stomach sink. None of them would be hurrying to investigate dead animals. As she reconsidered the dark shapes she began to make out human forms.

"How long ago, do you think?" she heard Werrin ask Dakon.

"Not long. A day at the most." Dakon looked around and his gaze settled on her. His face held a grim question. Suppressing a sigh, she directed her horse to move alongside his and looked down at the first corpse, forcing herself to notice only the colour of the skin and condition of the flesh.

"More than half a day," she said.

"These people aren't dressed in clothes warm enough for the night," Narvelan said. He had moved into the field and was riding back and forth, glancing from side to side. He came back to the road and turned his horse full circle. "Nor are some of them wearing shoes good enough for walking long distances. I think they had carts with them, probably stolen. There are trails of crushed curren moving out in all directions from this point. They must have seen their attackers and scattered."

"More than one attacker?" Werrin asked.

"Have to be. They've all been killed with higher magic. One attacker would have to gather them together in order to kill them one at a time. This looks like at least four or five."

"If these people scattered, then someone might have got away," Werrin said. "We should follow all the trails and see if any don't end with a corpse."

Apprentices and magicians looked at each other in silent dismay, then each magician chose a trail and, with apprentices following, began to ride along it. As corpses were discovered calls of "found it" were heard. Dakon continued on towards a line of trees. Tessia heard the sound of running water and realised they were heading towards a stream.

Just before it they found the trail's maker. He lay face down over a log. He turned his head to the side and stared up at them, eyes full of terror and pain. His breath came in short, painful gasps.

"He's alive!" Jayan exclaimed.

Together they leapt to the ground and approached the man. Dakon spoke reassuringly, dropping to his haunches. Slowly the fear in the man's face changed to hope.

"What happened here?"

"Told to leave," the man whispered. "Magicians. Sachakans. On road." He paused, the effort of talking clearly painful. "They . . . Elia. She told me . . . keep run . . . then . . . hit . . ."

Tessia gently examined him. "What hurts?"

"Back," he gasped. "Front. Everything."

She gently felt around his body. His ribs had broken in several places, some by an impact from behind and some from landing on the log, she guessed.

"Let's get you off that," Tessia said. She surrounded him with magic and eased him back off the log and onto his back. He groaned loudly, eyes wide and breathing fast. *At least there's no sign of the ribs piercing his lungs. He's a very lucky man.*

"Can you fix him?" Jayan asked. Tessia frowned at him, then was saved from having to choose between lying or voicing her doubts in front of the man by Dakon.

"Did you see which way they went afterwards?"

"Te . . . Tecurren."

Dakon straightened, his face creased with worry. "I should tell the others." He looked around. "It is not safe for you to stay here, if one stayed behind."

"I doubt any would, if they were headed for Tecurren," Jayan said. "They haven't targeted anything that big or far from the mountains since Mandryn. If any of them are about they won't risk drawing the attention of eight magicians."

Dakon looked from Jayan to Tessia, then nodded. "You won't have long. Werrin will want to get to Tecurren quickly."

"I won't take long," Tessia assured him.

As Dakon strode away, Jayan stood up. "I'll get your bag."

"Thanks," she said. As he hurried to her horse she turned her attention to the injured man. He stared back at her. Normally she would have known there was no way she could save him in the time she had. Most of the patients her father had treated for broken ribs had still died, despite being treated sooner and for less severe wounds.

But she had magic. Using it, she didn't have to cut him open. She could move bone and cinch pulse paths. Placing her hands on his chest, she closed her eyes and concentrated on the flesh beneath the skin.

At once she knew that the damage had been worse than she had first realised. Most of his ribs had been shattered. Though the bones hadn't pierced the lungs, they'd torn through pulse paths and damaged other organs. Drawing magic, she reached inside and tried to squeeze shut one of the ruptured pulse paths.

The man gasped in agony. Drawing away, she considered him again. What she had to do was going to be extremely painful. Footsteps behind her drew her attention. She sighed with relief as Jayan threw himself down beside her, her father's bag rattling as it hit the ground.

"Careful with that," she said. Opening it, she drew out her strongest cure for deadening pain. To her surprise, Jayan took the bottle from her.

"I can do the mixing," he said. "Just tell me how much."

He followed her instructions carefully while she cut away the man's clothes, then they gave him the dose and watched impatiently as it took effect. Tessia placed her hands on his chest again.

Drawing magic, she pinched broken pulse paths and shifted broken bones back into place. But even as she worked she knew it wasn't enough. There was already too much blood pooling inside him and too little in his pulse paths. Flesh that had been cut could not be held together by magic long enough to heal. *If only I could make the flesh heal faster*, she thought.

Even as she removed blood from within him to give room to his organs, she knew that too much had been lost. Then a shock went through the man's body. She felt the rhythms essential to life become irregular, then fail.

When Dakon's call interrupted her thoughts, she was not sure how long she had been staring at the dead man, trying to think how she could have saved him. *There must be a way.*

"Come on, Tessia," Jayan said, his voice uncharacteristically gentle. "We have to go. You gave it your best try." He looked down. "Better wash your hands first, though."

She looked down at her bloodied hands and nodded. Moving to the stream, she squatted and let the water rinse her clean. Jayan picked up her father's bag and waited for her.

Then she gave the dead man a last thoughtful, sorrowful look and headed across the field to join the magicians.

CHAPTER 27

Eight magicians and eight apprentices waited at the edge of the forest, silently looking at the cluster of houses several strides away. The village was quiet. None of the buildings bore any sign of damage. It was a scene of deceptive peace that might have proved a fatal trap to any visitor or passing traveller.

Would it have been the same had Takado intended to stay and occupy Mandryn? Dakon wondered. *Did he kill my people and destroy my home only to make a point, and was that point directed only at me or to prove he could do what he did?*

A family who had managed to hide from the Sachakans, then slip away during the early hours of the morning, had told the magicians what had happened in Tecurren. The tale they'd related, taking it in turns to pick up the story whenever the one speaking faltered, had brought back the horror and anger Dakon had felt when he'd learned what had happened to his own people. With the horror and anger came guilt and frustration that he could not have done anything to prevent it. And the knowledge, which brought no comfort, that he, Jayan and Tessia would have been tortured and killed along with everybody else if they hadn't been absent.

None of the four Sachakans who had taken possession of Tecurren matched Takado's description, however. Their leader was the most vicious of all, tormenting his victims after taking their power and then dismembering them.

363

Sounds familiar, Dakon thought darkly, *though we can't assume there is only one Sachakan with that habit.*

The young women, according to the escapees, had been taken away together into the largest house, owned by the now deceased town master. The rest of the villagers still alive had been locked up in a small hall used for social gatherings, probably in order to be drained of power each day. Scouts sent ahead to investigate had seen glimpses of figures in the main house, but couldn't get close enough to confirm if the hall was occupied. But they did report no sign of villagers elsewhere, though the Sachakans' slaves were keeping watch or raiding houses for food or drink.

Werrin looked from left to right, nodding to indicate that the magicians should take up their positions. They split into two groups. Separating into smaller, weaker forces had been a risk, but not a great one. They weren't going to be out of sight of each other for long, and never out of earshot.

"We are eight and they are four," Werrin had said the previous night, in summing up the situation. "The numbers are in our favour. We do not know their strength, however, so we must be ready to retreat at any moment."

They had anticipated three responses from the Sachakans: that they might flee in the face of a larger enemy, that they would scatter and try to ambush the rescuers, or that they might stand together and confront the Kyralians directly. The idea of splitting into two groups had first been suggested to prevent the first possibility. Nobody wanted the Sachakans to escape.

I fear nobody wants them to live, either.

Dakon wasn't sure how he felt about that. But he had to agree with Werrin. Until the pass was in Kyralian control again, any Sachakan they caught would have to be kept prisoner, which would be dangerous and take attention and resources they couldn't spare.

As Narvelan led his group out of the forest and angled towards the town, Dakon realised his heart was racing. Yet he wasn't as frightened as he expected. Instead he felt a cautious eagerness. *We've been chasing them too long. It is good to be able to take action at last. But I hope we don't make mistakes out of pent-up frustration.*

They neared the first house. No sign of life. Not even a patrol of slaves. All was quiet. Moving into the shadows between two houses, Dakon thought he heard the faintest sound of screaming, but it was hard to be sure. *Probably my imagination.*

A man stepped around the end of the building.

For a moment everyone stood frozen. The stranger was wearing nothing but a pair of dirty trousers, Dakon saw. *A slave.*

Then the man gasped and buckled in the middle, the force that struck him tossing him back out into the main road. Dakon looked at Narvelan and the other magicians. All but Bolvin were doing the same. The tall magician shrugged. "He surprised me."

A shout came from further down the road.

"Have they seen Werrin's group?" Narvelan murmured, peering round the corner of the house. "I think they have. Now we'll see if they flee or fight."

Magicians and apprentices waited. More shouts came from within the village. The distant sound of screaming stopped and Dakon's stomach turned over. He hadn't been imagining it.

Then a booming sound rang out and Dakon's heart skipped a beat.

"The signal," Tarrakin breathed. "They're coming out together to confront us."

Then another boom, doubled to indicate ambush, came. "Are all four of them there?" Dakon asked Narvelan, who was still peering around the corner.

"No. Just three. One could be doing what we're doing, hoping to sneak up and surprise our opponents."

Somehow calling the Sachakans "opponents", as if they were mere game pieces, sounded foolish and inappropriate. Narvelan backed away from the corner.

"Werrin's ready to come out. We need to get behind the main three. But we'll have to keep a look out for the missing fourth one."

A lot of skulking and dashing between buildings followed until they were behind the line of Sachakan magicians advancing down the street.

"Come out and face us, cowards!" one of the Sachakans called. "We know you're here."

Dakon felt his heart jump as a strike shot out from behind a building and stopped abruptly an arm's length from the lead Sachakan. The man's shield flashed, revealing that it encompassed only him.

"Shielding only themselves," Narvelan muttered.

"Werrin's out!" Tarrakin exclaimed.

Sure enough, the other group of Kyralians had emerged. They spread out across the road, as if barring the way, and began advancing, magicians in front and apprentices following close behind. The Sachakans threw strikes, but the Kyralians' shields held. The air sizzled as both sides exchanged bolts of power.

A confrontation like this ought to be a simple matter of one side running out of power faster than the other, Dakon knew. It only occurred when both sides were confident of their superior strength, or underestimated that of the enemy. But usually there was some other trickery at work. Like

Narvelan's group waiting for the right moment. Or some new use of magic.

"They look distracted enough," Narvelan said, glancing back at them. "It's time."

As planned, Dakon and the other magicians crowded behind Narvelan and placed their hands on his shoulders. Dakon readied himself to draw power and send it out at Narvelan's instruction.

The sound of footsteps came from somewhere close by. Dakon heard Tessia's indrawn breath and Jayan's curse. He looked round to see a man standing in the gap between the houses, staring at them in surprise. A Sachakan. Who was not dressed like a slave.

"Now!" Narvelan snapped.

Not knowing if Narvelan had registered the Sachakan, Dakon drew power and sent it through his arm anyway. Heat rushed past his face towards the Sachakan, and he flinched. The Sachakan's shield held for a moment, then crumpled inward. His face, blackening, stretched as he tried to scream, but the heat of firestrike must have burned away his voice instantly.

As the man fell to the ground Narvelan muttered a wordless exclamation. "I didn't think it would work *that* well!"

"For a moment I was worried you hadn't seen him," Jayan muttered.

"Only at the last moment. I figured we'd better deal with him first." Narvelan looked out at the battle still raging in the street. "Well then. Time to show the rest of them what we can do now."

As they all crowded close again, Dakon felt a tiny twinge of anxiety. *I can't help wondering how much power I'm using. How long will what I've gathered last? How long will it take to replace it? I guess that's the great uncertainty of magical warfare.* He felt his resolve harden. *But I'd rather end up as depleted as an apprentice than risk letting these bastards continue harming Kyralians.*

"Now!" Narvelan said again. Power flowed and the faintest shimmer in the air betrayed the path of his strike. It pounded the shield of the closest Sachakan. The man gave a yelp and staggered forward, then froze with his arms raised and face taut with effort.

"More!" Narvelan cried. Dakon closed his eyes and increased the flow of magic from himself to his friend.

He heard a shout of anger from the road, then a triumphant laugh from Bolvin. "That did it!"

"Now the last one," Narvelan muttered.

Last one? Dakon opened his eyes and looked out. Two Sachakans lay still, a curl of smoke rising from one, in the road. The leader now faced Narvelan, his face twisted in fury – *or is that fear?* – and began striding towards their hiding place.

"Let's show ourselves," Tarrakin said.

"Tempting," Narvelan said. "But we don't want anybody seeing us using Ardalen's method unless we have to. Not even a slave. Quickly now. Let's finish him off."

Dakon pressed his hand on Narvelan's shoulder and gathered more power.

"Now!"

The strike halted the Sachakan, but did not overcome his shield. He attacked in return and Narvelan flinched under the strike. The enemy's strike was bright, revealing the huddle of Kyralians in the building's shadows.

"Keep sending power," Narvelan said between clenched teeth. "Need it for defence too, remember." Narvelan's shield flared outward as it abruptly strengthened. He gave a little gasp of relief.

"He's getting nervous," Jayan said.

Sure enough, the last Sachakan was glancing from Narvelan's group to Werrin's. He started to back away from them both.

"Let's give him one last blast," Narvelan said. "Before he can get away from us."

Dakon wondered how his friend could stand under the pressure of hands. He drew power. Narvelan spoke. Power flowed out. At the same time a strike came from Werrin's direction. The Sachakan gave a crazed scream of anger as he staggered backwards.

Then he flew through the air in a spray of blood, twisting and then landing with a crunch. And was still.

Dakon's ears rang with whoops of triumph. Magicians and apprentices pushed him out into the street in their eagerness to have a closer look at their fallen enemies. Narvelan was grinning as he strode forward to meet Werrin. The two grasped arms in formal greeting. Dakon did not hear what they said to each other. He was aware of figures further down the street darting out of houses and racing away.

Slaves. To his relief, nobody tried to strike them or prevent them leaving. He noticed Tessia peering down at the Sachakan leader's body, her expression a mixture of fascination and revulsion. She looked up at Dakon as he moved to her side.

"Magic causes unique and terrible wounds," she said.

He looked at the corpse. The man's body had been crushed and distorted by the two forces hitting him from two different directions.

"He would have died instantly." She looked back down the street. "Better than what he did to others. I may need my father's bag."

369

"Shall I signal to the servants?" Jayan asked, looking at Dakon.

Dakon felt the elation of victory drain way. For a moment he wondered how Tessia could be so cool and practical. *She learned it from her father. He didn't let emotion cloud his judgement. But he never needed his skill as much as Tessia has lately.*

"Yes – but check with Lord Werrin first."

Jayan nodded and hurried away. Tessia barely noticed, her attention on the small hall down the street. Dakon smiled crookedly. She would seek out the Sachakans' victims alone if he didn't go with her. He gestured for her to follow, and set out to find and free the survivors of Tecurren.

At dusk Dachido's group arrived at Takado's camp. The magician had been the first one Takado had suggested choose some allies and travel separately. Hanara believed that his master had done so because he trusted Dachido, whereas Dovaka had decided to do so himself. Takado had raised no protest. He seemed almost encouraging. Hanara knew better, and worried what the mad Ichani might do on his own. But he was glad to be spending less time in the man's company.

As the camp swelled, Hanara realised that Dachido's group had grown. He looked around, counting, and found it was now three times the size it had been last time Takado and Dachido had met. The newcomers included a woman, he noticed. She approached with Dachido as Takado rose to greet his ally.

"I see you've gathered some new friends, Dachido," Takado said, then turned to the woman and smiled. "Asara. It has been a long time since we last met."

Her smile was faint. "Indeed. Too long. If I'd known about your plans I might have paid you a visit earlier."

"To support me or try to talk me out of them?"

"Probably to try to talk sense into you. But that was when I thought Emperor Vochira a strong man."

Takado's eyebrows rose. "And you no longer do?"

"No." Her dark eyes flashed. "He sent me here to deal with you."

They gazed at each other, both smiling knowingly. Then Takado chuckled. "Who was he trying to insult, me or you?"

"You doubt I could do it?"

His smile widened. "Of course not. But does he?"

She made a dismissive gesture. "It doesn't matter," she said. "I came here to join you, not drag you back to the Imperial Palace."

"And your companions?"

"Agree with and follow me."

He nodded. Hanara felt a prickling sensation run down his back. *She's just told him plainly that her people will only follow him if she does.* He chewed his lip thoughtfully. *He'll probably have her group travel separately, too. That will mean of the four groups, he has two not truly in his control. Though Asara is probably smarter and more sensible than Dovaka.* He sniffed quietly. *That wouldn't be difficult.*

Dachido and Asara joined Takado at the campfire, and the rest of the magicians followed. They set the slaves to the chores of setting up camp and bringing out food and drink. As Hanara worked he caught snatches of conversation. First Asara asked about Takado's progress — was it true he had destroyed a village? Why hadn't he kept it? What was the advantage in splitting into smaller groups?

Then he heard her ask Takado what his next move would be. He smiled broadly, clearly pleased but also amused.

"I am not quite ready to decide."

The next time Hanara returned to the fire they were

371

discussing confusing and convoluted stories about crumbling and new alliances, mysterious favours and oblique references to unexplained murders.

"The emperor may never forgive me for this," she said, shrugging. "But at least when I turned disloyal I didn't try to kill him, as others have."

"Surely you know that won't stop him having you killed?"

"Of course. But I do suspect he sent me here hoping I'd fail. I figure, if he didn't mind that, then he doesn't mind me remaining here with you and helping you retake Kyralia."

Takado looked thoughtful. He opened his mouth to reply, but a call from within the forest stalled him. All rose as the call came again, from closer. Then a slave staggered out of the trees and threw herself at Takado's feet.

"Dead," she gasped. "They're all dead!"

"Who?" Takado snapped.

"Dovaka, Nagana, Ravora and Sageko. They . . . they took a village and the Kyralians came and killed them."

Dachido muttered a curse. Takado glanced at him, then he looked down at the slave again. "They invaded a village."

"Yes."

"And stayed there. They didn't leave?"

"Yes. No."

"And the Kyralians took exception to this. How unfriendly of them."

"They killed Dovaka." The slave began to sob. "My master is dead."

"Go." Takado nudged her with his toe. "Get yourself some food and water and rest over by that tree. We will decide what to do with you later."

As she obeyed he turned to Dachido and Asara. To Hanara's surprise, he was smiling broadly.

"*Now* I am ready to make my decision. Tomorrow we will not travel separately. We will move southward together. We will destroy everything, strengthening ourselves as we go. But we will advance slowly so that others may still come through the pass and join us. We will take over Kyralia, piece by piece, magician by magician, until it is all ours."

There was a pause as all the magicians stared at Takado in surprise. Then they gave a cheer and raised their cups in agreement. Asara glanced at Dachido, then shrugged and raised her cup. Dachido did the same, gazing at Takado in thoughtful admiration.

Dovaka is dead! Hanara thought as he rushed to refill Takado's cup. *The madman is dead. Was that Takado's plan all along? Did he only want to get rid of Dovaka? And demonstrate to the rest of these allies why they should take his advice and follow orders? But then, maybe he needed the Kyralians to kill some Sachakans before he could get the full support of his allies. And if some Sachakans had to die then it might as well be the ones he couldn't rely on . . .*

Hanara's mind swirled with wonder. Truly his master was a genius. And while he had just lost four allies, he had gained considerably more.

CHAPTER 28

All night Jayan could not shake the thought that he was sleeping in the bed of a dead man.

Rather than squeeze all the magicians into the master's house, the villagers had found room for them in the unoccupied houses of the village. Jayan had been longing to sleep in a real bed, but when he realised that he, Dakon and Tessia were taking up residence in the home of a family who had died he found he could not relax.

At first he lay awake with memories of the day repeating before his mind's eye. Then sleep came, but was chased away time after time by nightmares.

We won, he thought. *So why am I suddenly having bad dreams?*

It might be the memory of the bodies of the villagers the Sachakans had tortured that was putting his mind in dark places. And the stories the survivors told, and the haunted eyes of the women rescued from the rooms where the enemy had imprisoned them, some of them far too young to have endured such an ordeal.

Or it might also have been the battle itself, frightening and thrilling all at once, that had excited his mind too much for sleep. He kept finding himself analysing everything – every step and choice. But another thought kept creeping in that disturbed him more than he expected.

It was the first time I've killed. Oh, I only contributed some of

374

the power, and did not direct the strike, but I still had a part in the deaths of other people.

It wasn't guilt or regret that bothered him. The Sachakans were invaders. They had killed Kyralians. And after seeing what the Sachakans had done to the villagers, Jayan knew he wouldn't have hesitated to deal the fatal blows himself.

But he couldn't help feeling that something in him had changed, and he wasn't sure if it was a good change. He resented the Sachakans – all the invaders – for causing it to happen. There was no going back, no undoing the change. Ironically, that made him want them gone from Kyralia even more – even if it meant killing again.

When dawn came, Jayan rose, washed himself and his clothes, dried his clothes with magic and put them on again. He waited in the kitchen until Dakon and Tessia emerged from their rooms and joined him. Dakon moved to a cupboard and opened the doors.

"It feels wrong to be eating their food," he said.

Jayan and Tessia exchanged a glance.

"Either someone will eat it or it will go bad," she said.

"And it's not as if we're stealing it from them," Jayan added.

Dakon sighed and brought out some stale bread, salted meat, and sweet preserves. Tessia rose and found plates and cutlery. They ate silently.

She looks exhausted, Jayan noted. Dark marks shadowed the skin under her eyes and her shoulders were slumped. He wished he could cheer her up, or at least see some of the familiar spark of interest in her eyes again. *Even a bit of healing obsession would be better than seeing her all glum and sad.*

"So how did the villagers fare?" he asked her. "Are they well?"

She blinked at him, then shrugged. "Surprisingly few

injuries – mostly the girls. They'll heal, but . . ." She grimaced and shook her head. "Otherwise, the Sachakans killed anyone injured in the attack, and once they decided to torture someone they always finished them off. Eventually."

Jayan nodded. It matched what he'd been told. He felt his stomach turn. *I thought what happened to Sudin and Aken was cruel, but they were treated kindly compared to some of these villagers. Tormented for hours. All out of some distorted idea of fun.*

"Not all Sachakans are so depraved," Dakon said quietly.

Tessia and Jayan looked at him. He smiled tiredly.

"I know it's hard to believe right now, and I admit I'm finding it difficult to make myself remember the fact, but it is true. Unfortunately it's the greedy, ambitious and most violent who are most likely to be attracted to Takado's side. I—"

A knock on the front door of the house interrupted him. Dakon rose and left the kitchen, then returned and beckoned. Jayan and Tessia rose and followed him out into the street, where Narvelan waited.

Two groups had gathered on the other side of the road. One was of magicians and apprentices, the other was a painfully small gathering of villagers. Narvelan gestured for the trio to follow and led them towards the magicians.

"They've offered to give us strength," he told Dakon.

"Hmm," was all Dakon uttered in reply.

"I thought you'd say that."

As Dakon joined the magicians and the debate, Tessia moved close to Jayan.

"It makes sense, and if they're willing to give it why shouldn't we accept?" she asked. "We've just used a lot of power. Taking theirs wouldn't harm them, but it could help us regain some strength." She frowned. "I would advise against taking power from the girls, though. They've gone through enough."

"Aside from the fact we'd be breaking the king's laws, it's not that simple," Jayan told her. "Dakon explained it to me once." He paused, trying to remember his master's words. "He said no good magician is completely comfortable with using higher magic. It's essential to the defence of the country, and enables us to do more than we can with just our own powers, but he said that in the hands of an ambitious or sadistic magician it can be dangerous. Or in the hands of someone desperate to justify its use. He said, 'Self-right-eousness can be as destructive as unscrupulousness.' Yes, I definitely remember those words. Got me thinking. Still does, sometimes."

She turned her head to the side slightly and considered him. "You're a very contradictory man, Jayan."

He blinked and stared at her. "I am?"

"Yes."

He could not think of anything to say to that, so he turned his attention back to the magicians' debate. Then he rolled his eyes. "Here we go again. It could be days before the villagers get an answer. Weeks even. Perhaps we should warn the villagers not to wait, or they might starve."

"Perhaps their offer won't be necessary," Tessia said quietly.

He realised she had turned away, and that some of the other apprentices were staring in the same direction. He followed their gaze and saw that a group of men on horse-back were riding into the village. The magicians' voices faltered and faded.

"Reinforcements?" someone asked.

"That's Lord Ardalen. This must be the group headed for the pass," another muttered.

"That's Lord Everran — and Lady Avaria!" Tessia exclaimed. Sure enough, the couple rode behind Lord Ardalen. Beside Ardalen rode Magician Sabin, sword master and friend of the king. Jayan began counting. If all the well-dressed newcomers were magicians – his idea for a badge to mark members of his imagined guild would have made it certain – then there were eighteen magicians arriving to either regain the pass or join Werrin.

The newcomers dismounted and Magician Sabin stepped forward to greet Werrin, Ardalen at his side. Jayan edged closer and strained to hear the conversation.

"Magician Sabin," Werrin said. "Please tell me you're here to join us. We could do with your insight and advice."

"I am here to join you," Sabin replied. "As are twelve of this company. Five will go with Ardalen to retake the pass." He looked at the villagers. "Your scouts told us you have won a battle here."

"Yes, we have," Werrin's tone was grim. "Four Sachakans took the town. We regained it."

"They are dead?"

"Yes."

Sabin pursed his lips briefly, then nodded. "You must tell me in more detail."

"Of course." Werrin glanced back at the villagers, who watched the newcomers with nervous interest. "We were just debating how to respond to a noble offer made by the survivors. They want us to take strength from them, both out of gratitude and so that we may use it to fight."

Sabin's eyebrows rose. "A noble offer indeed, if they have already been subjected to that unwillingly." He looked thoughtful. "The king has been examining the law against taking magic from anyone but apprentices. He acknowledges that there may not be enough magically talented young men in the higher classes to supply all the magicians needed to remove Takado and his allies. He is also worried that we may lose many of our magical bloodlines if things go badly. So he has decreed that servants may be employed as sources if a magician has no apprentice, so long as they are paid well."

"They should be tested first, as there would be little point if they had little or no latent talent," Werrin said. "I guess this means we can't accept the villagers' offer."

Sabin's eyes narrowed. "The law against taking magic from people other than apprentices does not apply in time of war. Sounds like what happened here qualifies as an action of war."

As Werrin and Sabin exchanged a silent, meaningful look, Jayan felt a chill run over his skin.

I think that means we're officially at war.

"I don't see how walking around the same old mansion is going to cheer me up," Stara told Vora as the woman led her down the corridor. "It might be a large prison, but it's still a prison."

"Don't dismiss what you haven't tried, mistress," the slave replied calmly. "This place won't keep a mind like yours entertained for long, I agree. But it has many interesting little corners, and finding them may provide some temporary relief from the boredom."

I'm not bored. How can I be bored? I've been too busy thinking about the monster my father is, and what he's going to do with me now I'm "unmarriageable", to be bored. If I'm wearing grooves into the floor with my pacing, it's because I want to go home. Stara sighed. *Pity I had to come here to find out where "home" really is.*

"Are there any walls here that aren't white?"

"No, mistress."

Stara sighed again. It had taken Vora some days to talk Stara into leaving her room. Stara wouldn't admit it to her slave, but she was afraid of encountering her father. Vora kept badgering her, and in the end Stara had agreed out of disgust at herself for letting him turn her into a coward. Though she imagined it would be difficult to talk him into sending her home, it would be impossible if she never encountered him again.

A curious smell had entered the air. It wasn't unpleasant, or sickly sweet like the fragrances Sachakans preferred. Vora led Stara into a curved corridor. Arched windows on the inside wall opened onto a mass of green. Stara stopped, surprised to see so much plant life before her.

As she moved to one of the windows she realised that the garden on the other side was enclosed within a circular room, whose roof was a segmented circle of woven fabric stretched between metal hooks fixed in the walls.

"Yes, this is rather nice – and unexpected," she said aloud.

Vora chuckled. As the woman moved to a doorway into the garden, Stara considered the slave. *I'm almost sure she likes me. I hope so. I've come to like her, and it would be a shame if it wasn't mutual.*

She still couldn't bring herself to treat Vora as anything less than a servant. The woman's bossy manner hardly emphasised her slave status, either. *I probably trust her more than I should*, Stara thought. *If her descriptions of Sachakan politics and intrigue aren't exaggerated then I should consider the possibility that an enemy might recruit her to poison me or something. One of Father's enemies, more like it . . . or Father himself.* She shivered. *But he wouldn't do that. Even if only because Mother would refuse to send her profits to him any more. Still . . . if she never knew it was him . . . I should think of something else.*

A small stone-lined creek wound across the garden, crossed by a bridge at the centre. At the far end water emerged through a pipe protruding from the wall. It was so pleasant that Stara was disappointed when Vora led her across the corridor and into an empty room. Here the walls were lined with grey stone.

"So the walls aren't all wh——" Stara began, but stopped as Vora indicated she should remain silent.

Intrigued, Stara followed the slave to a wooden doorway on the other side of the room. Vora stopped and beckoned for Stara to come nearer. The faint sound of music filtered through the door. Stara looked at Vora in surprise. She hadn't heard any music since coming to Sachaka. The woman smiled and repeated her gesture for silence.

Stara listened. The musician was playing a stringed instrument she was more used to hearing in the homes of rich Elynes. And the musician was good. Very good. As the player shifted from one tune to another, sometimes repeating a phrase to fix a mistake or alter the speed, Stara grew more impressed. Finally she could not stand the suspense any longer. She moved away from the door.

"Who is it?" she whispered to Vora.

The woman's smile widened. "Master Ikaro."

Stara straightened in shock. "My brother?"

"Yes, mistress. I told you. He is not who you think he is."

"How did he learn to play like that?"

"Listening. Practising." Vora's smile faded. "When Master Sokara found out he smashed Master Ikaro's first vyer. I don't know how your brother managed to get hold of another. He won't tell me, for fear your father will read my mind."

Stara looked at Vora, then at the door, unable to reconcile the picture she'd created in her mind of a handsome young vyer player come to make her prison more bearable with that of her memory of a hard-faced young man who thought women were useless.

"You two have more in common than you realise," Vora said firmly. "You should be allies."

Stara looked at the woman again, then stepped past her and pushed through the door.

"Wait, mistress!" Vora exclaimed. "It's a—"

Bathing room, Stara finished as she took in the scene before her.

A man sat at the edge of a pool of steaming water, naked except for a length of cloth draped over his lap. He was staring at her in horror. She looked down at the large hump in the cloth.

"Did you really think you could hide it under that?" she blurted out. "Surely you could have come up with a better plan. And you do know that playing in damp air could ruin a vyer, don't you?"

Ikaro's gaze slid away from her to somewhere behind her left shoulder, the surprise in his face changing to annoyance.

"Vora," he said disapprovingly, but with no great force. "I told you not to meddle."

"As you've always said, Master Ikaro, I'm not very good at obeying orders I don't like," the woman replied. She moved to Stara's side. "Though I wasn't expecting your sister to take my advice so literally."

Stara looked at her and shrugged. "Well, I'm here now. You want us to talk?" She looked at Ikaro and crossed her arms. "Then let's talk."

He gave her an unreadable look, then slid the vyer out from under the cloth and put it gently aside. Then he tied the fabric around his waist, retrieved the vyer and stood up. "There are better places than this," he said, gesturing for her to follow. "Places where we can still talk privately, but much drier."

They moved down the room beside the pool to a door at the far end. The next room was smaller, with stone benches on either side. A neat pile of clothes lay on one. Ikaro indicated the women should continue to the next room, which was an ordinary, white-walled one with a few chairs and tables.

He did not follow immediately, but appeared a moment later fully dressed. And not carrying the vyer, Stara noted. Where in those stone-lined rooms was he keeping it?

I suppose if it's always kept in a moist place, and never dries out too fast, it shouldn't split.

Still silent, he led them into a corridor then out into a walled courtyard. Potted plants shaded the area and a fountain in the centre filled the air with the constant patter of water. They sat at the edge of the pool.

Ah, yes. The old fountain trick. Hides the sound of voices. Good to know Elynes aren't the only ones who do this.

"We can talk safely here," he told them.

"None of the slaves are mouth-readers, then."

He looked at her oddly.

"Mouth-reading," she explained. "The trick of reading what someone is saying by the movements of their lips."

"I had no idea anyone could do that," he admitted, glancing nervously around the courtyard. Then he shrugged and turned back to her. "So what would you like to talk about?"

She searched for any sign of the aloof, cold man who had ignored her at the dinner a few weeks back. He looked a little anxious, but there was no animosity or distance in his face. He almost seemed a different person.

"Vora tells me you're not like the person I thought I knew," she told him, deciding to be blunt. "But you barely looked at me the one time I've seen you since I arrived."

He grimaced and nodded. "I wasn't to show any feeling towards you, good or bad, or it might affect the outcome."

"It might put my prospective husband off?"

"Yes."

She let out a short, bitter laugh. "I might have wanted him put off. But, of course, what my father wanted was more important than what I wanted."

His eyes were dark and haunted as he nodded and met her eyes. "There is not much point resisting him."

She looked back towards where she thought the bath was situated. "You don't seem to be giving up."

"A small victory that could be lost at any moment, any day. The larger issues . . ." He sighed and shook his head. "I've been so jealous of you, living with Mother and able to do whatever you wanted."

Stara stared at him. "You were jealous of *me*? I thought you . . . You said women weren't important and I figured that had to include me. Why would you have given me any thought at all?"

"I was sixteen when I said that, Stara," he chided her quietly. "You can't hold anyone responsible for the opinions they form at that age, especially growing up in this place. Everything is at the extreme here. There is no middle ground. When I met my wife I learned that things weren't that simple."

"*I* was jealous of *you*," she told him. "All my life I worked towards learning what I thought I'd need to know when Father finally called me home." She clenched her fists. "And when he did it turned out all he wanted was to marry me off like a piece of stock."

Ikaro chuckled. "He was furious that you'd learned magic. Nachira and I laughed so hard when I told her. You must meet her — you'd like her. I know she wants to meet you. How did you manage to learn and keep it a secret?"

She shrugged. "Friends in Elyne. Mother wouldn't let me become an apprentice, and I didn't want to leave her to do all the work alone. So I learned from a friend and from books."

"Father said you'd lacked any good training. I took that to mean you didn't know higher magic."

She held his gaze for a moment, then looked away. "You've been to Elyne. You know the laws."

"All magicians are bound by some oath before they're allowed to learn higher magic, right?"

"Yes. My friend said she wouldn't teach me higher magic, because it was a law she respected. Not that I resent her for it." She shrugged. "What I had learned was precious enough. Do any Sachakan women learn magic?"

He nodded. "Sometimes. Usually because they're the only heir to a magician's property, but there are tales of husbands who foolishly taught their wives and came to regret it, or of women who received training in exchange for some favour."

"Does it really mean no one will marry them?"

He raised his eyebrows. "I thought you didn't want to be married."

"Just not to someone I don't know and like."

"I see." He looked away, frowning. Stara looked at Vora. The woman was watching him closely, her face creased with worry.

"Having magic doesn't make a woman unmarriageable, but it is unlikely anyone of high status would take her." He looked up at her quickly. "Father has chosen someone of lower status than he wanted. That's all I know."

"He's chosen . . ." Stara echoed. A chill ran across her skin.

Ikaro frowned. "You didn't know?"

"I thought . . . I hoped he'd given up on the idea and . . . I hoped he would send me home."

He shook his head and looked away again. "No, he's accepted the man's proposal."

Standing up, she began to pace in a small circle. "Do I get any say in this?" She looked at him and saw the apology in his expression as he began to answer. "No. I know." She cursed. "What can I do? Run away? Tell him that if he marries me off against my will I'll make sure I never have a child?"

Ikaro winced, a reaction that made her stop pacing and consider him. *Father said his wife couldn't bear children. He's been married a few years now. From the sound of it, he likes and respects his wife. But if she's infertile . . . and Father said he needed an heir. To prevent the emperor from gaining the family assets when Ikaro dies.*

"Tell her," Vora said, her voice low and urgent.

Ikaro put his head in his hands, then straightened again. "If you don't bear a child, Father will make sure I do. By freeing me to try another wife."

Stara stared at him as the meaning behind his words sank in. *He'll murder Nachira. That's why Ikaro winced. He loves Nachira. He needs me to have a child in order to give Father no reason to murder her.* A wave of horror swept over her. *Someone get me out of this country!*

But if someone did, Nachira would still die. Though she had never met the woman, Stara knew she would always feel responsible if something she had done – or hadn't done – had led to someone's death.

Was she willing to marry a stranger and bear his children to avoid that?

Is there any chance I'd make it out of Sachaka, anyway? Father can still have me marry whoever he's picked, whether I want it or not. I get no say in it.

"So Father is willing to have Nachira murdered just so the emperor won't get the family assets?"

"Yes."

She shook her head. "He must really dislike the emperor."

"It's more a matter of pride for him," Ikaro told her. "It's certainly not a concern for me, but for the fact that if I die first Nachira will have no money or home."

He looked guilty but his eyes pleaded with her.

"I know I'm asking you to do something you don't want to do and I wish there was another way. If there was something I could give you in return, I would, but I know the things you want most are the ones that would still lead to . . . still leave her . . ."

Taking in a deep breath, Stara let it out slowly. "Sounds as if I need to meet Nachira."

Ikaro's eyes brightened. "You'll like her."

"So you said before. I won't agree to anything until I've had time to think about it." She paused as an idea came to her. "When you said you would give me something in return . . ."

He hesitated, frowned, then smiled. "If I can give it, I will."

"Teach me higher magic."

Again she saw surprise, concern, then amusement. Then he began to nod. "I will have to think about it, too. And ask Nachira. She often sees consequences where I don't."

"Of course," she said. Looking at Vora, she saw the woman was smiling broadly. "What are you looking so smug about, Vora?"

The woman's eyes widened in an unconvincingly innocent look. "I am a mere slave, mistress, and have nothing to be smug about."

To Stara's amusement, Ikaro rolled his eyes. "I don't know why Father doesn't sell you, Vora."

"Because I am so good at keeping his children in line." She rose and took a step away from the fountain. "Come now, mistress. Too much exposure to the sun will age you before your time."

As they began to walk away from the fountain, Ikaro called out quietly.

"We can't take too long to decide, Stara. There are rumours about that Emperor Vochira may go to war with Kyralia. If Father sends me off to fight I won't be able to protect or teach anybody."

Stara looked back and met his gaze, nodding soberly. Then she followed Vora back into the mansion, her thoughts turning slowly but ceaselessly with the choices she now faced.

CHAPTER 29

It came as a relief to Tessia, the next morning, to learn that the magicians had decided to move on to the next town. Vennea was a larger town on the border of two leys and, being on the main road to the pass, was a good place to base themselves for a few days. Sabin wanted to send out more scouts and locate the rest of the Sachakans before he and Werrin decided on their next move.

Tecurren was a town in mourning, which was too sharp a reminder of the fate of Mandryn and her parents. The survivors had begun to behave strangely towards the magicians. Their fascination and gratitude had only increased after the magicians took the strength they'd offered (though not from the girls, as Tessia advised). Some began following them around. All agreed it was time to leave and let them begin rebuilding their lives.

The road to Vennea descended in graceful curves along the sides of a widening valley. The forests around Tecurren had been patchy, held back by the spread of fields and relegated to a narrow band of trees hugging rivers and creeks. Now the group descended into a near-treeless landscape, giving them a clear view of fields, clusters of tiny houses, a river and the shiny surfaces of lakes and reservoirs.

As a horse drew alongside Tessia, she glanced up and saw that Lady Avaria was riding beside her. The woman smiled.

"How are you getting along, Tessia?"

"Well enough."

"I was saddened to hear about your parents, and the people of Mandryn."

Tessia felt something inside spasm as grief suddenly sprang to life again. She nodded, not trusting herself to speak, and resolutely pushed the feeling away.

"The girls all send their greetings – especially Kendaria. She wanted to come with me and try out her healing skills, but doubted the guild or the magicians would let her."

Tessia grimaced. "I'm not sure it would be what she expected. I've been failing to heal more often than succeeding. We don't have the time to treat serious injuries. I don't know if she's experienced being unable to save a patient. It's shocking the first time."

Avaria frowned. "Sounds as if the king ought to be sending a few healers to join this group. Lessen the burden on you."

"We haven't needed them so far. The Sachakans don't tend to leave their victims alive. But if there are more attempts to take over villages there will be more people with injuries from houses falling down and fires."

"Let's hope the war never escalates to the point where Kendaria has a chance to try out her skills. Though I imagine you'd have liked her company. Any womanly company. I can't imagine what it's been like for you travelling with all these men."

Tessia smiled. "It has been interesting." She looked at Dakon and Jayan, and the other magicians and apprentices ahead of them. "You know, I'm glad there's another woman now, but when I think about it I wonder why. I've spent all this time acting as if it doesn't matter that I'm female. I'm living as roughly as the boys – though I do get a tent all to myself – eating the same food and even dressing the same. Oh, I do have some physical requirements different from theirs, but it's not as if I haven't been dealing with that by myself for years already. A bit of extra privacy is all that I've needed."

Avaria glanced at her, an eyebrow raised. "You must tell me the arrangements you've made. I've been wondering what I'll do when . . . when that time of womanly inconvenience comes."

"Magic makes it easier, of course. Think how badly we'd all smell by now if we weren't able to wash our clothes because we didn't have time for them to dry."

Avaria chuckled. "I'm surprised your clothes haven't turned to rags in the process."

"We've bought or been given new clothes and shoes in the villages. Not always to the taste of some, but I think even the fussiest of us has had to acknowledge that fine cloth doesn't last long when you're riding every day."

"It would be a waste of fine cloth, too."

"Yes." Tessia chuckled. "We can't have that."

"What's this cloud ahead . . . ?" Avaria began, her voice tailing off. Tessia looked at the woman and saw she was staring into the distance. Following her gaze, she saw smoke billowing up from a cluster of tiny shapes in the valley below. At once she felt a sinking in her stomach.

A murmur of voices flowed through the magicians and apprentices as they saw the smoke. Though their words were too quiet to catch, Tessia heard the grimness in their voices and felt her stomach sink even further.

"Is that Vennea?" someone asked.

"I think so."

The rest of the morning passed slowly and painfully. Sometimes the road led them out of sight of the smoke below. Every time the valley came into view again, the smoke always appeared worse. Nobody spoke, but the pace had quickened and the silence was only punctuated by the huffing breath of the horses.

At last they reached level ground at the valley bottom and the road straightened. Though they no longer had a view of the town, the smoke cloud was now a stark shadow against the clear sky. At the same time, what had been a near-empty road ahead of them was suddenly full of people – both walking and riding – carts, and small groups of domestic animals.

Her stomach sank as she saw the numbers coming towards them. As she began to make out detail, she saw heads turning to glance behind and recognised the haste in their movements. When one of a group of reber skittered away from the rest, the herder made no attempt to stop and chase it.

The magicians fell silent. Expressions were grim. Slowly the gap between the two groups shrank. Several strides before the crowd reached the magicians people began to call out, some pointing back the way they'd come.

"Sachakans!"

"They've attacked Vennea! They've wrecked Vennea!"

"They're killing people!"

Tessia watched as the refugees stopped and formed a crowd before Werrin. The magician's questions were followed by a dozen answers, and she was unable to make out much. After several minutes she heard Werrin call over the voices.

"You must travel south. This way will take you towards the mountains and more Sachakans."

"But we can't go back!"

"You must go around," Werrin replied, pointing to the west.

After more discussion, the refugees moved to the side of the road so the magicians could ride on. Narvelan, who had managed to keep a position close to the leaders of the group since the reinforcements had arrived, turned his horse and rode back to join Dakon, Everran and Avaria.

"The townspeople say about twenty Sachakan magicians attacked Vennea less than an hour ago," he told them. "They're destroying the place, so it's doubtful they'll try to occupy it as they did Tecurren."

"I imagine scouts will confirm the number before we form a plan of attack," Everran said.

"Yes. It's likely they—"

—*Lord Werrin? Magician Sabin?*

Tessia jumped at the voice in her mind. She looked around to see her own surprise reflected in the faces around her. The voice had been familiar . . .

—*Who are you?* Werrin replied.

—*Mikken of family Loren. Ardalen's apprentice. He told me to report when I reached a safe place.*

—*Then report.*

—*They're dead. All of our group. Ardalen. Everyone.* He paused. *We were so careful. Silent. Travelled at night. But the pass . . . it was full of Sachakans. By the time we came close enough to see it was too late. Ardalen told me to run and hide, so I could tell you. I climbed the cliff . . . There are about ten of them. They have tents and carts of food and other things that indicate they are planning to stay there and hold the pass for themselves.*

Tessia realised her heart was racing. The Sachakans would be hearing this and would know he was still in the area. He was taking a great risk. *Be careful, Mikken!* she thought. *Don't give yourself away!*

—*Is there anything else you must tell us?* Sabin asked. *Anything vital?*

—*No.*

—*Then stay silent. Travel quick and quiet. May luck be yours.*

—*Yes. I'll do that. Goodbye.*

In the silence that followed, furtive, grim looks were exchanged. A few shook their heads. *They don't think he'll survive*, Tessia thought. Her heart twisted. *Poor Mikken.* She thought back to the apprentice's first and only attempt to charm her. Despite – or perhaps because of – her rebuff, he'd remained charming, but only in a friendly, light-hearted way. She felt an unexpected wave of affection for him. *It was like a joke between us. I knew he wasn't serious. After all, he wouldn't have looked at me twice if there had been prettier women around. But it was nice to have someone flirting with me, especially when Jayan is so serious all the time.* She sighed. *I hope he finds his way back to us.*

Then she remembered Lord Ardalen teaching them the method of giving magic to another that they had used to defeat the Sachakans at Tecurren. Such a valuable piece of knowledge. What other knowledge had been lost when the magician died? How much more would be lost in this war? And would any of them survive to form this guild of magicians that Jayan had thought so much about?

The grey-haired woman sagged in Takado's grip. He let her drop to the ground then extended a hand in Hanara's direction. Hanara handed his master a clean, damp cloth, watched Takado wipe the blood off his hand, then took it and stowed it in his pack for cleaning later.

"A surprisingly strong one," Takado said. Looking up at Dachido, he smiled. "You can never tell with these Kyralians."

Dachido shook his head and looked round at the corpses littering the street. *The ones who didn't run fast enough*, Hanara thought. *The ones who dared to confront us.*

"If they were slaves, the strong ones would have been found and made useful. I can't believe the wastage here."

A crash drew their attention. The front wall of a house

nearby collapsed and the heat of the fire within beat at Hanara, searing his skin. To his relief, Takado moved away.

"How do these Kyralians survive?" Dachido asked. "They should be wallowing in rebellion, the fields untended and thievery everywhere. Instead they prosper."

"Lord Dakon tried to convince me that slavery was inefficient," Takado replied. "That a free man will take pride in his work. That a craft worker is more likely to experiment and invent better ways of doing things if it is for his own benefit and his family's."

"I don't see how that would be any greater motivation than the threat of a whipping, or death."

"Nor did I, until I came here."

Dachido's eyebrows rose as he looked at Takado in surprise. "So you agree with him?"

"Perhaps." Takado turned at the creak of an opening door. Smoke gusted out, followed by a man. The man saw them and tried to run, but he crumpled against an invisible wall. He began to yell as magic drew him towards the two magicians. "Not enough to try to make it work myself."

"What would be the point of taking over a land only to let the people keep all their wealth and freedom?" Dachido said.

The failed escapee collapsed to his knees but the magic dragged him over the stone-paved ground. He whimpered as the force deposited him in front of Dachido, knees red and bleeding.

"Please," he begged. "Let me go. I've done nothing wrong."

"You have him," Takado said to Dachido.

"Are you sure?"

"Of course. Do I ever make an offer I'm not sure of?"

"No." Dachido drew his knife. Gems glinted in the sun as he stepped up to the man and touched its edge to the exposed skin at the back of the neck. A fine red line of beaded blood appeared.

Hanara waited, bored. He'd seen this too many times to count in his life, though it had not often resulted in death before now. Seeing an approaching figure out of the corner of his eye, he turned to see Asara coming towards them. She said nothing as she reached them, politely waiting for the strength-taking to finish. Dachido let the failed escapee fall to the ground, then started as he realised she was standing beside him.

"Asara," he said. "Had a good harvest?"

She chuckled. "That's an interesting way to put it. Yes, I must have replaced what I used, and more. You?"

"Easily."

She looked at Takado. Hanara saw respect in her eyes, not quite hidden behind her cool, restrained demeanour. "What next, Takado?"

Takado looked around them, considering. They were standing in the middle of a square area surrounded on all sides by houses and bisected by the main road. "We have achieved all we need to here. A start. A message. A beginning to our advance towards Imardin."

"Will we stay here tonight?"

"No." Takado's eyes were dark. "I believe the next major town on the main road is called Halria. If we move quickly we will stay ahead of our pursuers."

"Another town on the main road? What if they anticipate that and gather together another group of magicians to confront us?" Dachido asked. "We may be caught between two forces."

"We will move off the road before then," Takado told him. "But for a time we can take towns that are still full of people. Towns that haven't been warned of our coming. Towns they won't expect us to attack." He smiled. "There has to be a little randomness in war. Otherwise it wouldn't be as interesting."

Asara smiled. Hanara felt a shiver run down his spine. He felt a strange emotion, part fear, part pride. It made him want to get away from these three people, yet it also made him want to stay and watch what they did. Never in his life had he seen magicians demonstrate their full powers. Today they had burned and ruined a town while barely showing more effort than a stare or a frown. But he knew they hadn't been stretched to use their powers to the limit yet. It would be terrible and magnificent when they did. His heart swelled even as it pumped faster.

And I will be there to see it.

CHAPTER 30

The typical Sachakan home was a sprawl that contained clusters of rooms known as quarters. Stara's father lived in the master's quarters. She lived in the adjoining family quarters. Ikano and Nachira lived in the son's quarters – an area reserved for the heir to the master.

In the centre of the son's quarters was a large main room from which all other rooms were accessed. These smaller rooms were empty but for the couple's bedroom. The lack of furniture seemed to exude an air of sadness and disapproval. They ought to contain her nephews and nieces.

It would be bad enough failing to live up to that expectation, Stara thought as Vora led her into the main room, *but to be reminded of it every day would be awful – especially with the extra fear of murder as a consequence.*

Then her insides curled with a growing dread. *And Ikaro is asking me to become the focus of that expectation. What will happen if I can't produce a child either?* She knew what Vora would say. "Best not waste time dwelling on troubles until you have to, mistress." Stara disagreed. She preferred "Better to be prepared than be caught unready" as a motto.

Nachira rose to greet Stara, kissing her on both cheeks, her jewellery jingling pleasantly. Stara returned the gesture. They sat down on cushioned stools at the centre of the room. After prostrating herself, Vora took her usual position on a floor cushion behind Stara's seat. Though this always made the old woman grunt and rub her joints, she resisted invitations to sit "at their level" and if ordered to looked uncomfortable and made unhappy remarks until Stara let her return to the floor cushion.

"Is my brother here?" Stara asked, looking around.

"He's checking that Ashaki Sokara is not coming back early," Nachira said in her low, husky voice. "He heard one of the slaves speculating."

"I still can't believe Father would object to his son and daughter conversing."

"Oh, he will." Nachira frowned. "If he hears about it from the slaves. We are going to tell him that we felt we should keep an eye on you, and provide a distraction so you don't try to go out again."

"Won't he read your mind and find it isn't true?"

The woman blinked. "No. At least . . . I hope not. He hasn't before. Well, not since that one time, after the wedding, when he wanted to be sure I didn't have some secret mission to do him harm. But he was kind about it."

Stara looked away. "I'd have thought he'd do it *before* the wedding, if he thought there was justification for it."

"My father would have called off the wedding. It would be rude to show such distrust then."

"But not after?" Stara turned back to meet Nachira's eyes.

The woman lowered her gaze. "Not as much. And he was kind about it . . . as I said. I didn't think it was worth bothering Father over."

Stara nodded and sighed. This confirmed her suspicion that reading a free person's mind – even family – was not an everyday, accepted act.

Vora had brought her to her brother's rooms every day since that first meeting in the baths. Sometimes Stara visited in the morning, sometimes later in the day. The handful of visits weren't enough for her to consider she knew Nachira well, but she had judged the woman to be a straightforward sort of person. The idea that Ikaro's wife might have some secret mission – or any secret other than her infertility – was unlikely.

I like her well enough, Stara mused. *I haven't seen anything to dislike, except perhaps her utter passiveness. If I thought my father-in-law was likely to kill me, I'd be demanding or at least begging my husband to take me away from danger.*

Maybe there was no "away". Where would Ikaro and Nachira go? Without Stara's father's good will and protection, they would have no money, trade or land to inherit.

But that would be better than death, wouldn't it? They could go to Elyne. Even as she thought it, she knew it was not an option likely to be considered. Nachira would not be able to comprehend living in another land, and Ikaro would worry that his father would still be able to make their lives a misery from across the border, since he had trading connections through their mother.

Mother would never do anything to harm us, Stara thought. *But she may not know she is doing so. She could be tricked into it.*

Hearing footsteps, they both tensed and looked towards the doorway. When Ikaro entered Nachira let out a sigh of relief.

Ikaro smiled. "He hasn't returned and they don't expect him for another few days." He sat down and his expression became serious as he looked at his wife. "But I heard other news, just arrived. The emperor has officially declared his support of the invasion of Kyralia and is calling for magicians to join his army. When Father learns of this he will send me away to fight."

Stara heard Nachira catch her breath. The couple stared at each other for a moment, then their gazes shifted to Stara.

"You will have to make your decision sooner than we hoped, Stara." Ikaro reached out to take Nachira's hand. "We have discussed it, and agreed that the least we can do is give you what you asked for. I'll teach you higher magic."

Stara glanced at Vora. The woman smiled and nodded her approval. Stara felt a wave of emotions rush through her. First helplessness, then disgust at herself. *I'm going to give in to this. I'm going to marry some stranger and have his child because my father is a monster. How pathetic am I?* Then a strange pride followed by determination. *But I'm not just giving in, I'm making a choice – saving a life.* Finally, dread came and didn't leave her, settling into her as if it had found a home in her bones. *If Father has chosen someone horrible I will not sit there and accept it. Ikaro may help me, but if he can't I will find a way to help myself.*

She realised then that she had decided to help them from the first moment she learned of Nachira and Ikaro's dilemma. Foolishly, perhaps, because she had to trust they were telling the truth and not inventing the threat to Nachira's life to get Stara to co-operate. But all her senses told her their fear was real. She could see it in their slightest gesture, almost smell it in the air.

"Then I'll do it," she told them. "I'll marry and try to provide Father with an heir."

Both smiled, then sobered, then smiled again as they alternately thanked and apologised to her. Nachira began to cry; Ikaro consoled her. Stara felt her heart lift at their obvious affection for each other, but then it sank again.

Oh, Mother, I am going to marry and have a child, and you won't be there to help and share the experience. Stara knew then that the dread she felt was not just at the prospect of putting her life in the hands of a stranger, but of becoming trapped in Sachaka with nothing familiar and nobody she could trust

401

and talk to. It was hardly the sort of place she'd hoped to bring a child up in.

Nachira abruptly rose. "We must share some raka to seal the agreement," she declared.

"I'll get the raka," Vora said, her joints creaking as she rose. She looked at Ikaro. "You should honour your side of the agreement now, master."

He chuckled. "You're right, Vora. We can never know if and when we may be interrupted." He narrowed his eyes and smiled. "Be quick with the raka, too, as we need someone to practise on."

Vora's lips thinned, but her eyes were warm with fondness. Soon they had settled back onto the cushions, sipping the hot drink. Ikaro told Vora to move her cushion between them, and kneel. He drew the short, curved knife from the sheath at his waist, then looked at Stara, all humour gone from his face.

"First you must break the skin," he told her. "The natural magical barrier that protects us all from the will of others lies there when not extended to form a shield." He turned the knife and offered the handle to her. "Take it. The only way to show you is for you to sense it yourself."

She took the knife. The handle was warm from his touch. Vora rolled up her sleeve and held out her arm.

"Just the lightest touch should be enough. The blade is very sharp."

For a moment Stara could not bring herself to move. Vora eyed her, her gaze judgemental. Suddenly determined the old woman wouldn't see yet another moment of weakness, Stara pressed the blade gently against the woman's skin. As she drew it away a red line appeared. At one edge a bead of blood formed. Stara bit back an urge to apologise.

"Now place your hand over the cut," Ikaro continued. "Close your eyes. Send your mind out and locate Vora."

Doing as he instructed, Stara was startled by the intensity of what she sensed. Many of Nimelle's magic lessons had involved the meeting of their minds, but it hadn't been like this. Stara was aware not only of Vora's presence, but of her entire body, and even her mind. When she concentrated, she could hear the woman's thoughts.

Most keenly of all, she could feel the magical energy within the slave, imbuing every part of her body.

From a distance, she heard Ikaro speaking.

"Do you feel the strength within her?"

She made herself nod.

"Good. Now draw from it. Tap into it as you would tap into your own power."

Carefully, tentatively, she reached for the energy within Vora. It flowed to her, but she felt it slip away.

"Where'd it go?"

"You channelled it out of yourself, unformed. Don't worry. That is what most people do initially. Try again, but this time connect with your own power. Draw her power in to join yours."

Keeping an awareness of Vora's energy, she sought her own power. Suddenly she had an impression of two glowing human forms connected where one touched the other. She could feel the barrier about Vora's energy, sense the break where her skin had been cut.

Then she focused her will and pulled in energy from Vora's body. It responded to her will, flowing into her own body.

"I have it," she said. "It's working."

"Good. Now, to avoid others sensing what you are doing, you must strengthen your barrier. It will only hold the power you naturally contain if you don't. Father will sense the leakage and know what I have taught you. You must also learn to draw power without leakage, too."

He made her start and stop drawing power several times, alerting her whenever he sensed leakage. She was aware that some hours had passed before he pronounced her proficient enough to use black magic without alerting others. Looking at Vora, she searched for signs of weariness, but the old woman looked no different.

That's good. I don't want to drain Vora of too much energy. She isn't young, and uses enough running around after me and Ikaro.

"Will I need more lessons?" she asked.

"No." He smiled. "You're a fast learner."

Stara tossed her head in mock pride. "I guess I'm a natural."

Ikaro smiled briefly, then turned thoughtful. "Perhaps you would have been, if you hadn't learned magic in Elyne. Then Father would have been forced to teach you anyway."

"Or had you killed," Vora murmured. "Like most naturals."

Stara stared at them in disbelief, then shook her head. "Surely not. I know Sachakans kill slaves who are naturals, but do they really kill their own family members?"

"Naturals are . . ." Ikaro searched for a word.

"Dangerous," Vora offered, rising and moving her cushion back to its former position. "Freaks. Ashaki don't like not being able to decide who has magic and who doesn't."

"Sounds as if they ought to call them *un*naturals," Stara mused.

"Well, it's best not to use the word," Ikaro warned. "You will also have to be careful how you strengthen yourself, too, if that is your intent. By law, a magician can't take power from another's slave without the permission of its owner. Even I can't strengthen myself here without permission. All the slaves here are Father's."

"Including Vora?"

"Including her."

"So we just broke a law."

He shrugged. "We didn't use higher magic to strengthen anyone, just to teach."

"Well, gaining power isn't my aim right now. I only want to be sure I have all the abilities I might need when . . . well . . . later."

"I understand," Ikaro said. He smiled crookedly. "After all these years envying you, I find I want you to have as much freedom as possible, so you may survive and be happy."

She smiled and patted his hand. "And I want the same for you two."

"Well, in that case –" Vora said.

They all turned to look at her.

"– there is another ability that Stara needs. One that may save her life one day."

Ikaro looked at Stara questioningly. She shrugged to show she had no idea what the woman was talking about. *But I really want to know!* she thought.

"What's that, then?" Ikaro asked.

Vora's smile was sly. "How to kill someone while bedding them, master."

Nachira put a hand to her mouth and looked at her husband, eyes wide. Ikaro was smiling, but his face had reddened slightly.

"How am I supposed to teach her that?" he asked Vora.

"You tell me," the woman replied, a challenge in her gaze. "Presumably it's possible without resorting to incest or offending your wife."

Ikaro nodded. "You're right. Father told me how it was done, though I've never had cause to use that particular trick so I have no idea if I'd get it right." He turned to look at Stara. "Apparently it is easier for women than men. Timing is crucial."

She looked back at him expectantly. "How so?"

"At the moment of . . . er . . . highest pleasure the natural barrier we spoke of earlier disappears. Do you . . . know what I refer to?"

"Yes," she replied. "I know the peak you're talking about." His face had reddened more, she noted. "I gather I'll sense when the barrier disappears."

"So I've been told." He drew in a deep breath and let it out slowly, then glanced at Nachira, who was looking amused. "As with the usual method of higher magic, once the drawing begins the source is helpless. But once you stop the natural barrier restores itself, so if you intend to kill then you must not stop drawing until you have taken all his energy. Of course, we'd appreciate it if you left killing your husband until after you have a child."

Stara laughed. "Of course."

"You never know," Vora injected. "Stara may like her husband."

The three of them turned to look at the slave woman suspiciously. Vora raised her hands to indicate her innocence.

"Oh, I don't know who he is. But you shouldn't discount the possibility." She looked at each of them, then shrugged. "I suppose if you insist on expecting the worst you can only be right, or pleasantly surprised."

It's all right for her, Stara thought. *She's not being forced to marry anyone.* But then she checked herself. *Am I jealous of a slave? No, there are worse fates than being married off . . . though Vora seems to have done well for herself. I hope she continues to serve Ikaro and Nachira after I'm gone.*

To her surprise, Stara realised she would miss the bossy old woman.

The air was laden with smoke, the smell of it suggesting all the different things that had been burned, some of which turned the stomach. Wooden beams, scorched black and still glowing, jutted towards the sky. Bricks, wood and metal fragments were scattered everywhere. Not a single building in Vennea remained standing.

In among the rubble lay the dead. Their clothing fluttered in the wind. There was no blood. Somehow that made it more chilling.

Or perhaps it was the silence. There were noises here. The crackle of flames. The howling of a baby somewhere. The footsteps of the magicians and apprentices. But all sound was muffled and distant. *Perhaps the horror has made me deaf*, Dakon thought. *My mind doesn't want to believe this, so it refuses to take it all in.*

"The Sachakans left," the village baker said. He'd locked himself inside his oven, which had cooled just enough since the morning's baking not to cook him, when the Sachakans searched his house, and had burns on his hands and scorched shoes. "When I knew I needed air I got out. There were people in the street. They were stealing from the houses that weren't on fire. They told me the Sachakans had left."

"Which direction did the Sachakans go?"

"I don't know."

Werrin nodded and thanked the man. He looked at Sabin. "We must find out. What do you think they're up to now?"

"This has the feel of a proper invasion," the sword master replied. "The numbers of them, the harvesting of strength. There is no advantage to them in holding a town, but they can gain strength and supplies from it. They know we are too few to defend all the outer villages and towns, so they strike and move on."

"Learned their lesson in Tecurren?"

"Probably."

"Where will they strike next?"

Sabin shrugged. "Our best strategy is to withdraw people to a more defendable location. Clear the outer villages and towns so there is nothing for them to take."

"Sounds as if you're suggesting we abandon the outer leys," Narvelan said, frowning.

Sabin nodded. "We may have to. I know this is disappointing after all the work the Circle has done these last few years, but can you see any way we can protect them?"

Narvelan shook his head and sighed. He looked at Dakon. "Looks as if you and I are about to become landless. Will we have to give up our title of Lord, I wonder?"

"Better that than let all the people we govern perish," Dakon replied.

"For now we may not need to abandon entire leys," Sabin said. "We can withdraw the populations to places the Sachakans can't approach in stealth, that can be evacuated easily."

"And how will we tackle the Sachakans?" Narvelan asked.

Sabin frowned. "From what we know from scouts' reports and villager's stories we are equal in number to the invading force, but are we equal in strength? Those of us who fought at Tecurren will be diminished in strength, though the generosity of the villagers will have compensated a little for that. The Sachakans, however, have taken the strength of whole towns. I do not like our chances." He shook his head. "For now we should do what we can to help here. People may be buried or trapped. I will contact the king using our code of mental communication again. Be ready to leave at any time."

As the magicians split apart and headed in all directions,

Dakon looked for Jayan and Tessia. Neither was standing behind him. He scanned the village square and eventually located the pair sitting either side of a small boy several paces away.

As he drew closer he realised the child was wounded and Tessia was treating him. Jayan had the boy's arm cradled in a bundle of cloth. Despite the support, the forearm was bent at an unnatural angle. Tessia touched the skin gently.

Then, as Dakon watched, the arm slowly unbent.

The boy cried out in pain and surprise, then burst into tears. Tessia quickly cast about, then drew a fragment of wood towards her with magic. Splinters flew off and the fragment split into two. She took the pieces, wrapped them in cloth, then instructed Jayan to hold them in place as she bound them to the boy's arm.

I have never seen anything like that, Dakon thought. He'd stopped, frozen in amazement at what he'd witnessed. The memory of the forearm straightening, seemingly by itself, played out over and over in his mind. *Magic. Clearly she used magic. In such a logical and beneficial way. And only a magician can do it. Oh, the healers' guild is not going to be happy to hear about this!*

As Tessia consoled the boy, telling him what the supports did and how long to keep them on, Jayan looked up and blinked in surprise as he saw Dakon.

They were both so absorbed, Dakon thought, *that a whole army of Sachakans could have sneaked up on them. Still, I can hardly blame them. They're only trying to help people.*

Nevertheless, Jayan's involvement was interesting. The young man barely left Tessia's side now. Dakon suspected he saw himself as her protector, but perhaps there was more to it. Perhaps Jayan understood how important Tessia's use of magic in healing could be, and was trying to give her the chance to keep developing her skill. He found he could manage a smile.

Sharing of knowledge, healing with the help of magic, and Jayan supporting and encouraging another apprentice. Who'd have thought there'd be such benefits to be found in this war we've found ourselves in?

PART FOUR

CHAPTER 31

The first thing Stara did when she woke was to marvel that she had been asleep at all. Her last memory of the night before was of telling Vora she would probably lie awake all night as she lay down on the bed. Instead she was blinking and rubbing her eyes, feeling disappointingly fresh and rested.

A familiar figure prostrated herself on the floor, her knees cracking audibly.

"Did you put a herb in my drink?" Stara asked, sitting up.

"You said you wished today would hurry up and be over, mistress," Vora replied as she rose to her feet. "Did the time speed by as you wished?"

"Yes. You're an evil woman, Vora. And I'm going to miss you."

The old woman smiled. "Come on then, mistress. Let's get you washed and dressed. I've brought your wedding wrap."

Stara couldn't help feeling a small thrill of excitement, but it was followed by a more familiar annoyance and frustration. In Elyne, a bride spent weeks with her mother, sisters – if she had them – and friends selecting fabric, embellishments and a design for her wedding dress. In Sachaka women wore yet another wrap, though for once it was a sober colour, and a headdress to which a veil had been attached. This traditional wedding costume had barely changed for centuries.

Stara rose and eyed the bundle of black cloth in Vora's hands. "Let's see it, then."

413

As the woman let the wrap unfurl, Stara caught a ripple of tiny reflections. She moved closer and examined the cloth. Fine stitchwork covered the front, incorporating countless tiny black disc-like beads.

"Pretty," she said. "Elyne women would love this. I wonder why it has never made it to market?"

"Because it is only used on wedding gowns," Vora told her. "The quans are carved from quannen shell. It's a slow process and the shell is rare, so they are very expensive. It is also traditional to reuse those on a mother's gown for her daughter's. But since your mother took hers to Elyne with her, your father had to buy new quans for this one."

"That was generous, considering he thinks I'm of no value as a wife." Stara straightened and moved to the washbasin. Her stomach had started doing that sickening fluttering and sinking thing again. "Either that, or he was forced to because he doesn't dare tell my mother he's marrying me off."

"I doubt any message would get to your mother at the moment," Vora reminded her.

Stara sighed. "No. Blasted war." She stripped off her night-clothes and washed, then let Vora envelop her in the wrap. The slave fussed with Stara's hair, arranging and pinning it carefully. When she was satisfied, she stepped back and looked Stara over.

"You look beautiful, mistress," she said, then shook her head. "You look beautiful when you first wake up, in a bad mood and your hair a-tangle. I only have to make you look like a bride. Ah, I wish my orders were always this easy to follow."

Stara had noticed that Vora had placed a large box on the table. Now the old woman opened it and lifted out a heavy mass of cascading cloth and jewels. The cloth was gauzy and covered in an elaborate pattern of quans.

"This is the headdress," the slave explained, then let it fall back into the box. "Before I put it on, would you like something to eat?"

Feeling her stomach clench, Stara shook her head. "No."

"How about a little juice?" Vora moved to a side table and picked up a glass jug. "I brought some in case."

Stara shrugged. She accepted the glass of juice the slave poured for her and sipped. Against her expectations, her stomach did not rebel. She felt a cool, calm sensation spread through her, and looked at the drink speculatively.

"Did you put herbs in this as well?"

Vora smiled. "No, but creamflower and pachi juice are known to be soothing." She eyed Stara. "Drink up. We don't have all morning."

As she continued to sip, Stara looked around the room. Vora had assured her that the few possessions she'd brought with her from Elyne – mostly mementos to remind her of her mother and friends – would be sent to her new home, along with all the clothing that had been made for her since she arrived. As she swallowed the last of the juice she took her last look at the rooms she'd lived in these last few months.

Then she turned away and handed Vora the empty glass. The woman put it aside and returned to the headdress. She lifted it out, carefully raising the cloth at the front. Stara had to bend over so the woman could slip it on over her head. At once Stara felt stifled. She could barely see through the cloth, and her own breath quickly warmed the air within the canopy.

"Stop tugging at it," Vora said. "You'll pull it out of place."

"I can't see."

"It will be easier when we get outside."

"Will the ceremony happen outside?"

"No."

"How am I going to avoid tripping over or walking into walls?"

"Walk slowly. I'll tug on your gown to direct you. On the left side if you need to go that way, and vice versa."

"And if I need to stop?"

"In the middle."

"And if I need to move again?"

"I'll poke you."

"Great."

"Now you need to follow me. Ready?"

Stara laughed bitterly. "No. But don't let that stop you."

She couldn't tell if Vora smiled or did the characteristic lip-thinning that showed she was worried or annoyed. The woman turned and started towards the door. Stara followed, her heart suddenly beating too fast and her stomach flipping in a way that made her wish she hadn't drunk the juice.

Just as she'd begun to grow used to seeing through the gauze, Vora led her into a dark room.

"Stara."

The voice was her father's. She turned to face a shadow she hadn't noticed until he'd spoken.

"Father."

"I have found you a husband. You are very fortunate."

Silence followed. She wondered if he had expected her to agree with him, or thank him. For a brief moment she considered saying something to that effect, then decided against it. He'd know she was lying, so what was the point?

"Be an obedient wife and do not shame me," he said finally. Then she felt a movement of air on her right hand, and felt a simultaneous tug on her robe and light press of a finger in her back. Suddenly she had to fight to smother a laugh. *I'm being directed like one of those puppets that were so popular in Capia's markets last year. I wonder what Father would think if I started jerking about as if my arms and legs were on strings.*

Then she sobered. He wouldn't see the humour in it. He'd probably never seen a puppet. *He and I are of two different worlds. Unfortunately I'm the one stuck in his world, not the other way around.*

With Vora guiding her, she followed her father through the house, then out into the courtyard. A wagon waited. She could not see whether it was plain or fancy. Her father climbed inside. She followed and settled opposite him, finding her place mainly by feel. Where Vora went she couldn't see. For a moment she felt panic at the thought that Vora might not be coming to the ceremony. Taking a few deep breaths, she told herself that she would be fine without her. *So long as I walk slowly.*

The wagon jerked into motion. She heard the clunk and squeak as the gates to the mansion opened. The wagon turned. The sound of another vehicle passed by them as they rolled down the road. Her father said nothing, but she could hear his breathing. Was he breathing faster than normal? She had no idea what normal was, for him. What was he thinking? Did he have any regrets? Or was he happy to be rid of her?

Abruptly the wagon slowed. Voices called out. They turned again. The wagon speeded up, then slowed again. As it stopped her father stood up and moved towards the door.

Stara remained in her seat, wondering what the stop was for and how long she'd have to wait before they continued on their way.

"Get out, Stara," came her father's voice.

Mystified, Stara felt her way to the wagon entrance and climbed out. Through the gauze she could see they were in another courtyard. She felt a tug on her gown and turned to see Vora standing beside her. Relief flooded through her.

"Is this it?" she whispered.

"It appears so, mistress," came the answer.

So my husband lives close by, Stara thought. *Is this so Father can keep an eye on me?*

She could hear her father exchanging formal greetings with another man. The voices stopped, then a light pressure in the middle of her back urged her forward. She and Vora moved towards a dark patch in the white walls. They passed through into a golden light.

Vora's directions guided her through this into another bright room. She heard doors close, then Vora let out a long breath.

"We're in the bride room, mistress," the slave explained. "All mansions have them, but they are closed up except during weddings. Take a peep, if you like. It will be a while before the men finish their negotiations."

"What negotiations?" Stara asked as she lifted the gauze. They were in a small room, furnished with only a long bench. Lamps burned in each corner, filling the space with brightness.

"Part of the ceremony. Though all the details will have been worked out before now, they'll do a bit of mock bartering. Your husband-to-be will pretend to have doubts, pretend that your price isn't low enough. Your father will list your virtues and threaten to take you home."

"Ha!" Stara exclaimed. "I'd love to hear that!" She looked more closely at the walls. Scenes had been painted straight on the render. Depictions of men and women. As she realised what they were doing she laughed. "How scandalous! If anyone in Elyne – oh, my! I've never heard of anyone doing *that* before!"

"It's meant to make you ready for your wedding bed," Vora told her.

418

Stara looked at the woman, her amusement fading. "Seems a little, ah, *advanced* viewing for someone who is supposed to be a young virgin. More likely to frighten them than excite them."

Vora shrugged. "Men and women have all sorts of strange ideas about each other, and most of them are wrong." Her gaze shifted to the door as the sound of footsteps sounded beyond it. "Quick! Put the head covering down and come over here," she hissed.

Plonking herself on the bench, she felt Vora tweak the gauze into place. The door opened.

A lone man entered. He was too young to be her father.

"Stara," he said. She felt something in her mind spark. The voice was familiar, but she wasn't sure why. "Welcome to my home."

"Thank you," she replied.

He moved forward until he stood in front of the bench, then took hold of the edge of the gauze and lifted. As the cloth tumbled down her back she stared at him in surprise.

"Ashaki Kachiro!"

"Yes," he said, smiling. "Your neighbour."

But my father dislikes you, she wanted to say. *He read my mind because we spoke.* But Vora had said Kachiro was not an enemy of her father either, she remembered. She turned to look at Vora. The slave shrugged.

"Ah, your slave. I have bought her, so that you will have a familiar face here as you begin your new life."

Stara turned back and found herself smiling at him in delight. "Thank you! Thank you, again."

He smiled back and held out his hand. "Come and join me. I have arranged a celebratory meal. I hope it is to your liking."

She reached out and let him take her hand. He led her out

of the bride room back into the room of golden light. Looking around, she saw several floating globes of light hovering near the ceiling. *Magic. I never saw Father bother with globe light.* The room was furnished sparsely with elegant pieces, the floor covered in a dark blue rug. They moved to two chairs.

In the next few hours Stara found herself treated to delicious food cooked in the styles of both Elyne and Sachaka, while talking to a man who not only seemed interested in her but was also interesting to her. He owned several plots of land from which he gained an income from crops and animals. He also maintained a few forests, and traded in the furniture made from the wood. His customers were mainly locals, but he wanted to see if he could expand his trade to Kyralia and Elyne. The war with Kyralia was making this impossible at the moment, however.

She could not believe her luck. *This is too good to be true. I can't forget that, though I do find him attractive and he does seem nice, I didn't agree to this. I wonder if he knows . . .*

Long after they had finished eating, the servants began to bring another, smaller meal, and she realised just how much time had passed. They ate sparingly, then Kachiro rose and indicated she should follow suit.

"It is time I showed you to your – our – rooms," he said. Taking her hand again, he led her through another door into a corridor. Looking back, Stara saw the globe lights blinking out, one by one. She took a deep breath and let it out slowly. *He's a good-looking man. So long as he doesn't have any nasty habits in the bedroom it shouldn't be an unpleasant night. It might even be enjoyable. After all, I did fancy him the first time I met him . . .* Hearing footsteps behind, she knew Vora was following. Relief was followed by a nagging worry. *I hope she isn't supposed to stay and watch!*

At the end of the corridor they entered a large white room.

Like the main room, its few pieces of furniture were graceful and well made. Another blue rug covered the floor. Small, plain squares of cloth hung on the walls. She made herself ignore the bed and turn to him.

"This furniture is all from your workers?"

He nodded. "A friend of mine draws the shapes, and my slaves make it. He has a good eye."

"He has," she replied. "It's beautiful."

He was still holding her hand. She was too aware of it, and the warmth of his touch. *I've hardly touched anyone since I got here. Everyone's so touchy-touchy in Elyne, but Sachakans act as though touching is an affront . . .*

"I'm afraid I must leave you here," Kachiro said. "I have urgent business in the city to attend to. I will return tomorrow, however. My slaves will attend to you, and your slave will be given a room of her own close by so she can respond quickly to your needs."

He's leaving? Stara felt a stab of disappointment, then amusement. *Was I looking forward to this after all? Did I give him the impression I was too nervous?* All she managed was a slightly puzzled. "Ah. Yes. Look forward to it."

He let go of her hand, smiled again, then turned and left.

She watched him walk down the corridor, then when he had turned out of sight she moved to the bed, sat on the edge of it, and looked at Vora.

"So. My father's neighbour. The one he's supposed to dislike."

The slave shrugged. "It would not make sense for him to marry you to an enemy, mistress, and he would not offer a daughter with magic to an ally because it might be taken as an insult and endanger an agreement."

"So he chose someone he has no links to."

"Yes. And though he dislikes Kachiro, you did say you thought him decent."

Stara nodded. It almost made her father sound as if he wasn't the monster she thought he was. *No. He read my mind. That still makes him a monster.*

"Why do you think he left?"

"Ashaki Kachiro?" Vora frowned. "He probably does have pressing business to attend to. I can't imagine any man walking away from your bed willingly. A lesser man would have made it quick. Perhaps he doesn't want to rush you."

"We spent the whole day eating and talking. Is that part of the tradition?"

Vora smiled. "No. None of it was."

Stara sighed. "Ah, well, at least Father let me keep you."

At that, Vora's brow creased into a frown. "Yes," she said, but she did not sound happy.

"Oh." Stara grimaced and tried to smother a pang of hurt. "I'm sorry, Vora. I didn't realise you wanted to stay behind."

The woman looked up at Stara and gave a wry smile. "I am delighted to remain your slave, mistress, but I am worried about Master Ikaro and Mistress Nachira. I can't do anything to help them here."

Stara felt her heart skip a beat. "Are they still in danger?"

Vora grimaced. "We can never be certain."

"Do you think Father worked out what you were doing? That he sold you to Kachiro so we were both out of the way?"

"It's possible."

Stara sighed again, then lay back on the bed. "Then I had better hurry up and have a baby." Staring up at the ceiling, she wondered how long it would take. If Kachiro running off to take care of business would be a common occurrence. If she would grow to like the confined life of a wife and mother.

"Come on then, mistress," Vora said. "Stand up and I'll help you get out of that gown."

*   *   *

422

The streets of Calia were abuzz with activity. Dakon strode down the main road looking for Tessia, who had gone in search of cures and their ingredients several hours ago. Seeing a shop selling herbs and spice, he turned and took a step towards it.

And felt a stone slip through the hole in his shoe.

He muttered a curse and kept walking, but the movement rolled the stone under his heel and at the next step he felt it gouge into his sole. Shaking the stone to the front of his shoe, he walked back to the side of the road and into the shadow of a gap between two buildings.

I should get these resoled, he told himself. But as he grasped the shoe to take it off he took in the frayed stitching, the tears and the worn-out soles. *No, I'm going to have to get new ones.*

He had put off replacing his shoes for as long as possible, despite knowing it made him look shabby. The other magicians believed they had to look dignified and well groomed in order to persuade ordinary Kyralians to obey them. But Dakon did not like taking from the very people who were suffering most in this war.

We turn up, tell them to pack up their belongings and leave, and then say, "By the way, you'll have to do without your shoes and your best coat."

As the shoe slipped off he heard women's voices in the house beside him, through an open window.

". . . same thing happened there. First the people come from the last village that was attacked, running away from the Sachakans. Then the magicians turn up and tell us to leave."

"I can't see why we should leave until we have to. My ukkas will die if nobody waters and feeds them. What if the Sachakans never come here? It would have been a waste. A complete waste."

"I don't know, Ti. The things I've heard about those Sachakans. It's said they eat the babies of their slaves. Breed them for it. Fatten them up, then whack them in the oven alive."

Dakon froze in the middle of shaking out the stone.

"Oh! That's horrible!" the second woman exclaimed.

"And since they can't take babies to war with them, they've been eating Kyralian babies instead."

"No!"

As Dakon shook his shoe again, the stone rolled out onto the ground. *Where did those women hear that?* he wondered as he put his shoe back on. *Surely they don't believe it. Nothing I've ever been told or read mentioned such habits.*

More likely it was a rumour started either in revenge or to ensure nobody considered turning traitor. Or perhaps to persuade those reluctant to leave their homes to comply with the order to leave.

But what will the consequences be, when all this is over? Will people keep believing it? If we lose it will do nothing but make occupation and a return to slavery more terrifying. But if we win . . . it will be just another reason to hate the Sachakans. How far that hate takes us I can't guess. It's hard enough imagining us defeating the Sachakans, a far older and more sophisticated people and our former rulers, in the first place.

He started across the road again only to find a long line of riders and carts blocking his way. Looking to the front of the line, he saw the backs of several well-dressed men. The people passing him were servants, he guessed, and the carts contained much-needed supplies.

More magicians for our army, Dakon thought. *I hope there are new shoes in those carts.*

"Oh, good," a familiar voice said at his shoulder. "I hope they brought a healer or two, or at least some cures and clean bandages."

Dakon turned to Tessia. "There you are! Did you find what you were looking for?"

Her nose wrinkled. "More or less. The town healer has upped his prices so much he ought to be jailed for it. I had to visit a crazy widow on the edge of town. She puts all sorts of ridiculous things in her cures that haven't any provable benefit, so I bought ingredients instead." She lifted a basket full of vegetation, both fresh and dried, under which he could see jars and wrapped objects. "I'll be up all night mixing my own."

The smell of the plants was strong and not particularly pleasant. As the last of the servants and carts passed Dakon gestured for her to follow, and started after them.

"Should we hire this healer?" he asked. Despite the Sachakans' efforts to kill everyone they encountered, some people were managing to escape the towns they attacked. Many of these escapees had injuries and Tessia had spent every spare moment treating them.

"No. Even if he wasn't too old for it, he'll charge you so much he'll be the only rich man left by the end of the war, no matter who wins."

"We could order him," Dakon told her.

A gleam entered her eyes, then faded and she shook her head. But then she betrayed her doubts by biting her lip. "Well, we could do with all the hel—"

"Lord Dakon, is that the tail end of what I think it is?"

They both turned to see Lord Narvelan striding towards them.

"Our army," Dakon confirmed.

"About time," the young magician said. "How many do you reckon have joined us this time?"

"About fifty."

"The king has done well, then. Let's see who's here."

Quickening their stride, they overtook carts and servants and gradually caught up with the magicians at the head of the column as it reached the house Werrin and Sabin had taken over as the magicians' meeting place. The two leaders were already standing on the steps, waiting to greet the newcomers.

The new arrivals stopped, dismounted and exchanged greetings with the king's representative and the sword master. Three disappeared into the house with them.

"And so the levels of power shift again," Narvelan said. "Pushing us further down the hierarchy."

"You've done well up to now," Dakon said. "Werrin still listens to you."

Narvelan nodded. "I think this time I may graciously step back into my proper place and stay there. Not because of anything anyone has said," he added quickly. "But after listening to Sabin these last few weeks . . . he is far smarter and more qualified than I. A true warrior. Everything I've thought of and suggested seems trite and naive next to his grasp of strategy. And it is nice to see some responsibility move to others."

Dakon glanced at his friend, then looked away. Narvelan had changed since the confrontation in Tecurren. Though they'd won that fight, the magician had become hesitant and doubtful. He talked of the victory with a touch of regret. Dakon suspected he had realised, for the first time, that he might die in this war and he hadn't worked out how to deal with the fear. Or perhaps it was the knowledge that he had killed another man. Narvelan had quietly admitted to Dakon that he could not help feeling uncomfortable about that victory, even after finding out what the Sachakans had done to the villagers.

Perhaps it would be beneficial for Narvelan to take a rest from the pressure of decision-making.

"I saw the wisdom of retiring to the sidelines a while back," Dakon said. "After all, there's plenty of other work requiring magicians. I'm concentrating on teaching apprentices instead. Want to join me?"

Narvelan grimaced. "Avoiding having to teach is why I've resisted taking on an apprentice for so long. I'm too young. I don't enjoy it. And I'm not good at it. Which is probably why I don't enjoy it. Praise the king for letting us have a servant as our source."

"Don't get used to it," Dakon warned. "I doubt anyone will approve of his relaxing the law permanently. It's too much like slavery."

"We'll see," Narvelan replied. "So long as we pay the servant in some way it seems reasonable to me. And if too many magicians like the idea it will be hard for King Errik to reinstate the law."

Dakon frowned, not liking the hopeful tone in Narvelan's voice. He still hadn't decided how to respond to the young magician's comment when a servant hurried over to them.

"Lord Werrin requests your presence at the meeting, Lord Narvelan," the man said. He turned to Dakon. "And yours too, Lord Dakon."

Surprised, Dakon exchanged a look of puzzlement with Narvelan. Then he remembered Tessia and turned to her.

"I'll be fine," she told him. "I have plenty of work to do and Jayan has, perhaps foolishly, offered to help. We're both going to stink of husroot by tomorrow."

"At least it'll make you easier to find," Dakon replied. She grinned, then headed away towards the house where they'd taken up residence, the owners, like many in Calia, having offered the use of it to the magicians after they evacuated to Imardin. Dakon looked at Narvelan, who shrugged, then nodded to the servant to indicate that he should lead them to Werrin.

From the greeting hall, the servant led them into a corridor then stopped in front of a closed door. He knocked and a voice called out. Opening the door, he stepped aside so they could enter. Lord Werrin was standing beside a large table strewn with paper.

"Ah, good," Werrin said. "I was hoping he'd find you two, sooner rather than later. I have propositions for both of you." He rubbed his hands together and looked from Dakon to Narvelan and back again. "I don't want country magicians like you being overlooked and under-represented now that we have so many city magicians in the army, especially not if you lose your entire leys. At the least, we need you around to remind city magicians what we all will lose if they do not co-operate. You must remain part of all planning and discussion, and to reinforce this I am giving you both official roles. Lord Dakon will be in charge of teachers and organising the lessons of apprentices. Can you think of a good title? Teacher Master, perhaps? I don't think Apprentice Master will go down well."

Dakon chuckled. "No, I'd be suspected of taking charge of everyone's apprentices. Teacher Master implies anyone volunteering to teach has to become a subordinate, and I can't imagine that would encourage involvement. How about Training Master?"

Werrin nodded. "Yes. I like it. Very good. Now," he turned to Narvelan, "your role is to liaise between country and city magicians. To head off conflict or settle it when it arises. Are you willing to take on the responsibility?"

Narvelan paused, then nodded slowly. "Yes." He smiled crookedly.

"What shall we call you, then?"

"Country Master? No, that won't do. Is this title thing necessary?"

"Sabin believes so. The king has nominated him war master."

"How very grand."

Werrin eyes sparkled with amusement. "I've managed to keep to 'king's representative', thankfully. How about we call you the ley representative?" Werrin looked thoughtful. "Yes, then I can call the magician speaking for city magicians the house representative."

"Sounds good to me," Narvelan agreed, nodding.

"Good." Werrin moved around the table and straightened his clothes. "Now it's time to meet and discuss our experiences and strategies. We have some new contributors to introduce to the harsh realities of war, and to our way of doing things. I can rely on your support?"

Dakon glanced at Narvelan, who smiled. "Of course."

"Naturally," Narvelan replied.

Werrin smiled. "Then let's go strip a few well-meaning magicians of their delusions and see if they don't flee back to Imardin." He walked past them to the door, then paused and looked over his shoulder. "Though you can be sure the king would send them scurrying back again," he added. "If it weren't for some firm and sensible advice, he'd be here himself. Sabin wants the chance to whip us into some semblance of a cohesive army before the king comes out to lead us."

"He does, does he?" Narvelan said.

"Yes." Werrin looked at Dakon. "So there's going to be a lot of instruction required in our new fighting techniques."

Dakon sighed in mock despair. "I knew I shouldn't have agreed so quickly. There had to be a catch somewhere."

Werrin turned back to the door. "Don't worry. You'll have plenty of assistants. I'll make sure of it. My only concern is that the Sachakans won't give us any time for preparation.

Sabin thinks they may have left the road to avoid being caught between us and our reinforcements. But he believes they will only roam about in the farms and villages of Noven ley long enough to gather more strength before heading towards Imardin. We need to be ready to stop them."

CHAPTER 32

I n a large walled courtyard behind one of the grander houses in Calia, twelve apprentices had separated into six pairs. Each was taking turns practising the trick of sending magic to another. Only small amounts of magic were being channelled, and to make the exercise more interesting Dakon had them knocking broken tiles off the top of the back wall.

Leaning against the side of the courtyard entrance, Jayan sighed. Only three magicians had volunteered to teach Ardalen's method to the magicians and apprentices who had arrived the day before. It made what should have been a fast exercise into a day-long task.

They'd taught the magicians in the morning easily enough. In the afternoon they'd tackled the apprentices. Unfortunately, many of the magicians had resisted having their apprentices taught by other magicians. Dakon had told Jayan that though he'd managed to convince most of them of the benefits, a few had only agreed to it when Sabin had pointed out that the apprentices' families might not look favourably on their sons and daughters dying in battle for the lack of training that had been offered to all.

The apprentices had not been easy to teach, however. Some of them had barely begun their training and two hadn't even achieved full control of their powers yet.

After an inexperienced one burned the young man he was trying to send magic through by mistake, Dakon had decided to rearrange the three groups by splitting them based on experience: one group of those who had been only recently apprenticed, one for those who had been training for a few years, and one for those close to being granted their independence. Dakon, assisted by Jayan, had chosen the inexperienced group to teach, and it had taken a lot longer than the others.

Jayan had found teaching both frustrating and rewarding. It depended on the apprentice. Some were attentive and talented. Some were not. The former were gratifying to instruct, but he also found that if he managed to encourage – or bully – one of the latter into grasping something it was also very satisfying.

I always thought I'd put off taking on an apprentice for as long as possible, but I can see now there are benefits – other than the obvious one of gaining power.

The inexperienced apprentices ranged in age from twelve – much younger than the usual age for apprenticeship – to eighteen. He suspected the older ones had been chosen because their masters preferred to teach someone less gifted from their own family than someone more gifted from outside.

One of the apprentices giving power to another yelped, then turned to regard the other pairs suspiciously. A young woman – the only one in the group and one of two who had arrived with the reinforcements – tried to hide her smirk, but her victim obviously knew her well enough to guess where the attack had come from. Jayan assumed she'd let loose a strike in his direction that was only powerful enough to sting. The victim and the apprentice he was giving power to exchanged a look, then scowled.

Jayan glanced at Dakon. His master was watching the tiles flying off the top of the wall, and probably hadn't noticed.

There was a low laugh of triumph, this time from the

432

companion of the previous victim. A moment later the girl yelped. She turned to glare at the pair. Seeing the look of anger and calculation in her eyes, Jayan decided it was time to intervene.

Before he had a chance to speak, a messenger hurried into the courtyard and spoke quietly to Dakon, who nodded. As the messenger left again Dakon turned to face the group.

"That will be enough, I think. You all seem to have grasped it now. If you have a chance, practise what you've learned, but only use small amounts of power. You may return to your masters." He walked towards the courtyard entrance, smiling ruefully as he passed Jayan. "Another meeting. Will you tell Tessia, when she returns?"

"Of course."

The apprentices had gathered into one group to chat, and as Dakon left they started towards the entrance. All nodded to Jayan as they passed through. The last was the young woman. She was, he guessed, two or three years younger than him. A good-looking girl, but by the way she smiled at him it was clear she was well aware of it.

"Master Jayan, isn't it? I hear you were at the battle in Tecurren," she said, regarding him from under long eyelashes.

"Apprentice Jayan," he corrected her. "And yes, I was there."

As she tipped her head to one side and smiled at him again, he felt an unexpected wave of annoyance and disgust. He knew that look. He'd encountered enough female magicians to know when one was sizing him up.

"What was it like?" Her eyes widened. "It must have been *so* scary."

"We knew we outnumbered them and would probably win." He shrugged.

Moving to the entrance, she looked outside. The alley was empty. "Look. They've not bothered to wait for me. Escort me to the meeting hall?" She hooked a hand around his elbow. "You can tell me all about the battle on the way."

He took her hand and removed it from the crook of his arm, then let it go.

Her eyes flashed with anger, but then her expression softened again and she nodded as if chastised. "That was too forward of me. I am just trying to be friendly."

"Are you?" he asked, before he could stop himself.

She frowned. "Of course. What else would I be doing?"

He shook his head. "We're at war, not a party. This is not the city. Not the place for . . . for flirting and looking for a husband. Or lover."

She rolled her eyes. "I know that, but—"

"And there are other young women here. Younger, less experienced women. Do you realise how your 'friendliness' may affect them? How it may encourage young male apprentices to think all female magicians are . . . available? Or older magicians to assume women are too foolish and distractable to make good magicians?"

Her eyes went wide with astonishment. Her mouth opened, then closed again. Then her eyes narrowed and she spoke through gritted teeth.

"You are assuming too much, Apprentice Jayan."

She lifted her chin and stalked out of the courtyard. Then she stopped and looked over her shoulder. "Young men will always entertain stupid ideas about women, no matter how demure or *friendly* they are. You've just proved that yourself. Before laying blame, take a good look at yourself. You might be surprised to find who is the foolish, distractable one."

Then she strode away.

Drawing in a deep breath, Jayan sighed. The anger that had risen at her flirting ebbed too quickly, leaving him feeling ashamed of his outburst.

"Well, that was entertaining."

The voice came from behind him. He turned to see Tessia standing over by the door to the house, and winced as he realised she might have heard only the end of the exchange.

"I object to being sized up like a prize," he told her. "If she knew my father she would not be so keen on my bloodlines."

Tessia smiled and walked towards him. "It may not be your bloodlines she's so keen on. Apparently, or so Avaria's friends assure me, you're rather handsome. And you've also experienced battle, which gives you a certain kind of glamour that some women are attracted to."

He stared at her, unable to think of a response that wouldn't sound foolish or vain. She smiled.

"Well, I'm glad I'm not, if that's the way you react." She glanced around the courtyard. "How did the lessons go?"

Relieved by the change of subject, he nodded to the courtyard entrance and they both stepped out and started towards the main road. "They took a while, but I think most of them have grasped it."

She sighed. "Dakon finally gives another lesson, and it's something I already know." She grimaced. "We're not going to get any more training, are we?"

He shook his head. "Not now that Dakon is one of the army's advisers. Any time we're not riding or fighting, he'll be at meetings."

"It must be so frustrating for you, being so close to the end of your training."

"It is. But if I had finished, then I might only be a higher magician for a matter of weeks, or days if we are defeated. At least this way Dakon has two apprentices to draw from."

"But if you were a higher magician, you'd have your own source to draw from, and there'd be another fighter in the army." She chuckled. "And the women would have even more reason to annoy you with their flirting and their interest." She paused and looked at him. "I wouldn't be surprised if Dakon taught you higher magic soon, for that very reason."

Jayan felt his heart skip. She might be right. But the possibility roused an unexpected reluctance. *Why? Am I afraid to stand on my own? To be responsible for my own life?*

Tessia was smiling at him knowingly. *I've never said anything to her about my frustration at the delay in finishing my training,* he thought. *Yet she's worked it out for herself. She understands me. And I think she's finally stopped hating me.*

And then it was obvious why he was reluctant to end his apprenticeship with Dakon. It would take him away from Tessia.

He blinked in surprise. *Is that really it? Do I truly feel that way about her?* He felt a strange sensation, both pleasant and painful. Amazing how the admiration he'd always felt was suddenly enhanced by his recognition of it. Then he remembered what she'd said earlier.

"... *gives you a certain kind of glamour that some women are attracted to. Well, I'm glad I'm not* ..."

His heart sank.

It was possible his feelings would change. *Then it's possible hers might, too.* He pushed that thought aside. *No. Leave it be. War is not a good time to be caring too much about anyone, or having them care about you. At any point either one of us could die. I'd rather not make it more painful – for either of us. In fact, she'd be better off hating me.*

Which is just as well, because I'm very good at making women do that.

As Hanara headed towards the house Takado had claimed in the tiny village, he passed two slaves carrying away the remains of the reber that had been roasted for the night's meal. Pausing, he ducked in close and grabbed a large chunk of meat. Only half of the animal had been eaten, he saw, so the slaves would eat well tonight. But Takado was often awake late into the night discussing strategy with his closest allies, so if Hanara and Jochara didn't grab what food they could, it would be gone by the time Takado retired.

He gnawed away at the meat as he hurried to the house, where he retrieved a bottle of wine from the store of them he'd found in the cellar. He paused to finish the meat, chewing and swallowing quickly, so that he could wipe the grease from his hands and not risk dropping the bottle on the return trip.

To make up for the lost time, he jogged back, nursing the bottle carefully. Only Takado's three closest allies remained by the campfire they'd set up in the middle of the road: Rokino, his old Ichani friend, Dachido and Asara.

Hanara prostrated himself and held up the bottle. He felt it taken from his grasp. Takado said nothing. After a short wait, the slave crawled backwards on all fours, then sat on his haunches and looked around. Jochara was nowhere to be seen.

"You don't have enough slaves," Asara said, looking at Takado. "A leader ought to have more slaves than anybody else."

Takado shrugged. "I could try to bring a few more over, but I can't go myself and those I'd trust with the task I need here. It would be such a menial favour to ask it would be insulting."

"Then take one of mine," Asara offered. "No, take two." She turned and called out. "Chinka! Dokko!"

Turning to look over his shoulder, Takado looked at Hanara, his expression thoughtful and amused. "You'd serve me better if I didn't wear you out all the time, wouldn't you, Hanara?"

Hanara bent forward to place his forehead on the ground. "My life is yours to use as you wish," he said.

The woman laughed. "Ah, here they come."

Stealing a quick glance, Hanara saw that Takado's attention had moved away from him again. All the magicians were looking at a pair of slaves who had thrown themselves on the ground in front of Asara. A woman, lean and strong, and a large, well-muscled man.

"They are two of my best," Asara said proudly. "They're in good condition. Chinka used to work in the kitchens, but she is also useful at cleaning, mending clothes and shoes, treating minor hurts, light carrying duties and other general tasks. Dokko is a good maker – useful for more than just heavy work – and he's good with horses." She turned back to Takado. "Which I am surprised you haven't acquired yet. We would travel faster with them."

"Would we?" Takado shook his head. "Horses need feed, rest and slaves to look after them. And unless we have horses for our slaves we will travel just as slowly as we are doing now."

"But we don't always have to keep our slaves with us. We could attack rapidly, without warning, and return to them."

Takado nodded. "Yes, there may be times when the risk of leaving them alone and vulnerable will prove worthwhile. Still, for now I prefer not to have to take care of a horse."

"You won't have to, if you take my slaves."

Takado fell silent, his expression thoughtful. Hanara held his breath. How would two more slaves change his own situation? There would be less work. He would certainly welcome having less to carry each day, though that would not remain the case if Takado gained more belongings. But Hanara had no skills to make up for the man's brawn, or the woman's usefulness. And if Takado took the woman to bed . . . Hanara knew he could never compete with that.

But I am a source slave, he thought. *I will always have higher status because of that.*

Takado was nodding. "I accept. I thank you, Asara. It is a thoughtful gift. They are clearly valuable slaves for you to be losing."

The woman waved a hand gracefully. "I will miss them, but I can see now that I brought too many slaves with me. You need them more than I."

"Chinka. Dokko," Takado said. "Get up and sit behind Hanara."

As the pair obeyed, Hanara kept his eyes downcast. He heard them settle behind him. For a moment he thought one had disobeyed Takado, taking a position beside him, but when he looked he saw that Jochara had returned. The young man carried a metal tube that contained the map of Kyralia that Takado had brought with him.

"You are both – and you, too, Jochara – to follow Hanara's orders unless they conflict with mine. Do you understand?"

Murmurs of affirmation followed. Hanara stared at the ground, his eyes wide. *He's put me in charge!* His heart began to pound. It was a frighteningly important responsibility. *What if they won't obey me? What if they do something wrong? Will I be punished for it? What—*

An unfamiliar voice interrupted his panicked thoughts.

"Magicians . . . coming . . ." a slave was panting even as he threw himself on the ground. "Many. Fast. From. Emper . . . or. Wear. Rings."

The magicians hadn't moved, but their smiles had vanished. None voiced the worries written on their faces. Had the emperor sent forces to stop Takado? Were they about to attack? Whistles came from scouts to one side of the village.

Takado rose. He snapped out orders, sending Hanara and the other slaves scampering about to alert all the magicians, or the slaves of the magicians who were asleep since they knew best how to rouse their masters. Soon there were magicians and slaves crowding the road. Hanara positioned himself a step behind Takado, who stood between Dachido and Asara.

Interesting, Hanara thought. *Rokino has known Takado the longest, but he is an Ichani. Dachido and Asara outrank him and are a lot smarter than Takado's other Ichani friends. Lately Takado is favouring their company and opinions above the others'.*

As the last stragglers joined the crowd around Takado a large group of men rode into sight around a bend in the road. Globes of light hovered over them. The brightness set weapons and beaded clothes aglitter. Hanara looked for the rings of the emperor and caught a glint of gold here and there.

There must have been at least forty magicians. Of their slaves there was no sign.

The man at the head of the group was tall and wrinkled, with white in his dark hair. He led the men forward and stopped ten strides from the crowd. Back straight and head high, he scanned the crowd once before his gaze returned to Takado.

"Emperor Vochira sends his greetings," he said. "I am Ashaki Nomako."

"Welcome, Ashaki Nomako," Takado replied. "Should I send my regards to the emperor through you, or are your intentions to stay and join us?"

The man somehow managed to straighten himself even further. "Emperor Vochira has decided to support your efforts to bring Kyralia back under the influence of the empire, and has ordered me to provide what assistance and guidance is needed, including this army of magicians loyal to Sachaka."

"That is most generous of him," Takado said. "With your help we can conquer Kyralia faster and with less risk to our fellow Sachakans. If it is done with the support of the emperor, then all the better. Does the emperor support my leadership of this army?"

"Of course," Nomako said. "He gives credit where it is due."

"Then be doubly welcome," Takado said. He moved forward, closing the gap between them, and held out a hand. Nomako dismounted and grasped it. Then they let go and Takado nodded towards his crowd of supporters. "Have you eaten? We roasted a reber earlier, and there may still be some left."

"No need," Nomako replied. "We ate at sundown. Our slaves are waiting for us to send for them . . ."

As Nomako discussed practicalities, Hanara noted the way the man's gaze changed whenever Takado looked away. *Calculating*, Hanara thought. *He's not come here because he agrees with Takado. We always knew that Emperor Vochira would not like Takado taking matters into his own hands.* Hanara felt a shiver of premonition run down his spine. *This one is going to try to take back control for the emperor. And he won't find it as easy as he thinks.*

CHAPTER 33

The number of magicians, apprentices and servants in pursuit of the Sachakan invaders was now many times larger. Over seventy magicians, as many apprentices and servants employed as sources, and all the servants, carts and animals that were required to tend to the army's needs made quite an impressive sight.

It really feels like an army now, Tessia thought. Since Dakon was one of the army advisers, she rode near to the front. Before her rode Werrin, Sabin, Narvelan and a few city magicians. When she looked behind, a sea of magicians and apprentices filled the road. Only when the road turned did she glimpse the servants and supply carts.

She knew that Sabin and Werrin believed that having the army strung out like this wasn't as safe as bunched together, but the road was often confined between low rock field walls. There had been some trouble with a few of the younger magicians riding off to raid an orchard and then, ignoring Sabin's attempts to explain the danger, galloping out into fields to jump fences and race each other.

I'd have thought seeing victims of Takado and his allies would have sobered them up, Tessia mused, *but I suspect most of them still think this is a grand adventure.*

At mid-morning the new army encountered the first signs of destruction. The Sachakans had left a swathe of destroyed villages and houses across the ley, but left the main road to avoid the Kyralian reinforcements. Scouts had reported that Takado had headed east from the main road, through Noven ley – Lord Gilar's land – until he encountered the next main thoroughfare. It was the same road Dakon had taken to Imardin but the enemy had travelled in the opposite direction until it encountered a village, and settled there, leaving burned farm houses and storage buildings, and occasional corpses, in its wake.

"Tessia!"

The voice was female, coming from behind. Tessia turned to see Lady Avaria riding towards her. Others also turned to watch, as a wailing came from a bundle the magician held cradled in one arm. Avaria's servant and source, a practical young woman Tessia had instantly liked, followed close behind.

"Can you have a look at him?" Avaria asked as she drew alongside Tessia. "I asked the healers to, but one refused and the other told me it would be kinder to smother him."

A small, red face screwed up tight, the mouth from which the wailing poured stretched wide open, appeared as she tilted the bundle in Tessia's direction. Tessia carefully took the baby and examined it. There was a livid bruise on the scalp.

"He's had a knock, but nothing's broken," she said. "He's probably got a stinker of a headache. Where'd you find him?"

"I didn't. One of the others did, then decided that, because I'm a woman, I would be able to take care of him at the same time as riding into battle." A tone of annoyance had entered Avaria's voice, but it didn't override the concern. "Shhh," she said soothingly as Tessia handed the child back. "Poor thing. Found still strapped to the back of his dead mother. I guess this proves the rumours about Sachakans eating babies aren't true. Not that I believed it," she added hastily.

Tessia felt something inside her twist painfully. "Is leaving him to die of starvation any less cruel?"

"No. Shush," Avaria said, then rolled her eyes as he only bawled louder.

"He's probably hungry," Tessia said. "And from the smell I'd say he needed a change a long time ago."

Avaria sighed. "Yes. He can't stay with us. I'd have Sennia take him back to Calia if I could spare her, but I can't."

"Can any of the other servants take him?" Tessia asked.

A look of distaste crossed Avaria's face. "Sennia suggested we give him to the unmentioned ones."

"*Unmentioned*" *ones?* Tessia frowned, then smothered a laugh. "The women following the army? I suppose one might take him . . . for the right price." She looked at the boy and considered. "Try the servants first. We may find survivors willing to take care of him, too." The baby's wails grew suddenly louder. "But he won't last if you don't get him fed."

Avaria nodded. "Thank you." She looked at Sennia. "Could you ask . . . ?"

The servant smiled, turned her horse and started riding back down the line. Avaria looked ahead and her expression changed from concern and annoyance to one of horror.

"What . . . ?"

Following Avaria's gaze, Tessia looked past the magicians and felt her stomach sink. Corpses littered the road. Not one or two, but dozens, perhaps even hundreds. As the army drew close she saw that the victims were men and women of all ages. Children, too. She heard exclamations and curses from all around.

"They must have been on their way south," Jayan said quietly. "Doing what they'd been told – to evacuate. Only they ended up in the path of the Sachakans."

Dakon made a low noise. "Look." He pointed at broken furniture at the side of the road. "They probably took these people's carts and threw out what they didn't have a use for."

444

Avaria hissed quietly. "They're having no trouble replenishing the powers they're using to burn and wreck our villages and towns."

"No," Dakon agreed, his gaze dark with worry.

Suddenly a head appeared above the low stone wall on one side of the road. Then a small girl climbed over and ran to the head of the army. Werrin reined in his horse, and everyone began to stop.

"Help! Can anybody help? Father is hurt." The girl pointed towards the wall.

Werrin spoke to one of the servants travelling with the army's leaders. The man hurried down the line, his gaze pausing on Tessia, then sliding away. Tessia felt a small pang of hurt. For months she had been the one people turned to for healing. Now that there were guild-trained healers in the army, she had returned to being merely an apprentice.

But he did consider me, she thought. *It's not been forgotten, or remained unnoticed, that I do have some skill.*

Werrin nudged his horse into a walk again, and the rest began to follow. Jayan turned to look at her.

"Let's wait and see what happens."

Surprised and pleased, she followed as he drew his mount aside so the army could pass. Dakon glanced back once and nodded to indicate his approval. She felt a fond gratitude. He did not need her to ask his permission. He understood, even supported, her healing.

I am so lucky to have him as my master, she thought.

The wait for the healers seemed long, and she realised why when, long after the last magician had passed, the two men peeled away from the column.

They couldn't be bothered breaking from the line and riding ahead, she realised with disgust. The girl pointed over the wall, and the men dismounted with unconcealed annoyance. A servant

445

stopped to hold the horses' heads. Tessia and Jayan swung to the ground and gave the servant their reins as well. Tessia unhooked her father's bag, and they followed the girl and the healers across the field.

It was not hard to find her father. A great swathe of blackened vegetation led to him, and past. His clothes were also black. He lay in a furrow, face down, unconscious but still breathing.

The two healers bent to examine the man, then shook their heads.

"He is too badly burned," one told the girl, gently but firmly. "He will not live through the night."

Tears filled her eyes. "Can't you stop him hurting?" she asked in a small voice.

The healer shook his head. "Bathe him with cool water. If you have any strong drink, give him that."

As the healers walked past Tessia and Jayan, the one who hadn't spoken to the girl looked at Tessia. "Don't waste your cures," he told her.

Jayan cursed quietly under his breath as the pair strode away. He looked at Tessia. "Do you want to have a closer look?"

"Of course."

Moving to the man's side, Tessia knelt on the ground. She realised with a shock that there wasn't blackened cloth on the man's back. It was his skin.

"When the strangers came we ran," the girl said.

The man's breath was coming in short gasps. *The healers were right. He can't survive this.*

"When the fire came he fell on top of me," the girl said. "I didn't get burned."

Despite her misgivings, Tessia tucked her hands under his head, touching the unburned skin of the man's forehead, and closed her eyes. As she had all the times in the past, she focused on the pulses and rhythms of the body beneath her hands. She gently sent her mind out of herself and into his. But this time there were no broken bones or torn flesh to manipulate. The damage was more subtle. Her father had taught her how a heart reacted to a severe burn, and about other changes in the body. She sought a sense of these changes.

Suddenly she could feel his pain.

It was terrible. She recoiled. Opened her eyes. Realised she had cried out.

"What is it?" Jayan said, alarm in his voice.

"You'd better start mixing up the pain blocker now," she told him, then forced herself to close her eyes and send her mind forth again.

I've never sensed anything like that before! Knowing that if she hesitated, she'd lose the courage to face that pain again, she delved back into her awareness of the man's body. Eagerness and reluctance warred within her, and it took a long, long moment before she felt the pain sweep over her again. This time she forced herself to stay and endure it. To examine and gently probe.

Within moments she'd worked out where to apply magic to block the pain. But she hesitated.

Should I? Father always said pain was the body's way of making a person sit still and heal. This man is still going to die, but how shocking would it be for his daughter if he started walking about, all burned, only to collapse and die?

Perhaps if she could *lessen* the pain . . . she cautiously drew power and blocked some of the pathways. The body under her hand relaxed a little. Unsure if she had done enough, or too much, she drew away and opened her eyes.

The girl's father was awake. He made no attempt to get up. She realised that he was exhausted, and probably would not have had the energy to rise.

"There," she said, glancing at the girl and Jayan. "That's given him some relief." She looked at Jayan, who had measured out powder into a mixing jar. "Don't worry about it. I've worked out how to block the pain with magic."

His eyes widened and he stared at her in amazement. Then he shook his head and began to replace the items in her father's bag.

"Who are you?" a voice croaked.

They both jumped and looked down at the burned man.

"Magicians," Jayan replied. "And Tessia has some knowledge of healing."

The man looked at her. "Magicians who are healers. Never heard of that before."

Tessia smiled. "Me neither."

"You off to fight then?"

She felt the smile fade. "Yes."

"Good. Now get on with you."

"But—" Tessia began. *I haven't even tried to heal him yet . . .*

"Don't worry about me. Best thing you can do now is kill those bastards before they do this to anyone else. Go on." He lifted his head slightly, his eyes moving beyond them. "Your army's getting further ahead of you."

Jayan looked towards the road and frowned.

He's right, Tessia thought. *I can't save him and we shouldn't stray too far from Dakon.* The man spoke a name and his daughter moved closer. "You go to your aunt Tanna, right? You know the way."

As the girl began to protest, Tessia stood up. Jayan followed suit. Drawing in a deep breath, she let out a long sigh, then forced herself to walk back towards the road.

"You didn't try to heal him?" Jayan asked.

"No. There was no point trying. I couldn't save him."

"There's always a point in trying. Even if you can't save

448

someone, you might learn something – and you did. You stopped the pain with magic."

She grimaced. "It's still not healing with magic, though."

"But it's something new. Something no magician or healer has managed."

She frowned. "And I have no idea if I can undo it. What if I stopped the pain while doing something minor, but couldn't unstop it. Would I leave someone permanently numb?"

He shrugged. "You'll work it out. I know you will."

She sighed and looked at him. "I couldn't do this without you, Jayan. Not without your help."

His eyes widened and he quickly looked away. "I'm only doing it because I know you'd be running off on your own if I didn't keep an eye on you, no matter what Dakon said." He stepped over the walls and started towards their horses. "We'd better catch up."

Amused, Tessia watched as he roughly hooked her father's bag on her mount's saddle and then, without looking at her, swung up onto his own horse. He didn't wait for her to mount, and set a swifter pace than she liked, as it jostled the contents of the bag too much. When they were halfway along the line he abruptly kicked his mount into a fast trot, not even glancing back to see if she followed.

What did I say? she wondered as he left her behind. Then she noticed how one of the female apprentices stared at him as he passed her. He gave the apprentice a quick glance, and smiled. *Ah. Is that it? Has our little conversation yesterday made him reconsider what he thinks of female magicians? Being too openly friendly with me might ruin his chances with them.*

A pity, she thought. *We were getting along so well.*

Keeping her expression neutral, Stara walked into Kachiro's bedroom. *Or more accurately,* my *bedroom.* At once Vora jumped up from the low stool she had been sitting on and prostrated herself. Stara sat down on the end of the bed, thought of several different approaches to describing what had happened, and could not decide which to take.

"Can I get up, mistress?"

"Oh! Sorry. Of course." Stara felt her face flush. *Am I ever going to get used to having slaves? Though I suppose the fact that I forgot she was there is a good sign that I'm beginning to. Or a bad sign.*

Vora returned to the stool and looked at her expectantly. "Well?"

Stara shook her head. The slave's shoulders slumped. "What went wrong this time?"

"Not your plan," Stara assured her. "I went to the baths, as you suggested. He was there. He wasn't angry at me. He was . . . I think he expected me to try something like that, though perhaps not so soon." *Funny how I was surprised he didn't seduce me on the night of the wedding, but he's surprised I've only left it for a week. I wonder how long I'm supposed to wait?*

Vora was frowning now. "And?"

"I . . . I did what you suggested." Stara shook her head. "No reaction."

"Nothing? Perhaps he was pretending."

Stara smiled wryly. "I have no reason to doubt. He wasn't wearing any clothing. And neither was I."

"Oh." Vora looked away, her brow creased deeply. "What happened then?"

"He told me he's never been able to bed a woman, or even wanted to. He was very apologetic about it. I asked him why he married me and he said he'd hoped it would be different with a woman as beautiful as me."

Vora gave a quiet snort. "That, I suspect, is a lie. What happened next?"

450

"I told him I was hoping for children. He told me not to worry, that we would find another way. He made me promise not to tell anyone. Then he got me to put my clothes back on and leave."

The slave's eyebrows rose. "Interesting."

Stara frowned. "Do you think Father knew Kachiro couldn't . . . ?"

"That he'd marry you to a man he knew couldn't sire children?"

"Or because I can't kill him while bedding him."

Vora blinked. "I hadn't considered that. It wouldn't do Ashaki Sokara's reputation any good if his daughter had a habit of killing husbands. But the first reason is possibly more likely. Your father cares a great deal where his wealth and land will go when he dies. I'd assumed he would prefer it to fall into the hands of a man he disliked than the emperor's – especially since Kachiro's the same age as Ikaro and unlikely to outlive him by very long, so that everything would soon pass on to your son or daughter. But maybe I am wrong. Maybe this is more complicated than that." She looked thoughtful.

"Kachiro said we'd find a way to have a child. Is he lying?"

Vora shook her head and smiled. "There are other ways to 'baste the bird', as they say."

Stara grimaced. "Why are all Sachakan sayings so crass?"

The slave shrugged. "It probably started as a slave saying. We're nothing if not honest about the processes of life."

"Then . . . if there are other ways I can become pregnant by Kachiro, then it's still possible for Father's assets to go to my husband's descendants."

"Yes." Vora rose and began to pace the room. "If your father doesn't intend you to have a child, then he has to have considered that you may become pregnant by other means. Your father must know he can contest the paternity of any child of yours, and succeed. Either more people know about Kachiro's inability than he realises, or your father has other evidence. Someone willing to verify it. Or unwilling but powerless to prevent a mind-read." Vora's voice trailed off. She stopped pacing and her expression became thoughtful.

Rising, Stara began pacing in Vora's place. "So, if Father doesn't mean me to have a child, or plans to contest its legitimacy, then who does he want to have inherit?" She felt her heart skip and looked up at the slave. "He still means to kill Nachira!"

Vora looked up, and her expression became grave. "Ah."

A wave of frustration and anger rushed through Stara. "I agreed to marry for nothing! He was getting me out of the way. Argh! This is crazy!" She stopped pacing and turned to face Vora. "Why doesn't Father want a grandchild by me to inherit? It's not like Kachiro can take anything before Ikaro dies."

Vora shrugged. "Part of it is pride. Inheritance in direct line through male sons is considered the ideal, and your father is nothing if not a traditionalist. He also sees his trade as another son or daughter. He wants to make sure it has a healthy future in the hands of people who will maintain it."

"And this justifies killing Nachira?"

"Yes." The slave sighed.

Stara sat down, suddenly filled with helplessness. "I wish we could sneak Nachira out of there and send her somewhere safe."

"I too," Vora said sadly. "And I'm no longer in a position to help." Her eyes narrowed in thought. "Though I might be able to get a warning to Ikaro, if he hasn't left."

"Left? Ah, the war in Kyralia." Stara shook her head. "If Father is so set on having an heir through his son, why would he send Ikaro off to war?"

Vora grimaced. "Pride again. Any ashaki who do not fight will lose respect and status. He has most likely joined the army too."

"They must be *very* confident of winning – and surviving." Stara frowned. *Does Mother know any of this? She can't know her husband plans to kill her daughter by marriage. She hasn't even met Nachira, though she must wonder why she has no grandchildren yet. Does she know her son is going to Kyralia to fight? How is a war between Sachaka and Kyralia affecting trade in Elyne? She may not be able to receive dyes from here, but she did have a few arrangements locally. Eventually the war must end and life go back to normal. Then she'll find out I'm married . . .*

"Is me having a child really going to threaten Father's trade?" she asked aloud.

Vora blinked as Stara's question dragged her out of her thoughts. "Well . . . If Kachiro is gaining a bad reputation that might put people off trading with him or his offspring . . . so it's possible. But then if your father knew this he wouldn't marry you to him. In fact, if the arrangement was so damaging, why didn't he simply lock you up for the rest of your life?"

Stara scowled. "Because I'd have blasted my way out of there."

"And you'd have been caught and dragged back here. Which would be easy since you have no source slave with which to strengthen yourself." Vora pursed her lips for a moment. "You know, it would have been far easier for your father to have you killed. He must have enough family feeling to want to avoid that. He's taken quite a risk marrying you to Kachiro."

Stara shuddered. "All the more reason to ask: is having a child so great a threat that I should consider *not* having one?"

Vora began to shake her head, then she stilled and a familiar expression of deep and careful consideration took hold of her features.

"Perhaps. But you've told Kachiro you want to have them. He will think it odd if you don't attempt to." She grimaced. "Let's hope he does intend to be the father, by other means, because it could be a little awkward if he suggests you use a lover."

Stara sighed. "How much worse can this get?" she wondered aloud. Then she winced. "I guess I could be murdered for being infertile." She sighed and flopped back onto her back. "Why, oh, why did you let me come back to this crazy, crazy country, Mother?"

"You wanted to," she imagined her mother replying. "You couldn't wait to return to your father."

At least the man she was married to was kind and decent. Even if he had a secret or two. *Hopefully only the one*, she thought. *And I guess that's fair enough, considering how many I have. I don't even know if Father told him I can use magic. I'm beginning to suspect he didn't.*

For now, until she knew how he was likely to react, or unless she faced a life-threatening situation, she was going to pretend she couldn't.

CHAPTER 34

The scout's face had been smeared with ash and grease, and his clothes were dark with dried mud. Dakon had seen this man report many times now, but he still hadn't picked up his name. *He must be good at his job. We always seem to be recruiting new scouts, and old ones keep disappearing . . .*

"A few hundred people used to live in Lonner," the man told Magician Sabin.

"Any of the villagers alive?"

"Not that I could see. There's a pile of dead out in a field, but it doesn't account for all of them."

"The rest left in time?"

The man shrugged. "Hope so."

"How many Sachakans?"

"Just over sixty."

"And how many are magicians?"

The scout grimaced. "I only counted the magicians. There's two or three times as many slaves, I reckon."

Sabin frowned and looked at Lord Werrin, who shrugged.

"Perhaps they have dressed some of their slaves as magicians, to fool us," Werrin suggested.

"Perhaps," Sabin repeated. "We'll see what the other scouts say. Thank you, Nim."

The scout bowed, and moved away. All eyes looked towards the village ahead. Lonner was a typical small settlement, built on either side of a road with a river to one side.

Just like Mandryn, Dakon thought, and felt a pang of grief and loss.

The Kyralian army was waiting off the road, concealed behind a farmhouse and a copse. Servants and the supply carts waited several hundred strides further back down the road, though some servants had volunteered to stay with the army to tend to the horses while the magicians were fighting.

Dakon was standing among the seven advisers and leaders of the army.

"We shouldn't discount the possibility that more of Takado's friends may have joined him," Narvelan said.

Sabin nodded. "Though for his army to grow so large, he must be able to claim friendship with half the magicians in Sachaka. No, I am more worried that those who *don't* consider themselves his allies or friends are joining him, because there are a *lot* more of those across the border." He scowled and turned to stare at the village.

"What should we do?" Hakkin asked. "Will we still confront them?"

Sabin's frown deepened. "We still outnumber them, though not by much."

"We have Ardalen's method. That may give us an advantage," Dakon added.

"I suspect the benefits will be reduced in a direct confrontation," Sabin said. "Our strength is the same, whether we fight in teams and direct our strikes through one, or fight individually."

"But our defence will be more efficient. Those who run out of strength are protected by the shield of their team, and live to fight another day," Hakkin pointed out.

"Can we avoid a direct confrontation, then?" Bolvin asked.

"Not from the look of it," Werrin replied. He lifted an arm to point towards the village and everyone turned to look.

456

Streams of people were spilling out between the houses, slowly forming a wide line stretching out into the unfenced fields on either side of the road. Dakon felt a chill run down his spine. If these were all Sachakan magicians, their numbers had, indeed, swelled alarmingly.

"I gather their own scouts have reported our approach," Werrin murmured.

"And they don't think our greater numbers are a problem," Narvelan added.

Sabin drew in a deep breath, then let it out. He looked at the other magicians. "Then, unless any of you disagree – and if you wish to debate it you had better make it quick – I say it is time we demonstrated the effect of both our greater numbers and our improved fighting skills." As Sabin looked around at the other six magicians, they nodded. He smiled grimly. "It is decided."

Turning, he faced the rest of the magicians, milling around in groups as they waited for the leaders to decide their next move. "Ready yourselves," he called out. "The Sachakans are coming to us for a fight and we are going to give them one they'll never forget. Gather into your fighting teams. Spread out to match their line. Shield yourselves and be ready. It is time we went to war!"

To Dakon's surprise, the magicians responded with a cheer. He knew that some were too young or naive to realise the danger they faced, but most would not have been looking forward to this magical confrontation.

Yet we have been skulking about for too long, avoiding confrontations or not being able to find the enemy. There is a strange satisfaction in finally being able to engage the Sachakans. To test our strength against theirs – and vent our anger – whatever the outcome.

With the rest of the advisers, Dakon followed Sabin round the copse, past the farmhouse and onto the road. The rest of the army followed. Ahead, the Sachakan force was a wide, advancing wall. Glancing back and to either side, he saw that the Kyralian army had broken into teams of five or six magicians. These groups had moved out into the fields on either side to form a broken line as wide as the Sachakans'. Each group had nominated one member to strike and one to shield, and the others would add their power to either, or both, according to need.

For an endless time, the only sounds were of boots swishing and stomping through crops and on the road, the breathing of those close by and the faint whine of the wind. Dakon could feel his own heart racing.

He found himself worrying about Jayan and Tessia. Much debate had raged over whether the apprentices should stay with their masters, or remain behind. Traditionally, apprentices stayed close to their masters, both for their own protection and in case the magician needed more power. But if a magician took as much power as was safe from his apprentice just before battle, he didn't need one with him. Unless, like a Sachakan, he killed to gain every last shred of power. As far as Dakon knew, the king hadn't revoked the law against Kyralian masters killing their apprentices for magic. Since most apprentices were offspring of powerful families, it was unlikely he would. *Would he, if things got desperate enough?*

Lone apprentices whose strength had been tapped were vulnerable if parted from their masters. But in a direct confrontation, the enemy magician was too engaged in fighting to find and attack apprentices. The danger came most often from the enemy's apprentices or slaves. Any attack would be physical if it came from slaves, who were unable to use their own magic.

But as a large group, the apprentices were less vulnerable to attack. A few had been left with their power undrained, so that they could defend the group. Dakon had volunteered Jayan for the task since, unlike most magicians, he had a second apprentice to take power from. Jayan was one of the older and more experienced apprentices, and had been nominated their temporary leader.

So I have nothing to worry about, Dakon told himself, and then continued to fret. Only when he realised he could make out the faces of the Sachakans did his attention return fully to the enemy. Then he heard Sabin mutter a curse.

"Is that . . . ?" Werrin murmured.

"Yes," Sabin replied. "Emperor Vochira's most favoured and loyal magician, Ashaki Nomako."

"That explains the sudden increase in numbers."

A voice called out and the Sachakans stopped. Seeking the speaker, Dakon felt a jolt as he recognised Takado. He felt hatred well up inside him.

Takado. My former houseguest. A traveller supposedly come to satisfy his curiosity about a neighbouring land. All along he planned to return in force. We were right to be suspicious. Dakon scowled. *We should have arranged for him to die in some accident.*

"Halt!" Sabin called. Dakon stopped, as did the sound of movement around him.

A quietness followed. The air vibrated with expectation. *How can such near silence carry so much tension?* Dakon wondered. *Quiet is supposed to be calming.*

"Magicians of Kyralia," Takado shouted. "You make a fine army. I am impressed." He took a step forward, looking from left to right. "No doubt you are here to put a stop to our attacks. To seek retaliation for the deaths of your people. To send us back to our homeland." He paused and smiled. "I tell you now, that you can only succeed in one of these aims. We are not going home. We came here to conquer you. To reclaim what was foolishly given up in the past. To make our lands one again. Which, though painful in the beginning, will ultimately benefit us all." He smiled. "Naturally, we will not allow you to take out your revenge on us. But . . ." His eyes moved from left to right as he met the eyes of individual Kyralians. He paused briefly when he saw Dakon, and a faint smile twitched his lips. That fleeting expression of smugness sent anger burning through Dakon. "You can put an end to our attacks. All you need do is give over rule of your land peacefully and we will take it peacefully. Surrender and join us."

"And who will rule us? You, or the emperor?"

Sabin's voice cut through the air. Turning a little, Dakon saw the war master look from Takado to another Sachakan. Perhaps the man with narrowed eyes, Dakon guessed. *What do the emperor's magicians wear to indicate their status? A ring, isn't it?* There were many bands around the man's fingers, as was the fashion among most Sachakans, and he was too far away to see if any bore some mark of the emperor's.

"Emperor Vochira supports our reclaiming of former territory," Takado told them.

Sabin paused, but when it was clear that was all the answer he would get, he chuckled and turned back to Takado. "I don't know who is the greater fool, you or your emperor. It will be interesting to see which of you remains alive after this war. My bet is on Emperor Vochira, since we have no intention of letting you take Kyralia, and I can't imagine you'll survive long if you escape us and manage to crawl back home."

Takado smiled. "Then my bet is on us both being alive, since if you insist on fighting me I'll be free to rid Kyralia of its magicians, and nothing would please Emperor Vochira more. I have no desire to rule in his place when I, and my friends, can have all this." He stretched his arms wide. Then he let them fall at his sides. "Do you surrender?"

"No," Sabin said, simply and firmly.

Takado looked from side to side, at his allies. "The fools want a fight," he shouted. "Let's give them one!"

Turning abruptly back to face Sabin, Takado let loose a brilliant strike. It scattered an arm's length from Sabin's nose. A moment later the rest of the Sachakan army let loose their power, and the air suddenly vibrated and flashed with magic. Dakon grasped Sabin's upper arm and began drawing power from within himself and giving it to the war master. The other magicians in the group of advisers either followed his example or took hold of Werrin, who was shielding them all.

Shields held. Strikes flew in return, then filled the space between the armies. No magician, Sachakan or Kyralian, fell.

But the heat and vibration was so intense, both sides began to back away. Retreating slowly, maintaining their lines, the opposing armies reached a distance apart that was bearable. The exchange of strikes intensified and the tumult of magic seared the air again, but this time all stood their ground.

For a long time nobody spoke. Dakon could not take his eyes off the enemy. Every time Werrin's shield vibrated from an attack his heart jumped. Every time Sabin directed a strike at the enemy he felt hope rise, then fade as the power shattered against a shield. He could see Narvelan's head moving back and forth as the young magician watched how the fighting progressed elsewhere. But Dakon could not bring himself to look away.

I think I'm afraid I won't see the strike that kills me, Dakon thought.

"They certainly aren't saving their strength," Narvelan remarked.

"No," Sabin agreed. "How are we doing?"

"Holding," Narvelan replied. "Not striking as much as they. Nor as strongly, I suspect."

"Are we holding back?" Hakkin asked. "Is there a way we can tell other teams to fight harder?"

Werrin nodded. "There is, but—"

"There! The signal," one of the city magicians said. "We've got one exhausted magician – no, two!"

"One in most teams now," Narvelan added.

Dakon forced himself to look at Sabin. *He's probably thinking that those magicians would be dead if their teams weren't protecting them. The Sachakans aren't protecting each other – as far as we can tell – and none of them are dead yet . . .*

"We got one!" Narvelan exclaimed. Dakon looked in the direction his friend was pointing, but his view was blocked by Werrin. A moment later there was a dull thump and crack, and one of the closer Sachakans was thrown backwards. He landed on the ground, but was quickly dragged away by the slaves hovering behind the enemy line.

Three more Sachakans fell. Dakon felt his heart lifting in triumph. *Ardalen's method works!* he thought. *Soon they'll be dropping like rain.*

"We must retreat," Sabin said. "Signal the others."

Dakon gasped with disbelief. He cast about, watching as the message was relayed down the line of Kyralian teams. But as he counted the number of magicians holding a white strip of cloth in their left hand – the signal they had used all their power – he felt disbelief turn to fear.

We're nearly finished, he realised. *We've lost.* Some of the teams held only two members with power in reserve. These teams backed away the fastest. As the seven leaders began to retreat, Dakon turned his attention to the enemy, watching anxiously to see if they would follow.

Crouching on the ground behind his master, Hanara felt his heart pounding. He'd seen two of Takado's allies fall, and

462

three of the magicians who'd come with the emperor's representative. One had exploded in flames. Another's face and chest had crumpled into a bloody mess just before he was knocked back off his feet and sprawled on the ground. He'd also seen a slave broken in two by stray magic, and felt pride and gratitude that Takado had foreseen the danger and ordered him to lie on his belly and keep his head low.

Hanara had seen the surprise and horror on the faces of the Sachakan magicians still fighting. Seen the doubts, and the determination as they kept fighting. *How many will question whether the conquest is worth the risk after this?* Hanara wondered. *Surely their lives aren't so bad at home that a bit of land is worth dying for.* But owning land was one of the greatest symbols of freedom. Owning land and wielding magic. Of the former there was too little. And perhaps there was too much of the latter in Sachaka. *Now that's an interesting thought . . .*

A murmur rose among the magicians now. Lifting his head, Takado saw that the Kyralians were moving.

They are retreating! We have won!

He saw Takado's allies begin to move forward. Takado hadn't given an order yet. Hanara could not see his master's face, but something in Takado's posture told him his master was deliberating.

"Hold!"

The voice rang out, stalling those edging forward. It was not Takado's voice. Hanara felt a rush of anger and indignation. The emperor's representative, Nomako, had spoken. He was stepping out before Takado's army and turning to face them.

"Let them go. We have shown them who is the stronger. Let them ponder the future a while and consider the benefits of surrendering to us."

Hanara's blood boiled on behalf of his master. *How dare he! It's up to Takado to decide! Up to Takado to give the orders!*

He felt his heart leap with mingled terror and glee as Takado stepped forward to face Nomako, his face dark with anger.

"*I* lead this army, Nomako," he snapped. "Not you. Not even the emperor. If that isn't to your satisfaction – or his – then go home and leave the fighting to us."

Nomako stared back at Takado and his face tightened with annoyance and dislike for a moment. Then his gaze dropped to the ground. "I apologise, Takado. I thought only to save you more losses."

"Then you are a fool! They are spent." Takado turned away and called to Dachido and Asara.

"They have not lost a single magician," Nomako protested. "And we have lost nearly a dozen. It is a trick. A trap. I promised the families of Sachaka that we would not spend lives needlessly. We must analyse what they are doing and find a way to combat it."

Takado looked at his army and frowned. Hanara tried to read the mood of the fighters. Many looked uncertain. Some had backed away several steps and appeared to be expecting Takado to confirm Nomako's order. None seemed eager to pursue the Kyralians.

They did not expect us to lose fighters without the enemy suffering the same.

Sighing, Takado shrugged his shoulders. "We stay," he said.

The relief on the faces of his followers and Nomako's was clear. Some gathered into pairs or groups to talk, others headed back towards the village. Nomako joined the three men who appeared to be his most trusted companions.

Dachido and Asara reached Takado's side.

"What were they doing?" Dachido said. "Why did none of them fall?"

"They are protecting and supporting each other. Something we should be doing. Though I doubt we can expect it from one quarter," he added in a quieter voice. The three allies began talking in murmurs. Hanara crept closer, straining to hear.

". . . not retreat if they weren't," Asara was saying.

"We cannot be sure," Dachido replied. "It may be a trap."

Asara nodded, then turned to Takado. "I like your idea last night," she said. "Let's do that instead."

"We need horses," Dachido warned.

Asara shrugged. "We could demand some of Nomako's as reparation."

"And give the impression we need his assistance?" Takado asked, his eyes narrowing as he glanced at the emperor's representative.

Asara grimaced and said nothing.

Takado looked towards the village. "Are there any horses left in the area?"

Dachido followed his gaze. "There was one, but it was old and we slaughtered it to feed the slaves."

"If we look further afield we might find some," Asara said.

"Further west, where they do not expect us to go." Takado smiled.

"So we'll try it?" Asara asked, her eyes gleaming.

"Yes. And I have a first target in mind."

The pair looked at him expectantly.

"Did you notice their apprentices were not with them?"

"Ah," Dachido said.

"Ah!" Asara exclaimed.

"Yes," Takado replied. "It seems they have forgotten one of the key rules of battle, and we are going to remind them."

CHAPTER 35

By the time the army stopped for the night, exhaustion had almost overcome Jayan's curiosity to know what had happened when the magicians had confronted the Sachakan invaders. All Dakon had said was that the enemy had been stronger than the Kyralian army. Sabin had ordered a retreat. The Sachakans hadn't pursued them, but the possibility they were following at a distance couldn't be discounted. The Kyralian army needed to gain some ground between themselves and the enemy, so they had a chance to recover some magical strength before the next confrontation.

It was amazing to think that, despite losing the battle, nobody had died. But from the uneasiness and haste of the magicians, Jayan guessed that was due to luck or the ignorance of the enemy.

All day Jayan had seen the flashes of blades and hands briefly linked as magic was transferred on the ride. Though the apprentices and servants had given their strength only that morning, and so did not have much to offer, the magicians feared attack at any moment and wanted to be as prepared as possible.

Dakon, however, shook his head when Jayan suggested they do the same. "I am fine," he said. "The benefit of having two apprentices. I'd rather you and Tessia had a chance of defending yourselves if we are attacked. And you may need to take charge of the apprentices again, if we do engage the enemy."

466

The army had moved off the main road a while before in a weak attempt to confuse any pursuit, and followed a smooth road into a fold between two hills. They were hidden from the sight of anyone travelling down the main road, but Jayan suspected they'd left so much evidence of their passing that even the most unskilled scout would have been able to locate them.

The road wound through low hills and shallow valleys, all striped and divided by fields. Dusk settled like a growing mist, then darkness fell. Scouts galloping along the road reported no pursuit. The Sachakans had returned to the village of Lonner and appeared to be settling for the night.

Then, long past nightfall, the ghostly white walls of buildings appeared ahead. Several were storehouses, one had many doors and Jayan guessed it was accommodation for servants, and the two-storey mansion was clearly the owner's residence.

"What is this place?" he asked Dakon.

"Lord Franner's winery."

"Oh." Jayan grimaced.

Dakon chuckled. "His wine may not be particularly good, but he has plenty of food to offer. As he pointed out, better we have it than the Sachakans."

"Is there another exit from this valley?"

"Yes." Dakon smiled approvingly. "Sabin made sure of that. We won't be trapped here."

As the army gathered between the buildings, Jayan saw Werrin turn in his saddle, searching the crowd. His gaze snapped to Dakon and he beckoned.

"Ah, the inevitable meeting," Dakon murmured. He looked at Tessia, who had been silent the whole afternoon, then at Jayan. "Will you two be all right alone?"

Jayan grinned. "Of course. And we'll hardly be alone." He gestured at the army around them.

Dakon nodded, then rode away towards Werrin and the small group of magicians gathering about him. Looking at Tessia, Jayan shrugged.

"Want to explore this place?"

She shook her head. "Avaria asked me to see her tonight."

Jayan shrugged off disappointment. "I'll see you at dinner, then, whenever that turns out to be." He looked up at the stars. "I'll make sure our old fellow apprentices are behaving themselves."

Tessia rolled her eyes. "You're not in charge any more, Jayan."

"Is it so hard to believe that I enjoy other apprentices' company?" he asked.

Her eyebrows rose. "The more important question is whether they enjoy yours."

Turning her horse, she sent it trotting away too quickly for him to think of a retort. He watched her go for a moment, then pushed away the wistfulness that was threatening to creep in, and began to search the crowd for the faces of familiar apprentices. He longed for sleep, but he was hungry and rest could wait until after he'd eaten.

Refan was standing with four other apprentices over by one of the large storehouses, so Jayan made his way over to him. One of the youngsters looked familiar. As Jayan approached the newcomer looked up and grinned, and with a shock Jayan recognised him.

"Mikken!" Jayan exclaimed, slipping off his horse. He looked around and caught the eye of a servant, who stepped forward to take the reins. Then he ran up to Mikken and grasped his arm in greeting. "When did you get here?"

Mikken returned the gesture. "A few hours ago. Fortunately before the army turned off the road, or I would have ridden into the Sachakan army."

"How did you escape the Sachakans at the pass? No, wait. I bet that story is a long one."

"Long, but not particularly interesting." Mikken shrugged. "Unless you find stories about scavenging for food and hiding in caves and abandoned houses interesting."

Jayan grinned. "You can tell them when we're trying to get to sleep tonight."

"You watch out, I might just do that. How's Tessia?"

A traitorous flash of jealousy shot through Jayan, but he ignored it. "Still healing anyone she can get to sit still long enough."

"Lots of those, I'd imagine." Mikken's gaze became haunted. "I began to wonder, on the way back, if the Sachakans had left anyone alive. I wouldn't be surprised if Tessia hasn't had many patients to work on."

"She's had plenty," Jayan assured him. He thought of the burned man, and shuddered. Deciding to change the subject, he looked up at the storehouse. "Apparently this is a winery."

"Yes," Refan replied. "And they don't just make wine here."

"What else do they make?" one of the other apprentices asked.

"Bol."

Jayan grimaced, and saw a similar expression on all faces but Refan's. The boy looked thoughtful.

"You know, by the time all the magicians get their share of Lord Franner's wine, there probably won't be any left for apprentices. I bet we could find a barrel or two of bol for ourselves in one of these storehouses. Bol may be a poor man's drink." Refan smiled. "But it's a lot stronger than wine so we wouldn't have to drink as much."

As much as what? Jayan wondered. To his dismay, the other apprentices looked interested.

"Where do you think it's stored?"

Refan looked around, his eyes narrowing as he considered. "Let's have a look around." He started along the side of the storehouse they were standing beside.

As the group began to follow, Jayan considered leaving them to it. *But I ought to make sure they don't get into trouble. For their own sakes and mine. Dakon might think twice about making me a higher magician if I let these boys make fools of themselves.* He hurried after them.

Reaching the end of the storehouse, Refan rounded the corner and started along the next wall. He stopped where two huge, sturdy doors were bound together with a large iron lock. To Jayan's amusement, he sniffed at the crack between them.

"Wine," he said, then shrugged and turned his back, heading across open ground to another storehouse.

The same examination and conclusion were applied to two more storehouses. The fourth was so far from the main gathering of magicians that their voices were a distant hum and the group had to illuminate their way with small magical globe lights.

Refan's sniff at the doors made him smile.

"Aha! Definitely bol."

There was a different sort of smell in the air around the storehouse, but the lock was similarly large and robust. Refan glanced towards the gathered magicians in the furtive manner of someone about to do something mischievous, then took hold of the lock. Jayan felt alarm rising.

"What are you . . . you're not going to break in, are you?" one of the younger apprentices asked anxiously.

"No." Refan laughed. "I'm not going to break anything. Or take anything not already offered to us."

He stared at the lock, then something inside clicked and the mechanism opened. *Despite his reasoning, this is wrong,*

Jayan thought. *I should put a stop to it.* One of the doors swung outward and Refan slipped inside. Before Jayan could decide what to say, the other apprentices had followed.

A wordless exclamation of disappointment followed. He heard a clink, the murmur of voices, and the apprentices stepped back outside. Refan was holding a bottle.

"It's not bol. It's whitewater. For cleaning things. Smell." He held it out to each of them, and they grimaced as they sniffed the open neck. Jayan recognised a smell he associated with servants and wooden furniture. Refan suddenly grinned. "Watch this."

He glanced back at the magicians again, then strode round the back of the storehouse. Moving a hundred strides or so he flung the bottle on the ground. It smashed. As the others stopped beside Refan, he sent a tiny burst of firestrike toward the remains.

A wave of heat burst over them as flames shot up into the air. The fire died as quickly, leaving small flames spluttering where there were weeds in the hard, dry ground.

"That was fantastic!" one of the younger apprentices gasped. "Let's do it again!"

"Wait." Mikken was staring at the smouldering ground. "I have an idea."

Everyone turned to look at him, but he remained silent, staring at the ground.

"Well?" someone asked.

Mikken shook his head. "Can you hear that?"

Surprised, they all stood very still and listened. A rhythmic beating, faint but clearly from some sort of four-legged animal, came to Jayan's ears. More than one animal, perhaps. Whatever they were, they were coming closer. Turning towards the noise, he found himself staring towards the dark shapes of trees a few hundred strides away.

Slowly, out of the gloom, three horses appeared, carrying three riders. The distant light reflected back from exotic coats, knife handles and gleaming eyes.

"Sachakans!" Refan hissed.

"Run!" Mikken wailed.

"Stay together!" Jayan shouted, throwing up a shield and racing after them.

Then he cursed as the first strike nearly shattered his barrier. He strengthened it. *How long can I hold against three higher magicians? Who've probably got the strength of thousands of source slaves.* He winced as another strike beat against the shield. *Or have they? If they've followed us, they probably didn't have time to regain much power after the battle.*

Refan was nearly at the storehouse, too far ahead for Jayan to be sure he was shielding him. He skidded to a halt before the door, grabbed it and hauled it open. Then he vanished inside with unnatural speed.

"Not in there!" Jayan gasped. "If they use firestrike . . ." But Refan had disappeared within and the others were racing after him. Jayan sighed and followed. In the darkness someone stumbled and there was the sound of glass breaking and the smell of whitewater. Then a globe light flared into existence. Jayan cast about, taking in the huge interior filled with racks of bottles, the apprentices panting and staring at each other as they finally realised how dangerous this place was for a fight – and then the whimpering figure on the floor.

"Refan?" Jayan moved to the boy's side and knelt.

"Hurts," Refan panted. "Back. Hurts. Can't . . . can't move my legs."

Jayan cursed as he realised that Refan hadn't thrown himself inside the storehouse, but had been knocked in by forcestrike.

The sound of hoofbeats came from outside the doors. They

stopped and were replaced by footsteps. Jayan looked around, at the bottles, then towards the back of the interior. *Trapped. They only need the tiniest spark of power to set this place burning. And it will take a lot more to protect us.*

Protect us . . . or them? The glimmer of an idea set his heart racing with excitement.

"Quickly," he hissed to the others. "Drag him to the back and wait – and do it gently. When I say 'Now', break through the wall."

Refan yelled in pain as they began to move him. They let go as if he'd burned them. Jayan saw movement in the doorway.

"Pick him up and get him out!" he found himself roaring. Their eyes widened in shock and surprise. Grabbing Refan, ignoring his yells, they carried him away. Jayan followed, walking backwards, not taking his eyes from the three Sachakans entering the storehouse. He threw up a shield to protect himself and the apprentices behind him.

Two men and one woman, he noted. *One is familiar. Surely . . . surely that's not Takado. Surely he wouldn't leave his army and risk sneaking up on us with only two others to support him?*

The Sachakans stared at him. They smiled. They came closer, strolling as if they had all the time in the world. He could hear the apprentices retreating. Refan's yells had turned to whimpers. Someone else was also whimpering. Or crying.

"We're at the back," Mikken said.

At the same time the Sachakans stopped. He saw their heads start to turn as they began to look at each other, to gain silent agreement that it was time to strike.

"Get out! *Now!*" Jayan yelled. At the same time he strengthened his shield and sent several firestrikes fanning out on either side.

White light filled the space before him. He felt scorching

heat, then the ground hit his back. Something grabbed his collar and hauled him backwards. He found himself sliding across the ground, through a gap in the storehouse wall. The wall suddenly crumbled and heat enveloped him again, but not as ferociously.

Then he wasn't sliding any more. Looking up, he saw Mikken grinning down at him, the apprentice's chest heaving and face flushed with effort. Mikken released his collar.

"You're heavy," the young man told him. Then he grinned. "And I think it worked."

Climbing to his feet, Jayan quickly took in the other apprentices standing beside a prone and silent Refan, then turned back to the storehouse. It was burning with a more natural fire now, the flames eating wood rather than whitewater.

Then he saw movement. Three figures running towards the trees. *So they're not dead.* He didn't feel as disappointed as he expected. *I never really thought it would kill them, but they must have used a lot of power protecting themselves.* He considered himself and felt a new kind of exhaustion on top of mere physical tiredness. *As did I.*

"Their horses will have run off," Mikken said. He turned. "Here come the magicians. We're going to have a lot of explaining to do."

Jayan turned to see the crowd hurrying towards them and nodded.

"Yes. Let's not tell them why Refan was so keen to explore, shall we?"

"I won't if you don't. And I'll make sure the others stay silent."

As he moved away, Jayan smiled. Then he remembered the price Refan had paid for their little adventure and all satisfaction at weakening the Sachakans fled.

474

I should have protected him better. I should never have let him lead us away from the protection of the army in the first place. This is all my fault. He saw Dakon hurrying towards him and felt his heart sink. *He's not going to want to make me a higher magician now. And I won't blame him.*

When the boom shook the air, it seemed like the answer to Tessia's silent, heartfelt wishes.

Avaria had taken her to meet two other female magicians, Magician Jialia and Lady Viria. Both women had been questioning Tessia closely.

"Have you really been travelling with the magicians in pursuit of the Sachakans right from the start?" Viria asked.

"Yes," Tessia replied, suppressing a sigh at the question. Did the woman think she'd been making it all up?

"Have the other apprentices been polite to you? Have they made any inappropriate suggestions?" Jialia paused and leaned forward. "None of them have tried to force themselves on you, have they?"

"No, they've been very well behaved," Tessia assured them. "Besides, Lord Dakon would do something about it if they weren't."

The two women exchanged glances. Viria frowned and regarded Tessia closely.

"Lord Dakon hasn't . . . ah . . . made any inappropriate advances, has he?"

Tessia stared at her, appalled. "No!" she replied firmly.

Viria spread her hands. "It's not unheard of. A master seducing his female apprentice – or the other way around. When I was a girl I knew a young woman who married her master, after she conceived a child by him. We thought she'd been taken advantage of, but it turned out to be the other way around, though I imagine he couldn't have objected *that* much. It's not uncommon for young female apprentices to fall in love with their masters."

This is worse than talking to my mother! Tessia thought. Then she felt a wrench and a pang of guilt for thinking of her mother that way. *Still, she wouldn't have thought there was anything wrong with me falling in love with and marrying Dakon.*

Looking over to where her master was sitting with the other army leaders and advisers, she considered her feelings for him. Many times she'd felt an affection for him. And admiration. But both feelings were for his good nature. There was no deeper feeling. No physical longing.

"Don't be silly, Viria," Jialia said. "Young women prefer men closer to their age. If Tessia is infatuated with anyone, it's more likely to be young Jayan of Drayn." Her gaze became speculative. "I do hope Lord Dakon has taught you how to avoid conceiving."

Tessia shook her head and sighed. *If you knew Jayan, you'd know how unlikely that is*, she thought. *Though he has improved. It would be unfair to say he was completely loathsome.*

"Jialia," Avaria cut in. "It's hardly something a male magician is going to teach a female apprentice."

Viria nodded, then looked from Avaria to Tessia and back again. "So will you teach Tessia yourself?"

"I . . . if she wishes me to."

Tessia decided to say nothing. It was taking all her will to stop herself grinding her teeth. *Someone please come and take me away from these insane women*, she thought.

And then the sound of an explosion had assaulted their ears, coming from behind Tessia. She and Avaria jumped to their feet and turned around.

"What was that?" Avaria asked.

Magicians began moving towards the noise, their faces hard

with fear and determination. Tessia took a step away from the women.

"No! Stay here," Jialia said, a note of command in her voice despite the fear that made it waver. Tessia turned to find the pair still sitting on their blankets. "Don't get in the way."

A surge of rebellion fought common sense and her habit of obedience. Tessia looked at Avaria. *If she says I should stay, I will.*

Avaria glanced at Tessia, frowned and reluctantly sat down. "Yes, we should wait for orders." Her eyes narrowed as she watched the magicians disappear behind the storehouses.

Tessia sat down, but turned so that her shoulder was to the women and she could keep watching the magicians. Time dragged by. The women tried to resume the conversation, this time targeting Avaria with their questions.

"Well, they'd have ordered us to fight or flee by now if it was an attack," one of them said. She turned to Avaria. "So, when are you going to give Everran some boys to indulge?"

Tessia saw Avaria wince and smothered a smile.

"When there isn't a good chance the Sachakans will eat them before they grow old enough to talk," Avaria retorted.

"Well," the woman said, her eyebrows rising.

"I thought that was only a rumour," the other murmured to her.

Tessia didn't hear what they said next. Lord Werrin's servant had rounded the end of a storehouse and was hurrying towards her. Perhaps Avaria would ask for news as he passed. But as he came closer she realised he was looking at her.

"Apprentice Tessia," he called.

She rose. "Yes?"

"Your services are required."

Picking up her father's bag, she hurried forward. He led her back towards the end of the storehouse.

"What happened?" she asked.

"Sachakans attacked," he said, breathing heavily. "Only three, but gone now. They sneaked up on a group of apprentices exploring the estate." As she followed him round the corner she nearly stopped in shock. One of the huge buildings had collapsed, and the remains were burning.

"Anyone hurt?" she asked. *But of course someone is. Why else summon me? Unless . . . unless I know them.* She felt her insides clench with fear and dread. *Jayan? No. Surely not Jayan. He's too annoying to have been killed. Besides, this one said my "services" were needed. That can only mean healing.*

"The apprentices lured them inside," the servant continued. "The storehouse was filled with whitewater. Apprentice Jayan set it alight." He glanced back, grinning. "Must've cost them a bit of power shielding from that."

"But they survived."

The servant nodded. "Ran off into the night. Some magicians have gone off after them."

She'd meant the apprentices, but was glad he'd told her that bit of news anyway. He was leading her towards a group of magicians and servants standing around something. Recognising the two guild healers, she felt her stomach sink. Someone saw her approaching and all turned to stare at her. Then she saw Lord Dakon and Jayan.

Jayan looks unharmed. The relief she felt was stronger than she'd have thought warranted. *So who are they . . . ah. Refan.*

The young man was lying on the ground, face down. He was groaning with pain. As she reached the magicians, Lord Dakon moved to her side.

"It's his back," he told her quietly. "Hit by forcestrike. He can't feel his legs. The healers say the paths to those parts of his body have been broken. He'll live for a while, in pain, before those parts die and poison the rest of him."

She nodded. A broken back was a terrible injury. The healers were right, though it depended on where the break was, and whether the patient had constant, specific care. They could live for a few years, if they were lucky.

But even if Refan was so lucky, he couldn't ride. He probably couldn't travel in a cart, either. The jostling would worsen the injury. If he stayed, the Sachakans would kill him. She looked at Lord Dakon.

"Why call for me?"

He smiled faintly. "Jayan suggested it. He says you've found a way to use magic to stop the pain."

"Ah." She looked at the magicians and healers. They wore expressions of curiosity, mostly. Some looked doubtful. "I can't promise anything, but it's always worth trying."

Moving to Refan's side, she knelt beside him and placed a hand on the side of his neck. His skin was hot. She closed her eyes and for a moment struggled to put the thought of all the eyes watching her out of her mind.

Concentrate. Look inward. Inside. An awareness of Refan's body came to her. She gently probed beyond the skin, letting the signals and rhythms guide her. Spreading her awareness down his spine she found the source of the body's alarm.

The bones had been knocked out of alignment. Swelling around them radiated heat and pain. And once she became aware of that pain, it swamped her senses. She felt herself go rigid to match Refan's own agony-tensed muscles, and the same desperate need for the pain to stop that Refan must be feeling. But her need was *not* desperate. She could do something to stop it. Searching for the right place, she exerted her will and *pinched*.

The pain ended.

Relieved, she paused to rest and regain a sense of herself. As she did, she noticed something about the injury. The areas of swelling were acting as blockages. They were compressing the cord that threaded the bones, and some of the pathways that sprouted from it.

Then she realised that none of those pathways had been severed. Looking closer, she saw that none of the bones were broken or cracked, either.

It must have been a weak or glancing blow. Forcestrike should have made a much worse mess than this. Still, if the Sachakans had wanted to prolong his agony, they couldn't have chosen a better way to do it other than to stay and torture him. And the pain . . .

Abruptly she realised the pain was returning. Returning to the pathway she had pinched, she saw that it was recovering.

He's healing.

For a moment she marvelled at the futile but persistent efforts his body was going to in order to try to fix itself. Then she felt her skin prickle. *I've never noticed this before. I've never seen a body healing so fast I could sense it.* Curious, she looked closer, trying to understand the mechanism that was driving this unnaturally fast healing.

And she sensed magic.

The meaning of this came to her in a jolt. Dakon had told her that magicians were more robust than people who had no or little latent ability. Even those people with magical talents who never learned magic tended to heal faster and resist disease better. It made sense, then, that magic was, literally, the reason.

Am I the first person to watch this process? she wondered.

Unfortunately, it was acting against her intentions. The pain of the injury was returning as the pinched pathway recovered, and when she concentrated on the injury itself she saw that the speedy healing wasn't going to succeed. The bones would remain in the position they'd been forced into.

Refan would not be able to walk, and it was even possible his internal organs might not work properly.

But I can fix that, she realised.

Taking a deep breath, she thought her way through the task. First she must pinch the pain pathway again. Then she would have to gently encourage excess moisture to leave the swollen areas. Finally, when she had enough space, she must nudge the bones slowly and carefully back into their correct positions. All the interconnecting tissues should then return with them.

When she had thought her way through the process a few times, deciding what to move first, she set to work.

It was a slow process. As she pinched and squeezed and nudged, she wondered what the magicians and healers watching her were thinking. Did they think she was taking a long time, for the simple task of blocking pain? Could they see any of the change she was making? Or had they grown bored and left? After all, the much anticipated and very late meal they were all waiting for must be cooked by now.

Finally everything was back in place. She noticed that Refan's body was now applying magic to healing him in much more effective ways. *He's going to survive*, she realised. *He might not even be crippled.* A thrill of pride ran through her, and she immediately suppressed it. *This still may not work. It's the first time I've done it – maybe the first time anyone has – and I can't know the full outcome. And besides, it will still take days or weeks for him to heal properly and he's still going to be a burden to the army.*

After one last check, and pinching the pain pathway one more time to delay what would be an unpleasant revival despite her efforts, she drew her consciousness back into herself and opened her eyes.

Looking around, she saw that all the magicians were still

481

there. And the healers. They were staring at her, some frowning in puzzlement. Then Refan groaned and all attention returned to him.

"What . . . what happened?" he said. "Pain's gone . . . but I still can't feel my legs."

"You will soon," Tessia told him. "And you're not going to like it." She looked up at Lord Dakon. "His back wasn't broken, but it was all out of place and the pathways were being squashed."

He smiled, his eyes shining. "Will he recover?"

"If he has the time to." She grimaced. "If he has the time to, he'll even walk again."

His expression became grim, and his eyes shifted to Lord Werrin. The king's magician frowned and nodded. "I'll see what I can arrange."

That appeared to be a signal for the onlookers to leave. Tessia beckoned to some servants standing nearby and instructed them to get a long board of wood, then slide Refan onto it, still face-down and without flexing his back too much, so they could carry him somewhere sheltered. As they hurried away, Dakon and Jayan moved closer.

"That was well done. Very impressive," Dakon said.

"Thank you." She felt heat come to her face and pushed away another surge of pride.

Dakon looked at Jayan. "I've been proud to be the master of both of my apprentices tonight," he said, smiling broadly. Jayan looked doubtful, Tessia noticed. "Both of you are far too clever for a humble country magician like me."

She voiced a protest and heard Jayan do the same.

"Ah, but it is true," Dakon said. "That's why I have decided that, as soon as we get the chance, I am going to teach Jayan higher magic and send him off into the world as his own master."

Tessia smothered a laugh at Jayan's open-mouthed astonishment. *I was right. Clearly he didn't believe me.*

Then she felt an unexpected pang of sadness. *I think I may actually miss him.* Then she wrinkled her nose. *For a few hours, anyway. Then I'll realise nobody has said anything annoying to me in a while and I'll realise how nice it is to be rid of him.*

CHAPTER 36

The wagon rolled slowly through Arvice. Kachiro had ordered the flaps to be tied open so Stara could enjoy the scenery. Warm spring air lingered as the sun dipped towards the horizon. Flowers covered the trees that lined the larger, main roads of the city, and the air was sweet with their scent. Insects also abounded – in swarms that darkened the air as they passed and set slaves to slapping themselves – but at the wagon openings they vanished in a sizzle and spark of light as they encountered Kachiro's magical barriers.

The barriers only protected those inside the wagon. Stara thought of Vora clinging to the back. It must be hard and unpleasant for the old woman to ride that way, her hands gripping handholds and her legs braced on the narrow foot ledge.

Stara had suggested Vora stay behind, but the slave had shaken her head. "This is your first experience of Sachakan society outside your father's house," she'd said. "You'll need my guidance."

"Here we are," Kachiro said. The wagon slowed as it neared a pair of impressive double gates standing open to allow passage. He turned to look at her, smiling as his eyes travelled from her shoes to her headdress. "You look wonderful," he told her, and she could detect nothing but honest admiration. "As always, an excellent combination of cloth and decoration. I am lucky to have a wife with not just beauty, but good taste."

Stara smiled. "Thank you. I am lucky to have a husband who appreciates such things." She met his gaze, knowing she could not hide the fact that his compliment filled her mind with doubts and questions.

"I do," he said. Then he looked down for a moment. "I would also appreciate it if you did not mention . . . my difficulty, to the wives," he added in a murmur.

"Of course not!" she replied quickly. "It is our secret."

He smiled. "My friends' wives love a good secret," he warned her.

"Not this one," she assured him.

"Thank you." The wagon was now turning through the open gates into a large courtyard abuzz with slaves. Kachiro helped her climb down to the ground, then turned to the slaves waiting nearby, who had prostrated themselves. "We're here to join Master Motara in celebrating his birthing day. Take us to the gathering place."

One of the slaves rose. "It is this way," he said.

They headed inside, Vora and one of Kachiro's slaves following. Stara recognised the restrained decoration and beautiful furniture immediately. As she slowed to admire a long cabinet full of drawers of different sizes, Kachiro chuckled.

"Of course, Motara keeps all his best pieces. I've tried to persuade him to sell that one to me many times. He won't even risk it when gambling."

"So Master Motara is your friend who designs the furniture?"

"Yes."

"I must compliment him on it, then."

Kachiro looked surprised, then thoughtful. "He would like that. Yes – do it. Women do not usually take an interest in such things. At least, not when they are around men."

Stara frowned. "Should I say nothing? Would it offend him

485

more to voice an opinion?" She felt a moment's disbelief that she was asking this. Since when had she cared whether anyone wanted her opinion or not?

"He won't be offended. Only surprised," he assured her. Then he gave her that admiring smile that was so infuriatingly puzzling. "I am liking your unconventionality more and more, Stara. It is refreshing. Women are too secretive and reserved. They should be more like you, open and interested in things."

"I can also be stubborn and nosy. You might not like that sort of unconventionality."

He laughed. "For now, I choose to believe that is the price I paid for marrying a woman who is not only beautiful, but clever too."

Stara felt her heart flip over. Then she felt herself begin to scowl and forced herself to look down to hide her expression, hoping he thought her embarrassed by the compliment. *There would be no harm in falling in love with Kachiro*, she thought. *But it would be very, very annoying. And frustrating. But then, I might not mind his "difficulty" if I were in love with him. If the romantic tales are right.*

The slave stopped at the entrance to a large room and stepped aside, his head bowed. Kachiro led Stara past him, then took her arm. Five men turned to look at them. All had the broad shoulders and wide face of the typical Sachakan male, but one was fat, another was skinny, and one had dark pigmentation under his eyes. They ranged in age from not long past youthful boyhood to middle age. The skinny one rose and stepped forward.

"Kachiro! You're even later than usual!"

Kachiro chuckled. "I confess it is my fault, Motara. I didn't think to tell my wife we were visiting until it was nearly time to leave, forgetting that she would need time to prepare. This," he gestured gracefully toward her, "is the lovely Stara."

Stara smiled. She could have been ready in minutes, but Vora had insisted on taking an hour "to teach your husband that he needs to be more considerate in plans that include a wife".

The other four men had risen and now joined Motara in approving of her. She kept her gaze lowered as Vora had taught her, but could tell they were examining her closely and appreciatively.

"She is exquisite," Motara said. "Knowing you so well, I was confident you would apply your eye for beauty to even the difficult task of finding an appropriate wife. But even I am impressed at the result." The others murmured agreement.

Kachiro looked at her and smiled. "She is more than that. She has a sharp mind and wit, and an eye for beauty and taste to rival my own." He nudged her gently. "What did you say to me before?"

She looked up fleetingly to meet Motara's gaze. "That Master Motara's furniture, here and at home, is exceptional. Graceful in proportion and shape. The cabinet with the drawers . . ." She sighed. "So beautiful."

Motara seemed to grow a little taller, and for a moment he bounced on the balls of his feet. Then he chuckled. "You didn't tell her to say that in another of your attempts to get hold of it, did you, Kachiro?"

"Oh! No!" Stara protested. "He did not!"

"No," Kachiro replied, a hint of smugness in his voice. "She stopped to admire it on the way in. You can ask your slave to confirm it."

Motara laughed again. "I may just do that, though you still could have described it to her before arriving. Now, on to more important matters. Dashina has kept his promise. We have a bottle each! Vikaro and Rikacha were hoping you weren't coming, so they could share yours. Chavori wanted it all for himself, but we know how bad he is at drinking." Motara turned towards the chairs the men had been sitting on.

"And Chiara?" Kachiro asked.

Motara made a dismissive gesture. "With the other women, no doubt whining about us." He looked at Stara, and she dropped her gaze. "Don't believe half of what they say," he warned her.

She looked up at Kachiro questioningly, and he smiled. "They're not as scary as he makes out. Go and join them. They're probably itching with curiosity about you."

He made a gesture and she turned to see a slave step forward. Glancing back at Vora, who nodded, she moved towards him.

"Take me to the women," she ordered quietly. The slave bowed, then led her towards another exit from the room and into a corridor.

So I don't get to talk to Kachiro's friends, she thought. *Not that I expected to. He didn't so much want me to meet them as to show me off to them.* She considered whether this bothered her. *It does, but I can forgive him that. It's nice that he considers me clever, but even nicer that he's willing to tell people that he thinks I am, in a way that shows he thinks it's a good character trait and not a bad one.*

The women were in a room not far away from the men, sitting on cushion-covered wooden benches. There were only four of them, which she guessed meant one of the men was unmarried. They turned to regard her as the slave prostrated himself.

"And who is this?" a slim woman with a protruding belly

asked, but with the tone of someone who knows the answer and is following a ritual.

"She is Stara, wife of Ashaki Kachiro," the slave replied.

"Go," she told him then, rising and moving forward to meet Stara.

"Welcome, Stara. I am Chiara," she said, offering a hand and smiling. Stara took it and was led to the rest of the women. "Here is a space for you," Chiara told her, gesturing to the end of a bench, beside a woman who would have been beautiful but for the scars that marred her skin. "Your slave can stay in the next room with ours. She'll hear you if you call out."

As Vora slipped away, her lips pressed in an unhappy line, Stara sat down. She felt a prickle of self-conscious nervousness as the four woman gazed at her with obvious interest.

"Aren't you a pretty one?" one of them said admiringly.

"She is, isn't she?" another agreed. "Quite an exotic beauty. Her skin is so lovely."

"Kachiro said you had Elyne blood, you lucky thing," a third said wistfully. Though Stara's mother had told her mixed bloodlines were seen as a strength in Sachakan society, she could not help feeling disbelief at the envious looks of the women.

"Don't overwhelm her with compliments," Chiara said, laughing. "Or at least let me introduce you all first." She turned to the scarred woman. "This is Tashana, wife of Dashina. Next is Aranira, Vikaro's wife." She gestured to a rather plain, tall woman who looked to be the youngest. "And finally, this is Sharina, whose husband is Rikacha." The last woman was appealingly plump and flashed a bright but shy smile.

"Do you like your new home?" she asked.

"And your husband?" Tashana added. Her eyes sparkled

with mischief as she smiled. "Don't feel you must dress up the truth, if you're not pleased. We were all given to men not of our choosing. That gives us the right to complain as much as we want."

Stara chuckled. "And if I did choose him, am I still allowed to complain?"

"You *chose* him?" Aranira asked, her eyes widening in surprise. "Not that he isn't handsome . . . ."

"Of course you are," Tashana said. "Though you'll have to allow us to be jealous."

"I didn't," Stara said quickly. "Choose him, that is. I was just curious to know what I should expect if I met someone who had chosen her husband." She paused to gather her thoughts. "Now I'm not sure if you'll believe me if I say anything good about him."

Tashana laughed, and the others joined in. "Give it a try and see what happens."

"He's not what I had been led to expect of Sachakan men," she began, noting how this brought a wry twist to their lips. "He's considerate and respectful. He's happy to tell me about his trade and listen to suggestions. He's . . . he's surprisingly good company."

A short silence followed as the women exchanged glances.

"But?" Aranira asked hopefully.

Stara shrugged. "Nothing. Yet. Give it time."

They chuckled and nodded. "Good to see you're not too naive about marriage," Chiara said. "Not like I was. Though . . . I was a lot younger, I suspect."

"How old are you?" Sharina asked.

"Twenty-five."

"Rikacha said you were younger."

"I suspect my father lied about my age."

Tashana nodded. "Have you been married before?"

490

Stara shook her head. The women exchanged looks of surprise. "I expect you think I'm a little old to be marrying for the first time." They nodded. "I hadn't planned to get married at all."

They frowned and looked at her closely. "Why not?"

Suddenly Stara was not sure what to say. Would they think her odd if she admitted to ambitions in trading? They knew she had Elyne blood, but did they know she had spent half her childhood and her early adult life in Elyne? Should she tell them? It was probably safe enough to, she decided, especially as Kachiro knew and would probably tell his friends. *Should I admit I had lovers? They'd love that, but it might get back to Kachiro. I'm not sure he'd find that so "refreshing".*

"Perhaps that is too private a subject to discuss so soon," Chiara suggested. "You barely know us." She turned to look at the others. "Perhaps we should tell her more about ourselves. Our stories."

They nodded.

"I'll go first," Aranira said. She looked at Tashana, who smiled and nodded. "Tashana was married at fifteen to Dashina, who was twenty. He approved of his wife greatly, but also of his and other men's many pleasure slaves, some of which were never properly cared for. From them he caught slavespot, which he passed on to her and to her first child — who died — and since she began to scar he won't bed her."

Tashana nodded, smiling despite the pain in her eyes. "At least I kept my figure." She turned to Sharina. "Sharina was married at eighteen to Rikacha, a man fifteen years older than her. A man with no heart who beats her like a slave. She lost her first child after he hit her in the stomach. Motara threatened to stop talking to and trading with him if he ever hurt her again. Now he hits her only where it won't show. She has two boys."

Sharina glanced at Stara and shrugged. "But I am so lucky

491

to have them." She turned to Chiara. "Chiara was fourteen when she married Motara, who was eighteen. Though he is sweet and generous and appears to be fond of her, he refuses to see what we all can see. She has swelled with child twelve times, birthed eight times, and her body is worn out and broken. Each time she grows sicker and we fear it will kill her. He should let her be – let her rest, at least. How many children does a man need?"

Chiara smiled. "How can I deny him them? He does love them all – and me."

"You don't have any choice," Tashana said darkly.

Sighing, Chiara turned to Aranira and her smile was strained. "Aranira married Vikaro when they were both sixteen. For the first few years all was well. She bore two children, a girl and a boy. But he lost interest in her too quickly. And in the children. It all sounded too strange, until friends of ours discovered the reason. He is infatuated with another woman. A powerful, beautiful woman who desires him in return. A widow whose husband died of an illness the slaves say was too much like poison."

"He does not have the courage to risk my family's anger if he is found out," Aranira said. But there was doubt in her voice.

Stara saw the fear in the plain girl's eyes and nodded to show her understanding. *Her situation is much like Nachira's, except at least Ikaro loves Nachira and is trying to protect her.* The women turned to regard her. *This is like a ritual to them*, she thought. *They tell each other's stories. It is as if they all gain something from the ritual. Acknowledgement, perhaps. Yet each has made light of her own situation, too. Perhaps it helps them hold on to the good in their lives.*

She wondered, then, at how willingly they had offered up their private lives to her. Perhaps because, as Kachiro's wife, they had no choice but to include her in their group. Yet it felt as if they were challenging her as well as revealing themselves. Challenging her to be honest, perhaps? Or to accept their ways.

"We do what we can to help each other," Tashana told her. "If we can, we will help you, too. So if you need help, don't fear to ask."

Stara nodded again. "I understand. If I can help any of you, I will," she promised. "Though I have no idea how I could."

Abruptly she thought of magic. It was one asset she had that they didn't, as far as she knew. But she would not mention it unless she needed to, or could see how it might be of use to them. *And though I do like what I've seen of them so far, I still barely know them. I'm not going to tell them any secrets until I know I can trust them.*

"Admittedly, most of the time all we can offer is sympathy," Chiara said. "But we have learned that friendship and someone to talk to is worth more than gold. Perhaps more than freedom."

I'm not sure many slaves would agree with that, Stara thought. *Still, a life with no friends or family – no loving, supportive family, that is – would be a sad one, no matter how rich and powerful you were.*

Tashana began telling Stara about a friend they had helped, who had moved away with her husband to the north, to a place on the edge of the ash desert. The conversation turned to travel and Stara was surprised to find that all of the women had visited different parts of Sachaka, and most had moved to the city after they were married. Stara decided it would be safe to admit she had grown up partly in Elyne, and they bombarded her with questions about the country.

The conversation shifted and changed, sometimes informative, sometimes sad and often funny. When a slave came to announce the men were leaving Stara felt disappointment and realised she had been enjoying herself. *And not just because I've been starved for company. I think I like these women.* Which made it harder to know about their individual troubles. When she thought about their stories she felt anger stir deep inside. *I do want to help them. But I have no idea how. I have magic, but what use is it here?*

Magic couldn't heal Chiara's worn-out body, or rid Tashana of her disease. It couldn't stop Sharina's husband beating her, or stop Aranira's lusting after another woman and contemplating murder. At this moment, magic seemed like a useless and pointless indulgence.

But it might discourage Kachiro from beating or trying to murder me, if he was so inclined, she thought. *I wonder if I could teach Sharina and Aranira magic . . .*

She followed as the women streamed out of the room, down the corridors and into the main meeting room. The men were on their feet, laughing at something. As the women entered they separated, moving to their wife's side or beckoning their wife to join them. Kachiro slipped a hand lightly around Stara's waist. He smelled of something sweet and fermented.

As the men began to voice their farewells, she forced her gaze to the ground. What she had learned about the other men made her want to stare at them. Then she noticed Chavori. The women had said nothing about the young man, except that he had recently returned from a journey to the mountains and would talk for hours about it if allowed to. He looked very drunk, she noticed. Even leaning against the wall he seemed unable to keep his balance easily.

She felt Kachiro stir. "What do you think of our young friend?" he murmured.

"I haven't spoken to him."

"But he is good-looking, don't you think?"

494

She glanced up at Kachiro. Was this a poorly disguised test of her loyalty?

"He might be, if he wasn't completely drunk."

He laughed. "Indeed." Looking up at Chavori, his eyes narrowed in assessment and approval. "I do not mind if you find him attractive," he said, very quietly. He looked down at her again.

She looked back at him. His expression was expectant and curious. And, if she was reading him correctly, hopeful.

"I could never find him as handsome as you," she told him.

His smile broadened and he turned away as Motara spoke his name.

What is he up to? she wondered. *Is he testing me, or looking for a way for me to become pregnant? Does he have a reason to avoid siring a child?*

She pondered this through the last of the farewells, on the way through the house to their wagon, and all the way home. During the journey she was acutely conscious of Vora clinging on to the wagon behind her. She itched to discuss everything with the slave. When she finally extracted herself from Kachiro's company and retired to the bedroom, the information she'd planned to give spilled out too quickly and all jumbled together.

"Wait!" Vora exclaimed. "Are you saying he's picked out a lover for you?"

"Not . . . exactly. He just said he didn't mind if I found Chavori attractive."

Vora nodded. "Ah," was all she said.

"You don't look surprised," Stara observed.

"I have learned a great deal about your new husband's friends and their wives."

"About Sharina's husband beating her, and Dashina's having a taste for diseased pleasure slaves?" Stara asked.

"Yes." Vora nodded. "And it's no secret among the slaves that Vikaro wants to get rid of Aranira. They don't like Chiara's chances of living through this pregnancy, either."

Stara sighed and nodded. "I thought my situation was bad, but now I can see that other Sachakan women have far worse lives."

"They're still better off than female slaves," Vora reminded her. She looked away. "Cursed to be used for pleasure if beautiful, bred like animals if not. Their children taken and set to work too young. Girl children killed if there are too many already. Beaten, whipped, or mutilated as punishment, with no effort taken to find out if they committed the crime or not. Worked to death . . ." Vora drew in a deep breath and let it out, then straightened and turned to face Stara. "Or, worse still, handed over as a wedding gift to tend to the whims of a magician's wife with no idea of Sachakan manners or her proper place in society."

Stara made a rude noise. "You enjoy it. Admit it." She paused. "How are your hands? I hope you weren't stung too badly."

Vora's lips thinned, but Stara could tell she was pleased. "My hands will be a little stiff tomorrow. I have a paste for the stings."

Yet Vora did not seem at all pained. Her movements suggested a repressed excitement. Stara watched the woman move about the room, restless and efficient.

"You seem unusually pleased with yourself tonight," she remarked.

Vora stopped and looked up in surprise. "I do?"

Stara considered the woman's expression. Was that surprise, or dismay? She couldn't tell.

She shook her head. "So what should I do?" she asked. "If my husband does want me to bed pretty Chavori, should I?"

Vora's expression became thoughtful. As the woman began to list the possibilities aloud, and their consequences, Stara felt an unexpected surge of affection and gratitude.

One day, she thought, *I am going to repay her for all her help. I'm not sure how yet. I'd give her her freedom, but I'm not sure she'd take it. And besides, I need her with me.*

She smiled. *The best I can do for now is consider all her advice, and treat her as little like a slave as possible.*

To Jayan it felt as if they had been travelling in circles. The last day had been a repeat of the same scene, over and over.

The army had risen at dawn, packed and waited while the leaders deliberated. Then a message spread that they would retreat further south-east towards Imardin. Magicians, apprentices and servants travelled west until they reached the main road, then continued on towards Imardin, setting a pace that always seemed both excruciatingly slow and immorally fast. Slow, because all were conscious of the Sachakan army following. Fast, because every step they took meant giving up land to the enemy.

Each time they passed through a village or a town, the occupants came out to greet them, awed at the number of magicians visiting their home but anxious about what it meant. They did not always take kindly to orders that they leave their homes and flee the advancing army. But most understood warnings that every person who stayed behind would not only be killed, but add to the enemy's strength. People had begun to regard avoiding evacuation as an act of treachery, as bad as returning to steal from abandoned homes. More than a few times, Jayan observed villagers chasing down those who refused to leave, tying them up and throwing them into carts.

The magicians encouraged the villagers to collect what food and livestock could be gathered quickly and take it with

497

them. They didn't want to leave the enemy anything that could be eaten or provide magical strength. *More important, we'll need supplies to feed our people,* Jayan thought. *The Sachakans don't have increasing numbers of ordinary folk to care for. They'll probably manage to scrounge up enough food, but we aren't going to make it easy for them.*

Hearing a smothered sound, Jayan turned to look at Mikken. A glint of light reflected out of the corners of the apprentice's eyes.

"Are you all right?" Jayan asked.

Mikken glanced at him. "Yes." His jaw tightened, then he sighed. "We just passed the place my family used to visit in summer, when I was a boy. How much more are we going to let them burn and wreck?"

"As much as we have to," Jayan replied.

"I can't help wishing the king would hurry up."

Jayan nodded in agreement. Dakon had told him the army would have to keep retreating until it met the king, who was bringing the last of Kyralia's magicians with him. Jayan suspected they might also retreat further in order to give the Elyne magicians, travelling down from the north to offer their assistance, time to reach them.

Looking ahead, Jayan saw that Tessia was riding beside Lord Dakon, as she had these last few days. It was to be expected: she was Dakon's sole apprentice now. Jayan felt a tiny thrill. *I am a higher magician now. Independent. In charge of my own life. Able to earn money in exchange for magical tasks.*

A pity it had to happen in the middle of a war.

A new weight rested against his chest, within his tunic. He had no idea where Dakon had found the decorated knife he'd presented to Jayan as part of the ceremony. Blades of that style, with fine scrollwork along the handle, were usually made solely for the use of higher magicians, but where would

Dakon have found a craftsman to do it, or the time? Had he been carrying it all along, anticipating that he would grant Jayan his independence soon?

Jayan considered the information Dakon had given him. Higher magic had been surprisingly simple to learn, once he'd stopped trying to work it out intellectually and consciously, and simply *felt* how it was done. But it would take some practice before he could use it efficiently.

Mikken had volunteered to be the source for Dakon's demonstration of higher magic. Jayan had been glad it was not Tessia, as the thought of taking power from her had made him strangely uncomfortable. Yet he also found taking power from Mikken disturbing, too. It felt wrong to be sapping the strength of people he knew, even if it didn't affect them physically.

When Mikken had then offered to be Jayan's ongoing source, Jayan had fought off a strong reluctance to agree. At first he suspected he didn't want to out of jealousy. He often saw Tessia and Mikken talking now, and couldn't help questioning his resolve not to get too attached to her while Kyralia was at war. The only thing that kept him from refusing was the knowledge that, as a new higher magician, he was weak and vulnerable. He needed to build up his strength so he could fight in the next confrontation with the Sachakans.

But then, so did most of the magicians in the army. More than half of them had been exhausted by the confrontation with the enemy. The only consolation was that the enemy must also have depleted much of its strength, too.

If the conclusion of the next battle was decided by a race between the two armies to recover their strength, then the Kyralian side had the advantage. By removing as many sources of strength from the Sachakans as possible, they were preventing the enemy from recovering.

But we are doing no better than they. It's taken all our time and persuasion to get the people to leave, leaving no opportunity to gain any power from them. None of the magicians wanted to round up the villagers and forcibly take their strength from them. Jayan kept hearing them muttering that they would have to find time to convince the people to co-operate later.

His attention was drawn to a rider who galloped past and pulled up alongside Werrin and Sabin at the front of the army. Recognising one of the scouts, Jayan watched as a short conversation followed. Then the rider steered his horse away.

He watched as information melted back through the army. One by one the magicians riding before him looked over their shoulder at those riding behind, lips moving. Narvelan turned to speak to Dakon. Then Tessia's horse moved to the side of the road and slowed. She looked back at him.

Stop it, he told himself as his heart suddenly began beating faster.

"What are you scowling at?" she asked as she guided her horse in alongside his.

"I'm not," he told her. "But everyone else is. What's got them stirred up?"

Her brows lowered and she glowered at the back of her horse's neck. "News has come that another group of Sachakans have been attacking villages in the north-west. They might have headed west to cut off the Elynes, or they may be taking advantage of the fact that the people in the western leys weren't evacuated."

"Oh," he said. He opened his mouth to say more, then realised he had nothing to say that wasn't obvious or didn't involve cursing. Not that Tessia wasn't used to cursing. But he wasn't about to break a long habit of avoiding it around women just because she was used to it.

They continued in silence for a while.

"Sorry," she said eventually. "I keep forgetting to call you 'Magician Jayan'."

"So do I," Mikken inserted quietly.

Jayan looked from one side to the other, then shook his head. "It doesn't matter. You're my friends. I'd rather nothing changed between us."

Tessia looked up at him, her eyebrows rising. "Really? Nothing?"

"Yes."

"How wonderful." She looked across at Mikken. "I guess that means he wants to continue to be as rude and annoying as ever."

Mikken laughed, then, as Jayan shot him a glare, covered his mouth.

Jayan turned to her. "If I have been rude I apologise. I do believe, as a higher magician, I have an obligation to . . ." He stopped. Tessia's eyes were bright with humour and anticipation. Relaxing, he allowed himself a rueful smile. "Yes, I promise to be as rude and annoying as before."

She sniffed with disappointment. "You were supposed to promise to *not* be rude and annoying."

"I know."

"Hmph!" She urged her horse forward, leaving him and Mikken behind as she returned to Dakon's side.

"You two are like old friends, or brother and sister," Mikken said. Then he added: "Magician Jayan."

Jayan stopped himself from wincing. *But I don't want us to be. Curse this war!* Sighing, he resolutely set his gaze on the road ahead.

CHAPTER 37

Towards the end of the day, reports of the distance between the army and the king grew more frequent. At first both forces were on the road, closing the gap between them steadily. Then news reached them that the king had camped outside Coldbridge. He would wait for them to arrive. Dakon could not help feeling annoyance that the king was giving up more ground to the Sachakans, probably for the convenience of having a town nearby to service the army.

But it made sense. The army servants were exhausted. Several were ill and were travelling in a cart. With all the best food served to the magicians, some of the servants had cooked meat kept too long after slaughter for themselves. Two had died, and neither the guild healers nor Tessia had been able to help.

"What water or sustenance we give them goes straight through their bodies," she'd told him. "We'll see more of this, if we begin to run short of food."

It was incredible that she could mend a broken back, yet was helpless to stop simple gut sickness claiming lives. Refan had the advantage of magic giving him resilience, though. Tessia's description of sensing magic repairing Refan's body had fascinated Dakon. It confirmed what all magicians had long believed without any proof, except the observation that they lived long, healed fast and were resistant to disease.

A murmur among the magicians and apprentices around

him brought his attention back from his thoughts. Looking ahead, he saw what the others were remarking on. A town lay ahead, houses dotted along each side of the road.

Coldbridge. Spread before it were lines of tents and wagons, with tiny figures roaming about the space between them. *The king and the rest of Kyralia's magicians*, he thought. *Which should increase the size of our army to just over a hundred.*

At the centre, beside the road, was a large tent striped in the colours of the king's family. Already a crowd was gathering around the tent, no doubt in expectation of meeting the advancing army.

The pace quickened and the sound of voices rose around Dakon. He glanced around, noting the excitement and relief in the expressions of magicians and apprentices alike. Tessia, however, was frowning.

"What are you worrying over, Tessia?" he asked.

She looked up at him. "I'm not sure. Every time we gain more magicians we have to teach them so much. Not just Ardalen's method, but not to wander off, or who's in charge. Do we have the time, this time?"

Dakon looked at the tents ahead and considered. "We may have to give up more ground in order to gain the time we need."

She nodded. "There is another thing I've been wondering about."

"Yes?"

"Lord Ardalen taught us how to give power to another magician. He died at the pass. Would the Sachakan who killed him have had the chance to read his mind and discover the trick?"

Dakon shook his head. "Mikken said his master was killed instantly, once his shield was overcome."

She grimaced. "I guess we should be thankful for that."

He sighed. "Yes, I guess we should. Though . . . I'm not sure a Sachakan would have paid much attention anyway. He or she would not have known the significance of what he saw, since we hadn't fought them in direct battle at that time. If a Kyralian magician were captured now, however, I'm sure their mind would be thoroughly searched."

"Let's hope they don't get the chance, then."

The front of the column had reached the edge of the field of tents now. All fell silent as the leaders of the army approached the king's tent. Dakon saw that a line of three men stood waiting. He recognised the young man standing at the centre. The two men on either side of King Errik were magicians more than twice his age, regarded as two of the most powerful and wealthy men in Kyralia.

Werrin and Sabin signalled for the army to stop several paces from the king. Slowly the long column widened as magicians and apprentices gathered before the tent. Then, as all movement ceased and sounds quietened, Werrin and Sabin dismounted and bowed, and the rest of the army followed suit.

"Lord Werrin," King Errik said, stopping before them. "Magician Sabin. My loyal friends and magicians. It is good to see you again." He grasped their arms in turn, then straightened and faced the army, raising his voice. "Welcome, magicians of Kyralia. You risked your lives to face our enemy, responding quickly and bravely to the country's need. Though the first battle was lost, we are far from beaten. We have the rest of Kyralia's magicians with me, bar those too feeble to ride and fight. We are now one army, and as such we must ready ourselves to face the enemy with our full strength. We have the assistance of magicians from other lands." He turned and gestured towards five men standing nearby. Dakon saw, with surprise, that two were tall, well-tattooed Lans and the other three were of the less imposing Vindo race. Between them stood Magician Genfel, looking pleased with himself.

The king had paused, and his expression grew more serious as he scanned the faces of the newcomers. "There is no time to lose. The leaders are to join me to discuss our strategy. The rest of you may rest, eat and make camp for the night. By tomorrow we will have decided what our next move will be."

As he turned back to Sabin, the army stirred and began to disperse. Dakon looked at Tessia.

"Duty summons me yet again," he said.

The corner of her mouth twitched in a half-smile. "I expect a full report later, Lord Dakon," she said loftily, then nudged her horse after the crowd.

He chuckled, then rode up beside Werrin's horse, dismounted, and handed his reins to a waiting servant. Narvelan was already hovering nearby. Dakon moved to the young magician's side.

"That's Lord Perkin. And Lord Innali," Narvelan choked out.

Dakon looked at the two older men who had been standing beside the king. "The unofficial patriarchs of Kyralia?" He shrugged. "They had to show their faces eventually. And they're hardly going to be excluded from this discussion."

"I guess not," Narvelan said, his voice thin with resignation.

"Don't let them intimidate you," Dakon told him. "They may have money, and ancestry that goes back before the Sachakan occupation, but neither will matter in battle. You have fought and killed Sachakans. That makes you far more impressive than a pair of old men with only fancy names to speak of."

"I suppose you're right," Narvelan said. He sighed. "I almost wish it weren't so. Though it was easier the second time. And the third."

Dakon frowned at his friend. "What was easier?"

"Killing Sachakans." Narvelan glanced at Dakon nervously.

"I'm not sure whether to be relieved or worried that it gets easier."

"Choose relieved," Dakon advised. "If all goes well we will kill many more Sachakans. If it doesn't, I doubt we'll have the chance to worry if it was easy or not. Ah, we're heading inside."

The king, Werrin and Sabin were moving towards the tent. Dakon saw that the rest of the army advisers were edging after them. The king beckoned to the two patriarchs, who strode forward to follow him inside. Dakon, Narvelan and the rest came after.

Wooden chairs had been arranged in a circle. The king took the larger, fancier one, and the others settled into the rest. Magician Genfel introduced the Vindo and Lans magicians.

"I have some reports of the first battle," Errik told them. "But not a detailed account." He looked at Sabin. "Describe it to me."

Sabin obeyed, and Dakon was struck by how much the army leader had actually missed. Sabin's attention had been on attacking the enemy, relying on those around him to tell him how the rest of the Kyralian army fared.

Another advantage to our new methods of fighting, Dakon thought. *His attention did not need to be divided. But the disadvantage is this lack of the whole picture.*

To fill in the details he could not relate himself, Sabin turned to Werrin. After a while the king interrupted.

"This strategy of fighting in groups shaped much of what you were able to do. Tell me more."

Dakon smiled as Werrin related how Ardalen demonstrated his magical trick of giving power to another, and the advantages and drawbacks of the method. He then explained how setting the apprentices to playing Kyrima with themselves as pieces and using only strikes of light had led to fighting in groups, with one given the task of striking and another of shielding to focus concentration.

A message arrived for the king then, and servants brought food and drink. The king returned quickly, his face grim.

"The Sachakans have overtaken Calia," he told them. "They have not wreaked the destruction they have in the past, however."

Dakon shook his head. Calia was a major town, prospering from its position near the meeting point of two major roads.

"They aren't wasting their strength," Innali said. "At least there are no people left for them to take more from."

The king frowned. "Then why did I receive reports of bodies?"

Werrin sighed. "There are always some who refuse to leave, who hide to avoid being taken away against their will. Some even skirt around the army and return home."

"Why?" Innali asked. "Do they not understand the danger?"

"Some do, some don't. They think they can hide from the Sachakans – and some do manage to. To them protecting their property from thieves is more important. Or else their plan is the thievery itself."

Innali scowled.

"The enemy isn't keeping them alive to continue using them as a source," Sabin added. "So to them they are a limited resource." He looked at the king. "The Sachakans have their slaves, but we have the people of Kyralia. If they are willing, they could be our best resource."

"But they are a resource we haven't been using," Werrin pointed out. "It has been difficult enough getting villagers and townsfolk to leave their homes, giving them a chance to gather what food and possessions they can. We haven't had time to persuade any of them to let us take their magical strength."

Lord Perkin shook his head. "And the people of Kyralia aren't here for us to take power from. Instead they are arriving in Imardin in droves. The supplies they bring won't last long and most have no roof to sleep under. We will soon begin to lose them to starvation and disease."

The king frowned. "If the Sachakans decided to, they could ride here in a few hours. The towns and villages between here and Imardin are yet to be evacuated, and as you've said, that takes time. More than usual, since they contain not just their normal occupants, but those who have not travelled as far as Imardin but chosen to stay in these villages instead. I am reluctant to give any more ground.

"Then there is the news of another group of Sachakans in the north-west, travelling this way," he continued. "If we wait too long they may join with the main army. Are we strong enough to confront the Sachakans now? Tonight?"

The magicians exchanged glances.

"Let's sum up," Sabin said. "After the battle more than half of us were exhausted of power, the rest depleted to some degree. We each have had one day's recovered power from our apprentice or servant. Tomorrow we will have had two. And we have over thirty magicians who have not used up any power in battle yet. Together, we number over a hundred.

"We have no idea how depleted the Sachakans were after the battle, but we did kill twelve of them and we can assume several more were near exhaustion. They have more slaves per magician than we have apprentices or servants. They have been taking power from those people who foolishly remained in their path. As far as we know, no reinforcements or new allies have joined them. They number something over fifty."

"It sounds as if we have the advantage," the king said.

Sabin nodded. "We do."

The king nodded. As his expression turned to one of determination Dakon cleared his throat. There was one issue they had overlooked, which had to be tackled before this new army threw itself into battle too quickly.

"There is one other matter we have to address, your majesty. We need time to train the rest of the army in our new methods."

The king's stare was direct and challenging.

"How long will that take?"

"A day last time," Sabin told him.

"Which was longer than it should have been," Dakon added. "Too few of us volunteered to teach the newcomers." He shrugged. "We had the luxury of time."

The king looked at Werrin.

"I'm sure it could be done faster," Werrin said, "if all were willing to teach. Perhaps a few hours."

The king looked at Sabin. "Is it worth denying a few magicians their sleep for?" he asked, smiling wryly.

Sabin nodded. "Though we lost the last battle, it proved the value of Ardalen's gift. Though the Sachakans were stronger, they lost some of their number. We may have been weaker, but *none of us died*. Had we fought as we used to – as they do – all those who exhausted their power would have perished. Not a dozen, not two dozen, but more than half our number. We lived to strengthen ourselves again. We lived to fight again. That is worth giving up a few hours' sleep for."

Errik nodded, then he sighed and looked at Perkin. "Gather up those who need to be taught." He looked at Dakon. "You will have the unenviable task of rousing some volunteers."

Dakon bowed his head.

"I would like to make request," one of the Vindo magicians said in halting Kyralian.

The king turned to him. "Yes, Varno? What is it?"

"Would I and my fellow Vindo be welcome to learn new magic?"

Errik paused and looked at Sabin. "I must consult with my advisers, of course . . ."

"We can make exchange," Varno said, smiling. He reached into his jacket and drew out a small object. A ring, Dakon saw. A simple loop of gold holding a smooth red bead. All looked at it in curiosity and puzzlement.

Surely he doesn't mean to buy the knowledge with this rather unimpressive bit of jewellery, Dakon thought.

"It is call a blood gem," Varno explained. "Not stone; it glass imbued with blood of Vindo king. It allows him to reach wearer's mind." He smiled. "Very good if ships trading far away."

That revelation had roused murmurs of surprise from around the table.

"I check with him short time ago if I may tell you this," Varno added.

"Communication by mind," Sabin said. "But others cannot hear it."

"Yes," Varno replied. "My people keep knowledge of making many, many hundreds years."

"Communication in battle, without the enemy knowing or guessing your signals," Narvelan breathed.

The king looked at Varno. "How fast can you teach the making of these?"

The Vindo spread his hands. "Some moments, no more."

Errik smiled. "Then we have a trade. I suggest that the fastest way to do this is for your companions to join Lord Dakon for lessons in Ardalen's method, and then teach you later, while you come with me and teach the making of these blood gems."

Varno bobbed his head. "That faster."

The king rose, and gestured for them to follow suit. "Aside from Magicians Sabin, Werrin and Varno, who are to come with me, you are all to follow Lord Dakon's instructions." Dakon saw the two Lans magicians exchanging looks of uncertainty. Sabin leaned close to the king and murmured something, and the king turned to consider the pair. "Your help and willingness to risk your life for the good of our land is payment enough," he said quietly. "Go with Lord Dakon."

As the king and his companions left, the rest turned to regard Dakon expectantly. He found himself momentarily unable to speak. Then, recovering from his surprise, he smiled grimly and began to give instructions. To his relief, the magicians began to nod. Soon all were marching out of the tent, intent on the task at hand.

When Hanara opened his eyes again he noticed no change at first. It was still dark. He was still lying beside the entrance of Takado's tent. His master was still on the pallet in the middle, snoring faintly. Hanara pushed himself up and peered outside. The three shapes of the other slaves were still where they had been before he'd fallen asleep, on blankets laid on the ground outside. He knew he had been asleep, but for how long?

Then he realised someone was shouting, in the distance, but close enough to allow him to make out the words.

"Wake up! They're coming! The Kyralians! They're attacking!"

Muffled sounds of movement and voices raised in protest came from within other tents. Hanara heard a low groan behind him. He turned away from the tent opening and moved to Takado's side.

"Master," he said, quietly but urgently. "Wake up. The Kyralians are coming."

An eye opened. Takado blinked. He muttered something.

"The Kyralians, master," Hanara repeated. "They are attacking – or will be soon. I do not know if it is a trick or not. Do you want me to check?"

Takado's brows lowered, then abruptly he pushed himself up into a sitting position.

"No." He closed his eyes tightly and rubbed his face. "Get me a drink."

Hanara dashed to a small chest Takado had taken from one of the towns. On top were a half-empty bottle, a gold jug and a matching goblet.

"Water or wine?"

"Wine," Takado snapped. "No . . . water." He shook his head. "Just give me both. Quickly."

Hanara grabbed the bottle and the jug and brought them both to Takado. His master drank from the bottle first, then from the jug, then splashed water over his face. He thrust bottle and jug back into Hanara's arms, moved to the tent entrance and disappeared outside.

Taking the opportunity, Hanara drank some water. It tasted of silt. He considered the wine and decided against it. He'd need a clear head if he was to serve his master well in battle. But what should he do next? *If the Kyralians are about to attack he'll probably want to take as much power as he can, so I'd better wake the others.* Hanara felt remarkably calm as he moved outside and prodded the other slaves awake. As he explained, the slaves began to glance around the camp anxiously. *They do not have what I have,* Hanara thought, smiling. *I have achieved the long-life feeling, in serving Takado. It doesn't matter if I die tonight. Perhaps that is why I am calm.*

Yet doubts began to creep in again, as they had since the

night after the battle, when Takado had disappeared with Asara and Dachido, then returned with new horses, but in a foul mood. Hanara did not know what had angered Takado so much, but his master hadn't regained his confidence and good humour. Takado had taken magic from his four slaves two or three times over the next day, and hunted down the Kyralians foolish enough to cross his path with a frightening savagery. He'd even chased down domestic animals.

At least we ate well last night.

Takado's mood had swung back to its normal confidence when, at sundown, twenty Sachakans had ridden into Calia to join the army. They had been preparing themselves for battle by roaming about in north-west Kyralia, attacking villages and towns. But they brought news of a group of Elyne magicians travelling south to join the Kyralians. Takado had roused the army and set forth, intending to find and defeat the Kyralians before that help could arrive.

After a few hours' travelling, however, he had stopped the army and ordered them to make camp. Nomako's scouts had brought news that the Kyralian army had grown larger, and the Elynes would not arrive for another full day. He wanted to gather more information and debate tactics, and threatened to withdraw his assistance. Instead of engaging in a debate, Takado had retired to his tent, saying they could argue about it in the morning.

It wasn't morning. Hanara estimated morning was still several hours away. But the camp was alive with activity. Magicians strode about or gathered in tense knots. Slaves dashed here and there. Hanara saw Takado talking to Asara and Dachido. Nomako approached them, pointing south. Takado glanced in that direction, said something, then turned on his heel and headed for Hanara. Recognising the look on his master's face, Hanara dropped to his knees and held out his wrists. Takado's knife flashed into his hand.

The taking of power was rapid and left Hanara reeling. He saw the other slaves sway as they endured the ritual. Then Takado barked Hanara's name and strode away.

Hurrying after, Hanara looked beyond the camp and saw a sight that set his heart racing. A long shadow stretched across the southern end of the field. A dark ribbon of movement blown steadily closer, by a wind he could feel only in his imagination. The slip of moon skulking within the trees allowed only hints and glimpses of the Kyralians' approach.

White faces in the dark, he thought. *They look like what the barbarian tribes of old must have looked like, but they've grown clever and strong.*

As in nightmares, his feet felt weighty and encumbered as he walked towards them, but he forced himself to follow Takado. Memories of slaves struck by stray magic slipped into his mind, despite his attempts to keep them out. *I will stay close to Takado. I will keep close to the ground. If he holds I will be protected. If he fails I will not want to live anyway.*

Or would he? Again, traitorous doubts crept in. He pushed them aside.

From all around him, Sachakan magicians and their slaves hurried forward. As Takado stopped, they fell into a line stretching out on both sides of him. Asara and Dachido, instead of standing among their own people, took their places by his side, showing Nomako who they considered the leader of the army to be.

A globe of light flared into existence far above Takado's head, brightening the pale faces of the Kyralians. They had stopped advancing, Hanara saw. Once again they'd formed knots of five or six magicians. Many, many more knots than had been at the last battle.

514

"Have you come back to surrender?" Takado called out.

"No," a voice replied. "We have come here to accept yours, Ashaki Takado, though I expect you will take some persuading."

All eyes fell on a young man stepping forward from a knot of magicians near the centre of the Kyralian line.

Takado burst into laughter. "King Errik! The runt himself has scurried out of his castle to squeak at us. Which is about all he can contribute to a fight," Takado glanced at his fellow Sachakans on either side, "from what I've been told."

"I have plenty to contribute," the king replied. As if copying Takado, he looked up and down the line of Kyralian magicians. "I have my people. I have magicians, united in knowledge and strength. I have ordinary people, willing and ready to defend their country any way they—"

"Magicians who have already failed you once," Takado said. "And will again."

The Kyralian king smiled. "How many of your allies died in that last battle?"

Takado shrugged. "A mere handful. Nothing compared to how many we will slaughter in revenge tonight. You'll make a good start."

From him burst a sizzling flash of light. It pounded the air just in front of the king, who staggered backwards. Hanara saw a magician step forward to steady his ruler, then the air began to flash and ripple between the Sachakans and the Kyralians.

Throwing himself to the ground, Hanara shivered as magic once again seared the space between the two armies. He peered through the remnants of whatever trampled, half-grown crop had been sown in the field. Mostly he watched in case Takado signalled for him, or snapped an order, but he could not help stealing glances to either side, dreading the moment when the first Sachakan fell.

It happened much sooner than last time. Hanara flinched and felt his heart jolt as a magician a mere twenty strides away burst into flames. He felt the heat, cringed at the screams. Then slaves surged forward to put out the fire, but after the magician stilled he did not rise again. He heard the slaves' fearful lamenting as they realised they were now masterless and unprotected.

When the next magician fell, Takado made a disgusted noise. "What will it take for us to trust each other?" he muttered. "Do as they do," he called out. "Protect each other."

Looking down the line of magicians, Hanara saw one take a step back, then glance at both of his neighbours indecisively. Then he staggered to his knees as a strike pounded his shield. He quickly crawled behind the magician to his left and rose to his feet, looking uncomfortable but relieved.

Now magician after magician began to either slip behind his or her neighbour, or die before managing to. Hanara's stomach sank ever lower as more and more died or stepped aside, and he grew nauseous with dread. *How can we win at this rate?* Then a cry of triumph rang out. Lifting himself up on his elbows, Hanara saw that one of the Kyralian groups had disintegrated. Two corpses lay on the ground, and three magicians were running away. As he watched, one buckled in mid-stride and dropped. The other two swerved out of sight behind the enemy's line.

Now Hanara watched the Kyralians intently, refusing to look when one of his own people fell. Laughter broke from Takado as one of the enemy shrieked in pain, his face blackened and clothes alight. All but one of the magicians around the victim fled to either side, hiding in the protection of other groups. The one who stayed tried to drag the burning man aside, but then both were knocked off their feet and fell to the ground, where they lay still.

Seeking the enemy king, Hanara found him within another group, scanning the two lines and scowling as another magician spoke rapidly to him.

They're worried they're losing, Hanara thought, his heart lifting. *They're going to try retreating again. But this time Takado won't let them go. He'll chase them down.*

A sound beside him threatened to drag his attention away. He saw someone in the corner of his eye, crawling closer. It could only be a slave. He resisted looking back.

"Hanara? Are you the one called Hanara?"

Annoyed, he glanced back quickly. It was one of Nomako's slaves. Hanara grimaced.

"Yes. Why?"

"Message. For Takado. He requests Takado retreat. Nomako's men are nearly exhausted."

Hanara nodded. "I'll tell him."

As the other slave crawled backwards, Hanara edged forward, slowly closing the gap between himself and Takado.

"Master," he called. "Master Takado."

He waited, but Takado was rigid with concentration. In case his master hadn't heard, he called again.

"What is it?" Takado snapped.

Hanara repeated what the slave said. Takado scowled, but said nothing.

"My people are signalling that they are tiring," Asara said after a moment.

"But so are the Kyralians, I think," Dachido said.

"Yes," Takado agreed. "We are too closely matched."

"It doesn't matter if these Elynes are an hour away or half a day," Asara said. "Even if we win here, they will find us exhausted and have no trouble finishing us off."

Takado gave a low growl. "If they find us."

"Look at their faces," Dachido said, nodding towards the

Kyralians. "They're worried. Either they know the Elynes will arrive too late to save them, or they don't yet know the Elynes are close by. Let them be the ones to retreat."

Takado straightened. "We have only to bluff them. Intimidate them." He smiled. "When the next group falter, turn all your power on them so none have a chance to seek shelter."

The three allies fell silent. Hanara searched the enemy line, looking for groups that might be reaching the end of their combined strength. He noticed that one group did not appear to be striking.

"That one with the tall magician at the front," he said, loud enough for his master to hear. "Are they attacking at all? Or just shielding?"

Takado looked in the right direction. "Ahhh," he said. "We have our target." He sent a streak of light towards the tall magician and his group. It scattered off a shield. Hanara saw the man turn to see who had attacked him, and turn grey with terror.

In the next moment, the five magicians in the group fell under a barrage of magical strikes. Not one of the group survived.

Hanara watched realisation and horror spread across the faces of the Kyralians. He realised he was giggling, and felt a rush of loathing at himself, followed by a contradictory pride. *I found the target. Takado won't forget that.*

Then all smugness evaporated as several Sachakans fell, one after another. Looking in the direction of the attackers, he saw five magicians calmly separate and walk behind their neighbouring groups.

They expelled their last strength deliberately, so they could hide before anyone could kill them. He could not help admiring them for that. *It's this cool, calculating approach that makes them more formidable than they should be.*

The Kyralians now stood in groups of ten to fifteen magicians. As Hanara watched, magicians in the king's group shouted orders. The smaller groups moved together to form five larger groups.

But they did not retreat.

He looked up at Takado. His master's teeth were set in a grimace. Hanara hoped nobody could see this but Asara and Dachido. Perhaps from a distance it looked like a smile. On either side, two more magicians fell.

Then the Kyralians began to back away.

Takado gave a cry of triumph. "At last!"

"Now we give chase?" Asara asked.

"Not yet," Takado said. "We must wait until they break into smaller groups."

"But they're not."

Sure enough, the Kyralians were retreating in an ordered formation, protected by those still strong enough to shield the rest of the army.

Takado hummed in thought. "They'll probably keep that up until they reach their horses. Then we might have our chance."

Asara drew in a sharp breath.

"Ah! I have an idea," she said. Looking at Takado, she grinned. Then, as she told him, he also began to smile.

"A bold idea," he said. "Go. Try it if you dare."

She chuckled, then turned and sprang away from the fight.

CHAPTER 38

I t was growing clear that staring at the roof of the tent was not going to send Tessia back to sleep. Sighing, she turned on her side and looked at the other young women asleep on their pallets. Someone had decided that, now there were more female apprentices in the army, they should all share the same tent. There were five of them, not including herself, ranging in age from fourteen to twenty-five.

Is this really all the female apprentices in Kyralia? There must be more than seventy male apprentices, though she was not sure if that number had been skewed by magicians taking on new apprentices in order to strengthen themselves as preparation for war. *How many women have magical talent, but never develop it? How many never know they have it?*

She wondered why these particular girls had become apprentices. They were all a little frightened to find themselves at war, Tessia suspected. Even those who had been flippant, or enthusiastic about seeing a fight.

Yet nobody complained that we apprentices get to sit around waiting while our masters go off to fight.

Tessia felt a rush of apprehension. No magicians had died the last time, but that didn't mean none would this time. Mistakes could be made. The Sachakans might not let the Kyralians retreat this time, if it came to that.

But at least she didn't have to worry about Jayan. Once again, despite now being a higher magician, he'd been left in charge of the apprentices. He was a logical choice for the role, since he'd led them before and they all regarded him as a hero since "defeating" three Sachakans "all on his own" in the bol storehouse. She had to admit his solution had been clever, and admire his quick thinking.

And now the girls are even more inclined to swoon over him. She thought back to the previous night's conversation with the female apprentices. *They've started with Mikken, too, sighing over his tragic but brave escape from the pass, making his way back all alone, and re-joining the army when he could have gone back to Imardin.* She smiled to herself. *Still, you can't help admiring him for that.*

Tessia sighed. She was not going to fall back to sleep again. *I may as well get up and see if I can make myself useful.*

As quietly as she could, she rose and wrapped her blanket around her shoulders. Picking up her boots, she took them outside the tent and sat down on a box to pull them on. It was not quite the full darkness of night, nor the brightening gloom of dawn, but she could see figures pacing the boundary of the camp in the distance, and the pointed shapes of other tents. Fires glowed with dying embers. Lamps flickered, thirsty for oil.

Rising, she began to wander, no destination in mind. Just a circuit of the camp, she decided. The male apprentices either slept in their master's tent, or had their own individual shelters. She passed a small group of them playing a game of some sort. They saw her and beckoned, but aside from smiling politely she ignored them and continued walking.

A gap of about ten strides curved through the camp, and it wasn't until she had crossed it and passed a few more tents that she realised it divided the magicians and apprentices from the servants' area. The tents here were certainly plainer, and rectangular. She saw tables covered in pots, pans and kettles, as well as baskets and boxes filled with sacks, fruit, vegetables and other foodstuffs. She glimpsed people sleeping shoulder to shoulder with only blankets or mats of dried grass between themselves and the ground. She noticed the smell of animals, held within pens or cages.

Then a familiar mix of odours caught her attention. She stopped, recognising the twin scent of illness and cures, then quickened her pace. A large rectangular tent appeared ahead. She paused at the entrance, taking in the makeshift beds of dried grass matting covered in blankets, the sick men and women, the bowls for excrement or washing water, and the table covered in cures, some mixed, some not, some in the process of being prepared.

In the shadows at the back of the tent someone was bending over a patient. Tessia could hear the rasping sound of breathing. She moved into the tent and approached.

"I have some briskbark ointment back in my tent," she said. "Shall I go and get it?"

The figure straightened, then turned to face Tessia. Instead of the surprised face of a man, she was confronted by a beaming, familiar smile.

"Tessia!" Kendaria exclaimed. "I heard you were here. I was going to seek you out, but the healers put me on night duty."

"Alone?" Tessia glanced at the other patients. "Without even an assistant?"

Kendaria scowled. "It's my punishment for daring to be a woman. Besides, most of them are managing to sleep, except for this fellow here." She took Tessia's arm and led her out of the tent. "And he's not going to live much longer, no matter who watches over him," she added quietly. "Poor man."

"I can get my bag," Tessia offered. "Might ease his pain."

Kendaria shook her head. "What I've given him will do the job well enough. So, how are you? I've heard so many stories of chasing Sachakans, battles and such, and you've been there right from the start. How have you managed it?"

Tessia shrugged. "I don't know if management has been part of it. Wherever Lord Dakon went, I went too. He has gone wherever Lord Werrin then Magician Sabin and now the king took him. And they've gone wherever the Sachakans forced them to go." She looked back at the tent. "You've obviously managed to convince the guild to let you do a little healing."

"Only the boring or unpleasant work that they don't want to do." Kendaria's face darkened. "They treat me like a servant most of the time, sending me off to get them food or drink. One even thought he could help himself to my bed, but he was so obvious about his intentions I put some papea spice under my pillow and blew it into his eyes. They were streaming for days afterwards."

"That's terrible!" Tessia gasped. "Did you complain about his behaviour?"

"Of course, but the guild master told me that since most people think the only women who hang about armies are there to service the men, I should not be surprised if men make assumptions about me."

Tessia gaped at her. "He said *what*? Does he make that assumption about me? Or the other female apprentices or magicians?" She shook her head. "Or the servants? Do they work hard to feed and support us only to be treated like . . . like . . . ?"

Kendaria grimaced and nodded. "I've had more than a few women come to me asking for a preventative for conception. Who do you think got me the papea spice? It's not a cure ingredient."

Appalled, Tessia could not speak. She considered telling

Lord Dakon. He would tell Magician Sabin, she was sure. But would anybody do anything about it? Even if they forbade it, would the men taking advantage of the servant women pay any attention?

"Is it true what they're saying about you?" Kendaria asked, a little hesitantly.

Snapping out of her thoughts, Tessia turned to look at the healer. "What are they saying about me?"

"That you can heal with magic. That you mended a broken back."

"Oh." Tessia smiled. "It is and it isn't. I've been trying to use magic to heal, but haven't found a way yet. What I've been able to do is things like moving broken bones back into place, or holding a wound closed while it is stitched, or stopping bleeding. And I've recently worked out how to pinch the pain paths to numb an area of the body. That's all, though."

"So how did you mend the broken back?"

"It wasn't broken. It was all out of alignment. Once I put it right all the pathways straightened and unblocked. Though there was a lot of swelling that had to be discouraged."

"But . . . how did you know it wasn't broken?"

Tessia paused. Of course, ordinary healers couldn't see into their patient's bodies. *I hadn't realised how great an advantage that was. I've been thinking less of the healers for misdiagnosing their patients, when they really can't help it.*

"I'm able to see inside people," she explained.

Kendaria smiled. "You might not be able to actually heal magically, but what you can do is marvellous." Then her smile faded a little. "Which is why the healers aren't happy about what you're doing. Don't be surprised if they try to stop you. They're worried that if magicians can heal then they'll lose their richer customers."

"How could they stop me?"

"By convincing the king that, because you're not guild trained, you might do more harm than good out of ignorance. Or that magicians will take all the work from the healers, which will leave them less able to afford to do charitable work with people who can't afford to pay magicians. Not that they do much of it, anyway."

Tessia laughed quietly. "In other words, they're afraid they'll end up no better than a lowly village healer."

"Yes." Kendaria gave her a serious look. "Don't dismiss them. They are the most powerful guild in the city. They won't give up what they have without a fight."

"I'll be careful," Tessia assured her. "I'm not going to stir them up then disappear like my grandfather did. He used to say the mistake he made was to try to change them too quickly. He'd have had more success making changes so slowly that they didn't notice them. But he was young and impatient, and people were dying . . . what's that shouting?"

The calls in the background were growing rapidly louder and more numerous. Kendaria frowned as she listened.

"Go! Get in the carts!"

"They're coming!"

"Leave it! Just go!"

Suddenly there were people everywhere, darting between tents and shouting. Servants were emerging. There were questioning calls from within the healers' tent. A man strode up to Kendaria and placed a hand on the woman's shoulder. She yelped in fright.

"The army is coming and the Sachakans are close behind. We have to get everyone onto the carts and leave. No packing. Just get the people out." He looked at Tessia and blinked. "Apprentice Tessia? Master Jayan is looking for you." He pointed towards the centre of the camp.

"Thank you," Tessia said. She looked at Kendaria. "Good luck."

"You too."

Turning away, Tessia jogged through the tents. She was forced to dodge several times as men and women raced towards the outskirts of the camp where horses and gorin were most likely being harnessed to carts as quickly as possible. Once she crossed the gap between servant and magicians' tents, she found herself following apprentices all moving in the same direction.

As she emerged onto the road, into the space before the king's tent, she saw Jayan standing on a large box. He was shouting orders and repeating the same information again and again, in response to the apprentices' frantic questions.

"Our army is retreating. The Sachakans are following. They will be here soon. We must be ready. The servants are bringing horses." He paused and frowned at one of the apprentices. "Stop wasting time asking stupid questions and see if your horse is here!" he snapped. He turned away and pointed. "You! Arlenin. I can see someone bringing your horse. Yes, I'd hardly miss that ugly beast if it were on the other side of the country. Go and get it."

Tessia put a hand to her mouth to stop herself laughing, then felt a wave of affection for him. He had no patience with fools. While it was not always a good trait in times of peace, right now it was just what the apprentices needed to snap them out of their panic and get them organised.

It seemed to take for ever, but within a few minutes they were all mounted and waiting. As the crowd around Jayan diminished she was able to get closer. A servant came to tell Jayan that the carts were loaded and ready. Jayan paused for a moment.

"Then go. You'll travel more slowly than us. Is there any

road you can take other than the main one, to get you out of the Sachakans' path?"

"Yes. It has already been chosen, in case there was need."

"Good. Then go."

The man bent into a short bow then hurried away. For some reason this sent a shiver down Tessia's spine. *It's hard enough getting used to Jayan behaving and being treated like a higher magician, but watching him in the role of leader is very strange indeed!*

"Jayan," she called. His head turned in her direction, then another shout drew his attention away. Someone tapped her on the shoulder. She turned to find Ullin, Dakon's servant and former stable servant, holding the reins of her horse out to her. As she took them he smiled then raced away.

Only then did she glance at the saddle and realise that her father's bag was not there. It was back in the tent.

"The army!" someone shouted, and the call was taken up by several voices. Tessia tried to see past the apprentices to the road, but there was no hope of seeing anything with a crowd of horses milling before her. She turned away and swung into the saddle, then looked back.

A dark shadow filled the road ahead, and it was advancing rapidly.

For a moment an eerie quietness descended, through which she could hear the distant shouts of the cart drivers and bellows of gorin somewhere behind the sea of tents, and the thunder of galloping hoofs. Tent walls snapped in a lively breeze. She realised that the sun had come up and she hadn't noticed it.

"Where's your father's bag?" a familiar voice asked.

Turning, Tessia found Jayan beside her, Mikken on his other side.

"Back in the tent. I had no time to go back for it."

Jayan gazed at her intently, then turned to look at the advancing army. "There might be."

"No," she told him firmly. "There's nothing in it I can't replace."

He looked at her again and opened his mouth to speak, but another apprentice drew near.

"What are we going to do?" he said. "Start galloping ahead of them? Or move aside and let them pass?"

"They're slowing down," Mikken said.

He was right. The lead horses had slowed to a canter. She watched as they dropped into a trot and then a walk. Lord Sabin and the king rode at the head. She scanned the faces, sighing with relief when she saw Lord Dakon. He was riding a different horse, she noticed.

But something wasn't right. Where was the rest of the army? With sinking heart, she began a new search – of her memory. For the names of those who must have fallen. The names of the dead.

As the magicians stopped they turned to regard each other, heads swivelling as they took stock of their number. Tessia read the same shocked realisation in their faces. Some even blinked back tears.

A third, she found herself thinking. *We've lost a third. And where is Lord Werrin?*

She saw the king lean towards Sabin and gesture back down the road. Sabin nodded and stood in his stirrups.

"Apprentices, join your masters," he shouted. "We ride to Imardin."

As he urged his horse forward Tessia heard Jayan curse. He had risen in his stirrups to peer over the heads of the magicians.

"What?" she asked.

"They're coming," he said, dropping back into the saddle.

528

"The Sachakans are coming. We should have evacuated Coldbridge. Too late now."

Together they hauled on the reins and slapped their heels, and their mounts raced forward with the army.

The slave had said Stara was to appear in the master's room in an hour, well dressed, to help her husband entertain their guest, Chavori. Vora had been amused, since it was the same length of time she had made Stara take to prepare for the trip to Motara's house. "He's a fast learner," she said as she laid two elaborately embroidered wraps on the bed. "The blue or the orange?"

"Blue," Stara said.

"I wasn't asking you, mistress," Vora said, chuckling. "Though I agree. The orange is more suited to larger gatherings, where you might want to draw attention to yourself. The blue is a calmer colour, better for quiet evenings with single visitors."

Stara wondered briefly if "single" meant unmarried, or merely that Chavori would be arriving on his own. She decided not to voice the question. It might lead to another unnecessary lecture on the perils of following her husband's possible hint she take Chavori as a lover.

When Stara was dressed and laden down with jewellery, Vora pronounced her ready. "Don't forget my advice, mistress," the slave said, shaking a finger at her.

Stara chuckled. "How could I? He's handsome, but he's not *that* handsome. Have you heard anything from Nachira?"

"Not since her last message." Vora sighed. "The slaves say she is sick, but they are reluctant to say anything more."

"Not surprising, if Father might read their mind and kill them for betraying his plans. I still can't believe he and Ikaro left for Kyralia without telling me." She shook her head.

"They must have left right after my wedding, but Father didn't say anything."

"According to the slaves, Nachira fell ill the day after your wedding, too."

Stara looked at Vora. "Is there anything we can do?"

"Not give up hope?" Vora sighed, then gestured to the door. "Your husband and his guest await."

Though Stara knew the way now, the slave still led her through corridors to the master's room. Reaching the doorway, they stepped inside and Vora prostrated herself. Within the room, Kachiro and Chavori were looking at one of the pieces of furniture Motara had designed. Stara moved an arm so that her bracelets chimed against one another. The two men looked up.

"Ah," Kachiro said. "My wife has finally arrived."

Smiling, he extended his arms towards her and beckoned. She walked forward and took his hands. He kissed her knuckles, then let one hand go and turned so they faced Chavori. The young man smiled, a little nervously.

"A pleasure to see you again, Stara," he said.

"And for me to meet you once more," she replied, lowering her eyes.

"Let's sit down and talk," Kachiro said, leading Stara to the furthest of the three stools in the room. A small table stood in front of them, bowls of nuts gleaming in the light of Kachiro's magical globe light. He stepped back and indicated that Chavori should sit in the middle, then sat on the other side of the young man. "Tell us about your journey to the mountains. Stara knows nothing of your skills and adventures, Chavori, and I'm sure she would like to hear something of them."

The young man glanced at Stara and actually blushed. "I . . . we . . . I guess I should explain what I do, first. I make

530

charts and maps, but instead of copying what others have done I travel through the places I am mapping and measure – as best I can, using methods taught to me by a shipping merchant and some I've developed myself – the distances and positions of everything. Well, not everything, but the features that are important to people who use maps."

Stara noticed that he glanced a few times at a large metal cylinder leaning against a wall. It looked very heavy.

"Do you have any maps here?" she asked.

"Oh, yes!" He leapt up and strode over to the cylinder. Lifting it, he carried it back to the stools and sat down again. But he did not open it. He caressed the metal with his long fingers. *He has elegant hands for a Sachakan*, Stara thought. *So many of them have hands to match their shoulders, broad and strong. In fact, his build is more like that of a Kyralian, though his colouring isn't. I wonder . . .*

"Have you finished the map you were drawing for the emperor?" Kachiro asked.

Chavori nodded. "At least, as much as I can with the information I have." He turned to Stara. "Most people find maps confusing, so I have compiled everything into one, simpler map. But there are blank areas. I refuse to include any information I haven't confirmed for myself."

"Show us," Kachiro urged.

Chavori beamed at him, then grasped the end of the tube. The cap came off with a musical pop. Reaching inside, he drew out a thick roll of paper.

Peeling this back, he unrolled until a large sheaf fell away. It automatically recurled. Kachiro lifted the table and put it aside, so that Chavori could smooth the map out over the floor rug with his elegant hands. Kachiro looked around, then picked up the bowls of nuts and weighed the two far corners down with them. Then he slipped off a shoe and placed it

531

on the near corner at his side, which made Chavori's nose wrinkle. Stara took off a bracelet and dropped it at the other corner, earning an approving smile from the young man.

The paper was covered in fine ink lines. Looking closely, Stara gave a little gasp of delight at all the tiny drawings of mountains, houses and boats, and the fancy decorative border framing the map.

"It's beautiful!" she said.

"Chavori is quite an artist," Kachiro agreed, looking fondly at his friend.

Chavori shrugged. "Yes, people prefer this sort of thing, but I find it rather silly. It is difficult to be accurate."

Stara pointed to a large group of buildings, bisected by a drawing of a wide avenue and the Imperial Palace. "So this is Arvice – where we are."

"Yes."

She looked at the lines of mountains. At the top of the map was a large blue shape, and some of the mountains had red lines curling out of the top and down the sides. "What are these?"

"Jenna Lake," Chavori told her. "And the northern volcanos. They expel fire and ash, and what the Duna tribes call earthblood."

"The red?"

"Yes. It sprays out and runs down the sides of the mountains, so hot you'd burn if you got near it. When it cools it solidifies into strange rocks."

"Do people live there?"

"No. It is too dangerous. But the tribes risk it now and then, to harvest gemstones, which they say have magical properties. I found the same gemstones in some of the caves further south, and sensed no magic in them."

"I want to mine them," Kachiro told her. "If we can get

the secret of their use out of the Duna tribes we may be able to sell them for high prices. But even if we can't, we can still sell them to jewellers for a good profit."

"You should see if Motara can design jewellery as well as furniture," she suggested.

His eyes brightened with interest. "There's an idea . . ."

Chavori shrugged. "Just so long as we make enough to enable me to continue my work. Now, let me show Stara what a proper map looks like."

Taking the roll of paper, he peeled off another sheet and placed it over the first. This one was not as artistically drawn, and half of the map was blank. Instead of pictures of mountains, there were bursts of radiating lines. Where there had been drawings of buildings there were mere dots.

"This shows you not just where each mountain is, but where the valleys are between them," Chavori told her. He ran his finger along the spaces between the radiating mountain shapes. "I can not only show the valley, but indicate the width of the valley by leaving wider spaces. See this one?" He pointed to a large white gap with a blue line meandering along it. "It's the most beautiful valley you might ever see. No fields, just wild enka grazing. This river cascades along the middle. Mountains on all sides." He made a graceful upward gesture, then spread his arms. "And the biggest blue sky above."

His eyes had misted over at the memory, and Stara felt a pang of longing. Would she ever roam beyond the city again? Was her journey from Elyne the last taste of travel she would ever have?

Looking down, she sought and found the letters that spelled out "Elyne". They were drawn sideways, along a red line that followed the mountains at the top left of the map. The red line must be the border, she realised. And if a blue line meant a river, did this thick black line roaming through the mountains from the Elyne border to Arvice indicate the road? She looked at the mountains again and suddenly the map looked as if it had gained depth.

"Ah," she said. "I see the illusion now. It's just as if we are looking at the land from above. The centre point where the mountain lines meet is the peak."

"Yes!" Chavori turned to Kachiro. "You were right: you have an exceptionally clever wife."

Kachiro smiled broadly. "I have, haven't I?" he replied smugly.

Chavori glanced at Stara, then back at Kachiro. "What else can I show you?"

Kachiro considered the map thoughtfully. "Did you bring any maps of Kyralia?"

The triumphant smile on Chavori's face fell away, turning into a tolerant grimace. "Of course. Everyone wants maps of Kyralia these days."

"We are at war with them," Kachiro pointed out.

"I know, I know." Chavori sighed and picked up the roll again. Peeling off several more maps like the last, he finally spread out another of the beautifully decorated ones, with drawings of cities and mountains.

Kachiro pointed at the pass then spread his hand over the mountains that split Kyralia from Elyne. "From what I've been told, the Ichani gathered under the leadership of Ashaki Takado around here. When there were enough of them to form an army, they moved into the northern rural areas and took control of the villages and towns."

Chavori shook his head. "The reports I've heard said that they don't bother staying to control the people. Instead they've been destroying the towns and driving the people out."

"I doubt they're driving them out," Kachiro said. "They're

probably killing them and taking their strength. Driving them towards the Kyralian army will just give their adversary more people to take strength from. Why give them more strength, when you can take it for yourself?"

"Yes, they'd have to be." Chavori made a sweeping gesture from the mountains to the cluster of buildings labelled "Imardin". "They'll be heading for the capital. But I can't help wondering . . ." He looked up at Kachiro. "Do you remember I said I passed Nomako's army on my way back to Arvice?"

Kachiro nodded. "Yes."

"I noticed at the time that the army was split into three. Nomako at the head of the first group, and two others leading smaller groups." Chavori looked back down at the map. "It was almost as if he planned to split the army up once it crossed the border."

"Why would he do that?" Kachiro asked.

Chavori shrugged. "If you are right, so they can sweep through different parts of Kyralia and take strength from the people as they go. The Kyralians will not want to split their forces into three – or four if none of the groups join Takado's – in order to tackle them."

"Then all groups will arrive at Imardin at the same time."

"Those who haven't met any resistance still strong and ready for battle."

"Hmm." Kachiro narrowed his eyes at the map. "And which group is most likely to have met resistance?"

Chavori's eyes went wide. "Takado's! He was there first and, if Nomako times things right, will have been the target of the Kyralians. By the time he joins with Nomako's armies, his will be the weakest."

"So Nomako will conquer Imardin and ride home the hero instead of Takado. Emperor Vochira will be admired for outsmarting Takado." He looked up at Chavori, admiration in his gaze. "You have a good head for battle strategy. Perhaps you should be leading the army!"

The young man blushed again. For a second the two looked at each other, then both dropped their gaze to the map again.

Stara frowned. She felt as if she had just missed something. But then, she was no expert on warfare. Though she felt sure she'd understood everything Chavori had said, she might have missed some nuance that they had both appreciated.

"Can I ask a question about the war?" she asked.

"Of course," Kachiro replied.

"Why are neither you nor your friends part of the army?" Kachiro's face fell. "I am relieved that you are not risking your life," she assured him. "I'd much rather you were here. But I suspect it is political and I wish to understand Sachakan politics better."

Kachiro nodded. "Some of the reasons are political, some are not. My father was unable to fulfil an order taken out by the emperor many years ago, due to a fire, and spent years paying back the debt. He died soon after he made the final payment. So my family has been out of favour for some time, though rebuilding trade connections has grown easier with time."

His expression was so sad, Stara regretted asking the question.

"Others of my friends are similarly out of favour, though Chavori's family has good standing," he continued. Then he smiled. "The advantage is that if we have no family honour or respect, we do not need to join the army to protect it, though I expect our help would have been accepted if we had volunteered."

Chavori nodded. "I told my father that if he won't give

536

me the respect I deserve, there's nothing to risk my life to protect. He called me a coward." He shrugged. "I suspect he hoped I'd go and be killed, and he'd be rid of me."

Stara felt a stab of sympathy for this young man, so talented but clearly as unappreciated by his father as she was by hers.

"Can I buy this map off you?" Kachiro asked.

Chavori's mouth dropped open. "Buy it?"

"Yes. Or do you need it?"

"No," Chavori said quickly. "I make these to sell. I sell them all the time. Well, not *all* the time – maybe a few each year."

"Then can I buy it?" Kachiro looked up at the far wall of the room. "I think I will buy more, too. Perhaps one of every country, to put up on that wall. It would be good for starting conversations with guests, especially if Sachaka continues to reclaim the lands it used to rule. How much do you want for it?"

Stara felt a chill run down her back, and did not hear the price Chavori asked, or how much extra Kachiro offered. *Does he mean Elyne? Well, of course he does. It was part of the empire, just as Kyralia was. They both were given independence at the same time.* The thought of Elyne at war made her heart sink. *So many of the wonderful things about Elyne rely on the freedom of her people.*

Kachiro rose. "I'll get it now." He strode to the door. Pausing in the opening, he looked back at Stara and smiled at her, before disappearing.

The smile left her both amused and uncomfortable. It had a hint of mischief in it. A hint of challenge. Was he hoping she'd seduce Chavori right there and then?

I'm not that stupid, she thought. She turned to the young man.

"When will you be taking your maps to the emperor?" she asked.

He grimaced. "Just as soon as he grants me an audience. I've been trying to see him for weeks. I guess the war is taking all his attention. But the war is why he needs to see them."

"Why is that?"

His expression became serious. "Because there are places in the mountains where an enemy could easily hide and live. Caves and valleys where they could grow crops and raise animals for food, and live independently of the rest of us. They could attack the Sachakan people, then disappear again. If the Ichani found those places . . ." He shivered. "Once the war with Kyralia is over Emperor Vochira will be too busy establishing his rule over that country to deal with attacks from the mountains."

Stara frowned. "That is a frightening thought. But if these places exist, why isn't anyone living there already? Why haven't the Ichani already established themselves there?"

Chavori's expression was grave. "Access is through a cave through which a river flows. I suspect the river path changed recently – I found signs of a dry bed where a landslide blocked the river some years back. The water must have created or widened the cave . . ."

"Here you go." Kachiro strode into the room, carrying a small pouch that clinked in his hand. Chavori rose and smiled with embarrassed gratitude as Kachiro pressed the bag into his hands. "Now, there is something I want to show you." Kachiro looked up at Stara. "I'm afraid you would not find it interesting, Stara dear," he said apologetically.

She smiled. "Then I will return to my room, if you wish."

He nodded.

"Thank you for showing interest in my maps," Chavori said, looking at her a little plaintively. "I hope you were not bored."

"No, not at all," she assured him. "They were fascinating. I look forward to seeing more on our walls, and hearing how they are made."

He beamed at her. Smiling, she turned away and walked out of the room. A moment later, Vora slipped out of a side corridor and fell into step behind her.

"How was our guest, mistress?"

"Surprisingly pleasant company." Stara chuckled. "An intelligent man, though a little awkward socially. He will grow out of that in time, I expect."

Vora hummed non-committally. They reached Stara's room, and the slave closed the door.

"So, mistress, do you think he's the sort of man who would admit to being the father of your child, if bribed or blackmailed?"

Stara laughed ruefully. "As subtle as ever, Vora. Yes, he would," she said. "Whether at the threat of being discredited, or the temptation of having his work funded, he would do it. Don't worry. I am not going to fall in love with him."

"That is good. Though . . ." The slave frowned.

"What is it?"

Vora looked up at Stara and her eyes narrowed in thought. "The reason for you remaining childless may have been removed."

Stara felt her heart stop for a moment, then start racing. "Nachira? You heard news? Is she . . . is she dead?"

Vora smiled and shook her head. "No."

Sighing with relief, Stara sat down on the bed. "Then what?" As a possibility occurred to her she felt a thrill of excitement. "Is she pregnant?"

"Not as far as I know." Vora chuckled.

"Then *what*?" Stara scowled at the slave. "Stop playing with me! This is serious!"

Vora paused, her gaze becoming thoughtful and, to Stara's alarm, wary. Then she sighed. "Nachira has vanished. Either left or been taken from your father's house."

Stara stared at the old woman. "I see. You don't appear as alarmed by that as you should be."

"I am," Vora assured her.

"No. You're not." Stara rose and moved to stand in front of the slave. "What aren't you telling me?"

A hint of fear entered Vora's eyes. "Do you trust me, mistress?"

Stara frowned. *Do I?* She nodded. "Yes, but there are limits, Vora."

The slave nodded, then looked down. "There are some things I have learned through . . . through new connections with your husband's slaves . . . that I cannot tell you because if I do, and your mind is read by your husband or your father, people will die. People who do good things. People they've helped, like Nachira." She looked up at Stara. "All I can tell you is that Nachira is safe."

Stara searched the woman's gaze, which did not waver. *Do I trust her enough to accept this?* she asked herself. *I believe she loves and is loyal to Ikaro, and therefore Nachira. I'm not as sure she loves me as much, but it would be reasonable if she didn't since she does not know me as well. Yet I think she would try to avoid choosing between us. Which might mean keeping information from me.*

I could try reading her mind. But I don't want to do that to her. And is it worth the risk of endangering Nachira just to find out what happened to her?

"She had better be safe," Stara said. "And as soon as you can tell me where she is, I expect you to do so."

Vora's eyes filled with tears, but she blinked them away quickly. "I will. I promise. Thank you, mistress."

540

"Does Ikaro know yet?"

"That would be impossible. She only disappeared last night. No messenger could have got the news to him so fast, even if he knew where in Kyralia Ikaro was."

Stara moved back to the bed and lay down. "Poor Ikaro. I hope he is all right."

"I too," Vora assured her. "I too."

CHAPTER 39

*W*ho would have thought that horses could turn out to be so vital to the survival of the army? Dakon thought.

Thinking back, he remembered the discussion among the leaders, prior to battle, about whether to leave magicians with the horses or not. All had agreed that they needed as much of their magical strength engaged in fighting the Sachakans as possible. It would be no consolation to have saved their horses, if Kyralia was lost to the Sachakans because of it.

Leaving the apprentices in the protection of one magician had been a risk, too, Dakon thought. *But at least they have a little magic of their own, their wits, and the ability to tell us if they're being attacked.*

According to the servants who had been tending to the horses, only a handful of Sachakans had attacked them. It took only a few to wreak so much havoc. Fortunately, the Sachakans had set out to steal the mounts, not kill them. They could have slaughtered them quickly, but instead each had taken one horse, then gathered up the reins of as many others as possible, and left.

Once the servants had realised what the enemy's intentions were, they had bravely emerged from hiding to untie and cut lead ropes, setting horses free and encouraging them to run away. Then, when the Sachakans had left, the servants had rounded up the scattered mounts as best they could.

I hope the king rewards them for their courage and quick thinking,

Dakon thought. *Nobody thought to tell them what to do if they were attacked. They acted all on their own.*

None of the magicians knew the horses had been taken until they tried to retreat. Sabin had restricted the blood gem rings he'd made to the leaders of each team, saying too many minds connected to his was too distracting. He hadn't given one to Jayan, for the same reason.

As the army had retreated, the Sachakans had followed. Having to wait until horses were rounded up delayed their escape. Several more Kyralians had died when the magician protecting them ran out of magic. Eventually fewer than ten magicians had been left with the burden of protecting the entire army. The enemy continued to attack and pursued the Kyralian army step for step.

They were determined to press their advantage. But they should not have had the advantage. Their numbers were smaller, even with the addition of new allies. They should not have had enough opportunities to regain the strength they lost in the last battle.

But they had. With more slaves to draw strength from than the apprentices and servants the Kyralians relied upon, plus the lives of those killed in villages and towns, the Sachakans had managed to fend off the attack and chase their attackers all the way to Coldbridge, where they broke off the pursuit to hunt down any villagers who hadn't managed to flee fast enough.

They lost plenty of fighters, though. We lost nearly a third, but they lost more.

Dakon looked up at the road stretching ahead, curving and leading his eye towards the jumble of walls and roofs ahead. Imardin. Kyralia's capital. *I can't believe they've driven us this far.*

Abruptly, his horse skittered away from the side of the road. Tightening his grip on the reins, and bracing himself, he glanced back. Nothing. Just crops swaying in the breeze. No strand of curren looking any different from or more dangerous than any other.

He sighed and shook his head. He'd lost his favourite riding horse at Mandryn; then, while pursuing the invaders, he had changed mounts whenever possible as it had been impossible to care for them properly. Once the army had grown large enough, and they had access to better feed and took time to rest, he'd found himself growing to like the quiet brown gelding he'd ended up with, and had named him Curem for the colour of his coat. It irked him to know Curem was now in the hands of the Sachakans, or had been killed for his strength.

Tiro, the new horse, had an irritating habit of trying to bite him. And he was ugly. Dakon did not know which of the magicians who had died had owned Tiro. Whoever he'd been, he must have had great patience.

He looked over at Narvelan. The young magician's expression was dark and brooding. It was always dark and brooding these days. The light-hearted friend Dakon knew still surfaced now and then, but Narvelan's sense of humour now had a nasty edge to it. He had been the only magician willing to take Lord Werrin's horse. Nobody else had wanted to, knowing she would remind them constantly of her former owner's sacrifice.

Dakon shivered as he remembered. As the last of the magicians' power began to fail, Lord Werrin had shielded the army as all struggled to mount and leave. The king had led a horse to him. The magician had murmured a few words to the king, who had turned white and stared at him for a moment. Then Errik's face had hardened. He'd nodded, grasped his friend's arm, then turned away, taking the horse with him.

Werrin had still been shielding as the last of the magicians rode away. Dakon had paused to look back, before Narvelan shouted at him to leave and they both galloped off.

Werrin could not have lived much longer than that.

Later that day, the Elynes had joined the army.

Ah, the bitterness of bad timing, Dakon thought. *If only they'd come a day or two earlier. Or if we'd known they were coming, we might have waited another day before confronting the Sachakans.*

So much tragedy had happened because information had not been gained in time. He would not have left Mandryn if he'd known Takado was going to attack. He'd have evacuated the village. If the king had been certain the Sachakans were going to invade, and when, he'd have been able to prepare for it. Perhaps even prevent it.

Nobody could predict the future. Not even magicians. And even magicians could only guess at their own strength, or their enemy's. Dakon had been so sure that, with an army larger than the enemy's, they would win the battle. He, and many, many others, had been wrong.

Would they be again? They had no choice but to guess at the strength of both sides again, based on what they knew. More Sachakans had died than Kyralians, despite their efforts to emulate their adversary's ploy of protecting each other. So though many Kyralians had been lost, their numbers were still larger.

Once more they had lived to strengthen themselves again. So far they had only one day's strength gained from their apprentices. The Sachakans had slaves and whoever happened to be unlucky enough to cross their path. Unfortunately there hadn't been time to evacuate the villages between Coldbridge and Imardin effectively. And then there were the servants of the army, abandoned at Coldbridge. Though they had been given a little more warning to flee than the townspeople, the Sachakans could easily have caught up with them.

Kyralia had new allies, though: the Elynes.

Sent by the Elyne king, their leader was a small but sharply intelligent magician named Dem Ayend. The Dem was riding at the front, with the king and Sabin. Looking up, Dakon's gaze was drawn immediately away from the leaders to the scene ahead. They had crested a low rise approaching the city, and could now see the land surrounding it.

Which was covered in a great spread of makeshift shelters, and people.

His heart ached as he realised what it was. The slums around the city had bloated to ten times their former size as the people of the country had arrived, owning little more than what they could carry, and settled where they could find the space. As the army drew closer a stench grew stronger. He'd noticed it earlier, but assumed it was the excrement of the many domestic animals grazing on the slopes of the wide valley, no doubt brought by those fleeing the invaders. Now he recognised it as that particular smell of people living in close quarters with no sanitation. A smell he already associated with the city's slums, now much worse.

As the army drew closer, people began to move through the shelters, and a crowd rapidly formed on either side of the road. *What do they know? Have they heard we were defeated? Are they expecting a triumphant announcement of victory?* Dakon saw that people were already lining the streets within the city.

Thousands of expectant faces watched as the king led the army through the expanded slums. Voices rose in a roar of sound. Dakon could not make out whether people were cheering or jeering, merely shouting at each other over the din or yelling at the army, but the sound was full of expectation.

The army made its way to the Market Square, where the king stopped. Lord Sabin gestured for the magicians and apprentices to gather behind him, their backs to the docks. A cart was rolled forward, and the king dismounted onto it. There he stood straight and silent, gazing at the crowd gathering before him with an expression of sober patience. Lord Sabin stepped up beside him.

"Please be quiet, so the king may speak," he called out, repeating the request several times.

Slowly the noise diminished.

"People of Kyralia," King Errik began. "Your magicians have been fighting for your freedom. They have been fighting, and they have been dying. Twice they have engaged the enemy in battle; twice they have retreated."

Watching the faces in the crowd, Dakon saw dismay and fear. The king paused long enough to let the news sink in, then continued. He smiled.

"But, as is the way with magic, nothing is simple or straightforward." Dakon was amused to see people in the crowd nodding as if they knew what the king was talking about. "The Sachakans may have overcome us, but each time at a price. At the first battle many of them died, but all of our magicians lived to fight again. At the second both sides bore losses, but we were closely matched. We lost by the smallest margin. And we survived to fight again."

He paused again, scanning the crowd, his expression grim. "The third battle will decide our future." A hint of a smile returned. "I think we can win it. Why? Because our fate now relies not only on the magicians behind me. It relies on *you*."

Dakon saw people frowning, but mostly in puzzlement. He caught a few sceptical looks. A murmur rose but quickly faded. The king spread his hands wide as if he would wrap his arms around the crowd.

"It relies on you giving your strength to your magicians. A strength all of you have, no matter how rich or poor. I say 'giving it' because I would not demand this from any man or woman. You are not slaves – though if the Sachakans have their way you soon will be. I would rather die than lower myself or my people to the barbarity of their ways."

He straightened his shoulders. "But if you choose to give your strength to your magicians, it will not just be magical strength we use to defeat the Sachakans. It will be the strength of unity. Of trust and respect for what we can all do together, magician and non-magician, rich and poor, servant and master. The strength of freedom over slavery." His voice rose. "You will prove that one does not have to be a magician to have the power and influence to defeat our enemies."

Hearing the passion in the king's voice, Dakon felt a thrill run through him. He searched the faces of the people again. Many were gazing at the king in hope and awe. As he lifted his arms and spread out his hands again in appeal, voices rang out in agreement.

"What do the people of Kyralia say?" the king shouted. "Will you help us?"

The response was a mix of affirmation and cheering.

"Will you help yourselves?"

Another cheer, louder, roared out.

"Then come and give your strength to those charged with the duty of protecting you."

The crowd surged forward. Dakon saw Sabin's smile turn to a look of alarm. A few strides from the cart the wave of people crashed into an invisible barrier. But they didn't appear to mind. Arms stretched out, wrists upturned.

"Yes! Oh, yes!" came a voice beside him. Dakon turned to see Narvelan gazing at the crowd, his eyes bright, almost hungry. He looked at Dakon. "How can we lose now? Even if Takado finds the servants . . . how could they match what

548

we have here? All these people, begging us to take their power. The king . . . I never knew he was so *good* at this."

"He probably didn't either," Dakon pointed out. "It's not as if he's had to do it before."

"No," Narvelan agreed. "But if it's the result of good training, I want to hire his teacher."

Dakon chuckled. Sabin turned to address the magicians, explaining how they were going to organise themselves in order to take power from the crowd. Dakon sobered. They were going to have to work fast, before doubt or impatience dulled the people's enthusiasm.

And we have no idea how long we have before the Sachakans arrive to finish us off.

The idea of taking power from hundreds of ordinary men and women had discomforted Jayan so much at first, that he had to force himself through every step of the somewhat simplified ritual. The volunteers were nervous to begin with, but once those behind the first man saw how easy it was, and how he shrugged and grinned as he walked off, they relaxed and began chatting among themselves.

The magicians had spread into a wide line. The crowd hovered, someone stepping forward to face a magician as soon as the previous volunteer moved away. Almost all those who approached Jayan voiced encouragement, urging him to "give the Sachakans some of their own treatment" or "wipe out the lot of them".

He nodded each time, assuring them he'd do everything he could. He also thanked them. Time passed in a seemingly endless stream of support, reassurance, and taking of strength. Simmering beneath the civility was a sense of urgency. A tension that would have had him looking over his shoulder constantly, if he could have seen outside the city.

The king moved up and down the lines, thanking people and giving encouragement. Jayan saw the families of magicians come to greet them and express their relief that they were alive. He also saw the grief of those who came only to learn that their loved ones had perished. His own father and brother did not appear. He would have been astonished if they had.

As the day wore on a weariness stole over him, and he stopped worrying or pausing to watch these emotional encounters, and fixed his attention on the task of taking power. Face after face appeared and disappeared. He no longer noticed if the arms stretched towards him in offering were dirty or clean, clothed in rags or decked in fine cloth. But then a particular pair of very thin arms made him pause and look twice at the volunteer before him.

A boy no more than nine years old stared back at him.

Behind the boy, the volunteers had thinned to a few people, so that he could see through them to where a crowd now lingered around the edges of the square, watching and waiting for the final battle to begin. The dim light of dusk shrouded all. The day had passed. What power the people could offer was nearly all taken. He was thirsty. Mikken had brought him food and water earlier, but the apprentice was no longer near.

Looking at the boy, he shook his head. "You have courage, young one," he said, smiling. "But we don't take power from children."

The boy's shoulders drooped. He gave a deep, comical sigh. Then he reached into a pocket and thrust his hand at Jayan.

What is this? Is he trying to give me money? Or something else? Something dirty . . . Pushing aside doubts, Jayan opened his palm. The boy dropped something small and dark into it. He smiled.

"Give you luck." Then he turned and darted away.

Jayan looked at the object. It was an unglazed square of pottery, chipped at one corner. A hole in the top had been made for a loop of leather or rope, and into the surface had been carved lines to form a stylised insect that he recognised from one of Dakon's books.

An inava, he thought. *I wonder if he knew inavas are found in northern parts of Sachaka? Probably not.*

Pocketing it, he looked up and realised that the reason nobody had stepped forward to take the place of the child was that the crowd was now gone. Magicians were striding about, or gathering in groups. Looking around, he located Dakon and Tessia, and began walking towards them, but before he reached them the magician turned and hurried away. Tessia saw him and beckoned.

"The Sachakans have been seen from the palace towers," she told him. "They'll be here in an hour or so." She frowned. "Do you think we're strong enough to defeat them this time?"

Jayan nodded. "Even if they managed to hunt down all the servants, and people from the villages, that's only a few hundred people. We've just taken the strength of thousands."

"The healers arrived an hour ago. They said the servants split up and headed in different directions so it would take a lot of time for the Sachakans to track them all down. The healers had their own horses, of course, so they rode straight here."

He could hear the disgust in her voice.

"It's unlikely anyone the Sachakans found would need healing," he pointed out.

"Yes, but there were sick people the healers were tending. I'd have waited until the Sachakans had moved on towards Imardin, then gone back to see if my patients had survived." Then she flashed a wry smile. "But I have to admit to being selfishly glad to see Kendaria again."

He smiled. "I expect the two of you will go around trying to heal people tonight. Safely inside the city, I hope."

Tessia pulled a face at him, then her frown returned. "While you'll fight the Sachakans for the first time."

He felt a flash of fear, but pushed it aside. *The strength of thousands*, he reminded himself. *We can't lose.* "At least this time I have something to contribute."

"You will be careful, won't you?"

She was staring at him so intently, and the concern in her voice had been so obvious, he found he could not meet her eyes. *I can't hope that this is more than the concern of a friend,* he told himself. *It is still good that someone cares if I live or die, though,* he found himself thinking. *I doubt my father and brother do.* "Of course," he told her. "I haven't spent nearly a decade studying and itching to be independent only to die just after becoming a higher magician."

Her eyebrows rose. "Good. Just making sure the sudden independence and recent taste of leadership hasn't gone to your head and given you more silly ideas."

He looked up at her. "*More* silly ideas? What—?"

"I'll be watching you," she warned him. "Though . . . where do you think the battle will take place? In the city?"

"No," he replied. *Does she mean my guild of magicians idea?* "That would put the people in danger, from both our magic and the enemy's, and rubble from any houses that are struck. We'll go outside to meet them. What do you mean, sil—?"

"Where do you think the best place to watch would be?"

He felt a pang of concern. *She should stay out of sight — out of any danger.* But he doubted she would, so he had better think of a safe place to suggest. "Somewhere elevated, so the closer to the palace the better. Avoid houses. You don't want to be inside a house if a bit of stray magic comes your way."

"But magic could come my way anyway."

"If your feet are on the ground, all you'll need to do is shield. If you're in a collapsing house you have a bit more to deal with."

"Ah." She grinned. "I see what you mean."

His heart seemed to shiver within his chest. *I don't think I could endure it if she died . . .* He pushed the thought away. "So what did you mean by—?"

A gong rang out, drowning out his words. Tessia turned away. Sighing, Jayan followed her gaze to the cart in the centre of the square. The king had returned and was climbing up onto it. Sabin followed, holding a large striker. A large golden gong hanging within a frame had been placed beside the cart, probably wheeled down from the palace.

Magicians and apprentices shuffled closer. Dakon appeared with Narvelan and the other leaders. Seeing Jayan and Tessia, he beckoned. Together, they wove through the crowd to his side where, curiously, they found Mikken. The young man grimaced apologetically at Jayan.

"Sorry for disappearing. They recruited me as a messenger," he murmured.

Dakon leaned closer. "There are more Sachakans," he told Jayan. "They appeared in the south a few days ago and made their way here."

Jayan felt his heart sink.

"How many?" he asked.

"About twenty."

Surely it won't be enough. Not against the strength of thousands. But then he realised that if Takado thought his army wasn't a match for the Kyralian army, strengthened by its people, he wouldn't be attacking again.

Dakon looked at Tessia. "The king has said that if we lose this battle, apprentices should leave Kyralia."

She opened her mouth to protest, but Dakon lifted a hand to stop her.

"The Sachakans will kill you all. Your only chance is to seek safety in other lands. Then, perhaps, you might work towards winning back Kyralia in the future."

She closed her mouth and nodded. The crowd had quietened now, and everyone turned towards the king.

"People of Kyralia," Errik began.

As the ruler addressed the crowd, in a speech similar to the one he'd made on arrival, but full of thanks and praise, Jayan's attention strayed to the small group of Elynes standing nearby. They looked relaxed and unworried. Some of them looked bored, though the leader was watching King Errik with thoughtful attentiveness. Dakon had told him that Ardalen's method had been no revelation to the Elynes.

I wonder what other magical tricks they've known all along that we haven't yet discovered? Could they be persuaded to share them with us? Perhaps in exchange for being part of a magicians' guild? He glanced at Tessia. *Does she really think it's silly?*

Suddenly everyone was cheering. Jayan joined in.

"Tonight Sachaka will learn to fear the people who once feared them," the king shouted. "Tonight the Sachakan empire ends for ever!"

More cheers followed. The king jumped down from the cart, Sabin following. As he strode forward, magicians began to follow. Dakon paused to look at Tessia. She patted his arm and shooed at him. Then she looked at Jayan and her eyes narrowed.

"I'll be watching," she told him, barely audible over the noise.

Then she hitched an arm in Mikken's and led him away. Jayan quashed a sudden flare of jealousy and hurried after Dakon as the magicians of Kyralia started towards the edge of the city, and their last chance to defeat Takado and his allies.

CHAPTER 40

Tessia wasn't able to take Jayan's advice at first. Once the magicians had passed, the crowd fell in behind and she was carried along with it. Her arm slipped out of Mikken's and when he looked back at her anxiously she waved to show she was fine. Whenever she could, she resisted moving left towards the river side of the road, and took every opportunity to move right, where the land sloped upwards.

Soon the last of the city buildings slipped by and the crowd was moving past the slum houses and makeshift shelters of the poor and homeless. Tessia finally made it to the edge of the crowd. As she stepped out of the tide of people, she joined a thick wall of spectators. Back towards the city, she noticed a group dressed more finely than the rest, and then her heart skipped a beat as she recognised them.

The healers, she thought. *And Kendaria!*

Her friend had seen her, and was beckoning. Weaving and dodging between the spectators and the edge of the moving crowd, Tessia made her way back. A few of the healers nodded to her politely, but they said nothing. She saw one lean close to another and whisper something, and they both stared at her with narrowed eyes.

"Apprentice Tessia," Kendaria said, shouting over the noise. "What is going on? Why are the people leaving the city?"

"Probably to watch the battle," Tessia shouted back.

555

"Which is not a good idea. They should stay inside. Keep their distance."

Kendaria grimaced. "Can't stop people being curious. Where are you planning to watch from?"

Tessia smiled. "Jayan recommended I go up there somewhere." She pointed uphill. "Near the palace. Can I get there from here?"

"Sure, but you'll have to cut through the slums. Can I come with you?"

"Of course." Tessia looked at the other healers. Kendaria glanced at them, then shrugged.

"Don't worry; they don't care where I go." She hitched a hand through Tessia's arm. "Let's go."

The makeshift shelters were a disordered, confusing maze, but Tessia kept heading uphill, keeping a globe of magical light hovering above them. She was surprised to see how many people were here, either unaware or not caring that a battle to decide their future was about to take place close by. Many looked too sick to care. Some were drunk, slouching or staggering about, or asleep. At one point they stepped over a dead man lying across a gap between shelters. She exchanged several looks with Kendaria, each time seeing that the woman was as dismayed as she by what they encountered. *Someday I'll come back here and try to help . . .*

At last the number of shelters began to thin and the slope grew steeper. Twenty or so paces past the last, collapsed shelter, Kendaria turned.

"Do you . . . think . . . this will do?" she panted.

They were still nowhere near the palace. Tessia stopped and looked back. "I think it will."

The slums, road and land before the city spread before them. The crowd had spilled out on either side of the road, stretching from the edge of the river in a widening arc that reached up the slope of the hill, in front of the shelters. Lamps had been set around the entrance to the city. Beyond it was the Kyralian army, now split into groups of seven magicians and moving out to form a line.

Several strides further away was the Sachakan army. It was two-thirds the size of the Kyralian one. To most of the people watching, this would appear to put the advantage firmly on the Kyralian side. But the group of newcomers to the Sachakan army had been making its way, unresisted, through the south of Kyralia, strengthening itself as it came. Who knew how powerful they'd become?

But we have the strength of all these people, she reminded herself. *Surely that will be enough.*

Lights floated above the two armies, creating two pools of brightness. Two figures moved from the Kyralian side towards the enemy. Tessia recognised them as King Errik and Magician Sabin.

From the opposite side a lone figure stepped forward. She narrowed her eyes, then felt a chill as she recognised Takado. A memory of him leering at her flashed into her mind. Thinking of the harm he had done since that moment, she knew she had been very lucky. Not just to find the magic in herself to push him away, but that he hadn't been able to risk killing her at that moment.

Oh, but I wish I had killed him, instead of throwing him across the room. I would have hated myself for doing so, not knowing that he planned to invade Kyralia, but it would have saved us so much death and pain.

With the thought came anger and for a moment she imagined herself down there, throwing the final strike at Takado. The one that reduced him to ashes, or shattered all the bones in his body. She shuddered then, repelled by her own imaginings.

557

How can I think about wounding and killing, when what I most want to do is heal people and save lives? She sighed. *I guess I have a bit of the fighter in me after all.*

"What do you think they're saying?" Kendaria asked.

Tessia shrugged. "Pointing out their strengths and the other's weaknesses? Calling each other names?"

"Swapping threats, I suppose."

"Yes. That sort of thing. Perhaps inviting the other side to surrender."

Abruptly a flash of light shot from Takado to King Errik. A moment later the air began to flash and vibrate. A sound like thunder echoed over the hillside, forming a constant rumble as the last boom never quite fell silent before the next. Through the dazzling streaks of light, Tessia saw Errik and Sabin step calmly backwards, rejoining their group. Tessia recognised Dakon among them.

Suddenly her heart was racing with fear. The apprentices hadn't witnessed the last two battles, instead keeping safely out of the way. She had been full of impatience and frustration at not knowing what was happening. But now she almost lamented that ignorance. Now, if Dakon or Jayan died, she would see it, and she wasn't sure she wanted to.

Jayan! Where is Jayan? She began looking for him.

"The crowd is having second thoughts," Kendaria observed.

"What? Oh." Tessia realised that the arc of spectators was retreating hastily, some people tripping over others in their eagerness to put some distance between themselves and the heat and vibration of magic.

Yet not one strike, stray or deliberate, escaped the battlefield. Were the Kyralians shielding the city? On the other hand, she had not caught any obvious Sachakan attack directed beyond the army.

Destroying commoners and buildings will come later. For now it will be more important to direct all their power towards fighting. It won't count as a victory if they've smashed a few walls but not defeated the army.

"It's quite spectacular," Kendaria said quietly. "If it weren't for the fact that they're trying to kill each other I'd find it quite pretty."

Tessia looked at her friend. A flash of light illuminated Kendaria's face for a moment, showing an expression of awe and sadness.

"Oh . . . there goes one of the enemy."

Tessia looked down and searched the enemy line. Sure enough, one Sachakan had fallen. A slave was trying to drag him away. Looking beyond the enemy line, she noticed tiny figures lying in the grass, faces rising now and then to watch the battle.

Their slaves. I wonder if Hanara is among them? Thinking back, she remembered his shy, nervous smile. *Did he really betray us, by leaving to tell Takado the village was unprotected? I thought he was happy, or at least relieved to be safe and free. I guess I never really understood him.*

"Oh, there goes another, and another," Kendaria murmured. "Has anyone on our side fallen yet?"

Tessia searched the Kyralian line. "No." There was something familiar about a figure at the far end of it. Her heart leapt as she recognised him.

Jayan. There he is. Alive.

He stood with a hand pressed to the shoulder of Lord Everran. Lady Avaria also stood in the same group. Other magicians were giving her power, Tessia noted. She wondered which of the couple was striking and which shielding.

Turning to look at the other side again, her eyes were drawn to a slave who had begun to run away from the battle. As Tessia watched, he stumbled and fell onto his front. Then his foot rose and he began to slide back toward the Sachakan line, clawing uselessly at the soil. As he came within reach of his master, the magician grabbed an arm. A blade flashed. A moment of stillness passed. Then the Sachakan turned to face the battle, the slave remaining motionless behind him.

Tessia could not drag her eyes away from that tiny figure. *I've just seen something talked about in lessons and acted out in mock battles so many times. A Sachakan killing a slave for power. But that means . . .*

"Are we winning?" Kendaria asked, a little breathlessly. She looked at Tessia, "We are, aren't we? More of them have fallen."

"It's hard to tell."

A Sachakan master only killed a source slave if he was running out of power. If he was desperate. As she watched, the Sachakan who'd killed his slave stepped behind another magician, no longer fighting.

But not all the Sachakans were seeking the protection of their allies. Though over half were now dead or seeking the protection of fellow magicians, the rest were fighting confidently. She forced herself to examine the Kyralian side, and her heart lifted.

None had died. She looked closer. Only one group had sought the protection of another. From the clothing they wore, she recognised them as the Elynes.

Ah! The Elynes wouldn't have taken magic from the Kyralian people. It would have been too presumptuous of them or the Lans or Vindo to take magic from people not of their own country. And Kyralians might not have volunteered to give magic to foreigners, either. Even foreigners who have come to help us.

She felt a surge of excitement. "It does look promising," she said.

Kendaria chuckled. "It does, doesn't it?"

* * *

No crops hid Hanara from the sight of the Kyralians, or gave an illusion of protection from the magic that blasted towards him. He ducked every time a strike flashed his way, but each time it was deflected by Takado's shield.

Only a dozen paces away, a Sachakan magician exploded in flames. Those sheltering behind him scattered hastily to either side. One tripped over slaves groping towards their dead master. He turned and cursed the men, then a thoughtful and calculating look crossed his face. Stepping forward, he grabbed a slave's arm and drew his knife in one fluid movement. The slave's wail of protest ended abruptly as the man began to draw power.

The other slaves rose and fled. By the time the magician was finished, they had sought refuge among the slaves holding the horses. The magician scowled and retreated to shelter. Hanara saw that the eyes of the dead slave were open, staring towards his dead master, and shuddered.

He looked up at Takado. *Is he strong enough? Can he match Nomako's reinforcements or will he be forced to take shelter behind the emperor's fighters?*

After the last battle Takado and his allies had ridden down the road, stopping at each town or village then roaming about the area hunting down and killing as many people as they could find. They must have killed hundreds.

But later that day they had encountered another group of twenty Sachakans, who claimed to have come to join Takado. While Takado was welcoming to these newcomers, he told Asara and Dachido later that he had recognised some of the fighters.

"They are Nomako's allies," he'd said. "Did you notice how some of them are being so friendly with the last group that joined us? Who, coincidentally, also numbered twenty."

"Their timing worries me even as it pleases me," Dachido admitted. "Do you think Nomako sent them south?"

Takado had nodded. "To join us just when we have spent much of our strength on previous battles."

Asara scowled. "They mean to steal our victory."

"Not if I can help it," Takado growled.

So the three had delayed the journey to Imardin a few more hours, so that they could hunt for more strength. They killed people and animals. Anything that might give them the slightest scrap more of magic.

But it hasn't done them any good, Hanara thought. Looking past Takado, he could see that no Kyralians had fallen. They were not tiring and seeking the protection of their neighbours. Their attack was not failing.

In the next three breaths, two more Sachakans fell.

"Jochara!"

From a few steps away the young slave rose and hurried to Takado's side. He started to prostrate himself, but Takado's hand snaked out and grabbed his arm. Hanara saw the flash of a blade and a shock went through him. Jochara stared at Takado in surprise, and kept staring, and was still staring when he slumped, lifeless, to the ground.

"Chinka!"

Hanara looked up to see the female slave, her shoulders back and her expression grim, walk to his master. She knelt and held out her wrist. Takado paused only briefly. Then his knife touched her skin. She closed her eyes and died with a look of relief on her face.

That is how I should die, Hanara found himself thinking. *Accepting. Knowing that I served my master well. So why is my heart beating so fast?*

"Dokko!"

A wordless protest came from Hanara's left. He turned to see the big man scramble to his feet and break into a run. But he did not get far. An invisible force pushed him backwards.

He fell to the ground and yelled as he slid across the ground. Takado's face was a mask of anger.

He is annoyed at having to waste power.

The slave's yells stopped. Takado turned away to access the battlefield.

"Hanara!"

A warmth spread over Hanara's groin. He looked down, appalled at his loss of control. At his inability to push aside terror and accept his fate. He tried to force his shaking arms to lever his body up.

"Hanara! Get the horse!"

Sweet, sweet relief flooded through him. Strength returned. He scrambled up and raced back to the slaves holding the horses. His hands hadn't yet caught up with the news he wasn't to die, and shook as he grabbed the horse's reins. Fortunately it did not cause him any trouble, though it was not happy to be led towards the noise and vibration of magical battle. He realised other slaves were bringing horses forward. Those magicians who had noticed were looking at Takado, their faces taut with horrified realisation, panic and anger.

"Master," he called as he drew near.

"Wait," Takado ordered.

Looking beyond, Hanara saw several magicians in the Kyralian army take a step forward, then stop.

Perhaps it had been a collective reflex. Perhaps it was a quickly reversed order to charge. But the effect was like a gust of wind. Suddenly the Sachakan line broke. Magicians were running. Slaves were fleeing. All were dying.

A great roar came from the city. The ordinary Kyralians were cheering. The sound was deafening.

Takado turned and strode towards Hanara. He took the reins of the horse and swung up into the saddle. Then he paused and looked down at Hanara.

"Get on."

Hanara scrambled up behind his master, all too conscious of the dampness of his pants pressing against Takado's back. He felt Takado stiffen, then heard him sniff.

"If I didn't need a source slave, Hanara . . ." Takado said. He didn't finish the sentence. He shook his head, then kicked the horse into a gallop and then all Hanara could do was cling on and hope his master's power lasted long enough to see them beyond the enemy's range of attack.

As the sound rolled up the slope towards her, Tessia realised the people of Kyralia were cheering. Beside her Kendaria whooped with delight. Grinning, Tessia let out a yell. They looked at each other and both laughed. Then they were both leaping on the spot, throwing their arms around and shouting with abandon. "We beat them! We beat them!" Kendaria chanted. Something inside Tessia relaxed, like a knot released, and she felt the fear and tension of the last months flow out of her. They had won. They had finally overcome the Sachakans. Kyralia was saved.

Growing breathless, Tessia stopped, and as weariness overcame her elation she felt a sadness return. *Yes, we beat them. But we have lost so much. So much death and ruin.*

"They're going after them," Kendaria said.

Looking down the hill again, Tessia saw servants hurrying forward with horses for the magicians.

The healer was no longer smiling. "I hope they find them quickly. We don't want them roaming around preying on anybody."

"There's hardly anybody out there to prey on," Tessia said. But she knew that couldn't be true. People had been evading the Sachakans, staying behind to protect their property from looters, or to tend sick loved ones who couldn't travel.

"Let's go down and join in the celebrations."

Tessia grinned and fell into step beside her friend. "Yes. I suspect most Kyralians are going to have one very bad hangover tomorrow morning."

"You can count on it," Kendaria said. "I hope you still have some pain cures in your father's bag."

Tessia flinched as a familiar ache returned. "It was left behind after the last battle."

Her friend looked at her and grimaced in sympathy. "I'm sorry to hear that."

"It doesn't matter, really." Tessia forced herself to shrug. "I can always get another bag, new tools and more cures. It's what my father taught me that matters most." She tapped her forehead. "This is worth something to others; the bag only meant something to me."

Kendaria gave her a sidelong look. "And I expect you won't need tool or cures soon, when you find out how to heal with magic."

Tessia managed a smile. "But that will take a while. If I ever manage it at all. Until then I think I had better stick to doing things the old-fashioned way."

PART FIVE

CHAPTER 41

As the wagon rolled through the gates, Stara looked up in surprise. Though they had entered the familiar court-yard entrance of most Sachakan homes, a two-storey house dominated one side and it was not rendered in white. Smooth white stone, veined in grey, stretched across the longer side of the courtyard.

"It's one of the oldest houses in Arvice," Kachiro told her. "Dashina claims it is nearly six hundred years old."

"There's no sign of deterioration," Stara said.

"His family have always repaired and maintained it well. A great deal of the front had to be replaced after an earth-quake a hundred years ago."

Inside, the house had high ceilings and opened quickly onto a large, sunken master's room. Openings on either side revealed corridors running parallel to the room, and above them were more openings onto second-storey corridors directly above the lower ones.

The usual ritual of greeting followed. She and Kachiro were welcomed by Dashina, and her husband's friends drew close to take their parts. While the others ignored her, Chavori caught her eye and smiled at her. She nodded politely in reply. He had visited her husband's house (she hadn't quite got used to calling it "home" yet) three more times, always bringing more maps. Though he always took the time to show and explain them to her, at each visit he spent less time with her and more time with Kachiro. Her husband had not made any more comments to suggest he might not disapprove if she took the young man as her lover.

Looking around the room, she found her eyes drawn to the slaves. All were women, she realised, and all were young and beautiful. They wore very short wraps and were draped in an excess of jewellery. She thought of Tashana's story and how her husband had a taste for pleasure slaves. *Is that what these women are? But of course they are. They're all too beautiful to be anything else.* For a moment she worried about Kachiro. If Dashina was bedding these women, they could all carry the disease he'd given to his wife, and if Dashina invited Kachiro to . . . but that couldn't happen. Not if Kachiro truly was incapable, as he claimed.

What a strange place I've ended up in, she mused. *With a husband I like enough to feel jealousy over, but with no reason to be jealous!*

Tashana appeared in one of the corridor openings, then stepped into the room. She crossed quietly to Stara and took her hand.

"Can I steal your wife now, Kachiro? Please say yes."

He turned and laughed. "Of course. I know she has been looking forward to seeing you again." He smiled at Stara. "Go," he urged quietly. "Enjoy yourself."

Drawing Stara out of the room, Tashana led her down the corridor, which stretched long past the main room. Out of habit, Stara listened for Vora's steps behind her. The slave walked so quietly, Stara sometimes worried she'd left the woman behind and glanced back to check, which always earned her a disapproving frown. She wasn't supposed to show so much concern for a slave.

"Are you well?" Tashana asked. "Finding the summer too hot?"

"Healthy and happy," Stara replied. "And I'm used to hot summers. Elyne is the same, though it rains more and the damp makes the heat more uncomfortable. How are you? Your skin is looking good."

Tashana shrugged. "Well enough. The spots go away from time to time, but they always come back. I do enjoy it when they're gone." She smiled at Stara, then turned through a doorway into a spacious room.

The other wives were sitting on benches covered in cushions. They rose as Stara and Tashana entered. The usual greetings were exchanged, but when they were over the women didn't return to the seats.

"We thought it would be nice if Tashana showed you around the house," Chiara told Stara. She looked at Tashana. "Lead the way."

As the hostess beckoned and moved through a doorway, Stara noted that the wives' slaves had emerged and joined Vora in following. Women and slaves together made for quite a crowd roaming the corridors and rooms of Dashina and Tashana's house. This became even more obvious when they left the large, luxurious rooms and entered a plain, narrow corridor, which echoed with their voices and footsteps.

This doesn't look like part of the house its master and mistress would venture into, Stara thought. *It looks more like a part slaves would use. Not that I've seen many slave quarters since coming back to Sachaka.*

At the end of the corridor Tashana entered a large room containing robust wooden tables and occupied by several slave women, all of whom turned to stare at her and the other wives. Stara nodded to herself. She'd guessed right. But why were they here? She turned to look at Tashana. The woman smiled, then nodded at something over Stara's shoulder. Turning back to face the slave women, Stara realised that one, a woman with grey in her hair but a sturdy frame, had risen to her feet and was walking towards her.

"Welcome, Stara," the woman said. Though a slave, she looked Stara directly in the eyes. Neither she nor the other slaves had prostrated themselves before the mistress of the house, either. "I am Tavara. As you can see, I am a woman and a slave. But that is not all that I am." She gestured at the women beside Stara and those sitting at the tables. "I am a leader of sorts. I speak for these women, and others, who are all bound together by a secret agreement to help other women, in exchange for the help we all need."

Stara glanced at the wives, who nodded at her, serious but encouraging. She looked at the slaves and saw how they regarded her with suspicion . . . and something else. Hope?

A secret group, she thought. *Of women. Are these the people who saved Nachira?* She turned to look at Vora. The old woman chuckled.

"Yes. These are the people I asked you not to ask me about."

Stara turned back to Tavara. "You have Nachira?"

The woman smiled. "Yes. We took her away from your father's house and nursed her back to health when it was clear nothing else could save her. Save, perhaps, the death of your father." The woman grimaced. "But we prefer to avoid such extreme measures."

"And we didn't think you'd think fondly of us," Chiara added.

Stara shrugged. "Quite the opposite, actually. Though . . . to be honest I'd rather not commit patricide, even if he is a heartless monster." She met Tavara's eyes again. "So clearly you have the means to, if you need it."

"Yes. There is much we can do, yet much we can't. We were all slaves, to begin with. Slaves are invisible, and so can move about, delivering messages, easily. But we came to recognise that free women are often as helpless as we, sometimes even more so since they are not invisible and cannot roam beyond their homes. Yet they do have some advantages that we do not. Money. Access to some places forbidden to slaves. Political influence, through family or access to powerful ears. We came to trust them and they us."

"And you trust me?" Stara looked around. "You must do, or else you would never have brought me here."

"We had Vora's mind read," Tavara told her. "She trusts you. That will have to be enough."

"You read . . ." Stara looked at Vora, who shrugged. "Then you must have a magician in your group."

"Yes." Tavara nodded. "And hopefully we still do. She was obliged to join the army and left to fight in the war in Kyralia. You will no doubt see that this means we can't have your mind read."

"Yet you're still willing to trust me."

"We are." Tavara crossed her arms. "You should also have realised by now that we know something about you that your husband does not yet know — that you are a magician."

Stara nodded. "I hadn't quite got to working that part out, but it makes sense, since you read Vora's mind." She paused as a possibility occurred to her. "You want me to read minds for you? I haven't tried it yet. Not deliberately, anyway."

Tavara smiled. "Perhaps eventually. We do expect that, if you join us, you will work for us. Although you'll still have the right to refuse a task, if it is objectionable to you."

"If I'm too squeamish to commit murder, for instance."

"Exactly."

"That's a relief. What else?"

"We are all equal when we are together. Slave, free woman, magician."

Stara let out a sigh. "Oh, what a relief!"

The woman looked at her oddly. "You may not find this as easy as you think."

"I spent most of my life in Elyne," Stara retorted. "You have no idea how hard it has been to get used to having slaves. So when are you going to rise up and end it?"

The woman's eyebrows rose and she regarded Stara thoughtfully. "It wasn't among our plans," she admitted. "All our energies go towards trying to save women's lives. Your brother's wife lives in a place outside the city we call the sanctuary. Removing women from their homes is dangerous, but that is not the end of it. We have to transport them there, at the risk of exposing both the sanctuary and ourselves. Keeping the sanctuary stocked with food is difficult. We have plenty of money, but must ensure no transaction is traceable to us. Only a few women can know the location, and those who stay there cannot leave, for if their minds were read our work would be discovered."

Tavara looked at the other wives. "This is why we prefer not to take women from their homes. We try to make their lives better by other means. Sometimes by manipulating politics. The right rumour in the right ears can kill the emperor, as they say. Sometimes we use trade to change a family's fortunes. Sometimes, as I mentioned earlier, we are willing to go further: to make someone sick, or even have them killed." Tavara's gaze shifted back to Stara. "Knowing this, would you still be willing to join us?"

Stara nodded. "Oh, definitely. But are you sure you want to recruit me? What if my father visits, and reads my mind again? What if Kachiro decides to?"

Tavara smiled and reached into the tunic-like dress she wore. From some secret place within she drew out something that shone silver and green. She took Stara's hand and dropped the object into her palm.

It was an earring. Silver threads encircled a clear, vibrantly green stone. A thicker circle of wire protruded from the back, turning back on itself to fix securely into the setting again.

"It is a storestone. We buy these from the Duna tribes in the north. They make several types for different purposes, but will only sell us this kind. It protects the wearer from mind-reading – and not just by blocking all thoughts. Once you learn the trick of it, you can feed whoever is reading your mind the sorts of thoughts he is expecting, while still hiding what you don't want him to see."

Stara stared at the gemstone in amazement. "I've never heard of anything like this before. Not here or in Elyne."

"No. Magicians do buy stones from the Duna tribes, but they don't believe they have magical properties. So the tribes only sell them the ones too flawed to be useful. But they sell these to us, the Traitors."

Stara looked up. "The Traitors? You call yourselves the Traitors?"

Tavara nodded and looked away. "Yes. Twenty years ago the previous emperor's daughter was raped by one of his allies. She spoke openly of the crime, calling for him to be punished. But the emperor decided that the support of his ally was more important, and he had plenty of daughters. He called her a traitor and had her killed." Tavara met Stara's eyes again. "She was one of the first free women to help us. Through her efforts many women were saved. But we failed to save her. So we call ourselves the Traitors in her memory."

"Even an emperor's daughter . . ." Stara shook her head, then straightened. "I want to help, but what can I do?"

Tavara smiled. "For a start, there is a simple vow, and we put this earring in for you."

Stara looked down at the earring and grimaced. "I've never

liked the idea of piercing my ears, or anything else for that matter. Won't my husband be suspicious if he sees this?"

"No. Free Sachakan women love jewellery and give it to each other all the time. It will hurt, but it will be over in a moment." Tavara plucked the earring from Stara's hand. "Who has the salve?"

From somewhere Chiara produced a small jar. Stara felt her stomach sink as Tavara took hold of her ear lobe. She stiffened, worried what would happen if she moved while the pin went through.

"Repeat after me," Tavara said. "I vow that I will never willingly reveal the existence of the Traitors, their pledge and plans."

Stara repeated the words, wincing in anticipation.

"And to help all women, whether slave or free."

She knew she was speaking faster and at a higher pitch than normal, her heart beating fast in dread. *I'm not going to yell*, she told herself, biting her lip.

"And do what I can to save them from the tyranny of men."

As she uttered the word "men", Stara felt a flare of pain in her ear lobe and let out a stifled squeak. Then her entire ear went hot. Chiara and Tavara were fussing with the earring. Something cool spread over her ear lobe. Tavara stepped back.

"Here." Chiara pressed the jar into Stara's hand. "Put this on twice a day until it heals. But remember, the gem has to touch your skin to work and the salve can act as a barrier."

Tavara was smiling. "Well done, Stara. You're one of us now. Welcome to the Traitors."

At that Stara found herself the object of many welcoming hugs, from both wives and slaves. And none quite so tight as that from Vora.

"Well done," the slave murmured.

"Hmph," Stara replied. "You could have warned me about the piercing part."

"And miss the look on your face?" The old woman grinned. "Never."

Though it was cooler in the mountains, it was always a relief when the blinding summer sun eased into golden evening light. Dakon looked ahead and was unable to suppress a twinge of anxiety. Scouts had reported that the road leading up to the pass was clear. No Sachakans, magicians or otherwise, lingered there.

It still felt unwise to camp there overnight, but that was the king's intention. Dakon suspected most of the magicians needed to stop at the border in order to feel sure and satisfied that they'd finally driven the last of the invaders out of Kyralia.

Whether they truly had, nobody could say with complete confidence. For several weeks the Kyralian army, with the assistance of the Elynes, had split up in order to pursue the survivors of Takado's force. A handful had been found and killed. None had surrendered, though Dakon had doubts about the last one his group had tracked down. The man had emerged on his own, hands waving frantically, before being struck down. Dakon had resisted asking if the others also wondered whether the man had been trying to give himself up. He did not want to cause them to doubt themselves unnecessarily. Especially not Narvelan, who had suffered enough doubt in himself after the first time he'd killed.

A small number of Sachakans had survived by keeping far enough ahead of their pursuers to reach the northern pass and escape into Sachaka. Dakon knew Takado was among them.

As the different groups of Kyralian magicians swept across the country they eventually joined together in the north, on the road to the pass. Timing their simultaneous arrival had been easy with the use of the blood gems.

Only two magicians had been taught the trick of making the gems. Sabin was one, Innali the other. Sabin had made a blood gem ring for the leaders of every group that left in search of the surviving invaders. Innali was their link to Imardin.

Narvelan, as the leader of the group Dakon had been a part of, had worn one of Sabin's blood gem rings. He had not worn it constantly, as the rings communicated a continual flow of the wearer's thoughts and if too many rings were worn at once it was overwhelming to the maker. Dakon was not sure he'd have liked giving anyone constant access to his mind. Not even Sabin.

He sighed and looked ahead. The road had been climbing the side of a steep slope, cut into the rock by someone long forgotten – perhaps back when Sachaka had ruled Kyralia, perhaps even earlier, when the two countries had begun trading. It now curved to the right and wound through a near-level ravine. The road was relatively clear of stones and rock, swept clean by hundreds of years of traffic. But as Dakon rode round a fold in the wall he could see that the king and magicians ahead of him had stopped. Beyond them was a pile of rocks several times the height of a man.

"Takado's parting gift," Jayan said, moving up beside him.

Scouts carrying blood gem rings had warned Sabin of the obstruction. Dakon looked up at the rock walls stretching above them. He could see where the rock had been blasted.

"Hopefully such a waste of power means he is not waiting in ambush for us."

"Hopefully," Jayan agreed.

Dakon glanced at Tessia, who was gazing up at the walls. Abruptly a memory rose of the moment Jayan had caught up with them, some weeks back. He'd taken a side trip to the abandoned servants' camp, now being scavenged by people returning to the country, and found her father's bag dumped in a pile of rubbish with most of the contents missing. As he'd handed it to her she'd burst into tears, hugging the bag to herself and apologising for her outburst at the same time. Jayan had looked embarrassed and unable to think of anything to say, yet afterwards he had seemed very pleased with himself.

The bag was now restocked with a new burner and surgery tools, and cures made by Tessia or donated by village healers.

As they reached the magicians standing before the rocks, Sabin looked up at them.

"We'll camp here tonight," he said. "And decide what to do next."

Having dismounted, Dakon sat on one of the boulders and watched as the rest of the army arrived. A few magicians decided to sweep the area clear of rocks and stones from the fall. As soon as the servants reached the pass they set to work. Horses were tended to. The ground was too solid for tent hooks, so it was decided that everyone would have to sleep in the open and hope it didn't rain. Cooking smells began to waft about and made Dakon's stomach rumble.

As what little sunlight made its way into the ravine began to dwindle, the king, his advisers and the foreign magicians moved boulders into a circle and sat down. The rest of the magicians followed suit, arranging themselves outside the circle.

Lord Hakkin looked up at the rocks. "Since we got here and I saw this, I can't help wondering if we'd be better off adding to it rather than clearing it."

"Block the pass?" Lord Perkin asked.

Hakkin nodded. "It wouldn't prevent them coming back if they were determined enough. But it would slow them down."

"It is the main trade route, though," Perkin reminded him.

"Who's going to trade with them now?" Narvelan asked, narrowing his eyes and looking around the circle.

"An end to trade would harm us as much as them," the king pointed out. "Perhaps harm us more. They have better access to other lands."

"I have to agree with you, your majesty," Dem Ayend said. "When news came that Sachaka had invaded Kyralia some of my people took it upon themselves to murder the Sachakan traders based in Elyne. We will come to regret that, though I'm sure trade links will be re-established in time."

"Perhaps instead we should build a fort here," Lord Bolvin suggested. "Control who passes into Kyralia. It would have the same advantage of slowing an invasion, and we would know it is happening. Instantly, if we post a magician here."

"We could charge Sachakan traders a fee, as well," Hakkin added. "It might go some way towards helping our people recover."

Heads were nodding, Dakon saw. *The fee could never be high enough*, he thought. *It can't be set so high that it discourages trade. And it would go straight into some magician's coffer, most likely, not into the common people's hands.*

"How likely is it that we will be invaded again?" Lord Perkin asked, looking around.

Nobody answered for a long moment.

"That depends on two things," Sabin said. "The desire to, and the ability to. Will they desire to? Perhaps we have frightened them into leaving us alone. Or maybe, by killing so many members of their most powerful families, we have set a desire for revenge blazing that could lead to endless conflict."

"They invaded us," Narvelan growled.

"True. But Sachakans are nothing less than utterly convinced of their superiority over other races. We have dared to defeat them. They won't like it."

"How many Sachakan magicians are left?" Bolvin asked.

"I have kept count of the fatalities as best I could," Sabin said. "I estimate at least ninety Sachakans have died in this invasion."

"There were over two hundred in Sachaka, according to my spies," the king said.

"So over a hundred remain," Hakkin said. "We number no more than eighty."

"Some of their magicians are too young or too old to fight effectively," the king added.

"The odds don't sound good, even so," Perkin said.

"I think we've learned the hard way that it is not the number of magicians that matters, but their strength," Narvelan said.

"And their skills and knowledge," Dakon added.

"It is not only their strength to begin with, though that is important, but their *access* to strength later," Sabin said. "They can only bring so many slaves into Kyralia. We have the support of most of our population."

"I think they've learned their lesson," Hakkin said.

"But how long before they forget it?" Narvelan asked. "Will our children fight and die in another war? Or our grandchildren?"

"Can we prevent its ever happening again?" Sabin asked. He shook his head. "Of course we can't."

"Or can we?" Narvelan said. All turned to look at him, many frowning. His eyes were dark as he smiled back at them. "They wouldn't invade us if we ruled them."

That sent a ripple of murmuring out from the circle. Dakon saw eyes widen at the possibility, and heads shake.

"Invade Sachaka?" Hakkin scowled. "Even if we had a chance of success, we've just fought a war. Do we have the energy for another?"

"We might, if it would ensure Kyralia's future," Lord Perkin said.

The king was frowning. "Can we afford to lose more of our own magicians?" he asked, his gaze fixed on the ground. "We may return victorious only to find ourselves vulnerable to attack from elsewhere."

"Who else would dare, or bother, your majesty?" Narvelan spread his hands. "Lonmar? They are too busy worshipping their god and barely pay attention to what we do. Lan? Vin? Elyne? They are here, supporting us." He turned to regard Dem Ayend, smiling but with a hint of seriousness in his gaze.

The Dem chuckled. "Elyne has always been a friend of Kyralia." He paused. "And if you allow it, we would join you in your endeavour. We know we will not last long if Kyralia ever falls to Sachaka. I know I have my king's support on this."

Sabin hummed in thought, then looked at the Dem. "Your offer would have to be discussed, but I can see one problem to be overcome. If we are to invade Sachaka, we must do it without hesitation. We have only our apprentices and servants to draw strength from. Like us, the Sachakans will evacuate their slaves so that we can't gain strength from them. We must give them no time to."

"We should not kill the slaves, but free them," Dakon said. He smiled as heads turned towards him. "We couldn't hope to win without taking their power, of course, but after a country is taken it has to be ruled, and it would be easier if the majority of people were co-operative because we had treated them well." Dakon was pleased to see the king nodding, his expression thoughtful. "If we must invade Sachaka in order to save Kyralia, let's not become Sachakans."

Sabin chuckled. "Their way of doing things didn't work for them, so it won't work for us."

More murmuring echoed around the ravine. The leaders were silent, lost in thought. Then Bolvin sighed.

"Must we invade? I'm tired. I want to go home, to my family."

"We must," Narvelan said, his voice full of certainty. "So that your children will have the freedoms we have."

"Perhaps I can help you decide," Dem Ayend said.

All turned to look at the Elyne. He smiled wryly as he reached into the satchel he always carried. He glanced down and drew out a small drawstring bag. Untying the knot, he tipped out into his palm a large milky-yellow stone the size of a fist, cut like a precious gem.

"This is a storestone. It's the last of its kind. It and others were found in ancient ruins in Elyne, built and abandoned by a people we know little about. We don't know how they are made – and believe me, many magicians have tried to find out over the centuries."

He held the stone out so all in the circle could see. "It stores magic. Transferring power to it is not unlike sending power to another magician. Unfortunately the magic within must be used in one continuous stream. If not, it will shatter and release the remaining magic in a devastating blast. And once the magic is all used, the stone turns to dust. So, as you can imagine, you must choose the moment such an object is used very, very carefully. Especially since when this one is used, there will be no more left."

Dem Ayend looked up. His eyes were bright. Dakon saw awe and excitement in the faces of the magicians around him. Looking closely at the stone, he felt something at the edge of his senses. Concentrating on the feeling made his head spin.

The stone was radiating a feeling of immense power, unlike anything he had ever felt before.

"My king gave it to me to use only in the most desperate moment, and fortunately that moment did not come. I have consulted with him via messengers, anticipating this moment. He said if the chance came to conquer Sachaka, then we should seize it. Because I, and my king, can see no cause more worthy of the last of the storestones than ending the Sachakan empire for all time."

Looking at the faces of the magicians around him, Dakon knew, without a doubt, that he would not be going back to Mandryn to rebuild his life for some time yet.

CHAPTER 42

The morning air was crisp, but Hanara knew that once the sun rose above the mist that shrouded the hills below, baking the air dry, the day would be a hot one. The place Takado, Asara and Dachido had chosen to camp was several strides from the road, out of sight on a rock shelf. If they moved to the edge and looked down they could see the road twisting back and forth down the side of the mountain, curving over hills and eventually straightening and pointing, like an arrow, toward Arvice.

Hanara's master was not enjoying the view. He was being served by Asara's remaining slave, while Hanara kept watch on the road. Dachido's slave was packing up his master's belongings. The three slaves took turns at these tasks every morning, until all were ready to travel on.

But for the first time, none of the magicians were in a hurry.

Hanara looked up. The pass itself was not visible, but he could see where the road emerged from it. They had fled through it the previous morning, aware the Kyralian army was only a half day's ride behind them.

"Why send a whole army after us?" Asara had asked, a few nights before. "It doesn't make sense."

"Because they want Takado," Dachido had replied. "It was his idea to conquer them, after all. And they fear he will come back for another try."

Takado had chuckled. "I would, if it were possible."

The three magicians had argued over what to do when they reached Sachaka. Takado wanted them to stay together and gather supporters. Hanara wasn't sure if this was in order to invade Kyralia again, or in order to gain enough status and allies to return to his former life.

"None of us can expect to walk into our old homes and continue as if nothing happened," Takado had pointed out.

Asara had nodded. "We need to know if Emperor Vochira has learned of our defeat and taken our assets for himself, or given them to someone else. It'll be easier to regain them if he hasn't given them away."

It hadn't occurred to Hanara that he might not be returning to the place of his birth. Since he'd realised how unlikely it was, he'd woken with an ache in his stomach every morning, and a nagging uneasiness. *Where will we go, even if it is just until Takado gets his home back? And how likely is that?*

Though none of the magicians had stated it, the lack of conviction in their voices when they discussed regaining the emperor's favour told how much they doubted it would happen. Last night, as if standing on the soil of their own country had broken them out of a trance of denial, they had finally discussed what they would do in the short term.

"I've decided I'm going north," Asara announced. "I have contacts there. People who owe me favours. And . . . I must go alone. They will not help me if there are others with me."

Both Dachido and Takado had looked at her in silence, but neither of them argued against her choice. Dachido had turned to Takado then, his expression almost apologetic.

"I, too, am going to call in a favour. With a sea trader. How do you fancy sailing the seas of the south?"

Takado had grimaced, then patted Dachido on the shoulder. "Thank you for the offer, but I think I'd rather Emperor

Vochira cut out my heart than spend the rest of my days stuck on a ship." He sighed and looked out towards Arvice. "I belong here."

"In hiding?" Dachido asked. "An Ichani?"

"I have always regarded Ichani – most Ichani – as my equals," Takado said, with a hint of pride. "It will be no shame to me to wear the term. After all, I began this for their benefit, so they would have a chance to own land and throw off their outcast status."

"I hope they remember that, if you encounter any," Asara said. "Those that remained here were clearly not impressed enough by you to join your cause. And you led a lot of their kind to their deaths."

"Perhaps if I found them another place to make their own . . ." Takado began, but then he shook his head. "Unless they don't mind living on a volcano, I doubt there's anything I can offer them."

Having decided their futures, the three magicians had slept soundly for the first time in weeks. Hanara and the other slaves had taken turns keeping watch.

Hearing movement behind him, Hanara looked over his shoulder to see that Takado, Asara and Dachido were now standing, regarding each other with expectant looks. Then Takado grasped the others' shoulders.

"Thank you for answering my call," he said. "I would rather we were arranging Kyralia to our liking right now instead of parting ways, but I am proud to have fought beside you both." He paused, his eyes flickering to Hanara.

Hanara forced himself to turn away and look at the road, but his eyes itched to witness the moment taking place behind him. At least he could hear it.

"It was a grand idea, your plan to conquer Kyralia," Asara said. "And it almost worked. I'll never regret the attempt."

"Nor I," Dachido agreed. "I have fought beside great men – and women – which is more than my father or grandfather could claim."

"It was fun, wasn't it?" Takado laughed, but then he sighed. "I am glad I had you two to advise and support me. I'm sure I'd be dead if it weren't for you. I hope we will meet again some day."

"Is there a way we can keep in contact safely?" Asara wondered aloud.

"We could leave messages somewhere. Send slaves to deliver or check for them," Dachido suggested.

"Where?" Takado asked.

Something shifted before Hanara's eyes. He blinked and stared at the road winding down the side of the mountain. Then he blinked again.

Men. Horses. At least a hundred of them so far, turning into sight around a curve in the road. He should have seen them when they had first emerged from the pass. Turning, he rose and hurried over to Takado, threw himself on the ground and waited.

The three magicians stopped talking.

"What is it?" Takado asked, his voice low with annoyance.

"Riders," Hanara said. "Coming into Sachaka."

"*Into* Sachaka?" Dachido repeated.

Hurried footsteps led away to the edge of the rock shelf. As Hanara rose he heard Takado curse. The other two slaves exchanged glances, then tentatively hurried after their owners. Hanara followed.

"What are they doing?" Asara asked.

"I doubt they're paying the emperor a friendly visit," Dachido replied.

"*They're* invading *us*?" Her voice was strained with disbelief.

"Why not?" Takado said darkly. He sounded tired. Resigned. "They defeated us easily. Why not invade us in return?"

"Are they after revenge?" Asara sounded angry now.

"Probably, but I doubt that's their only reason. Beating us has given them confidence." He paused. "Perhaps a little too much."

"If they lose, there'll be nothing to stop us returning to Kyralia," Dachido pointed out, a hint of excitement in his voice.

Takado turned to his friend and smiled. "That is true."

Looking at them both, Asara became thoughtful. "So we wait here until they pass, then go back and take over Kyralia?"

Takado frowned. "And in the meantime, they invade Sachaka. No. We can't abandon our homeland."

"Surely there's no risk the Kyralians will succeed," Asara said.

"If we warn Emperor Vochir there's an army coming . . ." Dachido began. "If we help in the fight . . ."

"He might forgive us for getting him into such a mess in the first place?" Asara asked. As Takado frowned at her, she shook her head. "I think he would kill us first and discover the truth of our warning later." She looked out at the army and sighed. "But I can't run away from this. I can't abandon our people. We must warn them."

Dachido nodded. "At the very least."

They both turned to Takado, who nodded. "Of course we must." Then he smiled. "And I'm sure we'll find a way to come out the heroes and saviours in this. We only need to stay alive long enough to arrange it."

I can't believe I'm in Sachaka, Jayan found himself thinking yet again. *I always thought if I visited another country it would probably be Elyne. Definitely not Sachaka!*

589

At first there had been little vegetation to block the view of the land below. Jayan had traced the lines of roads, noting where they intersected or vanished in the distance. He'd studied the courses of rivers and positions of houses, trying to create a map in his mind. Though there were clusters of houses, they didn't follow the familiar layout of Kyralian villages. They were positioned off the road, enclosed by walls.

Eventually the road from the pass descended into forested slopes similar to those on the other side of the mountains. They could have been travelling in Kyralia, then. Everything looked the same, from the types of trees to the colour of the rocky ground. The air grew steadily warmer, until it was as hot as the hottest summer days he remembered while living in Mandryn.

Hearing a sigh, he glanced at Mikken. The young man was wiping his brow with his sleeve. He met Jayan's gaze and grimaced.

Smiling crookedly, Jayan looked ahead. How well was Tessia coping with the heat? She was riding alone, he saw. Dakon was further ahead talking to Narvelan. Urging his horse into a trot, Jayan caught up with her. She looked at him, her brow creased by a frown.

"How are you?" he asked.

She shook her head. "Worried."

Jayan felt a flash of concern. "About Dakon? Yourself?"

"No." Her eyes narrowed as she looked at the riders ahead. "About us all. About the future. This . . . this invasion of Sachaka."

"You're worried we'll lose?"

"Yes. Or that we'll win."

Jayan smiled, but her expression remained serious. "What's the problem with winning?"

She sighed. "They'll hate us. We already hate them. We're

590

seeking revenge for them invading us. They'll then seek revenge for us invading them. It'll go on and on. Never ending."

"They can't invade us in revenge if we win," Jayan pointed out. "We'll be in charge."

"They'll rebel. They'll find ways to make controlling them cost us more than we gain." She paused. "Dakon has been telling me what Kyralians and Elynes did in order to get Sachaka to grant us independence last time."

"Ah." Jayan nodded. "I've had those lessons too. But the situation is not the same. They imposed slavery on us. We'll end it here. They made the strong weak, we'll make the weak strong."

"The slaves?" She shook her head. "We're relying too much on the idea that Sachaka's slaves are going to rejoice at us marching in and changing their lives. They may not want us to. They may be loyal to their masters. Hanara returned to Takado, after all. They may not co-operate. They may resist us. Non-magicians can fight, too. You don't need magic – as you showed when you set fire to the storeroom to save the apprentices."

She may be right, he thought. "But not all slaves will be like Hanara," he reasoned. "If he had been truly loyal to Takado, he'd have left Mandryn as soon as he was well enough. He probably only returned to Takado because he knew his master was close by, and that Mandryn wasn't safe any more. If he didn't think he could escape, he'd think he had no choice."

Tessia gave him an oddly approving look. "Even so, Hanara did not adjust to freedom well. He did not make friends or trust anyone . . . except me, I think." She looked away. "I don't think Sachaka's slaves are going to trust or befriend us just because we free them. They won't know what to do with themselves. Without someone ordering their lives, fields won't be harvested, food won't be prepared. They'll starve."

"Then we'll have to help them learn a different way of doing things."

Tessia looked back at the magicians riding behind them. "Do you think enough of us will want to stay here, afterwards, to help Sachaka's slaves adapt to freedom? Or will everybody go home?"

Jayan doubted many would stay, but he did not want to admit that. He shrugged instead.

"I can't help thinking what we're doing is wrong." Tessia sighed. "We're so convinced that all Sachakan magicians are bad. But not all of them joined Takado. Those who did are nearly all dead, so the magicians we're going to fight will be mostly those that didn't want to invade us."

"Just because they didn't fight doesn't mean they didn't support the idea of invading," Jayan reminded her. "Some might not have been able to fight. Perhaps they were too old, or not well trained enough. Perhaps some were too caught up in something else to leave Sachaka. We can't assume they were all against their country taking back lands that they once considered theirs."

Tessia nodded, then glanced at him sidelong. "So how do we tell who was and who wasn't in favour of the war?"

Jayan considered this. "I expect that if most were against it, they'll get together and meet with us peacefully."

"But if only a few were against it?"

"There are always a few people who don't agree with the majority — or their rule. We can't let Sachaka recover and return to invade us again because a few of them might be nice people." He felt frustration rising. "Surely you can see that we must do this to stop Sachaka invading again."

"I can," she replied. "But I can also see that it could be

disastrous if we lose. Should our invasion of Sachaka fail, Kyralia will be left with a handful of magicians to defend it. The Sachakans will invade us in turn, again, and nobody will be able to stop them."

Jayan felt his stomach sink at the thought, but as he considered it he realised she had nothing to fear. "Even if the Sachakans win, they'll be weak as well. The magicians in Imardin have a whole city willing to give them strength. Whether that strength is taken by a few magicians or many, it's still enough to deter a few Sachakans."

"Even if those Sachakans have the strength of all the slaves here?" She turned to look at him.

Darn it, she's right. He bit his lip. "Are you suggesting we kill the slaves, just in case we lose?"

"No!" She glared at him. "We shouldn't be invading in the first place. It's justifiable to kill in defence, but saying we're here to protect ourselves from future invasions is . . . you could justify *anything* saying that. It's . . . wrong."

Jayan stared back at her. He remembered what Dakon had said the night before. "If we must invade Sachaka in order to save Kyralia, let's not become Sachakans."

Perhaps he could dismiss Tessia's worries as those of someone whose morals were good, but impractical. Even as he disagreed with her he could not help admiring her for her desire to do right. He could not so easily dismiss the opinion of his former master and teacher, either.

"Strategically, we should kill the slaves, but we won't. We have the luxury of doing things differently from the Sachakans because we have the storestone. And our different ways . . . our better morals . . . maybe they're something we can give to them. Freedom for the slaves and better morals for the magicians. Surely that's something worth fighting for?"

She glanced at him then looked away, her expression full

of doubt. Whether it was at what he said, or at her own opinions, he couldn't tell. She said nothing, and they rode on in an awkward silence for some time, before Jayan gave up and dropped back to ride next to Mikken again.

CHAPTER 43

The road into Sachaka had stretched across the bare skin of the mountains first, twisting this way and that as it descended steeply. Then, abruptly, it reached the hills below, where it took the easier route along flat valley floors, going wherever the watercourses went.

But the Kyralian army did not venture into the gentler landscape at first. It had camped in the shelter of a forest. Though it had been late afternoon, all but the first watch lay down to sleep. *Or attempt to*, Tessia thought wryly. She had lain on her pallet, listening to the other women breathing, wide awake and unable to stop worrying about Jayan and the outcome of this conquest.

Now, as the army rode silently into the populated lowlands of Sachaka, she ached with tiredness and wished she'd managed to sleep. *Tired in my body; tired in my mind. Tired of worrying; tired of arguing with Jayan over what we're doing.*

They'd talked twice more, once after he'd volunteered to go with the group of magicians who would investigate the groups of buildings they encountered on the way, and again, briefly, as they had neared the first settlement.

Now he was gone, riding with twenty or so other magicians, led by Narvelan, down a side road towards distant white walls glowing in the moonlight.

What I suspect bothers me the most is that I know he's right, she thought. *But I'm also sure he isn't. Invasion is wrong. It makes* us the aggressor. It makes us more like the Sachakans. Less certain we are better than them.

Yet I also can't help thinking we would have to do far worse to be as cruel and immoral as they. Perhaps the harm we do will be balanced by the good. We could make Sachaka a better place. We could end slavery for good.

It's going to come at a cost. It's going to change the way we see ourselves. How much are we willing to restrain ourselves in order to be right and moral? If we justify this, then how much easier will it be to justify worse? If Kyralians believe a little wrongdoing is excusable for the right reason, what else will we excuse, or assume others will excuse?

She sighed. If Jayan is right, then we are risking our future for the benefit of a people who have torn our country apart. I'm not sure many magicians would be putting their lives in danger if they saw it that way. A few may be that noble, but not all. No, most magicians are here to take advantage of our sudden magical superiority and, I suspect, to have their revenge.

A faint murmur among the magicians roused her from her thoughts. She looked down the side road towards the faint shapes of the distant buildings. Shadows moved before them. Though she could not make out recognisable shapes, they moved in the rhythmic, jolting way of riders coming at speed. Something about this haste filled her with dread.

As the riders came close they shifted from shadows to familiar figures. She was relieved to see Jayan among them, and that nobody was missing. Jayan wore a grim, unhappy expression. So did most of the others. Narvelan did not. His straight back suggested defiance or indignation.

Or I am reading too much into this? she thought, watching Narvelan and two others meet with the king, Sabin and the leader of the Elynes. The rest of the group split up, some staying to listen to the men talking, some moving away.

596

Tessia saw Jayan shake his head, then direct his horse towards her, Mikken and Dakon.

"So," Dakon murmured. "Did our neighbours give you a friendly reception?"

Jayan didn't quite manage a smile. "The master of the estate wasn't home. Just . . . slaves." He looked away, a haunted look in his eyes.

"And the slaves?" Dakon prompted when Jayan didn't continue.

Jayan sighed. "Weren't happy to see us and didn't much like our plans for them."

"So Narvelan offered them their freedom?"

"Yes." Jayan frowned and looked at Dakon again. Tessia glimpsed pain, guilt and a darkness in his eyes, then his expression became guarded. "When we arrived they opened doors for us, then threw themselves flat on the ground. Narvelan told them to get up. He told them we were there to free them, if they co-operated with us. Then he began to ask questions. They told us their master was away, and who he was, but when he asked where he was it was clear they were lying."

He grimaced. "So Narvelan ordered one to approach, and he read the man's mind. He saw that they had sent messengers to their master, who is visiting a neighbour, and that they were loyal to him. Afraid of him, but loyal. They did not understand what freedom was. Our offer was meaningless to them.

"We started to argue about what to do next, but Narvelan said we had no time. The slaves were already spreading word of us. We must stop them and we must take their power. So we did, while he left to catch up with the messengers." He stopped to take a deep breath. "When he returned he found we had done what we'd agreed – left the slaves alive but too exhausted to move. He looked at them and said we had to kill them. In a few hours they would have regained enough strength to leave and warn of our approach. So . . ." Jayan closed his eyes. "So he killed them. To save us the . . . from feeling responsible."

A shiver of horror ran down Tessia's spine and she heard Mikken curse under his breath. She tried not to imagine the slaves, too exhausted to move, realising as the first of their number died that they faced the same fate and knowing they were helpless to stop it, to even run.

Dakon looked at Narvelan and the king, then back at Jayan.

"Ah," he said. Instead of anger, Tessia saw sadness in her master's face. Then his eyes narrowed. She looked over at the army leaders. They had begun to move forward, Narvelan riding at the king's side, smiling.

Smiling! After just killing so many . . . How many? She turned to Jayan.

"How many? How many slaves?" she asked, then wondered why it was suddenly so important.

He looked at her strangely. "Over a hundred." Then his frown faded and he managed a weak smile. "Not even your healing will help, I'm afraid. Not this time." He looked away. "I wish it could."

I wasn't thinking it could, she thought. *But from the look of him, I don't think pointing that out will help much.* Dakon nudged his horse into a walk and hers and Jayan's followed suit. They rode in silence. Jayan's words repeated over and over in Tessia's mind.

"What I don't understand," Mikken said after a while, "is why Narvelan thought killing the slaves would prevent the Sachakans realising we were here. Once their master returns home it will be obvious something is wrong. And surely the Sachakans are going to notice a few hundred Kyralians riding through and camping in their land."

"Yes," Dakon agreed. "I'm wondering why we ever thought we'd be able to sneak up on them. Or why those who should know better even suggested it."

"Do you think they said whatever they thought would get the army here, knowing that once we were we couldn't change our minds?" Tessia asked.

Neither Dakon nor Jayan answered. But they didn't need to. The anger she had expected from Dakon earlier was now clear in his face. Jayan looked worried. For that, she felt a pang of sympathy. He must feel as if he'd taken part in the slaughter of the slaves.

"I think," Jayan said, so quietly that Tessia was only just able to hear him. "I think Lord Narvelan may be a little mad. And the king knows it, and is letting him do what the rest of us might not."

Dakon nodded slowly, his gaze still on his neighbour and friend. "I'm afraid you may be right, Jayan."

From within the corridor, Hanara watched as another man entered the master's room and was greeted by Ashaki Charaka. The man wore a knife at his belt, so he was also a magician. He greeted Takado, Asara and Dachido with friendly curiosity and a touch of admiration. Hanara felt a familiar pride. The long-life feeling.

My master is a hero. It doesn't matter that he failed to conquer Kyralia. He is a hero because he tried.

Beside him, Asara's slave stirred. "Something's not right," she whispered.

His stomach clenched and the long-life feeling vanished. He scowled at her. "What?"

She shook her head, her eyes dark with fear. "I don't know. Something."

He turned away. Foolish woman. He looked at the magicians

who had gathered to meet his master. Ashaki Charaka was old, but moved with the confidence of a man used to power and respect. The others were from neighbouring estates. Most of their domains weren't in the path of the Kyralian army. Unable to take the road, since the Kyralians were using it, and travelling on foot, Takado and his friends had spent two days descending the mountain. They took a direct route that put them in land a few estates away from those most likely to be invaded first.

The magicians didn't know about the enemy army yet. Takado was clearly waiting for the right time to tell them. Instead he had begun relating stories of the early days in Kyralia, of villages of people left to their own devices, working the land belonging to their master as they pleased, without his protection. How easy they were to take.

The other magicians listened closely. Hanara watched each of them in turn. None of the five hesitated to ask questions, and Takado answered with an honesty that clearly surprised them.

"They have developed new fighting strategies," Takado told them, while Asara and Dachido nodded. "In groups, so that when one member is exhausted he or she relies on the others for protection. When the whole group is exhausted they join another group. It is surprisingly effective."

"What happens when they are all exhausted?" one of the listeners asked.

"They never got to that point, though they came close," Asara replied.

"I suspect we would have an entire army of exhausted magicians to kill off as we pleased." Takado shrugged.

"But you never got to that point?"

Takado shook his head and began describing the first battle. When he reached the point where the Kyralian army began retreating he stopped.

"But . . ." one of the listeners said. "If they were retreating they must have been close to finished. Why didn't you follow?"

"Nomako," Dachido answered, his voice low and full of derision. "He tried to take command at that point."

"He made a fool of himself," Asara said. "We would have won then, but for the delay. The Kyralians removed their people from the towns in our path, so we weren't able to boost our strength as well as we should have."

"But in the next battle . . ." Takado began.

Hanara did not hear any more. Footsteps in the corridor covered the voices. He watched as slaves filed past, taking platters laden with food into the master's room for hosts and guests to feast on. At the smell of the food Hanara's stomach ached and groaned. For days he'd eaten only scrawny, magic-roasted birds and what herbs and edible plants he could find in the mountains.

When the magicians had finished and the last of the platters had been taken away, he felt a nudge at his elbow. Turning, he saw a child slave holding out one of the platters. Scraps of roasted meat and vegetables lay in congealing sauce.

Hanara grabbed a handful and ate quickly. Such opportunities had to be seized, whether in the midst of war or in the peaceful mansions of home. Dachido's slave ate just as hungrily, but Asara's slave was hesitating. He looked at her questioningly. She was frowning at the food in suspicion, but he could hear her stomach rumbling.

As he reached for the last morsel of food, she suddenly snatched it out from under his hand. Even then she didn't eat straight away. She looked at him closely, then at Dachido's slave. Hanara shrugged. He turned back to watch and listen to Takado. After a moment he heard her eating and smiled to himself.

"Now the last battle," the host said. "What went wrong there?"

Takado scowled. "Bad timing. Nomako hadn't told me that he'd sent two groups to the west and south to subdue those areas and gather strength before meeting up with us outside Imardin. Nomako convinced us that we should wait for the southern group to arrive so we were as strong as possible before facing the Kyralians. He said the Kyralian people would not submit to giving their strength to their masters, since they were not slaves." He shook his head. "I had doubts, but since most of the fighters were now his men, and he had threatened to withdraw their support . . ."

"He was wrong. We believe the entire city gave its strength to the Kyralian army," Dachido said.

The listeners looked surprised. "I'd have said it was unlikely, but not impossible," Ashaki Charaka said.

"I thought it a risk," Asara agreed, "but I didn't think they'd have time. An entire city of people giving power in a few hours? I have no idea how they managed it."

"But they did," Charaka said. He stared at Takado in an unfriendly way. Hanara frowned as the man said something else, but a buzzing in his ears drowned out the words.

"I told you something was wrong," a female voice said behind him, faint and weak. He heard a thud and turned to see her lying on the floor. Moving his head sent it spinning sickeningly. He stilled and closed his eyes.

What is going on? But he knew even as he asked himself. In the master's room, voices were raised. He opened his mouth and tried to voice a warning, but all that came out was a moan. *We have been drugged. And Takado . . . he is not strong enough to fight his way out of here.*

". . . fight us or you can co-operate."

"We have no time for that." Takado's voice was confident

and full of warning. "The Kyralian army is *here*. The fools have—"

"If they are or not is no longer your concern." The host. Commanding voice. More words, but they were distorted and lost behind more buzzing. Hanara felt the strength go from his limbs. He felt the wall slide across his chest, the floor stop his fall. Blurry shapes moved before his eyes.

Then rough fabric slipped over his head and all he saw was darkness.

CHAPTER 44

The sky had been brightening for the last hour, slowly turning an eerie red while the land was still a black flatness, interrupted here and there by the shapes of buildings and trees. The colour lit the edges of faces and was reflected in eyes, giving familiar figures a strangeness somewhat appropriate, Dakon thought, after the deeds of the night. People he thought he knew, whom he'd believed of gentler character, had shown a darker side. Or a weakness for copying what the majority did, though they did not agree with it.

The king had decided that Narvelan would lead every attack on the Sachakan estates, but that each time he should take a different group of magicians. *An interesting decision,* Dakon had thought. *He's forcing us all to take part in the slaughter, so the responsibility is spread among us. If we all feel guilty, none of us is going to start blaming others.*

Dakon was wondering what would happen when it was his turn, and he refused to participate.

So far there had been no shortage of volunteers. Lord Prinan had joined the third group, confessing to Dakon beforehand that he feared if he did not strengthen himself he would be useless in the battles to come.

Will I be useless? Dakon wondered. *If I only take power from Tessia I will be weaker, but not useless. Should that mean I am one of the first to fall in the next battle, then that is how it will be. I will not kill slaves for their power.*

"You could leave them exhausted instead," Tessia had suggested, no doubt realising what his refusal to participate might mean.

"And Narvelan will check afterwards and ensure they are dead," he'd replied. "Don't worry. It is only a matter of waiting. Once the king realises that we can't possibly keep our presence in Sachaka a secret, he won't care if we let the slaves live or not."

The estates were a few hours' ride from each other, so they had only attacked seven. In all the houses following the first one they had encountered magicians. Each had fought the attackers and been defeated. Nobody had mentioned if any family of these magicians had been present, and what their fate had been. Dakon doubted all the estates had been empty of their owner's family and that any had been left alive.

The sound of multiple hoofbeats drew the army's attention to the side road Narvelan's latest group had ridden down. Sure enough, the band was coming back. It broke apart as it met the army, the magicians returning to their former positions in the line and Narvelan approaching the king yet again.

Instead of riding on, the king turned to Sabin and nodded. The sword master turned his horse and rode back along the line. As he passed he met Dakon's eyes.

"The king asks the advisers to meet with him."

Dakon nodded, then, as Sabin passed out of hearing, sighed.

"Good luck," Jayan murmured.

"Thanks." Dakon glanced at Tessia, who offered him a sympathetic smile; then he nudged his horse forward.

He stopped beside Lord Hakkin and watched as the other advisers made their way to the front of the line. The leader of the Elynes joined them. When Sabin returned with the last of them, all turned to face each other, a ring of horses and riders.

"We need a safe place to camp," the king said. "But there does not appear to be anywhere nearby where a group our size could hide. Magician Sabin suggests we ride on."

"In daylight, your majesty?" Hakkin asked. "Won't we be seen?"

The king nodded.

"What we have done this night will eventually be discovered. Perhaps in a day or two, but we should assume we aren't so lucky and that the news of our arrival began to travel after our first stop. We should keep moving. We may not be able to keep pace with news of ourselves, but for a while we may arrive too soon for our enemy to prepare to meet or avoid us."

"But when will we sleep?" Perkin asked. "What of the horses?"

Sabin smiled grimly. "When the news has outpaced us, we will find a defensible position and take turns resting. And we will take fresh horses wherever we find them. Each estate has a stable, with between four and twenty horses. This one," he nodded towards the distant white walls, "had over thirty. I will send servants back to collect them."

"What will we do when the news has outpaced us? What will *they* do?" Bolvin asked.

"Advance as quickly as we are able. Give them as little time to unite and prepare as possible."

"Would we be more successful at keeping pace with the news if we did not stop to attack the Sachakan homes along the way?" Dakon asked.

"We would," Sabin said. "But we need to strengthen ourselves as well."

"But we have the storestone," Dakon pointed out.

Sabin glanced at Dem Ayend. "Which we should not use unless we absolutely have to. It would be a waste if we used it, but still failed because we had not gone to the effort of seeing to our own strength."

At this the Dem's lips twitched, but he said nothing.

"And prevented the Sachakans from strengthening themselves," Narvelan added. "It would be foolish to leave them any source of strength to use against us. We don't want to be attacked from behind, or have our path of retreat blocked."

Now it was Sabin's turn to look amused. Dakon looked around at the other magicians, who were all nodding in agreement, and felt a chill run down his spine, to gather as a knot of cold somewhere in his belly. *They're going to keep killing slaves*, he realised. *All the way to Arvice. Because they're too proud to use the Elynes' storestone. Because they're afraid.* He could not speak for a moment, and when his shock passed the conversation had moved to other matters. *Not that anything I say will make a difference. They want to give us the best chance of winning. The lives of a few thousand slaves aren't going to seem so important next to that.*

"Lord Dakon," the king said. Dakon looked up, realising he hadn't heard the last part of the discussion.

"Yes, your majesty?"

"Would you gather and lead a group to find food for the army?"

He felt a belated relief. "Yes, I can do that." Here was a task he could participate in without any challenge to his conscience.

"Good." The king's eyes narrowed slightly. "I would like to discuss this with you further. The rest of you may return to your positions."

As the others rode away the king urged his horse closer to Dakon's.

"I have noticed you have not joined any of the attacks on

607

the estates," the king said, his eyes sharp and level. "You do not agree with killing the slaves, do you?"

"No, your majesty." Dakon held the king's eyes, his heart beating a little faster with dread.

"I remember you saying, at the pass, that we should take care not to become Sachakans. I have not forgotten." The king smiled briefly, then became serious again. "I do not think we are in any danger of that."

"I hope you are right." Dakon glanced at Narvelan deliberately. The king's eyes flashed.

"So do I. But the decision is made and I must stick to it. I will not make you join the attacks, but I can't be seen to accept your refusal too easily. Fortunately, all who have noticed it have said that it is not in your nature, and remaining weaker is penalty enough. They are more worried about you than angry."

There was genuine concern in the king's voice. Dakon nodded again. "I understand."

"I hope you truly do," the king said. He looked over his shoulder. "Now, we had best get this army moving. Speed, as Sabin pointed out, is of utmost importance now."

Giving Dakon one last piercing look, he turned his horse away and rejoined Sabin. Dakon was not sure whether to be relieved or worried by what the king had said. As he rode back to join Tessia, Jayan and Mikken, he considered the king's words.

"... *remaining weaker is penalty enough.*"

How long would his friends and allies continue to think so, as the army delved deeper into Sachaka and closer to the battle that would decide both countries' futures?

The sun was high in the sky when Narvelan and his latest round of helpers returned along yet another side road. Jayan watched as Narvelan spoke briefly to the king, then turned and rode towards him. A mixture of feelings stirred deep inside him, and dismay joined them as he realised fear was among them. Disgust, resentment, betrayal and fear.

You were Dakon's friend, he thought. *Always talking about caring for the people of your ley and country. Always defending the common man and woman and complaining about magicians who used their power and influence to abuse those weaker than them.*

Then he realised that Narvelan was looking at Dakon. The magician reined in a few strides away.

"Hello, old friend," he said, grinning wearily, his eyes strangely bright. "We found a big storeroom full of food back there. Don't know why, since the place is half empty and run down, and hardly any slaves were about. I'd take two carts."

Dakon forced a smile. "Thanks for the tip."

Narvelan shrugged, then turned his horse's head and set off after the king.

"Well then." Dakon turned to look at Jayan and grimaced. "We had better work quickly, or the army will leave without us."

Jayan smiled. "They won't, unless they've taken a sudden dislike to eating."

Riding back along the line, they collected the magicians and servants who had agreed to help them, and two carts that the servants had readied. Then they set off down the side road toward the distant white walls, leaving Tessia and Mikken behind.

The magicians remained quiet as they rode. It could have been from fear of attack, though Narvelan should have dealt with any potential aggressors already. More likely it was out of the grim knowledge of what they would see.

But there were fewer corpses than Jayan expected. Narvelan had not been exaggerating when he'd said the place was half empty and run down. Many of the rooms within the house were bare. Others held old battered furniture. In one room a broken wooden chest stood open. He stepped inside and examined the contents. It was full of bundles of richly embellished fabric. A spicy fragrance wafted up from them.

"These look like women's clothing," he said aloud, feeling the fabric. "I've never seen the men wearing anything this fine."

Dakon met Jayan's eyes and frowned. "I've seen only corpses of slaves."

A chill ran down Jayan's spine. "Let's find this storeroom and get out."

Not long after, one of the magicians appeared and told them he'd found the store. Dakon left with the man to move the carts up to the building, while Jayan gathered together the rest of the helpers.

The store was a separate, squat building at the back of the estate. Inside it was lined with shelving. Huge pottery jars labelled with different types of grains stood in a cluster at the centre of the room.

"They're too heavy to put on the carts," Dakon said. He moved to the shelving and began investigating the contents. Vegetables, dried meats, jars of preserves and oils, and sacks of dried beans lined the shelves. "Take these – and these. Not those . . ."

The magicians and servants worked quickly. They could have used magic to move the food, but all were reluctant to waste even the slightest bit of power. Soon the first cart was full, and it was moved aside so the second could be rolled closer to the doorway.

"If only we had smaller containers or bags to put this grain in," Dakon murmured, opening the lid of another jar. He paused, then quickly replaced the lid and looked up and around, his eyes snapping to Jayan's. Then he shrugged and started helping to carry food out to the cart.

At last the cart was loaded, and Dakon ushered everyone out of the storeroom. The cart began to move away, but as it rolled over a discarded sack it tilted and food tumbled out onto the ground. While the magicians began to repack the cart, Jayan slipped back inside the store.

Moving close to the jar Dakon had opened, he caught a whiff of the same spicy scent the fabric had smelled of. He grasped the knob of clay at the centre of the lid and lifted.

And looked down at several terrified faces.

The pot had no base. It opened onto an underground cavity of some sort – a clever hiding place for these women so long as nobody thought to look inside the pot. Jayan felt a wry admiration for whoever had created the hiding place, then it occurred to him that it must have been made for some other danger than Kyralian invaders.

What do they have to fear other than us?

One of the women whimpered. Fascination changed to concern. He had no intention of revealing these women to the other magicians. He placed a finger to his lips, smiled in what he hoped was a reassuring way, then closed the lid again. When he looked up, he found Dakon standing just within the doorway, frowning in doubt and fear.

He worries because he has already seen one friend turn bad, and can't help fearing it will happen again.

Jayan walked to the door and patted Dakon on the shoulder.

"You're right. Much too heavy to take with us," he said, and moved outside to join the others.

CHAPTER 45

So this is the sort of house owned by a man who plans to murder his wife, Stara thought as she and Kachiro were led down a corridor to the master's room of Vikaro's home. Looking around, she felt a strange disappointment. She had expected to see something out of the ordinary, even if only subtly, that might hint at the dangerous nature of the owner.

Nothing strange caught her attention. The house had the usual white-rendered walls. The furniture was obviously designed by Motara and the other furnishings were typically Sachakan. Nothing unusual.

Maybe the lack of anything unusual is the clue, she thought. Then she shook her head. *Thinking like that, I could go a little crazy. Better to accept that a murderer can't be detected from his possessions. Well, unless he has a collection of poisons somewhere . . .*

As Vikaro's slave led them into the master's room they were greeted by the host and Kachiro's other friends.

"Have you heard?" Vikaro asked, his eyes bright. "The Kyralian army has entered Sachaka!"

"They think that, having beaten Takado, they can beat the rest of us," Motara said, smiling. "Victory has gone to their heads."

Stara looked at Kachiro. He was frowning. "How far have they got?"

"Nobody knows exactly," Vikaro said. "But the news must have taken a few days to get here. They might be halfway to

612

Arvice. They might be taking their time. Or they might even have been dealt with already."

"Has anyone heard if the emperor has gathered another army to meet them?" Motara asked.

The others shook their heads. Stara noticed Chavori wince and remembered how he'd said he had refused to join the army.

Kachiro looked thoughtful. "So . . . once they're defeated there'll be nobody left in Kyralia to stop Sachaka taking over."

Vikaro's eyebrows rose. "I hadn't thought of that."

The magicians fell silent as they considered this, so Stara took advantage of the pause.

"Has there been any news of the Sachakans who went into Kyralia?" she asked.

"All killed," Rikacha said, waving a hand dismissively. "Fools for going in the first place."

Stara felt something inside her recoil, as if a fist had just struck her in the chest. *Ikaro. Surely he can't be dead. We only just came to know and like each other.*

"I heard some survived," Chavori told her, his expression both hopeful and sympathetic.

She managed to smile at him briefly in gratitude. Kachiro patted her arm gently. "I'll see what I can find out," he murmured. "Why don't you see if the women know any more? They have their own sources of information."

"Gossip?" Vikaro rolled his eyes. "As reliable as rumour." He smiled at Stara. "Aranira's slave will take you to them."

He gestured to one side, and she saw that a female slave had prostrated herself a few paces away. As she took a step towards the woman, the slave leapt up, beckoned and headed towards a nearby doorway. Stara found Vora waiting in the corridor. The old woman's lips had thinned, and there was worry in her eyes.

She's even more anxious for news of Ikaro than I am, Stara thought.

Several corridors later Stara found herself in a garden shaded by a large wooden framework covered in vines. Chairs had been arranged underneath for her four new friends, and a slave brought another for Stara.

There were several slave women standing around the garden. More than was necessary, Stara noted. The one standing closest to Tashana was familiar.

"How is your ear healing up, Stara?" Tavara asked.

Stara touched the earring. "Well, I think."

"She whined about it every night for a week," Vora added.

"Vora!" Stara protested. "You don't have to tell them *everything* about me!"

"No, but it is so much fun," Vora replied, smiling slyly.

"You've heard about the Kyralians?" Chiara asked.

"Yes," Stara replied. "Is it . . . ?"

"Serious? Yes." Chiara sighed. "According to our messenger slaves, they are halfway to Arvice."

A shock of cold went through Stara. "Why hasn't the emperor stopped them yet?"

Chiara's expression was grave. "Because our army was wiped out in Kyralia."

"All? Everyone?" Stara felt her heart constrict with dread.

"There is a rumour circulating that Takado returned to Sachaka a few days ago and was captured by the emperor. Perhaps if he's only just managed to return, others are still to come."

"But it's not likely," Stara said, looking down. *I should harden myself to the likely truth. Ikaro is dead. Father is, too.* She felt a little regret at the thought of her father's death. Regret that he had proved to be so different from the loving father she had worshipped for most of her life. But Ikaro had turned out to be far kinder than she had always believed. It was unfair to lose him now. It hurt in a way that she had never felt before, a pain so strong it took her breath away.

I suppose I'll inherit Father's estate now. The thought came unexpectedly, and she was surprised to feel a mild excitement. *Could I take over the trade? Would it be as impossible as Father said for a woman to run it?*

But then she remembered Kachiro. As her husband, he would control anything she inherited. If he didn't want her running the trade, she couldn't be able to.

"Stara."

She looked up at Tavara. "Yes?"

"We need you to do something for us."

Stara blinked in surprise. "What is it?"

"The Sanctuary was attacked by the Kyralians. While most of the slaves died, a few survived, along with the women we are protecting. They had no choice but to flee. They are heading to Arvice and will be here tomorrow. We need a place for them to stay. Do you think Kachiro would allow you to have them as guests?"

Stara considered. "Perhaps. I've never asked anything of him before, but I can't think of any reason he would refuse."

Tavara moved out of the shadows and stopped behind Tashana's chair. Her expression was serious as she held Stara's gaze. "There is something you need to know about your husband."

Stara felt a chill run down her spine. *Of course there is*, she thought. *He is too nice. People that nice can't exist in Sachaka. They have to have some terrible flaw. Some dark secret that only their wives know about, and suffer for.*

She sighed. "I knew there had to be some bad news eventually. What is it?"

The women exchanged glances, then Chiara grimaced and leaned forward.

"Kachiro prefers the company of men over women," she said. "And I don't mean conversation. I mean he takes them to bed."

Stara stared back at Chiara and found herself smiling. *That's it? That's all?* It certainly made sense. His "inability" wasn't some physical flaw at all. He just didn't find women exciting. Relief swept over her. She watched the women exchanging glances, frowning and shaking their heads.

"You knew this already?" Tavara asked.

"No." Stara stifled a laugh. "I was expecting something, well, *bad*."

"This doesn't bother you?" Chiara asked, her eyebrows raised. "He beds *men*. It's . . ." She shuddered.

"Maybe in Sachaka," Stara told her. "But in Elyne men like that are neither mocked nor despised." *Most of the time*, she added silently. *There are some people who do plenty of mocking and despising, but they're generally unpleasant people and it's not just lads they hate.*

"Well . . . this is Sachaka," Tavara said. "Such things are considered wrong and unnatural. He will not want it publicly known."

"So you're suggesting I blackmail him?"

"Yes."

Stara nodded. "How about I try using my charming nature to appeal to his good character first? And save the blackmail for desperate situations."

Tavara looked taken aback. "Of course, if you think you can persuade him, then try that first. Elyne or not, it is still surprising that you are not angry with him. It was not fair of him to marry you, knowing he would not give you children."

Stara nodded. "It wasn't. And that will be far better leverage with him. He'll do what I ask out of gratitude for my staying silent, rather than resentfully obliging out of fear of exposure."

But she has a point. Even in Elyne, it is considered a low act for a man of his inclinations to deceive a woman into marrying him. I had no choice whom I married, but Kachiro did. Though . . . I do wonder how secret his secret is. Did Father know? Was that how he knew Kachiro would not produce an heir?

She might never know, now that her father was dead. And now he was and Nachira was safe, it didn't matter any more.

Plonking her father's bag on the ground, Tessia sat down beside Mikken. She looked at the bag and sighed.

"What's wrong?" Mikken asked.

She shrugged. "Nothing. Everything. The fact that I haven't needed this bag once other than to bandage a cut hand, brace a twisted ankle and treat one of the servants' headaches."

"You want people to injure themselves, or for the Sachakans to fight us, so you have someone to heal?" he asked, smiling crookedly.

"Of course not." She smiled briefly to let him know she understood he had been joking. "I just thought that healing would be my part in us helping the slaves of Sachaka."

Mikken nodded. "I know. At least all the houses are abandoned now. Nobody left to kill, slave or other." He frowned. "But I have to admit it's making me a bit scared. The Sachakans have got to be taking their slaves' strength instead. And we're taking none."

"We should have befriended the slaves. We'd have thousands of them by now, following us and giving their strength every day."

Mikken shook his head. "I don't think they would have been that easy to win over. What Narvelan said was true. They're loyal to their masters."

"They just don't believe anybody would free them. We should have at least tried to convince them we intended to."

Mikken shrugged in that way people did when they didn't agree, but also didn't want to argue. She considered him for a moment, then looked away. For a time there she had found him charming and attractive. Now she was too tired and too disappointed in everything to find anyone appealing. Except Dakon, and then only as a teacher and protector. And Jayan too, possibly, though she couldn't say why. He had become a friend of sorts. Or maybe just someone who agreed with her occasionally. Though he was an unreliable supporter, as likely to oppose her as to take her side.

"Tessia."

She looked up to see Dakon striding towards her across the courtyard. He'd gone in search of food supplies with Jayan as soon as the army had moved into the collection of buildings. The homes abandoned by the Sachakans had proved to be the best places for the Kyralian army to stop and rest. As Dakon drew near she rose to her feet. It was impossible to guess his mood from his face. He wore a frown, but these days he always wore a frown.

"Two magicians have fallen ill," he told her. "Could you have a look at them?"

"Of course." She bent and picked up her bag.

He led her through the entrance of the house, then down one corridor after another. Tessia had noticed similarities in the houses they'd stayed in, and recognised aspects of them from the Sachakan-made houses in Imardin, though those had been larger and grander.

The collections of buildings had grown more frequent as the army drew closer to Arvice, but they hadn't encountered any towns or villages. Jayan believed the estates were mostly self-sufficient, with trade for those goods not available on the estate happening directly with other estates.

The wood for furniture and such must come from somewhere, Tessia mused. *We've also encountered no forests since we left the mountains. Just trees lining roads or forming avenues alongside roads, and the occasional copse sheltering domestic animals.*

Dakon turned into a large room from which many smaller rooms opened. She had seen this arrangement before, too. Fine clothing of both adults and children was usually found stored in them, so she had come to think of them as family rooms.

Several magicians were standing in the larger room, and when they saw her they regarded her thoughtfully. She recognised Lord Bolvin and Lord Hakkin. And Dem Ayend was there.

Then a man stepped out from behind the Dem and she felt her heart skip a beat as she recognised him.

"Apprentice Tessia," King Errik said. "I have heard much praise for your healing skill." He gestured towards one of the smaller rooms. "These two magicians fell ill a short while ago. Could you examine them?"

"Of course, your majesty," she replied, hastily bowing. He smiled and drew her into the small room, Dakon following. The sick men were lying on beds too short for their tall frames. Beds for children, she guessed. Their faces were creased with pain and their eyes appeared to be struggling to focus. She moved to one and felt for heat and pulse. "Exactly how long ago did they fall ill, and in what way?"

The king looked towards a middle-aged female servant standing beside one of the magicians' beds.

"Half of an hour at most," the woman told them. "He complained of cramps in the stomach. They emptied their stomachs and bowels and I thought the food might have been bad, but they got worse. That's when I went for help."

Tessia looked up at Dakon. "Better make sure nobody else eats whatever they had."

Dakon nodded and beckoned to the servant. "Did you serve them?" The woman nodded. "Come and tell me what and where you got it from."

Conscious that the king was watching her closely, as well as the magicians in the other room, Tessia placed a hand on the brow of one of the magicians. She closed her eyes and breathed quietly to calm her mind. Then she sent her senses out into his body.

As soon as she attuned herself to what he was feeling, pain and discomfort drew her to his stomach. Cramps sent ripples through muscle. His body was reacting and as she looked closer she saw that it was trying to expel something unwanted. That unwanted substance was acting on the body like a poison. And it was acting faster than the body could expel it.

Faster than when the servants were dying from bad food. They must have eaten something truly terrible or . . . or else they have been poisoned!

At this revelation she drew her senses back and opened her eyes. She looked up and found herself staring into the eyes of the king.

"Unless the food they've eaten is truly foul, I suspect this is the effect of poison," she said.

His eyes widened, then he turned to look at Dakon, who had returned to the room. Tessia felt a pang of alarm and guilt. As the magician in charge of finding food, he could be held responsible for feeding poisoned food to the army. He met the king's eyes and nodded.

"I'll make sure nobody eats a bite until we find out whether all the food we have is safe."

"All of it?" the king asked. "Surely only what we have found today."

Dakon shook his head. "These magicians may have eaten

something we've been carrying for a while, which hasn't been cooked until now. The servant is fetching the cook who made the dish they ate."

The king nodded, turned to Tessia, and then looked down at the magicians. "Will they live?"

"I . . . I don't think so."

"Can't you heal them?"

He looked at her, his eyes staring into hers and seeming to plead with her. She looked away.

"I will try, but I can't promise anything. I wasn't able to save the servants who ate the spoiled food during the war, and this is far worse."

"Try," he ordered.

Loosening the neck of the tunic the magician wore, she placed her palm on the bare skin of his chest. Once more she closed her eyes and sent her mind forth. She saw immediately that the situation had grown worse. His heart was labouring; he was beginning to struggle to breathe.

First I should get rid of as much of the poison as I can, she thought. *But not through the throat as he's having enough trouble breathing as it is. I don't want to choke him.* Sending out magic, she created a flexible barrier around the contents of his stomach shaped like a scoop, and gently eased it through his bowels, gathering all residue on the way. She could not help feeling a wry amusement as she eased it out of his body. *This is not going to smell good.*

Now for the poison that has entered the channels and paths. She considered his systems carefully. All of the blood was poison-laced. Even if she could remove it all without killing him, how was she going to get it out? Clearly this was not the right approach to take.

Before she could think of another way, the man's heart began to falter. Alarmed, she drew magic and reached out to it. Concentrating intently, she began to squeeze, timing her pulses in a rhythm that felt natural and familiar for a healthy, relaxed body.

Then she realised that his lungs had also stopped working, seemingly giving up all movement. Drawing more magic, she forced them gently to expand then let them relax. It took all her concentration to keep the two parts working.

I can't do this for ever, she thought. *I have to think of something else.*

But as she managed to spare a little attention for the lower systems again, she realised she could feel a familiar energy at work. Magic flowed. Magic not her own, but imbued in the body of the magician. Magic that worked to combat the effect of the poison. Magic concentrated on the liver and kidneys, helping to purify blood and filter away the toxin.

And she realised that it had been working all along. It just hadn't been strong or fast enough to combat something as potent as the poison. Now that she was working the heart and lungs, she was giving it the time it needed.

All I need to discover is how to boost that natural flow of magic . . .

But even as she thought it, she found she didn't need to. The magician's heart regained animation and strength and suddenly strained against her magic, so she let it pump for itself. The lungs soon did the same.

I have saved him, she thought, feeling a rush of relief and triumph. *Thanks to his own ability to heal himself with magic.* Which meant that she would never have been able to heal a non-magician from this poison.

She drew away from the magician's body and opened her eyes. The man was sleeping now, his breathing deep and even.

"I think he's going to be fine," she said.

"Ah!" The king moved to her side. "Are you sure? Will he recover?"

622

"Yes. As best I can tell, anyway," she added.

The king nodded and patted her on the shoulder. "You are a remarkable young woman, Apprentice Tessia. When we get back to Imardin you must teach others your methods."

She smiled. "Not quite yet. There is another . . ." But as she turned to face the other sick magician she felt her heart sink. His face was deathly white and his lips were blue. Dakon stood beside him. Then she noticed the cut on the dead man's arm and the blade in her master's hand and her heart turned over. Surely Dakon hadn't . . . ?

Then realisation dawned as she remembered what Dakon had taught her, early in her training. If the magician had died with magic still locked within his body, it would have escaped in a destructive force. She, the king and the man she had just saved might have died with him, or used a great deal of power shielding themselves.

At least the power he held has not been wasted, she thought. *Though I can't imagine Dakon is too happy taking magic that was gained through slaughtering slaves.*

"Unfortunately there is only one Tessia," the king said, his expression sad.

"Indeed," she replied. "Perhaps I should have started teaching others earlier. To be honest, I didn't think anyone would be interested."

"There is plenty of interest," he told her. "But I suspect that between being too occupied with other matters to spare the time, uncertainty over whether it is better to wait until you are no longer an apprentice and can legally teach, and the strangeness of the prospect of learning from a young woman, many magicians have hesitated to express it." The king paused and smiled. "After what I just witnessed I am tempted to send you back to Imardin with a guard to ensure the knowledge you have is kept safe, but I fear you would be in more danger returning there than staying with us. And I need every magician and apprentice here with me."

"And you'd never persuade me to abandon Lord Dakon," she told him.

The king smiled again. "Not even if I ordered you to?"

She looked away. "I guess I'd have to go, but I'd be *very* annoyed with you."

He laughed. "Well, I can't have Tessia the magical healer annoyed with me. Who knows when I might need her services?"

CHAPTER 46

For eighteen days and nights Hanara and the other slaves had been chained to the back of a covered wagon. By day they walked behind the wagon as it made its way towards Arvice. By night they slept wherever it stopped, on ground that was sometimes mud, sometimes dry earth, and sometimes hard cobbles. He was glad it was summer, and the nights were relatively warm, though the exhaustion of walking all day would have helped him sleep even if it had been cold.

They were given water twice a day, and whatever leftovers were roused up from the estates they stayed at. Sometimes this was stale bread, sometimes congealed, cold soupy slops or the burned crusts from the bottom of cook pans.

Three men rode in the wagon: the driver, who also tended to the prisoners, and two free men whom Hanara only glimpsed when they got in or out of it. He sometimes imagined that Takado was in the wagon, too. If he was, he did not leave it at night and never spoke loudly enough for the slaves to hear. Now and then Hanara caught himself wanting to call out and tell Takado something, like that they had reached the outskirts of Arvice. And that they'd reached the high walls of the Imperial Palace.

He's not in the wagon, Hanara told himself firmly. *They've taken me far away from him, so he has no loyal source slave to call on if the opportunity came. He could be back at the estate where we*

*were taken prisoner, or already in the palace. Or he's been clever
enough to talk someone into helping him escape.*

The wagon abruptly turned into a low opening in the
side of the palace wall and entered a small courtyard. Doors
boomed shut behind it. Two large muscular slaves stood
on either side of the doors, holding spears. The two free
men clambered down from the wagon and spoke to the
palace slave who emerged to abase himself before them. A
headband indicated this slave was of higher status than
those who guarded the doors. He rose to snap orders at a
doorway, from which three lesser slaves emerged. They came
forward and, as the cart driver unfastened the chains from
the cart, took hold of a prisoner each. Hanara was pushed
and guided into the palace, followed by Asara's and
Dachido's slaves.

A long journey through dark corridors followed, descending
first one level, then two, below ground. The magicians had
vanished. The air was moist and heavy with a mixture of
odours that grew steadily less pleasant, finally becoming a
choking mix of excrement, sweat and mould. The doors they
passed now were no longer wooden, but iron grates that
allowed a glimpse of men and women of different ages, some
dressed in slave garb, some in fine but soiled clothes.

Are they going to lock us up here? Hanara wondered. He'd
tried in vain not to consider the future, but too often had
caught himself wondering if he was to be executed once he
arrived wherever his captors were taking him. *Surely if they
meant to kill me, they'd have done it already.* So they must want
something from him first. Or perhaps he would find himself
owned by some new master. He'd considered whether he'd
try to escape and find Takado if that happened. Perhaps only
if he found out where Takado was.

It won't be like Mandryn, he thought. *No chance at freedom to tempt me. My place is with Takado.* He smiled as he felt pride and the long-life feeling again.

At last they stopped in a large room and were forced to lie face down on the floor before another, rather fat high-status slave.

"Whose are these?" the man rumbled.

"The Ichani rebels'."

"Which is Takado's?"

"This one."

"He's to be questioned. Take him upstairs. The others are to go to the waiting cells."

As Hanara was dragged to his feet again he saw Asara's and Dachido's slaves being taken through a doorway. They didn't look back. He found himself being guided out of the same door he had come through into the corridor they had arrived by.

Then they were climbing, ever upwards. Stairs and corridors followed by more stairs and corridors. At every level the air smelled sweeter and the walls were whiter. Yet this only made the knot of dread in his belly grow larger and tighter. The rattle of his chains sounded louder the quieter the corridors became.

At the top of yet another staircase a well-muscled slave emerged to block their path.

"Who?" the man asked.

"Takado's slave."

The man narrowed his eyes at Hanara. "Follow me."

Though Hanara felt a sense of relief and freedom as the first slave let go of his arm and the new one didn't take hold of him, he knew it was an illusion. If he tried to run he would be caught and beaten. So he obediently trailed behind this new slave. The corridors here were decorated with carvings and hangings, and in places the walls themselves had been painted with colourful scenes.

They stopped before a carved wooden door. The slave knocked quietly. As the door opened a crack Hanara glimpsed a face and an eye.

"Ichani Takado's slave," his new guide murmured.

The door closed and they waited. Hanara examined the wall decorations, trying to slow his breathing and heartbeat. When the door opened again he jumped and all the calm he'd managed to summon evaporated.

Before he got a look at the room beyond, he was inside it.

"So. You are the Ichani Takado's slave," a voice echoed.

The man who had spoken sat on one of many bench seats arranged around the walls. His cropped coat glittered with gold and jewels, which matched the room's elaborately decorated furniture. Hanara threw himself on the floor.

The emperor! He must be the emperor! He didn't dare answer. The man's words had been pitched as a statement, not a question.

"Get up," the man said.

Reluctantly, but not so slowly as to anger the emperor, Hanara got to his feet. He kept his eyes on the floor.

"Come here."

He forced his legs to move, taking him closer but ready to freeze at any moment. The instruction to stop did not come and he found himself standing a mere two or three paces from the seated ruler, not daring to look up, fearing the consequences if his gaze even fell upon the man's shoes.

"Kneel."

Hanara dropped to the floor, the rattle of his chains echoing loudly in the room. The impact jolted his spine and bruised his knees, but he quickly forgot the pain as he felt hands press onto either side of his head.

Of course, he thought. *This is what they want from me. Information about Takado. Everything that happened. Well, I will show him how clever Takado was. How he wanted to help Sachaka.*

Sure enough, Emperor Vochira combed through Hanara's mind, skilfully drawing out memories of Takado's tour through Kyralia, Hanara's stay in Mandryn, Takado's return and then every stage of the war, from the wooing of allies to the morning when, having seen the Kyralian army entering Sachaka, Takado and his last two friends had put aside plans to disappear in order to warn Sachaka of the impending invasion, and help repel the invaders. *See!* Hanara could not help thinking. *His motives aren't selfish. He always wanted the best for Sachaka!* He felt the long-life feeling returning.

—*You little fool*, Emperor Vochira said into his mind, shattering the feeling. *It has been known for centuries that Sachaka could not risk a battle with Kyralia or Elyne. When we first conquered these lands they contained few magicians. Under our rule and influence they adopted our ways, and gained many more. That is why my predecessor granted them independence so long ago. Since then we have enjoyed a beneficial peace. If Takado had only spoken to me of his plans, I would have told him this.*

But Takado had never respected the emperor enough to let the ruler veto his grand plan, Hanara knew. His allies had mostly been Ichani at first – outcasts who hated the emperor and anyone with a position of power in Sachaka.

—*Why didn't you tell him?* Hanara asked. *Why did you never explain this?*

—*Would he have listened? Would he have believed it?*

Hanara could not stop a traitorous "no" forming in his mind.

—*It was knowledge that was only revealed, when needed, to those we could trust with it. We did not want Kyralia and Elyne discovering they were stronger than they believed. I doubt I would have trusted Takado with it willingly, even had he consulted me. I doubt he would have obeyed me if I had. He is disloyal and disobedient by nature.*

—He was loyal to his friends, Hanara pointed out.

—Friends who are now dead. Emperor Vochira's anger was palpable. *The man you are so loyal to has taken an ally of this country and done so much harm to it we may never be anything but enemies again. He has led half of the magicians in this land to their deaths. He has forced the Kyralians to discover strengths they didn't know they possessed, handed them a victory they didn't expect and given them the confidence and reason to seek revenge for the harm he did to them.*

—He didn't mean to! He never meant to lose! At least he had the courage to try!

—The courage of an ignorant, greedy, disloyal fool. Emperor Vochira's mental voice grew dark with something more frightening than anger – bleak resignation. *He has doomed us. And I have doomed us by failing to stop him. The Kyralians will soon arrive at Arvice. They will meet the last of the Sachakan army and they will defeat it. Within days we will be the conquered, and they the conquerors. Only then will we know the true extent of their revenge. All this because of your master. Takado the Betrayer. That is how he will be known. Do you still have the long-life feeling now, Hanara? Betrayer's slave?*

He could not help it. He reached for the feeling and felt it splutter and die. The emptiness that followed was unbearable and drew him deep into despair. It was worse, he realised, than finding out Takado had died. At least then Hanara could have remembered his master with pride. But was Takado dead?

—No, the emperor replied. *Though I would like the satisfaction of killing him myself, I must sacrifice that in the hope that handing him over to the Kyralians will save some of what survives of Sachaka.*

—When he dies, will you tell me?

The emperor paused and Hanara felt a hint of surprise. And was that jealousy, too?

—I will give orders that you be present when he is handed over. That is all I can offer.

"Thank you," Hanara whispered. But he did not know if the man heard. The sense of the emperor's mind lifted and Hanara felt the man's hands slide from his head.

"Take him away," Vochira said, his voice hoarse with disgust.

Hanara kept his eyes on the floor as footsteps hurried close behind him. Someone grabbed his arm and drew him away. He did not resist, too caught up in the knowledge that his master had brought about the fall of Sachaka, and the traitorous hope that Takado would escape to retake his homeland from the Kyralians.

The Sachakan estates they passed had reduced in size in the last few days, Jayan noticed. He'd learned to identify the markers that indicated a fence was a boundary as well as containment for stock. However, though the land each estate covered was growing smaller, the buildings were growing rapidly larger.

It's obvious we're getting close to Arvice, but everything is deserted, he thought. *The quiet is . . . eerie.* He'd felt tense and uneasy since they'd set out that morning.

"I heard a rumour about you last night," a familiar voice said from behind his shoulder.

Recognising Narvelan's tones, Jayan resisted turning around to look at the magician.

"What this time?" Dakon asked.

Narvelan laughed. Jayan winced at the sound. Narvelan's light-heartedness and joviality seemed out of place, and a painful contrast to the rest of the army. *We're about to fight our final battle with our ancient enemy, and he's behaving as if we're taking a nice ride in the sunshine.*

"I overheard some magicians speculating whether you arranged for those two magicians to be poisoned," Narvelan said. "They wondered if you'd heard the pair criticising you for being too scrupulous to kill slaves."

"I see," Dakon said calmly. "Did they see the irony in suspecting someone had done something so unscrupulous because he was accused of being too scrupulous?"

Narvelan chuckled. "I didn't stop to ask. Have you noticed anyone treating you with increased, ah, respect?"

"No."

Jayan shook his head. But then he remembered how quiet and obedient the servants had been that morning, as he and Dakon had supervised the preparation of the meal. As a precaution they'd kept a few rassook alive to feed samples to, watching to see if any poison affected the birds. They also mixed supplies from different estates together, in the hope that if one had been tampered with it might be diluted enough to not be lethal.

"Ah," Narvelan said. "They have finally come out to greet us."

The magician surged past Jayan, galloping towards the king and Sabin. Looking after him, Jayan realised the walls of the estates ahead were no longer a distance from the road, but instead hugged it. The roofs and upper floors of the buildings within were all that were visible and suggested that most of the area inside was filled with dwellings and other structures.

Where these walls started, a road bisected the one they were riding along. Along this stood a line of people. Sunlight glinted on jewelled and decorated clothing. Jayan counted and realised there were more magicians in this line than in the Kyralian army. He felt his heart sink.

But as he drew closer to the Sachakans he noted other details. Many were old, stooped and grey-haired. Others were as young as a new apprentice. A few were cripples, missing limbs or carrying walking canes. The few women among them looked either terrified or determined, most standing close to a man of their own age or one old enough to be their father.

Jayan exchanged a look of dismay with Dakon. Nearly a third of the enemy were clearly not suited to fighting.

This is a pathetic sight, Jayan thought. *And yet instead of feeling relieved that we might have a better chance of winning, I feel sad for these Sachakans. And I can't help admiring them for being prepared to defend their city.*

Magician Sabin and Dem Ayend were riding close on either side of the king now. King Errik was looking from one to the other as they talked, his brows lowered into a frown. The army slowed as it approached the line of Sachakans, finally coming to a halt less than twenty strides away. By then the leaders had stopped talking. They sat, regarding the enemy in silence for a long moment. Then the king nudged his horse a few paces forward.

"Magicians of Sachaka," he called out. "We know not all of you supported Takado's invasion of Kyralia. If you surrender to us, if you can prove you were no supporter of Takado and his allies, if you co-operate and show no resistance, we will spare you."

No voice rose in answer. No Sachakan stepped forward, or left the line. Jayan watched and waited.

"Get on with it, then," one of them shouted. "You came for a fight. So fight. Or are you going to wait until we die of old age?"

A faint sigh of nervous laughter spread across the enemy line. Jayan saw a few strained smiles.

"Do you speak for the emperor?" the king asked.

"The emperor is waiting at the Imperial Palace. If you get that far he might spare a moment to see you."

Magician Sabin rode forward to join the king. "I don't think we have any choice," Jayan heard him say.

"No," the king replied. "And we didn't come all this way for nothing."

He raised a hand, palm outward, to signal that the army should move into position. A flash seared Jayan's sight as one of the Sachakans took this to mean the start of the battle. The strike scattered off a shield and Sabin sent off a strike in return. As the Kyralian army spread out into formation, groups forming out of habit as much as intention, the air between the lines filled with flashing, vibrating magic.

As Dakon moved away to take his usual place among the advisers and leaders, Jayan found Everran and Avaria nearby and lent his strength to the pair. He realised he felt neither fear nor confidence. All he felt was the same disquiet that had nagged at him all morning.

At about the same time as the first Sachakan fell, Jayan's strength ran out.

Unlike the rest of the army, he'd only taken part in one attack on an estate. Even Dakon had more power, since he'd taken the strength of the magician who'd died from poisoning. *I am probably the weakest Kyralian magician here. Strange that nobody questioned my decision to not kill slaves, when they clearly questioned Dakon's.*

He remained in the shelter of Everran and Avaria's group. Instead of feeling useless, as he'd feared he would at this point, he felt as if he wasn't really there. Absent. An observer at most.

The Sachakans were not protecting each other, he noticed. The lessons Takado's army had learned had not been taken back into Sachaka. *Where is Takado?* Jayan wondered. *Why isn't he leading this last, desperate force? I can believe Emperor Vochira is hiding away, letting others fight for him, but I think*

Takado would face us if he had the choice. For all his nasty ways, he did have pride in himself and his homeland.

If the king had been correct about the number of magicians in Sachaka before the war, then there must be more of them elsewhere. The force facing the army was large, but it didn't approach a hundred. And some of them looked like unlikely candidates for being taught magic. They might only have had their power loosed and been taught to strike in the last few days. If so, then they might not even have achieved full control yet.

Looking over his shoulder, he saw the apprentices and servants waiting several paces behind, as close as they dared to come to the battle, but not so far away that the army couldn't protect them if they were attacked. Between them, the apprentices had probably recovered enough power overnight to ward off a few strikes, but not a concentrated attack from higher magicians.

"What are they . . . ?" Lord Everran exclaimed quietly. Jayan glanced at him, saw he was looking at the Sachakans, and followed the man's gaze.

The enemy line had fragmented. Sachakans were dashing sideways, or back along the main road. Disappearing into doorways, though a few were caught by strikes before they could reach them.

They're running away.

From the bodies on the ground Jayan guessed about a third had fallen. He saw that the leaders and advisers of the Kyralian side were talking, and strained to hear.

"I guess that's it," King Errik said, looking at Sabin. "Shall we go after them?"

Sabin shook his head, his voice too low to hear.

"So on to the Imperial Palace," the king concluded.

Everran straightened, then looked down at the ring on his

finger. "We're to maintain shields. Keep alert and be ready in case of ambush."

"I have no magic left," Jayan told Everran quietly.

The magician nodded. "Ride in front and I'll shield us both."

Jayan nodded to show he understood. The army formed a protective ring around the servants then started forward, apprentices riding as close as possible to their masters.

Once again, they travelled in an eerie silence. The high white walls loomed over them, stark and threatening, and Jayan knew he would not be the only one worried about what they could be hiding.

"How are you doing?"

He turned to see Tessia riding beside him.

"Fine," he said. "Other than having no magic left. How is Dakon?"

"Better than he expected."

The army proceeded slowly and cautiously. The road stretched on, the white walls continuing towards hazy buildings in the distance. They crossed several intersecting roads, all deserted. At first there was the occasional shout as someone caught a glimpse of a face, an arm, or a human-like shadow above the walls, but eventually no further signs of life were seen – or else nobody bothered to draw attention to them any more.

The buildings in the distance grew larger and sharper. They gave a hint of impressive size and grandeur. Tessia wondered aloud if one was the Imperial Palace.

Then everything exploded in a rush of light and roar of sound.

There were shouts of surprise, and screams from both humans and horses. The wall beside Jayan bulged outwards, and he felt himself thrown sideways. As his mount toppled

636

he fell with it. Something heavy landed on his leg as he hit the ground. He tried to pull free but could not. The horse lay still, either stunned or dead, pinning his leg under it.

Trapped under my own horse! he thought, amused at the situation he found himself in despite the deadly magic sizzling through the air around him. *And with no magic to free myself with.*

Smoke billowed out from beyond one of the broken walls. "Ride!" a voice bellowed, and was taken up by others. Hoofs rapped on the road. Carts rumbled by. Jayan felt hands grasp his shoulders. He looked up. Tessia frowned at him, then began pulling. After several heaves she managed to drag him out from under the horse. They collapsed, leaning up against an upturned cart.

The eerie quiet of the city had returned. Looking down the road, Jayan saw the rear of the army hurrying away.

Thin cheers rang out from the houses around them. Tessia turned to look at Jayan, her eyes wide. His heart was racing. *Should we run?* From behind the cart came voices.

"Did we get any of them?"

"Nah, just those over there, and I think they're servants."

"We'd better hurry then, or we'll miss the next one."

The sound of running followed, fading into silence. Tessia let out a long sigh of relief. They both got to their feet. Jayan tested his weight on the leg that had been stuck under his horse. It felt bruised, but wasn't broken.

He peered around the cart. He had no magic and Tessia did not have enough to defend herself against a higher magician. If Sachakans were lurking behind the walls, waiting to ambush the Kyralian army, then an exhausted magician and an apprentice had no chance of catching up with the army alive. They would have to hide.

There were gaping holes in the walls around them. Behind one a house was burning, though not as much smoke was billowing out now. The closest gap was a few steps away — where the blast that had killed his horse had come from. Hopefully whoever had sent the strike had left to continue the fight elsewhere.

If he or she was still here, they'd have seen us already. "Let's get out of sight," he said.

Tessia followed as he dashed towards and through the gap, and then they both skidded to a halt.

Lush greenery surrounded them. Wide-leafed plants fanned out over paved pathways. Vines clung to a lattice roof. In the centre a large stone-edged pool brimmed with water.

"It's beautiful," Tessia whispered.

They exchanged a look of wonder, then moved further into the garden, moving as silently as they could. Jayan hoped that the owners of this place, and their slaves, were gone, or staying as far from the battle as possible. They found a small, sheltered alcove and slipped inside, then sat down to wait.

"What do we do now?" Tessia asked.

Jayan shrugged. "Wait."

She nodded. "Do we wait until night, or until someone comes back for us?"

"Whatever comes first."

CHAPTER 47

It seemed like years since Stara had been in a crowded room. Nine women sat around her, some chatting, some quietly listening. The youngest was only twelve, though far too wise and self-possessed for her age. The oldest was near Vora's age, with more grey in her hair than the slave had, but an energy Stara envied. Stara suspected she would have found it hard to keep her entertained if it weren't for the work the women had brought with them.

Since the Traitors treated all women as equals, free women had contributed in practical ways to the running of the Sanctuary. They were not given unpleasant or physically demanding tasks, however, as that would have been too great a shock to women who had never worked before. Instead they were taught skills like sewing and weaving, cooking and preserving foods. Though they'd fled the Sanctuary in a hurry, they'd each managed to pack tools for their work among the clothes and food they'd brought, and soon took up new projects when they arrived at Kachiro's house.

Talking Kachiro into letting the women stay had been easy. She'd told him they were friends of his friends' wives who had fled their estates in the country, and would leave when the Kyralians had been dealt with. Since his friends didn't seem to know or care exactly how many friends their wives had, he had accepted the half-truth without question.

She'd had to gamble that he wouldn't recognise Nachira,

but he tended to avoid the women as much as possible and had barely spared her brother's wife a glance. He was distracted by the news that the Kyralians were nearing the city, and often disappeared for hours to discuss plans with his friends.

Nachira had been distraught when she'd learned that Ikaro was probably dead. They'd wept together, Stara surprised at the extent of her own grief. She'd expected to have to soothe and reassure Nachira constantly, but the formally passive woman appeared to have gained some confidence now that she wasn't under the constant threat of murder. The loss of her husband clearly hurt deeply, but she was alive and determined to stay that way.

Stara looked at her sister by marriage. *What will I feel, if Kachiro doesn't come back?* He'd left a few hours before to join his friends, who were all determined to do what they could to defend the city. *He said the Kyralians haven't got a chance, but I can't help worrying. After all, they wouldn't have come here if they didn't think they could defeat us. I hope he's careful. He may not have been completely honest with me, but he's not a bad man. Just a man surviving in an overly judgemental society. Like me — and I haven't exactly been honest with him either.*

She'd never been so tempted to tell him about her magical ability. If it weren't for her obligation to protect the women, she'd have left with him to throw what little magic she had at the invaders. When loud booming and cracking noises had penetrated to the room it had taken all her willpower to stay seated. Slaves had reported that they'd heard fighting a few streets away, but it had moved on.

"Are you worrying about Kachiro again?" a voice said at her elbow.

Stara jumped and looked down. "Vora! You're back!" The other women looked up and exclaimed, saving Stara from answering Vora's question.

"Yes." Vora moved into the circle of women. "And I have news."

"Tell us," one of the women murmured. All were gazing at Vora eagerly.

"The Kyralians have entered the city," Vora confirmed, her expression grave.

"No!"

"But . . . how?"

"Are many dead?"

Vora raised her hands and they quietened. "A third of the defenders fell." She looked at one of the women, her expression grave. "I am sorry, Atarca." The woman hung her head and nodded, but said nothing. "The rest . . ." Vora continued. "When it was clear they would be overcome they retreated. Fortunately they'd planned for such a situation. They started attacking the Kyralians from hidden positions. I followed at a distance for an hour or so. When I knew they were getting close to the palace I came back here." She stopped to take a deep breath. "I think we should leave the city while we can."

The women stared at her in silence, then broke it with question after question.

"So the enemy has won?"

"Where will we go?

"Does Tavara think we should go?"

"What would happen if we stayed here?"

Stara felt a chill run down her spine, then another. The women were already in danger of being discovered and recognised by those people in the city they'd fled from in the first place. Now there was the possible threat of the invaders taking their revenge upon the people of Arvice. Without magicians to enforce laws there was the danger of attack from lawless free men taking advantage of the chaos, who would rape and rob them and later claim it was Kyralians. And slaves might stop working once there were no masters to order them about, and with nobody raising or delivering foodstuff Arvice would eventually starve.

We are probably safe here . . . so long as Kachiro returns. But what will the Kyralians do to the magicians who survive the battle? Even if they let him live, I doubt he could protect us from them . . .

So should they leave? It might reduce the dangers. They might encounter lawless free men or slaves. *I should be able to fend them off with magic. But where can we go?*

She thought of Elyne and her mother. But she had promised to help the Traitors, and she couldn't take them there. Not when stories of the murder of Sachakan expatriates in Capia were circulating in Arvice. *Hopefully nobody remembered that Mother was married to a Sachakan, and has decided that makes her Sachakan too.* Kachiro had sent a message to Elyne hoping to find out her mother's fate, but no reply had come.

"Many, many other Sachakans are leaving," Vora told them. "There's a line of carts and people on every road out of the city."

"Where are they going?"

"Who knows?" Vora replied. "To stay with friends on country estates? Out of Sachaka entirely?"

"Have we got friends on country estates? Or will we go back to the Sanctuary?"

"The Sanctuary is too close to the road to and from Kyralia," Nachira said. "If there was anywhere else, Tavara would have sent us there instead of bringing us back to the city."

Vora nodded. "I'm afraid that is most likely true." She paused. "Wherever we go, we will have to fend for ourselves for a while."

"We are used to work," the older woman stated.

"Not tilling fields or handling stock," Vora reminded her. Then she smiled. "But I'm sure we'll manage. Stopping other people from taking what we have will be harder."

"Stara has magic. She can stop them."

Stara felt her face warm as all the women turned to smile at her.

"She has only her own magic," Vora warned them. "Magicians who have taken strength from slaves will be stronger than her."

"Then why don't we give her our strength?" Nachira said. The women fell silent as they exchanged questioning looks. Then they all nodded. "There," Nachira continued. "Most magicians will have used up their power during the battle anyway. Stara will quickly end up stronger than them."

The older woman frowned. "Better that they never know we have anything they want," she said darkly. "Better we find somewhere to hide, out of sight."

"Oh," Stara said.

Somewhere to hide. Somewhere out of sight . . .

"Oh?" Vora repeated.

"I know of a place." Stara felt her pulse quicken. "A place in the mountains. But I don't know how to get there." Her heart sank. *I wonder. Could I follow Chavori's maps? I'd have to get them first.* She blinked as she realised she had risen to her feet. The women were looking at her expectantly. These amazing women. Adaptable. Strong. *We're going to do this. We're going to leave and make our own Sanctuary.* She turned to Vora.

"Can you get the wives?"

Vora's eyebrows rose. "I can try."

"Then try. Explain that we're leaving and see if they want to come. I'm going out to get . . . something. While I'm gone, everyone," she looked at the women, "pack as much as you can carry and put on travelling clothes. When I get back . . ." She paused to take a deep, calming breath. "When I get back we'll leave Arvice. For the mountains."

As the women scattered to collect their belongings, Stara hurried to her bedroom. She opened chests and searched for dark clothes. It would soon be night and she didn't want to be seen. She heard footsteps behind her.

"I have sent a message to the wives," Vora said, moving to another chest. "Are you planning what I think you're planning?"

"What do you think I'm planning?"

"A little evening thievery. For which you'll need to cover that Elyne skin of yours." Vora took something from the chest and held it out. It was a dark green wrap, long enough to cover her legs. Stara took it and began to change.

"I'd say I was borrowing without permission, except I'd never convince you." Grabbing a dark blue blanket woven by one of the women and given in thanks for her help, Stara wrapped it around her shoulders. She stuffed her feet into a pair of sandals and hurried out of the room, Vora following. "Are you coming with me?" she asked.

"Of course."

Stara looked over her shoulder and smiled. "Thank you."

The air outside was pleasantly warm, though it held the scent of smoke. The sun hovered near the horizon. Soon the city would be shrouded in a concealing darkness. *Which will be the right time to slip away.*

The courtyard was deserted. Stara wondered where the slaves had gone as she and Vora slipped out of the doors into the street. Keeping to the shadows cast by the city's high walls, they hurried away. The slave's darker skin and drab clothing made her even less noticeable than Stara in the dusky light.

An eerie silence was broken now and then by the sound of running feet, or wailing, or the passing of a cart. They reached a main road and suddenly the air was full of noise. People crowded the thoroughfare. Carts laden with belongings and people rattled past, all heading out of the city.

She and Vora had to weave their way across, dodging animals and people. On the other side they found themselves on empty streets again, though at one point doors opened and a stream of carts spilled out, heading towards the main road.

"Perhaps by night there will be less of a crowd," she remarked aloud.

"I doubt it," Vora murmured in reply.

Finally they reached the house Stara remembered from her one visit to her husband's friend's home. She'd been surprised to learn that Chavori lived in such a spectacular house. But it turned out that the house belonged to his father, and Chavori lived in a single room located at the rear of the property, out of sight and reached most easily through a slave entrance. It indicated with painful clarity what his family thought of his dedication to drawing maps.

Stara found the door to the slave entrance open and unlocked.

"This is odd," she murmured.

Vora shrugged and peered inside. "The slaves may have fled. They'd hardly stop to make sure to close the door after them."

They slipped inside. Stara's heart was pounding now. If anyone found them . . . well, she could pretend to be looking for somewhere to hide. It was obvious from her clothes she was a free woman. Or she could pretend to be looking for Kachiro. They might not remember her, but Kachiro was a regular visitor.

Chavori's room was located down a long corridor that looked long overdue for repainting. She crept along it as quietly as she could. Reaching the door, she was relieved to find it, too, was ajar. No need to break it to get in. But what if someone else had already stolen the maps? The thought made her pause, one hand on the door. And realise she could hear sobbing and a man repeating a name.

And that the voice was familiar. All too familiar.

She exchanged a look with Vora, then pushed open the door. The room was as small and neatly arranged as she remembered. A large desk covered in parchment and writing tools took up one side of the room. Along the opposite wall was a narrow bed. Sitting on the bed was her husband, cradling an unconscious Chavori.

Not unconscious, she corrected herself as she saw the bloodied mess that was his chest. *Dead.*

Kachiro looked up at her and she felt her heart spasm at the grief she saw in his face. He blinked and recognition came into his eyes, then they widened with surprise.

"Stara?"

"Kachiro," she breathed, hurrying forward and kneeling before him. "Oh, Kachiro. I am so sorry."

He looked down at Chavori and she could see the internal struggle that followed. Fear that he'd been discovered, she guessed. Then hate, probably at himself for the fear. And then his eyes filled with tears and he covered his face with one bloodstained hand. She reached out to stroke his head.

"I know you loved him," she told him. "I know . . . everything." He flinched and stared at her. "Remember that I grew up in Elyne." She smiled crookedly. "You won't receive any judgement from me. I even understand why you married me."

"Sorry," he croaked. "I am a terrible husband."

She shrugged. "I forgive you. How could I not? You are a good man, Kachiro. You have a good heart. I am proud to be your wife." Standing up, she held out a hand. "Come home."

He looked at Chavori again, then sighed deeply. "I want to give him a proper death burning. The Kyralians won't know who he is. They'll put him under the ground."

Stara felt a shiver run over her skin. She'd forgotten the Sachakan custom. Then she shuddered again. *Even Kachiro believes the Kyralians have won.*

"Is his family here?" she said.

"No. All gone. Or dead. So are the others. Motaro. Dashina. All of them. I am the only . . ." He closed his eyes and grimaced.

"Do it," she urged. "If you don't mind, I'll wait here. I'm not sure I'm ready to see that."

He nodded, then gathered Chavori's body up in his arms and carried it out. The young man suddenly seemed very frail and small, and Kachiro taller and broader.

Once he had gone, she turned to the maps and began looking through them.

"I want to be sure there are no copies left behind," she whispered to Vora. "No notes or sketches. Nothing to tell anyone this place he described exists."

The maps on the table were of the volcanos in the north, with flows of lava indicated with rippling red lines. She paused as she realised how close he must have climbed to make his measurements. *He's braver than he appears. Or appeared.* She felt a pang of loss. *What else would he have invented and discovered, had the Kyralians not ended his life too soon?*

Several tubes like the ones Chavori had used to transport his maps stood on end in the corner of the room. Stara took one and opened an end, then tipped the rolls of parchment out onto the table. She unrolled them, one by one. They were of the coast of Sachaka. She cursed under her breath. How long was it going to take Kachiro to burn Chavori's body and return?

Hearing a sigh of frustration from Vora, she turned to see that the old woman was leafing through bundles of parchment in a small chest, opening the covers and shaking her head.

"He has terrible handwriting," the slave said. "It could take weeks to read all this."

"Can we take them with us?"

Vora looked into the chest and grimaced. "It'll be heavy."

Stara reached for another tube. "Can we send someone back for them?"

"What are you doing?" Kachiro's voice came from the doorway.

Stara froze, her back to him. "We can't let all his work be lost," she said. The lie tasted sour in her mouth. *But in an odd way, it's true. Who knows what would happen to them, if they were left here? We may be saving them from destruction.*

"No," she heard him say. "He wouldn't have liked that. Put them back in the tubes."

Hearing his footsteps approaching, she turned to smile wanly at him. He took the maps on the table and rolled them up, then slipped them into the tube. Picking up half of the tubes, he handed them to Stara. The other half he gave to Vora. Then, with a grunt, he picked up the chest.

"Let's get these to a safe place," he said, then strode out of the door.

The pace he set on the return journey was hurried, and though Stara and Vora were less heavily burdened they struggled to keep up. The sun had set and a deepening twilight was leaching everything of colour. Finally they reached Kachiro's house and slipped inside. Stara saw the surprise on his face as he took in the crowd of women in the master's room, all dressed ready for travel. The other wives were there, with their children. Stara had no idea if they knew of the fate of their husbands. That news would have to be delivered later. Several women Stara knew to be slaves were in the crowd, wearing similar clothing to the free women. Tavara was not among them. For some reason this filled Stara with relief.

He put the chest down. "Where are you going?"

"Out of the city," Stara told him. She put the maps down, moved to stand in front of him and searched his gaze. "I didn't know when or . . . or if you'd come back, so I started organising it. I think we'll be safer out of Arvice for a while. Chiara has friends in the country." That last was a lie, of course.

His eyebrows rose and he began to nod. "Yes. It would be safer for you all. And you should take these too." He gestured to the chest.

She frowned. "What about you? You're not coming with us?"

Kachiro paused, then shook his head. "No. The Kyralians can't kill every Sachakan magician and expect the slaves to keep working – whether as slaves or not. We'll starve. Someone has to stay and try to save something of what we have." He grimaced. "And though I'm better at negotiation than fighting, if the chance comes to drive them out, or even take a little revenge, I want to be here for it."

Stara felt a wistful pride sweep through her. She kissed him on the cheek, and then, as he stared at her in surprise, gave him a stern look. "You take care of yourself. I'll send word when we've reached Chiara's friends."

He nodded and smiled wearily. "You take care of yourselves, too. I should go with you, to protect—"

The women all voiced a wordless disagreement. "We'll stick together, and we have slaves to defend us," Chiara assured him.

649

"Now, it's dark outside and we want to get some distance between ourselves and Arvice before we stop," Stara said, turning to the women. She picked up the tubes and handed them out. "Take one each, and spread the weight of these out between you." She bent and opened the chest, handing out bundles of notes.

"Surely the slaves will carry those for you," Kachiro said.

Stara didn't have the heart to tell him how many slaves had run away. She already felt guilty at leaving him here, in the city. For a moment she was tempted to talk him into coming, but her dream of a true Sanctuary did not include men.

"I'd rather they carried food, and other necessities," she told him. "Don't worry, they're not much trouble spread out." The women were now looking at her expectantly. She smiled at Kachiro, and touched his cheek. "Goodbye."

He smiled faintly, took her hand and kissed it. "Thank you."

They gazed at each other for a moment longer, then she tore herself away. "Come along," she said, gesturing to the door. The women managed smiles and even a few light-hearted comments as they followed Stara out, making it sound as if they were setting out on a pleasure trip. Stara didn't look back, not wanting to see Kachiro standing, alone, watching them go.

Once outside she breathed a deep sigh of relief, then set a quick but not too tiring pace along the road. The women quietened, all pretence at joviality abandoned. Vora began to walk alongside Stara.

"Which way out, do you think?" the slave murmured.

"The main road," Stara replied. "All the other roads will be crowded. It's obvious we're a bunch of free women travelling with no protectors. I'd rather not have to use any magic until I have to. People might avoid the route the Kyralians took."

"I guess if the Kyralians won they won't have reason to leave the city."

"And if they lost, they're dead."

They hurried on, the only sound the rustle of clothing, the patter of footsteps and the breathing of the women. Distant sounds echoed from around the city. A dull boom. An angry shout. A scream that made them all stop and shiver. Stara felt a tension growing inside her. She resisted an urge to start running. *Just a jog*, her mind urged. *Not an outright race.* But she did not want to tire herself or the women out. They might need the energy later.

She found herself reaching in to the store of magic within her, giving it the lightest of touches to reassure herself it was still there, ready to be drawn upon. It was tempting to try covering them all in a shield, but while she had learned to do that as part of her basic training, she hadn't bothered to practise in years and wasn't sure how much power she'd use stretching it to protect so many people. Still, she was ready to throw up a wall. Ready to strike out, too, if she had to.

They were coming up to the main road now. She slowed as she saw rubble scattered over the highway. Houses on the other side of the road were burning, casting a flickering, hot light. The women made low noises as they noticed the damage. All stopped at the corner to gaze about in grim silence.

Stara heard the faintest of sounds to her right. Then her heart jumped as she realised that the movement she'd seen in the corner of her eye was not the flicker of shadows cast by the fire. She threw out her arms and moved backwards, pushing the women back.

But they had not seen the danger, and moved too slowly.

Two figures appeared on the road ahead, walking slowly and staring around. A man and a woman. Their dress was Kyralian. Stara froze and heard the women catch their breaths.

Then the man spun to face them. Stara felt a surge of fear and let loose magic, instinctively shaping it into a force to sweep the invaders away.

And it did. The two strangers were thrown across the road and landed like dolls tossed upon the ground.

Are they dead? Stara stared at the Kyralians, waiting for them to move. As time stretched on she became aware of the gasping, frightened breathing of the women around her. Even Vora was panting with fear.

"They're not moving," Chiara said. She took a step forward. "I think you got them."

"Better make sure," Tashana advised.

Stara took a deep breath and moved forward. The women followed. They reached the man. She felt her heart skip as she realised he was conscious, and put up a wall of magic. He'd landed on a section of wall. As she approached he moved, pushing himself up then rolling onto his back. His front was covered in blood, which seeped out as she watched. Looking back at the wall, she saw the mangled end of a lamp hook, glistening wetly.

His eyes flickered from face to face. Stara reached for magic, preparing to finish him off. But then a look of recognition and surprise stole over his face.

"You . . ." he said, his voice catching with pain, his eyes on the women behind her.

"It's the one who let us go," Nachira said. "The one who found us, at the Sanctuary, and left us without telling the others."

Stara felt horror wash over her. Why, of all the invaders, had she struck down the only one who had shown any compassion?

652

"I didn't see a girl, though," Nachira added.

Looking past the young man, Stara saw that the woman was lying on her side, eyes closed. *They didn't defend themselves. Perhaps they had no power left.* It was impossible to tell whether the woman was unconscious or dead. She grimaced. *With the luck I'm having, she'll turn out to be someone else I shouldn't have killed.* Sighing, she turned away.

"Let's get out of here," she said.

Feeling tired in her heart, but pushing doubt aside, she started down the road. As she left the city of her birth, she did not look back. Instead, she lifted the map tube so it rested over one shoulder, and set her mind on her dream of a Sanctuary for women, where all were equal and free. And the women she had befriended and championed here followed.

Rows of trees surrounded by beds of flowering plants lined the wide road to the Imperial Palace. Once the army had reached this thoroughfare the attacks had stopped. Dakon doubted it was because the local magicians didn't want to ruin the streetscape. Most likely they were rushing to join in a last line of defence at the palace gates.

He looked over his shoulder again, seeking where the road they had fought their way down had met this tree-lined thoroughfare. He found it and searched for movement.

"Don't worry about them," Narvelan said. "They're a smart pair. They'll keep out of sight until we can go back and fetch them."

If they're alive. Dakon sighed and turned back to face the front. *But if they aren't . . . my mind knows Narvelan is right but my heart says otherwise.*

"I should go back," he said for the hundredth time.

"You'd die," Narvelan replied. "Which won't do them any good at all."

"I could go," another voice said.

Dakon and Narvelan turned to look at Mikken, riding to Dakon's left.

"No," they both said together.

"When it gets dark," the apprentice said. "I'll keep in the shadows. It doesn't matter as much if I die – and I was supposed to stay with Jayan—"

"No," Narvelan repeated. "You're a better asset to Jayan alive. If anybody is going to slip back at night, it will be all of us plus a few more as extra protection."

Mikken's shoulders slumped and he nodded.

They were nearing the palace now. Looking up at the building, Dakon saw that it was a larger, grander version of the mansions they had seen before. The walls were rendered and painted white. They curved sensually. But they were far thicker and taller, and formed dome-topped towers here and there.

As the army neared the gates the magicians shifted into fighting teams without a word spoken. No sound came from the building. No one emerged to challenge them.

There was a muffled clunk, then the gates swung open.

"The emperor invites you to enter," a voice called.

Dakon watched as the king, Sabin and the Dem discussed their options. *We could stay here and wait until someone comes out. We could all go in. Or one of us could go in wearing a blood ring, and communicate if the way is safe.*

Sabin turned to scan the faces around him. Looking for a volunteer. *Should I? Why not? If Tessia and Jayan are dead, who needs me? My Residence is gone and it's clear I am of no use as a protector to the people of my ley, who are going to recover their lives quite well without me.* He opened his mouth.

"I'll go," Narvelan said. "I already have a ring, anyway."

Dakon watched as the magician strode up to the gates and

654

disappeared inside. Long, silent minutes passed. Then Sabin chuckled.

"The way is clear. He's read a few minds. The emperor has ordered that no obstruction or trap be put in our way." He turned to look at the servant and the carts. "Even so, I think half of us should stay outside to protect the servants, and be ready to fight if this does turn into a battle."

More time passed as the arrangements were made. Then finally they were ready. Sabin gave the order, and Dakon walked, with forty other magicians, into Sachaka's Imperial Palace.

CHAPTER 48

H anara had been in the middle of a nightmare when the guard slave came to get him, and now, as he was dragged, pushed and shoved through increasingly wider and more opulently decorated corridors, he was not entirely sure if he was truly awake or still caught in the dream. He'd travelled this route many times in his sleep, after all.

There was a lack of strangeness in this journey that told him he was back in the waking world. No monsters lurking in side corridors or rooms full of tortured slaves. No Takado rushing out to rescue him. No Kyralians.

But Takado is sure to feature in this version, at least, he thought. *Unless the emperor wants to read my mind again. Or someone else does . . .*

He did not recognise the corridors from the previous journey. They had been narrower than these, and far less populated. Slaves hovered around doors or hurried back and forth. Many wore similar trousers, in a yellow fabric finer than any Hanara had seen on a slave before. They all looked fearful and harried.

A large crowd of slaves hovered round one particular door. Hanara felt his stomach flip over as he realised the guard was taking him towards them. The slaves were frowning, some wringing their hands, and he could hear a frantic, rapid chatter.

They fell silent, however, as the guard pushed Hanara

through them to the door. A slave standing next to the door eyed Hanara, then smiled grimly as he looked at the guard.

"Just in time," he said, then turned to open the door.

Pushed through, Hanara found himself at the side of a huge, narrow room filled with columns. Before him, in the centre, was a large and spectacular throne. The emperor was looking at him, his nose wrinkled with disgust. Hanara threw himself to the floor.

"Get up," the guard whispered, and Hanara felt a toe jab his leg. He rose slowly, looking towards the emperor. The man had turned away, his attention now somewhere down the long room. Hanara stared down between the columns, but the space was empty. Then he noticed something on the floor.

A man. A naked man lying on his back, covered in cuts and bruises. Hanara looked closer and saw the chest rise and fall. He saw a faint movement and looked at the face. The eyes were open.

And recognition rushed over Hanara like a hot burst of steam.

Takado!

A terrible pity and sorrow rose up to grip his heart. With it came dread. *If Takado dies today, what will happen to me? Will I die, too?*

Something slammed at the end of the room, making Hanara jump. Footsteps filled the room. Lots of footsteps. Faint but growing louder. He found himself leaning forward to get a better view between the columns, and felt the guard jerk his arm to pull him back.

When the white-faced men marched into sight the room seemed to grow cold.

They made it, he thought. *They got through the city and into the Imperial Palace. After all that Takado did to them, they fought back and then kept coming, all the way to Arvice. All the way to here.*

He couldn't help admiring them for that. The barbarian race of Kyralia had come a long way.

Hanara recognised King Errik and the face of the magician at his right. An Elyne stood on the king's other side. The other men around the king were also familiar from battles. One face jolted him with recognition. The face of the man who had given him freedom and a job. Lord Dakon.

The magician hadn't seen him. His eyes were on Takado. His expression shifted from horror to anger and back again.

King Errik slowed to a stop several strides from Takado, his eyes moving from the supine man to the emperor. He waited until the rest of his army of magicians stopped and quietened before he spoke.

"Emperor Vochira. This is a strange way to meet a conqueror."

The emperor smiled. "Does it please you, King Errik?"

The king eyed Takado, his lip curling with hatred and disgust. "He is alive. You expect that to please me?"

"Alive and helpless, near all his strength taken from him. A gift to you, or perhaps a bribe. Or a trade."

"For what?"

The emperor rose, slowly and gracefully, and stepped down from the throne. "For the lives of my people – at least those whom you haven't yet taken. For the lives of my family. For my own life, too, perhaps."

The hoarse, rasping sound of laughing drifted up from the floor, sending a shiver down Hanara's spine.

"Who is the traitor now?" Takado coughed. "Coward."

Emperor and king looked at the supine man, and then back at each other.

"Why should I let you live?" the king asked.

"You know I did not initiate the invasion of your country. If your spies did their job well, you should also know that I tried to stop it."

"But you did endorse it, eventually."

"Yes. It was a necessary deception. The army I sent was meant to split in three, two parts held in reserve to overcome this . . ." the emperor sneered down at Takado, "this Ichani rebel when he was at his weakest."

"It looked, to me, as if your intention was to take over at that point, and claim victory for yourself," the king said.

From Takado came a weak cry of triumph. "See?" he rasped. "Even the barbarian king sees through you!"

"Yet you didn't," the emperor reminded him. He looked at the king. "Would you prefer I kill him, or that you do it yourself?" He smiled. "As no doubt you will have your magicians do now?"

The eyes of the king became cold and hard. Then his mouth curled into a smile.

"A foolish ruler bases his rule on magic alone." His hand moved to his waist and slipped inside the long-sleeved tunic he wore, then came out gripping a long, straight blade. "A wise one bases it on loyalty and duty. And rewards those, magician or not, who serve him well in whichever way suits them best." He glanced over his shoulder. "All of them have earned my loyalty and gratitude, so I find it impossible to choose who should have this reward." He turned back to face the emperor.

The king took the blade of the knife between his fingers and held it up to one side. "Whoever takes the blade may make the kill."

Hanara saw the magicians behind the king hesitate and exchange glances. A tall young magician stepped forward, then hesitated as another followed suit. The young magician turned to stare at the second man in surprise. Hanara's heart skipped as he saw the other was Lord Dakon. The older magician's face was dark with unreadable emotions. He stared at the younger man, who bowed his head and stepped back again.

Lord Dakon grasped the handle of the knife. The king let go of the blade, and as he turned to see who had taken it he, too, stared in obvious astonishment.

"Lord Dakon . . ." he began, then frowned and did not continue.

As the magician who had given Hanara freedom stepped up to Takado's side, Takado hissed.

"You? What joke is this? Of all the Kyralians you choose the most pathetic of all to kill me?" He shook his head weakly. "He won't kill me. He's too squeamish."

Dakon nodded. "Unlike you, I don't relish killing. I asked myself many times why I joined in this invasion of Sachaka, why I said nothing against the unnecessary slaughter. Now I see it was to get to the necessary slaughter. And I find I'm not squeamish at all." He dropped to one knee and raised the knife above Takado. Hanara felt the hand on his arm tighten. He realised he had begun to move forward.

"I only did it to help our people," Takado shouted, straining to look at the emperor.

"Don't we all," Dakon replied, and his arm jerked downwards.

Then it was just like Hanara's nightmare, yet all the details were wrong. His imagination had conjured far more gruesome and magical deaths for his master. Not this one, clean stab.

As Takado gasped and spasmed, Hanara cried out. He strained against the guard's arm, but didn't struggle. His eyes took in every twitch Takado made, how his muscles slowly relaxed, how a thin stream of blood spread across his chest and trickled down to pool on the floor. He felt liquid run down his face, as if in mimicry. He knew that several of the magicians had turned to stare at him, but he didn't care.

Dakon rose and waited, then as Takado stilled he leaned forward and removed the knife. The king reached for it, wiped the blade on a cloth he'd produced from somewhere, then stowed it back in its hidden sheath. Dakon returned to his place behind the king.

Errik looked up at the emperor and smiled. "You and your rebel have, through seeking to conquer us, made us stronger than we have ever been. Without you we'd have remained weak and unco-operative, distrustful of each other. You forced us together, forced us to make magical discoveries that we will be refining and developing for years to come. I would not be surprised if the Sachakan Empire is eventually forgotten, eclipsed by the new age that begins in Kyralia."

The king's eyes narrowed, though he kept smiling. "And for me you have done a great favour. Before this war I doubt my people would have accepted a king with no magic. But now I have proved that a king can still lead, still defeat an enemy, still *conquer* an empire despite having no magic of his own. The ordinary people of Kyralia have, themselves, contributed to the defence of their country. After that I doubt any will dare to suggest their king is not fit to rule." He paused. "But there is one more decision to be made here. One last step to be taken. You know what it is."

The emperor's shoulders dropped. "Yes, I know it," he said, his voice low and dark. "I *am* a magician, as you know. I have the strength of the best source slaves of this land. Many of them, many times. But it will not be enough to defeat you. So I will not fight you." He straightened. "I surrender, myself and all Sachaka, to you."

"I accept," the king replied.

Someone muttered something. The two leaders frowned and turned to look at the other magicians. The one who had always been at the king's side shook his head.

"We can't trust him. He most likely has the power he claims he holds. While he does he is dangerous."

The king spread his hands. "He has surrendered. Must I force him to give us his magic as well as his power? It is too much to ask."

Hanara stared at the king in surprise. The emperor was regarding his conqueror with a knowing look.

"Yes," the Elyne replied. "But there is another way. Have him transfer his power into the storestone. Not directly, of course. Someone should take it from him and then transfer it."

"What if he attacks the one transferring it?" someone asked.

"If he hasn't attacked us already, why would he do so during the transfer?" the Elyne reasoned.

"I volunteer to do the transferring." The young magician who had stepped back so Dakon could take the king's knife stepped forward.

"Thank you, Lord Narvelan." King Errik nodded. "Do it."

A strange scene followed, in which the young man took the emperor's hand in one hand, and the Elyne's in the other. The Elyne brought out a large gemstone which he held in his fist. A long, silent moment passed, then the three broke apart.

I have no idea what happened, Hanara mused. *What is a storestone?* Clearly it was capable of holding magic. But why put magic into a stone?

Discussion had begun on practical matters. Hanara stopped listening and found himself gazing at Takado again.

His master's eyes still stared at the ceiling. His mouth was slightly open. What would happen to him now? Would someone burn the body with the proper rites? Hanara doubted it. He felt the hand holding his arm squeeze, and looked up. One of the magicians was pointing towards him. The others had also turned to regard him.

"Him? He is the slave of the Betrayer," the emperor said, nodding at Takado's corpse.

"Really?" the young magician said. Hanara felt his heart sink as the man walked towards him and stopped a few steps away. "Hanara, isn't it? I think Dakon would like to have a chat with you." He smiled, but there was no friendliness in it. Hanara looked down, avoiding the man's eyes, which looked a little crazed.

"Let him go," the magician ordered.

The hand slid from Hanara's arm. Surprised, Hanara glanced up, then quickly away from those strange eyes.

"I think I might need a slave of my own while we sort things out here," the magician said. "You'll do for now. Come with me." The magician spun on his heel and walked away.

Swallowing hard, Hanara glanced back at the guard. The man shrugged, then made a shooing motion.

"Come on."

Hanara looked up. The magician had stopped, and was beckoning. Taking a deep breath, Hanara forced himself to obey.

Forgive me, master, he thought as they passed Takado's corpse. *But I'm only a slave. And a slave, as they say, doesn't get to choose his master. His master chooses him.*

Pain throbbed through Tessia's head. She wanted to sink back into oblivion, but the sharpness of it gave her no choice. She snapped into full consciousness.

Opening her eyes, she lifted hands to her head and instinctively felt for damage. There was a swelling to one side, but

663

nothing more, and her hands did not come away stained with blood.

Haltingly, cautiously, she shifted other limbs and pushed herself up onto her elbows. She felt more bruises, but nothing worse. Her head swam for a moment, then cleared.

I'm fine. Uninjured.

She could not recall how she had ended up like this. She remembered having to leave the garden after they heard sounds of people moving about inside the house. She recalled hurrying down the main road, trying to keep to the shadows. She remembered passing burning houses. After that . . . nothing.

Had they been attacked? She'd not even been shielding. Jayan had told her to avoid using any magic unless she needed to. She hadn't seen what had knocked her out. Her and . . .

Jayan? Where? She sat up and cast about. It was dark, only a glow of red from a fire burning low nearby lighting the road and rubble. Everything smelled of smoke and dust. Not daring to create a light and risk revealing her position, she got to her feet and felt her way forwards, circling about.

Suddenly her hands felt soft cloth rather than harsh stone. She recognised the shape and resistance of a leg beneath the fabric. A familiar smell teased her nose. Metallic. Like blood. But then all she could smell was smoke.

Maybe she had imagined it.

"Jayan?" she whispered. "Is that you?"

Feeling her way up the leg, she reached the waist, and wet stickiness. Her stomach sank. Whoever it was, they were bleeding. Her nose had been right.

I need light. I have to risk it.

Concentrating, she created the tiniest globe of light, cupping it between her hands. At once she knew two things: she had found Jayan and he had terrible injuries. Her heart lurched with dread. Was he dead or alive? She moved her hands further apart so the light spilled out. At once she saw the wound, a hole in his abdomen that seeped blood. Her heart filled with a wry hope. If blood was still flowing, he wasn't dead yet.

"Jayan," she said, reaching out and shaking his shoulder. "Wake up."

His eyes fluttered open and struggled to focus. Then he grimaced, squeezed his eyes tight then opened them again. This time his gaze locked onto her face.

"Tessia?" he croaked. "Are you all right?"

A wave of affection washed over her, almost overwhelming in its strength. *For all his infuriating arrogance, and inability to empathise with others at times, he does think of others before himself.*

"I'm fine. A bit bruised." She paused. "You're not."

He grimaced. "I certainly don't feel all right."

"I'm going to heal you," she told him.

He opened his mouth as if to protest, then closed it again and nodded. "I'd be disappointed in you if you didn't try, at least," he said.

She pulled a face at him, then pulled the fabric of his tunic up to expose his belly. Placing her hands either side of the wound, she closed her eyes and sent her mind forth.

At once she knew the damage was far worse than it appeared from outside. Something had penetrated deep into his abdomen, perforating the tube that snaked and coiled out from the stomach. Liquids had leaked from these into places normally protected from them, and were causing more damage. Blood had filled spaces between organs and was crushing them. Too much blood. He could die of blood loss alone.

For a moment she despaired. How could magic fix this? It was impossible. Jayan was doomed.

No! I can't let him die. I have to try!

Drawing magic, she blocked the openings in the tubes to stop the contents seeping out. Then she gathered up the muck that had escaped and forced it out of his body via the wound. Turning her attention to the blood expanding the cavities it was leaking into, she channelled it out as well. That helped her find the sources of the bleeding, and clamp shut the damaged pulse paths.

What now?

She could feel his body weakening. Remembering how she had sensed the poisoned magician's body using magic to repair itself, she looked for the same process happening within Jayan.

There. I see it. But there is still no way it is going to heal him in time. There is too much damage.

—Help me.

Surprised, Tessia's mind nearly slipped out of his body.

—Jayan? Are you talking to me?

—Tessia? Oh. Sorry. I didn't mean to distract you. I think I was dreaming . . .

He was delirious.

—Hold on, she urged. *Don't give up yet.*

—I'll never give up on you.

Turning her mind back to the damage, she considered it carefully. There must be some way to mimic this healing magic. She tried to send magic into him, but could not shape it into anything but heat or force. Something nagged at her. Jayan's words echoed in her mind. *"Help me."* She would never forgive herself if she could not save him. There must be a way to do what his body was doing. *"Help me."* Or at least speed his body's healing up . . .

Wait . . . Perhaps she didn't need to copy his body, just give it more magic. Boost the healing process with a lot more power. Drawing magic, she sent it in a gentle, unformed flow to mingle with that already flowing from him to the wounded areas of his body. It became part of that flow, was shaped in whatever mysterious way his body shaped it for healing.

That's it!

She had doubled the flow, and saw double the effect. Now she sent greater amounts of power in, and saw the healing increase rapidly. She concentrated on the rents in the tubes and watched them slowly shrink and close. She sent power to the torn pulse paths and felt a rush of triumph as they all but snapped shut. The general damage to his insides from the toxic liquids was more subtle, but soon she could feel a sense of rightness return.

As she channelled power into him she began to feel the way his body used the magic. She understood it in an instinctive way that she could not have explained to another. *Perhaps if I somehow memorise the way this feels and flows, I can apply my own magic to a non-magician and heal them, too.*

Soon the damage within his abdomen was all but gone. She concentrated on the tear in his skin, boosting the magic until flesh drew close to flesh and knitted itself together. But even as she saw the scar tissue form, she knew that he was not completely healed.

He had lost a lot of blood. Delving deeper, she wondered if there was anything she could do to replace it. Healers did not agree on which organ produced blood. But if he rested, ate and drank some water perhaps his body would recover by itself.

—*Tessia?*

—*Yes, Jayan?*

—*I felt that. I felt you healing me. I wasn't imagining it, was I?*

—*No. I've found it. The secret. It's—*

—*Don't tell me.*

—*What? Why not? More people need to know. In case you've*

667

forgotten, we are both still in the middle of a war, stuck on our own in a city of people who want to kill us. If I die this discovery will be lost.

She felt a wave of emotion from him. Fear. Protectiveness. Affection. Longing. All mingled, yet something else.

—*Don't talk about dying,* he told her. *You have to survive this war. I've waited too long and it's almost over.*

—*What are you talking about?*

But she knew even as she asked. She felt it leaking through the cracks of his self-control. Even as she recognised it and felt astonishment, she felt her own body respond in a way that no healer had ever been able to explain in a satisfactory matter. One of the mysteries. One of the more delightful mysteries, her father would have once said. What was the heart for but to pump blood? Why then did it do this other, inexplicable thing?

And why me? Why not some rich woman? Some pretty apprentice?

—*I love you,* he told her.

Sweet joy rushed through her. But there was a distinct smugness about his words. He'd sensed her feelings in return, and was pleased with himself for doing so.

—*Turns out I love you too,* she replied, communicating her wry amusement. *Of all the annoying people in the world.*

—*Poor Tessia,* he mocked.

—*I'm sure as soon as we get back to Imardin you'll be off flirting with rich, pretty girls. Maybe I shouldn't tell you the secret of healing. It'll make you even more appealing to them.*

—*More appealing than I already am?* He didn't pause to let her retort. *Actually, you are right. It would be safer if another person knew.*

So she told him, and when she was sure he had grasped it she withdrew her mind from his body. As she opened her eyes she felt a hand slip behind her neck and draw her down. Jayan rose and pressed his mouth to hers. Surprised, she resisted a moment. Then a shiver ran through her, not cold but warm and wonderful. She kissed him back, liking the way his lips moved against hers, and responding in kind.

I could get to like this.

She almost protested when he let her go. They stared at each other for a moment, then both began to smile. Then Jayan's smile faded again. He pushed himself up onto his elbows and looked down at his bloodied clothes, then grimaced and put a hand to his forehead.

"Dizzy," he said.

"You'll be faint and weak for a while," she told him.

"We can't stay here."

"No," she agreed, standing up. Looking round, she saw that the fire in the house nearby had almost burned itself out. "Let's hide in there until morning. Nobody will bother entering because anything valuable will have been burned, and the walls might fall in. I can protect us with a shield."

"Yes. This is the main road, after all. We can keep watch, and come out when someone we know passes by. It might take a while, but someone is sure to come along eventually. Where's your bag?"

"I don't know. It doesn't matter, though. If I can make this healing work on non-magicians, I won't need cures or tools any more."

He nodded, then rose to his feet in stages, first sitting up, then rising into a squat, then leaning over, and finally straightening. As they started towards the house she felt a wave of tiredness and stumbled. Healing had taken more magic than she'd realised.

"Are you sure you're all right?" Jayan asked.

"Yes. Just tired."

"Well, wait until we get inside before you fall asleep, won't you?"

She gave him a withering look, then let him lead her into the house.

CHAPTER 49

A nagging thirst dragged Jayan out of sleep. He opened his eyes and saw charred walls bathed in morning light. They looked no softer than the surface he was lying against. His body ached. There was a pressure on his arm. He looked down.

Tessia lay curled up against his side, asleep.

His heart lifted and suddenly the hardness of the wall and ground wasn't so unbearable.

I should have waited until the war was over and we were safe, he thought. *But she was there, too close to my mind, and I couldn't hide how I felt.*

Yet he couldn't bring himself to regret anything.

She loves me. Despite all the stupid things I've said. Despite me pushing her away. He realised he hadn't expected her to. That he'd thought that, when they returned to Imardin and he gathered the courage to let her know his feelings, she'd turn him away.

Maybe she would change her mind. When she was famous for discovering healing. When she grew older. She was still young. Seventeen or eighteen? He couldn't remember. When he considered what he had been like at that age – constantly changing his mind – he couldn't delude himself that she would never grow tired of him and find some other person to be interested in.

But she is not like me at that age. She fixes on something and remains true to it — like healing. Perhaps she will be the same with *people. With me. And I wasn't completely incapable of sticking to* *one thing back then. Nothing ever took away my interest in magic,* *or my loyalty to Dakon.*

He reached for the bowl of water she had brought him last night, after disappearing into the burned house for a while, and drank deeply. The water tasted of smoke. He closed his eyes and let time slide past.

After a while something roused him. In the distance the sound of hoofbeats echoed. Several horses, coming closer. Jayan felt his heart skip a beat. He and Tessia had meant to take it in turns to sleep, the other watching for passing Kyralians, but they had both succumbed to exhaustion. He suspected the healing had used a lot of Tessia's power. She had probably needed the sleep as much as he had.

The hoofbeats were growing rapidly louder.

As he shifted, intending to disturb Tessia as little as possible, her eyes flew open. She blinked at him, then frowned.

"Is that horses?"

Instantly awake, she pushed herself to her feet. Jayan rose and they both moved to the broken wall. Peering out, they saw twenty or so Kyralian magicians riding towards them. Jayan looked around, checking for signs that anybody might be watching. The road and nearby houses appeared deserted. He stepped out and waved an arm at the riders.

The magicians slowed to a stop. Jayan smiled as he recognised Lord Bolvin at the front, Lord Tarrakin beside him.

"Any chance of a ride?" he asked.

Bolvin grinned. "Magician Jayan, Apprentice Tessia, it is good to see you both survived. Dakon will be relieved. He came back last night but couldn't find you." He looked over his shoulder. "We're heading to the edge of the city first. You'll have to ride double."

Two magicians came forward and Jayan and Tessia climbed up behind them.

Jayan looked around. "Has anyone seen Mikken?"

"He's back with the army."

Bolvin urged his horse into motion and the rest of the riders followed suit.

The city was quiet, but now and then Jayan noticed someone scurrying away down a side road. They passed the place where Jayan and Tessia had been separated from the army. Soon after, when walls no longer lined the road, and fields surrounded buildings, the group halted. Five of them, including Bolvin, separated from the rest, each accompanied by a servant and an apprentice and leading a riderless horse laden with baggage. Jayan caught enough of the conversation to understand that they were returning to Imardin. At first he assumed it was to deliver news of the victory, but then he realised that the news would already have reached Kyralia via the blood gem rings.

The thought sent a shiver of excitement down his back. *I wish we were going with them.* He realised he was tired of war. *I want to be home, wherever that is now, with Tessia. I want to start a magicians' guild and help Tessia develop magical healing.*

As Bolvin and his companions rode into the distance, Lord Tarrakin turned his horse around.

"They're on their own now," he said. "The king said we should return as quickly as possible."

The remaining magicians turned and headed back into the city. Soon they were riding through parts of Arvice Jayan hadn't seen yet. He admired the tree-lined avenue leading up to the Imperial Palace. The palace was, surprisingly, undamaged. Servants came out to take the horses. Jayan dismounted, relieved to no longer be riding on the uncomfortable edge of the saddle.

Moving to Tessia's side, he followed the magicians into the palace. Just like the Sachakan-built houses in Imardin, a corridor led to a large room for meeting and entertaining guests. But the corridor was wide enough to ride ten horses through, and the room was an enormous column-lined hall. Voices echoed inside.

"We can't abolish slavery entirely," a voice declared. "We must do it in stages. Start with personal servants. Leave the slaves that produce food and do the least pleasant work to last, or else Sachaka will starve while drowning in its own refuse."

Narvelan, Jayan thought, a familiar chill running down his spine. *Why doesn't it surprise me that he wants to keep slavery going?* Yet he couldn't help agreeing with the magician. Freeing all slaves at once would cause chaos.

As Jayan neared the end of the room he saw that several magicians were sitting in a circle. The king wasn't using the enormous gilt throne in the middle of the room, Jayan noted, though the chair he was sitting on was large and had a back and arms, while the rest were backless stools. Beyond them, other magicians were standing around the room, some listening to the discussion, others talking.

One of the magicians began to rise from his seat, then glanced at the king and sat down again. Dakon. Jayan smiled at his former master's relieved expression.

"We must also keep the populace here weak," Narvelan continued. "But not so that we are weakened along with them. Freeing the personal slaves means that the remaining magicians will have to pay the people who serve them."

Jayan saw the king nod, then look up at the newcomers. "Lord Tarrakin. Have Lord Bolvin and the others left?"

"Yes. We also found Magician Jayan and Apprentice Tessia."

The king looked at Tessia, then Jayan. "I am glad to hear you both survived the night." He frowned and looked from Tessia to Dakon. "Since you have agreed to stay and help rule Sachaka, will your apprentice be staying with you?"

Jayan drew in a quick breath. *Dakon is staying? Surely not! He has a village to rebuild, and a ley to run.*

But he found he could easily believe Dakon would choose to stay and help the Sachakans. Perhaps in order to redress the harm the army had done.

And Tessia will have to stay with him . . .

"I have been considering that," Dakon said. "If Tessia does not want to stay here she is free to go."

"I couldn't leave you, Lord Dakon," she said.

The king turned to regard her. "You have a gift, Apprentice Tessia. A gift of healing that you might teach others. If I asked you to return to Imardin with me, would you agree?"

She bit her lip. She glanced at him, then at Dakon.

"Who . . . who will take over my apprenticeship?"

Jayan felt his heart skip. Could he . . . ?

"I will."

All turned to see Lady Avaria stride towards the circle from the side of the room.

"Dakon mentioned that he was considering staying," she explained. "I thought of Tessia, and how she might not want to remain here, and that perhaps it is time I took on an apprentice of my own." She looked at Tessia and smiled. "I can't hope to match Lord Dakon's experience, but I promise to do my best."

All eyes shifted to Tessia. She looked at Avaria, then at Dakon, then at Jayan, then turned to face the king.

"If Lord Dakon wishes it, I would be honoured to be Lady Avaria's apprentice."

Dakon smiled. "Though I would like to finish your training,

Tessia, I think it is more important that your knowledge of assisting healing with magic be shared with others."

The king smiled broadly and slapped his thighs. "Excellent!" He then turned to Jayan. "What are your plans now, Magician Jayan?"

"I will return to Imardin," Jayan replied. "And, if you approve, begin work on forming a guild of magicians."

The king smiled. "Ah. The magicians' guild. Lord Hakkin is exploring this guild idea as well." He nodded. "You may join him in the endeavour. Now." He looked around the circle. "Who is going to stay and help Lord Narvelan and Lord Dakon rule Sachaka?"

A shock of cold rushed through Jayan. *Lord Narvelan? Rule Sachaka? Is King Errik mad?* He turned his attention to Narvelan. The young magician wore a smile, but it looked fixed and strange. It didn't match the intensity of his gaze. As something distracted him – a slave tugging at his arm – a savage anger crossed his face, to be quickly smothered behind the smile again.

Jayan heard Tessia catch her breath.

"Hanara," she breathed. "It's Takado's slave!"

Looking closer, Jayan realised that the slave now prostrating himself before Narvelan was the man Takado had left in Mandryn. Whom Lord Dakon had freed. Who had betrayed the village to Takado.

"I told you, no throwing yourself on the floor," Narvelan said to Hanara, as the conversation of the magicians continued. "No wonder you get so dirty so quickly."

"Yes, master," Hanara replied.

"Hanara is Narvelan's slave?" Tessia choked out.

"Yes," Lord Tarrakin said. "Though apparently he's told the man he is free now, but he won't pay attention."

Tessia shook her head. She glanced at Jayan, then as Hanara

676

hurried away to do Narvelan's bidding she strode forward to intercept him. Jayan followed. She caught up with the slave near the side wall of the room. When Hanara saw her, his eyes widened and he froze.

"Tessia," he whispered. Jayan could not decide if his expression was one of horror or amazement.

"Hanara," she said. Then she said nothing, her mouth slightly open and her eyes suddenly tortured.

Hanara dropped his gaze.

"I am sorry," he said. "I couldn't do anything. I thought if I went to him he might leave. But I also knew he'd learn from me that Lord Dakon wasn't there. But . . . he would have worked that out anyway. I . . . I am . . . I am glad you were gone."

The slave's babble was about Mandryn, Jayan suspected. *I ought to want to throttle him, but for some reason I don't. The magician who had dominated his life had returned. I don't think anyone could have acted out of anything but fear at that moment. And now he's serving Narvelan. I'm not sure whether to think of it as a punishment he deserves, or to pity him. Or to worry at the combination of an invader's former slave and a ruthless, mad magician.*

"I forgive you," Tessia said. Jayan looked at her in surprise. She looked relieved and thoughtful. "You're free now, Hanara. You don't have to serve anyone you don't want to. Don't . . . don't punish yourself for your master's crimes."

The slave shook his head, then looked around furtively, bent close and whispered: "I serve him to stay alive. If I didn't, I would not live long." He straightened. "You go home. Get married. Have children. Live a long life."

Then he hurried past them and disappeared through a doorway. Tessia turned to look at Jayan, then let out a short laugh.

"I suspect I've just been given orders by a slave."

"Advice," Jayan corrected. He moved through the same doorway, glanced up and down the empty corridor, then shrugged. "Good advice. Add teaching magicians to heal to it. And helping me set up the guild." He shook his head. "I'm going to have to work with Lord Hakkin. I'm going to need all the help I can get."

"Yes," she agreed as they started walking along the corridor. "I noticed you didn't mention to the king that I'd worked out how to heal with magic."

"No. It didn't seem the right time. And now that I think of it . . . I'd rather the teaching of healing didn't begin in Sachaka. It should start in Kyralia, and be part of our new guild."

"Incentive for magicians to join?"

"Exactly."

Her eyes narrowed. "You know, for a moment there I was worried you were going to offer to take on my apprenticeship."

He blinked in surprised. "Worried? Why? Don't you think I'd be a good teacher?"

"A reasonable teacher," she replied. "But I suspect Kyralian society would frown upon a master and his apprentice being . . . well . . . romantically entangled."

He smiled. "Depends how entangled you want to be."

Her eyelids lowered and she regarded him in a way that made his pulse speed up. "*Very* entangled."

"I see." He looked up and down the corridor. It was still empty. Reaching out, he drew her close and kissed her. She tensed, then relaxed and he felt her body press against his.

Footsteps suddenly echoed in the corridor and he felt someone brush past him. Belatedly, he and Tessia sprang apart.

"I'm going to have to keep an eye on the two of you, aren't I?" Lady Avaria said, not looking back as she strode away.

Tessia smothered a giggle, and then her expression grew serious.

"Where are you going to live?"

"I don't know." Jayan groaned. "Not with my father!"

"Well, we have plenty of time to work these things out," she said.

"Yes. And plenty to sort out here, first. Like eating. I'm starving. Though I suppose we should find Mikken first."

She nodded. "That's what we'll do next. We'll do what's needed, one thing at a time, until there's nothing left to do and we're old and grey and we can leave it to someone else to fix."

He reached out and took her arm. "Come on. The sooner we start, the sooner we get to the good parts."

CHAPTER 50

Stopping to catch her breath, Stara looked up at the steep slope of rock before her. Like the one she and the women who followed her had just climbed, there were angled creases in the surface that a climber could shuffle along to get to the top. This slope was larger than the previous one, though. It ended at a jagged crest some way above her. Beyond that she could see the top of another sheer wall of stone, and another behind it. Past them, the peaks of the mountains loomed over all with cruel indifference.

Chavori was a tougher man than he looked, she thought for the hundredth time. *He must have climbed all over these slopes to take his measurements. And he must have had assistance. Definitely slaves. Possibly also other magicians or free men. We'll have to keep watch, in case any ever return.*

As the other four women caught up, panting and gasping, Stara decided they could all do with a rest. She shrugged her pack off her shoulders. Strapped to it was a tube made of a hollow reed – much lighter than Chavori's metal tubes. She unstoppered it and drew out the map.

Spreading it out over the flat rock face before her, Stara held the corners down with magic. The women crowded close to examine it. She could smell their sweat. Only the fittest of them had joined her for this exploration, after it became clear what the path to the valley demanded. She'd left the others in Vora's capable hands at a camp further down the mountain.

One of the women, Shadiya, pointed to the zigzag path they were following.

"I think we're nearly there."

Stara nodded in agreement, then rolled up the map and stowed it away. "Let's have a drink and a bite to eat first."

The women were quiet as they rested. With backs to the rock wall, they gazed out at the Sachakan plains, stretching into the haze of the distance. Stara stared at the horizon. Somewhere beyond it was Arvice. After two months, how had the city fared under the rule of the Kyralians? Was Kachiro still alive? She felt a weak pang of sadness and regret, then a vague guilt for not feeling more. *I would if I wasn't so tired,* she told herself, though she knew it wasn't true. *It wasn't as if we married for love. But I did like him and hope he survives.* She wondered if he'd received news of her mother. *I'll have to send my own messenger, once we're settled. Perhaps she can come and live with us.*

All the women ate sparingly, not having to be reminded how low their supplies were. Stara had been able to supplement their meals by catching birds with magic, but the vegetation that grew in this harsh place was sparse and inedible. She was beginning to worry that Chavori had exaggerated when he'd described the valley they were heading for.

Rising, she hauled her pack onto her back. The others followed suit. Without speaking a word, they sought the start of one of the long creases in the slope, then began to shuffle along it, Stara in the lead.

After a seemingly endless stretch of time, she finally reached the top of the ridge. Dragging herself over the edge, she crawled forward, relieved to have the weight of the pack off her shoulders. She paused to catch her breath, then realised the air she was sucking in wasn't the dry air that had parched their throats these last weeks. It tasted of damp and mould. Her heart skipped a beat and she pushed herself up and onto her knees.

The next wall was a few strides away. At the base of one of the creases in it was a dark triangle. A gap. She moved closer. From inside came the sound of water, and a gust of damp air.

The entrance was low – she would have to crawl to enter it. Hearing a sound behind her, she restrained her curiosity and moved back to the edge to watch over the next two women as they climbed up to join her. As they reached the top, their eyes went immediately to the opening.

"Sounds like a river inside."

"Shall we go in?"

"No. Wait until we've all made it up," Stara said.

Finally the last of the women had been helped up over the edge. They stood back and waited to see what Stara would do. She smiled and dropped to the ground like a slave, then crawled through the opening, sending a globe of light ahead of her.

The roof was low for several strides, then it and the floor curved away. She slid forward, then pushed herself up into a crouch. Her light failed to penetrate far in two directions, and from the way the sound of her movements echoed she guessed she was in a tunnel. It was like being inside a long, squashed tube, wider than it was high and on an angle that matched the creases in the rock walls. Along the bottom water rushed.

"Chavori said he thought this was recent, caused by the river changing course upstream," Stara told them. "So let's go upstream."

A few hundred strides later they saw light ahead, then

after a few hundred more they stood at the opening of the tunnel. The stream sparkled blue and white. Along its sides grasses stood almost as high as a man, but further from the water were low and dry. A few squat, ancient trees enjoyed a more sheltered position near the steep walls of the valley.

"What do you think?" Stara asked.

"Not quite what I expected," Shadiya replied. "But we were hardly going to find cultivated fields, were we?"

"It needs the worst weeds removed. Then a few reber to get the grass down. Then water channels. Then we have to sweeten the soil before we can plant crops." Stara turned to look at the speaker, Ichiva, impressed at her knowledge of farming. The woman shrugged. "When you're not allowed to talk around men, you do a lot of listening."

The others nodded in agreement.

"Yes, it needs a lot of work," Stara said. "And it will be interesting getting reber up here. And then there's the building of houses to do. We have much to learn. Shall we explore further?"

They smiled at her and nodded. Splitting up, they roamed in different directions. Stara headed out into the valley, examining the soil and wishing she knew enough to tell if it was fertile. The trees proved to be a lot larger than they appeared from a distance. Looking up into the branches, she found herself imagining children climbing along them.

Children. If we want them we can't ban men from our lives completely. Perhaps we can avoid bringing them here, though. Those who want to can visit a town down on the plains and spend the night with someone they fancy.

But what of male children? There was no way any woman was going to agree to send her child away. She shook her head. Perhaps it didn't matter so much that the Sanctuary was free of men, only that women controlled it.

"Stara!"

She turned to see Ichiva waving to her. The woman turned to point at the wall of the valley. Stara searched the rock surface, frowning as she tried to find what Ichiva was drawing her attention to.

Then suddenly she saw it. And it sent chills down her spine.

The wall of the valley was not natural. Not only could she see where the original slope abruptly changed to a man-made wall, but she could see the lines and curves of deliberate human carving all over the face.

With heart pounding, she hurried forward. The carvings had deteriorated badly, and in places sections had fallen away completely. Whoever had made this had done it many, many years ago. Hundreds. Perhaps thousands.

She felt a rush of excitement. Clearly, if someone had lived here once, others could do so again. The arches and lines looked like highly decorated frames of doorways and windows. Perhaps the ancient occupants had lived within the wall, in caves. As she reached Ichiva she saw that she was right. There was a rectangular hole in the wall. She shared an excited grin with the other woman.

"I don't think we're the first to take up residence," she said. "Get the others. I'm going inside."

Creating another globe light, Stara stepped through the doorway. Inside was a long corridor, and she could see light coming through the vegetation that covered other doors and windows. Roots splayed and wove together in tangles for the first few strides, but after that all was bare stone. Wide openings on the far wall beckoned her further inside.

She chose the closest. It was a wide corridor with rooms on either side. The walls between were almost as thick as the spaces. In places they were wet from seepage, but most were dry. Hearing footsteps, she waited for the women to catch up with her, then they all went on. After passing six rooms the corridor ended.

Returning to the main corridor, they continued exploring. One of them noticed shallow carvings of people and animals on some walls. Most rooms had one or two, but then they discovered a wide corridor covered in them. It led to an enormous cave. A crack in the roof high above them let in a weak stream of light and straggling roots. It had also obviously let in the rain, as there was a pool in the centre of the cave. Behind this was a raised section of floor, and on it a crumbling slab of stone.

They skirted the pool and climbed up on the dais to examine the slab. On the surface was the faint outline of a human shape, surrounded by lines radiating out from the chest area.

Shadiya peered closer. "What do you reckon that's about? Is it a coffin cover? Or an altar for human sacrifice?"

Stara shuddered. "Who knows?"

"There's another doorway behind here," Ichiva said, pointing to the wall behind the dais. Then she looked to one side. "Do you think that was the door?"

They all stopped to look at a great disc of stone, split in two, that lay in front of the opening. There was a deep groove in the floor before the doorway. It was as wide as the disc, Stara noted.

"Perhaps it was rolled into place, and out again," she said.

The women hummed in speculation, then turned to examine the opening. Stara directed her globe light inside. A narrow corridor continued into darkness. She stepped inside.

Before too long the corridor split into two, then again. Stara slowed. "This is becoming a bit of a maze. We should mark our way."

They traced their steps back, then scraped an arrow symbol on a wall at each intersection pointing back the way they'd come.

"We'd best stay together, too," Stara said. "Don't stray. Don't let anybody fall behind."

"Not likely," one of them replied nervously, and the others laughed in agreement.

Going on, slowed by the need to mark the way, they explored the maze of passages. Some led to small rooms, some to dead ends. Then abruptly the corridor changed from smooth, carved stone to rough natural rock. It continued for several strides, then opened up into another cave.

The surface of this cave glittered, drawing gasps of amazement and appreciation from the women. Stara moved closer to the wall. There were crystalline shapes all over the surface. In some areas they were the size of her fist, in others as small as her fingernail.

"These look a bit like the gemstones the Duna sell us," Ichiva observed. "Do you think they're magical?"

"Magical or not, they are worth a fortune," Stara replied. She straightened and looked at them all. "So long as we are careful, we can trade them for anything we can't make or grow ourselves."

They were all smiling and hopeful now. For a while they lingered, touching the gemstones and competing to find the largest. But hours had passed since their previous snack and hunger drew them out again. Following the markings, Stara was relieved when she had them safely returned to the first cave. They sat on the edge of the dais and unpacked some food. Stara chewed on one of the dry buns, laced with seeds and nuts, that Vora had cooked for them.

"I think there's another doorway next to that," Shadiya

said, pointing to the left of the opening to the maze. "See the lines in the wall?"

Putting aside her bun, Stara rose and moved closer. Shadiya was right. There was a door-shaped groove in the wall.

"I wonder how you open it," Shadiya said, coming closer. "There's no handle or keyhole."

"That suggests magic, doesn't it?" Stara said. She stood before the door and drew power, then sent it out and into the cracks. It wrapped around the back with no resistance, so she knew there was a hollow beyond. Probing further, she sensed that there was a hollow above the door. It curved up and to one side, so the door would rest on its side within the cavity.

Exerting her will, she lifted the door. It scraped loudly as it rose and slid sideways at her direction, then settled into place.

The women crowded around the opening Stara had exposed.

Faint walls were visible. Stara sent her globe light inside and all gasped. Every surface of the room within, apart from the floor, was carved. And unlike the rest of the carvings they'd seen, these had been painted in vivid colours.

Stara moved inside. She stared at the scenes depicted. Painted people carved stones from cave walls. The stones were brightly coloured and lines radiated from them. One man, always dressed in white, appeared in several of the scenes. He tended to the gemstones as they grew, before they were cut, and they were given to him afterwards. He also gave them out to others. In all depictions he wore a single blue stone on a chain around his chest, radiating lines.

On another wall a man tied with ropes was presented to this white-dressed man. He was bound to a rectangle marked the same way as the slab in the big cave. The white-dressed man then held the blue stone against his chest. In the next scene the victim was dragged away, clearly dead, and the white man radiated power.

"I was right about the human sacrifice," Shadiya murmured.

Beneath all the scenes were lines of markings. Some sort of ancient writing. *Do they explain what is going on?* Stara wondered. *Clearly these gemstones have magical properties. Like the stones the Duna make. I wonder . . . would the Duna be able to read this?* She would have to have some phrases copied and taken to them.

Moving out of the room, Stara returned to her pack and her abandoned meal. She watched the women return one by one, all looking awed and giving the slab a sober second look. She listened to their chatter and thought about all they had discovered.

The valley needed a lot of work before it would be habitable, and even more before the women could live here, entirely self-sufficient. But they had wealth now, in the form of the gemstones. From what she could tell from the paintings, the stones needed special tending as they grew to become magical. Those on the walls now could be sold by the Traitors without any risk of putting anything dangerous in the hands of the Kyralians or Sachakans.

She paused. *Already I'm thinking of Sachakans as people other than us. We are going to become a new people. Perhaps a small people, like the Duna, but not as primitive. Will we still call ourselves the Traitors?*

She nodded to herself. *Yes. We should. We must not forget why we came here. Not because of the war, but because as women we were invisible, undervalued and powerless. Sachakan society put us in a place little better than a slave's. Now we have found a new place, where we make the decisions, where nobody is a slave and all work for the good of everyone. I doubt it's going to be easy, or that we won't make mistakes, or perhaps even fail in the end. It'll probably take more than a lifetime. But this is more exciting than running Father's trade. It isn't just an escape for me, Vora, Nachira and my friends. If it works, it'll help many, many women in the years to come.*

And that's something I'm willing to dedicate a lifetime to.

EPILOGUE

Hanara ran a hand through his hair and sighed. He could feel dirt and sweat, and the wiriness of grey hairs. The pack he carried was heavy and made his joints ache. His breath came in gasps.

The man ahead of him stopped and looked back. The crazed, hard look on Lord Narvelan's face softened.

"Take your time, old friend," he said. "We're both not as young as we used to be."

Only thirty or so, Hanara thought. But like many slaves he had aged faster than free men. *Except I haven't been a slave for ten years. I've been a servant. Not that there's been much difference.*

He could have left Narvelan and sought work in another household, but who would have given it to him? Who would want the Betrayer's slave? Nobody. No, he was stuck with Lord Narvelan. The Crazy Emperor, as the palace servants called him. Crazy, but clever.

Narvelan had all but ruled Sachaka for most of the past decade. Though he was supposed to come to a consensus with two other magicians for all decisions, nearly all the Kyralians who had taken the roles of co-rulers hadn't been smart or determined enough to oppose Narvelan. Lord Dakon had prevailed for a while, until he was assassinated, his body drained of energy but not a cut or scratch on him. Only Lord Bolvin, who had taken up the role most recently, had ever managed to successfully stand up to the Crazy Emperor.

When Narvelan's plan to remove the children of Sachakan magicians and have them raised by Kyralian families was thwarted by Bolvin, Hanara's master had become angry and paranoid. He'd refused to attend meetings for three months, only coming back when decisions began to be made in his absence.

Things had gone downhill from there, with fighting between the magicians and appeals sent to the king. Finally, a week ago, a message had arrived from the king "retiring" Narvelan from his position. A day later, Narvelan had ordered Hanara to pack for a journey. They would be travelling on foot.

Far ahead, Narvelan had stopped. Hanara guessed his master had reached the top of the hill. He trudged on, forcing his aching legs to carry him up. When he finally reached the crest, Narvelan was sitting, cross-legged, on the stony ground.

"Put your pack down," Narvelan said. "Have a drink. And some food."

Obeying, Hanara watched his master gazing about. The hill lay at the end of the plains, where the endmost roots of the mountains rippled the ground. They had come more than half the distance to the border, but probably only half the journey time if the slower travel rates on the steep roads nearer the mountains were taken into account.

Are we going to Kyralia? Hanara wondered. *Is Narvelan hoping to talk the king around?* They weren't headed for the pass, though. He looked at his master, but remained silent.

Narvelan glanced at him. "You're wondering where we're going," he stated.

Hanara said nothing. He'd learned that asking questions was pointless when his master was in this mood. The man would hear the question he expected, not the one that Hanara voiced.

"Ten years," Narvelan said. "Ten years I've worked, every

691

day and most nights, to keep this country in Kyralian control. Ten years I've strived to keep our ancient enemy weak, to prevent an invasion happening again."

He looked back towards Arvice, which was far beyond the horizon now. His eyes were afire with anger.

"I could have gone home, married and had a family. But then, would I have enjoyed the peace and safety that everyone else has because of me? Without my work here, Sachaka would have recovered, grown powerful, then attacked us again. No. I had to sacrifice a normal life so that others would have one.

"And did I get any thanks?" Narvelan stared at Hanara, then looked away. "No! Not once! And now they're undoing everything I did! All my work, all my sacrifices, for *nothing*. They're going to free the farm slaves. Let Sachakan magicians marry and breed more invaders. They're going to let them come here," he swept his arm out to indicate the area, "and start farming again. Letting this land grow wild was intended to reduce the food the Sachakans could grow, keeping their population small and manageable. It was to be an extra layer of protection between Kyralia and Sachaka. It was my great idea. My *vision*!"

Hanara looked down at the local farmhouses and fields. Though they were supposed to be abandoned, he could see signs of cultivation and occupation. Narvelan's vision had only led to bandits and Ichani taking up residence. *We're lucky we haven't been attacked*, he thought, then pushed the thought away. Narvelan was powerful. He'd had several servants as source slaves. He was strong enough to fight off Ichani, who had only one or two slaves to take from.

"I don't blame the king for retiring me," Narvelan said, his voice laced with sadness and regret. Hanara looked at him in surprise. "I shouldn't have stopped attending meetings. If I'd been reasonable, he'd have had no good reason to get rid of me."

He frowned. "They made me angry because they wanted to undermine the plans I'd worked on for so long. I didn't realise that there was a way to make them happen anyway. A faster way. I hadn't thought of it yet. If I'd thought of it earlier . . . maybe they'd have agreed with me. If what I planned hadn't been so difficult."

Narvelan's gaze was distant. He fell silent and stared towards Arvice for a long time. Brooding. Then abruptly his attention snapped back to his surroundings. He drew in a deep breath and sighed, then smiled and slowly turned to look at the plains, the hills, the mountains, and then the hill they were sitting on.

"This is a good place. I don't know how far its power will reach, but how far it does will have to be good enough." He looked at Hanara.

Hanara shrugged. Narvelan often said unfathomable things, especially when he was having one of these one-sided conversations. He watched as his master reached into his pack and dug around.

"Where is it? I know it's here somewhere. Ah!"

He drew out his arm. His fist was clenched around something. Looking around, Narvelan fixed his gaze on a large, flat rock. It slid towards him, settling before his crossed legs. Then he picked up a smaller rock and hefted it, testing its weight.

"That should do the trick."

He opened his fist and, with a musical clink, a bright, glittering object landed on the flat rock. Hanara felt his heart stop.

It was the storestone. The one the Elynes had left with the Kyralians, in case they ever faced conflict with Sachakans again. Narvelan must have stolen it. The other magicians certainly wouldn't have approved of his taking it.

Narvelan looked up at Hanara, and a look of realisation crossed his face.

"Oh. I'm sorry, Hanara. I hadn't thought what to do about you. Guess we're in this together."

Hanara opened his mouth to ask why.

Then Narvelan's arm rose and fell. The rock hit the storestone. A crack appeared. Hanara had a moment to wonder why the crack was blindingly white.

Then all sensation and thought ceased.

The path was narrow and steep. It twisted and turned around the precipitous side of the mountain, climbing and descending in order to pass enormous boulders, or wide cracks in the ground. Hunters had advised Jayan and Prinan that the way was too difficult for horses, and though they wished they could declare it unpassable for humans, the truth was it was merely hard work.

Jayan sent healing magic to his legs and felt the ache fade. He'd needed to do this less and less often over the last few days. *I might actually be getting fitter*, he mused. Looking back, he saw that the dust that covered Prinan's clothes, skin and hair was only broken by darker patches of sweat under his arms and on his chest and back. *And I look just as bad*, he mused. *I doubt anybody at the Guild would recognise us, and if they did they'd gain much amusement.*

Prinan looked up and grinned. "I wish Tessia could see you now. She'd have a good laugh."

"I'm sure she would," Jayan agreed. He felt a pang of affection for her, followed by an equally strong pang of anxiety. *She'll be fine*, he told himself yet again. *She's still the best healer in the Guild. Of all the women in Kyralia — or the world — she has the best chance of surviving birthing a baby.*

But she'd not had a child before.

Yes, but she's assisted in the birth of plenty. She knows what to expect.

Maybe they'd waited too long.

But there had been so much work to do first. Developing healing and teaching it to others. Getting the Guild established and sorting out all the problems. And magicians certainly have a talent for creating problems . . .

The path rose and turned round a ridge before him. To stop yet another endless argument in his head, he set his mind on navigating it. He scrambled up, grasping at protruding rocks for extra leverage. His calves protested. His thighs strained. Then at last he'd reached the top. He sat on the ground, gasping for breath. Then he looked up and felt his entire body go rigid with cold.

For many heartbeats, all he could do was stare.

What had been green, fertile land ten years ago was now a blackened, scoured desert. From the foot of the mountains to the horizon stretched nothing but bare, blasted earth. His skin prickled as he realised he could make out lines radiating from somewhere to the north. Lines that were made up of gouges in the land, or the flattened trunks of trees. He barely registered the sound of Prinan reaching the top of the ridge and stopping beside him.

"Ah," Prinan said. "The wasteland. No matter how many times I see it, I can't get used to the sight."

"I can see why." Jayan glanced up at the magician. "The magicians who investigated still think it was the storestone?"

"We know of nothing else that might have caused so much destruction."

"And Narvelan did it?"

"He disappeared a few days before, the same time the stone was stolen. And he'd been trying to convince us that we should weaken Sachaka by spoiling the land."

"But we'll never know for sure if that was what happened."

"No." Prinan sighed. "And the last chance of working out how to make storestones is gone."

Jayan drew in a deep breath, then rose. "Well, if that's what storestones can do, maybe it's better that nobody found out."

Prinan shook his head in disagreement, but did not argue. "So, do you think we need to build another fort here?"

Turning to look back down the path, Jayan considered. "I will have to think about it. This pass is by no means easy or fast to traverse. The fort in the main pass will only ever slow the advance of an army, not block it. If we cause a few land slips and carve away the path in a few places, this pass may not need anything more than watching."

Prinan frowned, then nodded. "I suppose you are right. Though Father will feel we are being foolishly neglectful not building a big stone fort to block the way."

"I understand," Jayan assured him. "But surely if he has seen this," Jayan waved a hand at the wasteland below, "he knows there is little chance of another invasion from Sachaka."

Prinan nodded. "Narvelan may have been mad, but I suspect he was correct in his belief that destroying the Sachakans' land would weaken the people. What Father fears is retribution. It would only take a few Sachakan magicans to cause havoc in Kyralia."

"Then I will recommend we post a watcher on the Kyralian side."

"I guess that's the best we can do," Prinan said. He sighed, then looked over his shoulder. "And there's not much point us continuing on into Sachaka. Shall we head back?"

Jayan smiled and nodded. "Yes." *Back to Tessia. Back to await the birth of our son.* Then he grimaced. *And back to the never-ending work and arguments of the Magicians' Guild.*

GLOSSARY

ANIMALS

aga moths – pests that eat
   clothing

anyi – sea mammals with short
   spines

ceryni – small rodent

enka – horned domestic animal,
   bred for meat

eyoma – sea leeches

faren – general term for arachnids

gorin – large domestic animal
   used for food and to haul boats
   and wagons

harrel – small domestic animal
   bred for meat

inava – insect believed to bestow
   good luck

limek – wild predatory dog

mullook – wild nocturnal bird

quannea – rare shells

rassook – domestic bird used for
   meat and feathers

ravi – rodent, larger than ceryni

reber – domestic animal, bred for
   wool and meat

sapfly – woodland insect

sevli – poisonous lizard

squimp – squirrel-like creature
   that steals food

yeel – small domesticated breed
   of limek used for tracking

zill – small, intelligent mammal
   sometimes kept as a pet

PLANTS/FOOD

anivope vine – plant sensitive to
   mental projection

bellspice – spice grown in
   Sachaka

bol – (also means "river scum")
   strong liquor made from tugors

brasi – green leafy vegetable with
   small buds

briskbark – bark with decongestant
   properties

cabbas – hollow, bell-shaped
   vegetable

chebol sauce – rich meat sauce
   made from bol

cone cakes – bite-sized cakes

creamflower – flower used as a
   soporific

crots – large, purple beans

curem – smooth, nutty spice

curren – coarse grain with robust
   flavour

dall – long fruit with tart orange,
   seedy flesh

dunda – root chewed as a
stimulating drug
gan-gan – flowering bush from
Lan
husroot – herb used for cleansing
wounds
iker – stimulating drug, reputed
to have aphrodisiac properties
jerras – long yellow beans
kreppa – foul-smelling medicinal
herb
marin – red citrus fruit
monyo – bulb
myk – mind-affecting drug
nalar – pungent root
nemmin – sleep-inducing drug
nightwood – hardwood timber
pachi – crisp, sweet fruit
papea – pepper-like spice
piorres – small, bell-shaped fruit
raka/suka – stimulating drink
made from roasted beans,
originally from Sachaka
shem – edible reed-like plant
sumi – bitter drink
sweetdrops – candies
telk – seed from which an oil is
extracted
tenn – grain that can be cooked
as is, broken into small
pieces, or ground to make a
flour
tiro – edible nuts
tugor – parsnip-like root
ukkas – carnivorous plants
vare – berries from which most
wine is produced

whitewater – pure spirits made
from tugors
yellowseed – crop grown in
Sachaka

CLOTHING AND WEAPONRY

incal – square symbol, not unlike
a family shield, sewn onto
sleeve or cuff
quan – tiny disc-shaped beads
made of shell
undershift – Kyralian women's
undergarment
vyer – stringed instrument from
Elyne

COUNTRIES/PEOPLES IN THE REGION

Duna – tribes who live in
volcanic desert north of
Sachaka
Elyne – neighbour to Kyralia and
Sachaka and once ruled by
Sachaka
Kyralia – neighbour to Elyne and
Sachaka and once ruled by
Sachaka
Lan – a mountainous land
peopled by warrior tribes
Lonmar – a desert land home to
the strict Mahga religion
Sachaka – home of the once
great Sachakan Empire, where
all but the most powerful are
slaves

Vin – an island nation known for their seamanship

TITLES/POSITIONS

Apprentice – Kyralian magician under training, and who has not been taught higher magic yet

Ashaki – Sachakan landowner

Ichani – Sachakan free man or woman who has been declared outcast

Lady – wife of a Kyralian landowner

Lord – Kyralian landowner, either of a ley or a city House, or their heir

Magician – Kyralian higher magician ("Lord" used instead if magician is a landowner)

Master – free Sachakan

Village/Town Master – commoner in charge of a rural community (answers to the ley's lord)

OTHER TERMS

the approach – main corridor to the master's room in Sachakan houses

blood gem – artificial gemstone that allows maker to hear the thoughts of wearer

earthblood – term the Duna tribes use for lava

kyrima – a game played by magicians to teach and practise strategic skills in battle

master's room – main room in Sachakan houses for greeting guests

slavehouse – part of Sachakan homes where the slaves live and work

slavespot – sexually transmitted disease

storestone – gemstone that can store magic

ACKNOWLEDGEMENTS

The first half of this book was written during a very stressful and frustrating year, then the second half, rewrites and polishing in a tight six months. So I would like to thank Darren Nash and the team at Orbit for their understanding and patience, and Darren and Tim's sympathetic ears when I poured out the whole house-extension saga on their visit to Melbourne.

I also want to thank Fran Bryson, my agent, and her assistant, Liz Kemp, for their support and great work, and the agents all over the world who bring my books to readers who speak languages other than my own. Another thank you also goes to Phillip Berrie, who I hired to do a professional consistency check on the manuscript, that was well worth the investment.

Thanks to my partner, Paul, who read the book, chapter by chapter, over the course of a year and a bit and kept encouraging me to write more, even though he was as demoralised over the house saga as I.

And to my friends and family, who provided valuable feedback on part or all of the book: Mum and Dad, Donna Hanson, Fiona McLennan and Kylie Seluka.

Lastly, but always most fondly, thank you to all the readers of my books who have sent lovely emails, left enthusiastic messages on my website's guestbook, and recommended or given my books to friends and family. You make my day.

extras

about the author

Trudi Canavan published her first story in 1999 and it received an Aurealis Award for Best Fantasy Short Story. Her debut series, the Black Magician trilogy, made her an international success, and all three volumes of her Age of the Five trilogy were *Sunday Times* bestsellers. Trudi Canavan lives with her partner in Melbourne, Australia, and spends her time knitting, painting and writing bestselling fantasy novels.

Find out more about Trudi Canavan and other Orbit authors by registering for the free monthly newsletter at www.orbit-books.net

look out for book one of the Traitor Spy trilogy

THE AMBASSADOR'S MISSION

the exciting new sequel series to the
Black Magician trilogy

by

Trudi Canavan

CHAPTER ONE

The Old and The New

The most successful and quoted piece by the poet Rewin, greatest of the rabble to come out of the New City, was called *Citysong*. It captured what was heard at night in Imardin, if you took the time to stop and listen: an unending muffled and distant combination of sounds. Voices. Singing. A laugh. A groan. A gasp. A scream.

In the darkness of Imardin's New South Quarter a man remembered the poem. He stopped to listen, but instead of absorbing the city's song he concentrated on one discordant echo. A sound that didn't belong. A sound that didn't repeat. He snorted quietly and continued on.

A few steps later a figure emerged from the shadows before him. The figure was male and loomed over him menacingly. Light caught the edge of a blade.

"Yer money," a rough voice said, hard with determination.

The man said nothing and remained still. He might have appeared frozen in terror. He might have appeared deep in thought.

When he did move, it was with uncanny speed. A click,

a snap of sleeve, and the robber gasped and sank to his knees. A knife clattered on the ground. The man patted him on the shoulder.

"Sorry. Wrong night, wrong target, and I don't have time to explain why."

As the robber fell, face-down, on the pavement, the man stepped over him and walked on. Then he paused and looked over his shoulder, to the other side of the street.

"Hai! Gol. You're supposed to be my bodyguard."

From the shadows another large figure emerged and hurried to the man's side.

"Reckon you don't have much need for one, Cery. I'm getting slow in my old age. I should be payin' *you* to protect *me*."

Cery scowled. "Your eyes and ears are still sharp, aren't they?"

Gol winced. "As sharp as yours," he retorted sullenly.

"Too true." Cery sighed. "I should retire. But Thieves don't get to retire."

"Except by not being Thieves any more."

"Except by becoming corpses," Cery corrected.

"But you're no ordinary Thief. I reckon there's different rules for you. You didn't start the usual way, so why would you finish the usual way?"

"Wish everyone else agreed with you."

"So do I. City'd be a better place."

"With everyone agreeing with *you*? Ha!"

"Better for me, anyway."

Cery chuckled and resumed the journey. Gol followed a short distance behind. *He hides his fear well*, Cery thought. *Always has. But he must be thinking that we both might not make it through this night. Too many of the others have died.*

Over half the Thieves – the leaders of underworld criminal

groups in Imardin – had perished these last few years. Each in different ways and most from unnatural causes. Stabbed, poisoned, pushed from a tall building, burned in a fire, drowned or crushed in a collapsed tunnel. Some said a single person was responsible, a vigilante they called the Thief Hunter. Others believed it was the Thieves themselves, settling old disputes.

Gol said it wasn't *who* would go next that punters were betting on, but *how*.

Of course, younger Thieves had taken the place of the old, sometimes peacefully, sometimes after a quick, bloody struggle. That was to be expected. But even these bold newcomers weren't immune to murder. They were as likely to become the next victim as an older Thief.

There were no obvious connections between the killings. While there were plenty of grudges between Thieves, none provided a reason for so many murders. And while attempts on Thieves' lives weren't that unusual, – an expected part of a Thief's life – that they were successful was. That, and that the fact that the killer or killers had neither bragged about it, nor been seen in the act.

In the past we would have held a meeting. Discussed strategies. Worked together. But it's been such a long time since the Thieves cooperated with each other I don't think we'd know how to, now.

He'd seen the change coming in the days after the Ichani invaders were defeated, but hadn't guessed how quickly it would happen. Once the Purge – the yearly forced exodus of the homeless from the city into the slums – ended, the slums were declared part of the city, rendering old boundaries obsolete. Alliances between Thieves faltered and new rivalries began. Thieves who had worked together to save the city during the invasion turned on each other in order to hold onto their territory, make up for what they'd lost to others and take advantage of new opportunities.

Cery passed four young men lounging against a wall where the alley met a wider street. They eyed him and their gaze fell to the small medallion pinned to Cery's coat that marked him as a Thief's man. As one they nodded respectfully. Cery nodded back once, then paused at the alley entrance, waiting for Gol to pass the men and join him. The bodyguard had decided years ago that he was better able to spot potential threats if he wasn't walking right beside Cery – and Cery could handle most close encounters himself.

As Cery waited, he looked down at a red line painted across the alley entrance, and smiled with amusement. Having declared the slums a part of the city, the king had tried to take control of it with varying success. Improvements to some areas led to raised rents which, along with the demolition of unsafe houses, forced the poor into smaller and smaller areas of the city. They dug in and made these places their own and, like cornered animals, defended them with savage determination, giving their neighbourhoods names like Blackstreets and Dwellfort. There were now boundary lines, some painted, some known only by reputation, over which no city guard dared step unless he was in the company of several colleagues – and even then they must expect a fight. Only the presence of a magician ensured their safety.

As his bodyguard joined him, Cery turned away and they started to cross the wider street together. A carriage passed, lit by two swinging lanterns. The ever-present guards strolled in groups of two – never out of sight of the next or last group – carrying lanterns.

This was a new thoroughfare, cutting through the bad part of the city known as Wildways. Cery had wondered, at first, why the king had bothered. Anyone travelling along it was at risk of being robbed by the denizens on either side, and probably stuck with a knife in the process. But the road was wide, giving little cover for muggers, and the tunnels beneath, once part of the underground network known as the Thieves' Road, had been filled in during its construction. Many of the old, overcrowded buildings on either side had been demolished and replaced by large, secure ones owned by merchants.

Split in two, vital connections within Wildways had been broken. Though Cery was sure efforts were underway to dig new tunnels, half the local population had been forced into other bad neighbourhoods, while the rest were split by the main road. Wildways, where visitors had once come seeking a gambling house or cheap whore, undeterred by the risk of robbery and murder, was doomed.

Cery, as always, felt uncomfortable in the open. The encounter with the mugger had left him uneasy.

"Do you think he was sent to test me?" he asked Gol.

Gol did not answer straightaway, his long silence telling Cery he was considering the question carefully.

"Doubt it. More likely he had a fatal bout of bad luck."

Cery nodded. *I agree. But times have changed. The city has changed. It's like living in a foreign country, sometimes. Or what I'd imagine living in some other city would be like, since I've never left Imardin. Unfamiliar. Different rules. Dangers where you don't expect them. Can't be too paranoid. And I am, after all, about to meet the most feared Thief in Imardin.*

"You there!" a voice called. Two guards strode toward them, one holding up his lantern. Cery considered the distance to the other side of the road, then sighed and stopped.

"Me?" he asked, turning to face the guards. Gol said nothing.

The taller of the guards stopped a step closer than his stocky companion. He did not answer, but after looking from Gol to Cery and back again a few times he settled on staring at Cery.

"State your address and name," he ordered.

"Cery of River Road, Northside," Cery replied.

"Both of you?"

"Yes. Gol is my servant. And bodyguard."

The guard nodded, barely glancing at Gol. "Your destination?"

"A meeting with the king."

The quieter guard's indrawn breath earned a glance from his superior. Cery watched the men, amused to find them both trying – and failing – to hide their dismay and fear. He'd been told to give them this information, and though it was a ridiculous claim the guard appeared to believe him. Or, more likely, understood that it was a coded message.

The taller guard straightened. "On your way then. And . . . safe journey."

Cery turned away and, with Gol following a step behind, continued across the street. He wondered if the message had told them exactly who Cery was meeting, or if it only told the guard that whoever spoke the phrase wasn't to be detained or delayed.

Either way, he doubted he and Gol had chanced upon the only corrupted guard on the street. There had always been guards willing to work with the Thieves, but now the layers of corruption were stronger and more pervasive than ever. There were honest, ethical men in the Guard who strove to expose and punish offenders in their ranks, but it was a battle they had been losing for some time now.

Everyone is caught up in infighting of one form or another. The Guard is fighting corruption, the Houses are feuding, the rich and poor novices and magicians in the Guild bicker constantly, the Allied Lands can't agree on what to do about Sachaka, and the Thieves are at war with each other. Faren would have found it all very entertaining.

But Faren was dead. Unlike the rest of the Thieves, he had died of a perfectly normal lung infection during winter five years ago. Cery hadn't spoken to him for years before that. The man Faren had been grooming to replace him had taken the reins of his criminal empire with no contest or bloodshed. The man known as Skellin.

The man Cery was meeting tonight.

As Cery made his way though the smaller, lingering portion of the split Wildways neighbourhood, ignoring the calls of whores and betting boys, he considered what he knew of Skellin. Faren had taken in his successor's mother when Skellin was only a child, but whether the woman had been Faren's lover or wife, or had worked for him, was unknown. The old Thief had kept them close and secret, as most Thieves had to do with loved ones. Skellin had proven himself a talented man. He had taken over many underworld enterprises, and started more than a few of his own, with few failures. He had a reputation for being clever and uncompromising. Cery did not think Faren would have approved of Skellin's utter ruthlessness. Yet the stories most likely had been embellished during retellings, so there was no guessing how deserving the man's reputation was.

There was no animal Cery knew of called a "Skellin". Faren's successor had been the first new Thief to break with the tradition of using animal names. It didn't necessarily mean "Skellin" was his real name, of course. Those who believed it was thought him brave for revealing it. Those who didn't, didn't care.

A turn into another street brought them out into a cleaner part of the area. Cleaner only in appearance, however. Behind the doors of these solid, well-maintained houses lived more affluent whores, fences, smugglers and assassins. The Thieves had learned that the Guard – stretched too thin – didn't look much deeper if outward appearances were respectable. And the Guard, like certain wealthy men and women from the Houses with dubious business connections, had also learned to distract the city's do-gooders from their failure to deal with the problem with donations to their pet charity projects.

Which included the hospices run by Sonea, still a hero to the poor even if the rich only spoke of Akkarin's efforts and sacrifices in the Ichani Invasion. Cery often wondered if she guessed how much of the money donated to her cause came from corrupt sources. And if she did, did she care?

He and Gol slowed as they reached the intersection of streets named in the directions Cery had been sent. At the corner was a strange sight.

A patch of green sprinkled with bright colour filled the space where a house had once been. Plants of all sizes grew among the old foundations and broken walls. All were illuminated by hundreds of hanging lamps. Cery chuckled quietly as he finally remembered where he'd heard the name "Sunny House" before. The house had been destroyed during the Ichani Invasion, and the owner could not afford to rebuild it. He'd bunkered down in the basement of the ruin, and spent his days encouraging his beloved garden to take over – and the local people to enter and enjoy it.

It was a strange place for Thieves to be meeting, but Cery could see advantages. It was relatively open – nobody could approach or listen in without being noticed – and yet public enough that any fight or attack would be witnessed, which would hopefully discourage treachery and violence.

The instructions had said to wait beside the statue. As Cery and Gol entered the garden, they saw a stone figure on a plinth in the middle of the ruins. The statue was carved of black stone veined with grey and white. It was of a cloaked man, facing east but looking north. Drawing near, Cery realised there was something familiar about it.

It's supposed to be Akkarin, he recognised with a shock. *Facing the Guild but looking toward Sachaka*. Moving closer he examined the face. *Not a good likeness, though*.

Gol made a low noise of warning and Cery's attention immediately snapped back to his surroundings. A man was walking toward them, and another was trailing behind.

Is this Skellin? He is definitely foreign. But this man was not from any race that Cery had encountered. The stranger's face was long and slim, his cheek bones and chin narrowing to a point. This made his surprisingly curvaceous mouth appear to be too large for his face. But his eyes and angular brows were in proportion – almost beautiful. His skin was darker than the typical Elyne or Sachakan colouring, but rather than the blue-black of a typical Lonmar it had a reddish tinge. His hair was a far darker shade of red than the vibrant tones common among the Elynes.

He looks like he's fallen into a pot of dye, and it hasn't quite washed out yet, Cery mused. *I'd say he is about twenty-five*.

"Welcome to my home, Cery of Northside," the man said, with no trace of a foreign accent. "I am Skellin. Skellin the Thief or Skellin the Dirty Foreigner depending on who you talk to and how intoxicated they are."

Cery wasn't sure how to respond to that. "Which would you rather I call you?"

Skellin's smile broadened. "Skellin will do. I am not fond of fancy titles." His gaze shifted to Gol.

"My bodyguard," Cery explained.

Skellin nodded once at Gol in acknowledgment, then turned back to Cery. "May we talk privately?"

"Of course," Cery replied. He nodded at Gol, who retreated out of earshot. Skellin's companion also retreated.

The other Thief moved to one of the low walls of the ruin and sat down. "It is a shame the Thieves of this city don't meet and work together any more," he said. "Like in the old days." He looked at Cery. "You knew the old traditions and followed the old rules once. Do you miss them?"

Cery shrugged. "Change goes on all the time. You lose something and you gain something else."

One of Skellin's elegant eyebrows rose. "Do the gains outweigh the losses?"

"More for some than others. I've not had much profit from the split, but I still have a few understandings with other Thieves."

"That is good to hear. Do you think there is a chance we might come to an understanding?"

"There's always a chance." Cery smiled. "It depends on what you're suggesting we understand."

Skellin nodded. "Of course.". He paused and his expression grew serious. "There are two offers I'd like to make to you. The first is one I've made to several other Thieves, and they have all agreed to it."

Cery felt a thrill of interest. *All of them? But then, he doesn't say how many "several" is.*

"You have heard of the Thief Hunter?" Skellin asked.

"Who hasn't?"

"I believe he is real."

"One person killed all those Thieves?" Cery raised his eyebrows, not bothering to conceal his disbelief.

"Yes," Skellin said firmly, holding Cery's gaze. "If you ask around – ask the people who saw something – there are similarities in the murders."

I'll have to have Gol look into it again, Cery mused. Then a possibility occurred to him. *I hope Skellin doesn't think that my helping High Lord Akkarin to find the Sachakan spies back before*

the Ichani Invasion means I can find this Thief Hunter for him.
They were easy to spot, once you knew what to look for. The Thief
Hunter is something else.

"So . . . what do you want to do about him?"

"I'd like your agreement that if you hear anything about
the Thief Hunter you will tell me. I understand that many
Thieves aren't talking to each other, so I offer myself as a
recipient of information about the Thief Hunter instead.
Perhaps, with everyone's cooperation, I'll get rid of him for
you all. Or, at the least, be able to warn anyone if they are
going to be attacked."

Cery smiled. "That last bit is a touch optimistic."

Skellin shrugged. "Yes, there is always the chance a Thief
won't pass on a warning if he knows the Thief Hunter is
going to kill a rival. But remember that every Thief removed
is one less source of information that could lead to us getting
rid of the Hunter and ensuring our own safety."

"They'd be replaced quick enough."

Skellin's frowned. "By someone who might not know as
much as their predecessor."

"Don't worry." Cery shook his head. "There's nobody I hate
enough to do that to, right now."

The other man smiled. "So are we in agreement?"

Cery considered. Though he did not like the sort of trade
Skellin was in, it would be silly to turn down this offer. The
only information the man wanted related to the Thief Hunter,
nothing more. And he was not asking for a pact or promise
– if Cery was unable to pass on information because it would
compromise his safety or business, nobody could say he'd
broken his word.

"Yes," he replied. "I can do that."

"We have an understanding," Skellin said, his smile broad-
ening. "Now let me see if I can make that two." He rubbed

his hands together. "I'm sure you know the main product that I import and sell."

Not bothering to hide his distaste, Cery nodded. "Roet. Or 'rot', as some call it. Not something I'm interested in. And I hear you have it well in hand."

Skellin nodded. "I do. When Faren died he left me a shrinking territory. I needed a way to establish myself and strengthen my control. I tried different trades. Roet supply was new and untested. I was amazed at how quickly Kyralians took to it. It has proven to be very profitable, and not just for me. The Houses are making a nice little income from the rent on the brazier houses." Skellin paused. "You could be gaining from this little industry, too, Cery of Northside."

"Just call me Cery." Cery smiled, then let his expression grow serious. "I am flattered, but Northside is home to people mostly too poor to pay for roet. It's a habit for the rich."

"But Northside is growing more prosperous, thanks to your efforts, and roet is getting cheaper as more becomes available."

Cery resisted a cynical smile at the flattery.

"Not quite enough yet. It would stop growing if roet was brought in too soon and too fast." *And if I could manage it, we'd have no rot at all.* He'd seen what it did to men and women caught up in the pleasure of it – forgetting to eat or drink, or to feed their children except to dose them with the drug to stop their complaints of hunger. *But I'm not foolish enough to think I can keep it away forever. If I don't provide it, someone else will. I will have to find a way to do so without causing too much damage.* "There will be a right time to bring roet to Northside," Cery said. "And when that time comes I'll know who to come to."

"Don't leave it too long, Cery," Skellin warned. "Roet is popular because it is new and fashionable, but eventually it will be like bol – just another vice of the city, grown and prepared by anybody. I'm hoping that by then I'll have established new trades to support myself with." He paused and looked away. "One of the old, honourable Thief trades. Or perhaps even something legitimate."

He turned back and smiled, but there was a hint of sadness and dissatisfaction in his expression. *Perhaps there's an honest man in there*, Cery thought. *If he didn't expect roet to spread so fast, maybe he didn't expect it to cause so much damage . . . but that isn't going to convince me to get into the trade myself.*

Skellin's smile faded and was replaced by an earnest frown. "There are people out there who would like to take your place, Cery. Roet may be your best defence against them, as it was for me."

"There are always people out there who want me gone," Cery said. "I'll go when I'm ready."

The other Thief looked amused. "You truly believe you'll get to choose the time and place?"

"Yes."

"And your successor?"

"Yes."

Skellin chuckled. "I like your confidence. Faren was as sure of himself, too. He was half right: he got to choose his successor."

"He was a clever man."

"He told me much about you." Skellin gaze became curious. "How you didn't become a Thief by the usual ways. That the infamous High Lord Akkarin arranged it."

Cery resisted the urge to look at the statue. "All Thieves gain power through favours with powerful people. I happened to exchange favours with a very powerful one."

Skellin's eyebrows rose. "Did he ever teach you magic?"

A laugh escaped Cery. "If only!"

"But you grew up with a magician and gained your position with help from the former High Lord. Surely you would have picked up something."

"Magic isn't like that," Cery explained. *But surely he knows that.* "You have to have the talent, and be taught to control and use it. You can't pick it up by watching someone."

Skellin put a finger to his chin and regarded Cery thoughtfully. "You do still have connections in the Guild, though, don't you?"

Cery shook his head. "I haven't seen Sonea in years."

"How disappointing, after all you did – all the Thieves did – to help them." Skellin smiled crookedly. "I'm afraid your reputation as a friend of magicians is nowhere near as exciting as the reality, Cery."

"That's the way with reputations. Usually."

Skellin nodded. "So it is. Well, I have enjoyed our chat and made my offers. We have come to one understanding, at least. I hope we will come to another in time." He stood up. "Thank you for meeting with me, Cery of Northside."

"Thank you for the invitation. Good luck in catching the Thief Hunter."

Skellin smiled, nodded politely, then turned and strolled back the way he had come. Cery watched him for a moment, then gave the statue another quick glance. It really wasn't a good likeness.

"How did it go?" Gol murmured as Cery joined him.

"As I expected," Cery replied. "Except . . ."

"Except?" Gol repeated when Cery didn't finish.

"We agreed to share information on the Thief Hunter."

"He's real then?"

"So Skellin believes." Cery shrugged. They crossed the road and began striding back toward Wildways. "That wasn't the oddest thing, though."

"Oh?"

"He asked if Akkarin taught me magic."

Gol paused. "That isn't *that* odd, though. Faren did hide Sonea before he handed her over to the Guild, in the hopes she would do magic for him. Skellin must have heard all about it."

"Do you think he'd like to have his own pet magician?"

"Sure. Though he obviously wouldn't want to hire you, seeing as you're a Thief. Perhaps he thinks he can ask favours of the Guild through you."

"I told him I hadn't seen Sonea in years." Cery chuckled. "Next time I see her, I might ask if she'll help out one of my Thief friends, just to see the look on her face."

A figure appeared in the alley ahead, hurrying toward them. Cery slowed and noted the possible exits and hiding places around them.

"You should tell her Skellin was making enquiries," Gol advised. "He might try to recruit someone else. And it might work. Not all magicians are as incorruptible as Sonea." Gol slowed. "That's . . . That's Neg."

Relief that it wasn't another attacker was followed by concern. Neg had been guarding Cery's main hideout. He preferred it to roaming the streets, as open spaces made him jittery.

The guard had seen them. Neg was panting as he reached them. Something on his face caught the light, and Cery felt his heart drop somewhere far below the level of the street. A bandage.

"What is it?" Cery asked, in a voice he barely recognised as his.

"S . . . sorry," Neg panted. "Bad news." He drew in a deep breath, then let it out explosively and shook his head. "Don't know how to tell you."

"Say it," Cery ordered.

"They're dead. All of them. Selia. The boys. Never saw who. Got past everything. Don't know how. No lock broken. When I came to . . ." As Neg babbled on, apologising and explaining, words running over themselves, a rushing sound filled Cery's ears. His mind tried to find some other explanation for a moment. *He must be mistaken. He's hit his head and is delusional. He dreamed it.*

But he made himself face the likely truth. What he had dreaded – had nightmares over – for years had happened.

Someone had made it past all the locks and guards and protections, and murdered his family.

if you enjoyed
THE MAGICIAN'S APPRENTICE

look out for

THE EDGE OF THE
WORLD

book one: Terra Incognita

by

Kevin J. Anderson

CHAPTER ONE

Off the Coast of Uraba

These foreign seas looked much the same as the waters of home, but Criston Vora knew the lands were different, the people were different, and their religion was contrary to everything he had been taught in the Aidenist kirk. For a twenty-year-old sailor eager to see the world, those differences could be either wondrous or frightening—he wouldn't know which until he met the people of Uraba, which he was about to do.

The Fishhook had made this voyage several times, and Criston's captain, Andon Shay, was confident in his abilities to negotiate another trade deal with the Uraban merchants. The young man kept his eyes open and studied the unfolding coastline as the ship sailed far, far south of everything he had known.

From his fishing village of Windcatch, he had always felt the call of the sea, wanting to see what lay beyond the horizon, yearning to explore. Though he had signed on for only a short trading voyage, at least he was seeing the other continent: Uraba. A place of legends and mystery.

Though connected by a narrow isthmus, the world's two main continents, Uraba and Tierra, were separated by a wide gulf of history and culture. Ages ago, at the beginning of time, when Ondun—God—had sent two of his sons in separate sailing ships to explore the world, the descendants of Aiden's crew had settled Tierra, while those from Urec's vessel colonized Uraba. Over the centuries, the followers of Aiden and the followers of Urec developed separate civilizations, religions, and traditions; despite their differences, they were bound together by ties of trade and necessity.

On a bright sunny day with a brisk breeze, Captain Shay called for the sails to be trimmed for a gentle approach to the city of Ouroussa, where they hoped to find eager customers. The hold of the Fishhook contained barrels of whale oil from Soeland Reach, large spools of hemp rope from Erietta, grain from Alamont, and, in a special locked chest in the captain's cabin, beautiful metal-worked jewelry made by the skilled smiths of Corag Reach. Though the bangles and ornaments would be sold to the followers of Urec, the Corag metal-workers had subtly hidden a tiny Aidenist fishhook on each piece of jewelry.

Captain Shay would sell his cargo at prices greatly reduced from what the other Uraban merchants and middlemen could offer. With fast vessels, intrepid Tierran sailors braved the uncharted currents and sailed directly to Uraba's coastal cities, bypassing the much slower overland merchants (much to their consternation).

Near the ship's wheel, Criston paused to look at the two compasses mounted on a sheltered pedestal, a traditional magnetic compass that always pointed toward magnetic north and a magical Captain's Compass that always pointed home. The silver needle of the Captain's Compass came from the same piece of precious metal as an identical needle in the

Tierran capital city of Calay. These twinned needles remained linked to each other by sympathetic magic, as all things in Ondun's creation were said to be linked.

Now, as the Fishhook closed in on Ouroussa, the crew saw a flurry of activity in the distant harbor; a ship with a bright red sail set out to meet them, sailing toward the open water. Captain Shay gestured to Criston. "Go aloft and have a look, Seaman Vora." Shay's dark hair ran to his shoulders, and instead of wearing a full bushy beard like most ship captains, he kept his neatly trimmed.

Nimble and unafraid of heights, the young man scrambled up the shroud lines to reach the lookout nest. During the voyage, Criston had enjoyed spending time high atop the main mast overlooking the waters; he had even seen several fearsome-looking sea serpents, but only at a distance.

As the Uraban ship approached, Criston noted its central painted icon on its square mainsail, the Eye of Urec. He spied additional movement in the harbor, where two fast Uraban galleys launched, their oars extended, beating across the water at a good clip. They spread apart, approaching the Fishhook from opposite directions.

Captain Shay called for a report, and Criston scrambled back down the lines to relate what he had seen to Captain Shay. "I couldn't see many crewmen aboard the main ship, Captain. Maybe they just want to escort us into port."

"Never needed an escort before. These aren't waters that require a pilot." Shay snapped orders to his crew, and all twenty-eight men came out on deck to stand ready. "Once they know what we're offering, they'll welcome us with open arms, but don't let your guard down." He turned back to the young sailor. "This could be a very interesting first voyage for you, Seaman."

"It's not my first voyage, sir. I've spent most of my life on boats."

"It's your first voyage with me, and that's what counts."

Criston's father, a fisherman, had been lost at sea, and Criston himself had served aboard many boats, working the local catch but dreaming of more ambitious voyages. Though young, Criston owned his own small boat for carrying cargo up to the Tierran capital of Calay, but the prospect of paying off the moneylenders seemed daunting. So when the Fishhook had passed through Windcatch on her way south and Captain Shay asked for short-term sailors to accompany him on a two-month trip to Ouroussa, offering wages higher than he could make on his own boat, Criston had jumped at the chance.

Not only would it help him pay off the debt, but it would give Criston a chance to see far-off lands. And when he returned to Windcatch with his purse full of coins, he would finally be able to marry Adrea, whom he had loved for years. Once the Fishhook unloaded her cargo in Ouroussa, Criston could be on his way home. . . .

As the scarlet-sailed Uraban ship closed to within hailing distance, he spotted a man standing near the bow dressed in loose cream-colored robes, his head wrapped in a pale olba. Only five crewmen stood with the man on the foreign vessel's deck. The robed man shouted across to them in heavily accented Tierran. "I am Fillok, Ouroussa's city leader. What goods have you brought us?"

Shay lowered his voice to Criston. "Fillok . . . I know that name. I think he's the brother of the soldan of Outer Wahilir, an important man. Why would he come to meet us?" He frowned in consternation. "Men who consider themselves important sometimes do brash things, and it's rarely a good sign." The captain raised his voice and called back across the water, "We are on our way to port. I can give your harbor-master a full list."

"It is my right to inspect your cargo here and now! How do we know your boat is not filled with soldiers to attack Ouroussa?"

"Why would we do that?" Shay asked, genuinely perplexed.

If Fillok did not change course, his ship would collide with the Fishhook within minutes. Captain Shay eyed the two swift war galleys coming toward them from both port and starboard. "This doesn't feel right, Vora. Go up there and have another look." The young sailor slipped away and scrambled back up the ropes to the lookout nest.

Tierran traders often made great profit from selling to Uraban cities, but many vessels vanished, more than could reasonably be accounted for by storms and reefs. If Fillok were an ambitious and unprincipled man, he could have attacked those traders and seized their cargoes. No one in Tierra would know.

When Criston reached the lookout nest and peered down at the foreign ship, he was astonished to see far more than just the five Uraban sailors standing at the ropes. At least a dozen armed men crouched out of sight behind crates and sailcloth on the deck; the hatches were open, and even more Uraban men crowded below, holding bright scimitars. Criston cupped his hands around his mouth and yelled at the top of his lungs, "Captain, it's a trap! The ship is full of armed men!"

Shay shouted to his crew, "Set sails! All canvas, take the wind now!" Already on edge, the men jumped to untie knots, pull ropes, and drop sails abruptly into place.

Criston's warning forced Fillok into abrupt action. The Ouroussan city leader screamed something in his own language, and hidden men burst into view, lifting their swords.

Shrill trumpets sounded a call to battle. Ropes with grappling hooks flew across the narrow gap between the two ships; several fell into the water, but three caught the Fishhook's deck rail. Answering horns and drumbeats came from the two closing war galleys, and the rowers picked up their pace.

Shay reached down to grab a long harpoon stowed just below the starboard bow of the Fishhook. The Tierran men armed themselves with boat-hooks, oars, and stunning clubs. Criston clambered back down to the deck, ready to join the fight. He held a long boat-knife to defend himself, though its reach was much shorter than that of a Uraban scimitar.

Criston ran to the straining ropes that bound the ships together, just as five Urabans jumped across the gap with an eerie inhuman howl. Ducking the wide swing of a Uraban sword, he sawed at the first rope until it snapped and immediately set to work on the second one.

The Fishhook's sails were fully extended now, giving her a much greater canvas area than Fillok's small Uraban ship. The ropes creaked as the Tierran vessel tried to break away. One of the Tierran sailors went down, bleeding from a deep gash in his head.

Ignoring the mayhem around him, Captain Shay cocked his arm back and let the long harpoon fly toward the other ship. Where its sharp iron tip plunged directly through Fillok's chest. The Ouroussan city leader staggered backward, grabbing the harpoon's shaft in astonishment, before he collapsed into a pool of blood on his own deck.

The Uraban attackers howled in rage upon seeing their leader killed. They piled against one another, preparing to leap across and slaughter the Tierrans. Racing in from shore, the two war galleys closed in a pincer maneuver.

Criston sawed with his knife until he severed the third grappling rope, and like a freed stallion, the Fishhook lunged free, separating from the Uraban ship as many of the enemy fighters leaped across. A dozen men tumbled into the deep water, and only two managed to cling to the side of the Fishhook, clutching nets and an anchor rope. Leaning over the rail, Criston lopped off fingers with a knife slash, and the screaming men slid into the water.

Though he was as white as a sheet, Captain Shay's voice did not waver as he shouted, "All speed—head north! Out to open sea!" The Fishhook began to pull away.

Only three enemy soldiers remained on the deck. Captain Shay's crew quickly dispatched them and dumped the bodies overboard.

With Fillok killed—the brother of the local soldan!—the remaining Uraban sailors were in a frenzy aboard his ship. The drums of the approaching war galleys beat furiously, but the Fishhook's sails pushed the cargo ship faster. The coast-line began to dwindle in the distance, but Criston knew the uproar would not die down. "Captain, what just happened? Why did they do that? We came only to trade."

"They wanted our cargo, and now they'll want our hides as well." Shay looked sick. "Fillok's brother will go to Soldan-Shah Imir and demand blood. I suppose the blood of any Tierran will do. We have to get to King Korastine as quickly as possible." He gave the young sailor a weary smile as he turned the wheel and aligned the course with the Captain's Compass. "When we pass Windcatch, I can drop you off, Mr. Vora. But for the rest of us . . ." He shook his head, still frowning. "I think we just started a war."

CHAPTER TWO

The Royal Cog, Sailing to Ishalem
Three Months Later

The royal ship sailed southward through the night, following the Tierran coastline. She was a single-masted cog with her square sails trimmed so that she made slow headway under the stars. Because the route down to the holy city of Ishalem was so well charted, with lighthouses to mark hazardous stretches, the captain was comfortable with proceeding in the dark.

Even so, King Korastine of Tierra could not sleep, caught between hope and anxiety about the upcoming meeting with Soldan-Shah Imir. After the disastrous clash between Captain Shay's trading ship and the Uraban privateers, he could just as easily have been leading warships down to ransack Ouroussa and sink enemy ships in the harbor.

Instead of leaping headfirst into war, the Uraban leader had dispatched his best ambassador, a man named Giladen, to search for a peaceful solution. Though neither leader would admit it, both knew that Captain Shay should not have gone where he did; they also knew that Fillok should not have attacked a peaceful trading ship, and that a harpoon in the heart was exactly what he deserved. Though their respective populations were inflamed, both the king and the soldan-shah believed they had a chance to salvage the situation.

Long past midnight, Korastine stood on the raised bow platform and gazed into the misty shadows that lay ahead, imagining their destination. *Ishalem.* The sacred city built on the narrow isthmus that connected the continents...the most ancient settlement in the known world, considered holy by both the Aidenist religion and the rival Urecari religion.

Korastine wrapped weathered hands around the wooden balustrade. He was a thin man, wise-looking, barely forty. His long hair and neatly trimmed beard were light brown, salted with graying strands. He could already see what he would look like when he grew old, and times like these aged a man more swiftly.

In Ishalem, he and the soldan-shah would sign a treaty blessed by the Aidenist prester-marshall and the head sikara priestess of the Urecari church. After so many years of turmoil, they would divide the known world in half, clearly defining the two spheres of influence. That would settle the matter for all time, and at last there would be peace.

So why couldn't he sleep? Why did his stomach insist upon knotting itself with doubts? With a heavy sigh, he tried to convince himself that he was just being a fool, stung by too many disappointments, too many misplaced dreams.

The mist intensified the salt-and-seaweed smell in the air. The whispering laughter of gentle waves against the hull planks was soothing. Though there were hammocks below, most crewmen chose to sleep on the open deck. A puff of breeze luffed the sailcloth, making the masts and rigging creak.

Korastine barely heard the soft barefoot tread ascending the steps to the forecastle platform. He turned to see his beloved eleven-year-old daughter rubbing sleep from her eyes. "Are we almost to Ishalem, Father?"

"We'll be there in the morning." He reached out to hug her, and she comfortably folded herself into his arms.

Princess Anjine had straight brown hair, parted in the middle. When she was at court in Calay, she brushed her hair many times nightly, as her mother had once insisted, but on the five-day voyage, the girl didn't bother with such silliness, and the king couldn't blame her.

Though Queen Sena had been dead from pneumonia for half a year now, Korastine and his wife had often disagreed on the raising of their only child; the queen insisted that Anjine ought to be ladylike and courtly, while Korastine wanted the girl to focus more on leadership—while also being allowed some measure of her own childhood. As an uneasy compromise, the princess had learned both.

Knowing how much was at stake with the upcoming treaty, the king insisted that Anjine accompany him now. He could never forget the responsibility he had to his people and to his daughter. One day, he would leave Tierra in Anjine's care, and he did not want to give her a broken, war-torn land.

Korastine glanced around for his daughter's constant companion. "Where is Mateo?" One year older than Anjine, the young man was Korastine's ward by virtue of a heartfelt promise made when Mateo's father, a captain of the royal guard, had died in the line of duty.

"Oh, he has no trouble sleeping." Anjine lounged back against the rail. "Should I go splash a bucket of seawater in his face?"

"Let him sleep. We're going to have a busy day when we reach port."

As the royal cog had sailed out of Calay Harbor, Anjine and Mateo had chattered with excitement about the exotic things they were going to see. Neither had ever been to Ishalem, though they had heard plenty of stories from sailors, presters, and teachers. By the second day, however, the excitement of the voyage faded, and Mateo made it his personal mission to entertain Anjine. After the king had scolded the two children for scrambling up the mast and hanging on the rigging, Mateo devoted himself to playing strategy games with her. They hunkered down together on the deck boards, sketching out a chalk grid and making their marks. Korastine noted, proudly, that Anjine won more often than the boy did.

Queen Sena would have argued against bringing Mateo Bornan along at all, claiming that the king had gone far beyond the requirements of his promise to care for the boy. Though he did not like to think ill of the dead, stuffy Sena was no longer with them, and Korastine could raise his daughter as he pleased.

Now, wide-awake and eager as the ship sailed on, Anjine stood next to her father. Though her head barely came to his chin, he could think only of how tall, how mature his little girl was becoming. Where had the years gone? He felt a hint of tears welling in his eyes. By signing the Edict, he would leave her—and all his people—with a better, safer world.

Anjine strained to see through the fog, then pointed. "Is that Aiden's Lighthouse?"

Korastine did see a flicker, like an ember suspended in the air. "If it isn't, then we're far off course." The tall tower of sturdy rock had been erected on a jutting point of land outside of Ishalem. Its light burned constantly, not just to warn ships of the reefs that lay farther south, but to represent the light of Aiden's wisdom.

A groggy Mateo hurried across the deck, and the twelve-year-old sprang onto the forecastle platform to stand between Anjine and Korastine. So full of energy, like his father had been! The dark-haired young man would make a fine soldier someday—a high-ranking officer, if Korastine had anything to do with it.

Before long, they could see a silvery fringe of dawn on the eastern horizon. The off-watch crewmen began to awaken, and the cook stoked his stove in the galley to begin cooking breakfast. Men worked the rigging, pulling ropes to stretch the sails, now that the captain could see his heading. Ahead and to port, the shore loomed out of the shadows.

Korastine stared at the western edge of the isthmus that separated the vast Oceansea from the calmer Middlesea. He remembered the first time he'd sailed down the coast at his own father's side, being trained to lead Tierra . . . He had made the voyage six times now, always on matters of state, always in response to a major or minor political emergency. After this time, though . . .

Finally the warm sun burned off the rest of the morning fog, and the whitewashed buildings of sprawling, majestic Ishalem came into view. Ah, he remembered the amazement and wonder with which he had first viewed the holy city. Anjine would be seeing the same thing now, through the clarity and optimism of youth.

On the Aidenist side of the city, the architecture showed familiar Tierran influence, similar to what one might find in any coastal village, while in the Uraban District on the opposite side of the isthmus, the buildings looked alien, with unusual curves and angles, stuccoed rather than timbered, the roofs tiled rather than thatched.

On the highest hill in the center of Ishalem stood the ruins of the Arkship, little more than a skeletal hull with one broken mast, like a giant beached sea beast, lying far from the water. Anjine pointed as soon as she spotted it. "That's the ship! Aiden's ship."

Korastine uttered an automatic awed prayer. "Yes, the actual one."

Prester-Marshall Baine appeared on deck, wearing a long, dark brown robe trimmed with purple silk. An Aidenist fish-hook pendant hung at his throat, nearly covered by his unruly red beard. King Korastine not only revered the energetic religious leader, he respected Baine as an intelligent, thoughtful friend. Though he was only in his mid-thirties, Baine had reached a high position of authority and responsibility, thanks to his forceful personality and his persuasive words. The prester-marshall closed his blue eyes as he bowed in silent prayer. "The holy Arkship."

"But how could such a big ship get so far from the water?" Mateo asked pragmatically, and Anjine gave him a brisk kick in the shin.

The prester-marshall chided her. "Some presters might tell you never to question, but that is tantamount to telling you not to think. Ondun There is no harm in raising questions, and Mateo a good one. That conundrum has puzzled scholars for many generations."

Mateo flashed a vindicated grin at Anjine, but the prester-marshall didn't exactly answer his query. "Now would be a good time to reflect upon where our people came from. You have heard the story all your life, but when you gaze upon Ishalem, you can see in your heart that it is more than just a *story*.

"At the beginning of the world, Ondun created the continents and the seas and the skies. He made His own perfect holy land, which He called Terravitae, and Ondun filled the land with crops and orchards, forests, animals, birds, and insects. He populated it with His own people. Then He made other people and scattered them across the remaining continents. When He was finished with all His work, Ondun created three special sons—Aiden, Urec, and Joron.

"Satisfied with all that He had done, Ondun bequeathed stewardship of the world to His heirs, for He had other worlds to create, and He would soon depart. Ondun instructed Aiden, Urec, and Joron that they must keep this world intact, improve it, make it thrive. While the youngest son, Joron, remained behind to rule Terravitae, Ondun commanded that His two older sons go out in separate ships to explore His creation."

Baine related the tale to Anjine and Mateo with an earnestness that village presters could never match. Korastine smiled: No wonder the man had risen so quickly in the church hierarchy. "Before the voyage, Ondun gave Urec a special map to show him how to find the mysteries of the world, and the key to creation. To Aiden, he gave a special compass to facilitate his return to Terravitae, for its needle was charmed always

⸻⸻ interrupted.

⸻ Captain's Compass," Anjine corrected.

"Aiden and Urec each constructed a giant Arkship, and taking their crews and families with them, sailed away from Terravitae on separate routes. But Urec was arrogant and sure of himself. He would explore the world, but considered the map an insult to his bravery, a way of cheating. Urec threw the chart overboard and chose his own course." Baine raised his bushy red eyebrows for dramatic effect. "Now, the Urecari will tell it differently, because such foolishness does not reflect well upon the man they consider their prophet! But we have the Book of Aiden to tell us the truth."

The prester-marshall looked up as the cog sailed toward the crowded maze of wharves. "We know that one of Aiden's crew members was secretly a spy for Urec, though the Urecari deny it. As soon as Aiden's ship passed well beyond sight of Terravitae, the Urecari spy damaged the sacred compass so that Aiden, too, became lost.

"After voyaging aimlessly for years, Aiden's ship came to rest here. The crew intermarried with the people of Tierra, and their descendants now populate half the world. When Urec's ship landed, he, his crew, and their children settled in Uraba to the south."

As the royal ship pulled into the harbor, Korastine saw the buildings clustered like devout worshippers kneeling before the many-spired Aidenist kirk built on the western side of the Arkship hill. The cog drifted up to a long dock festooned with pennants and garlands. Gulls greeted them with a raucous fanfare. Ishalem looked so glorious that Korastine could almost believe that their meeting was blessed by Ondun.

Anjine glanced up toward the gigantic wreck on the hill. "So how do we know that's Aiden's ship, instead of Urec's— as the Urecari say?"

"Because we *know*. Yes, we know."

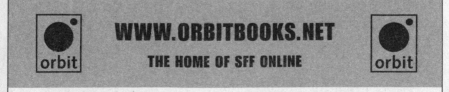